THE BRIDES OF PURPLE HEART RANCH

THE COMPLETE SECOND SERIES

SHANAE JOHNSON

THOSE JOHNSON GIRLS

CONTENTS

IN OVER HIS HEAD

ALWAYS ON HIS MIND

EVERY STEP HE TAKES

HIS STRENGTH TO STAND

HIS GRACE UNDER PRESSURE

IN OVER HIS HEAD

THE BRIDES OF PURPLE HEART RANCH
BOOK 6

AUTHOR'S NOTE

My favorite type of love stories are the ones when one or both of the love interests have a wound, be it internal or external. I love reading, watching, listening to how these two people will work out their differences and, most importantly, heal together. That's what's in store for anyone who visits the fictional Purple Heart Ranch; a place where Wounded Warriors find rehabilitation for their bodies and everlasting love to heal their hearts.

In order to make this particular story, work I had to take some liberties with how things work in the real world, particularly when it comes to the military. When you turn the page, you'll find out that the hero is headed to a bereavement visit. It is not protocol for enlisted men to make bereavement calls before someone who is trained to do so visits the family. I know that. However, leaving out the Bereavement Officer made the story work better. I hope you can suspend your disbelief on that front.

The stories in this series will deal with elements of Post Traumatic Stress Disorder (PTSD). These love stories will presume that love is the key to healing these internal wounds. I know that love is often not enough in matters of this disorder. If you, or someone you love, is suffering from this heartbreaking ailment, please know there is help in the real world. That real world help is often the best form of medicine, along with a side dose of a few sweet kisses.

Love,
   Shanae

CHAPTER ONE

It was the metallic smell of fresh blood that knocked him off his feet, not the blast from the bomb exploding behind him. Corporal Brandon Lucas got down, ducking and covering to avoid the deadly fragments that radiated from the center of the attack. From his training, he knew that most of the damage from an explosion was caused in the first few seconds of the blast wave. It was the shock that left a lasting impact.

Heat licked up his back. Screams pierced his ears. Even with his eyes closed, he saw the flames flicker on the inside of his eyelids. When the worst of it was over, he looked over his shoulder. But all he could see was black smoke and orange flames.

There was no one left standing. Not his commanding officer. Not the other two men on his team. That's when he lost his footing.

He'd been on his knees. As he tried to stand, the combination of smoke and blood knocked him onto his chest. Brandon went down hard.

His palms scraped the coarse desert sand. Dirt mixed with the metallic blood on his tongue constricting his throat. He couldn't speak, but he had to. There were orders to be followed. He was trained for this, though the simulations and drills never quite prepared any soldier for the realities of combat.

He inhaled. Blood wasn't the only chemical smell. Mixed with the synthetic smell of the explosive material were the charcoal scent of gunpowder, the rancid odor of burned flesh, and the toxic fumes of diesel fuels. He knew he had to push past the assault on his nose. It was a rookie mistake, and he was a seasoned officer. The unexpected smells of war typically startled privates who'd just gotten a bit of hair on their chests and dust on their polished boots.

Under orders, Brandon had given the command to proceed. Yet, when he had, there had been hesitation in his voice. Brandon never hesitated. Not once in his years in the United States Army. But something had been off. His gut had told him so. But orders were orders. And so he'd given them. Unfortunately, his team had heard his doubt, and they too had hesitated.

Then everything blew up in their faces. All that was left was blood, and burning flesh, and a blaze. And it was all his fault.

"Lucas, wake up."

Brandon jerked awake at the sound of his superior's voice. He'd only closed his eyes for a few moments. He knew that because the last time he looked at his watch it had been five minutes ago. But that was all it took for the scene to invade his dreams and assault his senses like he was back in that village with smoke and gunfire and the cries of women and children and enemies all around him.

That was not the scene before him now. The sun was peaking up past the horizon. He'd watched it go down the previous night and rise up as it brought forth a new day. The scenery outside the window moved slowly past him as the airplane made its slow taxi to the gate.

"We're here."

Sergeant Colin Chase looked back at Brandon from his seat. Beside him, Brandon felt an elbow from his seat companion. Private Mark Ortega had already unbuckled his belt and was ready to bounce out of his seat. Brandon knew that Ortega was more ready to get out of the confines of their metal transport than he was ready to carry out their latest orders. Brandon saw no reason to rush for that very reason. Also because he knew they had ample time to make their connecting flight.

"Ladies and gentlemen," said the pilot's voice from the overhead speakers. "Please allow our members of the United States Army to depart the plane first. We thank you for your service."

The three men in uniform rose slowly from their seats. Applause sounded from the back rows of the commercial airplane. Chase turned to the civilians at the back of the plane. He put on that thousand-watt smile that had been captured once or twice in military brochures. Brandon swore he heard a few feminine sighs of approval as Sgt. Chase saluted and waved.

Those sighs doubled when Private Ortega, now free from the confines of the window seat, smiled his dimpled grin from the aisle. There was a reason he was nicknamed Lady Killer back on the base. It had nothing to do with his sharp aim and everything to do with those twin bullets on the sides of his face.

For his part, Brandon gave a quick salute and turned away. He didn't want the praise, not today. Maybe not ever again. His gaze fell on the empty seat beside the one Chase had vacated. Brandon's mind went to the missing fourth member of their team.

"Hey." Chase's hand came down on his shoulder, a vise grip that Brandon knew he'd never escape. "It's not your fault. You did everything you could. We all did."

Brandon didn't nod his agreement. He turned from the empty seat. Reaching up to the overhead compartment, he grabbed his duffle bag and headed to the exit. His movements decisive now that he was back on his home turf.

It was his first time back in the United States in over a year. The heat of Atlanta felt like the same heat he'd confronted every day in the deserts of Afghanistan. Brandon wasn't from Atlanta. None of the men were. This was just a layover. Their final destination was the northwestern state of Montana.

After a favor pulled by Chase, their fire team was headed for some rehabilitation at a ranch run by vets. The Purple Heart Ranch it was called. There, the three remaining members of the team might heal from the ravages of their last assignment. Though Brandon doubted it.

All scrapes, burns, and bruises from the ambush had healed. Brandon's skin had reknit from the burns. His aches had dulled. It was only his mind that still had an open wound.

They all had open wounds on the inside. Classic symptoms of Post Traumatic Stress Disorder. Brandon's symptoms robbed him of sleep where every time he closed his eyes he'd relive the events of their last mission and his one mistake that had knocked their four-man fire team down to three.

It was supposed to be their last job before their separation from the army. He hadn't expected that separation to be so permanent. But it's what they all had signed up for.

Now they had one mission left before the separation was complete. In this final assignment, they had to tell the family of Private Reece Cartwright that the vibrant young man wasn't coming home again.

At the arrivals gate, people waved signs and held up posters thanking the soldiers for their service. Chase and Ortega put their winning grins on. Brandon forced a smile, but a glimpse in the glass window told him it did not meet muster. Still, he did what he was trained to do, he soldiered on.

CHAPTER TWO

The choir director's fingers struck the first chord on the ancient organ in the church's music room. Voices rose in praise and perfect harmony. It was a joyful noise.

Reegan Cartwright raised her voice alongside the small but devoted choir. This was her favorite song of the program. She closed her eyes as the words of the song penetrated her heart.

There was nothing like the sounds of the choir singing praises on a Sunday. This wasn't a Sunday. It was a Saturday night at choir practice. By the way practice was going, it was going to be a rapturous service come tomorrow.

As the music swelled, so did the passion in Reegan's heart. It lifted her voice. Unfortunately, the note was an octave out of step with the other singers around her. The organ music came to a crashing halt.

Everyone turned to Reegan since the dissonant note had come from her lips. Reegan pressed a hand to her throat, rubbing at the corded skin she found there. This was the third time that day where she'd hit the wrong note on a song she'd sang in perfect accord her whole life.

"Is everything okay, Reegan?" Barbara Bowen, the choir director, asked her. "Are you coming down with something?"

Reegan checked in with her body. She did feel out of sorts, but not the yucky feeling that accompanied a cold. She pressed the back of her hand to her forehead and was met with cool skin. She swallowed a couple of times, but there was no scratchiness in her throat.

"I'm fine," she said. But even those words hadn't felt quite right. "I'm just going to grab a drink of water."

Reegan stepped out of the group. Her friends and neighbors that she'd known her whole life all made room for her to take a moment to herself. These were the same people who had rallied around her after she'd lost her parents three years ago. They were the same people that invited her to family dinners every Sunday night or on holiday weekends now that her parents were gone and her brother was away. She loved each and every one of them and couldn't fathom her life outside this community, her extended family.

Her twin brother Reece was off overseas serving his country, just as he'd always dreamed. Reegan was also doing what she'd dreamed of. Singing in a choir was all she ever wanted to do in life.

Her mother had joked that she'd come out of the womb singing. That even when baby Reegan had awoken her late in the night, it had been the most resonant cries she'd ever heard, and she was tempted to listen to Reegan's wails rather than offering her comfort to get her quiet.

The moment she could join, Reegan had signed up for the youth choir. By the time she'd become a teen, she'd graduated into the full choir with the other adults. Reegan spent all of her time singing. But not just any singing. She might hum along to a pop hit or country song. But gospel and hymns were what brought her joy.

Singing in the church that she was raised in, the church her parents were married in, the church she and her twin brother were baptized in, that was the dream. And she was living it. Even though her parents had passed on and her brother was away saving the world in the service, Regan was living her best life.

She sipped from the cool water in the cup. The liquid slid easily down her throat meeting no obstructions or sore spots. When it reached her chest, it met with a rumble there.

Reegan rubbed at her chest. Her palm rested on her heartbeat. The organ raced, beating twice as fast as normal, as though she'd just run down the hall. But she hadn't. So why was her heart racing as though something was wrong?

Reegan took a few deep breaths. And almost instantly, her heart rate settled. She continued breathing deep as she made her way back to the music room. She even practiced some runs. Everything, her pulse, her vocal cords, all seemed to be back in working order.

When she rejoined the group, they tried the song again. This time Reegan hit all the notes with no problem. The song finished, and the choir was once more in perfect harmony. As she packed up to leave, Barbara pulled her aside.

"Do you think you'll be ready for the solo tomorrow?" Barbara asked.

Reegan loved adding her voice to the group's. But she never felt closer to heaven than when she got the spotlight on the stage. "Of course, I will. I think I just may be tired, that's why I missed the note."

"I'd have to agree, Reegan. You're always overextending yourself. If you're not here volunteering at the church, then you're out at someone's house giving them your time. Or you're off at the Purple Heart Ranch working their gardens."

That was Reegan's other passion. She had a small plot of land out back of her house that she and her mother had turned into a small garden. But on the ranch, she had acres she could plant and cultivate. In the last year that the ranch had been open, it had become her second favorite place in the world. The first being the home she'd lived in her whole life.

"I like being busy," she said to Barbara. "And I like giving my time to others. I have the luxury of not having to work since I live rent free and my parents left me a small sum to live off."

Reegan hadn't gone to college or pursued any work other than giving her time to others. She hadn't wanted to waste her parents' money on an overpriced education when she knew singing was her passion. And that the only place she wanted to sing was in her church choir. Plus, her parents' hard earned money had been reserved for her brother who had realized his dream of going into the Army.

To that end, they'd left Reece the house and Reegan a nice monetary sum. Being true twins, the siblings had decided to share their inheritance. They hadn't even needed to speak their decision. Being connected in the way that twins were, they just knew each other's decision.

So, Reegan stayed in the house while Reece went off to save the world. She invested a good portion of the money in repairs on the ancient home, though there was a lot more she had to do. But those repairs could wait until the next time Reece came home, which by her calculations should be soon. Her heartbeat sped up again at the thought of having her brother home again.

"I'll go home and get a good night's sleep," Reegan said to Barbara. "I promise I'll be rested and ready in the morning."

CHAPTER THREE

Brandon's eyes were wide open as their connecting flight began its descent. He looked over at Chase's and Ortega's faces in the two connecting seats. Blessedly, they were in three adjoined seats in the middle row this time. The fourth seat was occupied by an elderly woman.

Chase and Ortega had slept through the afternoon flight. Each man's eyes were shut, gripped in the peace of sleep. Ortega's mouth was slightly open, a quiet snore whistling out of his nose. Chase's head was tipped back against the headrest. His jaw a firm line that brooked no nonsense even in repose.

Not too long ago, Brandon had come upon a similar scene. Though back in the desert both men had lain in the dirt with their eyes closed. Their uniforms weren't pristine as they were now. Dirt, dust, and blood had covered them. Instead of the calm and soothing voice of the flight attendant giving landing instructions, screams and groans had sounded in the chaos after the gunfire and ear-wrenching explosion had died down.

Brandon hadn't known if the two were living or dead. He was hurt himself, but he managed to crawl to them. Ortega was closer, and Brandon reached out and found the pulse at the man's limp wrist. Before Brandon could get to Chase, the man was already rising to his feet.

The Terminator, Sergeant Colin Chase had been known as back on the base. His fellow soldiers swore he was more machine than man with how far he could go and his expectations that those behind would keep up. Also for his relentless pursuit of his targets. Their last mission was the first time he'd returned empty handed with no asset and missing one of his own.

When the smoke had cleared, Brandon had wanted to stay behind and at least look for Cartwright's body. But they had been compromised. The last Brandon had seen of the private had been the man headed directly into the line of fire. And then nothing.

It was as though he'd disappeared into thin air. It was possible he'd been taken out by the bomb. Brandon hoped that had been Cartwright's fate. If he'd been captured by insurgents, his end would have been far more gruesome.

Chase's eyes opened. His green eyes focused on Brandon like a heat-seeking missile. That strong jaw hardened into steel making Brandon wonder if he were built out of metal like the machine he was accused of being.

"You good?" asked Chase.

Brandon wasn't. Chase knew that. None of them were, but they didn't talk about it.

"I'm good." Brandon gave a quick nod of his head, not meeting Chase's penetrating gaze.

"Did I just wake up in a chick flick?" Ortega stretched his limbs over his head and arched his back with a loud yawn.

The captain's voice came on overhead, telling the passengers to prepare for landing. It was a smooth landing. Not even a bump as the wheels touched down on the tarmac.

They were there. Their final destination after three days of traveling first from a military base, and then the long flight across the ocean, and a somewhat shorter flight to the middle of the country.

They were travel weary. They each needed a shower and change of clothes. A hot meal was certainly in order.

All around them, travelers rushed to retrieve their bags and line up in the aisle to be the first off the plane. All three soldiers held their seats. Not one of them was anxious to complete this final mission.

Once the aisle began to clear, Chase took a deep breath and rose first. Ortega followed suit. And finally, Brandon rose to join the rest of his unit.

He'd never gone to a family to deliver a death notification. This wasn't the usual protocol, but Chase had pulled some strings. Reece had served under him since he'd strapped on his first pair of boots. The kid had been like a true younger brother. He'd been about to advance in rank before they'd lost him.

In his career in the United States Army, Brandon had lost people. But there had been more civilians who'd passed than soldiers. Far more deaths had happened back home due to illnesses and accidents than in war zones. Modern warfare was a different beast these days. Still dangerous, but with new tactics, casualties were down.

Private Cartwright should've still been here but for Brandon's hesitation. And now, he'd have to face the man's family and tell them that Reece wasn't coming home. But worse, they had no body to bury.

"There is nothing you could have done," said Chase.

They were alone on the plane now. Brandon's arms were raised in the act of retrieving his duffle, but he hadn't brought his belongings down to him. He'd just stood their frozen, lost in the memories and guilt.

"There is nothing any of us could have done," Chase continued.

Brandon nodded, though he didn't believe the other man's words. Just like they were all fine.

The walk through the terminal was blessedly quiet as the hustle and bustle of the airport whirled around them. Chase's gaze remained alert as his eyes darted here and there. The instinct to look for threats would never leave any of them.

Ortega's dimples were hidden behind a stern look as he gripped his bag with one hand and balled his fist with the other. Sweat threaded his dark brow. Walking in civilian areas were always the hardest. It was always possible that a threat could materialize out of a child or a woman.

Finally, they made it to the glass doors that spilled out into warm Montana sunshine. The landscape had been breathtaking from the air. It reminded Brandon of the beauty of Afghanistan.

The middle eastern land was a beautiful oxymoron. Filled with demanding deserts as well as lush valleys. Tall mountains and stunning cities. It wasn't until driving through the human settlements that the ugly underside was revealed. Bombed historic sights, toppled monuments, and decrepit homes where civilians hid, trying to carve out a semblance of life.

Back on U.S. soil, the buildings he could see from the airport were all intact. Cars made their way down the streets with little to no obstruction. Pedestrians walked without a care.

Standing on a curb, a man held up a sign with all three of their names on it. He didn't wear fatigues. He didn't need to. That he was a soldier was clear in the way he stood and the seriousness of his features.

Chase stuck out his hand. "Good to see you again, Sergeant Banks."

"You too, Sergeant Chase."

The two men clasped hands. Dylan Banks held on a moment longer. Chase took a deep breath and let it out slowly. It was the most emotion Brandon had ever seen the Terminator display.

"You didn't have to come all this way," said Chase after he released his friend's grip.

"It's my honor," said Dylan. "We're all excited to have you at the ranch."

"I'm excited to see what you've built."

Dylan nodded with clear pride. "You'll find a state-of-the-art rehabilitation center. Everything from horseback riding to strengthen injured or missing limbs, gardening to increase the dexterity of injured fingers or improve hand-eye coordination. We even have a therapist. The Purple Heart Ranch treats both external and internal wounds."

Brandon frowned at that. He'd accepted the invitation to stay at the ranch for a short duration of time. More of a decompression time before he made his way back into civilian life if, in fact, that was the route he was going to take. He was still leaning more toward re-enlisting and redeploying.

He couldn't deny he needed a few weeks of R&R. But Chase had said nothing about internal healing. He was fine. They all were.

Ortega looked to have the same sentiment. But both Ortega and Brandon held their tongues out of respect for the men of superior rank. Chase would get an earful later.

"We'll head out now then," said Dylan.

"We do have to make one stop," Brandon spoke up for the first time.

"Oh, don't worry," Dylan chuckled. "There's plenty of food waiting for you."

"No," said Brandon. "We need to notify a family." He didn't need to elaborate.

Dylan's face sobered in understanding. "Here in the city?"

Chase nodded. "Yes, for Reece Cartwright."

Dylan winced.

"You knew him?" asked Chase.

"Not him, his sister. She does volunteer work on the ranch. His parents died three years back before we arrived on the ranch."

Brandon remembered that. Reece had been given leave during their training to mourn his parents. He'd come back hardened, even more dedicated to his job in the service.

"Reegan sings in the choir. In fact, she'll be at church right now. It's best to take you there. I think it will be better for her to be surrounded by those she loves when you deliver this news."

Brandon wasn't so sure. He preferred to suffer in silence, in private. But he didn't argue. It would be fine.

CHAPTER FOUR

On Sunday afternoon people flocked into the church's open doors as though it were an Easter Sunday service. Many of the worshippers lingered in the doorways catching up with their neighbors. They stood in the aisles and bent over pews to gossip or extend well wishes or kiss newborn babies. The conversations weren't overlong as most people had seen each other either the day before or a few days ago. But this was the way of their community, and Reegan reveled in it.

The church members in this congregation were lifelong friends. Everyone knew everyone. People of every age took their seats amongst the pews. Some in their Sunday's best, which might have been a suit and tie or frilly dress and patent leather shoes. Others were donned in the best that they could do, which might be pressed jeans and a collared shirt or a hemmed skirt with a little scuff to their second-hand shoes.

Reegan watched as the senior pastor, Pastor Barrett made his way to the pulpit. The man gave her a secret smile as he always did. Pastor Barrett had been the youth pastor when she was a girl. He had been there for her whole life, and she'd spent a lot of time not only under his wing but in his nest making a mess with his young daughter.

Elsbeth Barrett stood at the doors to the church, greeting the stragglers as they made their way in. The pastor's daughter and Reegan had been best friends from the cradle. They'd shared their toys, their clothes, and their dreams. They'd even shared a best friend between them.

Reece was the third part of their trio. It made sense that because Beth and Reegan got along so well, and Reece was a carbon copy of Reegan but with boy parts, that they should get along too. And they did.

Reece looked at Beth as a second sister. Unfortunately, he never looked at her any other way. Even though somewhere around middle school, Beth's view of her bonus brother had shifted.

Thinking about Reece made her heart pound. Reegan was missing her brother more and more each day. It had been over a month since the last time she'd heard from him.

The twins had always had a connection. Reegan swore she could feel when he was upset or hurt. She didn't feel that now, but she still felt ... off.

They'd gone longer stretches where he couldn't communicate. It didn't make it easier. She knew he'd be home soon for some downtime when his enlistment with the army was up. But she also knew that Reece had every intention of re-enlisting. Service was her brother's passion, and she was a proud Army Sister.

"You good, Reegan?"

Reegan turned to look beside her. Cassie Ramos sat beside her, her hand resting on her belly bump. The slight young woman was more belly than anything else these days.

"I'm fine," said Reegan. "Don't worry. You won't have to step in for me."

Cassie, who had the soprano voice of an angel, had been doing her fair share of solos since joining the choir only six months ago. But her voice had changed during her pregnancy. It would often pitch lower in the middle of a song. It was as though she were going through an adolescent boy's puberty.

"Good, cause this kid is kicking up a storm today," Cassie said. "He's got too much of his daddy in him."

Her husband, another armed forces vet, looked up from his place in the congregation as though he'd heard his wife invoke his name. With their young daughter in his lap, Xavier Ramos kept an ever watchful eye on his wife. Reegan had to look away as a secretive smile crept across his face, causing his dimples to make an appearance.

The doors to the church opened again, letting in the last of the setting sun. Four men came in. The first man she recognized.

Dylan Banks walked smoothly down the aisle. Only someone who knew the man would know that his right leg was a prosthetic one, put in place after he lost his leg in the service. The man strode with easy confidence until he found space for himself and the three soldiers behind him.

The other three men were dressed in the familiar green uniform her brother wore. Their faces were serious. Their postures stiff.

Reegan was certain they had likely just come off a base where they'd been steeped in training. Or perhaps they'd come from time overseas. They had that look about them that her brother had when he returned home for his short stretches.

As they sat, their bodies were ever alert. Backs straight. Gazes roaming, darting here and there. Sizing up everyone and everything in their periphery for a sign of threat.

It had alarmed Reegan the first time she'd seen her brother react that way to the people he'd known all his life. But he'd explained that hyper-vigilance was a soldier's greatest defense.

All three soldiers had dark hair, but Reegan's gaze caught on the one lagging behind. There was no height difference making him taller or shorter than the other two. His body wasn't broader or leaner than the others either. Though one soldier had striking dimples that rivaled Xavier's, and the other had striking green eyes which had already caught the attention of a few of the single women in the congregation.

Reegan's gaze caught and held on the third soldier precisely because he did not look up. He looked bone-weary tired. The dark circles under his eyes called out to her, begging her to run her thumbs beneath them to clear some of the dusk away. The firm set of his jaw urged her to say something to tickle his funny bone. He looked like he definitely needed a good laugh, but she knew that even a grin would be hard won.

The tap of the microphone brought her attention back to the service. Looking over, Reegan noted the new youth pastor Walter Vance was taking the pulpit. Pastor Vance nodded at Pastor Barrett. The young man of God's enthusiasm at giving his first sermon was hard to miss.

"The reading today is from Genesis 2.18." Pastor Vance waited while everyone found the place in the Bible. "The Lord God said 'it is not good for the man to be alone. I will make a helper suitable for him.'"

Pastor Vance gave a pointed look to Elsbeth who had taken her seat in the front pew. Reegan knew the man was interested in the pastor's daughter. She knew the two had gone on a few dates. But Beth had kept a tight lip on the relationship … or perhaps it was only a friendship? Reegan wasn't sure of Beth's level of interest in Walter.

"The companionship of women was designed by God," Walter continued. "God made Eve, but that wasn't the end of it. Adam and Eve made sons and they begat sons, who begat sons, who begat sons, who begat …"

The audience giggled and chuckled as Pastor Vance took a deep inhale to replenish his lungs after all the begetting. Reegan couldn't deny that the man knew his way around a pulpit.

"Until eventually we were all here. We are all made up of different chords of the same music. We are meant to be played together. In our community, in our relationships, we are called to come together in harmony and unity. You're not meant to be alone."

Pastor Vance paused for effect. He repeated that last phrase, pointing to people in the pews for effect.

"We are meant to serve. It is His design. He called for us to come together in harmony and unity with one another and be one. I don't know about you, but that makes my heart sing."

A chorus of *amens* sounded through the hall, rising to the rafters. Reegan chanced a look at the three guests clad in uniform. The green-eyed man smiled politely, but it wasn't clear if the message penetrated. The dimpled soldier nodded his head and mouthed the word, *amen*. But the third soldier, his head stayed bowed. Reegan knew it wasn't in supplication. Though she could no longer see it, she knew he was still looking discreetly at his phone.

With the sermon delivered, the chords of the piano began. The choir rose. Reegan took her place out front to perform her solo.

She inhaled deeply, asking the butterflies gathered there to settle. She'd sang in this choir, in this very spot, more times than she could count. But something was different about today.

At first, every chorister's voice rose in harmony, just as Pastor Vance had preached. But then accompanying voices died down, leaving Reegan's voice on its own.

Reegan took a deep breath and opened her mouth. She belted out the lyrics only to be slightly off-key. There were a few frowns amongst the congregation. They knew what she was capable of and waited for her to shine.

Her gaze found the soldier still on his phone. She had the misfortune of catching his right eye wince at her blunder.

He lifted his head then. Dark eyes met hers, and she felt as though they penetrated past her heart and into her soul. From somewhere beyond, an angel started to sing. Her voice was lighter than a harp's strings. It had more whimsy than a flute could muster.

The soldier's gaze widened. That firm jaw loosened, and his mouth went slack. He sat up taller, his phone forgotten as the voice continued its joyful noise. His eyes were locked on Reegan as though he'd just seen a wondrous sight. And then Reegan realized; that joyful, angelic sound was coming from her.

CHAPTER FIVE

*B*randon's stomach grumbled as he sat on the uncomfortable wooden bench. People in the pews in front of him turned to look back at him. He shrugged apologetically. What could he say? Church had never agreed with him.

As a kid, he'd tugged at his shirt collar which always had too much starch. He'd scrunched up his toes in the pinching dress shoes which he was never allowed to play in and only wore a couple of times a month. He only ever had to go to church services with his grandma. Mostly on holidays or if his grandma had someone to impress on a given Sunday.

Brandon's parents were happily holiday Christians who only ever went on Easter and Christmas. They called out to God a lot and not in a prayerful way. Typically, in elaborate, sailor-wincing curses, which Brandon had perfected during his time in the military.

But sitting still in a church? That was not his thing. He'd rather have to sit still in a foxhole.

However, this was his duty. And he'd do it. He owed it to Reece. And so he sat still ... for all of five minutes before pulling out his phone and looking for a distraction.

As always, his mind raced when he was forced to sit still. It went back to that village in Afghanistan. Back to the smoke swallowing Reece whole. Back to the explosion ringing in his ears. Back to the crushing guilt he felt for his moment's hesitation.

What he wouldn't give to take it back. To yank Reece back to him with certainty. Unfortunately, that was one thing in this life he was certain of, you couldn't go back and correct your mistakes. You had to face them and move on.

All around him, the congregation murmured praises and *amens*. Brandon should relax in the comfort of their exaltations. Pretty soon, their gazes would turn on him in despair and disappointment when they learned the news that their favored son was gone.

Brandon knew that Reece Cartwright was a devoted Christian. He carried a worn Bible with him wherever they went and wore a gold cross around his neck alongside his dog tags. He could imagine the young man sitting in the pews listening to the sermon and making notations in his book.

Listening to the young pastor speak, Brandon decided he liked that the man spoke to the congregation and not at them like the gray-haired men that had always lorded over his grandmother's church. However, the sermon wasn't one he felt pertained to him.

Brandon had no intentions of begetting or getting married. He still wasn't entirely sure he wasn't going back into the military. He knew for certain he wasn't cut out for this type of civilian life; one where he'd dress in slacks and narrow-toed shoes and sit on a hard bench for hours each week. And on a Sunday afternoon at that.

No, his life would be of more use in going back into the military. That was how he planned to be of service. That's where he would find his fellowship. That's where all of his relationships were forged. He wasn't suited for a life of musical chords or whatever. He'd find harmony within the ranks, unity within a unit.

He looked down at his phone, scrolling through the openings and re-enlistment data on the army's website. He knew Chase and Ortega were finished with their time in active duty, but Brandon decided then and now that he wasn't. How could he be after his last mission and his failure?

There was an itch to get back out there. To make a difference. He'd never felt more human than when he was in service.

It's just that he was so tired. Likely because he hadn't had a good night's sleep since the explosion. He would take advantage of this downtime. He'd relax at the ranch and try and quell the demons that kept him from sleeping. But make no mistake, he was going back.

His nightmares posed a disadvantage to his fitness to serve but not a big one. What soldier didn't have nightmares about what they'd seen in combat zones? He didn't have suicidal or homicidal thoughts. Just memories and guilt over what could have been, what he should have done.

The chords of an old organ began to play. A shudder went down Brandon's spine. This was truly his least favorite part of a church service. The part where regular folk who often were tone deaf raised their voices in an old, sleep-inducing hymn.

Well, on the bright side, maybe the song would send him off to some much-needed sleep.

At least the organ was in tune. And the lady playing it appeared to have the needed skill to command it. The group of singers wasn't half bad, and the song they sang, though not modern, was at least upbeat enough to keep him awake.

Then the soloist stepped forward and hit a wrong note. Brandon felt the impact of the note land somewhere in his gut. It resonated inside him, like a doorbell ringing in the middle of the night announcing the arrival of someone he wasn't expecting.

Brandon was already irritable from not having slept in over seventy-two hours. He tugged at his collar, feeling lightheaded. His fingertips and toes were numb. His heart rate kicked up. He felt as though he were back in a war zone with rockets flying overhead.

That type of adrenaline was normal in duty. But once in civilian life, where being on high alert wasn't necessary, it was disorienting. And then, like the sun breaking through a cloudy day, a voice rang clear through the cacophony of sound that had just assaulted his ears.

Brandon's heart rate began to slow and settle. The life returned to his fingers and toes as the blood pumped down to the ends of his extremities. He lifted his head and took a deep, filling breath. His eyes locked onto an angel's.

An angel with flaming red hair, so bright it looked like the most intense rays of the sun. Not just red but with hints of gold and orange. Blue eyes as clear as a cloudless day gazed back at him as pink coated lips moved, ushering words from a slender neck. From those lips came the sweetest melody.

Brandon's entire body relaxed. He felt light, as though he'd gotten a full eight hours of sleep every night for a week. He felt like he could float. In fact, he felt his bottom leave the seat as he stood.

A hand grabbed at him, pulling him back down. Brandon looked over to see Chase eying him quizzically. Still disoriented, Brandon retook his seat, but he didn't tear his gaze away from the songbird.

"That's her," said Chase.

Brandon wanted to tell the man to shut it. He didn't want to miss a note of her song. But he also wanted to know who she was.

"That's Cartwright's sister," Chase clarified.

The song ended. The booming sound of applause filled Brandon's ears. People got on their feet in praise of the choir and the soloist.

Brandon remained in his seat. Getting up and approaching the songbird was the last thing he wanted to do. He'd have to tell that angel that her brother wasn't coming home, and despite what his superiors and the report said, it was Brandon's fault.

CHAPTER SIX

here were hugs and congratulations as Reegan made her way through the crowd of people she'd known all her life. With the services over, most people were making their way to the banquet hall where a potluck was spread over the tables. Reegan held back, not just for the compliments. She held back because she saw that the soldiers had all remained at the back of the church instead of making their way off to the side door that would lead to the food.

All throughout her song, the stiff-jawed soldier hadn't been able to keep his eyes off her. Reegan had even seen him stand up as though he wanted to come to her during the song. He wasn't looking at her now. His gaze was fixed on the floor as he hung at the back of his group.

She knew because she kept sneaking glances at him. She willed him to lift his head and look at her. She ached for the heat of his gaze to touch her face again.

And if he did look at her, what then? Reegan wasn't sure she could ever date someone in the military. Not with her brother's long absences and infrequent calls.

She and her brother had a special connection. Not just because they were twins but because they were close. It tore at her that she couldn't reach out to him any time she wanted. Especially in the last few years without their parents.

It had been hard being on her own. Even though she was never truly alone. She had a community of people to look after who also insisted on looking after her.

Before her parents had died, they'd assumed Reegan would marry and start a family with her own husband. Her parents were traditional like that. Reegan just hadn't found anyone she'd wanted to marry much less make a home with. So, she'd stayed in the house while her parents were alive and after they'd passed on. She kept it for Reece while he was away. And the money that her parents had left her allowed her to fill her heart's delight which was to sing and help others.

Reegan spotted the soldiers speaking with Pastor Barrett and moving steadily forward. Beside the pastor, she saw Elsbeth. It was a perfect reason to go up and introduce herself to the newcomers.

Reegan took a step forward, only to have coldness shroud her shoulders. The looks on Pastor Barrett and Beth's faces weren't filled with the typical rays of joy they showered on anyone who came into the church's doors. Pastor Barrett looked disheartened. Beth looked pale.

Reality hit Reegan square in her chest. Three soldiers in uniform, sad faces, it could only mean one thing. Someone in the church had died. Someone whose family was at this service. There were only three people in the service. Aside from Reece, there was Arnold Bishop and Shelly Turner.

Reegan's heart broke to know that either Arnold or Shelly had been lost. Inwardly, she mourned for their parents. She'd just seen them make their way to the banquet hall. Perhaps she should go after them and bring them back. But she didn't know which family had suffered the loss.

Before she could take a step toward the doorway, her steel-jawed soldier looked up. His dark gaze found hers. His chin was steel once more. His gaze haunted.

The others looked to her too. Reegan couldn't fathom why? Before she could think too much, they were around her.

"These men have come to see you, Reegan," said Pastor Barrett.

"They have?" Reegan asked the question of the steel-jawed soldier whose gaze hadn't left hers.

"We should go to my office to talk," said Pastor Barrett.

"Why?" said Reegan.

"Ms. Cartwright," said one of the soldiers. "My name is Sergeant Colin Chase."

Reegan knew that name. "You work with my brother. I remember him telling me about a Sergeant Chase."

The man nodded. He wouldn't want to know some of the things Reece had said about him. They weren't mean or inappropriate. Her brother had a lot of fun stories to share about his four-man fire team.

Reegan counted the men. There were three of them. Ortega was on one man's shirt. Lucas was on another. She knew those names. They were Reece's fire team.

Her heart began to pound out of her chest. She clenched her fingers together in anticipation. She looked behind the men, but there was no red-haired private standing in the doorway.

Where was Reece? This had to be one of those internet videos where he'd pop out and surprise her. She couldn't believe she hadn't sensed him near. The two could never sneak up on one another. They were banned from playing hide and seek together when they were kids. They just had a sixth sense about each other. But Reegan didn't sense her brother.

"I'm afraid we have some bad news," said Sgt. Chase.

Reegan didn't look at him. Her gaze connected with the man who'd held her attention throughout her song; Lucas. Corporal Lucas's eyes looked haunted, not mischievous as though he were in on a surprise for her.

"Why don't you tell us the news here," said Pastor Barrett. "We're all family."

Sgt. Chase nodded.

Reegan's head was spinning. Something wasn't right. Her gaze went again to Lucas, searching for the answers there as though she was sure he had them.

"I'm sorry, Ms. Cartwright-"

"Reegan."

"I'm sorry, Reegan, but Private Reece Cartwright has been declared missing in action."

Reegan let out the breath she hadn't been aware she was holding. Relief flooded her, and she pressed her hand to her heart. "Oh, my gosh, you scared me."

The sergeant's eyes widened at her. So did everyone's. Beth's hand gripped hers as though to offer her support.

Reegan took a deep breath and let out another sigh of relief. "I thought you were going to tell me he was dead."

"Ma'am ..." Sgt. Chase looked uncomfortable. So much so that he looked beside him to Cpl. Lucas.

"Ms. Cartwright," said Cpl. Lucas. His voice was deep, resonant. Like a baritone's.

"Please, call me, Reegan," she said. "We're practically family as we both have to put up with my brother."

Reegan knew she should be feeling worried for her brother, but in the midst of his unit, she knew that all would be well. She knew they would find her brother wherever he went missing and bring him back home.

"Reegan," Cpl. Lucas began again. He spoke carefully, cautiously. "We can't give you the full details as the mission was classified. But your brother was caught in enemy fire. It was the last we saw of him, and nobody was recovered in the aftermath."

Reegan struggled to understand his words. Cpl. Lucas was telling her something important. Reece wasn't just missing. "You're telling me he's been captured?"

Once again, the men looked to one another as though they were at a loss.

"It's unlikely," said Cpl. Lucas.

"Then where is he?" Reegan asked.

The men looked at each other again. Cpl. Lucas looked as though he were battling an inner demon who wouldn't release his words. Sgt. Chase looked to the other man in warning, his features clearly shouted *hold it together.* But it was clear Cpl. Lucas wouldn't. He turned away from Sgt. Chase and faced Reegan fully.

"It's against protocol to classify someone as deceased when there is no body. But for all intents ... your brother ... is gone."

Cpl. Lucas's words were strangled, hoarse, as though he hadn't used his voice in days. He gave her his full gaze, letting her see into his soul. There was so much pain and guilt and— was that shame there?

Reegan wanted to comfort him. She wanted to pull him inside her arms and sing to him. He was clearly in such pain. But all she could offer was her certainty.

"No," she said. "He's not."

Instead of looking relieved at her words, Cpl. Lucas blinked at her in utter disbelief.

"If he were dead, I'd know it. We have a bond. We're twins. We came into the world together. I'd know if he'd checked out on me."

The hall was silent. Her community was used to the Cartwright twins. But clearly, these men weren't.

Reegan was sure Reece hadn't gone on and on about his connection with his sister on the base. But it was true. Reegan knew Reece's heart was still beating because hers hadn't skipped a beat. She'd felt off for days. And now she knew why.

"You're going back to find him?" She addressed this question to Cpl. Lucas. "Aren't you?"

CHAPTER SEVEN

For the second time since he'd come to stay on the Purple Heart Ranch, it was the sound of nature that woke Brandon up. Not the natural sounds of the base where he'd hear boots on the ground trudging through gravel. Nor the all-too-common sound of weapons being cleaned outside of tents. Or foul language being slung about as freely as *uhs* and *ums* to fill the flub between words.

No, these were the sounds of actual nature. There were birds chirping off in the distance. Dogs barking nearby. Was that a rooster crowing out back? And children giggling in close proximity. There were no children at camp.

Brandon was not in a war zone. He was not on a base. He was on a ranch.

And he'd slept.

All night again.

Well, most of it. Sunday night he'd slept four, nearly five hours. Looking at his watch, he saw that he'd nearly cleared eight hours Monday night. He couldn't remember the last time he'd gotten that much sleep.

And peaceful sleep at that. Instead of screams and the orange-red of an explosion, he'd dreamed of a red-haired angel singing a sweet tune as she floated down from a sunny, blue sky. The sight of Reegan Cartwright standing in the midst of the choir, the sound of her voice filling the cracks and crevices of his chest, had been the last thing he'd thought about before closing his eyes. That memory of her had carried over into his dreams.

Reegan had turned Brandon's unwanted nightmares into fulfilling dreams with just the power of her beautiful voice. Unfortunately, now that it was the bright light of day, the reality of the situation struck home.

Brandon knew the five stages of grief. For most people, when they were told of tragedy, disbelief was their first emotion. That denial would be followed by anger, bargaining, depression, and finally, acceptance. Reegan hadn't believed a word they'd told her about her missing brother. She was stuck in the first stage of grief, believing that Reece was still alive.

Brandon hoped that wasn't true. If by chance Private Cartwright had been captured, he'd be experiencing unbearable torture and certain death. For Reece's own soul, Brandon hoped the young man was safely ensconced with his Maker, leaning over the gates of heaven to hear his sister sing.

Reegan's voice had certainly sent Brandon off to heaven while in church and later when he'd rested his head on his borrowed pillow. But the sound of her song was already fading from his memory. And the sleep-stealing numbness was creeping back into his body.

He wondered if it would be possible to hear her sing again? He wasn't sure he was willing to go back through the church doors, sit on the hard wooden bench, make it through another sermon he didn't believe in, and face her denial of her brother's fate for another sweet note.

He had to admit that the notion was tempting. His body felt languid. His mind was clear. Though he could feel memories of the heat of that day crawling across his toes and pinching at his fingertips. It would be back.

For now, Brandon rose to greet the day. He'd been placed in a two bedroom, ranch-style row house all to himself. Ortega was shown to the connecting house on Brandon's left, while Chase was given the key to the one on his right. In addition to the bedrooms, the homes each sported a full kitchen and dining area, along with a living room.

It was a nice setup. Better than most housing on base. But they'd all been told they could only stay a maximum of three months. Something or other to do with zoning? Brandon hadn't been listening. He hadn't planned to stay that long. As soon as he was cleared, he'd be back on a base overseas where he was needed.

Washing and dressing quickly, Brandon stepped out of the front door and was greeted by a pack of dogs. The dogs didn't bark menacingly at him. They were each curious of him. He was curious of them. They were a scraggly bunch. They looked like a pack of wounded soldiers.

There was a tiny Irish Terrier with a wheelchair attachment. A quiet Chihuahua who was missing his front leg. And a Pug with a face only a mother could love who had patches of skin missing from her back.

"They don't bite."

Brandon looked up to see two pregnant women ambling down the way. The first was a brunette who Banks had introduced as his wife. Maggie was her name. She had a friendly smile that had put Brandon immediately at ease. There had been something in the woman's gaze that had told him that if he were ever wounded, she would be the one he'd want to turn to.

Beside her, he saw another woman he recognized. The blonde had been in the choir alongside Reegan. She had a pleasant voice, but it had a fullness to it where Reegan's was light and airy. She'd been introduced to him as Cassie, the wife of another soldier on the ranch.

"You missed breakfast," Maggie was saying. "So, we stopped by to bring you a muffin and some berries."

The dogs sat obediently. Each set of eyes on the food being offered to Brandon. So, the mutts weren't the welcome crew. They were hoping for a morsel of Brandon's breakfast. Well, that was too bad. He was far too ravenous to share. And besides, the animals looked well cared for.

"Sgt. Chase and Private Ortega have gone for a ride," Maggie continued. "Dr. Patel is waiting for you in his office when you're ready. It's just over that hill."

"Thank you," Brandon said as he took the offered food. The dogs' gazes now swung to him, tongues lolling out of their mouths.

Maggie snapped her fingers, and the dogs all came to attention like good little soldiers. Before she turned on her heel, she called out to Brandon. "I hope we'll see you for dinner."

Brandon gave a noncommittal waggle of his head. Not a nod but not a shake either. The truth was, he wasn't much interested in being in a crowd right now.

Understanding lit Maggie's brown eyes, but she didn't press. The fact that she hadn't pressed, the realization that she would likely give him space, and that the other soldiers and their wives would likely do the same, made Brandon curious to break bread with them. Maybe he would.

He'd been on base around military wives and families. He'd always enjoyed their company more than being back in civilian life. They understood him more. If he ever were to retire, he'd want to do it in a place like this.

Then he remembered Dylan's words. Every soldier who stayed on the ranch had to be married. That was the zoning edict Brandon had tuned out.

At dinner their first night, Brandon had given a firm shake of his head at the thought. He'd let everyone know that he would be re-enlisting in a few months, and likely re-deploying if he got the opportunity. He would enjoy his time while he was here. Marriage was not in his cards, especially not if he planned to re-enlist.

Brandon munched on the muffin and made his way over the hill. Having grown up in the city, he wasn't used to seeing trees and mountains as far as the eye could see. He jumped at the sound of a mooing cow. He had to wait until chickens crossed the path he was on.

Once he came to the medical building, things began to look more familiar. He walked down the hall until he saw the psychologist's name on the door. The door was open, and an unassuming, brown-skinned man sat behind a wooden desk.

Dr. Patel rose when he saw Brandon lurking in the doorway. "Corporal Lucas, it's nice to meet you."

Brandon looked down at the thin man with a smile bigger than his face. Patel clearly wasn't no nonsense like the military doctors on the base and at the VA Centers. His eyes looked patient and kind, like he had time.

That still didn't change the fact that the man was a head shrink. Sitting across from him, Brandon didn't feel comfortable under the man's gaze. He sat up straight in the plush chair, ever alert.

"I've already met with your other team members," said Dr. Patel. "I'm so sorry to hear about your loss. It's a loss to our entire community. I knew Reece well. His family were all devoted members of my church."

Brandon could only nod. He had no words to offer the man. He'd already botched any attempt to provide solace for Reece's sister.

"It seems you are all still suffering from the loss."

"It's part of the job," said Brandon. "War is dangerous. Not everyone comes back."

"Yet, when it comes to the living, sometimes they leave parts of themselves behind."

Brandon wanted to frown, but he schooled his features, waiting for the psychologist to make his speech plain.

"Sergeant Chase tells me you're having trouble sleeping."

Brandon chewed at the inside of his lip. But he soon realized that if he thought he'd wait out the doctor, he would lose that particular game of patience. Dr. Patel would be just the type of companion necessary for a stakeout.

"It's a common problem," Brandon said. "Soldiers are often sleep deprived in our line of work. Just like doctors on call."

"True." Dr. Patel nodded, seeming to consider his words. "But you're not on call any longer."

The doctor had him there.

"However, it seems you slept quite well the last two nights. Maybe there's no problem at all?"

Brandon recalled the reason he'd slept so peacefully. A beautiful songbird whose song he'd likely stolen with the news of her brother's demise. The numbness that had been missing the last two days was now creeping into the palm of his hands and up to his ankles. It would likely rob him of his sleep again by this time tomorrow.

"As you know, this is a rehabilitation ranch. I've set your other team members up on healing jobs specific to their injuries."

Again, Patel eyed him with that assessing gaze. Brandon wondered what duties he would be prescribed while on the ranch? He knew there was horse therapy there. He'd like to mount one of the powerful beasts. He'd even be fine with the physical, monotonous work of mucking out stalls. Anything to help numb his brain and his thoughts.

"While you're here, I'd recommend gardening."

"I beg your pardon?" Surely, Brandon had heard him wrong. "Do you mean you want me to pull weeds?"

"It's soothing watching something grow, caring for something other than yourself."

Brandon blinked. Gardening? Dr. Patel couldn't be serious?

"You'll find the gardens just over the bridge."

CHAPTER EIGHT

eegan dug her hands into the fresh soil of the earth and hesitated. She was about to pull up a weed. But then she questioned why she was doing it. Why should she end the plant's life just because it decided to start its life next to something others found to be more pleasing to the eye?

This weed was only guilty of trying to thrive in the best place in the garden. The wild plant had the audacity to sink its roots down in the midst of a group of plants whose seeds had been placed there by human hands. But the weed had found its way there through its own grit and determination. It had as much right to life as the other plants that were tended to and coddled.

Reegan let the weed stay for a second, before pulling it up at the root. If she didn't uproot it, it would take not only one flower's life, but likely a few more around it as it sucked up the meager resources of the plot of land. Sometimes things in nature killed for their own survival.

She took a deep breath, breathing in all the fresh life that was on the ranch. As much as Reegan loved going out and helping the people in her community, she loved coming here and helping tend this garden the most. The yard of her family's house wasn't so big, and she easily managed the flowers her mother had planted there since before Reegan was born. She liked the challenge of the acres of pastures that the Purple Heart Ranch provided.

Here she found solitude in all the acres. Here she could think in the quiet spread of land. Here she could tend to herself as much as she did the plants.

Most of the soldiers who came to the ranch for healing preferred to strengthen their bodies with farm work and ride horses to feel in control of something outside of themselves. Typically, it was only her and Reed out in the gardens. The soldier was within shouting distance today.

Reed preferred to work the plants and gain more dexterity with his prosthetic limb. But more and more when he was out there, he wasn't alone. Most of his time was spent making googly eyes at his wife Sarai to notice what needed to be pulled and what didn't.

For her part, Sarai, a former model, didn't get her hands dirty. She chatted with her husband, spoiling the peace and tranquility that Reegan craved. Outside of the garden, Reegan loved Sarai's chatty nature. Just not when she needed quiet and solitude like today.

The couple was quiet today. Sarai had her hands in the dirt, but she neither pulled at unwanted plants or planted any seedlings. Reed ran his fingers over flowers that needed no tending. Today, instead of making eyes at each other, the Cannons mostly snuck glances at Reegan.

Everyone was treating her as though weeds were springing up around her. People who she had been a source of strength for were all waiting at the ready to pluck away anything they thought threatened her light and sustenance. Everyone was treating her with special care, but she didn't need it. She didn't want it.

No matter how many times or ways they said it, Reegan just couldn't come to believe that her brother was dead. It didn't feel like a fact. And no one could prove it to her. Not when she felt the connection that had been between them while still in the womb beating so strong.

Earlier that morning, Reegan had been on the phone with the Department of Defense. But they didn't give her anything more than the soldiers had. In fact, she knew that Corporal Lucas had given her more than he was supposed to.

Reegan had seen the soldiers ride out on horseback when she'd pulled up. She hadn't seen Brandon Lucas's broad form atop one of the majestic beasts. She wondered where he was. Not that she was looking for him.

"Hey, how are you today?"

Reegan looked up to see Beth making her way to her. Beth was dressed in one of her flowery sundresses. But her friend's features were cloudy and gray. Beth's eyes were red and bleary. Her smile didn't come anywhere near her eyes.

Reegan held out her arms to her best friend. Beth sank down to her knees and brought her arms around Reegan. As the two friends held each other, Reegan saw Reed and Sarai make a quiet departure. It was another thing she loved about this community. They'd let one of their own suffer in silence but never alone.

The problem was that Reegan wasn't suffering. Sure, she was torn up that her brother was missing. She was gutted that she didn't know where he was or what he was experiencing. But unlike everyone else, she knew with every fiber of her being that Reece's heart still beat. If anyone should know Reece was still alive, she'd thought it would be Beth. But by the woman's silent tears, Reegan saw even their shared best friend didn't believe he was still with them.

"I wrote him a letter over a month ago, and he never responded," said Beth. "I suppose this is why."

Reegan opened her mouth to refute the conclusion of that statement, then closed her lips. She was too weary to dispute what she believed, what she knew.

"You know military mail can be delayed," Reegan said instead. "We both have gotten letters from him dated weeks in the past. Once I got one over a month old."

Beth pulled away, wiping at her face. "I hope he got the letter before … It was a confession."

Reegan didn't need to ask what kind of confession. Beth had been in love with Reece since she understood what the word meant. For his part, Reece was entirely oblivious.

He'd once promised to marry Beth so that they could all be real brothers and sisters. He'd been six when he'd made that promise. Reegan suspected Beth had never forgotten. She was sure their friend had been holding out hope that he'd make good on that promise someday soon.

But when Reece had chosen a military career instead of the call to the pulpit, Beth had had a wake-up call. She'd only started dating after Reece's first tour, and she realized they'd never be together. Reegan suspected that didn't change how her friend felt in her heart. It was evident in the redness of her eyes.

"I told Reece I loved him, that I always had. When he didn't respond, I took it as a sign to say yes to start dating Walter. And now Walter's asked me to marry him."

"Oh, Beth," Reegan sighed.

"I'm going to say *yes*." Beth sniffled as she spoke about her impending marriage. It wasn't a good sign when a bride to be was in tears over the proposal, especially not when she was crying over another man. "Walter is a good man. I can make him happy. Especially if I'm never going to be with the man I truly love."

Reegan wasn't sure what to say. Part of her wanted to tell Beth to wait, that Reece wasn't truly gone. But another part of her wanted her friend to move on. It was clear that Reece didn't feel the same way about her as she did about him. But Reegan couldn't lie, not to her oldest friend.

"I just don't believe Reece's gone," Reegan said. "I still feel him in my heart."

"I hope to God you're right." Beth took a deep breath. "But if you are, I've still got my answer from him. It was never going to be us. I need to accept that and move on."

Reegan knew she should feel relief at Beth's statement, but she didn't. She wanted her friend to marry for love, not to settle for anything less. And she wanted Reece to be there when Beth did walk down the aisle. He would insist that whatever man won his best friend's hand had also won her heart.

Reegan just needed to get someone to believe her and go back and look for her brother. The sun shifted in the afternoon sky and her gaze flicked over the hill. There a man appeared.

He rose up as though he were walking out of the sun. Corporal Brandon Lucas walked toward them like he was the answer to her prayers.

At that moment, Reegan knew what she needed to do. She needed to make Brandon Lucas see the light. She needed to make him believe so that he would help her recover her brother.

CHAPTER NINE

*B*randon looked down at the pick in one hand and shovel in the other. He'd held heavy artillery. He knew how to put together a rifle and take it apart in the dark. His skills with a firearm were deadly accurate.

And yet here he was reduced to a gardener. Sent off to battle weeds. Enlisted to sow seeds of string beans.

He didn't have time for this. He definitely didn't have any patience for it. He'd come to the ranch to relax and recuperate, not to tend and till.

He'd figured he'd at least get to ride the horses. He could see Chase and Ortega in the distance trotting on horseback with a few of the other soldiers in residence. And yet here he was walking away from that excitement to commune with nature.

Wasn't the whole point of this to get him out of his head? Not to leave him alone with his thoughts. He was near to tossing the tools down in the cursed dirt when he spotted a red flame up ahead.

It was her. Reegan. She held the same tools in her hands that he possessed. Her tools were buried in the earth. The flowers around her stretched their wiry limbs up for her attention. But she wasn't looking at the blossoms. Her blue gaze was latched on him.

Her gaze wasn't friendly. Those long lashes swept low as she narrowed her eyes. Her nostrils flared. Her arms crossed over her chest, and her shoulders squared off in determination.

She reminded Brandon of a disgruntled kitten. Part of him wanted to toss her a ball of yarn and watch her play. The other part of him recognized the lioness hidden inside that ball of fur.

For the first time in his life, Brandon contemplated running away from a battle line. Because make no mistake, there was a line drawn in the fertile ground. It ended where the weeds were wilting away, losing a battle to Reegan Cartwright's pruning.

He felt her fingers plucking at him. Sifting the soil of his being to get to the root of him. He held still for her, as though she'd taken one of those gardening sticks used to prop up a vine that couldn't hold its own weight.

Brandon stood tall, the tallest thing in the entire field. The sun's rays touched the top of his head first. But he wasn't interested in the star's light. He felt warmed through just being in Reegan's presence. Even though he knew that he was about to get burned, his feet kept moving closer to the heat source.

"Hello, Ms. Cartwright."

He didn't know if he was still allowed the use of her Christian name. When she didn't correct him or insist that he call her Reegan, he knew the privilege had been revoked.

"How are you today?" He tried for politeness. Anything to get a few words from her, to refresh his memory of the sound of her voice. Perhaps once he heard a few more notes, he'd have that peace he'd felt when she sang wash over him again.

Reegan lifted her chin. She inhaled through her nostrils, her lips still pursed. Brandon held very still. Any second she would give him words.

Her chin dipped. She tugged the left corner of her lower lip into her mouth. Her gaze bounced from place to place. His face, his shoulders, his chest, and back again.

Finally, she settled on his face. She let go of her lip and opened her mouth. Her lips trembled as the words came out.

"I have questions."

Brandon felt his chest sink. He felt the blazing heat of the desert lick over his shoulders. He felt the hairs on his neck prickle with awareness. Danger, his brain told him. Flee, was the response his body told him.

She had questions? Those were the only three words he didn't want to hear from this woman. He'd expected shouting. It had been two days.

He'd felt certain she'd moved from the stage of denial and was at anger, perhaps even bargaining. But it looked as though she were still in denial.

He found himself lowering his body until he was kneeling before her. She let out a little gasp at his supplication. Her features softened. Some of her nerve left her for a moment, and she looked unsure.

Brandon had the urge to pull her into his chest. He wanted to tell her that everything would be all right. But that would be a lie.

Reegan still believed her brother was alive. Brandon knew it wasn't possible. If there was even the sliver of a chance, he hoped Reece would meet his end soon instead of face any torture at the hands of the insurgents who they'd come up against.

"What happened?" Reegan asked, her voice a shaky whisper.

It was a simple question. It was also the root of Brandon's nightmares. Brandon swallowed a few times, but the lump in his throat wouldn't pass to let him speak.

"The last email I got from him, he seemed fine," she said. "He said he was training for an operation and that he would have to go dark for at least four weeks."

Brandon focused on the sound of Reegan's voice. She wasn't singing, but the timber of it soothed him. Even though she was using her melodic voice to speak his nightmare out loud.

"That was over six weeks ago."

Brandon nodded, meeting her gaze. He sat the shovel and pick down and leaned his elbow on his knee to prop himself up. "We did train. And then we went on an operation in Afghanistan. I can't get into the particulars of the mission. It's-"

"Classified."

Now Brandon bit his lip. Everything in him told him to tell this woman everything. But he'd been well trained. "I can't tell you where. But I can tell you that it was a counterinsurgency mission. We were trying to help keep the peace for the upcoming elections in the region."

The anti-coalition militias in Afghanistan were intent on disrupting the local and national elections. Having officials elected in a democratic fashion would undermine their authority. The insurgents detested the idea of unification of the country but more so a national government.

"Our team was sent to surveil a particular location which had reports of insurgent activity. We were nearing the end of the operation. Everything had run smoothly. And then ..."

Brandon took a deep breath before continuing. Reegan was staring at him intently. He noticed then that her eyes were the same blue as Reece's. It was like looking at the man, like the last time he'd seen Reece when he'd looked back over his shoulder.

Reegan reached out a hand to him. He'd expected her fingers to be pillow soft. But they weren't. There were calluses on her fingertips. The polish on her nails was chipped, and there was dirt in the nail beds.

There was no anger in her gaze as she looked at him. No accusation. Her eyes held so much compassion. That's what broke him.

"A group of women entered the perimeter. We weren't sure if they were friend or foe. Your brother spoke the language and asked permission to go down to them. I should've said no. But I hesitated. I wasn't sure."

Brandon expected her to recoil from his admission. She didn't. Her rough fingers squeezed his bicep like she was supporting him, like she was there for him.

He frowned at her. Didn't she understand what he was telling her? It was all his fault.

"I was wrong. I should have told him to hold his position. It was an ambush."

"The women were the insurgents?"

"I don't know. We never found out. We tried to get down to him, but there was an explosion. When the dust cleared, they all were gone."

She released her hold then. Her fingers relaxed their grip on his bicep. But her hand didn't leave him entirely. Her palm rubbed up and down his arm.

She wasn't looking at him anymore. She was looking skyward.

Beside them, Brandon heard a small sob. He'd known they weren't alone, but it was the first time he gave any attention to the pastor's daughter. Elsbeth Barrett covered her mouth with her hand and looked away. Tears streamed down her already red eyes.

Brandon was certain he'd get the same reaction from Reegan. But her jaw was firm, determined. Her gaze was clear. And her hand was still on his arm, offering him the support he should have been giving to her.

"So, you think he was blown up?" Reegan asked. "And that's why there was no body?"

Brandon hesitated. Explosions left traces. A recovery team had been sent in, and they'd come back with nothing. It was more likely that the insurgents had taken the bodies.

"Did you go back and look for him? Did they find his dog tags? What about civilians in the area? Did someone question them?"

"It doesn't work that way."

Brandon took a deep breath. He felt the heat of the desert licking over his neck at the rapid-fire questions. She didn't understand. He'd already said too much.

Her hand finally fell away from him. Brandon was left feeling cold, alone in the bright heat of the Montana afternoon. There were those blue eyes staring at him. Accusing.

"Well, how does it work?" That beautiful voice rose, shouting at him.

"I did everything I could." He shouted, shooting up to standing. He was on his feet, towering over her.

Reegan looked up at him. Not in fear. In shock, confusion, and hurt. The sob that broke from her tore what was left of Brandon's heart apart.

"I'm sorry," he said. But his voice was so raw, the lump so big, he wasn't sure the words even got out. Shame colored his vision until both women were a blur. He turned on his heel and, for the first time in his life, he ran away.

CHAPTER TEN

For the third time in three nights, Reegan's house was packed. Every neighbor from along her block as well as a couple of streets over was in her living room. There were many tears as friends came to grips with the news. There was much light laughter as remembrances of a young, mischievous Reece were told. There was also more food than she could ever hope to eat in a lifetime on the kitchen table.

This was how her community remembered those who had gone home to heaven. The house had been even more filled when her parents had passed on. Those had been the hardest days of her life, but she'd had Reece at her side then.

There were plenty of people by her side now. The problem was, Reegan didn't feel as though Reece had passed on. She could still feel him in her heart.

All of the mourning going on in the family room was making her itch. All use of the past tense when anyone spoke of her brother was giving her a headache. What she really wanted was solitude.

"Remember how he loved dinosaurs," said Mrs. Peterman from next door. "I brought him a T-Rex, but he wanted a Brontosaurus."

Reegan nodded. She didn't trust her voice not to ring with irritation or her words to be those of a mourning sister. Because she wasn't in mourning.

She felt numb but not empty. She knew what loss felt like. She knew what it felt like when a loved one's spirit left the earth and traveled on. She'd experienced it before times two. This was not that.

She still felt the link between herself and her brother. But she couldn't explain it to anyone else. No one else got it besides Reece. Her twin never spoke about it, but she knew he'd felt it.

Once when she'd broken her arm at Girl Scouts camp miles away, Reece had cried out in pain at baseball practice. He'd been walking out to left field and no one was on the mound.

Reegan didn't feel any phantom pain now. She just felt tired, and cold, and lonely. Was that what Reece was feeling wherever he was? She ached that she couldn't reach out and touch him, comfort him.

She needed to find someone to listen to her. That someone wasn't Corporal Brandon Lucas. Behind the anger in his eyes, she'd seen a haunted look. Whatever had happened to Reece, he'd seen it with his own eyes and it tore at him.

Reegan had poked at him, but she didn't feel ashamed. She had no choice. Her brother was alive and someone needed to go and find him.

"I put the casserole in the oven, dear," said Mrs. Russo. The woman owned a diner on the main street and made the best lasagna in the entire state. "I had some trouble with the flame."

"The wire's faulty," said Reegan. "I need to get someone out to take a look. I just keep putting it off."

The house was over a hundred years old. It had been passed down to her father from his father who had taken over from his father. Reegan's dad had been in the process of updating all the wiring when he'd passed on. Reece said he'd handle it when he got some downtime, but that was over a year ago.

She'd expected him home next month for some time off. She had a list of repairs they would tackle together. The wiring was at the top of the list.

"Well, I got it on," said Mrs. Russo. "It just needs to be there for ten minutes and then you can eat up. I know it's your favorite."

"Yes, she needs to eat," said Mrs. Peterman. "She's far too thin."

"You really shouldn't be staying here alone," said Mrs. Cottman. "You should come and stay with us. You know we'd love to have you."

Reegan loved her community, but she loved her independence more. When her parents had passed, her well-meaning neighbors had urged her to move in with them, to date their single sons and nephews. But

Reegan loved her home. She had no desire to move or live anywhere else. She did want to get married and have a family of her own. But she hadn't felt that special something with any man in town, and she'd met them all more than once.

The closest thing she'd felt to a spark was with a certain corporal. If she were honest, it was more than a spark. She'd felt her skin go aflame the first time she'd seen Brandon Lucas in the doors of the church. It had stoked higher that afternoon when he'd knelt before her in spite of their disagreement. When he'd gone down on bended knee, Reegan's heart had fluttered, and her first thought was that he was going to propose.

"All right everyone." Beth's voice broke through Reegan's insane thoughts. "Reegan's had a long day. Let's let her get some rest."

Reegan could've kissed her best friend for her intervention. In fact, when everyone had filed out of the front door, she did. Reegan pulled Beth into a tight hug and didn't let go for long moments.

"I can stay," said Beth.

But Reegan shook her head. "I just need some quiet."

With a long sigh and one more squeeze, Beth let Reegan go and filed out the front door. Her walk home was short. The Barretts lived just across the street from the Cartwrights.

Once the door closed behind Beth, Reegan rested her head against the wood frame. She felt bone weary. The house was tidy, bless the old biddies who cleaned up after the guests who'd come to pay their respects. There was nothing for her to do.

Reegan headed up the stairs. She wasn't tired. Instead of going into her room, she went into her brother's old room and flipped on the light switch. The electricity hummed in protest but eventually blinked on.

Everything was the same from the last time he'd been home. That had been at her parent's funeral. She'd made his bed after he'd left and left the comforter on. It had been winter when the funeral was held. The weather was warm now, but she still hadn't pulled off the familiar blanket.

She went to the shelves on the far side of the room and thumbed through his record collection. Reece preferred vinyl to CDs or digital files. He said he liked the scratch of the needle.

Reegan found what she was looking for and brought the record downstairs into the living room. She flicked the switch to the old turntable. The red ON light blinked a couple of times before going solid. Reegan placed the record on the B side with the instrumentals.

The old song was Reece's favorite. It was a duet. Her brother had a strong baritone to her soprano. They'd always sing this song together.

After the melodic intro came the high part. Reegan sang the words of the familiar tune. She went mute when the tune changed and made way for the lower notes that required a baritone's pitch. It was the silence that brought the tears to her eyes.

The lack of the strong familiar voice left Reegan feeling desolate. She searched her heart, looking for any signs that her brother was no longer of this earth. All she felt was alone.

Could she be wrong? Could Reece be gone? Could she just be in denial?

When the tune changed and came back around to her part, Reegan opened her eyes. She was facing the front window. Outside, just beyond the bushes, she saw something moving.

It was a big something. Like a man. There were old men and young boys on her street. No grown men. Only Reece.

Reece?

Could that be him?

Reegan raced to the door. She flung it wide open. Only to sag against the frame with disappointment when recognition dawned.

"I'm so sorry," Corporal Lucas said. "I didn't mean to scare you."

He held his hands up, as though trying to make himself look small and unassuming. It didn't work. He was the biggest man she'd ever met in her life.

His face shifted from placation to alarm. He lifted his head, his entire body going on alert. His nose went up into the air, and he inhaled deeply.

"Something's burning."

CHAPTER ELEVEN

Brandon hadn't meant to be a stalker. He'd meant to come and apologize for his behavior earlier that day. He'd said he was sorry before turning and hightailing out of the garden, but he couldn't sit still for the rest of the day. The heat of his memories from the ambush, the cold lick down his spine of the shame, the numbness of the helplessness he felt knocked into him like a missile.

He couldn't shake it. He had to see her. Not just to apologize, but also to hear her voice again. It was the only salve that had worked.

Not keeping silent about it. Not talking to one of the VA doctors or the ranch doctor. Not listening to gospel music of the exact same song she'd sang on streaming sites. None of it.

The only thing he wanted, the only thing he craved was the sound of Reegan's voice. When he thought of her, the tension throughout his body eased up. When he showed up outside her house an hour ago, just the sight of her through the open curtains loosened the grip of the stressors inside him.

He needed to apologize again for the tone he'd taken with her. But he also just wanted to be near her, to be there for her. That scene back on the ranch, all those questions she fired at him, he knew she was going through the bargaining stage. Pretty soon, she'd be at acceptance, but not before grief sank its claws in her and rung tears from her eyes.

Brandon had an insatiable need to be there when it happened.

He'd watched through the window like a stalker as she mingled with her neighbors and friends. All throughout the room people were crying or teary-eyed. Everyone except Reegan. She kept that stiff upper lip, much like her brother wore each day Brandon had known the man.

Though he wanted to be with her, the idea of wading through the crowd of people made him itch. Luckily, the house began to empty soon after he arrived, leaving her alone. Before he could take the steps to knock on the door, she'd started to sing.

He'd morphed fully into a creepy stalker, and standing outside her window. Peering inside and peeping in as she sang a haunting tune.

And then, as though she sensed him, she opened her eyes and looked right at him. Brandon felt like a bug on the wall. He held still, certain that if he didn't move, she couldn't see him. But she had, and now she was standing in the doorway.

Her curvy form filled the rectangular doorway. Her red hair flaming behind her, her blue eyes open wide with a look between fear and hope.

"Reece?"

She mouthed the name, her voice barely above a whisper. But Brandon heard it. What came out loud and clear was the disappointment when she realized that he wasn't her brother.

"I'm sorry," Brandon said coming closer. "I didn't mean to scare you. I just ..."

The night wind rushed him from the side. It brought a familiar smell. The noxious smell of burning gas. The foul smell of charred vegetation. The fetid odor of hot metal.

"Something's burning."

He didn't hesitate. He didn't wait to be invited in. He dashed past Reegan and into the house.

He saw the first spark coming from behind the oven door. The pop, crack, and fizzling sounds of electricity forced him to take a step back. When he did, he bumped into the warm flesh of Reegan.

He might have had time to put out the impending fire. He would never know. His first reaction, his only reaction, was to protect Reegan. He pulled her into his arms, putting his body between her and the short-circuiting appliance.

Brandon had heard men and women in the service talk about their partners back home as their other halves. Reegan Cartwright fit perfectly into his chest like they'd been one whole person who had been carved apart at birth. Now that she was in his arms, nothing would tear them apart.

Except maybe the encroaching flames that were licking their way out of the oven.

He picked her up in his arms and raced through the house. They were over the threshold of the front door when the loud bang sounded. The flames worked fast, eating through the kitchen and reaching for the living room.

Whipping out his phone, Brandon dialed 911. After the call disconnected, he felt the flames growing stronger as they made their way into the front of the house. Brandon expected Reegan to fight to get back, to try and get inside and save her belongings. But she hadn't struggled. There was no fight in her as she watched the flames eat at her house.

By now, the neighbors were coming out of the woodwork. People he was sure she'd known her whole life came up to her. Instead of accepting their comfort, Reegan stayed inside Brandon's arms. She rested the side of her head against his chest. The tears he'd expected the first day he met her finally streamed down her face. Her arms were around him, her nails digging into his back.

The firetrucks had arrived as the flames became visible in the second story windows. Brandon cradled Reegan as they sprayed the blaze. By the time the fire was under control, and only the moonlight lit up the night, the downstairs of the home was charred.

All around her, people made offers of sheltering Reegan in their homes. She didn't pay any of them any mind. She clung to Brandon, wordlessly. The only sound was her even breathing as her chest heaved, pushing out silent tears from the corners of her eyes.

He knew she was exhausted. Emotionally as well as physically. He held all her weight. He knew if he let her go, she would dissolve into a puddle. The last thing he wanted was for her to be out of his arms, out of his sight, out of his care.

"Come back to the ranch," Brandon whispered in her ear.

For the first time since she'd stood on her doorstep looking down at him in disappointment, Reegan blinked. Her head tilted back as she looked up at him. There was only a small light in her large blue eyes. It took her a moment to focus, and then she nodded.

Brandon had borrowed one of the ranch's trucks to make the drive back into town. He tucked Reegan into the passenger seat and strapped her in. When he climbed into the driver's seat, he wondered if he should reach for her hand. In the end, she curled away from him and rested her head against the passenger window.

Guilt hit him on the drive. It ratcheted up as the tires ate up the asphalt to lead them back to the ranch. All the while, Reegan was silent. It all must be hitting her now. Her brother's death as well as the loss of her home.

All Brandon wanted to do was give her cover and shelter as she felt the effects of her losses. He knew better than to offer her any words. For now, all he could give her was silence.

When he pulled up on the ranch, he parked the truck and came around to her side. After opening the door, he unbuckled her from the safety belt. She practically fell into his arms.

Bringing her into his borrowed home, he lay her down in the bed he'd vacated earlier that night. It was the only one made up. He'd find sheets and take the smaller room across the hall.

Pulling the sheets down now, Brandon placed Reegan's small body inside. She made no move to undress, so he pulled off her shoes and then her socks. It was so intimate to see her pink toes on the white cotton bedsheets.

He felt he should look away. Instead, Brandon tucked her under the covers. He prepared to leave her there to her thoughts when she reached for his hand. Her callused fingers felt fragile on his large palm.

"They're all gone," she whispered, her voice cracking as though it were dry from days in the desert.

Brandon didn't answer. He pulled up a chair from the side of the room. He kept her hand in his and settled down by her side for the night.

It wasn't like he'd get any sleep. He was certain he'd never sleep again. He'd taken not only her brother from her, but now he was responsible for her losing her home.

CHAPTER TWELVE

Reegan woke up in an unfamiliar bed. Unfamiliar sheets. Unfamiliar ceiling fan. Unfamiliar curtains. Unfamiliar view.

The funny thing was she didn't feel out of place. She also didn't feel alone. Somehow, the unfamiliar place felt like home.

She looked to her right and saw why. Corporal Brandon Lucas was fast asleep in a chair beside the unfamiliar bed she was in. His big body in the small chair looked very uncomfortable.

Realization hit her square in her chest. She was in Brandon's bed. He'd brought her here last night after …

Reegan closed her eyes. She wasn't ready to face that reality. As long as she kept her eyes shut, as long as she kept the sun out, she didn't have to remember what had happened.

"I'm sorry."

His deep voice penetrated the barrier she'd erected. The walls came crumbling down around her. She felt the heat of his gaze on her face. Reegan opened her eyes, and her heart nearly broke.

There were dark circles under Brandon's eyes. The whites of his eyes were red, not the way they would be from crying. The way they would be if he hadn't gotten any sleep.

"You don't sleep well?" she said.

He didn't answer. Instead, he took a deep inhale, his jaw tightening.

He rearranged his large form in the small chair. Had he been there all night? Without asking, Reegan knew that he had.

"Nightmares?" she asked.

Now he looked away. Reegan moved the sheet from her body. She pressed her bare feet to the cold floor only to recoil and tuck them back underneath herself. Brandon inhaled sharply, as though he'd felt the attack of the cold as well.

"Reece has them too," she said. "The nightmares."

Brandon's gaze came back to hers. She knew without him saying that he had fixated on the present tense she used when she spoke about her brother. Her home and everything she owned might be gone, but she was even more certain now that Reece wasn't.

She turned to face the dawning sun. Clouds moved lazily in the early morning sky. She marveled that the scene was so peaceful after the destruction she'd witnessed the other night.

She felt the loss of her home. The place she'd felt the safest all her life. The only place she'd known as home all her life.

She felt the loss of her things. She only had the clothes on her back, and they weren't her favorite. They still had the stains from when she'd been gardening the day before.

More importantly, she'd lost all her journals, her favorite books, her CD collection, irreplaceable picture albums of her family. All gone.

The loss hurt. But one thing remained true. She still felt in her soul that her brother's heart was beating.

That's why she wouldn't dissolve into a puddle of nothingness. She'd lost everything. But she hadn't lost it all.

Reece was still out there.

She turned back to Brandon. He leaned forward, watching her intently, as though he feared she might fall apart at any second. "Why did you say you were sorry?"

He gulped, the bob of his Adam's apple loosened the steel of his jaw. "The fire was my fault."

Reegan turned her body fully to him. She placed her feet on the floor, ignoring the shock of cold that her toes met. "What are you talking about?"

"If I hadn't been acting like a peeping Tom, you wouldn't have been distracted. You wouldn't have burned the food."

The food? And then she remembered; Mrs. Russo's casserole. "That casserole had been in the oven for at least thirty minutes before the fire happened. It wasn't your fault."

Brandon looked doubtful. In fact, he looked as though a ton of guilt were on his shoulders. Not just the fire that had stolen her home from her.

His shoulders looked rock hard as he sat straight. Reegan wanted to knead the worry out of him. How was it she'd lost everything, and all she wanted to do was comfort this man?

Before she could make a move to offer him solace, the doorbell rang. His body went on full alert. His gaze softened when he turned back to her.

"You don't have to see anyone if you don't want to," he said.

She didn't want to. All she wanted to do was sit quietly with him. She had to admit that a large part of her calm at this moment was due to the fact that Corporal Brandon Lucas made her feel safe.

"I'll get rid of them."

When he stepped out of the room, Reegan pulled her socks on but left her shoes off. She looked around the bedroom. She knew the layout of the row houses having been inside a few of them for dinner with the permanent residents of the ranch.

She knew each of the row houses sported two bedrooms. This room looked lived in but only sparsely. She could tell Brandon had claimed it.

His large, khaki, unpacked duffle bag was in the corner. There was a picture on the bed stand. It was of a younger Brandon and an older man and woman she had to assume were his parents. She saw his uniform hanging in the closet. His polished boots below them. He'd been in a plain shirt and jeans that morning. It was what he'd been wearing last night as well.

Reegan's head lifted when she heard raised voices from the main room. She opened the bedroom door and stepped out.

Brandon stood in the front doorway, his arms crossed like he was a great protector. He turned when he saw her. His look was fierce. Reegan pitied whoever was on the other side of the door.

Coming farther into the room, she recognized who stood on the porch. It was Fire Marshal Porter.

Seeing his orange jacket made all the memories of last night come crashing back to her. The fire. Her home in flames. The grim look on Mr. Porter's face was confirmation; she had nothing to go back to.

"It's all gone?" she asked.

Mr. Porter nodded. She'd expected it. She waited for the impact to hit her in her chest. She waited for her legs to give out. She waited for the tears to sting her eyes.

None of that happened. Losing her parents had been far worse. Learning Reece was missing was in second place. The house, it hurt, but at least she could replace some of what was lost there.

"It's just stuff," she said. "I know my parents took out insurance. It will be enough to rebuild the house and replace some of the things that have been lost."

"That's the problem I was explaining to Corporal Lucas," said the fire marshal.

"What problem?" asked Reegan. She looked from Mr. Porter to Brandon.

Brandon was standing in front of her, facing off against the fire marshal as though ready to fight. But that was ridiculous. Nathan Porter was in his fifties. It would be no contest. And what reason would Brandon have to be angry at the man?

"The house is in your brother's name," said Mr. Porter.

Reegan nodded. Reece had gotten the house. She had gotten cash. That was the way it was set up. She just wished she'd put the money into the wiring instead of waiting for her brother to get home for a DIY project. Then she wouldn't be in this mess.

"The problem is that Reece is declared missing and not dead. There's no death certificate. Without the certificate, the insurance company won't play ball. They won't give you the money to rebuild."

CHAPTER THIRTEEN

"I guess I'll have to move to California with my aunt."

Brandon's head shot up at Reegan's words. He sat next to her on the couch in the small living room. Her hand was in his. He wasn't sure when that had happened, but he did nothing to discourage her strong hold on him.

The fire marshal had long gone, but the news he'd delivered still singed the air. Reegan's house would be declared a total loss. The fire had destroyed the kitchen and severely damaged the living room. The integrity of the upstairs was in question, not to mention that the wiring had proven itself a total fire hazard.

Now, not only had Reegan lost everyone in her immediate family, she'd lost her home too. It was good that there was still an extended family that she could turn to. Brandon just didn't understand why that family had to be so far away as California?

"You'll stay with us," said Beth.

Elsbeth Barrett and her father sat opposite them. Both Barretts eyed Reegan and Brandon's joined hands. Brandon didn't make a move to let Reegan go. His grip loosened only slightly with Beth's offer.

Brandon wanted Reegan to stay right where she was so he could keep an eye on her. Or hold her hand if necessary. Or wrap her up in his arms when she grew weary.

He knew where the Barretts lived. Their house was in town and not at the edge of the country. If Reegan stayed with the pastor and his daughter, he could at least see her from time to time. Or every day.

Reegan shook her head. "You're getting married soon."

Beth blushed and looked away. Brandon had known a number of soon-to-be brides. He couldn't remember one not beaming with anticipation anytime their impending nuptials were brought up.

"And besides," Reegan continued, seemingly oblivious to her friend's discomfort, "I can't rain on Pastor Barrett's empty nest dreams."

The older man smiled good-naturedly. "Don't talk such nonsense. You've always been a second daughter to me. You're family, and you're welcome to stay as long as you like."

But Reegan shook her head again, shutting her eyes. "If I did, I'd have to … see it."

She didn't need to clarify what she didn't want to see. When she opened her eyes, she smiled. The smile didn't reach her eyes.

She turned her body to Brandon and squeezed his hand. There was a question in her gaze. Whatever her query was, she was uncertain of the ask. She needn't be. Whatever she wanted Brandon would do whatever it took to give it to her.

"Can I stay here for a while longer?" she asked.

Gasps escaped both Barretts's mouths. Both the pastor and his daughter's gazes widened as though they spotted Beelzebub sitting on Brandon's left shoulder.

"In the spare bedroom of course," Reegan clarified. "Just until I figure things out."

This was far preferable to California. It was even better than her being in town at the Barretts. If she were in the next bedroom, he could watch over her constantly. He could hold her hand. He could hear her sing.

When he didn't answer, Reegan's face fell. "Unless … of course … you don't … I didn't mean …"

"You can stay as long as you like." Brandon blurted the words out.

Relief touched her blue eyes. Her hold on him relaxed, but he held onto her tighter. He wanted to tug her to him, but he felt certain that would only confirm the presence of a little imp on his shoulder for the others.

"But, Reegan, he's a stranger." The pastor's tone was gentle, but his stern gaze was firmly set on Brandon.

"He was on my brother's team in the service," said Reegan. "Reece trusted him. He put his life in Corporal Lucas's hands. I see no problem with me doing the same, even if only temporary. Besides, you both know the garden is my happy place. I need a little happy in my life after all I've been through this week."

Pastor Barrett looked as though he still wanted to argue the point. Brandon had the urge to ask them to leave. He didn't want Reegan to be challenged, especially if that challenge meant she'd leave his presence.

Luckily, it was Beth who spoke first. "If you think it's best for you?"

Reegan gave her friend a firm nod.

Beth nodded too. "Well, then, all right."

Beth rose and opened her arms to embrace Reegan. When Reegan stood, Brandon found he had trouble unlinking their entwined fingers. In the end, he did let go of her hand. She was staying with him.

"I'll stop by tomorrow," said Beth. "And don't worry, no one's expecting you at choir practice tonight."

"No," said Reegan. "I'll be there. More than anything, I need to sing."

"Okay, why don't you come into town with us."

"I can bring her," said Brandon. The words came out a bit too forceful. He couldn't help it. The idea of Reegan leaving his sight unsettled him.

Beth gave him another glance over beginning at his booted feet and ending at his hairline. Finally, she gave him one last nod. Then after a stern, sixty-second long gaze from Pastor Barrett that made Brandon feel like a naughty schoolboy, they were gone.

When the door closed behind the Barretts, Reegan slumped back down on the couch and into Brandon's side. He held her, resting his head atop hers. She'd held a brave front these last few days.

Through it all, the news of her brother, her house burning down, she only showed her vulnerability when she was alone with him. Brandon's chest swelled that she trusted him with her worries and woes.

"I'm sorry," she said. "I keep breaking down around you."

"I've got you," he assured her. "No one should have this much put on them."

"I'm sure there's a lesson in here somewhere. Otherwise, what's the point?"

There was no point. Bad things happened for no reason. Or simply because men wanted power.

This woman needed a protector. Brandon had spent his life in service. He was sure he was the man for the job.

"Maybe a change will do me good," Reegan said. "I should probably consider California."

He stiffened beside her. He had to struggle to keep his hold on her light and not tighten like a vise. "But your life is here."

He felt her nod her head against his chest. "This community is my family. But I should probably go and be with my actual blood. Aunt Prudence has been after me to come and visit for two years now, and I've just never found the time."

"A visit wouldn't be so bad." The words were forced from his mouth. Maybe he could make a road trip out of it, and he could drive her there?

"I thought I'd have a family of my own by now and would have been moved out of the house."

A terrible thought went through Brandon's mind. "You're not ... I mean, there's no one ... Are you dating anyone?"

Reegan tilted her head back and looked up at him. She looked so soft and small. He shifted her head so that it was in the nook between his shoulder cap and neck. He could look down at this sight for the rest of his life.

"I'm not interested in any man in town," she said. "I watched them all grow up. I remember when they ate boogers. How can I kiss someone who ate his own boogers?"

It was funny, but Brandon wasn't laughing. He was too focused on the implications of that statement. "You've never kissed anyone?"

Reegan's cheeks reddened. She didn't lift her head from his shoulder, but she did tilt her gaze down. "I didn't say that."

By the way she looked away from him, Brandon got the feeling she hadn't. What was wrong with the men in this town? How could they resist the taste of the sweetness of her lips? They all were cracked in the head if they preferred boogers to Reegan Cartwright.

But he had to put that aside. He didn't want her thinking about other men. He definitely didn't want her thinking of California.

"But you'd rather stay here if you could?" he said.

She lifted her gaze back to his, and his breath caught. She was, without a doubt, the most beautiful woman he'd ever seen in his life. He would do anything to keep her close to him.

"I would," she said. "I love it here. I've never had any desire to leave. I'd miss the blooms. I'd miss my friends. I'd miss the choir."

All of a sudden, her words made complete sense to him. He couldn't see any reason for leaving this place either? Especially if he saw the blooms while standing at her side. He'd happily mix with her friends. He definitely wanted to hear her sing every day for the rest of his life.

"I mean, I could sing anywhere. But I love singing in that church surrounded by the people I've known all my life. It's all I've ever wanted to do. I'm afraid I don't have any other ambitions except to sing there. Sing solos, sing in a group, sing to myself."

"So stay."

"I will."

Reegan shifted her body until her forehead fit under his chin. Brandon's hold tightened around her.

"I'll stay for a while," she said. "But if the paperwork with my brother doesn't get sorted, I can't afford my own place. All my spare money went into home repair."

"So, stay here," he said.

Brandon's heart raced inside his chest. He was certain she could feel it. The organ was pounding so hard he was sure it knocked against her skull.

Reegan lifted her head and looked up at him, a question in her raised brows.

"Stay here with me." Brandon heard his mouth speaking. He didn't try to shut up. He agreed with every impulsive word he spoke. "You know how the Purple Heart Ranch works. Married soldiers get a house for their families, and then they can stay forever."

Reegan pushed away from him and sat up tall. Her lips parted as she regarded him. Had she stopped breathing as she waited for his next words?

Brandon knew he'd stopped breathing as he waited for her to say something, anything. But she just stared. And so he allowed what was in his heart to fill the silence.

"If we got married, you could have a home in your name. You'd be near the garden. You'd be near all of your friends. You wouldn't have to work a day in your life. And you could sing all you want."

Now that the words were out, he couldn't take them back. And the truth was, he didn't want to.

CHAPTER FOURTEEN

eegan let the dark, rich soil sift through her fingers. Once it was all gathered in a pile, she patted the mound to secure the tall plant. Instead of climbing, the thin part at the top of the large stalk drooped.

Reaching for a stick and some thin rope, Reegan bound the wilting vine to the sturdy stick to help keep it straight as it grew. Now that it could reach the sun's rays, the plant would definitely grow and thrive.

She sat back and admired her handy work. Looking down at the plant, she felt a kindred spirit. Reegan had been planted in fertile soil. She'd been nurtured by her environment. But she'd never thrived, not truly. In the last few days, she'd been dealt tragedy after tragedy. She hadn't wilted because there was a strong post at her side.

Stay here with me.

Her heart lurched the moment the words had left his mouth. Reegan wanted to stay by Brandon's side forever. Unlike what Pastor Barrett had said, Brandon Lucas was not a stranger. Reegan felt she knew him better than any man of her entire acquaintance. Except, of course, for her brother.

Reegan had never had that type of reaction with any other man. Heck, she'd never truly kissed another man. Well, if she wanted to get technical, there had been Kenny Pratt, but he hadn't counted. Why? Because he'd missed her lips and tongued her nose; an unhappy event neither of them ever brought up again. It was also what solidified Reegan's belief that the boys of this town preferred boogers.

There had never been a man like Brandon Lucas in this town or in her life. Even now, she wanted to close her fingers around his. She wanted to rest her head against the strong beat of his heart. She wanted to stay inside the safety of his arms. The world could crash and burn while she was with him, and it wouldn't matter. It would hurt, but she'd be safe in his arms.

"How are you holding up?"

Reegan looked up to see Maggie Banks waddling up to her. The woman was near the second trimester of her pregnancy, and she looked like she was having twins. Two dogs trailed at her feet, her ever watchful army. Reegan was surprised she didn't see Dylan, Maggie's overprotective husband, in his wife's wake. But she supposed the dogs were protection enough.

"It's a bit of a lot," Reegan said in answer to Maggie's question.

The Irish Terrier, Spin, pulled up to a stop next to Reegan. The dog's hind legs hung limp in the wheelchair apparatus that Maggie had fashioned for him. Now, instead of being disabled, the dog was a holy terror. But his bright eyes and enthusiastic sniffs made everyone who came in contact with him fall instantly in love.

Spin rested his head on Reegan's lap and looked up at her with those doleful eyes. Reegan scratched the little dog's head and heard him sigh in utter contentment.

Maggie folded herself down into a crossed legged position in the dirt. Reegan worried the woman might not be able to make it back up again. But Sugar, her Golden Retriever, stayed at her side. Once his mistress was seated, the large dog leaned into her back as though he were propping her up.

"You've been through more in the past week than anyone should have to manage in a lifetime," Maggie said.

Reegan took a deep breath, inhaling the crisp afternoon air. "I'm waiting for the lesson of it all."

Because there had to be a lesson, a silver lining. She knew her parents were in heaven and safe with God. She still wasn't convinced that her brother had met his glory. When her house had burned down, her faith had been shaken.

Reegan had been stripped of everything. Her family. Her possessions. Her belongings. But she had to believe it was all for a reason.

"You know you can stay here as long as you need," said Maggie. "We have plenty of room in our place."

"Brandon—Corporal Lucas—asked me to stay forever."

Maggie's brows rose. But not in alarm that a stranger had proposed a marriage of convenience to her. The soldier's wife's eyes shone bright with approval.

Reegan knew the story of Maggie and Dylan. Maggie had been a regular at the church since she was a girl. Though she'd never come with parents, always on her own. The veterinarian had had a tough beginning as a foster child, but she never lost faith. When Maggie had been kicked out of her apartment for having too many dogs, she'd walked right into a miracle. The miracle happened on this ranch where she met Dylan. They'd agreed to a marriage of convenience so he could stay on the ranch. In exchange, she could keep her dogs here and out of a pound where the disabled brood would've surely met their maker. In the course of events, after the wedding, the two fell madly in love.

That story had repeated four more times with the other soldiers who lived here on the Purple Heart Ranch. And it looked like the tradition would continue with Reegan and Brandon.

"Brandon asked me to marry him. You know, like you all did for the zoning."

The soldiers had thought the zoning regulations were a curse. But the rules had turned out to be a blessing in disguise as they'd each found the woman they'd spend the rest of their lives with. Maybe the same rules would now work in Reegan's favor?

"Oh, honey," Maggie beamed at her. But she shook her head at the same time, which confused Reegan. Those two words were cautionary, but she said them with joy. "They all say it's for the zoning; a marriage of convenience. It never is. It always winds up turning into lasting love."

Reegan's heart skipped at that thought. Her mouth became parched under the cloudy sky. Her fingertips itched as they sank into the rich soil.

"Is that what you want?" asked Maggie. "Do you have feelings for Corporal Lucas?"

"I barely know him."

Yet she'd spent last night in his bed with him by her side. In a chair. But it was still more intimate than she'd ever been with a man. And there was the way he'd held her that morning before he'd made his proposal. Reegan was certain she could stay in Brandon Lucas's arms forever.

"Eva and I barely knew Dylan and Fran before we said *I do*. And look at us."

That was true. It was all shaping up to be another purple-hearted love story. Except for one difference.

"Brandon feels guilty about what happened to Reece," Reegan admitted. "He even mentioned that he thinks the fire was partly his fault."

"Guilt is a powerful motivator," Maggie agreed. "But not enough to force a man into marriage. I've seen him looking at you these past few days. Especially that first day when you were singing in church. He looked like he'd found heaven."

Reegan went breathless. A light wind sent a shiver over her skin raising goosebumps. Maggie reached out her hand, and Reegan took it, needing something to hold onto.

"Just be sure it's what you want," said Maggie.

Was it what she wanted? Reegan knew she wanted to sing. She knew she wanted to stay in her home town. She knew she wanted to be held in Brandon's arms. With this arrangement, she could spend forever doing all those things.

She had her answer.

CHAPTER FIFTEEN

The tap-tap-tapping sound was incessant, like the clatter of rounds firing and shell casings falling to the ground. Brandon couldn't stop his restless legs from moving. His entire body felt hot and cold at the same time. He needed somewhere for the energy to go.

He took a deep breath, closing his eyes. He knew before his lashes touched the tops of his cheeks that the move was a mistake. Heat flared behind his lids. Tingling started in his palms. The muscles in his chest tightened.

He saw smoke in his mind's eye. But he didn't see brown and orange hues of the desert. He saw the lush green and sturdy red brick of suburban America. The fire raged, and the brick of the house melted as he stood gaping in the street. Instead of a red-haired Reece, he saw the flames of Reegan's long tresses as she looked up at her home in horror.

Her gaze went wide as the explosion rocked the foundation of her home. The blast knocked her off her feet. Before Brandon could move, smoke sank low to the ground and engulfed her body. He tried to get to her, but his body wouldn't move. He was standing instead of lying face down, but it didn't matter. His feet wouldn't move. They were mired in something dark, thick, and black as night.

It was guilt.

Brandon's stomach churned. His breathing came in shallow pants until he roared. Brandon fought with everything in him, but the shame had a vise on him. As his internal battle raged, Reegan was swallowed whole by the gray cloud.

"Corporal Lucas?"

Brandon's eyes slammed open to find Dr. Patel standing a few feet away. Having dealt with PTSD issues, it was clear that the man knew to keep his distance until he was sure the way was safe. Brandon was no threat to anyone other than himself.

"I take it sleep is still eluding you?" The man took slow steps until he came behind his desk. His brown features were smooth and placid as he spoke. He leaned back in his chair, his hands folded on the top of his blank notepad.

Brandon sighed, trying to shake off the daydream. His head felt light after he pushed out the last of his heavy breaths. The tightening in his chest didn't lighten. But his leg tapping slowed a bit.

"When's the last time you slept?" Dr. Patel picked up his fountain pen. His scribbles filled the spaces were his taps had slowed.

Brandon thought back to the last time he'd slept longer than a few minutes. It had been the first night he was there. Right after hearing Reegan sing at church. He'd awakened feeling a peace he hadn't known in months. Just the thought of it made his toe-tapping slow down even more, but he hadn't come to a complete stop.

"It's been a couple of days," Brandon admitted.

Dr. Patel pulled his notepad onto his lap, blocking Brandon's view of his notes. "That would've been your first night here?"

Brandon nodded.

"After you came from the church?"

Brandon's gaze narrowed at the man. He watched as the pen moved across the paper, but there were no scritch scratch noises filling the silent beats between his foot tapping any longer.

"Reegan was lucky you were in the neighborhood the other night," Patel continued.

"Maybe. Maybe not."

Dr. Patel looked up. The pen went still as he regarded Brandon.

"Maybe I distracted her, and that's why the fire happened."

Dr. Patel sat the pen down on the desk. And then the notepad. As Brandon had suspected, there were hardly any marks on the lined paper.

Brandon had the sudden urge to fill that blank sheet of paper with his truth. And so he opened his mouth, and the guilt that had been clawing at him spilled out. "First, I took her brother from her, and now, I've taken her home from her."

Dr. Patel was silent for a long moment. He didn't reach for the pen and paper. He didn't downplay or deny Brandon's claims.

After another long, silent moment, Brandon frowned. Why wasn't the shrink telling him he wasn't at fault? Wasn't that his job? To assuage him of his guilt?

"I read the fire marshal's report," Dr. Patel finally said. "The report said the fire was due to faulty wires."

Brandon chewed at the inside of his lip. The tightness in his chest moved up to his throat, closing off any words.

"I also read the military report on Private Cartwright's incident." Dr. Patel leaned forward, folding his forearms over the pad on the desk. The pen rolled off to the side. "You both followed protocol."

"I hesitated."

Dr. Patel steepled his fingers and rested his chin. His gaze was like iron as it held Brandon's. "Many a man has. Decisions are rarely black and white. There will always be shades of gray. It's the strong man that realizes that in a world of gradations, all he can do is what is right."

Brandon took a deep breath. He'd heard a Monday morning quarterbacking speech such as that before. It didn't change the fact that he couldn't stop wishing he'd made different decisions. If he hadn't let Cartwright go down and investigate, the man would still be alive. If he hadn't startled Reegan, she wouldn't have come to the front door, and her house wouldn't have burned down.

Dr. Patel shook his head slowly, as though he could hear Brandon's thoughts. "Until you let go of your guilt, you won't find peace or rest. That's why I wanted you to tend to something else. To work in the gardens, put the seeds in the soil, clear their paths, and watch the plants grow. But I see you found something else in the garden. News has spread of your proposal."

Brandon sat back in his chair, angling his body away from the doctor. Dylan and the others had joked that the man might be psychic. Brandon had never believed in unseen powers and reading people's minds, but now he wasn't so sure. "How did you find out?"

"Maggie."

So, it wasn't a psychic connection, just a gossiping pregnant woman. Reegan must have told her. Brandon had watched Maggie Banks waddling around the ranch. But apparently, she moved fast when she had a juicy tidbit to share.

"Pastor Barrett came to me," said Dr. Patel. "We are both pastors in the church. He wanted to know what kind of man you were."

"What did you tell him?" Suddenly Brandon's limbs and organs were still and silent. He cared very much what the two pastors thought of him.

Dr. Patel took a deep breath and picked up his pen again. "I told him that I'm not entirely sure your decision-making isn't impaired."

But hadn't he just said Brandon was blameless? That he was a strong man and shades of gray and ... what else had he said? Brandon couldn't remember the words from just a moment ago.

"You understand that lack of sleep leads to a myriad of impairments, one amongst them is poor impulse control and poor judgment?"

Brandon sat up stiff. "That had nothing to do with my relationship with Reegan. Proposing to her was a purely logical decision. She needs a home and a provider. She needs to be around those that care about her and not go to California. I can give those things to her if I marry her."

A broad smile spread across the doctor's face. He pushed the pen and the notepad off to the side of the desk. Brandon felt as though he'd passed some test he wasn't aware of taking.

"She would have a home," said Dr. Patel. "She'd also have a husband looking after her, tending to her. And she would look after and tend to you."

"Are you trying to say Reegan is my cure?"

Patel shrugged. But he did it with a smug smile. "I'm old fashioned, biblically old fashioned. Of faith, hope, and love; love is the greatest of the three. That's in Corinthians."

Brandon wasn't sure he had any of those three. He wasn't in love with Reegan. He didn't think?

But the thought of Reegan as his wife sent a shock of peace all through him. She would be his to provide for. His to protect. His to hold and keep safe. He wanted it more than a good night's sleep.

Maybe taking care of Reece's sister would assuage his guilt. Surely, that was more noble and useful than plucking weeds or talking about his feelings. Brandon was a man of action, a man who'd pledged his life to service and protection. More than anything, he wanted to serve and protect Reegan Cartwright. Not only because he loved looking at her, not only because he loved listening to her sing, but because he simply loved being around her.

Marriage had never been his plan. He'd had every intention of re-enlisting, of going back into service, and fighting for his country. But what if he found something else to fight for? What if he could stay on home turf and protect someone?

"You're a soldier to your core," Patel was saying, making Brandon think again about the man's psychic ability. "It's a different battle here. You have to decide what you're fighting for. And who."

CHAPTER SIXTEEN

"*A*ren't you going to stay?"

Reegan watched Brandon hesitate at her words. Oh, no. Had her voice been too needy? Was she being clingy?

They'd driven with Cassie and Xavier into town. The plan was for Brandon and Reegan to drive back in her truck which someone had brought from her house and to the church. So, it was entirely sensible that she ask him that question. He was her ride. She'd need to know where he was so they could ride back together.

Unless he hadn't planned to ride back with her. What if he'd planned to stay in town, see some of the nightlife? He was a soldier just off deployment. He'd been away for over a year. And even though he'd asked for her hand, he wasn't about to get his kicks with her.

Reegan was a modern woman but not that modern. She was considering marrying this man. She wasn't considering hopping into bed with him.

And maybe that's why he was thinking about heading out to sample some of the town's nightlife.

"You don't mind?" Brandon asked.

Just like that, all the tension left her shoulders. Gazing up into Brandon's eyes, she saw an eagerness there. He wanted to stay, but he was unsure if he was welcome.

"Of course not. I'd like it very much if you did. I want you to hear."

He smiled at her. Just a lift of the right corner of his mouth. But his eyes sparkled as he did so.

Reegan was lost. Her knees felt weak. Her heart fluttered like the butterflies flitting around the flowers she tended in the garden.

"I like hearing you sing," he said. "I love the sound of your voice."

"Oh? Well, that's good. Because I love to sing. I sing a lot."

"You won't hear any complaints out of me."

"Good."

Somehow, they were standing only an inch apart. Somehow, his fingers brushed her forearm. Somehow, his gaze was fastened to her lips. Reegan wasn't sure if she wanted to sing for him or pull him in for a kiss?

"I'm so sorry for your loss."

At the sound of the feminine voice, Brandon pulled away from her. His face, so open a second before, shuttered like blinds being closed on a sunny day. Reegan turned to find Dakota Harris. The petite alto reached out her arms and folded Reegan inside.

For a moment, Reegan wasn't sure what was happening. And then she remembered. Reece. He was still missing, and everyone else thought him dead.

"We've taken up a donation for you," said Dakota. "Clothes and shoes and gift cards so you can replace other things."

Right. Her house had burned down. Reegan knew she should feel numb and devastated due to her losses. But she didn't. She felt blessed. She'd lost all her belongings, but her community was showering her with both material things and love.

"Thank you, Dakota," was all Reegan could manage.

Her brother was still MIA, but every day she didn't get a call that the military had found his body, her hope and faith remained intact.

"It's awful that the insurance company won't hand you the check," said Noah Harris, one of the baritones in the choir. The man's gray mustache touched the bottom of his nose, causing him to wrinkle it.

Reegan wasn't complaining. She'd take not getting a check if there was a possibility that her brother was alive. Reece was strong. He was stubborn. She knew in her heart, that if he was able to, he'd come through and find a way home.

Now she had Brandon, a man who wanted to protect her, and provide for her, and hear her sing. In truth, she hadn't lost anything. Her cup runneth over.

Brandon had taken a seat in the back of the room, but Reegan felt his gaze on her from the moment she left him. His face was no longer open as it had been when they were standing close. It remained closed, but not his eyes. His eyes were filled with admiration as he watched her. The butterflies in her heart were working overtime.

Could it be possible that she was coming to have feelings for this man? She didn't need to question. She knew it was true.

No one had ever given her butterflies. No one had ever made her feel warm and safe. No one had ever looked at her as though she were both special and desirable. Because that was desire in Corporal Brandon Lucas's gaze. She wasn't so innocent that she didn't know what a man's hunger looked like.

As rehearsal began, Reegan's voice sailed from somewhere in the depths of her soul. Her every note was pitch perfect. Her voice lifted above everyone else's until all eyes were on her and all other voices went mute.

Gone was the cold and emptiness that had robbed her of her voice a few days ago. Gone was the heaviness on her shoulders and the hollow feeling in her heart. Reegan felt full. The feelings spilled out of her heart and drifted over her tongue.

All the while, she held Brandon's gaze. He watched her as though he were in rapture. At one point, his eyes closed as though he were in ecstasy… and they didn't open again until practice was over.

One by one, the other choristers filed out until it was just Reegan and Brandon left alone in the room. She came to him on quiet feet. She sat down next to him, the wood of the pew creaking as she did so. But still, he didn't stir.

She wasn't sure what to do. She'd never had to awaken any man besides her brother. She tried calling his name quietly. But still, he dozed.

She laid a hand on his forearm. His skin was warm to the touch. The tiny hairs she found there tickled her fingertips.

Then her hand was snatched away from his arm. Her fingers wrenched. Brandon looked at her wild-eyed.

It took him a second before recognition dawned. And then his dark eyes filled with horror. His cheeks went beet red, and he groaned.

"Sorry," he said gruffly. "I wouldn't have hurt you."

"I don't doubt it."

She had been startled. But not frightened. She knew better than to come upon a soldier unaware. Her brother had warned her. But just as she felt no fear from Reece, she felt none from Brandon.

"Reegan, you can't … you can't …" There was so much shame, and guilt digging into the features of his face, making grooves and leaving frown marks.

"I'm sorry," she said. "I know better. You just looked so peaceful."

"I'm not." His gaze darkened. "There's a war raging in my mind."

"You have PTSD?"

The muscles in his neck worked. "It's not severe, like some others. But when I close my eyes, I see …"

He was silent for so long. Reegan ached to reach out to him, to take him into her arms. And so she did.

She wrapped her arms around him and held him tight. He was stiff at first, but then he relaxed in her hold. His own grip became a vise around her.

"Listen, Reegan," he said into her hair. "About that thing I asked you—"

"That thing? You mean to marry you?"

"Yes."

She felt his breath at the cone of her ear. The single word was like a match. Her ear was the fire. The flame tunneled through her entire body. But then, it was doused by a single doubt.

"Are you taking it back?" she asked.

Reegan pulled back, but she didn't get far. Brandon's hold on her was absolute. She couldn't have gotten away if she'd tried. She did not try.

"No." His insistence was vehement.

Relief swam through her. The single word stoked the fire that had been lit a second ago. She felt the flames rising higher and higher.

"I just want you to know there's no rush," Brandon continued. "You've been through a lot. I don't want to add any pressure to you. The offer stands today, tomorrow, next week. However long you need. Whatever answer you want to give. I want you to know that I'll be here. For … whatever you need."

Reegan's muscles relaxed as the heat between them worked its way through her limbs. "Brandon, you should know that my answer is yes."

"It is?" His voice, so hot and sure a moment ago, came out on a dry croak.

She nodded. They were holding each other in a loose embrace. She would swear that she felt the heat of him rise a few degrees under her fingertips.

"Well." He cleared his throat. "Good." He swallowed. "Fine. I suppose I'll let Dr. Patel and Dylan know so arrangements can be made."

"Brandon?"

"Yes, Reegan?"

"You can kiss me. If you want."

"I could?"

"Well, we are going to be married. So …"

"That's true," he agreed. "Kissing is part of the ceremony. So, we should probably prepare for it."

"That's smart." Reegan pursed her lips, tugging them into her mouth to moisten them.

"They teach us to be prepared in the army."

"Sounds like good preparation."

Brandon took a deep breath. He leaned closer, pulling her body toward his. The bench squeaked again.

Reegan tilted her head up. She felt the warmth of Brandon's breath on her lower lip. It robbed her of the moisture she'd just licked into her lips. She didn't have time to prepare again. It was going to happen. Her first kiss. And not with some boy from around the block. It would be with a real man, a man who was going to be her husband very soon.

He was just an inch away now. Any second and she would—

The door to the room wrenched open. She saw Brandon's gaze slide away from his intended target, which had been her mouth, to scope out the intruder. Whomever he saw standing in the doorway must have been a threat because he pulled away from her.

Reegan looked up to find Pastor Barrett standing in the doorway. The older man glared at Brandon. Brandon stood to attention, leaving her alone on the bench. It looked like her first kiss would have to wait even longer.

CHAPTER SEVENTEEN

The sun was dipping down below the horizon when Brandon put Reegan's Ford F-150 in park outside their home.

Their home.

When had he switched over from thinking of the small row house as a borrowed home to claiming it as a homestead for him and his soon to be wife? Probably a second after she said yes to his proposal. He turned to her now, the last rays of the sun wrapped one of its tendrils around her cheek like a warm kiss.

Brandon wanted to take that trail. But he didn't. Not after the brief, but stern, chat they'd had with Pastor Barrett. It would seem that the senior pastor wasn't as enthused as Dr. Patel about their engagement.

The man had insisted on premarital counseling. Reegan had stepped forward. She'd agreed but on the condition that they receive their counseling from Pastor Patel and not the man who'd stepped into the role of father to her since her own father had passed away.

Pastor Barrett had clearly wanted to argue. But Reegan's jaw was set. Her chin was lifted high in defiance. Brandon hadn't necessarily wanted to spend hours each week under the man's disapproving glare, but he'd do it if that meant Reegan was the prize. Luckily, his bride to be was fierce, and the man of cloth acquiesced to her demands.

Now she sat comfortably in the passenger seat of her own vehicle, allowing Brandon to take the wheel. Something bloomed in Brandon's chest. He knew that he would protect this woman with everything in his heart. He would strive every day to ease her way in this life.

Reegan turned to him then, a small smile on her beautiful face. Brandon's breath caught. Though he still felt the claws of exhaustion right now, he pushed the feeling down. He didn't want to miss the opportunity to have his first taste of his soon to be wife. He'd been dreaming of brushing his lips against hers since … well, since the first night he'd met her, and he'd fallen into the first contented sleep in months.

He parted his lips to take a deep breath, only to exhale a long yawn.

"Oh, are you tired?" asked Reegan.

"No, I'm not." Yes, he was. He hadn't gotten much sleep at all last night.

"I'm surprised after that nap you took during rehearsal."

"I'm sorry about that." He wrinkled his nose.

"I know some of the songs are boring and—"

"No, it wasn't that. It was your voice."

Her brows shot up in surprise. "My voice is boring?"

"No, no." Brandon took another deep breath. This time it came out on a sigh and not a yawn. "Your voice is beautiful, peaceful."

He searched for the words to make her understand the numbness he felt throughout the day. The incessant buzzing that ran through his head like a radio tuned to a defunct station.

"I told you it feels like a war raging in my mind," he said. "The constant noise and images keep me on high alert, keeps my adrenaline up. But when I hear you sing, it all just stops. And because it stops, I can rest."

She nodded, understanding clear in her blue eyes. "We can go inside and lay down." The moment the words left her lips her cheeks flushed a crimson red. "I didn't mean like that. I mean—I know we're getting married. And it's a marriage of convenience—"

Putting his arms around her waist, he pulled her to him, effectively hushing her errant thoughts. But also putting a point on the statement he was making. "I need you to understand that this marriage is more than a convenience for me."

"It is?" Her voice was breathless. Her eyes kept dipping down to his mouth.

Brandon had to swallow when she wet her lower lip. He was fascinated with everything that came out of her mouth. Including the small pink of her tongue. She could probably start quacking like a duck, and he'd be rapt with attention.

"Reegan, I wanted to kiss you since the first time I heard you open your mouth."

"Oh." She looked down. "Because my voice puts you to sleep."

He chuckled. With his other hand, he tilted up her chin so that he could gaze directly in her eyes. His thumb brushed over her lower lip, giving himself a preview of what he was about to sample.

"Your voice gives me peace," he said. "Being with you gives me purpose. This marriage is more than about a home. Reegan, I want to give you the world."

"Oh," she sighed. Her warm breath brushed the tip of his thumb. "That's funny."

"Funny?"

"Maggie said it's never about the zoning."

It *was* about the zoning. Brandon wanted to mark Reegan Cartwright as his territory. In fact, that was exactly what he was going to do. There were no pastors around to stop him.

Her eyes fluttered closed as he leaned down. His bottom lip got the first taste as it brushed against her upper lip. Just that small hint was enough to knock him back on his heels. He wondered if he'd actually fallen down when he heard a knock behind him.

Brandon turned to look out the driver's side window. When he saw the man standing on two firm legs, he glared. Even the sight of his superior officer didn't wipe the murderous look off his face.

Chase raised his hands in surrender. Ortega, who stood behind him took a step back. Smart man.

"I need a word," said Chase through the closed window.

Unfortunately, Brandon could hear him clearly. "Right now? This actual second?"

"It's important." At least the man had the common decency to look apologetic.

Brandon let go of Reegan's chin and opened the car door.

Chase's eyes glanced over to Reegan. "In private."

Chase's smile was gentle toward Reegan. It was clear he didn't want to exclude her, but it must be army business that she couldn't know. Brandon circled around to the other side of the car and handed her out.

"I'll meet you inside," she said to Brandon.

She reached up on her tiptoes and kissed him on the cheek. It wasn't the first kiss he wanted with her, but it would hold him over until they were alone. He'd be sure and lock the front door behind him as soon as he was done with this private matter that couldn't wait.

"So, it looks like you're sticking around after all," said Ortega.

Brandon didn't respond. He watched Reegan as she entered the house. She'd turned the knob easily. The door hadn't been locked. No one seemed to lock doors here. Why would they with a ranch filled with veterans and soldiers? It was the safest place in the world, a place he would want to raise a family. A family he'd never truly even thought about. But now all he could think about was his marriage to Reegan and the life they'd have together.

"I got a phone call from the DOD about the mission," said Chase. "They found something."

That snapped Brandon back to attention. "Reece? They found his body?"

"Not exactly. They're not sure. An informant came through with credible information. They had his tags."

"So, they want to ransom the body?" Bile filled Brandon's throat at the thought.

"No," said Chase. "They said he's alive."

Brandon went entirely still. Everything in him went still as well. The constant buzzing sounds went on mute. The flickering images that flashed through his mind on a constant reel went dark.

"The information is still classified," Chase continued. "I sent Reegan away because I didn't want to get her hopes up, not after everything she's been through. Our orders are to wait until it's been confirmed."

CHAPTER EIGHTEEN

"*H*ave you set a date yet?"

Reegan sat two glasses of lemonade down on the kitchen table. Sarai wrapped perfectly manicured fingers around the tall glass and sipped carefully. Reegan knew the woman still struggled with an eating disorder and was very mindful of what she put in her body, which was why Reegan had gone light on the sugar.

Meanwhile, Eva DeMonti tossed her head back and tilted the yellow liquid until it was bottom's up. The co-ed then slammed the glass down for another, which Reegan happily refilled. Eva was constantly on the go between attending classes, wrangling her two tween siblings, and a husband who was also a busy body.

The two women had been walking by as Reegan had come out onto her front porch that morning. Reegan liked the sound of that; *her* front porch. She'd had an entire deck on her parents' house. And though it had been her home all her life, this small house that she'd only spent two nights in suddenly felt like her entire world.

Last night, Brandon had come inside. His features looked weary and tight. Reegan guessed that whatever private matter had been discussed between him and his fellow soldiers had weighed down on him. She decided not to press him on it. They were still getting to know each other, coming to trust one another with their secrets.

Brandon had walked her to his bedroom door. But after he'd

ushered her inside, he'd stayed at the threshold. He insisted she take the larger room while he went off to the spare. Before Reegan could protest, he'd shut the door and was gone.

He'd also been gone early this morning before she'd awakened. She knew he hadn't gotten much sleep. She'd heard him tossing and turning and then up and about all night.

Something was wrong. When she saw him later, she was determined to get him to open up to her. She knew he probably couldn't tell her the details of the matter if it was army related. Reece had often had a heavy expression on his features when he was home on leave. Despite her insistence, he explained he couldn't give her all the details on his missions.

Reegan didn't need the details now. She just needed Brandon to know that she was there for him. She'd be happy if he rested his head in her lap while she sang to him.

"I bet the wedding will probably happen as quickly as this weekend," Eva was saying.

That snapped Reegan back to the present. Married? This weekend?

But just as much as the thought stole her breath, it created an equal ache in her heart. She didn't want to wait. She wanted to be Mrs. Brandon Lucas as soon as she could. She wanted to be his wife, and she wanted to make this house a home.

There was nothing in this place that was hers, not even the clothing she wore. It was all gifts and donations. Neither was there much in there that belonged to Brandon. The two of them would get to paint this blank slate together and make it theirs.

Again, her heart filled with so much joy of how blessed she was even in the light of all the tragedy she'd experienced. There had been a reason for it all. There had been a masterplan that brought her to this moment.

From deciding to stay and take care of the house left to her brother, to getting up and singing in the choir at that particular service. She'd been there at the right moment when Brandon had shown up. True, he'd come to tell her that her brother was missing, but her faith was still firm that Reece was with her if not in body then in spirit.

It had all led her to this moment, standing in her very own kitchen, preparing to marry the man of her dreams. Her singing had pierced Brandon's heart. If she hadn't have raised her voice, Brandon wouldn't have heard her sing. And now they'd be spending the rest of their lives together.

Reegan doubted they'd spend forever in this house on the ranch. But it would be a good start for them. There were two bedrooms, one for them and one for their first child. She hadn't even had her first real kiss yet, and she was already thinking about, well, more.

"Brandon and Reegan don't have to rush like we did," Sarai was saying.

"None of us had to rush," said Eva. "They all had months before that zoning about this land being for families only kicked in. Every one of them married before time was up."

"She's right." Sarai turned back to Reegan. "You'll likely be hitched by the weekend."

That sounded perfectly fine to Reegan. The sooner, the better.

"And then you won't be alone when he gets deployed again," said Eva. "You'll have us."

It took Reegan running the woman's words in her head over and over again to comprehend. Each time she replayed Eva's words her blood grew colder and colder until the pitcher of lemonade slipped out of her hands.

"When he what?" Reegan breathed, her voice barely above a whisper.

Eva and Sarai looked to each other. Concern was etched on both their honey-golden skin.

"I …" Eva looked between Sarai and Reegan. "That's what he said his first night here."

"Brandon's deploying?" Reegan tested out the words. They tasted bitter on her tongue. "He's going back to war?"

"I could be wrong?" Eva's words rushed out. "That was his first day here before he met you."

"He met me before he came here."

"But he wasn't in love with you then," Sarai offered. "He is now."

The back door opened. All three women turned to the large figure standing in the doorway. Brandon's gaze swept over the scene at the kitchen table. His eyes were bright, hungry as they searched for her. But the light dimmed when he saw her. The two other women quickly excused themselves.

Reegan couldn't look at him. Instead, she grabbed a rag and began mopping up the spilled lemonade. As she squeezed the sugary beverage from the rag, she felt all the joy squeeze from her heart.

"What happened?" Brandon asked.

"What does it look like?" she snapped, her voice breaking.

"I see the obvious answer is that someone spilled lemonade. But I don't think it's the right answer." He bent down and took the rag from her, finishing cleaning up the mess she'd made.

Reegan watched him. She watched how the muscles of his arms moved as he dragged the rag over the floor. She watched how his lips pursed in concentration of the job. She looked at the dark bags under his eyes and ached to soothe him, even now.

"When were you going to tell me?" she said.

He frowned, looking up at her. She saw her own anguish reflected back at her from his dark eyes. His gaze turned guilty, and he turned away.

Brandon stood, tossing the rag into the sink and then washing his hands. He pumped soap into his palm and rubbed his hands together. Then he repeated the action as though he hadn't gotten clean enough the first time.

"So it's true?" Reegan asked coming to her feet. "You're re-enlisting and looking to deploy?"

"What?" Brandon whirled around to face her. "No. I'm not re-enlisting."

Reegan's relief was instant. So, it had been a misunderstanding? He wasn't leaving her. But then his gaze clouded over as he appeared to think about it more.

"Well, yes," he revised his answer. "I was. That was the plan. But then I met you and … everything changed."

Brandon opened his arms, and like she was a moth to his flame, she came to him. Her legs were shaky, and he caught her before she took the last step to bring them together. He wrapped her up in his warm embrace, and Reegan knew heaven.

"I have no idea what I'm going to do with my life now," he said into her hair. "Except for the fact that I want to spend it with you."

Reegan's whole being was a tornado of emotion. Everything was topsy turvy. Nothing was clear. She needed some clarity, something to hold onto. "So, you're not leaving?"

"No." He pulled away from her, gazing down into her eyes so that she saw the truth there. "I'm not leaving you."

The tears fell then. Reegan felt as though she'd been holding herself together, not just for days, but since her parents died. For his part, Brandon held her, he held her tight, whispering sweet-nothings in her ear.

She wasn't sure how they ended up in the bed. But his arms were around her. She felt his warm embrace even through the layers of clothing that remained between them. His large, strong body was a spoon behind her while she cried. He held her tight as though protecting her from all sides.

And cry she did, for hours, maybe even days, as she finally felt the effects of her world crashing down around her. But through it all, she knew she was safe. Nothing would ever hurt her again. Not while Brandon Lucas held her in his arms.

And hold her he did. He didn't loosen his grip for one second. Not when her tears stopped. Not when she fell asleep.

CHAPTER NINETEEN

It was the bright rays of dawn that awakened him. Not the whirring of a helicopter. Not the crunch of boots. Not the snore of someone sleeping next to him. Though someone was sleeping in his arms.

Reegan's back was tucked against his chest. They were both still fully clothed. His arms were wrapped firmly around her, holding her close. Against his forearm, he felt her chest rise and fall in the peace of sleep. Her fingers were entwined in his.

The last thing Brandon remembered was lying down with her in his arms as she cried herself to sleep. She'd finally reached the next level in her stage of grief. All because she'd thought he was preparing to leave her.

His hold on her tightened at the thought. He doubted he'd ever be able to be away from her for more than a few hours. In fact, in the bright morning light, even one hour felt excessive.

Brandon knew he'd carried Reegan in here when the sun was still high in the sky. Looking at the clock on the side table, he saw that it was the start of a new day. He didn't remember seeing the darkness of night.

Had he slept through an entire day? She hadn't even sung him to sleep. Her wails had pulled at his heart. He knew he hadn't closed his eyes until she'd settled. It must have been the act of holding her, of having her near that had brought him to the place of peace.

He had to have gotten at least ten hours of sleep, likely more. He hadn't wakened once in the night. Not even from a nightmare.

It wasn't her singing that gave him peace, it was her. He'd found hope in her. He'd found faith in her. He'd found love in her.

That young pastor was right; it wasn't good for man to be alone. Just as soldiers formed teams and units, Brandon had found his true calling with the woman in his arms. Holding the woman he would marry, he felt the chords of harmony settle over him. Pressing the palms of their entwined fingers together, he found an unbreakable unity.

For the first time in a long time, Brandon wanted to sink to his knees and say thank you.

Later.

Right now, he pulled the woman who completed his life to him. He pressed his lips to her temple. Reegan stirred, turning her face to him and slowly blinking open her bright blue eyes.

Recognition was swift in her gaze. The smile she gave him lent him the strength of a full army. Her sigh of utter contentment, had he not been laying down, would've knocked him to his knees.

"Good morning," she said.

"Good morning," he parroted.

"I don't think we were supposed to sleep together until after the wedding."

She turned her body to face him. Brandon loosened his hold only slightly. He had no intention of letting her go right now or ever. Moving his fingertips through her mussed hair, he brushed her strands aside so that he could have a clear view down into her lovely face.

Brandon had never expected to fall in love. He was glad he was lying down for the occasion. It was a dizzying event.

Reegan looked up at him with so much trust in her eyes. But there was still a vulnerability on her brow. He wanted to brush it away. Before he could have that right, he'd need to come clean about everything.

"I blamed myself for your brother's ..." He couldn't use the word death now, since it may no longer be accurate. "For losing Reece. He asked permission to investigate something that seemed off. There were a group of women headed into a danger zone we were surveilling. He wanted to warn them. I thought they might be setting a trap. He argued against it. I let him convince me to take the chance."

Brandon took a breath. He waited for the darkness to assault him, for the smoke to fill his nostrils. The sights, sounds, and smells were all there, but they weren't strong. They were no longer a visceral experience, just a memory.

"Were they the bad guys?" asked Reegan.

"We still don't know for sure," Brandon answered. "But some evidence has come to light that we may have been wrong."

"Well, you could always count on Reece to do the right thing. Even if that meant he'd sacrifice himself for the possibility of the good in others. If he is gone, then I'm glad he did it trying to save someone else's life. And his last act brought you to me."

Brandon closed his eyes. There were no flames, no smoke, no sand behind his eyes. There was only the glow of orange-red. He'd rested his forehead against Reegan's forehead, and her hair filled his vision.

She was a blessing come to life. He felt he could breathe again. He felt absolved.

He opened his eyes in time to catch Reegan tilting her head. Both of her soft pink lips closed around his bottom lip. Brandon relaxed into her sweetness. One of his hands came up and cupped the side of her face, tilting her head so that he could capture both of her lips with his.

As much as he wanted to hear her voice, to hear the sweet songs she made, he wanted the sweetness of her lips even more. His fingers tangled in her hair, holding her to him, and he deepened the kiss.

Reegan gasped. The sound of her voice, coupled with the sweetness of her lips, added onto the softness of her flesh broke something inside Brandon. The soldier in him threw up his hands in surrender.

Before he could wave the white flag, a pounding knock sounded at the front door.

They both groaned. Neither pulled away from the other. Reegan's hunger for him was reflected in her blue gaze.

Just as Brandon thought to ignore it, the knock sounded again. He knew it wasn't one of the women from the ranch. It was an authoritative knock. Like a soldier's knock. But he knew it wasn't one of the men on the ranch.

Rolling out of bed, he ran his hand through his hair as he left the bedroom. He took a few deep breaths as he approached the door so that he wouldn't bite off the head of the person on his doorstep. Throwing open the wood door, Brandon's suspicions were confirmed. Standing on the stoop were two uniformed officers. Alongside them was Chase.

"Corporal Lucas?" said one of the uniforms.

Brandon nodded. He glanced over at Chase whose look was grim. Brandon's first thought was to shield Reegan from whatever news they were about to deliver. But it was too late. He already felt her coming up behind him.

"We have communication that Private Reece Cartwright has been found."

Reegan gasped behind him. Brandon turned with his arms outstretched in case she was about to faint. But who was he kidding? This was Reegan. The woman had been thrown tragedy after obstacle, and she was still standing.

Her blue eyes were bright. Her lips tilted up in a smug smile. "I told you."

Yes. She had told him. He knew now never to doubt his future wife's intuition.

"We're putting together a team to retrieve him," the uniformed soldier continued. "We'd like you to be on it."

CHAPTER TWENTY

Reegan's emotions were being tugged in two different directions. On the one hand, she'd been right. Her brother was alive. Her heart felt like it was expanding, growing ten times as large as though it could hoist a sail and head overseas to retrieve her brother. And that's where the tug in the other direction came into play.

She turned to Brandon. His jaw was tense. His hands were balled into fists.

In order to get her brother back, she'd have to relinquish her hold on the man she loved. She'd lost so much in the last week. Could she take the gamble and possibly lose more? There truly would be nothing left if they didn't recover Reece and Brandon didn't return.

Her heart, so heavy from the joyful news of her brother, broke into pieces of shard at the thought of losing the love of her life. Her insides felt sliced up at the two directions she was pulled. She wanted her brother back safe, but she didn't want to let go of Brandon.

Her fingers found his. Slowly he unballed his fingers and clutched her hand in his.

"Is this the only way?" she asked the two uniform soldiers sitting on their couch. Sergeant Chase stood near a window looking out at the ranch. Reegan sat in a wingback chair with Brandon standing over her like some great, protective beast.

"No," Brandon answered. "I don't have to be the one to go."

She'd only known this man for a handful of days, but she heard it clearly in his tone. He was not the type of man to push his responsibilities off on others. To shun this duty would take something from him. That something was a major part of what had made Reegan fall in love with him so fast and so surely.

She gave his hand a tug until he met her gaze. The turmoil in his dark eyes told her she had gotten it right. He wanted to go, but he didn't want to leave her.

"Corporal Lucas knows the terrain and the logistics," said the uniformed soldier. "He's the best man for the job on such short notice. Sgt. Chase said so."

Chase pushed off the wall and came closer. "I assumed you meant to consult him. I didn't realize you wanted him to go back."

"He's our best chance at getting Private Cartwright back," said the soldier.

"Which is why he's going."

All eyes came to Reegan. But she only had eyes for Brandon. She stood, turning her back and shutting the others out. She placed her hands on his heart and looked up into the face she'd come to cherish.

His gaze narrowed as he peered into her eyes. Words were not necessary between them. Reegan understood this man perfectly. And now she was certain he understood her.

"I have to do this," he said. "I have to go and bring him back."

"I know."

She reached out to bring him into her arms and found herself swallowed up in his embrace. She felt his deep and shuddery inhale. His exhale blew strands of her hair away and caressed the cone of her ear.

Reegan rested her head under his chin. She'd had so much taken away from her, but this was the one thing she wanted to hold onto; the safe place just above Brandon's heart.

She straightened, looking him in his beautiful eyes. Eyes that knew her so well after such a short time. She felt bared to this man.

They were alone now. At some point during their embrace and intimate conversation, the uniformed soldiers and Chase had left. But she could see them waiting outside the front door. It let her know that her time with Brandon was short. The clock was ticking before he'd leave.

Brandon put his forefinger under her chin and turned her attention back to him. "I need you to do something for me before I go," he said.

"Anything."

"Marry me."

Her breath caught at the fierceness in his strong features. She lifted a hand and ran it down the side of that strong jaw. "I already agreed to do that."

"I want to give you my vow before I go." His dark eyes practically glowed with emotion. His hold on her was firm. If she'd wanted to get away, it would've been an impossibility. "Not because I want you to have everything I own before I go. Because I need you to know that you have my heart, you have my strength, you have everything that I have to offer. Reegan Cartwright, you came upon me like a sneak attack, and you broke down all my defenses. I surrender to you."

She rested her forehead against his. He wiped the tears as they fell to her cheek. "We're lucky these guys and girls on the ranch know how to throw together a quickie wedding. Let's do it so you can bring me back my brother."

CHAPTER TWENTY-ONE

randon opened his eyes. He blinked a few times and then he was wide awake. Sleep came to him with ease now that his spirit had found peace.

Nightmares still touched his dreams, but their grip was weaker. Dark thoughts flitted through his mind throughout the day, but he was overwhelmed by the bright blessings now present in his life.

He reached out across the mattress for the source of that wondrous warmth, but the space next to him was empty. It had only been two days since he'd slept with Reegan in his arms. The following two nights had been peaceful as he listened to her sing in their kitchen, as he listened to her hum in the gardens as they tended the soil side by side. She hadn't been in his bed again, but his body knew that her place was next to him.

Soon…

The night after the soldiers had made their visit had been a whirlwind of preparation for both his mission as well as his wedding. The women of the Purple Heart Ranch had whisked his fiancée away, and he hadn't seen her again until dinner. They'd whisked her away again for the night for an impromptu bachelorette party.

The next day, he'd had some time with Reegan in the gardens. But as the following day would be their wedding day, tradition dictated that they spend the night apart.

Brandon found he slept each night peacefully even knowing the dangerous mission he was about to undertake. His mind was rested, and his soul was at peace. Be it because he had a chance to save Reece or because he had given his heart over to Reegan, he wasn't sure? Likely a bit of both.

So, it was easy to roll out of bed each morning and greet the day with less weight on his shoulders. He pulled on his uniform and stared at his reflection. For so many years his self-worth had been wrapped up only in how he could serve his country, the livelihood of his unit, and his personal performance. It had never occurred to him to serve one person above others, to stick to one community, to evaluate himself on his relationship to others. But that would be his life moving forward.

"Ready?"

Brandon looked up to Chase and Ortega standing in the door to his home. Like him, the men were decked out in their uniforms.

"Man," said Ortega. "Who would have thought that when we came here for a little R&R it would lead to a wedding. In just a week."

"Dylan warned us," said Brandon. "You two should be on the lookout."

Ortega snorted. "Yeah, no. I'm pretty sure we're good."

The two single men raised their fists and tapped their knuckles. Brandon got the sense that those were famous last words.

The three men walked out of the front door and down to the pavilion near the small body of water in the center of the ranch. A white gazebo trimmed with vines and flowers was the focal point. The rows of white chairs spread out before the gazebo were filled with a few rows of standing individuals.

It appeared the entire community had gathered for the wedding. Brandon recognized the soldiers from the ranch and their wives seated in the front. He also saw some familiar faces from the church choir.

"Thank you for your service," a kid said. The words were said with a lisp as the little boy was missing two front teeth.

Brandon reached down and gave the kid's head a pat. He heard the sentiment a few more times as he made his way to the gazebo where his nuptials would take place. Instead of getting annoyed at the sentiment, his heart swelled at the gratitude displayed.

He had served his country well. He was proud of that service. Now he would serve this community. Starting with taking care of their favorite daughter.

Music started to play from a speaker, and he saw her. Brandon's heart stopped for a few beats as she walked toward him. She was a vision in white, but more importantly, she was his.

Reegan walked on the arm of Pastor Barrett. The man glared at Brandon as he came closer. Brandon stood with his back even straighter. He met the man's glare with wide eyes and an open heart. If the pastor didn't see that he would do everything in his power to cherish the woman coming toward him, then Brandon would spend the rest of his life showing it to the man of the cloth. He'd spend his life showing it to everyone in this town that he was the best man for Reegan.

At the end of the aisle, Pastor Barrett turned to Reegan. She beamed up at the man who was a second father. His stern expression broke. It softened into love and adoration. A small smile remained in place when he turned to Brandon and presented him with his bride.

Brandon nodded his thanks. He stuck out his hand. Pastor Barrett's grip was strong. It also felt sure.

Turning his attention to Reegan, Brandon felt a little unsteady on his feet. She looked up at him with such trust, such certainty, such love. How had he come to deserve her?

A light wind brought the scent of honeyed flowers from the gardens. Mixed with that was the hint of hay from the barns. He hadn't believed in anything magical before setting foot on this ranch. Now he was a believer that there was something special about this place.

Love was in the rich soil underfoot. It blossomed for those who came here. Chase and Ortega didn't stand a chance if they planned to stay here for any length of time.

Brandon tucked Reegan's hand in the crook of his elbow and turned them to face Dr. Patel. The delight in the doctor's features eclipsed that of any other attendee. The knowing glint in his eyes made Brandon wonder if the man had foreseen this scene playing out.

After all, it had been Patel who'd sent him to the gardens instead of horseback riding. The man hadn't even blinked when, just days later, Brandon had proposed marriage to the woman who'd been tending the soil on that same day.

"Before we begin," said Dr. Patel, "Corporal Lucas has prepared some words."

Brandon cleared his throat. Turning to face Reegan, he took both her hands in his. Once again, her beauty and trust shook something inside until his knees quivered, but he did not hesitate, he did not falter.

"There's so much we don't know about each other, but I'm excited for the rest of my life. What I do know is that you're loyal and fierce. You feel deeply. So deeply that you've reached inside and forged a connection. I feel it. It's beyond my heart. It's in my soul. Though we're about to be parted for some time, I understand that you are a part of me, and I'm a part of you."

It took a few moments for the gathered crowd to settle. Sobs and moans went up. Tissues were passed around. And all the while, Brandon gazed into Reegan's eyes seeing the same certainty that he felt in his blood.

He meant every word, and he would prove it with actions. After years of fighting, peace settled over Brandon. Once the official vows were said by the two of them, he bent down and sealed his promise with a kiss. He embraced this new duty where he was ready, willing, and able to serve for his lifetime.

EPILOGUE

His eyes wrenched open. Though he was surrounded by gray and black shadows, he winced. A dull ache spread through his limbs now that he was conscious. His mouth was dry, and his mind was a swirling vortex of darkness.

He heard a voice next to him. Looking up, he saw someone whose face was covered in dark cloth. Only her eyes were visible. He knew it was a woman because of the length of her lashes, the kohl around her eyelids, and the soft lilt of her words.

He knew that she was no threat. Her words were hushed but not urgent. They were gentle but urging him into action. The words were also said on a foreign tongue. The sounds jumbled in his mind, but a second later, he understood them.

"What is your name?"

Four words. He understood their meaning, but he didn't know the answer.

What was his name? He knew he had one. It was there, somewhere in his brain. He just needed a light to shine in the darkness.

When a shard of brightness from somewhere in the room met his gaze, he instantly shut his eyes. It was too late, a vision slipped through. His entire body shuddered at a pain that wasn't his own. No, he would not go towards that light. Any illumination would only bring pain.

But he couldn't keep his eyes closed forever. Especially since the voice asking him questions was growing louder, more insistent. And so he peeked out from under his lashes.

The woman held up an object. It was a bound book. Somehow he knew it belonged to him, and he reached for it.

It was small, brown, and leather bound. There were burn marks at the edges, and a few of the pages were charred. *Daily Devotional Bible* was written in gold letters on the front face.

With ginger fingers, he opened the book. A folded piece of paper fell out. The corners flapped like a bird's wings bringing it in for a landing.

His eyes scanned over the writing. He knew that writing. It was the first familiar thing. He picked out a few words.

Love you.

Always.

Marriage.

Beth.

Beth? He felt possessive over that name. It wasn't his. Beth was a woman. Was she his woman?

I will always love you, Reece. If there's a chance ... marriage ... always yours ... Beth.

A feeling of serenity came over him. He wanted to be Reece. He wanted to have Beth's love. He just wished he could remember who she was. He wished he could remember who he was.

———

You won't want to miss the reunion
between Reece and Beth.

Watch as true love is realized in
Always On My Mind
the seventh book in The Brides of Purple Heart Ranch!

ALWAYS ON HIS MIND

THE BRIDES OF PURPLE HEART RANCH
BOOK 7

CHAPTER ONE

He was dreaming, of that he was sure. But it was one of those dreams where he felt every sensation. The heat of the fire licked up his back as though his spine was a trail of gasoline. Sharp pebbles and debris bit at the fleshy underside of his palms and nipped at the cleft of his chin. The ear-piercing screams of women beat at his eardrum like the percussive section of a marching band in a small auditorium.

Then came the blood. Metallic and musty. Tinged with a burning, chemical smell. The stench gripped his gut, forcing his stomach to surrender its goods.

He felt, heard, tasted, and smelled all of it. But he saw nothing. All around him was a thick, suffocating blackness.

He was trapped in the darkness of his mind. Though he knew he was dreaming, he could not wake up. He could not move a limb, not even his pinky finger. Everything was bound, strapped down, and held tight. There was no escape.

His senses released their hold when voices rose around him in the darkness. He knew the urgent murmurs were not a part of the dream. The voices came from the real world.

The words were spoken in a foreign tongue. Harsh consonants, few vowel sounds. But he understood the meanings.

"We have to move him."

"It's too dangerous."

The voices were feminine, but there was steel in their tone. Whoever these women were, he knew they were very brave, strong, and capable. That knowledge would've made another man relax. Not him. He felt honor bound to rise to their aide.

The urge to reach out to them was a powerful one. He felt it was his responsibility to help them complete their mission. He got the sense that that was what he did. He completed missions, got things done.

Unfortunately, he couldn't do anything at the moment. He wasn't sure if his eyes were open? He was still bound in darkness. On the bright side, life was slowly returning to his limbs and extremities.

His right pinky separated from the rest of his fingers and wiggled. His head turned a fraction to the left. He took in a deep breath, feeling his chest rise high as his lungs expanded to their full capacity. And then it appeared.

A tiny light. Smaller than a pinprick. It grew to the size of a pencil tip. Then to the size of the surface of a spoon. Until, finally, it filled his eyes.

His eyes were definitely open now. He was awake, let loose from the dream world and his shadowy captivity. But there wasn't much to see.

The room he was in was dark. Just not the all-encompassing dark of the dream world. There were gradations of black from ebony to charcoal to slate gray.

His eyes were adjusting quickly now, and he began to pick apart his surroundings. There were more than two bodies standing over him. He couldn't make them out. Their heads and faces were covered in black cloth. Only their eyes were visible. But he knew they all were women.

"You are awake," one of them said. The language she spoke switched. It was more familiar, easier on the ears to hear. Easier on his brain to understand.

"We will have to move him now. It is not safe if he stays."

"It is not safe if we move him."

"We will not have a choice much longer. They will come for him. We cannot continue to shelter him."

"But he saved our lives. We owe him."

The silence was tense. He could see the worry in the posture of one woman, the one insistent on sending him away from ... wherever he was. He saw defiance in the one who spoke up.

He opened his mouth, but only a garbled sound came out. His throat was on fire. Like a blaze burning in the dry desert.

"We need to send him back to his own people."

"We have already sent word. No one has come. We cannot wait any longer."

His people? He had people? He tried to picture who he belonged to, but his mind came up blank. Just a black slate. Not absolute darkness like the dream. Not as many gradations as this darkened room.

He tried to sit up, but a pain in his shoulder prevented it. Now that he thought of it, there was pain everywhere. He let out a strangled cry. The sound was short-lived as it burned a path through his throat and over his tongue.

All three women went tense. Their gazes went to the far side of the room where a tiny sliver of light escaped. That was the way out. Or the way in.

He shrank from that light. But a shard found him, landing on his bottom lip. His lips trembled under the weight of the ray.

Inside his mind, he felt the dream world pushing at the real world. He knew he could not let that happen. He could not let the sharp heat or the blood-curdling screams enter this world.

But the ray of light was unrelenting. It moved up his face, touching his upper lip, then his nose. He knew that if it got to his eyes, he would be in trouble. The eyes were the windows into the soul after all.

The women moved in front of him, blocking out the light. He breathed a sigh of relief at the narrow escape. But the reprieve was short-lived. Movement sounded from the crack where the light intruded.

The other two women stepped in front of him as well. The sight of the protective barrier in front of him kicked him into action. It should be him standing in front of them. But he couldn't rise. The pain in his limbs prevented it.

Even though he was still lying down, he wanted to shout at the women to get behind him. He wanted to rise from the bed to protect them. This was all wrong. He might not know much, but he knew that was his duty; to protect.

Before he could get any words out, the sliver of light grew. It invaded the room, spreading across the floor and taking up stations in the corners. And then they were inside.

Large men carrying guns burst into the room. He wasn't sure how many. They filled the entire space.

The women gasped. But just as soon as they gasped, relief seemed to rush through the room. One woman put her hand to her chest and began chanting in that harsh language. Another sank to her knees and bowed, beginning a prayer of gratitude. The third, the one who had fiercely tried to protect him, stepped forward.

One of the gun-toting men peered around her. He had dark hair and dark eyes. He was covered in tan clothing that looked familiar. The way the man looked him over, with relief, and gratitude and guilt, tugged at a memory in the darkness of his mind.

"Thank God, we found you, Private Cartwright."

CHAPTER TWO

"*But* I thought the highest worship of the Lord was love. Wouldn't that mean that if we got married, it would only prove our devotion to God?"

It was a good argument, thought Beth Barrett as she gazed at the young woman with a high ponytail and flowery, plastic barrettes in her hair. Too bad the voice making it was high-pitched with a nasally whine.

Beth sat in the Youth Pastor's office. She didn't sit behind the desk. She sat just off to the side, next to the youth pastor as he attempted to counsel the young couple before them. Beth wore a placid smile on her face as the two teens put forth their argument that they be allowed to marry without their parents' consent.

"We love each other, and we want to be together," the young girl said.

Her whine raised an octave on the last word. Beth winced at the dog whistle note. Luckily, she was able to cover her discomfort with a sigh she hoped would be translated as sympathetic.

Pastor Walter Vance smiled over at her. Though Beth wasn't sure if it was at her sigh? Or if he was appreciative of her faked compassion?

She assumed the latter when Walter steepled his fingers and nodded at the young man and woman. Nathaniel Green, the hopeful fiancé, sat upright, holding Nathalie Brown's hand.

Yes, that was their names. Nat Brown and Nat Green. The similarities in their names had pushed them together all their lives. With their last names being close in the alphabet they were often seated next to or near each other in the public schools of their small town. Nat and Nat started dating just before high school and had never stopped. A romantic person might call it fate. Their parents called it too soon.

"You know my hands are tied until you're both eighteen," said Walter.

"He *is* eighteen," Nathalie insisted.

"Yes, but you're not," Walter said patiently.

"I'm seventeen and three months old."

"Plenty of time to start planning a wedding," Beth added helpfully.

In response, Nathalie cut her with a death glare. Beth sat back in her seat and resumed her silence. She dropped the forced smile. She rarely had to force her smiles in church. Only when, as part of her duties as the pastor's daughter, she had to sit and listen to those who cared more about their way than what was right.

Luckily, Walter was there to pick up the gauntlet. "Even when you reach the age of majority, don't you want your parents' blessing?"

"They're never going to give it to us," said Nathaniel. "My mom wants me to go to college, get a degree, explore the world and other people."

"I love it here," Nathalie was saying. "I've never wanted to live anywhere but here. I've never wanted to be anything but a wife and a mom. Is that so bad?"

Natalie looked to Beth for an answer. Beth wished she disagreed with the young girl. But they had the exact same aspirations.

Beth had her Associate's degree, which she'd earned from courses at the local college. Unlike many of her former schoolmates, she had no desire to explore the world outside of their town. More than anything in the world, she wanted to be a wife and a mom.

Walter gazed down at her, as though he knew the trajectory of her thoughts. He covered her left hand with his, resting his thumb on the rock he'd put there not long ago.

"I'm a traditional woman like you, Nathalie," Beth said.

"Thank you," Nathalie exclaimed as though Beth had entirely cosigned her argument.

"But," Beth continued. "I couldn't imagine walking down the aisle without my father at my side. Can you?"

Nathalie pursed her lips and wrinkled her nose like the child she still was. "But don't you believe in love? Don't you know when it's true and the only thing you want?"

Beth did know all about that. She'd been in love since before she understood what the word meant. She'd felt the feelings the first time she'd laid eyes on the man of her dreams. She'd loved nothing more than gazing into his blue eyes.

Walter's smiling brown gaze settled on her, shining with admiration. Beth cleared her throat, but words failed her.

"I mean, didn't you know that when you said yes to marrying Pastor Vance?"

Now all eyes were on her. Vocal Natalie, silent Nathaniel, patient Walter.

Beth was not a liar. What she was was a coward. She'd never told Reece Cartwright how she felt about him all the years of their lives. No, she'd wimped out and written him a letter confessing her feelings. He'd never responded. And then he'd gone missing.

Just thinking about him now Beth felt a burning in her heart for what it would never have. Her inner lip burned from biting down. All eyes remained on her, waiting for her response. In times like these, she did what she always did, she turned to the Lord.

"I'm reminded of 1 Corinthians 13:13 where it says that faith, hope, and love abide, but of those three, love is the greatest."

Nathalie's face lit up once again, likely assuming that Beth was championing her cause.

"However," Beth continued, "just because love is the greatest thing in the world, it doesn't mean you can ignore faith and hope. It's hard for faith to take root when you've planted doubts in someone's mind and heart. Ask yourself if you've done that with your parents."

Nathaniel looked far off. Beth knew she'd reached him as he nodded while pursing his lips.

Nathalie sighed and rolled her eyes. But she didn't argue Beth's point. It looked like Beth had gotten through to both of them.

"I think you should take some time to show your parents the truth of your commitment. Let their faith in you be restored. Give it some time to grow and hope that they will come around to see the path you both wish to take. But, no, I don't believe you can force it."

The two would-be newlyweds looked at each other. Nathaniel lifted a brow. Nathalie lowered her lashes and gave him a barely perceptible head nod.

Beth smiled, a real smile this time. These two were in sync. They knew each other. They would make it. They left the office hand in hand, walking at a more subdued pace toward their future.

"Have I told you how much I am looking forward to not only marrying you but sharing my duties with you?"

Walter brought her knuckles to his lips for a light kiss. When he gazed up at her, there was a brightness in his brown eyes, turning them more hazel than coffee. It was the bright look of love that shone from his eyes.

Beth knew the look because she'd seen it reflected back at her many a time when she'd looked into Reece Cartwright's clear blue eyes. She'd been only seeing her reflection. Reece had never looked at her that way. And he never would.

For weeks, she'd mourned the loss of her first love when he'd been declared missing in action by the military. Only to find out last month that Reece might be alive. Though that had brought her relief, she was still out of sorts.

She'd written Reece a letter three months ago; a letter confessing her love for him. He hadn't written back. He'd always written her faithfully be it over email or a handwritten note. But he'd gone silent after that revealing missive.

He might have never received it. Military mail could be delayed, especially when soldiers were deployed. Whether he'd received it or not, she hoped more than anything that he was still alive and would soon be found.

But for now, Beth had chosen to move on. She'd waited her whole life for Reece Cartwright to love her, and it was clear he did not.

She turned back to Walter, who was still waiting for her response to his compliment. Beth reached out and grasped the hand of the man who reached for her. It felt good to be wanted. It felt warm. It didn't burn like rejection, or worse, silence.

"I'm looking forward to our life together too," she said.

CHAPTER THREE

He found a Polaroid. Four people smiled back at him. All four looked alike. Two older, two younger. A family.

The redheaded woman smiling back at him was only familiar because of her hair. There was a rosy blush to her high cheeks. Her smile was big; nearly as big as her face. Her green eyes were big and bright. She had the type of friendly face that made others feel it was safe to tell her their secrets.

She stayed frozen in that smile, as though someone had told her a joke. The punchline was captured forever in the celluloid. A happy moment frozen in time.

She wasn't alone in that moment. Next to the grinning redhead stood a gray-haired man. His eyes were big, but bushy brows took up most of the real estate. His pupils were small and beady, like a wise, old owl. But they were the clearest blue. The man had long limbs that rivaled the wingspan of an owl. He stood with one arm around the woman and the other around two other people in the frame.

The two younger people were carbon copies. A girl and a boy. They both had flaming red hair like the woman and bright blue eyes like the man. Siblings. Twins.

The boy possessed the face he'd seen reflected back in the mirror that morning. Reece was the man's name. Reece was *his* name. Private Reece Cartwright of the United States Army.

"How are you holding up?"

Reece looked up from the polaroid of his family. Cpl. Brandon Lucas looked down at him with concern. Everyone Reece had encountered the past two weeks that he'd been awake looked at him with concern.

He'd only seen the eyes of the women who had taken care of him in the cave. In just that sliver of a glimpse, and in the short amount of time he'd been conscious, he'd discerned a mountain of worry in their features. The endless stream of men and women in tan, brown, and green uniforms that had poked, prodded, and questioned him for days on end all wore pinched expressions when they regarded him.

Corporal Lucas had always been nearby. His worry had taken time to develop. The first thing Reece had gotten from the man was an overwhelming sense of relief. But now, two weeks later, his brow was perpetually wrinkled each time he looked Reece over.

"I'm fine." Reece knew he said the expected thing when Corporal Lucas nodded.

"You're not fine," said Brandon. "But what else could you say?"

Reece had been taken from the bombed out structure where he'd been hidden. Apparently, the women had protected him at great peril to themselves after he had tried to protect them from insurgents. Reece and his four-man fire team had been stationed in the area on a surveil and reconnaissance mission. They were tasked with gathering intel on some structures thought to be in use by an anti-coalition militia.

From what they could gather, Reece had seen the women headed toward the area. There was some uncertainty of whether the women were in the wrong place at the wrong time or if they were a part of the militia. Reece was the only member of the team who spoke the language. With his team covering him, he approached the women. And then fire rained down on all of them.

Reece remembered none of it. Only waking up. Even though the two weeks that he'd been awake were a blur. It was difficult for him to hold anything, especially names and faces. His mind felt like it was rebooting and installing a new systems update, all while crashing at the same time.

Reece pressed his thumbs to his temples. The move didn't offer much relief. The pain was inside his head. He needed a way to let it out.

He closed his eyes, shutting out the bright light of the day. That helped. Darkness was the only thing that soothed him. A large hand clapped down on his shoulder, causing him to wrench his eyes open.

"Don't stress yourself, Cartwright."

Corporal Lucas sat beside him in the moving vehicle. The worry was gone from the other man's gaze. In its place was certainty. Reece wished he felt some of that.

"The doctor said the amnesia is likely temporary," said Corporal Lucas. "It'll all come back when you're ready."

Reece dropped his hands from his temple. The Polaroid was still on his lap. He looked again at the family, his family. They looked happy, without a care in the world other than the care for each other. He wished he could remember how to feel that way.

"You've been through a lot. We're all just glad to have you home."

Home. Reece was home. He looked out the window of the moving vehicle to see mountains and a blue sky. It looked somewhat like the valley that he'd been pulled out of. But the buildings were all erect and sturdy. Still, none of it looked familiar.

"Reegan is going to maul you when she sees you."

Reegan. His twin sister. Reece pressed his thumb and forefinger into the snapshot of the life he couldn't remember. He ached for something, anything familiar.

"She insisted you were still alive. She never gave up. She demanded we go back for you."

Reece felt gratitude toward the woman but still no familiarity. He reached for the duffle bag of his belongings and put the picture back inside. His fingers grazed a leather-bound book inside. He peered inside the dark bag and pulled out a small Devotional Bible.

The pages were worn. The spine broken. It looked well used and well cared for. Was he a religious man?

He thumbed through the pages. Many of the corners were dog-eared. There were highlights in yellow, pink, and blue. The margins were filled with notes in black and blue ink. In the Book of John, with the highlighted verse about friendship, there was a letter. Before he unfolded the letter, Reece read the verse.

Greater love has no one than this, that he lay down his life for his friends. John 15:13.

That felt familiar. But even more familiar was the handwriting inside the letter. A spark of recognition hit him. He knew this handwriting. It was familiar.

A warmth spread through his chest as his gaze slid over the carefully written script. The T's all had loops. The L's slanted to the right. The small case S's had fat bellies that made them resemble hearts.

I need to tell you what's in my heart. I love you. I've always loved you.

Reece's first instinct was to put the letter away. He felt as though he were intruding. It was obviously a love note. Then he scanned up and saw his name at the top.

My dearest Reece.

It's easier to write to you than it is to speak to you. We've been in each other's lives for so long, but my feelings for you have only deepened through the years. There has never been anyone else for me. There never will be. You are my best friend. I'd like to offer you my heart. I know that you care for me, but I'm asking if you could ever love me?

It was signed *Beth*.

Reece tried to picture Beth in his mind. He didn't get a face. But he did get a feeling. It was warm and cozy. Was that love? Did he love Beth?

He jolted forward as the truck came to a stop. The letter tumbled out of his hands, fluttering in the air. Reece caught it before it could hit the ground.

"We're here," said Corporal Lucas.

Whoever Beth was, and what she might be to him, Reece was about to find out.

ered between a rock causing her to gag. She
CHAPTER FOUR

*B*eth frowned down at the rich earth below her. Part of her was happy for the plants thriving in such nutrient-dense soil. Another part of her knew that it wasn't just little seedlings ready to poke their heads out of the fertile ground.

An earthworm slithered between a rock causing her to gag. She cringed and shuddered when a beetle lumbered over a long blade of grass. Beth forced herself to lower the gardening spade and pray for patience and compassion for all God's creatures.

"You know it's more afraid of you than you're afraid of it."

Beth wasn't afraid. She was grossed out and uncomfortable and wishing for hardwood floors and air conditioning. Clearly, gardening wasn't her favorite activity. She didn't like getting dirty. The picnic blanket she knelt on kept her yellow dress from getting messy. She'd switched out of heels and changed into running shoes. Unfortunately, her nails would suffer the consequences of girl time.

Reegan Lucas's smile was brighter than the sun. The tan on Reegan's left hand showed a visible band line where the ring should go. Beth's best friend wore a diamond ring around her neck as she dug her bare hands into the dirt. Reegan had been married for just over a month. It clearly agreed with her.

A lovely hum rose as Reegan sang a hymn. The sound of her voice wafting on the light wind made butterflies flutter. Butterflies Beth could handle. It was the slimy baby caterpillars that made her skin crawl.

"Any word from Brandon?" asked Beth.

Reegan's smile fell a bit, but only slightly. "Not for two weeks."

Reegan's husband, Corporal Brandon Lucas, had been on the original mission where Reece had gone missing. When the army announced they were putting together a retrieval operation, he stepped up. Beth had gotten the sense that Brandon felt responsible for losing Reece. The honorable man that he was, she hadn't been surprised when he'd stepped up in the effort to get his fellow soldier back.

The cold metal of the gardening utensil wasn't what made Beth shiver. It was the thought of seeing Reece alive and breathing and fine. No matter how awkward things might be between them, she wanted that more than anything in the world. She'd had trouble fathoming a world where Reece wasn't in it. She would happily live in a world where he was alive and well, even if their friendship didn't survive.

"Brandon prepared for the mission," said Reegan. "And he prepared me. He said there was a possibility of three dark weeks where I wouldn't hear from him. So, it should be just another six more days, then I should hear something."

Six days. They'd know something in six days.

Beth placed her palms in the dirt, needing something solid and warm to quell the jitters shimmying over her skin. With her right hand, she cleared a path for the string beans struggling to take root. She pushed the white roots back into the earth to give them purchase with her left hand.

"Let's talk about something else," said Reegan. "Let's talk wedding plans."

Beth's shudders were replaced with a rumbling in her tummy.

"Mine was quick but still perfect. I got my dream man." Reegan pressed her hand to her ring over her heart.

Beth carefully averted her gaze from her best friend. If Reegan looked in her eyes, she might see that she was dreaming of another man. Her own engagement ring caught the light. The small, colorless rock felt heavy on her hand. That had to mean it would sink deep into the foundation and make sturdy roots.

"But it's the marriage that counts, not the wedding," Reegan continued. "Just know that since we have time to plan, I will be living out my dream wedding through yours."

It wouldn't be the wedding Beth had dreamed about. That dream had featured another man. Beth had never told Reegan about her infatuation with Reece. The three of them had been as thick as thieves since they were in the cradle. Both Reegan and Reece were her best friends. Since they were girls, Beth had relied on Reegan for all things boy band, fashion, and feelings.

Reece was more of an academic. He loved all things scholarly, especially when it came to scripture. He'd even taken to learning the ancient languages like Arabic and Hebrew, which was a prized skill in the military.

When they were younger, the two of them would talk well into the night on a myriad of Biblical and spiritual topics. Beth had cherished those times as some of the most enlightening moments and enriching experiences in her life. Reece had always made her feel heard and important. He just hadn't known he'd also made her feel something more, something in her heart.

"Have you two set a date yet?" said Reegan.

"Not yet. I was thinking winter."

Beth looked up at the mountains and the sunny skies. The bare branches were just beginning to sprout new leaves.

"Winter? That's months away," protested Reegan. "At least we'll have time to plan."

"Reegan, Walter is only a youth pastor. We're just going to do something small."

"You might think you're just going to do something small, but you're this town's favorite daughter. And, thanks to the Purple Heart Ranch and its zoning, this town hasn't had anything except quickie weddings in months."

When the soldiers had moved onto the ranch and converted it into a place of rehabilitation for veterans, they hadn't read the fine print. A zoning regulation had stipulated that all permanent residents had to be families. That meant the men who'd been living there for a year and getting the much-needed care they required had to either fight through a wad of red tape or get married. Surprisingly, they all chose marriage.

"Beth?"

Beth looked up to Reegan, meeting her gaze for the first time that morning. There was concern in her best friend's clear blue gaze. Beth gasped a little. Sometimes it shook her how alike Reegan and Reece looked.

"Are you sure about this?" Reegan asked.

Beth set her mouth to assure her oldest friend, but her throat went dry. At the same time, she felt a desperate need to swallow down bile. Before she could give an answer, a golf cart pulled up with Private Mark Ortega behind the wheel. He hopped out of the cart looking very serious. His perpetual dimples were at ease today.

"Reegan, we need you to come to the medical center."

"Is something wrong?" Reegan asked as she stood, brushing the dirt from her hands.

Mark shook his head. But the corner of his lips tugged up, and his dimples gave it away.

"He's back," Reegan breathed.

The dimples went on full assault as Mark grinned his answer.

"And Reece?"

Mark's smile wavered, the dimples dimming.

Beth felt nauseous. Why a half smile? Either Reece was back. Or he wasn't. Or he was back but not alive.

"He's here," Mark confirmed.

Beth sagged down to the ground. Her fingers took root in the soil. Her rear came to the grass, staining her dress. She didn't care.

He was here. He was back. He was alive.

"Come on, Beth."

Beth looked up. Reegan was beckoning her into the cart. Neither her legs nor her hands would move. She'd taken root into the earth. A beetle crawled over her knuckles, and still, she didn't move.

"Beth, get in this car."

Beth shook the dirt and the bug off her hands. As she rose, she noted that her knees and the front of her dress had spots of dirt on them. On unsteady feet, she walked to the cart and slid in next to Reegan. They held onto each other as the small, unwieldy cart rolled over the green pastures.

Beth wasn't ready to see Reece. It was enough to know that he was alive. But she knew she needed to see him, to confirm it. But also, that would be exactly what she needed to truly let go and move forward.

In no time, they pulled up to the medical building. Reegan leaped out, hitting the ground at a running pace. Beth's unathletic friend took the stairs three at a time and bounded through the glass doors.

Beth walked slowly up the stairs beside Mark. "Is he injured?"

"In a manner of speaking, yes." Mark took a deep breath in that way when someone had bad news to deliver. He let it all out in a gush. "He has amnesia."

Beth stopped in her tracks. She ran those three words over in her mind, again and again, making sure she understood them. Amnesia?

Reece had amnesia.

She said the words again and again in her head, as though she were trying to be certain that she remembered them.

Reece had amnesia.

That would mean he wouldn't remember anything. Including her. Including the letter.

As she came closer to the door, she heard the sounds of Reegan's sobs. And then she heard his voice.

"I'm sorry."

Beth stopped in her tracks. He sounded exactly like himself. His soft, deep voice reached her from the hall. She'd always marveled that someone with a resonant baritone could also speak so softly.

"It's okay," said Reegan. "I don't care that you don't remember. You're alive and whole. I remember everything. I can tell you your entire life story."

Beth stopped at the threshold. Reece sat in a chair. He wore a T-shirt and khakis, looking like his old self. His hair was cut close to his scalp as he preferred it. His chin was cleanly shaven. His bright blue eyes were clear, but there were bags beneath them.

He was smiling, but it didn't reach his eyes. He was thin and gaunt. He looked defeated and lost.

And then his gaze rose and found her. Beth braced herself for her heart to shatter when he didn't recognize her. Instead, she felt her heart sink. Not from breaking. It felt like a house settling into its foundation.

It didn't matter whether he remembered her or not. It didn't matter how long they spent apart. It didn't matter who came between them. She would always love this man.

She was thankful he wouldn't remember her letter. She was thankful he wouldn't know what would have never been. She could go on loving him in secret. And best of all, they could start anew and be just friends.

And then recognition lit his blue eyes. He reached out his hand. He reached out for her.

"Beth?"

CHAPTER FIVE

 eece had long lost count how many different rooms he'd been in over the past two weeks. It wasn't that he couldn't remember them all. His brain worked fine at recording the details of everything he encountered from the moment he opened his eyes back in that cave. It was just that he was too exhausted and disinterested to keep track of what was going on around him.

His disinterest extended to more than just the rooms. He hadn't made much effort to remember the multitude of names and faces that paraded around him. There was an endless sea of people. They moved in and out of his vision. They asked him the same questions over and over again. Over and over again, Reece gave the same answers; *he couldn't remember.*

He had tried at first. However, every time he got close to the light of old memories, a blinding pain seared his mind. The backs of his eyelids burned. The smell of smoke choked his throat. His palms sweated, and his legs began to bounce. The only salve was to retreat.

He knew that retreat was not in his character. He admitted to being a weakened man right now. He was no longer in physical pain. All aches had left him before he'd left the base in Afghanistan. He didn't have a single bruise on his body. But his mind was weary. And that's what was asked of him day in and out: *remember, think, consider.*

That light of remembrance was far too powerful in his present state. He knew he'd have to face it. But later.

Now he just wanted to shut his eyes. Shut them all out and get lost in the darkness. That was until he saw her …

Sergeant Chase—Colin, his superior had insisted Reece call him— had driven them into town from the airport. Reece had caught flashes of some memories from his time in this town. Having an ice cream at the shop with the pink trim. He knew there was a cozy spot in the library he preferred. He had the strongest reaction to the church that sat at the end of the main street. That place called to him as though it were a second home.

None of the town memories were painful. But trying to pull them closer to him, trying to delve deeper into the flashbacks, brought on the threat of the bright, hot light. He'd backed off, slunk down in the rear seat of the truck, and closed his eyes.

Corporal Lucas—Brandon, he'd insisted Reece call him—and Colin had let him rest in the car. Though Reece had no memories of either man, he trusted them both immediately.

Reece knew he liked the ranch nurse and doctor as well. The pretty, brown-skinned nurse named Ruhi took his vitals. She spoke like they knew each other, but she hadn't pressed him to remember.

An older, male version of her appeared in the door next. Reece knew it was Nurse Ruhi's father. The connection was clear. Reece had no visual memories of Dr. Patel either, but he felt at peace around the psychologist.

Dr. Patel hadn't asked questions about the mission or his memory. He asked questions about Reece's health and wellbeing. The doctor's voice was familiar to Reece. It was soft and calm like his words could have been a lullaby. Reece was content to simply listen while the man spoke.

Reece settled back in his chair, near lethargic after the long days of travel when a red-haired tornado nearly bowled him over. Her impact pushed the front two legs of the chair off the floor as she crashed into his chest. She squeezed the life out of him and drenched his shirt front with tears.

"I knew you were alive," she sobbed. "I felt it in our connection."

She pulled away from him, and Reece looked into his own blue eyes. In his mind, there were flashes of her smiling over at him. Flashes of her nostrils flaring at him in anger. He remembered the sound of her laughter. But even more, he remembered the sound of her voice singing. The lyrics were imperceptible, but he knew that he'd know her song anywhere.

"Reegan."

It was as though a lightbulb went off behind her eyes. "You remember me."

Reece winced. "I'm sorry."

Before he could let her down, she shook her head and squeezed his shoulder.

"It's okay," she said. Her smile was wobbly, but he could see her resolve. "I don't care that you don't remember. You're alive and whole. I remember everything. I can tell you your entire life story."

It felt right to hold her to him. He did feel a connection to her, though he didn't feel comfortable vocalizing it as she had. He had the overwhelming urge to apologize to her again. The apology caught in his throat when the vision in yellow appeared in the doorway.

She stood in a shard of light that should've made Reece cringe had it been anyone else. But he couldn't look away from her. She glanced around the room, but not at him. There was uncertainty in her hazel eyes. She bit at her lip, tugging it into her mouth as though she wanted to speak but was afraid. And then her gaze met his.

Reece felt like something kicked him in the chest. He was convinced his heart began beating for the first time. Before that moment, the organ had only been a murmur. He'd been breathing shallowly, but he took his first deep breath. He had no choice. His lungs needed to expand to fit the sudden growth of his heart.

Like with Reegan, Reece saw flashes of this woman from times past. He saw her smiling, laughing, indignant, compassionate.

He felt connected to her as well, an invisible bond that felt all too real. Yet the bond he shared with her took a different route to his heart. A route that had been under construction and was now in the final stages of completion. When he spoke, the finishing touches were added.

"Beth?"

It wasn't a question. He knew it was her. She was the first thing he was certain of outside of his sister.

Beth's uncertain gaze went wide, like saucers filled with hope. Her lips shaped into a delicate O. Her fingers untangled and rubbed down her sides, smoothing the pleats of her skirt.

Reece felt parched watching her. The dress made her look like a young, fifties housewife. A vision of Donna Reed flitted through his mind. He remembered that he loved that show. That and another show about a boy named Beaver, but he couldn't recall the title. He didn't care to. His mind was wrapped around the vision in the doorway.

Beth was licking her lips again, in preparation to speak. Reece's gaze latched onto the motion. Had he ever kissed those lips? He wanted to fight the pain of the light to uncover one of those memories.

"You remember me?" asked Beth, her voice a shaky whisper.

Reece's gaze swept her body. Long brown hair that brushed her shoulders. Long legs that ended in—running shoes? That didn't seem right.

He continued his perusal to her long slender fingers. On her left hand, on the fourth finger, there sat a sparkling diamond. And now Reece's lips parted in an O.

The letter. He must've answered her plea of love. Now he knew what his answer had been.

"Yes," he said.

Yes, he did remember her. As much as he remembered his sister. Just a feeling of familiarity. But it was too hard to explain.

Reece wasn't certain of the expression that crossed Beth's features. Surprise? Happiness? Horror? Resolve?

Had they fought the last time they spoke? Had they argued? She was still wearing his ring. So, whatever disagreement they may have had, they hadn't broken things off.

He glanced at the ring again. The jewelry didn't suit her. It was small and colorless. That seemed wrong. But perhaps it was all he could afford at the time?

"How is it he remembers Beth and not Reegan?" asked Brandon.

Dr. Patel shrugged. "The mind is fickle. He may be simply remembering what is comfortable."

"What?" said Reegan. "I make him uncomfortable?"

Reece ignored his sister. He knew she wasn't upset. He felt certain that the three of them had always been close. Instead, he focused his attention on Beth, particularly on her dress. He spotted smudges of dirt on the front and green stains on the side.

"I remember ..." Reece fought the wince. He wanted this memory to come through. He took a breath and began again. "I remember swinging on the monkey bars while you and my sister sat on the side. I jumped down to the ground. It had been raining earlier, and it was a bit muddy."

He glanced up at Beth. She hadn't taken a step over the threshold. Her hand was on the door frame as she watched him. Her knuckles were white as she gripped the frame.

"I got mud on your dress. You got very angry with me. You don't like to be dirty." He frowned at the mud on her dress and knees.

Beth looked down and brushed at the smudges on her dress. "I was helping Reegan weed in the garden just now."

Reece's gaze went to his sister. "Reegan loves gardening."

His sister's smile was brilliant and wide. She nodded her head vigorously. "I do. I love gardening."

"There's a garden out back of our house." Reece saw the patch of green out back of the red brick house. He felt an overwhelming nostalgia to be in that place. That place would be safe. "I'd like to go home."

CHAPTER SIX

As the others took a moment and explained the tragedy of the Cartwright home to Reece, Beth gripped the frame of the doorway. Her breaths came up short, which was a problem because her racing heart needed more oxygen to pump blood down to her weakening knees.

Reece remembered her.

Selective memories, true. But look at what he'd selected. He'd pulled out times from their childhood when things were innocent and pure. He remembered small things about her, like the fact that, unlike most kids, she didn't like to get her hands or her clothes dirty.

She didn't have the mental capacity to determine whether this was a good thing or a bad thing. She simply gloried that it was a thing. She was important enough for his brain to hold onto as everything else went dark.

She'd always known she'd mattered to him. He'd told her many a time that her friendship meant the world to him. But now she knew that memories of her were a comfort, and that warm, cozy feeling of comfort was found in the heart.

He remembered the good things. He hadn't remembered the letter. He might not ever. That meant they could be friends again.

Beth tried to gulp down a deep breath, but her lungs didn't inflate all the way. There was a lot of empty space in her chest. It was as though her heart had shrunk down in disappointment.

Despair colored her vision. Her mouth went dry. The palms of her empty hands itched. She balled her hands into fists and met a sharp point on her left hand.

Common sense told Beth that it wasn't possible. Memories or not, she and Reece could never be the friends that they had been. She was still in love with him. And here she stood wearing another man's ring.

Reegan sat next to her brother. She took his hand in hers as she relayed the tragedy of the fire and the loss of all they held dear.

"Where will I stay?" Reece said.

"You'll stay with us," said his sister. "Here on the ranch. Now that you're here, we can rebuild the house, but it will take a while."

Reece frowned looking between his sister and her husband. Brandon stood behind Reegan's chair, just off to the right of her shoulder. He looked to Beth like a sentinel, ever watchful of a precious treasure.

"Aren't you two just married?" Reece asked. "No offense, but I'd rather not stay in the room next door to newlyweds."

Reegan's cheeks heated at her brother's words. Brandon cracked a grin.

"You could do what all the other soldiers did," Ruhi spoke up from her place next to the medical equipment. "You could get married. Then you could have your own home here on the ranch."

The nurse said it with a smile. It was likely meant to ease the tension that had clouded the room. But no one laughed.

Brandon's right brow lifted in consideration. Reegan pursed her lips, the way she'd done in math class when puzzling over a particularly tricky problem. Pastor Patel smiled in that way when Beth would come to talk to him about an issue and come to a resolution without him ever offering any advice.

Beth's knees solidified at that moment. She pushed off the wall and took one step into the room. But she stopped before she could take another step.

She'd been about to raise a protest. The idea was ludicrous. Reece marry a stranger? Or worse, an ex-girlfriend.

Mindy Engle was still in town. She'd just gotten out of a long term relationship. Beth had seen her nursing her wounds a few times at the ice cream parlor last month.

The idea of Reece and Mindy back together? Forever this time? It was more than Beth could manage.

But she had no say. She couldn't even mount a credible argument. Not with the rock on her finger holding her back.

"That's not a bad idea."

The sound of Reece's voice had always sent a flood of warmth through Beth. Now it just delivered chills. An icy cold that made her shiver and want to jump into a fire.

"Unless I'm mistaken," Reece continued. "I believe I'm already engaged."

Now Beth wanted the fire to form a pit and bury her alive. So, she and Reegan weren't the only women he remembered. There was someone else. Someone else he loved and had proposed to.

"I only hope she'll still have me."

Whoever this girl was, she'd be a fool if she didn't. Reece Cartwright was an amazing man. The best man. The man of her dreams who she was never meant to have.

"Will you, Beth?"

There was a tingling in her chest. That was the first sign that she was still alive after being dealt a deathblow. When Beth lifted her head, she felt dizzy. Had she been holding her breath the whole time?

Her gaze locked on Reece. He'd asked her to do something for him. Was it something to do with the wedding? Did he want her to go and find Mindy? She'd die again if he asked her to have any part of this wedding.

"Will I what?" Beth's voice croaked like a toad when it finally bubbled past her constricted throat.

"Will you still have me as your husband?"

Everything and everyone in the room went still. There had been a fly buzzing on the window. It held perfectly still, as though it also couldn't believe what had just transpired.

Had Reece Cartwright just said what she thought he said? To her?

"Can we have a moment in private?" said Reece.

Slowly, everyone filed out. Ruhi mouthed *OMG* to Beth as she followed out her father. Brandon had to practically lift Reegan off her feet to get her moving. Even the fly followed the others out of the room.

Once the room cleared, Reece turned away from her. He looked down at something in his lap. It was his father's old Bible, the one he'd given to Reece when he'd gone off to college. Reece opened the well-loved pages and unfolded a piece of paper. Beth's heart kicked up again when she recognized her handwriting.

"I've been reading and rereading it. Your handwriting was the first familiar thing to me. I couldn't remember your face, but I knew that I cared for you. Every time you wrote the word *love*, I felt it in my soul."

Somehow, Beth made it over to the chair beside him. It was just in time because the next words out of his mouth would have sent her to the floor.

"I love you, don't I? We love each other?"

She had to be dreaming. This was how it always happened in her dreams. His blue eyes gazing at her, only brighter as the light of realization dawned in them. He always scanned her entire face as though seeing her anew, just like he was doing now.

"It's the first thing that felt real to me."

Reece took her hand. The left one. Beth nearly jerked her hand back when he found Walter's ring.

"I asked you to marry me, and you said yes, right?"

He frowned down at the ring, cocking his head and squinting like he knew it didn't belong.

"I guess this was all I could find out in the desert."

"It's not yours." Beth choked the words out. "I mean, it's not what I wanted."

He nodded. "I know. There's no color. You like colorful gems."

"Yes."

"I can get you a ring with every gem imaginable."

"Yes."

"I know I don't have all of my memories. I have no idea what I'll do to support you. But, Beth, you're the only thing I feel certain about. Will you still marry me?"

"Yes."

There was no hesitation. Beth took off the ring and set it aside. Then she did what she'd been dreaming of since she was a little girl. She threw her arms around the man she'd loved her whole life.

CHAPTER SEVEN

*D*arkness settled all around him like a warm blanket. He swathed himself in it, pulling it tighter over his head, tucking the sheets beneath his chin, curling the edges under his toes so that the blackness could not escape.

Reece knew that outside the large, downy comforter the sun had risen. For the first time since he'd awakened to darkness, he wanted to greet the day. He was finally looking forward to something. Or rather someone.

Beth.

He ripped the sheets from his person and instantly recoiled. Though his body was ready for the day, his mind wasn't. The bright light made him wince as it threatened him with visions he wasn't ready to see.

An explosion of light. Ear piercing screams. The salty taste of panic. The metallic smell of fear. And finally, darkness.

The darkness was the only safe place. He had to hide in the darkness. Not forever, just for a moment.

As he made to settle back under the thick sheet, a quick succession of taps sounded at the door. Reece hit the floor. He threw his arms over his head as his knees impacted the solid wood.

"Cartwright, open up. It's Ortega."

The sound wasn't gunfire. It was knocking. It wasn't an adversary. It was company.

Reece noted that he'd reached to his side, but there was no weapon. He didn't need a weapon. He wasn't in a combat zone. He was on a ranch in his hometown. He was safe.

Opening his eyes wide, he yanked on a pair of pants and a T-shirt. Padding out of the bedroom in the small row house, he went to the front door. He pulled it open to reveal a young man his age, dark hair, bright eyes, and twin dimples.

A flash of memory featuring those dimples snaked through Reece's mind. Women smiled and giggled all around Reece and Private Mark Ortega whenever he flashed those dimples. But then the scene changed. Ortega wasn't smiling anymore. His eyes were alert as he watched Reece put distance between them. There was worry on his brow. And then abject horror as the blinding bright light separated them.

Reece stepped back from the sunlight shining in the doorway.

"You good?" Ortega clamped a hand down on his shoulder.

Reece shrugged out of Ortega's hold. He shook his head, shaking the memory loose until it went back in the darkness. "Yeah, I'm good."

Ortega looked as though he wanted to ask more, but like Brandon and Sergeant Chase, he didn't. There seemed to be an unspoken code between the four men that they only shared what and when they were ready. Reece wasn't ready.

"I'm here to walk you over to Patel's office."

"I can remember where it is." Reece's expression was pinched as he stepped into a pair of running shoes at the door.

Ortega punched him in the shoulder, lightly, but enough for him to feel. "Don't think I'll take your attitude 'cause you got knocked in the head."

Reece laughed, closing the door and rubbing his shoulder. The exchange felt familiar between the two men. He also appreciated that Ortega wasn't treating him with kid gloves like the others.

"You know you were up for a promotion," Ortega said as they walked the green path toward the medical offices. "You'll probably get it now. If you still want it. If you decide you want to go back."

"Go back?"

"Into the Army. Re-enlist. Though I hear you're thinking of a different title? Husband?"

Reece's mind went back to Beth. He was going to marry Beth. The idea of going back to the army held little appeal to him when placed beside that idea.

"Man, what is it about this place?" asked Ortega. "Single men drop like flies here. I need to get out of here soon."

Reece wasn't sure what the man was talking about. But confusion was a common enough occurrence with him these days. He decided to enjoy the crisp morning air and the stunning view of the mountains instead.

A few men were out riding horseback. A number of younger boys clustered around one of the barns looking up to a grown man with the countenance of a soldier and one prosthetic arm. A ragtag pack of dogs followed around a man with a long, angry scar on one side of his face.

With each step, Reece felt more and more at home. This was a place for people like him. People who'd been wounded by the ravages of combat and were now ready to heal.

They walked farther, and Ortega continued to chatter on. This seemed normal, as well. Ortega chattering on while Reece listened.

"So, you and the pastor's daughter?"

Reece frowned. "Beth is the pastor's daughter?"

Before Ortega could confirm, a memory came to Reece. He saw flashes of Beth; a young Beth in a bright green dress; a tall and gangly Beth in a slim pink dress with ruffles at the bottom of the skirt; and Beth as she was now in a stunning royal blue dress.

Each iteration of Beth in his mind had been standing beside a man at a pulpit. Reece couldn't see the man's face clearly. Still, he felt a deep connection to the man.

"Makes sense," Ortega was saying. "You were always a holy man with that Bible of yours. Always quoting verses and trying to help people find Jesus."

That sounded right. It sounded like the kind of man Reece wanted to be. Apparently, it was the kind of man he had been.

He felt a deep sense of trust in the Bible and in God. Though he couldn't remember much, he knew not to fear. He felt an unseen hand on his shoulder with every step.

"Look," said Ortega. "I'm sure you're not ready to remember a lot because of what happened back there. But when you are …"

Ortega took a deep breath. He tilted his head up to the dawning sun. When he turned his gaze back to Reece, Reece felt an ominous foreboding.

"I want you to know when you're ready to hear about your sordid past … don't trust me. I'll make it all up."

Reece laughed. He knew Ortega's words to be true. Mark Ortega had a serious side, but it was never the one he presented.

The two executed a complicated handshake. With another pat on the shoulder, Ortega took off. Reece made his way inside the medical building.

Instead of going into an exam room, he was shown to Dr. Patel's office. The ranch's resident psychologist smiled and rose when Reece came in.

"How are you feeling today?"

"Fine."

Dr. Patel's expression didn't shift a facial muscle from its serene expression. Still, Reece got the picture that *fine* wasn't the right answer.

"You look rested," said Patel. "Nothing wrong with your sleep?"

Reece preferred to sleep. Even though he'd apparently been in a coma for days and then in and out of consciousness in the cave, he welcomed the dark oblivion sleep afforded. It was the bright light of his waking thoughts and the memories trying to invade that unsettled him.

"So, you and Beth?"

Reece blinked. The other doctors had launched into questions to get him to remember. Not this one. "Did you know us both before?"

Patel's smile brought to mind one of the many times Reece had climbed up on Santa's lap as a child. Jolly and expectant and ready to spread joy.

"I've known you both your whole lives," said Patel. "It was clear she adored you from a young age."

Now it was Reece's grin that felt ready to spread joy. It thrilled him that Beth's feelings had a long tail. He wondered when the first time he'd felt something for her was?

"It was always clear you cared for her, though your feelings were late to bloom."

Reece pursed his lips to know that. He didn't like the idea of Beth pining after him without him returning her feelings. But at some point, he'd come to his senses and asked for her hand.

"Do you remember proposing to her the first time?" asked Patel.

Reece shook his head. "She wrote to me, confessing her feelings. I still have the letter. I don't remember responding, but when I read the letter, I felt something, the first real thing I'd felt since waking up. And when I saw the ring on her finger—"

"The ring?"

"The engagement ring. That's when I knew I had proposed, and she'd said yes."

Dr. Patel nodded again. He wasn't smiling in serenity any longer. There was a slight tick on the left side of his face, as though he were chewing something over. He inhaled and let out a long breath.

"Is there something wrong?" asked Reece.

"No. Just realizing I'm going to need to clear my schedule for some individual and couple's therapy."

"Individual? You want to see us both separately?"

"It's fine."

Reece felt his shoulders snap to attention at the F-bomb. It didn't sound truthful coming from the doctor's mouth.

"Really," smiled Patel. "It's nothing to concern yourself about."

"You don't agree with our engagement?"

"To the contrary, I've been pulling for the two of you for years. I've always thought you were a perfect match. We've all just been waiting on you. This is the right thing. It's just going to be painful for a minute."

"Because of my memory loss?"

"That, and other things. I won't worry you with that now. Now, we need to get you well both inside as well as out. We'll start with some EMDR treatments."

"What's that?"

"Eye Movement Desensitization and Reprocessing. It's a method where we manipulate the eyes to try and bring the left and right hemispheres of your brain into harmony so that you can recall events."

Reece winced. "Are you going to shine a light in my eye?"

"No. You just need to follow the movement of my finger."

"And that's going to fix me?"

"There's nothing wrong with you. Your memories are all there. You've simply locked them away."

Reece wondered if maybe his memories should stay locked away.

Dr. Patel sat back in his chair and folded his hands in front of him. Reece knew he hadn't said the words out loud, but he got the sense that Dr. Patel knew exactly what was on his mind.

"We'll start next week," Patel said. "Today, you'll do some occupational therapy."

"Do you mean something like taking apart and putting together a gun?"

"No, you're going to go and milk the cows."

CHAPTER EIGHT

"Are you sure?"

Reegan rubbed her palm up and down her bare shoulder. There was a light breeze outside, but they were inside the church hall where it was warm. It was the billionth time Reegan had asked Beth that question in the last twenty-four hours.

"Yes," Beth hissed. She didn't glance over at her best friend. Neither did she apologize for her short temper in the use of the single word. Beth knew Reegan would ask her again in another five minutes. The answer would be the same.

Yes, she was sure she was going to marry Reece. Yes, she was sure she was about to break up with her previous fiancé so that she could take on the suit of her new one.

Beth and Reegan sat outside the youth pastor's office. The door was closed, and a low murmur of voices wafted from the crack between the floor and the door frame. She didn't know who Walter was in there speaking with. She didn't knock to try and rush the conversation on. Although she was sure of the actions she was going to take when the door opened, she wasn't looking forward to having this conversation.

But she knew it was the right thing to do. She didn't love Walter. She might have grown to care deeply for him, but he would never have her heart. It had always belonged to Reece. It always would. And now, Reece wanted to accept it.

A quick pang went through Beth that Reece had only discovered he cared for her now that he couldn't remember anything else. But she shushed that fleeting feeling away.

This was all she'd ever wanted in her life; to be married to Reece Cartwright. She had no doubt that she'd make him happy. She knew more about him than he knew about himself. And that had even been true when he'd had his full faculties about him.

Beth would make him happy. This marriage would make her happy. Unfortunately, she'd have to hurt a good man to bring forth all the happiness.

The voices grew closer to the door frame. Walter and his guest were about to come out the other side. Beth gripped Reegan's hands. Thankfully, her best friend knew better than to ask if she were sure again.

The door cracked open to reveal Walter's jovial face. His smile spread when he saw her. Beth stood in greeting, letting Reegan's hand go and preparing to speak a hard truth.

She could do this. This was the easy part. The hard part would be telling her father.

The door to Walter's office opened wider. A second figure emerged. Beth came face to face with her father.

Behind her, Reegan swore, but only loud enough for Beth to hear. Beth prayed that if her best friend were about to be struck down for cursing in the house of the lord, that she go with her. Eternal damnation would be better than facing this present.

"There's the bride to be," said her father. "We were just talking about you."

Beth swallowed. Her stomach grumbled, not wanting to accept the bile collecting in her mouth.

"We were thinking of a fall date for the wedding," said Walter. He came up and planted a chaste kiss at her cheek. "What do you think?"

Beth opened her mouth, but nothing came out. Her throat had grown thick with saliva since her stomach was still in revolt.

"Hello, Reegan," said her father. "Any word from Corporal Lucas about your brother?"

Reegan had to clear her throat twice before her words were audible. "Yes. They found Reece. They brought him back yesterday."

Pastor Barrett opened his palms and looked skyward. "To God be the glory. That is wonderful news. When can we see him? Is he well?"

Before Reegan could answer, Pastor Barrett turned back to Walter.

"I can't wait for you to meet Reece. He's the son I never had. You two will get along famously. Beth was like a second sister to him. You'll bring him over as soon as he's well enough, Reegan? And I suppose you can bring that husband of yours too."

Beth's father had not taken to Brandon when he and Reegan decided to marry so quickly. He believed in couple's counseling and taking the time to court. Or at least he used to. Walter and Beth had only been dating for a couple of months, and now her father wanted to push the wedding.

"Well, I'll leave you two love birds to talk," said Pastor Barrett.

"No, Dad." Beth's voice rang loud and clear. Her mouth was now dry; her heart was now racing. "Don't go. You should hear this too."

Beside her, Reegan turned to step away. Beth grabbed her best friend's hand and held on in a death grip. Reegan's sigh of resignation was only slightly louder than her curse a moment ago.

The hall was empty, which was good. Beth didn't want to go inside Walter's office where the four walls would trap her. She preferred to be in the hall so she could run if cowardliness took over her, which was very close to happening.

Now that she had both men's full attention, and her voice was in working order, and her lifelong friend was bolted to her side by Beth's one hand, she wasn't sure where to begin.

"Reece is home, and he's ill."

Yes, that was a good tactic. Show how charitable this decision she'd made was. No selfishness in it at all.

"He's going to need someone to care for him."

"Of course," said her father. "You know his church family will be here for him."

Beth nodded. This was a good start. But she had no idea in which direction to continue the conversation. So, she just blurted it out. "I'm going to be the one to take care of him."

Her father's gaze glowed with paternal pride. "You are such a good soul. I have raised a truly giving and wonderful young woman here, Walter."

"That you have, sir. I'm a lucky man."

Beth cringed. She was making this worse. Beside her, Reegan tried to wiggle out of her hold. Beth turned and glared at her friend until she held still. Reegan's shoulders slumped in complete surrender, and she stopped wiggling.

Beth decided the best way to get to the point was to bulldoze a path forward. She turned to Walter. "I can't marry you. I'm going to marry Reece."

Both men's reactions were twin mirrors. They both widened their gazes as they considered her words. Then their brows frowned as though they were repeating her statement over again in their minds for clarity. Then each of their heads snapped up as realization dawned at the exact same moment.

"I'm sorry." Beth handed over the pale engagement ring. "I've loved Reece my whole life. I tried to get past it, but I see now that I never will. It would be unfair to you, Walter. You are so good and kind. You deserve someone who will love you with all her heart, and that's not me because my heart belongs to someone else."

Beth sat the ring in the palm of his hand. She could've sworn she heard a thunk as the band landed on soft flesh. The rock was heavy, and it would make a good foundation, just not for her.

Walter looked hurt and shocked and confused. Beth's heart ached as she took one last look at him, but she knew it was the right thing to do. She could've never made him happy, not truly.

She turned to her father. The look of disapproval on his face made her want to sink into the ground. "I'm sorry, Daddy."

"Reece is a good man," said Pastor Barrett. "He would never take another man's fiancée. Did you tell him you're engaged to someone else?"

"I ..."

Her father's head lifted until he was looking down his nose at her in total censure. "You're making a mistake."

"No." Beth shook her head; the certainty she'd felt before the door opened returning. "I'm not."

Holding Reegan's hand tight, Beth turned on her heel and walked down the hall.

CHAPTER NINE

"Hmmm." There was surprise in that rumble that had a moment ago been doubtful. "It looks like you know what you're doing there."

Of course, Reece knew what he was doing. He'd grown up in Montana, not some concrete jungle. He'd milked his fair share of cows in his lifetime.

Reece was surprised he knew that about himself. General memories were easy. It was the specific ones that hemmed him up. Those memories were still shaky, coming in wisps. But his motor actions were fine.

They'd put the cow in a head catch. Reece knew he hadn't needed the assistance of such a contraption since he'd been a boy. Though he couldn't remember the first time he'd actually performed this specific task, he knew what he was doing.

Reece sat on a wooden stool. Using his booted toe, he slid the tin bucket beneath the cow's udder. He firmly grasped the animal's teat and got an annoyed moo from the old girl.

Okay, so he was a bit out of practice. He gentled his touch and began again. Making a ring with his thumb and index finger, he tightened his pointer finger in and brought each finger towards his palm one by one. The creamy substance flowed with ease into the bucket.

It was just like riding a bike.

Hmm? He wondered if he'd remember how to ride a bike. He certainly knew what one was.

"Your talk with Patel go well?" asked Dylan Banks.

Now that the man was certain his cow wasn't in jeopardy, his stance had relaxed. Reece hadn't recognized Dylan when he'd met the man. That was because they'd only met once before in passing, but Dylan knew his sister. Reegan had spent a lot of time at the ranch in the last year tending to the gardens.

"Yeah, it went well," Reece said.

"Did he go on about healing your inside as well as your outside?"

"Yeah, he did."

Dylan had smirked when he said it. The truth was, Reece was actually more interested in healing his heart. Unlike Dylan, who was missing a leg, Reece's limbs and extremities were fine. Reece knew he needed to recover what he'd lost. Still, a large part of him wanted to ignore the light trying to break through in his mind and instead focus on his heart.

"Listen to him," said Dylan. "His tactics may sound crazy, but he's usually right. Some of us believe he has a direct line to the man upstairs." Dylan pointed up to the heavens. "Anyway, I'll leave you to it."

Reece watched him walk off. He was left alone with only himself, the cow, and the bucket. Reece didn't prefer the solitude. But he also craved it.

Since he'd been awake, every person he'd encountered looked at him with expectancy. He knew they all were waiting for his memories to return. Reece felt certain that the memories would come back if he'd let them. But that would mean letting in that blinding, glaring light, and he just wasn't ready to face that pain.

The sun was up high in the sky. Reece used the cow's body to shield himself from the rays. But the cow stepped back, and a shard of light pierced his eye.

Reece turned his face away, only to meet with another ray. He couldn't block out the memory that surfaced. It hit him square in the chest.

He heard the sound of a woman wailing. He couldn't see her face, but he recognized her voice. Looking back at the memory, he recognized the woman. She had been in the cave with him. She had stood in front of him when he was rescued.

Back in the memory, Reece felt his heart pumping. He felt his legs moving fast, hitting the pavement. The woman's eyes grew wider; her wails louder. Reece's arms came around her and then blinding red hot light. Then pain, blinding pain.

"Reece?"

His initial reaction was to jump, to jerk away, to put his hands up and ward off the intruder. But the sound of her voice, the touch of her hand, it was all a salve to his soul. Beth's hand rested on his shoulder. Her body blocked out the sun. The light and pain evaporated like a reverse tornado swallowing it all whole.

Reece opened his eyes wider to look upon his salvation. The shards of sunlight surrounding Beth were muted, but they were still there. The encroaching memories weren't done with him.

Beth's face went hazy before his eyes. Another memory came clearly into focus in his mind. But not of deserts and explosions. Instead, Reece saw her face.

A young Beth smiled up at him with adoration in her eyes. Another flash and it was her face again, only a few years older. She threw her head back and laughed. The sight made him catch his breath, the sound was a sweet tune. Then another flash a few years later. This time she looked at him with a softness in her gaze that Reece immediately recognized as love.

Beth Barrett loved him. Of that, he was sure. It was how she was looking at him now, once his vision had cleared and he was seeing the present moment.

Why hadn't he married her the first time she'd looked at him that way? What had taken him so long?

"Reece? Is everything okay?"

Reece pulled Beth to him. She was standing, and he was still on the stool. He didn't dare rise. He knew his legs would be shakier than a newborn calf after the assault inside his mind.

Beth came to him willingly, allowing his head to rest against her chest. The closeness thrilled him, and he tightened his hold. He pulled her out of the light, turning her around so that his back was to the light. He would not let it consume her.

She put her arms around him. Her fingertips were a balm on his hot skin. "It's all right," she said.

And it was. So long as she was near, everything was all right. Reece wanted her like this in his arms every day.

He lifted his head and looked up into her bright eyes. Her lips parted on a gasp as she regarded him. He reached up and brushed a strand of hair from her face, tucking it behind her ear. Her hair was like spun silk. He could spend his days touching it, resting his nose in it, running his fingers through it.

His gaze traveled back to her lips. He willed a memory to come to him of kissing her. But his mind was dark now that he was turned from the light. Only she filled his gaze.

Had they kissed before? His brain hurt from the effort to wrangle free a specific memory of the feel of his lips against hers, the taste of her tongue, or the heat of her breath.

It was no matter. He could make new memories. Starting now.

Standing, Reece snaked his hand around the nape of Beth's neck. The corners of her eyes widened, like a bird spreading its wings and preparing for its first flight. There was no resistance as he tugged her to him. She was a willing traveler on this journey.

Before he could touch her lips, the cow mooed. And then he heard a crash. The milk he'd gathered spilled over and onto the floor.

"I'm sorry," Beth said. As she'd stepped closer to him, her foot had caught on the pail. "I've made a mess of things."

Her hands went to her cheeks. Reece took a hard look at her then. He noticed the puffiness of her eyes. "Have you been crying?"

She shut her eyes. But that did nothing to hide the evidence. In fact, it only accentuated it.

"What's wrong? Tell me. I can't stand to see you upset."

Beth took a deep breath. When her gaze found him again, her smile wasn't bright. But there was a light coming from within. A light Reece wanted to bathe in for the rest of his days.

"I'm happy, Reece. I promise you. I'm just overwhelmed. I never thought I'd see this day."

"Because I went missing?"

She tugged her lower lip into her mouth. Her head tilted a little to the left, like a newborn bird considering the distance from its nest up high and the unknown world down below. Finally, she gave Reece a curt nod.

Reece brought her into his arms. He towered over her. If she rested her head against him, it would fit right over his heart.

"I made my way back to you," he said. "Now we can pick up where we left off."

She rested her head against his chest, nodding vigorously. "We're going to make new memories."

"Not just new memories." Reece tilted up her face, so that he could see her eyes, but also so that he might take his first taste of her lips. "I also want to remember everything about you."

He bent to kiss her again, but she turned away. Twisting out of his hold and heading for the doorway where the sun was high in the sky.

"Have you had lunch?" she asked. "We should go and join everyone. We have a lot of planning to do for the wedding."

"All right." Reece winced at the light, but he didn't hesitate to join her. This woman was his past as well as his future. With her hand in his, he was certain he could face the glare of each new day.

CHAPTER TEN

Rain poured down in buckets outside. Not the pitter patter of an April shower. Literal buckets as if the downpour were coming out of a fireman's hose turned on full blast. The deluge had been going on for the last three days, not letting up for a split second. And now it was Beth's wedding day.

That was supposed to be a sign of good luck, right? Rain on the day of the wedding? Beth doubted it. She was sure someone made up the old wives' tale to make the bride feel better about the one thing out of her control on her big day; the weather.

Every bride who'd gotten married on the Purple Heart Ranch so far had done the ceremony outside. Beth would be the first forced into the barn. And that was after all of her guests would get drenched running from the muddy parking lot and into the damp, hay-strewn barn.

It wasn't just the weather that wasn't cooperating. Nothing else was going right. She'd stepped into her mother's vintage wedding dress, the dress she'd dreamed of wearing since she was a girl and her mother had shown her the beaded gown in the back of her closet. It was finally Beth's day to unzip the garment from its protective bag.

Even after twenty-five years of being in the back of a closet, the dress hadn't lost its luster. It was as pearly, pure white as the day her mother had said I do. The fit was perfect on Beth's figure. Unfortunately, when she tugged at the zipper on the side of the dress, the metal clasp broke.

"Don't worry," said Sarai Cannon. "I can fix this."

Beth didn't doubt that the former model could work her magic on the dress. What she couldn't help wonder about was what the next catastrophe would be?

Would the food get ruined? Would the sound system short circuit? Would Pastor Patel change his mind and not marry them?

Beth had always dreamed of being married by her father. However, the two hadn't talked since Beth had walked out of the church after announcing that her engagement to Walter was off.

She hadn't called her father either. She was far too frightened of his rejection than anything else. She knew that Pastor Patel, one of her father's oldest friends, had spoken to him. Pastor Patel had looked glum when he'd returned from that visit. Her father hadn't extended his blessing on the union, but neither had he barred his friend from performing the rights.

Beth had hesitated when she'd received the news. Her father was not a stubborn man. He always gave an ear to reason. Except when it came to his girls; and that included Reegan.

Pastor Barrett hadn't approved of Reegan's hasty marriage either. But eventually, he'd come around. That eventuality had happened on Reegan's wedding day when the man who had been a second father her whole life had shown up and walked Reegan down the aisle.

It wasn't too late. Her father might still arrive to perform that honor. There was a rustle outside the door. Beth held her breath as she waited for the person on the other side to present himself.

The door to the house opened. Instead of the familiar broad shoulders of her father, she saw the smaller frame of her best friend. Reegan ushered herself inside, tossing an umbrella back out the door. A gush of rain came in after her. Beth looked at her friend, expectantly. Reegan caught her glance and shook her head.

Beth's head dipped. Her heart sank. Her father wasn't in attendance. He wasn't coming. Not even to walk her down the aisle.

Outside, the rain beat a vicious pattern. It showed no signs of letting up. Beth straightened her shoulders. She was still going through with her wedding.

The one thing she knew for sure was that she loved Reece

Cartwright. She always had, and she always would. Nothing would change that.

Especially now that she knew Reece wanted her too. He'd almost kissed her. She'd wanted that kiss more than she wanted this marriage. She'd turned away from him at the last second because there was one thing she wanted more than the marriage and the kiss. Beth wanted everything to be real with Reece.

So long as he had amnesia, they were living in a fantasy world and not reality. He didn't remember her, not really. He only had snippets of the whole. Tiny shards in a broken mirror. Beth wasn't sure if it was an adequate reflection of who she truly was, of who they truly were to each other.

At the same time, when she'd looked in his eyes these last few days, she'd seen something she'd only dreamed. Reece had always cared for her, of that she had no doubt. When he looked at her now, that affectionate glance held a spark of heat in its depths.

Reece Cartwright wanted her.

Beth knew that look well because she wanted him too. She knew that no one else would ever love him the way she did. She knew that no one else would care for him the way she could. That's why she would walk to him down that aisle. Come what may, memories or not, her feelings about him would not change.

This was the right thing. She didn't doubt that. She just wanted Reece, the old Reece, to know it for certain too.

"You're ready to go," said Sarai. The words were mumbled as she had a needle between her lips. Her fingers tugged up the zipper to the dress, closing Beth in and sealing her fate.

Beth looked at herself in the mirror. She took her own breath away. The beading of the dress sparkled back at her. The boning in the corset did wonders to her figure. She didn't look like herself. She looked like the woman she'd always dreamed of being on this day.

There was just one more piece to complete the look. The shoes. Beth stepped into her heels … and the right stem broke.

Gasps rang up through the room. No sooner than the breath left every woman, did they each charge into action. They were all military wives, after all.

Maggie went looking for more shoes, only to discover that they were all too small or too large for Beth's feet. Sarai took the heel and attempted to glue the stem back on. Reegan pulled out the tennis shoes Beth often wore when she came to sit beside her friend in the garden, which turned out to be the winning solution. The dress was long enough to cover them.

Luckily, the laces didn't snap, and she didn't poke her toe out of the fabric. But Beth was done with holding her breath. She was done with the preparations. She just wanted to get to Reece before the next catastrophe befell her.

And so with her reconstructed zipper, and her flat, rubber shoes, she made her way over to the door. She turned the knob, girding herself for the downpour. The first thing that greeted her was sunshine.

The clouds were rapidly clearing in the sky. The sun's rays were stretching through the white wisps, as though waking from a leisurely afternoon catnap. But nothing compared to the bright bit of splendor that was the man walking toward her.

Reece was dressed in his Army uniform. His hair combed back, his chin clean-shaven. Despite the nightmares of the day, it was another of Beth's dreams come true.

This was exactly how she'd pictured it all these years. Reece would walk toward her, a slight smile on his face. Then he'd take her in, and he'd stop, just as he was doing right now. His gaze would sweep over her, and his blue eyes would light with fire, like the inner flame of a stovetop burner. That was happening too.

The only thing that was out of place in this real life fantasy was the umbrella in his hand. In her dreams, he always had a colorful bouquet of flowers. And sometimes there was ice cream in the other hand.

He held the umbrella up lamely as he spoke. "I know you don't like to get dirty. But it looks like we won't need this any longer." He tossed the device to the side. "Are you ready?"

He held out his arm. Beth came down the stairs and took the proffered limb. The sun broke through the clouds now, shining down on them. Looking up, the saw the colorful strands of a rainbow in the sky.

"It's beautiful," Beth said.

"It's fitting," said Reece. "The only way that rainbow could shine is after such a violent storm."

CHAPTER ELEVEN

Her skin hadn't come into direct contact with his, but Reece felt a cool heat where Beth rested her hand in the crook of his elbow. They'd shared a few light touches over the past couple of days that led up to their wedding day. But they hadn't been alone again. They were always surrounded by others. And in the few, brief moments when they were alone, Beth demurred.

He might not remember much, but he was starting to doubt they'd ever kissed. He now believed their courtship had been entirely through letters. He hadn't asked Beth for confirmation. It didn't matter because he knew she wanted him.

He knew that each glance she slid his way was full of longing. He saw her breath catch each time his skin faintly brushed hers. She would always linger a few more moments when it was time for them to part and go their separate ways. However, if he leaned in, if he gazed too long, she became flustered. So, he'd kept a respectable distance.

They were standing on the threshold of the barn doors. Once they crossed inside, they'd begin their wedding ceremony. He didn't feel a moment's hesitation about that. He knew in his soul that this was the thing he was meant to do, to be Beth's husband. To stand beside her and protect her for the rest of their days. He may have never kissed this woman, he may have never embraced her the way a man takes the woman whose heart he's been entrusted with, but he was certain he'd spend his life doing just that.

Looking down at Beth, he saw the brightness of love in her eyes. She looked at him with trust and adoration. He might not be certain of much in this unfamiliar life, but of that, he was sure.

Neither of their steps faltered as they approached the barn doors. Inside the large room, Reece saw a sea of unfamiliar faces. They all turned to look at the bride and groom. That's when Reece did stop, pulling Beth up short beside him.

"Where's your father?" He knew the groom wasn't meant to walk the bride down the aisle. That honor was reserved for the father of the bride.

Beth's fingers trembled in the crook of Reece's arm. The sun shone down on her, but a cloud passed over her beautiful features.

"He's not coming." Her voice was small, her gaze downcast.

Her father wasn't coming? That didn't sound right. Reece knew that Beth's father doted on her. This, her wedding day, was not an occasion the man would miss.

"Is he ill? Should we postpone?"

Come to think of it, Reece realized he hadn't seen Pastor Barrett at all the last few days. He couldn't bring the man's face into view, but he knew he'd know him the moment he saw him.

Beth sniffed. Tears pooled at the corner of her right eye as she stared down at her hands. "He doesn't think we should get married."

Again, that didn't feel right to Reece. He couldn't pull up any specific memories, but he knew that Pastor Barrett loved him. Like a son.

With supreme gentleness, Reece put his forefinger under his bride's chin and lifted her face to meet his gaze. Their voices were hushed as they stood just outside the barn doors. Even more people had turned in their seats to stare. Reece ignored them all.

"Did I do something wrong?" Reece asked. "Is he angry with me?"

The clouds fled from Beth's features to be replaced with care and compassion. "Oh, no. Not at all. You didn't do anything wrong."

"Then, why?"

She took a deep breath. Then seemed to have trouble swallowing. "My father wanted me to marry someone else."

The thought of Beth and someone else lit a fire in Reece. The flame wasn't warm. It burned.

"The problem is that," she continued, "I've only ever loved you."

And just like that, the flame was extinguished with her words. Reece looked down at her, this woman who was pledging herself to him. Her lips were there for the taking. She wasn't demurring now. Her gaze slid to his lips in turn. She did not pull away. She did not turn away. Before he could take what she was offering, Reece had to make something clear.

"This might not sound genuine," he said, "because I don't remember everything about us. But I feel certain of this. I feel certain of us."

"Oh, Reece …"

The tears that had gathered at the mention of her father's absence collected more moisture. In another second, they poured down like the rains from earlier. Reece caught each and every one of them.

Beth's lower lip trembled as she looked up at him. He tilted her chin up. Her lips parted on a shaky exhale. The taste of her warm breath filled Reece with a mighty hunger.

He dipped his head for his first taste of this woman when a throat cleared in the distance. There was also a chorus of feminine sighs. An ensemble of masculine chuckles. And a few gleefully delivered *ewwws* by giggling adolescents.

The throat clearing is what both Reece and Beth heeded. Breaking apart, the two turned to face Dr. Patel, who was waiting for them at the end of the aisle. The man's lips were pursed, but there was an amused smile in the pinched expression.

"Sorry," Reece called to Dr. Patel.

"You're doing just fine on your own," he called from his place at the makeshift altar. "I couldn't do it better myself. But since my words will make it official, why don't you two come down here, and we'll get started."

Reece escorted Beth down the aisle. He looked to the right and left at the people gazing back at him. Everyone was smiling in approval at the two of them. A few handkerchiefs were pressed to eyes. Many hands were on hearts. A few of the soldiers held thumbs and fists up in the air.

In the features of every other face, Reece caught snatches of familiarity. The prickles of light began to overwhelm him. He turned away from the townsfolk and focused his gaze on Beth.

"I bless this union," Dr. Patel began, "because I know each of your hearts. Doubts will come into the light. Remember who you are and how you feel about each other when the light of truth gets too harsh."

The pastor tore his gaze from the couple and looked over their heads to address those gathered.

"God brought Reece back to us. Beth was the guiding light that brought him home. Their love was born in friendship, blossomed with time and maturity. This community has watched these two grow, and we will continue to nurture them and invest in their progress."

A chorus of *amens* rang through the barn rafters; the promises of a tight-knit community that Reece felt a connection to, even though he couldn't discern the individual threads.

"And now for the vows." Dr. Patel turned to Beth. "Repeat after me."

"In the presence of these, our family and friends, I, Elsbeth Elaine Barrett, do take you, Reece Joseph Cartwright, to be my husband, my partner, and friend. To join my life with yours, to share with you all that is to be, to laugh with you in joy, to comfort you in sorrow, to grow with you in love. I will honor you, I will be faithful to you, all the days of my life. This is my sacred vow."

Reece's fingers tightened around Beth's as she gave him her vow. When he was instructed, he slid the ring on her finger. She gasped at the perfect blue stone surrounded by a tiny sapphire, emerald, and ruby. When she looked up at him, her eyes shone with more tears.

Reece didn't have time to catch those ones. They would have to fall. It was time to give his own vow to the woman who'd indeed brought him back to life.

"With all my heart, I, Reece Joseph Cartwright, take you, Elsbeth Elaine Barrett, to be my wife. I promise to be your lover, your companion, and your friend. I will be your partner in joy, your ally in conflict, your greatest fan in all that you endeavor. I will be your comrade in adventure, your comfort in disappointment, your accomplice in mischief, your strength in times of need. I will listen with understanding and trust you completely for all the days of my life. This is my sacred vow."

Both Beth and Reece had allowed the elderly pastor to pick out their vows for them. As the other married couples on the ranch had informed them, the man had a way with vows. Each oath he swore made an imprint on Reece's heart as a solemn truth that he would defend for all his days.

"You may now kiss your bride."

Reece didn't need to be told twice. He gathered Beth to him, wrapping one hand around her waist and the other around the nape of her neck.

Beth took in a breath as she tilted her head back, opening for him. Reece brushed his lips lightly over hers. That first touch was like a match. The second touch caught fire. He ached to deepen the kiss, but the applause and shouts from the audience pulled him back.

That was their first kiss as husband and wife. It was the first kiss that he would remember. And it certainly wouldn't be the last.

CHAPTER TWELVE

The vows solidified it for Beth. This was definitely the right thing to do. Reece's words still echoed in her ears. It didn't matter that they were composed by another man. Pastor Patel had a knack for writing the vows of the ones he married. He always got to the heart of what the two people needed in their lives and crafted just the right words both needed to say to convey that.

She was Mrs. Reece Cartwright. All the doodling in her notebooks, all the pining each night in her childhood bed, all the wishing on stars falling from the skies, and pennies being tossed into wells, and prayers to God had manifested this.

Beth knew that when Reece said those vows, he'd meant them. If she hadn't believed his promises, then she would've known this was the right thing by that kiss. Oh, Lord in Heaven, that kiss.

The first brush of his lips against hers had been cursory. But the second taste had been filled with hunger. She knew because she'd felt it too. She'd wanted a third and fourth taste, but they weren't alone. They were in a room full of their closest family and friends. So, it would have to wait.

Until tonight.

Her wedding night.

Beth stumbled at the thought. Reece was there to catch her before she fell. They were making their way back down the aisle surrounded by the cheers and well-wishes of everyone they knew.

With her stumble, Reece looked at her with concern in his blue eyes. When he gathered that she was all right, he smiled at her. All worry about the night and what it held fled Beth's body to be replaced by the heat of desire.

As much as she'd dreamed of saying *I do* to Reece, she hadn't thought much about the wedding night. She'd been a girl with a crush. Then a woman with a broken heart. Now that she was Mrs. Reece Cartwright, her wedding night with her husband was all she could think about.

People came up and congratulated her, but all Beth could think was whether or not they knew what the blush on her cheeks really meant. Food was passed around the table during the reception, but Beth couldn't eat a thing as she worried how the extra slice of bread might make her look later.

She watched Reece as he piled mac and cheese on his plate. Then greens. And, finally BBQ chicken. She wondered if he would mix them up like he did when they were younger.

As Mr. and Mrs. Fowler came over to offer their congratulations, Reece absentmindedly mixed the three dishes on his plate. He waited to take a bite until after the couple had moved back to their table. As Reece chewed his food, a look of pure ecstasy came across his features.

"This is my favorite, isn't it?"

He asked no one in particular. He was remembering more and more. What would happen when he remembered everything? And that everything hadn't included the love he'd professed for her today?

But she hadn't made this all up. He did feel something for her now. Which had to mean he'd felt something for her always. Love didn't just happen out of thin air. Right?

Beth wasn't sure. What she did know was that now that she had his love, she wasn't going to give it up. She was determined to make her husband see that the love between them should've always been there.

"I know this song," Reece said.

The sappy love song blaring on the speakers had been the theme song at their junior prom. Her date, Steve Hudson, had gone off to kiss another girl midway through the dance when Beth hadn't offered her lips to him. Beth had been left standing alone on the dance floor. Until Reece came to her rescue.

Reece had come over to dance with her, even though he had brought

Lisa Webber to the dance. This was the song that had been playing during that dance. Beth had listened to it on repeat for an entire year after the dance.

"Would you like to dance?" Reece asked her now.

Beth placed her hand in his. The colorful gems of her ring sparkled next to the gold band on his left hand. Reece led her out onto the dance floor. Wrapping his arms around her and holding her closer than he had when they were teens, he moved in time to the beat.

A few bars into the song and Beth began to wonder if he was remembering more than he let on. His steps anticipated the changes in the music where he could turn her, much like he did when they were at the school dance. Near the end of the song, he hummed a few of the lyrics. She'd heard the lyrics of unrequited love so many times, but never in the voice of the man she loved. Now that she had, the original version would pale in comparison.

Just before the song was over, Reece stopped. His steps halted, but he did not let her go. He pulled her close. But he wasn't looking down at her, he was looking away.

Beth turned to look over her shoulder, trying to see what had caught his attention. She knew it wasn't dangerous, as no other soldier was on alert. And she was right. There was no danger. Still, her heart skipped a couple of beats as the man approached them.

A broad smile crossed Reece's features as her father came up to them. Reece released his hold on Beth and opened his arms to embrace her father. "Pastor Barrett."

Beth's father looked surprised. His body stiffened, but he allowed the hug. After only a couple of seconds, all stiffness and stoicism went out of the older man. He lifted his arms and wrapped Reece in a firm grip, holding on a second longer.

Pastor Barrett pulled away and stared into Reece's eyes. He began to say something and then choked up. Instead of trying to force the words, the older man hugged Reece to him again.

"I recognized you instantly," said Reece. "Just like I did with Reegan and Beth. I suppose that happens with the people I was closest too."

"It's good to have you home, son," said Pastor Barrett.

"I'm glad you made it," said Reece. "I know this was sudden, and I can't remember if I asked for your permission before I lost my memory, but know I'll cherish your daughter all my days."

Once again, the senior pastor of the church, the man who was never at a loss for words, choked on whatever he was about to say. Pastor Barrett took a deep breath and said his piece slowly.

"I practically raised you, so I know what kind of man you are. I couldn't want better for my daughter. You have my blessing. You always did."

And then father turned to daughter. Beth took a deep breath as her father regarded her. Even though it was her wedding day, she felt that she was about to be sent to time out for disobedience.

"May I have this dance?"

Beth let out the air she'd been holding. She literally flew into her father's arms. When he wrapped his arms around her, she buried her face in his chest and cried.

"I'm sorry, Daddy."

"I'm sorry I missed your vows. By the time I came to my senses, the ceremony had already started."

"You're here now."

"I am. I may not have agreed with how you got here, but I had always hoped that Reece would be your path."

"You did?" Beth glanced up at the man she respected more than any other in the world.

"Of course, I did." Her father brushed away the tears on her cheeks. "I know Reece would never hurt you."

"He's already made me so happy. And I'm going to make him happy, whether he gets his memories back or not."

"Then, you have my blessing."

The moment he said the words, Beth realized how much she'd needed to hear them. Now this, her marriage, her future, it all felt real.

CHAPTER THIRTEEN

The wedding festivities lasted far after the sun went down. Young and old continued to sway to the beats coming from the speakers. Plates and cups were refilled a few more times. Boisterous laughter could be heard from each nook and cranny of the enclosed yard just outside the barn.

Reece listened politely as unfamiliar faces came to tell him stories from his past. Stories he had no recollection of unless they featured Beth. If they brought up his wife's name, Reece would often get a sliver of vision of times gone by.

He'd reach out and try to touch those memories. He tried to pull the delicate strands closer. He wanted to hold onto anything that reminded him of her, his wife.

At times when his neighbors and friends brought up his parents, Reece looked away from the brightness of those flashbacks. The recollections didn't hurt like trying to remember the explosion back in the desert. Still, Reece knew that if he shone a light on those memories featuring his parents, those soft spots of light would only invite more glaring rays.

So, he listened politely without letting anything penetrate. Except, of course, for the times when someone mentioned Beth's name.

A next-door neighbor recounted the time when an adolescent Beth was bundled up in a parka out in her front yard. Apparently, Reece had come over to her, plopped down in the snow without his winter coat. The two had made angels in the snow. Reece had gone home shivering and had to stay in bed for two days with a head cold. Beth had made him a paper angel to watch over him until he was well.

One of his grade school teachers told of a field trip to the beach. Instead of getting in the water, Reece and Beth had built a sand castle half their size. Beth had declared herself a princess and Reece her prince. However, Reece had insisted he was a Knight's Templar.

Not all of the memories were of happy times. He felt her hand in his after her mother passed away when she was barely a teen. He felt her head resting on his shoulder. He felt the strands of her hair falling through his fingers as he gave her solace.

As the people who'd known them both their whole lives continued recounting tales, Reece's mind went on a trek of its own. A trek where each memory marker featured Beth. It appeared he'd been there nearly every major moment of her life. So, why had it taken so long for him to admit his feelings to her?

He wanted to ask her. But now wasn't the time. They weren't alone.

Reece's gaze swept the crowd looking for his wife. She'd been at his side most of the night. At some point, they'd become separated. He felt an emptiness beside him that was just her shape and height.

He found her sitting in a group of older women. The women spoke animatedly to her, over her head, and across her. For her part, Beth smiled politely, her eyes blinking slowly as though the lids were heavy.

It had been a long day. He knew that she was tired. He could see the exhaustion written across Beth's face, but the smile on her lips said she'd fight through it. It wasn't the first time he'd seen that expression.

More flashes of memory skittered through his mind. He saw Beth's face in the firelight. He saw her smile illuminated by a movie screen, a television screen, a computer screen.

With each instance, she looked up at him with the same heavy-lidded smile. Beth, he remembered, was not a night person. She was up with the dawn, eyes bright. But when the sun set, so did she.

"You ready to go?"

Beth turned to him. Her eyes lit when she saw him, the weariness receded to the corners of her gaze until all traces were gone. She nodded enthusiastically. His heart filled with knowing that he could incite that emotion in her, that she clearly wanted to be alone with him as much as he wanted to be alone with her.

Beth said their goodbyes for the two of them. Reece couldn't remember a single name of the people he'd been chatting with the entire day. No one appeared to take offense. They all gave him encouraging smiles and nods.

Reece took Beth's hand as they walked across the dark pastures. The newlyweds were silent, but it was a comfortable silence. A silence of two people who knew each other.

Arriving at their front door, Reece hesitated. Should he carry her over the threshold? He knew the answer was yes. Beth was traditional in that sense.

"Reece? What are you—ah!"

He swept her off her feet and into his arms. Her weight was slight. She felt right in his arms.

"You'll hurt yourself," she protested.

"I only hurt my head."

"You don't have to do this." She continued to wiggle in protest.

"I have to do it right," he chided. "We're only getting married the one time."

Reece carried his bride over the threshold. Once inside, he didn't want to put her down. There was so much he'd lost, but this he knew for certain; he never wanted to let this woman go.

Her arms were wrapped around his neck. Her face tilted back as she gazed up at him. Her lips were there for the taking.

He could take them. She was his wife now. She was also willing by the look in her eyes. So he took.

Their first kiss in front of the entire town had been sweet. This kiss warmed him down through his fingertips and down to his toes. His knees felt weak, and so he put Beth down. But he didn't stop the kiss. He deepened it, drinking from her like a man taking his first sip of cool water.

He felt alive for the first time since he'd woken up. This was what he was born for, kissing Beth Barrett.

No. She was Beth Cartwright. She was his wife. He could kiss her all night. He could even do more.

As though she'd heard his thoughts, Beth caught her breath. She pulled away from him. But only her mouth.

They both were breathing hard, chests panting from their shared desire. Beth rested her hands on Reece's chest. She didn't press against him, but Reece got the signal that she didn't want him to advance any further.

He could've pressed his suit. There was no fight in her, as evidenced by the way she laid her forehead against his chin. Having not had his fill of her, Reece pressed his lips to her forehead. He wrapped his arms around her waist. They stayed like that while he waited for another signal, either for his retreat, or hopefully, for him to advance further.

Though he wished for one outcome, he would honor either option. And then Beth did something he wasn't expecting. She giggled.

"I never thought this would happen," she said. "I can't believe I'm finally kissing you. I can't believe I'm your wife. It's a dream."

"No," he said vehemently. "Please, no. I was asleep for days. This has been the best part of waking up."

She gazed up at him, open and vulnerable. Her fingertips curled at their place on his chest. Her lips trembled as she spoke to him.

"I love you. So much. I've never said it to your face. I thought I'd never have the chance." She took a deep breath. The next time she spoke, there were no tremors. Her voice was resounding and sure. "Reece, I love you. I've loved you all my life. I'm ready to give myself to you."

Reece opened his mouth to say the same. She'd already said the words. He had the script for what he needed to say.

But nothing came out.

He took a deep breath. A tremor ran through him as he gulped down a breath. When he tried again, his voice caught on something. The only sound that came out was a squeak.

Beth's face fell. It was like watching a rose wilt in the moonlight. One by one, the petals fell, leaving the bare stamen of the flower exposed.

Her hands recoiled from their place at his heart. She stepped back. But Reece didn't let her get far.

"Beth, I ..."

"Don't." She stiffened her fingers and pressed her palms into his chest. "Don't say anything."

"I have to."

"Reece, please." Her hands balled into tight fists over his heart. "It was too much. I shouldn't have said those things. It's been a long day. We should get some rest."

She stepped toward the spare room. Reece wasn't sure what to do.

He knew that sleeping together was out of the question tonight. But he knew he couldn't let her go to bed thinking he didn't care for her.

"Beth, what you said was perfect. You're perfect. You're the first thing I wanted when I woke up. You're the first thing I've thought of each morning since I've been awake, even back in the desert. Tomorrow will be no different for me."

She turned to him, a bright ray of hope in her eyes. Reece closed the distance between them. He pulled her to him, pressing his lips to her forehead again and reinforcing his brand.

"I'm not the same man you fell in love with. I'm sure you've changed too. But I know with everything in me that you're the woman I'm supposed to be with. Please believe that."

"I do."

He smiled down at her. Then he pressed another kiss to her lips, just a small one. He knew that if he lingered, he would get no rest tonight.

"Sleep well," he said, releasing her. "We'll start our new life together in the morning."

CHAPTER FOURTEEN

*S*he was an idiot.

Reece had been kissing her. It had been better than her wildest dreams. Better than her waking wishes. Better than she could have ever imagined.

And then she'd opened her mouth and ruined it.

Did she really have to make her declaration of love right at that moment? It couldn't have waited until they had been married for, perhaps, a full day? She couldn't have maybe waited until morning to lay it on thick and then make him run for the spare bedroom?

But another part of her revolted. Reece already knew how she felt. She'd written it all down for him. He had the letter to prove it. But saying it all like that, while standing face to face with him, without giving him time and space to compose his own thoughts, it had been too much.

Beth tossed and turned under the coverlet in the unfamiliar bed. The full bed was far too spacious for her body. She felt drowned in the expanse of sheets.

The day had been perfect. Despite all of the gaffs. The dress, the shows, the vows, her father turning up and giving his blessing. But also Reece.

He had been so attentive to her throughout the entire day. He'd kept his hand at her back for most of the day. When they'd been separated, she'd often glanced up to catch him seeking her out. When he'd find her, he'd narrow his gaze, as though asking if she were alright. She would nod. Fifteen minutes later, he'd do it again; seek her out and inquire after her wellbeing.

Now she was alone, in a large bed, tangled in sheets, chiding herself for jumping to a conclusion during his hesitation. Beth ran her hand over her face. The cold touch of metal opened her eyes. She gazed at the ring that Reece had chosen for her. She wasn't sure how he'd gotten it so quickly nor where from. But it was perfect.

The colorful ring was exactly what she'd have chosen for herself. It proved that the Reece she'd known all her life, the one who knew her, was still in there somewhere.

Some part of him wanted her. The problem was she couldn't get that shell-shocked look he'd worn when she'd declared her love for him out of her mind. She'd hinted at her feelings to him once years ago. Just once. It was enough.

He'd given her the same look he'd given her tonight. Back then, she hadn't been as explicit in her ardor. His response had been to call her his sister. That had doused cold water on the flame she'd been trying to stoke.

She'd been able to laugh it off that one time. She couldn't laugh about it now. Not with his ring on her finger and him in the next room.

A choked sound came from the other room. A loud gasp, like someone who'd already let out a string of chuckles and was now trying to catch their breath.

Wait? Was he laughing? She could hear him in the next room. There were more gasps. Followed by a series of short bursts. It could have been coughing, but it sounded more like chortling.

Were the chuckles at her expense? There was something off about the sounds. They didn't sound joyful or chiding. They sounded painful.

Beth rose from the bed. She put her bare feet on the floor and held still to listen. She wanted to be sure. She'd embarrassed herself enough for one night.

The next burst of sounds confirmed it. Those weren't chuckles. They sounded like moans of pain.

Beth rushed out of the room. From the hall to the living room, the house was dark. As she stepped closer to Reece's room, she saw that no light shone from beneath his door.

She lifted her fist and knocked. No response. No acknowledgment.

She was on the verge of convincing herself that she'd heard things. She was about to turn away. But then she heard it again; the unmistakable cry of pain.

Beth tried the door. It was unlocked. She hesitated for only a second, wondering if she should invade his privacy without permission. She'd been hasty in everything she'd done so far, why stop now.

She pulled the door open to a thick darkness. It took her eyes more than a few seconds to adjust. And then she saw him.

Reece lay writhing beneath the sheets. His features were contorted in agony. With his next move, he kicked off the sheets, and Beth got a clear sight of his bare chest.

Her husband was in sweat pants and bare feet. She wasn't sure why his bare skin shocked her. She'd seen him in swim trunks more times than she could count.

He moaned again, the sound sent a shudder through her body. She felt the echo of pain run down her spine. Whatever was there in his dreams was not pleasant. His fists balled, and his legs pumped as though he were trying to get away from whatever was behind his eyelids.

Beth took a step toward him and stopped. Pastor Patel had told her to approach soldiers cautiously when they were unaware of her presence. But she couldn't bear to see Reece in misery.

Reece had never been a violent man. He'd never do anything to hurt her physically. She just needed to make sure he knew it was her.

She knew that awakening to the darkness would disorient him. Reaching out, she felt for the wall paneling. Her fingers hit pay dirt when she found the light switch. She flipped it up, and light flooded the room.

Reece roared awake. He threw his arms over his face. "Off. The lights. Off."

"Okay, okay."

Beth fumbled for the switch. Once the switch was down, the room was cast back into darkness. She heard Reece panting as though he'd been running for his life.

"Reece, are you okay?"

Stupid question. Clearly, he wasn't. He didn't answer. He was too busy gulping air into his lungs.

"Should I call Pastor Patel? Or Ruhi?"

Ruhi would be a better choice. The nurse, who lived on the ranch with her soldier husband and their infant, was just a few doors down.

"Beth?" Reece breathed. His voice sounded broken.

Caution told her to keep her distance. Her heart shut that idea down. It was Reece, and he was in distress.

"Beth?" There was a note of panic in his voice now.

"I'm here." She made her way to the bed in two strides.

Before she could climb on the mattress, his arms snaked out and grabbed her. Reece brought her down onto the bed beside him. His hold was a vise grip.

"Don't go," he murmured into her hair.

Beth lay on her back while he was on his side. Their bodies were flush together. One of his arms pressed against her shoulder blades to mold her body into his. Another hand was in her hair, holding her against him.

"It's okay," said Beth. "I'm here. I won't go."

"The light." His breathing remained harsh. "It brings back the memories. Some of them are blinding. They feel like a physical burn. But when you're near ... it doesn't hurt as much. It's like your light is brighter. It's how I knew it was right to reach for you on that first day. And now."

Reece's heart pounded against her chest. She was certain he felt hers pounding the same rhythm. The organ was trying to get out of her chest and go to him.

"Stay with me?" he begged.

"Forever," she agreed.

Reece wrapped himself around her and was asleep in minutes. For the remainder of the night, they rested peacefully inside each other's arms.

CHAPTER FIFTEEN

"Did I ever tell you how we ended up just outside an insurgency stronghold?" said Sgt. Chase.

All eyebrows were raised in incredulity. Except of course for Ortega and Lucas. Reece lifted one brow. Though he didn't remember the story, he knew the significance of nearly crossing into lands overrun by insurgents.

The five permanent male residents of the Purple Heart Ranch and the four men of Reece's fire team were gathered in one of the barns. That particular barn had been remodeled into a gaming room. There were three flat screen televisions. An array of gaming consoles from Play stations to Nintendos to an old fashion Atari.

Surprisingly, Reece remembered the game he was playing. He'd beaten Specialist Sean Jeffries a number of times. Jeffries could've grumbled that his lack of concentration was due to having a baby at home, but he didn't. He took his licks and got up again.

Reece liked the man. Jeffries was quiet and didn't ask him any questions. None of the men in the room tried to get Reece to talk about his memories. Not even when they recounted times in the military, like now.

"We were patrolling a border city, but something happened to the military charts." Sgt. Chase slid a sideways glance over to Ortega.

The man's dimples made an appearance as he spoke. "I still maintain they were in my bag when we left the base."

"So, this fool," Chase spoke over Ortega, "pulled up Google Maps."

"He didn't," groaned Sgt. Banks. The man rubbed his hands over his eyes.

"As you know," Chase continued, "Google Maps isn't known for its accuracy; hence, you're often rerouted. We just so happened to be a mile and a half off in accuracy."

All the men groaned now.

"We nearly caused an international incident because we used a navigation system that's best for locating the closest Starbucks and not military patrol routes."

"Hey." Ortega lifted his hands, as though in defense of his actions. "A good, dark roast is worth fighting over."

All the men laughed, Reece included. He couldn't remember the incident, though it would have happened during the time he was on the team. Still, Reece enjoyed being amongst the men. It felt right. Mostly. He couldn't shake the feeling that something was missing.

"Married life is agreeing with you," said Ortega as he came over and slumped down in the chair Jeffries had just vacated.

Reece nodded. His marriage to Beth was agreeing with him completely. He'd been enjoying wedded bliss for only two days.

He and Beth had developed a routine. They had breakfast together in the mornings, discussing various topics. None to do with his memories or lack thereof. They had quietly decided to start with the present and forge a new life together with new memories.

During the day, Reece milked cows, rode horses, and did other chores around the farm. Beth went off with Reegan to the gardens. Although she came back each evening without a spot of dirt on herself, so he wasn't sure exactly what form of gardening his wife was or wasn't doing. Then the two had lunch with the others in the afternoon.

In the evenings, they'd make dinner together in their small kitchen with produce from the gardens and meat from the farm. Afterward, they'd read the Bible together. That was Reece's favorite part of the day; listening to Beth recite passages from his worn devotional.

When it came time for bed, Beth made sure all the lights were extinguished before climbing into his bed. After a few chaste kisses, they settled their heads on their pillows and were asleep instantly. At least he was. Holding Beth in his arms brought him total peace.

They were taking things slow, getting to know each other for who they were in this time and not in the past. Yet, Reece felt he knew everything he needed to know about the woman he'd given his vows to. All that was left was becoming the man she needed him to be.

Reece wasn't sure who that was now that he'd been discharged from the service. He'd been told he'd had plans to reenlist, but with his current condition that wasn't going to be a possibility.

He and Beth had no worries financially at the moment. They lived rent-free on the ranch, and his pension covered any other expenses they might have. But it wasn't enough to give him a sense of purpose. He just wasn't sure where to look.

"Beth?"

"Hmm?" She turned the page of his Bible looking for the passage where they'd left off the previous evening.

"There's Wednesday Night Bible study at the church," he said.

"You remember that?"

Her thumb and forefinger pinched the page she'd been about to turn. Beth was the only person who didn't have hope in her eyes about his amnesia. She had caution when she thought he might remember something.

"No, I don't. I read it on the church's website."

"Oh," she said. "Yes, there is. It starts in about an hour."

"I'd like to go to church," said Reece.

"To … our church?"

Reece nodded. "I only have happy memories about the church. It's probably because you're in most of those memories. All of my memories of you are always good ones."

"I'm not perfect." Beth shut the Bible with a decisive thunk. "I have my vices. You and I have even had our share of disagreements in the past."

"I know."

That caution showed again in her eyes. Her jaw tightened as though she was holding her breath. She searched his gaze as though she might be able to see what he was remembering. Ever since he'd told her that some memories gave him physical pain, she'd been like one of those gargoyles over churches, watching and waiting to ward off anything that might trespass in his mind.

"I remember the strawberry versus chocolate ice cream debacle," Reece clarified.

Beth blinked. Then an unexpected giggle loosened her clenched jaw. "I can't believe you remember that."

"That was a brutal battle between the two of us. I seem to remember sprinkles being thrown."

"You started it." She grinned, pointing an accusatory finger at him. "We're still not allowed in Mr. Vincetti's ice cream parlor."

"I'm sure when you admit chocolate is best, you'll be welcomed back like a civilized person."

"Never." Her growl was that of a fierce kitten.

Reece loved these moments with her. He preferred nothing better than to remember the good times he'd shared with his wife or to make new memories with her in the safety of their home. But he craved a wider community and deeper relationship with God and church. His church.

As their laughter over the ice cream flavor memory died down, Reece noted the hesitancy return to Beth's features. He wasn't sure why? He thought she and her father had made up at the wedding.

"There's something you should know," she said. "I was engaged."

"To be married?"

She nodded.

"To someone else?"

"The youth pastor." Beth smoothed her hand over Reece's Bible. Peeking from the inside cover was the worn page of the letter she'd written to him. "When you didn't answer my letter, I took it as a rejection. When you went missing, I decided to try and carve out a semblance of a life without you. So, I said yes to Walter."

Walter? What man had a name like Walter? It was a grandpa's name. Reece disliked him instantly.

"When you said you *were* engaged …?"

"I broke it off when you came back," Beth said. "I knew I couldn't have married Walter the moment I saw you again. These feelings I have for you are permanent. They're so big. They can't be ignored."

Reece pulled his wife to him. He set aside the Bible with her love letter to him inside its pages. He took her chin in his hands and brought her lips to his in a kiss.

It wasn't one of their chaste kisses before bed. This kiss was a claiming kiss. Reece pressed his lips to Beth's firmly. He had every intention of leaving a mark. He wanted every man to know that Beth was his.

When he pulled away from her, her breath was ragged, and she appeared a bit disoriented. Reece wasn't. His mind was clear, and his point had been made. Her lips were swollen, and her hazy gaze was focused entirely on him, just where he would always keep it.

"Thank you for telling me," he said. "But what does that have to do with Bible study?"

"Walter preaches at the church. When I decided to marry you, I figured I'd give him some space. That's why I haven't been back."

"You said he was the youth pastor? He's not likely to be at a night-time Bible Study. Besides that, you shouldn't run from the place you love because of this."

"I do miss it."

"Me too."

"Then, let's go."

CHAPTER SIXTEEN

f course, Walter was at the church when they arrived. Because that was just Beth's luck. As Beth and Reece walked down the halls, hand in hand, Walter came out of his office followed by the young couple they'd counseled just a couple of weeks ago. In the fluorescent light of the hallway, a small diamond glinted on Nathalie's left hand.

"They said as long as I get my Associate's degree, and if I can save up enough for first and last month's rent, then we can get married next year."

Nathaniel beamed down at his fiancée. Walter nodded his head. He smiled at the young couple, but the smile didn't reach his eyes. In fact, his features looked a bit worn and haggard.

"We were ignoring faith and hope," said Nathalie. "We'd planted too many doubts in our parents' minds. Your fiancée was right."

Walter's jaw tensed. His smile dropped by degrees. Then he looked up to find Beth and Reece approaching, and his features went positively frigid.

Nat and Nat looked at Beth and Reece's joined hands. Confusion spread over the teenagers' faces. They looked to each other, then to Pastor Vance. Wordlessly, they made the decision to walk past the new couple and the odd man out.

"Pastor Vance, I'm Reece Cartwright." Reece stuck out his hand. "I'm pleased to make your acquaintance."

Walter looked at the proffered hand. The weariness in his features spread like wildfire. In the end, the man took a deep breath and clasped Reece's hand.

"I thought you lost your memory?" said Walter.

"I lost my memory, but not my way to the Lord. Beth was the guiding light that brought me back home, back to myself."

Walter took another deep breath. A slight sheen of sweat dotted his forehead as though this interlude was exerting him greatly. "God be praised that you are home and well. But I'll need to ask your forgiveness if I can't yet congratulate you on your marriage. I may be a man of the cloth, but I am by no means perfect. I'm suffering from a bout of both envy and jealousy at the moment."

Though Beth stood at Reece's side, their hands still clasped, Walter only looked at Reece. His words were meant for her, but he still hadn't acknowledged her.

"'And whenever you stand praying, forgive,'" said Reece. "'If you have anything against anyone, so that your Father also who is in heaven may forgive you your trespasses.'"

"Matthew 11:25," said Walter.

Reece nodded.

"You know your scriptures well."

"I was told that I have a B.A. in Biblical Studies. I can remember full passages of the Bible. It's just people and experiences that I'm having trouble with."

"I've only ever heard what a good man you are."

"Beth said the same about you," said Reece. "I hope that one day we might get to know each other better. And I hope that you can forgive her for my trespasses."

Reece inclined his head to Beth. He loosened his grip on her and draped an arm around her shoulder. Beth snuggled into his hold as Walter's gaze found hers for the first time. But only briefly before settling back on Reece.

"I wish the two of you well." Walter turned and went back into his office. He closed the door behind him with a quiet snick.

It was the best they were going to get. The wounds were too fresh. Beth hoped that one day soon Walter would come to forgive her her trespasses. But she knew that day would be far, far into the future.

"That went better than expected," said Reece as he turned her away from the door. "If I lost you to him, I'd be on the floor."

Beth gazed up at her husband. The statement seemed absurd now. No matter how much she would've tried, she would never love another man the way she loved this one.

Reece's blue eyes sparkled as he looked down at her. A warm smile tugged at the corner of his mouth. And then his lips were on hers, brushing lightly.

He hadn't pressed his suit on her these last few days. But neither had he kept his hands and lips to himself. His hands always rested softly, just a hint of weight. However, Beth felt the yearning need of possession in how his fingertips would curl ever so slightly into the fabric of her dress.

His kisses were soft, patient, fluttering touches. Yet the hot breath he'd exhale when they parted always told her the full truth; Reece wanted her as a husband wanted his wife.

Each night he held back. Waiting for … something. Beth wasn't sure what, and she wasn't sure how to ask. With each embrace, with every caress, she knew she wouldn't have to wait much longer.

They entered the Bible study room. It was a relatively full house. Ten people were gathered in the semi-circle of chairs. One of the junior pastors was in charge tonight.

Reece leaned forward as he'd always done in school classrooms. He'd always sat dutifully when he was in church services, following along in the leather-bound Bible that had belonged to his father. But he thrived in these types of lecture settings.

He offered up his thoughts on the night's readings, but in no way manipulated the conversation. He listened to the other parishioners with keen interest. He built on the ideas put forth by the pastor. He searched for deeper context, often pulling in other instances in the scriptures. Soon, everyone was leaning forward and listening to him before offering their own thoughts.

"Did I want to become a pastor?" he asked as they left the study group.

Before Beth could answer, a deep male voice beat her to it.

"No, I would've loved that if you did."

They both turned to the sound of Pastor Barrett's voice. The man was standing at the church's great doors. He was in his shirtsleeves, his jacket slung over his arm and his car keys in his hand.

"You liked the academic side most. The history around the scriptures, the development of the church. Not to mention the cultural aspects of the old world. That's why you began learning the old world languages."

"I speak four languages, don't I?" said Reece.

He repeated the sentence in three distinct languages. Beth couldn't make out any of the harsh sounding words.

"Why don't you two come over for dinner?" said her father.

"You cooked?" asked Beth.

"*Pfft.*" Her father let out a harsh breath. "Why do you think I'm inviting you over? So that you can make your old man a good meal."

Beth let go of Reece's hand and snuggled under her father's hold. The three of them walked out of the church and down the street together. It felt like old times. Beth's heart was ready to burst with the joy of it.

While Beth wrangled a meal of baked chicken breasts, roasted potatoes, and green beans, Reece and her father kept up the discussion in the other room. Their conversation lasted all through dinner and beyond. They didn't exclude Beth. In fact, they asked her opinion at many turns.

Beth wasn't interested in the topic. Talking seemed like a chore when she simply wanted to watch, listen, and soak in the scene before her. Her father and her husband at the dinner table, their bellies full from a meal she'd crafted.

A quarter of an hour later, when she saw that the conversation was still going strong, Beth decided to take on another duty that had been hers when she'd still lived at home. She loaded the dishes and wiped down the counters.

Poking her head into her father's office, she saw that it was in disarray since she'd last been home. Even though she was now married, she'd need to make her visits to her former home much more frequent. She knew her father could do without her. He just hadn't adjusted yet, and he didn't truly need to. Beth was happy to manage both households. She certainly had the time, now that she felt comfortable back in both her family church and her family home.

She straightened the books on the shelf, replacing texts he'd used in preparing a sermon last month. She straightened her father's papers, sorting the documents into various piles. There was a separate pile of unopened mail at the corner of the desk. A few bills, a few letters from parishioners, and a few pieces addressed to her. One envelope, in particular, stuck out.

It was army issue.

It was from Reece.

The post stamp was from over a month ago. Sometimes military mail was delayed, especially when it came from overseas. So this would've been from Reece before he lost his memory.

It could be one of his normal letters. They'd written to each other his entire military career, preferring the handwritten notes to emails and phone calls. Somehow, she doubted it was a normal correspondence.

Her fingers trembled as they set to the task at hand. Beth tore the lip of the envelope carefully. The first line tore at her heart.

Dear Beth,

You are my dearest friend. I love you like you were my sister...

She heard the words in her head in Reece's own voice, an echo of the one and only time she'd tried to tell him her feelings face to face. He'd let her down gently then. The letter was a repeat performance.

She didn't read the entire missive. She couldn't. She knew where it would end having been there before.

Beth looked down at the ring on her finger. The one he'd so carefully chosen for her based on the memories he did have of her. He had no recollection of this letter now. But one day, he would.

What was she going to do until that day?

CHAPTER SEVENTEEN

"It really is good to have you back, son."

Reece sat back in the recliner in the Barretts's living room. It felt normal, natural. He was certain he'd done this before. Many times.

The lights were dim. The memories breezing through his mind were easy and non-threatening. He remembered Christmas morning at the Barretts. He remembered Sunday dinners. But mostly, he remembered Beth.

"I admit I had fantasies of you and Beth getting together when you were younger," said Pastor Barrett. "But you always seemed more like siblings than anything romantic."

Reece frowned at the thought. His feelings for Beth were most certainly not brotherly. Though he wasn't about to admit that to her father. Reece hoped that he and Beth would soon take their relationship to the next level.

He'd taken his time with her. Sticking to a few chaste kisses. Tempering his touches and embraces to remain light. He wanted to be sure their relationship was firmly rooted in the present and not relying on the past, especially since he didn't have a full picture of the past. He wanted to be sure that Beth loved him for the man he was today, as he loved her for the woman that she was in this moment.

He felt certain that the mission had been achieved. He believed the next time he took his wife in his arms and kissed her they wouldn't be falling to sleep immediately. Just thinking about it, he felt his cheeks heating, which would not do while he was sitting in front of her father.

Reece turned his gaze to the window, hoping the moonlight scene would cool his ardor. Under the light of the moon, he saw a familiar structure across the street. He realized what the dark outline was.

"Have you been to see it?" Pastor Barrett asked.

Reece shook his head. His fingers gripped the leather cushion of the seat. "I think I should."

"Do you want me to come with you?"

"No," Reece said rising. "Let Beth know I'm outside."

Once outside, Reece barely made it across the street before his knees went weak. He smelled char. Patches of the roof were missing. There was no glass in any of the windows. Two black smears ran down the front of the house. It was as though happiness leaked out of the structure. It looked war-torn.

A light breeze blew on the wind, ruffling the ghosts of memories around his mind. Reece saw his parents sneaking kisses on the patio when they thought he and Reegan weren't looking. Another flash showed him and his sister running through the sprinklers on a warm summer's day. Another glimmer displayed him and his friends playing a game of soldiers where they lined up and marched across the lawn.

Reece walked closer, his feet making a slow march toward his past. The memories were calling to him, like a blow horn. They pushed at the back of his brain, trying to make their way forward.

And then an explosion broke the barrier.

Reece's logical brain knew that the sound was of a car backfiring. But the memories took the opportunity to charge forward. Down to his knees, he went, hard. The assault of his entire past flooding his temple shot pain throughout his entire body until he felt like his fingers and toes were the barrel of a discharging firearm.

He took a deep breath, fighting for air, fighting to maintain consciousness. Dirt touched his lips. Concrete abraded his palms. Blinding light filled his eyes.

And then he felt hands on his back. But when he looked up, it wasn't a face covered by cloth like when he'd woken up the first time. It wasn't the face of his sister that mirrored his own. It wasn't the face of his wife, whom his heart had known instantly.

"Mrs. Harrison?"

"Are you all right, dear boy?"

That's what she called everyone; *dear boy* or *dear girl*. Kids were dear to Mrs. Harrison because she'd never had any of her own.

Reece remembered that. He remembered her. Mrs. Harrison, the wife of grumpy old Mr. Harrison. Her husband had only ever scowled at the neighborhood kids, but his wife always smiled and had cookies in her apron.

"You remember me?" asked Mrs. Harrison.

"I remember everything."

He remembered his parents sending him off for training camp. The mix of worry and pride intermingling on their faces. He remembered his first tour and the apprehension he'd felt on the flight overseas. He remembered his first few months on base, making friends, and bonding with his team.

His team; Chase, Lucas, and Ortega. They were his brothers.

He remembered the look in Lucas's eyes just before the bomb had gone off. That look hadn't been in fear of his own life. It had been about Reece, and the knowledge Brandon wouldn't get to him in time.

But he'd come back for him. And now they were true brothers. Reece had lost consciousness in that explosion, and he'd woken with a whole new lease on life.

Now more than ever, he knew what was important. Family. Not just the family by blood, but the family that he'd chosen and those who had chosen him.

His fire team was his family. The men and women of the Purple Heart Ranch were his family. The people of this town were all his family. But most importantly, Beth was his family.

Beth.

He needed to get to Beth. He needed to tell her that he remembered. But first, he had to escort Mrs. Harrison back across the street.

As he deposited the older woman at her porch, she reached into her pocket and handed him a cookie. He returned the warm embrace she gave him, holding her tight as he'd realized he needed a motherly hug. After she was safely inside, Reece turned back to the Barretts.

It was when he passed the mailbox that a particularly unpleasant memory shoved its way to the forefront. The letter. After he'd received Beth's letter, he'd written a response.

The words he'd pressed to parchment seemed like a foreign language to him now. In response to the confession of her feelings for him, Reece had let her down. His words had been as gentle as he could make them. He didn't want to lose her. He prized her friendship above all others. But he didn't have those feelings for her.

Well, he hadn't. Not then. Now? Now she was all he thought about.

What had he been thinking back then? It had always been Beth. True, he hadn't realized it then. Would he have realized it had he not forgotten who he was?

It didn't matter. He didn't want to be anyone other than Beth's husband. That's where his new life began, and he had no intention of walking backward. Then a terrible thought hit him.

What if Beth had gotten that letter?

He remembered writing it. Had he actually sent it? He couldn't remember that.

He remembered his high school gym locker. He remembered his college roommate's middle name. But he couldn't remember if he'd posted a letter that would change his life if it fell into the wrong hands.

And then she appeared in the doorway. Beth peered out into the night. Backlit by the porch light, she looked like an angel. He would've followed her anywhere.

He came to her, needing to be near her but afraid to touch her. She looked so ethereal he was afraid she'd dissolve if he actually reached out to her.

"Is everything okay?" she asked.

She looked worried and unsure. Her gaze flickered behind him. Out of the corner of his eye, Reece saw what caused her distress; the remains of his house. She was worried that seeing the destruction of his family home had upset him.

She was wrong. It was just bricks and mortar. The only thing that could rip his heart out now was her rejection.

"What's past is past," he said. "You're my home now."

She closed her eyes and breathed a sigh of relief. Reece opened his mouth and inhaled her breath. Unfortunately, there was still the smell of smoke and char in the air.

CHAPTER EIGHTEEN

Since their wedding, the past nights they'd lain together Reece held onto her, tightly. To be sure, Beth had wanted her husband to press his suit and claim his marital rights. But he insisted on taking things slowly; on the two of them getting to know each other as they were now.

Beth had been content to play along. So long as he stole kisses from her after breakfast. So long as he opened his strong arms to her each night. So long as he pressed his nose into her hair when their heads hit the pillow.

She could spend the rest of her life receiving light caresses from her husband. She could wait forever in his attentive embraces. She could hold still and tamp down her desire for more interminably, so long as his lips remained pressed against her hair, her cheek, her lips. It was enough.

Tonight, however, he kept his distance.

Not physically. They lay side-by-side. Reece held Beth's hand in his own, but his fingers were not clamped down on hers. The hold was loose.

His head was turned away. He stared up at the ceiling. His brows were pinched together, making an M-shape. More than anything, Beth wanted to reach over and smooth the M out into a placid line. Instead, she kept her hand in his loose embrace.

A light shone into the bedroom. They forgot to turn off the hall light. But Reece hadn't made a single complaint about it. Beth doubt he'd even noticed it.

Had it worn off? Whatever had made him rush into her arms and away from the light. Whatever had made him decide he wanted her in the darkness?

Beth turned away from the light. She unraveled her fingers from his. He did not protest. He did not reach out to bring her back. He barely stirred from his quiet reverie.

She turned over onto her side. Pressing her palms together and resting her cheek against her hands, Beth stared out the window. She blinked, and it was dawn.

She hadn't slept a wink. She hadn't changed position in the night. Turning to face her husband, the bags under his eyes told her he hadn't moved his position or slept either.

She didn't know what to say to him. She wasn't ready to tell him the truth; that she'd received his letter telling her that he harbored no romantic feelings toward her. She likely wouldn't have to. By his avoidance of her last night, something inside him was already coming to that realization.

And then what?

Would they have the marriage annulled? There were grounds for it. Plenty of grounds.

Her husband wasn't in his right frame of mind when he said his vows. The bride had knowingly misled the groom. The marriage hadn't been consummated.

"Beth?"

Beth looked up to find Reece leaning over her. His handsome face gazed down at her, blue eyes filled with concern. His smile was soft, not containing hunger as it had been every night before he closed his eyes after their chaste kissing. He rested his head on the knuckles of one hand while his other hand boxed her in.

Beth wanted to stay in the cage of his arms. She wanted to reach out and press her hand over his heart and keep it there for the rest of their days. Or for just one more day. A few more hours. She'd settle for a few more seconds.

His hand came to her face. His thumb brushed her cheek, just under her eyelid where she was certain dark circles hung.

"You didn't sleep well?" he asked.

"Neither did you," she countered. "Nightmares?" She hoped it was nightmares and not memories.

Reece shook his head. "Too many thoughts."

Beth filled her lungs slowly, then let out the breath before he could speak. "What kind of thoughts?"

He didn't turn away from her. He peered into her. Past the windows of her eyes. Down into the chambers of her heart. Until his light touched her soul.

"You have always been there when I needed you," he said. "I'm very lucky to have had you in my life."

She was a balloon, stretching its confines with the breath of his words. One more syllable from him and she would burst open.

Beth shut her eyes. She was far too overwhelmed. Relief rushed through her, giving her a little room to wiggle.

Maybe it would be okay; when she told him about the letter. Because she had to tell him. She wouldn't have their relationship based on lies and secrets. Maybe he could still love her as more than a friend when he knew.

Reece's hand snaked around her waist. Beth opened her eyes as his long, lean body came in contact with hers from his chest on down to his bare toes. He pulled her to him … and kissed her on the forehead.

She let out a sigh. Her breath hit his Adam's apple. She had the urge to taste the bobbing bit of skin. Before she could act on the impulse, the doorbell rang.

Reece released her. Sliding out of bed, he pulled on a T-shirt to cover his bare chest. In a T-shirt, pajama bottoms, and bare feet, he went to answer the door.

"It's just Reegan," he called a moment later.

"*Just* Reegan," came his sister's indignant reply.

Despite the turmoil inside Beth, she chuckled at the siblings' banter. "I'll be out in a bit. Just gonna shower."

Beth took her time getting out of the bed. She wasn't ready to begin this day, not knowing how it would end. Walking over to the closet, she grabbed her purse from its hook. She took the letter from its depths. Unfolding the missive, she read the lines again.

Reece had said he was a new man the day of their marriage. Maybe he didn't harbor these feelings anymore? Maybe he had developed new romantic feelings for her. It was possible. But she wouldn't know until she brought it to him.

She knew today had to be the day she told her husband about his letter. But the day lasted until 11:59 pm. No need to rush it.

Stuffing the letter back in her purse, she padded into the bathroom on bare feet. The tiled room was cold. Beth decided to indulge and run the shower a few minutes to heat up the room. Realizing she'd forgotten her clothes, she headed back to the bedroom, closing the bathroom door behind her to keep in all the heat.

"Mrs. Clarkson brought these pictures over this morning," Reegan said from the other room. "Nearly everything was lost in the fire; all the photo albums. The neighbors have been looking through their albums and finding pictures with us in them so that we have some memories."

"Oh," laughed Reece. "Is that Martin Burns? He lived four doors down. He cheated at chess. He's working on Wall Street now, isn't he?"

"You remember Martin?" Reegan asked. "He was a cheater, and he does work in New York now. What else do you remember?"

Beth couldn't see Reece, but she felt his hesitation. The floorboards creaked as he rose. Beth ducked into the bedroom. Peering through the crack of the door's hinge, she saw Reece poke his head around the corner and look at the closed bathroom door. After a second, he turned back to his sister in the other room.

"I remember everything," he said.

Reegan squealed. Reece rushed out of Beth's sightline. She heard him hush his sister.

"I don't want Beth to know," he said.

"Why not?" asked Reegan.

Why not? Beth knew exactly why not, and it made her knees weak. It made her stomach knot. It made her heart shatter into a tiny million pieces.

Reece knew. He knew their marriage was all a sham. If he remembered weasely Martin Burns, then he surely remembered that he didn't love her. Clearly, Reece was trying to figure out how to let her down and get out of a marriage to a woman he didn't love.

Beth couldn't breathe. She had to get out of here. She pulled a dress over her head, sneakers on her feet, and then she opened the bedroom window.

Outside, the ground was still wet from the rain. A puddle of mud lay right under the window. With only a moment's hesitation, Beth plunged herself feet first into the pile of dirt.

Mud splattered all over her shoes, up her thighs, and on the folds of her sundress. She didn't spare a care. Her future was already in a ditch. The rest of her might as well join in.

CHAPTER NINETEEN

Reece shushed his sister, waving his hand at her in agitation. That feeling was another familiar thing; being annoyed by his twin sister. Oh, he loved and adored Reegan dearly, but her songbird voice often carried. This was not a song Reece wanted everyone to hear.

He held up his hand, his fingers splayed. His ears strained to listen for any sign of movement, feminine gasp, or floorboard creaking. He heard nothing, but he needed to be certain.

Balling his fingers into a fist, he looked meaningfully at his sister. Reegan frowned at him. The twin expression of annoyance she felt for him dripping off her features to be replaced with incomprehension.

She wouldn't know that his fisted hand signal meant *stop* in the military. Stop moving, stop talking. That there was possible danger afoot because something unknown was present.

Reece wasn't sure if Beth had heard his confession. He needed to be sure. Sound wasn't enough. He needed a sight line.

On quiet feet, he tiptoed toward the hall. Peering down the passageway, he saw that the bathroom door was closed. From within, he heard the clear sounds of the shower running and saw the steam wafting up from under the door.

She was in there. Had been in there for a while if steam was escaping. He let out a sigh and lowered his hand.

"What's going on?" asked Reegan once he'd turned back to her. "Are you and Beth fighting?"

"No, we're not fighting," said Reece. As a matter of fact, they hadn't said much to each other since dinner last night. Something was on her mind, something she hadn't cared to share with him.

A terrible thought arrested Reece's heart. He pinpointed the moment when Beth went silent. It was after running into her ex back at the church.

Just as quickly as the thought came to mind, Reece dismissed it. The few furtive glances the Youth Pastor had given to Beth had been filled with a mixture of pain and longing. Whereas Beth had looked at him with only shame and remorse.

There was no passion in her gaze as she looked up at her former fiancé. Not the way she looked at Reece. Not the way she'd looked at Reece their whole lives.

Beth had loved him her whole life. If her letter to him hadn't confirmed it, thinking back on all of their encounters now did confirm it. The woman of his dreams had been in arms reach his entire life, and he was only now coming to realize it.

So, why had she begun pulling away from him last night?

"You guys never fight," said Reegan. "Not for real. Not when you were kids, not when you were older. I don't think you two have ever had a real disagreement."

That was true. Reece remembered when he'd told Beth he was going to enlist. He'd expected her to jump for joy alongside him. Her feet had remained on the ground, her smile had turned upside down. She'd looked at him as though he'd told her there was no Santa Claus—which even as a teenager, she insisted that the jolly old man lived in everyone's hearts.

Aside from her adolescent view of Saint Nick and Christmas being her favorite holiday, Reece knew that the church was Beth's favorite place in the world. She hadn't strayed far from it or this community in all her life. Whereas he'd left and gone half a world away.

Before his accident, he'd planned to reenlist. He'd been convinced that a military career was his calling. He'd confided as much to Beth. It had been the first time she'd lied to him and pretended that she was happy for him.

Was that why she'd clammed up last night? Was that why she hadn't slept? Was she having second thoughts about her marriage to Reece?

Was she waiting for the day he announced that he was returning to the service?

He could return now that his memory was back. He could pass a psych evaluation, as well as a physical one. But the question was, did he want to?

"I love her," Reece said.

"I know," said Reegan in that annoying, know-it-all way of sisters.

"No, you don't get it. I *really* love her. Not like a friend or a sister. I love her like a man loves the woman he wants to spend the rest of his life with. The woman he wants as the mother of his children."

Reegan leaned forward, one brow quirked up. "I know. I'm just glad you finally figured it out. Especially before she married Walter. He's a great guy. He just wasn't right for her. It was only ever you for her."

It could've never been anyone else for him but her. He had to hope he'd have come to that realization eventually. He was just thankful that it hadn't been too late as well. He now had his answer on whether or not he would go back into the Army.

Losing his memory had saved his life. He'd always believed that serving his country was the most honorable thing a man could do. But there was a higher calling than that. Something that hit closer to home; serving his family, his community.

"When did you get your memory back?"

"Last night." Reece spared his sister the details about what had triggered his memories to all click back into place. He knew she was still having a hard time with losing their family home to the fire. But now that he was back, they would rebuild. It would take time, but they could all stay on the ranch until the job was done.

"And you haven't told Beth yet? Why?"

"I…"

Reegan was right. Why was he hesitating? He didn't need any secrets between him and his wife. He gave his sister a hug and peck on the cheek and then ushered her out his front door. With the house now empty except for him and his wife, Reece made his way back down the hall.

The muted sounds of water against tile could still be heard from the other side of the bathroom door. It was an unusually long shower. Beth wasn't as mindful of the environment as his sister, but neither was she wasteful.

He knocked on the door. After waiting a few seconds, he knocked again. Louder this time.

"Beth?"

Still no response.

Reece began to worry. His hesitation lasted all of two seconds before he pulled open the bathroom door. He averted his gaze, but he didn't need to. The bathroom was empty, save a thick cloud of steam.

Reece didn't bother turning off the water. A prickling sensation began at the bottom of his spine. As he took quick steps toward their bedroom, the prickling turned to sharp shards when he opened the bedroom door and found it also to be empty.

Panic set in when he saw the open window. Had someone taken her? No, that was preposterous. He would've heard something. Even if it were remotely possible, the ranch was crawling with soldiers and veterans.

Beth's purse sat on the bedsheet. A sheet of paper sticking out of its belly. A light breeze ruffled through the open window caused the edges of the paper to flutter. The crackling sound of the parchment in the breeze drew Reece closer.

He gave the edge a yank. Yet the moment his fingers came in contact with the page, he jerked his fingers away as though the paper seared his fingertips. But the sheet was already loose.

There, floating to the ground, was the missive he'd fired off months ago. It landed on the top of his bare foot like a silent explosion. The edges of the pages curled as though the fire of the ink had singed the corners.

Reece didn't pick it up. He wanted to stomp it out so that it couldn't burn the new life he'd woken up to. But clearly, it already had.

So, he had mailed it. And she had opened it. He wasn't sure what had made her run? The letter or overhearing that he'd gotten his memories back.

It didn't matter. All that mattered was that he found her and told her what was in his heart in the present moment, and what he wanted for their future.

He left the room, shouting her name. But she wasn't in the house. He looked in the front yard to see that her car was gone. She was gone.

CHAPTER TWENTY

*B*eth drove aimlessly. The mud from her skirt smeared her elbow as she turned the wheel in directionless circles. She brushed at the mess of her dress, but the stains weren't coming off anytime soon.

Her mind was blank as she felt her heart breaking into a thousand pieces. Meanwhile, Reece was whole once more. With all his memories back, Reece would surely be looking for a way out of their sham of a marriage.

She should have stayed and faced the mess she'd made. She shouldn't have gotten herself into this mess in the first place. She shouldn't have reached out to him when she knew his heart was not hers for the taking.

But truth be told, it had been worth it.

What was the saying? It was better to have loved and lost. Those words were true.

If she had it to do all again … well, she wouldn't give any of it up. The few days she'd gotten to spend as Reece's wife were worth the sharp points now piercing her chest.

The nights she'd spent in his arms, the furtive touches, the hungry kisses that were on a leash. Every second of it was worth the pain she was in now. Those memories would have to sustain her for the rest of her life because she was never walking down an aisle again. That would be the real lie; to let any other man believe that she could devote her heart to him.

But also, the thought of a life without Reece in it looked beyond bleak. Her stomach tightened with nausea. Her shoulders felt sore and began to droop. There was a sharp pain in the back of her throat. And her vision began to blur from unshed tears that were very near to spilling from every corner of her eyes.

Beth pulled off the main road. She could stomach being a hazard to herself, but she wasn't about to hurt anyone else. Pulling into an empty parking lot, she cut the engine, put her head on the steering wheel, and let the tears flow.

She cried every tear in her heart, every tear in her soul until nothing was left. She had no idea what she was going to do? She had no idea where she was going to go?

The ringing of bells pulled her out of her misery. Beth looked up to find that she had subconsciously driven herself to the one place where she always felt whole and sure: church.

Catching a glimpse of herself in the rearview mirror, she couldn't help but cringe. Elsbeth Barrett had always prided herself on her appearance. The woman looking back at her was a shell of the prim and perfect pastor's daughter.

Her hair was a rat's nest. She wore no makeup, and the red rim of tears around her eyelids did her no justice. Her clothes and skin were mud splattered.

Normally, she wouldn't be caught dead in the state she was in. Appearances did mean something to her. But right now, she was so far from the woman she'd always portrayed herself to be.

Beth climbed out of the car, not bothering to smooth out her sullied dress or her untidy hair. She went inside in search of her father. She knew now that her father wouldn't say *I told you so* when she confessed her sins about the foundation of her marriage. Pastor Barrett would do what he always did when one of his flock had gone wayward. He would guide her on the best course of action.

Sure, he'd be disappointed in her actions. But Beth was ready to atone for that. She was ready to do whatever was necessary to make Reece happy, healthy, and whole. Because even though she'd gotten the better end of the bargain, her heart had been in the right place. She'd only wanted to look after Reece and be certain he was cared for.

Beth opened her father's office door, preparing to confess her sins.

Inside, she didn't find her father. She found Walter at her father's book-shelves.

Twin, long, deep, uncomfortable sighs escaped both Beth's and Walter's lips. A heaviness settled over Beth's feet making it impossible for her to turn tail and run. The tightness in her chest from before made it difficult to take in a cleansing breath to get out any words. She slumped against the door in weary defeat.

Walter dropped the book he held in his hands, along with his own wary expression. He rounded the desk and came to her immediately. "Are you hurt? Are you injured?"

Walter's hands came to her shoulders, caressing lightly but urgently. There was no spark in his touch. Had there ever been?

"You're an absolute mess," he continued as he looked her over. "What happened?"

Beth looked into his eyes. She saw no desire, no passion. All that was reflected back to her was concern and compassion. Regardless of how she had hurt him, she knew that Walter would come to her aide if she were in need.

Beth unfurled Walter's fingers from her shoulder and took his hands in hers. "I'm so sorry for what I did to you."

Walter blinked, once, twice. He reversed her hold. Taking her hand in his, he led Beth over to her father's seat. Then he leaned against her father's desk peering down at her.

"This is about your husband?" Walter asked.

Beth winced at the word. "He's not my husband. Not really."

Walter was eyeing her with caution in his gaze. He held his tongue, just like he did in his marriage counseling sessions. But without the other party there, Beth had all his attention.

"It was all a lie," she admitted.

"Are you telling me you don't love Reece?"

The words were so ludicrous that she laughed. The sound hurt the dry patch in her throat. "I love him with all my heart and all my soul. But he never loved me. Not in that way."

"He seemed pretty full of love for you the other day."

"That was then. This is now."

"What happened in the space of a day?"

"He got his memories back."

"So, the man he was before is not the same man that he is today?"

The throb in Beth's heart moved to her temple. She closed her eyes against the oncoming headache.

"I've never believed in the old adage of love at first sight," Walter continued. "Lust is a spark. Love is a raging fire. It takes a while to start a fire."

"Sure," Beth agreed, rubbing her temples with her thumbs. "Unless you use gasoline."

Walter chuckled softly. It was a nice sound. She'd always liked his laugh. It set her at ease. She might not have loved Walter, but she'd certainly liked him.

"Either way it begins, there must be the necessary ingredients. A spark of lust. A match to capture the flame. Fuel to keep it going. Something must be there. I saw a spark in you that day you broke it off with me. I just realized too late that the spark wasn't for me."

The headache was receding, the more Walter spoke. Beth opened her eyes and took in the youth pastor with new eyes. There had been something between her and Walter. But there hadn't been enough fuel to get through a lifetime.

"That's why I didn't fight when you broke off our engagement. You were revved up, full of fuel. I knew you would never stop loving him, and there would never be room for me. When I saw the two of you together, I saw the same thing in him."

"You did?" Hope sprung like an oil geyser in Beth's heart.

Walter lifted an eyebrow as he regarded her. Beth was instantly chastised by that brow. She knew this conversation couldn't be easy for him. Still, he offered her the guidance she sought.

"I don't know the man he was. But whoever he is now, he loves you. You two were close when you were young. You're different people now, especially with his trauma. That wedding was hasty though. You should get to know one another. Perhaps marriage counseling."

Beth stood. But once she was back on her feet, indecision made her knees wobbly. She shut down her uncertainty and opened her arms to Walter. "I truly hope that one day we can be friends."

Walter reached out and put his hand on her shoulder. Both of his brows raised as his gaze traveled the length of her, taking in her state of disarray. "Maybe ... but not today."

Beth couldn't help herself. She burst out laughing. So, she didn't hear the door creak. She wasn't sure how long Reece stood there on the threshold gaping at Beth standing close and laughing with her ex-fiancé after running out on her husband.

CHAPTER TWENTY-ONE

*R*elief.

That's all he felt when he saw her standing with Pastor Vance. Reece ignored the hands that were on her shoulder. Beth was his, and he didn't doubt that. The only thing in doubt was what she believed he felt for her since she'd read that letter. By the shame and guilt that clouded her features, Reece could hazard a guess.

"Will you give us a moment?" Reece asked Vance.

The man looked at Beth, as though asking for her permission. Beth gave him a nod. With a squeeze of her shoulders and a nod to Reece, the pastor left the room.

Reece closed the door to the office before making a beeline for his wife. Before he could take her into his arms, she hopped out of his path and went to the window, standing directly in the sunlight.

The glare didn't give him a second's pause. He followed her, a moth to the flame of the woman that he would die for, live for.

"Before you say anything," Beth began, "I just need you to know I'm sorry I misled you."

"Misled me?"

"I know you remember everything, so you must remember the letter. You must remember that you don't love me."

Reece leaned forward, boxing her in. The sun cast her in an ethereal glow that he could not look away from. "Beth, I do love you."

"Not in that way." Tears pricked her eyes, and her voice trembled. "Not in the way a husband loves a wife. You told me before that you loved me like a sister. But I had to tell you what was in my heart, and when you didn't answer my letter …"

She took a deep, shuddering breath. As she let it out, her loose hair fluttered off her cheek. Reece brushed the tendrils tenderly away, tucking her hair behind her ear in a semblance of tidiness. He waited for her to finish, knowing she needed to confess as much, if not more than he did.

"Then I got your response in the mail. It came after the wedding. It was mailed to the house."

He nodded, waiting for her to go on. Instead of giving him more words, her head hung, her chest slumped in defeat. Reece gathered her to him, giving her his strength.

"Beth, my strawberry sweet girl, please let me explain—"

"No." She whimpered, but she didn't fight his hold. "I don't want you to explain. I don't want you to tell me that you'll always love me like a sister because I will never feel that way about you. I love you in the way God intended a wife to love her husband, and it will never change."

Reece saw that he wasn't going to get a word in edgewise unless he took action. His wife needed to be rescued from her insurgent feelings. So, he let his training kick in.

He cupped Beth's face in both of his hands. He pulled her to him and then he kissed her until she went senseless. Once she was gasping for breath, he could finally tell her what he needed to say.

"I wrote that letter. I remember writing that letter. I remember what my feelings were. They're not that now."

"They're not?"

"Beth, it was always going to be you. I didn't realize it until I forgot everything else. My first memory was of you. When I woke up, all I wanted was you. Now that I have my memories back, none of that has changed. I still want you. Forever."

He felt her heart racing alongside his. The only light he saw was the light of hope in her eyes. He could bathe in that for the rest of his life.

"I need to tell you what's in my heart," he said, echoing the words of her letter in his own voice. "I love you. I've always loved you. My feelings for you deepened while I was asleep. I woke up knowing there will never be anyone else for me but you. You are my best friend. I'd like to offer you my heart. But—"

"But?" Her fingers tightened into the front of his shirt a death grip. "No buts. I don't want a but."

"But," he chastised, pulling her closer, letting her know that there was no escape from his capture, "I think Walter was right. I think we need to take some time and get to know each other. I'm not sure about the marriage counseling, but I definitely think we should maybe date for a while first."

"Date?"

"Yes, I'll take you out to dinner and court you and—"

She nodded as though considering his proposal. Then the prim and proper pastor's daughter snaked her arms around his neck. She pulled his head down to hers and claimed him. That answered that question.

"We can date if you want," she said when she released him from a kiss that claimed his body and his soul. Beth's kiss took over his mind replaced each one of his memories with dreams of a future with her. "But every one of these dates will begin and end with a kiss."

"I give you my solemn vow," he said. And since he planned to take his wife out to lunch, he began their date as she requested, with the first of a lifetime of unforgettable kisses.

EPILOGUE

*T*here were couples all around him. At every turn. In every corner.

Mark had no problem with love. He could even be romantic when the situation called for it. But in this place, on the Purple Heart Ranch, even a casual glance could turn into a marriage. That was a situation he had no interest in.

At least not any time soon. He'd gone from his family's two-bedroom apartment, where he'd been one of three siblings crammed into the second bedroom until he was eighteen. It was all his parents could afford.

The Army had been his escape. Now, five years later, he was out of the military and wondering what to do with his life. More than half of his money during his time in service had gone to his family. With only one brother still at home, they had a more comfortable living, but they were still wedged firmly in the middle of the lower class.

Living on the Purple Heart Ranch had been the nicest accommodations he'd ever had in his life. But even with his meager savings, the price of living here was too high. He was not ready for a bride. He could barely take care of himself.

Still, he'd miss this place when he'd have to leave in a few weeks. Unless he put a ring on some poor girl's finger, his time was up, as per

213

the zoning regulations that came with the ranch. It would be the second time he was discharged from a place he wanted to be.

Mark hadn't wanted to leave his life in service, but his disability had forced the Army's hand. Now, he had no way of providing for his family, or himself. He had no idea what he was going to do with himself?

Going back to his parents' two bedroom apartment and sharing a bunk bed with his sixteen-year-old brother was out of the question. At least he hoped that wouldn't wind up being his only answer.

"Ortega, wait up."

Mark turned to see his commanding officer, Sgt. Colin Chase jogging after him. Unlike Mark, Chase's family was well off. His family's wealth aside, Chase had been lucky in the blast that had crippled Mark. The officer could return to service if he chose.

"I was thinking of setting up a recruitment office here," said Chase as he fell in step beside Mark.

That was the other think about Chase. He thought about others and how he could help them. The man many of the soldiers on the base called The Terminator actually had a beating heart.

"That's a great idea," said Mark. "A lot of these kids need the direction and the work."

It's how Mark had found his way into the military. Near the end of this senior year in high school, a recruiter had handed him a flyer during Career Day. Mark had read the pamphlet cover to cover. The next day, he'd walked into the recruitment office and signed up.

"I was hoping you might stay and help?" said Chase.

Mark stopped walking. It took Chase a second to realize he was no longer beside him. Chase turned and faced Mark fully.

Mark's palms opened and closed, as though he were grasping for something. "You want me to work with you recruiting men and women into the Army?"

"Yeah, I think you'd be a perfect fit. It won't pay much, but we'll be doing a service-"

Chase couldn't finish his pitch. He'd been attacked with a hug from Mark. It wasn't often that they showed any type of affection, but Chase had just offered Mark a lifeline.

"I'll take that as a yes then?" said Chase when Mark released him.

"Yeah. I'm ready. What do we need to do?"

"Well, we just need some start-up capital. There's a big society party coming up; a debutante ball. There will be lots of upper-crust society there. Those types are always looking for causes to put their money in. I should know."

Chase rolled his eyes. He didn't talk about his family much. Mark knew there was some tension there.

"Anyway," Chase continued. "We just need to put on our uniforms and schmooze some rich folks. Then we'll be up and running in no time."

Schmooze rich folks? As in talk to them and ask them for money? The poor kid that still lived inside of Mark recoiled. But he wanted to do this work. He wanted to give back in the same way that had saved him.

So it looked like he'd be off to the ball; a debutante's ball.

———

Are you a fan of historical romances?
Especially the ones where an innocent miss and a reformed rake are caught in
a compromising position during a ball?
Well, get ready for a modern day take on that story with
Every Step He Takes
the eighth book in the Brides of Purple Heart Ranch!

EVERY STEP HE TAKES

THE BRIDES OF PURPLE HEART RANCH
BOOK 8

CHAPTER ONE

"Left. Left, right, left."

The sounds of boots marching on the ground should've been thunderous, imposing. In reality, it was more like the sound of grade school children let out of the back of the school for recess. That was likely because none of the boys and girls assembled had reached their majority. They were also marching on fertile, green farmland and not pavement.

"Billy, I said right, not left," shouted Private Mark Ortega. "Do you know your right from your left, son?"

"Yes, sir," said the scrawny kid who was no thicker than a bean pole. "It's the one we say the Pledge of Allegiance with."

Mark resisted the urge to pinch the bridge of his nose when Billy started to raise his left hand, then yanked it down in favor of his right one. Mark couldn't help a glance at his watch. Not because he was ready for the hopeless training to end. He wanted more time to teach these cadets the drill. He knew that for most of them, the Army was not just a way out, it was the only way up.

"All right," said Mark. "Let's try it again."

There were less than a dozen kids gathered. They ranged in racial identity from porcelain skinned Jordan Scott to the tall cup of coffee that was Ayden Benson. The kids also ranged in socioeconomic backgrounds to the polished black oxfords worn by Janey Marsden to the worn sneakers of Billy Trent.

"Left," called Mark. "Left, right, left."

Once again, Billy lifted first his right foot and then his left foot. He collided into Janey, who then bumped into the brick wall that was Eli Wilson.

Janey halted. With clenched fists, she turned to glare at Billy in a way that made Mark wince. The young woman was going to make a fine Army soldier.

Billy, on the other hand, might make a great Marine. That bunch didn't need to know their left from their right out in the water swimming with the fishes.

"At ease, everyone," said Mark. "At ease."

The small group of seventeen and eighteen-year-olds relaxed their stances at Mark's command. For the past year, the Purple Heart Ranch had invited the town's youth to the land for enrichment programs. Aside from the original mission as a rehabilitation ranch for Wounded Warriors, the ranch had developed a specialty of working with troubled adolescents and teens. Which made sense since many of the soldiers there had come from a troubled past.

Mark's past wasn't troubled. He'd come from a loving, close-knit family. Though his family ties had been strong, life still hadn't been easy.

He'd come to the ranch broken after the dregs of combat. With a medical discharge, he'd found healing of his own after only a couple of months on the ranch. Mark hadn't wanted his military career to be over, but it would appear that it was God's will. With his time left on the ranch, he was determined to dole out as much of himself as he could to the next generation of service men and women.

"I'm sorry," Billy mumbled to Janey and Eli. "Sorry, sir," he said to Mark, not quite meeting Mark's gaze.

It was another thing Mark wanted to work on with the kids; building confidence. The soldiers manning the ranch put the kids through their paces taking care of the farm animals, learning to work with and ride horses, and tend to the lands. Those programs had flourished, making a positive impact on each kid that came on the ranch and turning more than one life around for the better.

In the last two months, they'd added a new program; a Junior ROTC program. Mark's hand had shot up as a volunteer to work with the kids.

He enjoyed nothing better than rising each morning and taking the would-be soldiers through their paces. Unfortunately, their pacing was part of the problem. His troops were constantly out of step with one another.

"The last drill of the day is to hit the pivot."

Mark saw a number of the kids wince. Marching wasn't as easy as it looked on television or in the movies. The kids struggled with staying in their simple formation and keeping their spacing. He knew pivoting, turning a corner, would be a challenge for them. But as he'd learned when he was in his high school's JROTC at their age, if you never pushed yourself, you'd never go anywhere.

And so, Mark gave the command. First to march. And then to pivot.

Just as he predicted, the pivot didn't go as planned. Billy turned left instead of right. Only this time he bumped into the wall of Eli. Down Billy went, nearly getting trampled by Janey who had perfect form, spacing, and pivot. Mark knew he had to get in there before Janey made the boy road kill. But before he could bark an order, he saw something else out of order. The sole of Billy's shoe was hanging on by a thread, or rather what looked like dried glue.

"All right, that's enough for the day," said Mark. "You all know what you need to work on for next time."

"Sir, yes, sir," the kids bellowed, nearly in unison. If unison sounded like an echo off a large cliff where the sound bounced around a few times before dying off.

Mark reached out his arm to Billy. The boy took it. Mark hefted the young man up, but Billy's gaze stayed cast down.

"I'm sorry, sir," said the boy. "I'll work on it some more tonight. I'll get it the next time, I promise."

"I have no doubt," said Mark. "It took me quite a while to get the hang of all this."

"It did?" Billy's gaze lifted, hope shining in his eyes.

Mark gave the kid a nod. "You headed back to the barn to get your stuff?"

"Yes, sir."

"Mind if I walk with you?"

"Yeah, that would be cool. I mean, yes, sir."

"It's fine," grinned Mark. "At ease."

The two took off. Billy had to march double time to keep up with Mark's casual gait as they walked the path from the pastures to the barn designated for the youth program. In the distance, Mark saw amputees mounted on thoroughbreds. Each man and woman wore content smiles on their faces. Mark understood why. He'd come from combat with all his limbs and most of his mental faculties, but he knew the power of commanding such a majestic animal restored something in a soldier's spirit.

"I'm glad you were able to keep coming," Mark said to his young charge. "I know you had a conflict, having to watch your younger brother."

"It got sorted," said Billy. "He's in the after-school program at the church. Pastor Patel set it up."

Mark knew that. The pastor had arranged for the fees to be paid so the younger kid could attend the program his wife ran. The Patels had done it quietly as Billy's mother had a reputation for being proud and not accepting handouts.

"I had to do that a lot when I was your age," said Mark. "Take care of my younger brother. The kid was a pain, but he was my pain."

Billy nodded but didn't offer any elaborations on his situation. Honestly, Mark hadn't expected him to. He had been the same way in his youth.

"You doing good in school?" Mark tried another way past the kid's defenses.

Billy shrugged. "I don't get the best grades, but I'm not failing."

This kid could've been living Mark's past life. Mark hadn't been a scholar by any stretch. His grades were normally just barely above passing. He'd only put in the effort because he didn't want to disappoint his parents. Plus, he had to graduate. His family didn't need another high school drop out with no job prospects to take care of. Money had been tight since before he was born, and the situation had never loosened up for a single day after.

They were the last to arrive at the barn. Most of the kids were already on the bus to take them back into town. Billy's well-used backpack sat on a patch of dirt just inside the door.

"Hey," said Mark, "you live near the consignment shop, right?"

Billy nodded uncertainly as he pulled the dingy straps over his shoulders.

"Would you mind dropping these shoes off for me?" Mark grabbed a shoe box off one of the tables inside the barn. "They were a size too small. I got them thirty days ago, so I can't take them back."

Mark took the pristine sneakers from their box. He had to maneuver quickly to hide the sales tag that still hung from the laces. Mark wasn't sure if Billy noticed as he placed the unblemished soles in the palms of the kid's hands.

"Actually," Mark continued, "they look like they might fit you. You want them?"

The accommodating smile fell from Billy's face. His skinny elbows had been bending as he brought the shoes to his person. With Mark's last words, he straightened his elbows and handed them back.

"No, thank you," said the kid.

Mark didn't take the shoes back. "You'd be doing me a favor."

"I know what you're trying to do." Billy placed the shoes back in the box on the table.

Mark sighed. Yup, this was his teenaged self to a T. Taking donations and gifts from strangers had always left him feeling dirty and inferior. As though he were a stain on society that someone with money had to wipe out. He preferred going through hardship than to confront that feeling.

But this was different. Mark wasn't a stranger to this kid. And this wasn't a handout. The kid needed the shoes to reach his dream. He certainly couldn't keep marching when his sole was damaged.

"Look, kid, it's not a handout. It's a leg up. I want you to succeed. We need men like you in the service. But you're not going to get ahead if you can't take a step in the right direction."

Billy pursed his lips. Mark could see he was wearing him down. He decided to try another tactic.

"You'd take them if we were family, wouldn't you?"

Billy hesitated. His features screwed as though he knew there was a trick on the horizon.

"It's what soldiers do for each other. When you're a unit, you're family. I'm the head of your unit, which means I'm pretty much your father. So, do as I said and take the shoes."

Huh. Look at that. It worked.

Under that command, the resistance went out of the kid's shoulders. Billy sighed, letting go of all his tension and pride. He took the shoes.

"Thank you," he said, once again not quite meeting Mark's gaze.

That was fine. Mark had some time to work on that. But it wasn't much time.

"Now, go home and practice that march."

"Yes, sir."

Mark watched the kid hurry to the bus. He felt a strong sense of pride well in his chest at what he'd done. When he shoved his hands in his pockets, they were empty. Those shoes had cost him a pretty penny that he hadn't had to spare. But that's what family did for one another, and the people on the ranch were all family.

Unfortunately, his time on the ranch was almost up. He knew he could come and visit the people there whenever he wished. Mark just wished he could be the one to keep leading these kids into the bright future they all were trying to get to.

CHAPTER TWO

The room was an explosion of white. Alabaster white walls boxed the ladies inside. Ivory white curtains hid them from outsiders' views. Cream colored carpeting ran under their heeled feet. A porcelain chandelier hung from the ceiling illuminating the lace, chiffon, and tulle that exploded from every corner.

Honey Dumasse smoothed the fabric of her pearl-white gown. The material was exquisite to the touch. She tried to keep herself from touching it over and over again for fear she'd leave a stain. But her hands were as pristine and clean as always. Every strand of her hair was in place, even though she'd been in and out of gowns all morning.

There had been the A-line ivory gown that flared from her hips. Honey hadn't had the bust line to support the gown. Then she'd tried on the eggshell-colored mermaid dress. Only her figure was more of a flat board and not the curvy hourglass that the dress shape demanded. Then she'd stepped into the pearl-colored drop down gown.

The strapless gown put the focus on her shoulders instead of her bust line. Her honey-blonde hair was lifted up to accentuate the dress's lines. The skirt had a flare, but that flare started at the calves and not her boyish hips. It was perfect.

All three gowns had been specially made for her. Each one had a price tag that was the down payment of a house, and there were no returns. Her father had told the seamstress to spare no expense, not that he ever looked at the price tag of anything.

It was appearances Sugar Daddy was most interested in. And he wanted his little girl looking picture perfect for her big day so that everyone could see. She was his only daughter to come out in the debutante ball, so he'd needed her to make a big impact.

"Where's your sister, Honey? Shouldn't she be helping you?" asked Mrs. Klein. The older woman had had three daughters come out already, each to a glowing success that had declared one after the next Klein sister the Belle of the Ball.

Honey plastered on a bland smile as she lifted her gaze in the mirror. Her smiles were always bland, never big and bright, never too small or pinched. Bland was just right. No one could say she was trying too hard or too little with this smile. They couldn't say she was trying at all.

"Ginger is out of town today."

"Oh, you mean she's off on the campaign trail?" Mrs. Klein wrinkled her nose in distaste.

The thought of working women always brought on such derision in this cluster. Yes, it was the twenty-first century. But they were society women. With the money in their bank accounts, there was no need to lift a finger outside of charitable work. Especially if you were as wealthy as the Dumasse family.

"I think what Ginger is doing for the community is admirable," Honey spoke up for her sister. Not because she believed in her sister's cause. It was because she knew that weakness was a liability.

Ginger insisted she was doing the highest form of charity work by serving her community. It was not a notion that the ladies of the society, or their father, shared. Henry Dumasse took his eldest daughter's political career as an affront to his wealth and position of power. If Ginger needed to work, then his company, Sugar Daddy's, would be seen as lacking.

Just another reason everything needed to be perfect for Honey's coming out in the debutante ball. Starting with the dress. Looking at the reflection again, she realized it was only *almost* perfect. Something was missing. She just didn't know what.

A mother would know. But her mother wasn't in the picture. Her father had erased her from their lives, quite literally. He'd even had her painted out of the commissioned family portrait.

"I think I know what that dress needs, my dear," said a kind voice.

Honey's gaze shifted in the reflective glass. She slipped, and a real smile broke through her bland expression as Mrs. Patel came into view.

"What do you think about these shoes?" asked Mrs. Patel.

"Yes," Honey breathed. "They would be perfect."

Mrs. Patel handed the beaded, white heels to Honey. She slipped them on and saw that they did indeed complete the outfit. In fact, she decided they had to make their debut at the Bachelor's Brunch tomorrow.

"It just needs one more thing." Mrs. Patel reached behind her back and unclasped a necklace resting there. It was a simple chain with a heart-shaped pearl at the center. When Mrs. Patel approached her, Honey shook her head.

"Oh, no, Mrs. Patel. I couldn't—"

"Nonsense," the elder woman said as she clasped the necklace around Honey's neck. "You should always have a family heirloom for these things. And you've been such a help to me raising money for the Sunday school program, it's the least I can do."

It was a stretch of the truth. Honey hadn't been that much help to the Sunday school effort. At least not with her presence. But she had worked her contacts and helped to raise a majority of the funds that would support the effort for another five years.

She'd had to do it quietly as her father didn't believe in supporting church efforts. Henry Dumasse had yet to find a way to bribe God, so he didn't give His house much attention. That meant the family didn't give the church much attention.

But Honey had fond memories of going to Sunday school while her mother did Sunday Bible study. Even though she hadn't been to church in years, much less Bible study, Honey always tried to find a way to help the church that had once brought her so much joy.

"That dress is a good choice on you," said Mrs. Dumbarton. "It gives the illusion that you have something in the way of hips. You want the gentlemen to see that so they know you can carry plenty of babies."

Honey inhaled and exhaled through the tight bland smile. "Thank you for the advice, Mrs. Dumbarton."

The funny thing was, the woman was truly trying to be helpful. The end goal of all this fuss was another piece of jewelry; a few carats worth of an engagement ring.

Most modern-day debutante balls were no longer about the

marriage mart. In New York City, many of the women coming out were already successes in their own right. In the big cities, the balls were more of a networking opportunity to meet and greet the movers and shakers of upper-class society.

But that was New York. This was Montana. And the truth was, Honey was husband shopping.

Jackie Onassis had been a debutant, and she'd married a Kennedy. True, John cheated on her, a lot. But it had happened after they were married, and she'd been locked into the security of the union.

Unmarried women had it hard back then and today. Divorced women had it harder. Honey had no intention of becoming one of those kinds of women.

She had her sights set on Beau Bryant, the most eligible bachelor in the whole state. His family was wealthy, so Beau wouldn't be after Honey's trust fund. He would be handed his own business once he finished college. And when he did, he would need a high society wife to be on his arm at events, to run his household, and to stand beside him in this society. Honey had been trained for just that job.

In fact, she'd been trained for only that job. At twenty-one, she had bypassed college in favor of spending time at high society dinner parties and charity events. It cost about the same, but she was far better educated to handle the role in life she'd chosen.

She was ready to leave the uncertainty of her home and find some job security. All she needed to do now was get Beau to escort her to the debutante ball. Then her future would be secure. She had the dress, she had the accessories, she just needed to ask the man.

It was the only non-traditional thing about the entire process. Tomorrow, there would be a Bachelor's Brunch. After mingling and getting a feel for each other, the women would take the initiative to ask out the men.

Honey had no plans to mingle. She'd walk in wearing the outfit she'd planned, zero in on her quarry, and monopolize all of his time. The competition was small but fierce. She truly only had a few girls to worry about.

Hayley Tyler was having an affair with the gardener, so she wasn't truly interested in marriage. Sienna Bell had her sights set on college and a career. Honey's only true competition was Quinn Ford.

"Honey, don't you look a picture," said Quinn as she sashayed in an off-white mermaid gown that accentuated her paid for bumps.

"Me? Don't be silly," said Honey. "You're going to outshine everyone in that gown."

Bland smile met bland smile. And it was on.

"I hear you still don't have a date to the ball," said Quinn.

"Well, no. Not yet. I'd like a chance to meet all the bachelors at the brunch." Honey knew better than to tell her frenemy the name of the bachelor she was most interested in. "At the brunch, I plan to see who would be most interesting and who I have the most in common with. It would be dull to spend the night of the ball talking with someone who had nothing in common with me."

"That's a very good plan," said Quinn. "Well, I'm headed off to brunch with Mrs. Bryant. She wants to introduce me to her son. Have you met him? His name is Beau. Our fathers go way back."

Honey clenched her teeth. Her bland smile dipped. But she grabbed hold and yanked it up before Quinn could see that she'd gotten under her skin.

"I think I'll try your tactic and see if Beau and I have anything in common," Quinn was saying. "If we do, you'll see us together at the brunch this weekend. Tah."

Honey pressed her hands to her dress, uncaring of whether she got a stain on the fabric. All was fair in balls and bachelor hunting. She just had to hope that Beau was smart enough to see through Quinn's facade on his own. But come tomorrow's brunch, the pearls were coming off, and it would be all-out war.

CHAPTER THREE

*M*ark brought the horse down from a gallop and back into the corral. He hadn't grown up riding the magnificent creatures having been born and raised in an inner city. But over the past two months, he'd taken to riding like he'd been born to it. Too bad he'd only have a couple more weeks to ride whenever he pleased.

"You're looking good up there, soldier."

Mark turned to grin at Dr. Patel. The man was one of the pastors of the town's church, but he was also the psychologist on the ranch. Mark had often wondered if the two professions contradicted each other. But Dr. Patel brought a certain spirituality to how he healed ailments of the mind.

He'd certainly helped Mark his first few weeks there. Now Mark was managing his PTSD symptoms. Too bad Dr. Patel wasn't a financial planner because that's where Mark really needed the help.

"I was just here for the ride," said Mark, as he brushed the horse down. "I let her take me where she wanted to go."

Dr. Patel laughed. "Keep that attitude with human women, and you will be successful in your love relationships."

Mark had no desire to be in a love relationship at the moment. Even if he had been looking for someone, he couldn't possibly take care of them financially. He would never have a wife and family without being able to take care of all their needs. He was, for all intents and purposes, unemployed and not easily employable.

With only a high school diploma and an honorable medical discharge from the military, there wasn't much he had to offer. What little he did have, he funneled right back to his family, trying to keep their heads above the rank waters of poverty.

"I'm gonna miss this place," said Mark, as he finished putting the horse back in its stall.

"You won't be going far," said Dr. Patel. "As I understand it, you and the sergeant are opening a recruitment center in town."

That was the plan. But they were having trouble securing a location. It was always something with the zoning in this town. Be it the zoning of the location they were looking for the recruitment center or zoning restrictions of the ranch that said all inhabitants had to be married if they planned to live on the land permanently.

Like all unmarried, enlisted soldiers and veterans, Mark and Chase had only been allowed to stay on the Purple Heart Ranch for three months to convalesce. As neither man had any intention of following the tradition of the soldiers who'd come before them and marry a woman for the keys to one of these houses, they would be out on their rears in less than a month's time.

Mark looked off into the distance where the cabin he'd been staying at rested. It was the nicest place he'd ever stayed in in his life. It housed two bedrooms, which he had all to himself. Even though he often found himself sleeping on the couch as he'd done back at home in his parents' two-bedroom apartment that they shared with his two other siblings.

"I wouldn't worry," said Dr. Patel. "Miracles happen every day in this place."

"We're working on the location," said a familiar voice.

Sergeant Colin Chase marched over to them. The man had a march that the JROTC cadets would envy. The sergeant moved with his shoulders back, head high, and long, evenly spaced strides. His walk was much like a certain terminator he'd been nicknamed after.

"See," grinned Dr. Patel.

"In fact," Chase said when he reached them, "I just found a possible building for us to put the recruitment center in. It's owned by the Sugar Daddy company and a man named Henry Dumasse."

Dr. Patel wrinkled his nose. It was a rare occasion to see the man show distaste. Mark had assumed the doctor's optimism knew no bounds. But a line seemed to have been drawn around the name of Dumasse.

Mark chuckled to himself. If someone placed a strong emphasis on the wrong part of Mr. Dumasse's name it would come out sounding highly inappropriate. Mark caught the smirk on Chase's face. Apparently, the ever-present middle schooler was alive and well in both men.

"You know him?" asked Mark.

"Not well," said the psychologist. "I knew his wife a long time ago. She and her daughters would attend church. But Mr. Dumasse never did."

Dr. Patel looked off into the horizon. He often did that in sessions when he was deep in thought. Mark had also caught him gazing off during his church sermons. After the pregnant pauses, he would say something profound that touched Mark and the rest of the parishioners deeply.

When Dr. Patel turned back to them, he simply shrugged his shoulders. It wasn't the reaction Mark expected. Not for a man of the cloth who believed every soul could be saved.

"His daughter, Ginger, still attends church," Patel continued. "She's a great asset to the community. And his younger daughter is very involved in charitable work. She helped fund the Sunday school program my wife runs."

"Maybe we can talk to them," said Chase. "Let them know what a great thing this center will be for the youth in the community."

"Dumasse is a hard man to get in to see," said Patel. "But I know where he will be. He'll be at a brunch tomorrow."

Mark frowned at the term. He'd never understood the purpose of brunch. Why take two meals and smoosh them into one? Especially if you weren't poor? Brunch was a rich man's meal.

"My wife happens to have some tickets to the event if you two would like to attend."

"That sounds great," said Chase volunteering the two of them.

Mark held back. The ever watchful sergeant had missed something in Patel's gaze. Mark had seen that look in the doctor's eye before. Right before Brandon Lucas met his wife Reegan Cartwright. And then again before Reece Cartwright proposed to Elsbeth Barrett. Patel had a hand in most of the marriages arranged on the ranch. It was a touch Chase and Mark had studiously avoided their time there.

"You'll have to wear your uniforms," Patel was saying.

"Not a problem," said Chase.

Mark stood quietly. He crossed his arms over his chest and waited for the other shoe to drop. Or rather, for the cupid's bow to let loose its arrow. He bounced on his toes in preparation to duck.

"You might get picked up by rich women," Patel grinned.

Now Chase was catching up. His eager grin turned upside down. "What exactly is this brunch?"

"It's called a Bachelor's Brunch. It happens before a debutante ball. It's where the young ladies who are about to come out into society go to find an escort for the ball."

Mark took two steps back. He'd already shut down when the good doctor had said they would be high society women. That was another phrase for stuck up, rich girls. Mark did not mix with that breed unless they were out slumming. He'd done that once and gotten burned for it when the woman pretended she didn't know him the next day.

He knew why she'd shunned him after their rendezvous. He wasn't from money, and the copper smell of the pennies he pinched clung to him like cheap cologne. But Chase held his ground. He turned to Mark with a look of determination.

"We gotta go," said Chase.

"You're welcome to go," said Mark, taking yet another step back. "But not me."

"We're in this together. I need you to have my back. Especially with those dimples."

Mark swatted Chase's hand away from his face.

"We don't even have to talk to any women," said Chase. "We can just go in and meet with Dumasse, tell him what a great thing the recruitment center will be, and ask for him to consider leasing the building to us."

"What if a woman asks us to be their escort to the ball?"

Chase raised an eyebrow.

Mark pursed his lips.

Then the two men burst out laughing.

"Yeah, right," said Mark. "Like they'd choose one of us."

"I don't see the joke," said Patel. "The two of you are good, strong, courageous men. Any woman would be blessed to have you as an escort."

That's why Mark liked the man. Dr. Patel was a believer when it came to love. Especially when he was trying to direct one of his patients to heal their wounds with the elusive emotion.

Mark's unit had come to the ranch as a four-man fire team. Brandon and Reece were both happily married, and those marriages had truly healed their wounds. But the ranch had already rehabbed both Chase and Mark without brides. They now had a different mission.

Unfortunately, it looked like their path would meander into a day of bumping elbows with the rich folks to accomplish their mission. Fine, he'd suck it up. Besides, there was no way a man like him would get chosen to escort one of the high society ladies anywhere.

CHAPTER FOUR

It appeared like a castle in the sky. Only there were no turrets. The Dumasse Estate was one of the first mansions built in the state of Montana. Honey's family's money was old, nearly as old as the state itself.

The Dumasses had started out as farmers but not humble ones. They'd bought up most of the fertile land in this and neighboring towns. Once they had a monopoly, her forefathers then leased the land to the farmers who made their way west. Later, during times of tumult and depression, the Dumasses bought back that land and raised the rents.

Landowning was only a small part of their fortune. Sugar beets were the family's bread and butter, or rather, bread and honey. The turnip looking plant was used to make granulated sugar, brown sugar, powdered sugar, and more.

That elixir was packaged up and sold as part of the Dumasse Sugar Daddy company. Sugar was a mainstay of modern life. It was in everything, which meant that walking out of a grocery store each shopper would be taking home a bit of Dumasse into their cupboards. Her father's reach was everywhere.

Honey's driver pulled the luxury car up to the gates of the sprawling property. Once upon a time, this land had been crops. But her grandfather had not preferred the working men and women of society be so close to his humble abode. So, the land had been turned and was now miles of private, manicured pastures.

It took a few minutes to drive the long road through those pastures to the massive plantation style mansion at the epicenter. Once at the massive front steps, the driver came and handed Honey out. He went to take her bags, but Honey stayed him. It was only four bags this shopping trip. She could manage.

She was eager to get inside to her room and decide which dress would go best with the shoes she'd picked out for the Bachelor's Brunch tomorrow. The one she had purchased yesterday would no longer do now that she knew Quinn was on the warpath. So, after her fitting for her ball gown, she'd made a couple of stops to find the perfect cocktail dress to fit her plans.

Honey did allow the driver to open the front door for her. It was a massive oak, likely one hundred years old. Even with her hands-free, she often had a hard time getting into the door of her home. The door made a creaking sound as the hinges gave way. The squeak died out beneath the raised voices coming from the hall.

Both Honey and the driver halted on the threshold. The driver, being a good servant, averted his gaze and affected a dispassionate smile as he bowed and closed the door behind them. Honey, being a dutiful daughter, plastered on her bland, unaffected smile as her father's booming voice shook the plaster.

"Do you have any idea what your little antics are doing to my reputation?" Henry Dumasse bellowed.

"Do you have any idea that my career has nothing to do with your reputation?"

Honey recognized the even-toned voice. Her sister had had the same upbringing as Honey. They both knew that women were not to raise their voices or show too much emotion, especially in the face of men. Most definitely not in the face of their father.

Like Honey, her older sister, Ginger, had been sent to finishing schools. There they learned manners and deportment. But only Honey had actually finished school. Ginger had always had a different vision for her life.

"I'm not asking you for any of your money," Ginger said, exasperation slipping through her inflection. "I'm not even asking for your vote."

"Good. Because I'm voting for your opponent," said their father. "Women have no place in politics. They don't have a head for business."

Honey stayed frozen in the foyer. Whenever people argued, she had a habit of staying as still as a bug in hopes that they wouldn't see her. Just like when her mother and father used to argue. Only, her mother never actually opened her mouth to defend herself. She'd just take whatever her husband had dished out to her in poised silence.

"You forget that I was at the top of my class in high school and college," Ginger countered her father's assertion.

"Useless degrees." Honey could imagine her father's meaty hand slicing through the air at the ridiculous notion. "Not worth the money I paid for them."

"You didn't pay for college, I earned a scholarship."

Ginger's words were clipped. Her voice had also raised an octave. Honey could hear them both breathing hard. Still, she held her place, clutching her bags tightly in her fists.

Though she would never run. Not like her sister had. Not like her mother had.

"I don't know why I even came here," said Ginger. "Maybe out of some delusional hope that you would support me, not with your money, but with ..."

Ginger let the sentence drift off into the abyss that had struck up between the two of them. Her older sister had reached her majority, so she didn't need her father's money. Her trust fund was now in her possession. Every once in a while, Ginger would return home to try and bridge the distance with her father. Henry Dumasse would always take another step back from his eldest child.

Honey knew her father had a good heart. He'd kept a roof over her head. He'd made sure she'd had the finest clothes. He'd made sure she ran in the most elite circles. Wasn't that how parents showed love? By providing.

Their father had provided for his two girls even through his disappointment of wanting boys to carry on the family name and business. He'd never let them forget that they'd failed him from the start at their births. That's why Honey was determined to be a success and marry the son he never had. Well, one of the reasons why.

"If a woman disagrees with you," Ginger was saying, "you cut her off. Just like you did with Mom."

"Watch your tongue." Her father's voice dipped dangerously low.

The air changed on the entire ground floor. It felt like a heat wave passing through a hot desert. It was safest when Henry Dumasse raised his voice. When he lowered it, it was time to take cover.

Ginger knew better than to challenge their father with that tone. "I'll show myself out."

Honey heard her sister's footsteps coming near. She didn't want to be in the middle of this argument. She always made it her business to stay out of any argument that involved the man who provided for her. Unfortunately, despite the heat of the argument, her legs hadn't unthawed from their frozen mode.

Ginger appeared in the hallway. She looked more like her mother than Honey. Despite her name, Ginger was a brunette, like their mom. But all three of them had the same crystal blue eyes.

Ginger's face softened when she saw Honey. "Hey, honey bunny."

"Good afternoon, Ginger."

Ginger's smile fell by a degree. She didn't mention the formality of her baby sister's greeting. Her gaze went to the bag's clutched in Honey's hands. "Shopping?"

Honey dipped her head. "For the Bachelor's Brunch."

Her sister's smile went down another degree. Honey knew Ginger detested the Debutante Ball and all its trappings. She had walked away from her come out ball in favor of campaigning to become the youngest state politician in the region at twenty-one.

"Whatever you wear, you're going to look beautiful, honey bunny."

Ginger came to her, arms open wide. Honey stiffened. If her sister noticed, Ginger ignored Honey's tense state. Ginger wrapped her arms around her as though they were little girls again.

Honey couldn't help it. Her bottom lip trembled, losing its grip on her bland smile. She shut her eyes for a brief moment and allowed herself to relax in her sister's hold.

A creak of a floorboard brought Honey's eyes open. Her father loomed in the doorway. Henry Dumasse narrowed his bushy, blond brows at the two. Under his glare, Honey wiggled in Ginger's hold.

"Goodbye, Ginger."

Ginger's smile was completely gone when she released Honey. She ran a hand down the side of Honey's face. "See ya, honey bunny."

The front door opened and closed with a quiet snick. When Honey looked up, her father was gone from the doorway. She was left alone in the quiet foyer. She was often left alone in this house. Soon, she was the one that would be leaving, she promised herself as she headed on quiet feet to her room.

CHAPTER FIVE

Mark had never considered himself to be socially awkward. He was always the life of the party. He'd just never been to a party where one wrong move could cost him his entire bank account, plus a few pints of blood. And maybe his right arm.

He'd never been inside a place so fine as the Chateau du Planturex. The carpet looked like it had been shaved off the backs of tiny chinchillas, sewn together using golden thread. The curtains were fine lace but such a high thread count that he couldn't see through the fabric. Intricate glass vases sat in every corner with long, lush, colorful flowers that looked out of this world.

Mark kept his arms at his sides in fear of making one wrong move. He moved in a straight line to ensure he didn't put a foot out of place and bump into something he couldn't ever hope to repay.

And then there was the food.

He'd never been to a brunch a day in his life. If he missed breakfast, he simply ate lunch. He didn't know what to do with this combination of the two meals.

There were mini dishes that looked like egg omelets, but were far too colorful and filled with vegetables that should not accompany a yoke. There were tiny pastries with intricate sugary decorations that all had a 3D effect. And he wasn't sure, but he thought he saw snails on one of the silver platters. The things that looked like tiny blueberries, he'd learned were fish eggs. With his stomach turned, he decided to skip eating and focus on the reason they'd come there so they could leave as soon as the task was complete.

"I'm glad we're not splitting the check," Mark said to Chase.

The sergeant looked more at home in the high-end setting. But Chase stood rigid, far more stiff and stoic than his normal stance in the military. Clearly, he wasn't comfortable being back in his former life.

"Don't worry, buddy, I would pay," he said. "You're a cheap date. You'd just order a bison burger."

The mere thought of one of Montana's bison burgers or elk burgers brought Mark's stomach back to life. He couldn't wait to get out of this she-she poo-poo place and get some real food. Along with a slice of huckleberry pie instead of the little girl's tea party dishes that were available here.

The two soldiers were inside a grand ballroom with overhead chandeliers. Everyone was dressed to the nines. Many of the men wore uniforms. Mark had learned many of them were from military schools. But there was an equal number of men in tailored suits and ties. Those men, he'd learned, were from Ivy League schools.

Mark kept his distance from both. He had nothing in common with the suits. And he couldn't stand the green noses in uniform who had yet to know a day of combat and might never.

The women were another story. They were like porcelain. Pretty to look at, but he didn't dare touch one of the delicate creatures. He'd had his hands in the mud that morning. There was still dirt in his nail beds.

He gave his cuffs a tug. The fabric fought back. His watch had caught on the lining. The timepiece was an heirloom passed from his grandfather to his father to Mark. It was old and crinkled, and it didn't keep perfect time. But he wore it because it reminded him of who he was and where he'd come from.

"There's our guy," said Chase, his back stiffening even more. "Henry Dumasse, the CEO of Sugar Daddy."

Mark looked over at the guy. He was a big bruiser of a man. He looked like a wrestler that had been stuffed into an expensive suit. But the suit, it suited him. Definitely custom made.

Henry Dumasse reminded Mark of a drill sergeant. He watched as the man cut the weaker men in his path with glares until they parted the floor for him. He silenced others with a downward turn of his lips until they sank down into seats. This was the man that stood between them and their recruitment center?

"Mr. Dumasse." Chase stepped directly in the man's path, back straight, gaze unflinching.

Mark fell in step at his back.

Mr. Dumasse peered down at Chase. Though both Mark and Chase were over six foot, the older man easily had a few inches on them in height as well as width.

"Sergeant Collin Chase." Chase stuck out his hand, aiming it for the man's middle. "I believe you know my father, Stuart Collins of Sunstone Banking and Financial."

Dumasse's glare didn't lose its hard edge. But there was a twinkle of recognition in his eyes. He took Chase's hand and engulfed it with his own. Mark could've sworn he saw Chase wince at the man's grip.

"This is my colleague, Private Mark Ortega."

Mark reached out his hand, preparing for a crushing shake of his own. But Dumasse didn't offer his hand. Instead, he wrinkled his nose, the flint returning to his gaze. He left Mark's hand hanging there.

Mark's empty hand curled at his middle. His feet shuffled until he was back behind Chase. Mark had no officer's title or rich family name to recommend him. Why was he there again?

"I did some business with your father," Dumasse was saying to Chase. "I don't recall meeting you during any of our interactions."

"I decided to go into service for my country," said Chase.

"Seems a man's first loyalty is to his family. But I assume you'll be taking over for your old man when you're done playing toy soldier?"

Mark had served under Chase for over a year. They had been dropped into some harsh conditions during those times. Mark had never seen the man flinch. At Dumasse's last statement, a slight tick began at the corner of Chase's right eye.

"No, sir," Chase said stiffly. "I think I can do more good serving my country on the home front than behind a mahogany desk."

Now Chase got the flint sneer. "Good?" said Dumasse. "What good?"

"My colleague and I are opening a recruitment center," said Chase. "It will be an opportunity to talk with the youth of the town about the benefits of enlistment and a career in the armed forces. It would give them a purpose."

"Let me guess, you're looking for a donation?"

"Not a donation." Chase shook his head. "A lease. It seems you own the property we're interested in letting. I'd love to make some time with you to-"

"Bryant," called Dumasse with a sharp toothsome grin. "Been waiting for you to arrive."

Dumasse walked past Chase, bumping him in the shoulder and putting an end to the conversation. He shook the hand of another gray-haired man. Beside the newcomer stood yet another young man in military dress. The rank on his pristine uniform marked him as a second lieutenant, the highest rank that could be achieved for a student in a military academy.

"That went well," said Mark.

"I know men like him," said Chase. "That was just the intro meeting. We need to show him we won't back down, gain his respect."

"So, we can go now?"

"Not yet. Let's not waste this opportunity. There are other movers and shakers in this room."

"Well, you go move into the crowd. I'm gonna go shake a leg outside for a minute and then head out."

They had brought separate cars as Chase had come from the location in town and Mark from the ranch. Mark clapped Chase on his back and then made his way to the doors that led out back. The moment he stepped outside into the warm breeze, he felt all the constraints of the last half hour he'd spent inside the chateau loosen. He took his first deep breath and stretched his arms without fear of collateral damage.

The sound of a frantic feminine voice brought his attention around. The voice spoke quietly, quickly as though asking questions and also answering them.

Peering around a sculpted bush, the deep breath Mark had just inhaled stuck in his throat. Standing on the other side of the rose bush was the most beautiful girl he'd ever seen in his life.

Blonde hair like sunshine. Blue eyes like the waters of a clean pool. She wore pink, the same shade as the roses. But her beauty made the flowers look dull. And she was indeed talking to herself.

It looked like she was giving herself a pep talk. Mark couldn't hear her words, but her actions spoke volumes. She opened and clenched her fists for emphasis. She nodded her head as though that would force the truth of the words down into her soul.

Finally, she took a deep, cleansing breath. Then she took a step forward, only to catch her heel in the cracks of the pavement. Her forward momentum halted. She very nearly toppled to the ground. Luckily for her, Mark rushed into action.

CHAPTER SIX

$\mathcal{E}$verything was perfect. The designer dress she'd had custom made highlighted all of Honey's best assets. Her hair was done up to sleek perfection framing her heart-shaped face. Her professional makeup job shimmered in the afternoon light. And the shoes were the knockout portion of the ensemble.

The golden straps crossed her petite ankles. The slim stem of the shoe lifted her arch and did wonders for her calves. She felt like Cinderella. If Cinderella had her father's credit cards and not a fairy godmother.

Also, unlike fairy magic, Honey's ensemble wouldn't vanish at midnight. These would stay in her closet after this momentous day. Not that she would ever wear the outfit again. Dumasses never did repeat showings.

With her chin up, her bust line high, and her feet strapped in, she prepared to go and meet her future. Her father would be waiting inside to introduce her to Beau Bryant. She'd learned that Beau had just gotten into town the other night. So, there was no way that Quinn Ford had had a chance to interact with him.

Honey still had the advantage. She turned on her heel. Her body lurched forward, but her foot didn't move. Her shoe had been caught in the cobblestones.

She tried to raise her foot. But the golden straps trapped her ankles inside the shoes. She'd have to bend down to undo the strap. Unfortunately, the boning of the dress made that difficult, and she almost toppled over. She immediately straightened.

She tried wiggling her foot but was so afraid that the stem would break. She was even more afraid that the smudges of dirt from the cracks would smear her stem. What was she going to do?

Even now, Quinn was probably inside talking Beau's ear off. They were probably even talking about her. Quinn would certainly drop Honey's name casually. With an innocent smile and guileless gaze, she'd match innuendos and allusions to Honey's name, meticulously picking apart her character with nothing but friendly chatter.

Honey is as lovely as a bee, always buzzing around in everyone's ear. Implying anything that he might tell her wasn't safe. Which wasn't true. Honey was not a gossip.

Have you ever been stung by a bee? Wait until you meet Honey. Implying that Honey was vindictive. But no, that was Quinn. The woman never met a grudge she didn't hold on to.

Honey knew the game. Everything was fair in love and husband hunting. She might have done the same. Only anything she might've said disparaging about Quinn would've been true.

"Can I give you a hand, ma'am?"

The voice sent a delicious buzzing sensation down her spine. The tone was deep and resonant. It washed over Honey's back like warm syrup. She turned to see where such a voice had come from. She let out a tiny gasp when she saw that the face did the voice justice.

Twin dimples stared back at her. They arrested her before his eyes did. Dark, coffee colored eyes that she could've gotten lost in. But it wasn't time to get lost. She had to get free.

She saw that the man was an officer with his uniform covering his very broad shoulders. He was a big man, but he wasn't as broad as her father. Her father's size was imposing. This soldier's size looked warm and welcoming, perfect for hugging.

But hugging wasn't what she needed right now. She needed to get her shoe loose and get into the banquet to snag herself an appropriate escort for the ball and for life.

"Yes, sir," she said. "If you please."

The soldier walked toward her. Honey had the impulse to step back. That is if she could've. Not out of fear. With every step this man took, she felt something big coming her way, something that would change her life forever.

"What seems to be the problem?"

"My shoe appears to be stuck."

"It's like you're Cinderella," he said. His grin was a bright planet with two twin stars on the polar opposites.

"Yes, but instead of fleeing the ball, I'm trying to make an entrance into brunch."

He wrinkled his nose at the word *brunch*. That was curious. What person didn't like brunch? It was breakfast and lunch foods all at the same time, the best of two worlds.

"Right," he said, rubbing his hands together. "Let's see what we can do. Two heads together will certainly win against a shoe."

He reached out toward her leg. His fingers nearly grazed her ankle before he jerked his hands back.

"I'm so sorry," he said. "May I?"

It was not at all proper, having a stranger put his hands anywhere on her body off the dance floor under the watchful gazes of plenty of chaperones. But Honey had no choice. She had to get free.

At least that's what she told herself as she gazed down at his strong, capable hands hovering around her bare ankles. She could've asked him to go get help from another woman. But, for some reason, she didn't want him to leave.

Honey nodded her head, giving him the permission he sought. With another three-point smile, the officer ducked his head and took hold of her ankle. Honey sucked in a breath at the first contact.

His fingers were warm and gentle on her skin. They set off trickles of sensations that ran the length of her legs. Her heart skipped a beat at the points of impressions that he made.

"Just loosen the strap, and I can step out," she said.

He cradled her ankle with his left hand. Though most of his palm cupped the back of the shoe, she felt a sense of security, of being sheltered by him. It was an unfamiliar feeling in her life with a volatile parental figure. The soldier's thumb fumbled and fiddled with the clasp.

"I'm afraid I'm not all too good at taking off a woman's shoe."

Honey wondered what he was good at taking off a woman?

She gave her head, and those errant thoughts, a shake. Looking down, she saw that her dress still covered most of her leg. He was having some difficulty managing her dress, keeping her modesty intact, and wrangling the shoe.

Her head shot up as someone walked past the door. If someone saw them in this position, it would not be good for her reputation. Especially if it got back to Beau. Or worse, Quinn.

"Get up, get up, get up," she urged the soldier.

The soldier shot up, but instead of moving away from her, he pulled her to him. This position would be even worse. So, why wasn't she pulling away from him?

His chest pressed into hers. Her hands fluttered down to rest on his biceps. She thought he might try and kiss her, but his head was turned away from her.

He wasn't trying to seduce her. He was trying to protect her. Of course, he was. He was a soldier.

"What is it?" he demanded. "What's wrong?"

"I ..."

He looked down at her. Coffee colored eyes bright and alert. Her heart pounded so hard, as though she'd had a triple espresso shot ... three times. She was sure he could feel her heart beating against his chest.

"Someone was walking by," she said. "If we're caught together, it wouldn't be good."

"Oh." He blinked. The strong, dark roast of his gaze dulled. "Right. We wouldn't want that."

He let her go. She wobbled in place. His dimples were no longer out, and his lips were drawn into a thin line. She felt she'd hurt him and that knowledge hurt her.

"They're gone now," she said.

He nodded. He hadn't looked behind him. He had taken his gaze off her. It was trained on the ground, and he worried his bottom lip. She wasn't sure why, but her strong rescuer looked vulnerable.

"I'm sorry," she said.

His gaze lifted to hers, eyes searching. She had no idea what he was looking for. But something deep inside her was rising to the surface, eager to give it to him.

"Would you mind?" She pointed back to the ground, down at the predicament she was still trapped in.

The soldier sank back to his haunches. With deft and sure fingers, he tugged the strap loose and freed her.

Honey stepped out of her shoe. She felt exposed with him being so close to her bare foot.

"All better?" he asked.

"Yes. Thank you."

He wiggled the shoe. "It looks like you got it good and wedged in here." He wrapped both hands around the shoe and was ready to pull when she stopped him.

"Don't hurt the shoe."

"Don't hurt the contraption that had you trapped?" The soldier let out a low chuckle. The dimples were back as he looked up at her.

"They're hand made." Honey gave a helpless shrug. She knew men didn't understand women's obsession with shoes. But she also knew that when the right shoe was present, they couldn't take their eyes off a woman's leg.

"So, we'll just leave it there?" he asked.

"I don't know?" She looked down at the shoe that completed her outfit. She couldn't go into the brunch without it. "This is a disaster."

Honey took a step. When her bare toe met with warm concrete, she hopped. He caught her in his arms before she could topple.

The feel of being in this man's arms felt right. She'd been right about the size of him being perfect for hugging. She was only in his loose embrace, and it was better than the hugs her mom used to give. But this was not the man she was supposed to be with. She took a step away from him, but something tugged her back.

"Sorry, it's my watch," he said. "It's got a chink in the band."

The fissure in his timepiece had caught in the side of her dress. First her shoe. Now her dress. Could this day get any worse?

"Hold still," he said.

But she was already tugging away. It was at the same time that he was trying to tug in the opposite direction. The sound of expensive, custom made fabric ripping was the sound of all her hopes and dreams turning back into pumpkin seeds at the stroke of midnight. The delicate fabric tore at her hip, exposing her thigh with a peek at her backside.

His eyes went wide, as did hers. They both stood frozen in place. But there was no way they could turn back time. This was a reality, and it wasn't done.

"Honey, are you out here?" Her father's voice boomed, overtaking the light afternoon breeze.

The soldier grabbed him to her again. He gathered the ruined fabric and put her back to his front. But it was already too late.

Henry Dumasse rounded the corner. The older man blocked out the sun. But even in the shadows he cast, it was clear something was afoot in the garden.

"What's going on here?" her father demanded.

Honey might've been able to explain this away to her father. She might've been able to sneak off and climb into the town car that had brought her here, get home, change into another dress, and arrive a little more than fashionably late to the brunch and still keep up appearances. Unfortunately, her father wasn't alone.

Honey's future flashed before her eyes as she saw another man in uniform walk up beside her father. Beau Bryant came to stand at attention next to her dad. But that wasn't the worst of it.

Coming up behind Beau was Quinn Ford. There was triumph in her nemesis' gaze. There would be no need for innuendo or allusions when the reality was too good to be true. Honey was ruined.

CHAPTER SEVEN

It went beyond getting her dress dirty with his unkempt hands. He'd now divested her of her shoe and ruined the fabric of the dress. Mark's hands continued to fumble as he tried to hold the material to her body while also shielding her from prying eyes. The only way he could win this particular battle was to turn her around, her back to his front, and keep her exposed body from the gathered crowd

But things went from bad to worse when he looked up at the onlookers to see the Sugar Daddy, Henry Dumasse, gaping at them. The older man's mouth moved like a fish out of water. His lips flopped around, gasping in the open air as though the air were choking him. His eyes were big, bugging out of his head as though he were straining like a cartoon character. His huge meat-grinder hands balled and curled into fists, also opening with the tips curled as though he wanted to reach out and dig his nails into Mark's neck.

Mark knew the situation looked bad. It looked as though he'd assaulted this poor, young woman. Not that she was poor. He'd seen the bottom of her shoe. It was blood red. He'd caught enough *Sex in the City* episodes to know what a red bottom shoe meant. It meant money. She was from money, and he had his lower-class hands all over her.

This could be explained. Surely, she'd tell the man he'd meant her no harm, that he was, in fact, helping her out of a jam. Luckily, things couldn't get any worse.

"Daddy?" his damsel said.

Now, Mark was the fish out of water. But instead of bugging out of his head, his eyes felt as though they had sunk down into his sockets. His lips puckered as though he tasted the salty brine of seaweed. This could not be happening.

"Take your hands off my daughter," growled Mr. Dumasse.

Mark obliged. His hands went up in the air, as though he were under arrest. Unfortunately, they hadn't completed the job of unsnapping his watch. So, the moment he put his hands up was the same moment that more fabric tore.

Mark immediately pulled her back to him, using his arms to cover her modesty. She was trembling now. Her small form shaking like a leaf in a storm in his hold. Mark's instinct was to pull her closer. But each time he touched her, it turned into an even bigger disaster.

"I was helping," Mark began. "Her shoe was caught. And I lifted her dress to-"

Not the best choice of words.

"I wasn't trying to undress her," he corrected. "I was only after her foot."

And there went another wrong turn.

"I don't mean I have a foot fetish or anything like that. I don't even like feet."

Why was he still talking? When he opened his mouth, he made it worse. When he moved his hands, he made it worse. The best course of action was probably to keep perfectly still.

By now, a crowd was gathering. There was the young officer Dumasse had ditched them for earlier. The man lifted a brow at Mark, looking between him and the girl. The young man's jaw tensed, revealing an aristocratic cleft in his chin.

Mark felt the woman in his arms stiffen under the young officer's perusal. In response to her discomfort, Mark pulled her even closer to him to get her out of the line of inquisitive eyes. For the first time in their encounter, she struggled in his hold.

"It's true what he said." Her voice trembled when she spoke. Defeat colored her soft-spoken words, as though she didn't believe anyone gathered would see the truth. "My shoe got stuck, and he was trying to help and ..."

Her words trailed off at the sound of someone giggling. No, that wasn't giggling. It was snickering. A better word would be cackling.

The girl standing behind the toy soldier threw her head back as though she were a witch and just needed her broom. She turned on her heel without the flying device. Once inside the doors, she stopped the first person she saw, another girl in an expensive dress. The cackler pointed at the woman in Mark's arms. Then she stopped another, and then another.

Mark felt the body of the woman in his arms deflating like she was a balloon whose ends had just been untied. He was certain that if he didn't hold onto her, she would float away on the soft breeze. He wrapped his arms even more tightly around her. Though she didn't seem to notice him anymore, she did sink into his hold.

Henry Dumasse's gaze was locked on the young women behind the glass pointing and jeering at his daughter. Then he turned to the young man in uniform. The toy soldier at least had the decency to avert his gaze. Finally, Dumasse turned to face his child. The glare etched into his features made Mark, a man who had faced down the Taliban, want to take a step back for his own protection.

"If you want to go off cavorting in gardens," said Dumasse, "then you're no daughter of mine. You're just like your mother."

Mark felt her sharp inhale of breath. She had been so deflated a moment ago that when her shoulders went back and they struck him right in the chest. Again, his hold tightened. He wanted her to know that she had his support.

For his part, Mark couldn't understand what he was hearing. He couldn't understand what he was seeing. Why wasn't her father coming to him and taking his daughter from his arms, putting her care and comfort into his own arms where it belonged. Instead, he left the matter to a stranger.

"I disown you," Dumasse said to his daughter. Then he turned to face Mark. "And you, you want to toy with what's mine to try and force my hand?"

"No," said Mark. "That is not what happened here. I didn't even know that she—"

"You won't get that property," said Dumasse. "I won't have trash like you turning the good young men in this town into scoundrels."

Mark wanted to correct the man, to let him know that the military was open to both men and women. But he felt now was not the time.

Especially not since Dumasse was marching out of the garden and around the path.

When Mark turned back, the crowd had grown larger. People pointed and snickered from behind the glass door. The toy soldier was making his way through them, not looking back at the scene he'd walked up upon.

The woman in his arms collapsed into him. A protective instinct came over him, and he swept her off her feet. She weighed next to nothing.

Mark cradled her in his arms so that she wasn't exposed to the leering crowd behind the glass. She turned her face into his chest. As he carried her away, the wetness he felt soaking into his uniform nearly broke him.

CHAPTER EIGHT

$\mathcal{D}$ark blue was the color of devastation. That was all Honey could see as the tears leaked out of her eyes. She wasn't a crier. She had been given too much in life to feel sorry for herself. Her father had given her the finest foods, the most coveted wardrobe, and a sprawling shelter. But he never failed to remind her that they were all his belongings that he gifted to her. Because all those items were gifts and not her earnings, he could always take them away.

"It's all right," soothed a deep voice. "I've got you."

She wasn't hearing the baritone notes with her ears. She felt them vibrate across her forehead and touch her eyelids. The words bypassed her ears entirely and sank into her heart.

"It's not the end of the world."

Blue was the color of deception. It was a cool balm against the tear that had ripped her life in half. One moment, she was on top of the world, at the cusp of her destiny. The next, her entire future was slashed from her hand like tattered lace.

"He'll cool down in a bit."

Blue was the color of desolation. Without her father's protection, without the hand of a man and his ring, she was alone and unequipped for the world. She had no place to go. No one to turn to.

Even now, she could still hear the echoes of the snickers and whispers of her peers. Upper-class society was not a community of caring individuals. It was a dog eat dog world, and Honey had just been stripped of her pedigree.

"You can stay right here with me until he comes for you."

Honey blinked her eyes once, twice, until the blue of her soldier's uniform came into stark focus. Seeing it clearly now, it looked far more black than blue. Looking up to meet his gaze, she saw that the center of his eyes was more hazel than coffee, as though there was a splash of cream to stave off any bitterness.

She knew there was no bitterness in this man. His insides were likely more sweet cream. He smelled sweet, earthy with a hint of something, well, sweet. Honey couldn't help but stare for a long moment as she drank him in.

He brushed a tendril of hair behind her ear, and she shuddered. It was more touch, more tenderness than she'd felt in years. And like a caffeine addict, she instantly wanted more.

"Your father was upset," the soldier said. "He couldn't have possibly meant what he said."

Yes, he could. Yes, he did. He'd meant every word and would enact everything he'd said.

Her father had divorced her mother, cut her off, and made her life unbearable for defying him. Even now, he barely tolerated his eldest daughter for choosing to live with her mother instead of him in the custody battle. He'd never forgiven Ginger for that embarrassing act, and he never would.

And now Honey had caused a scene in front of people he felt should be impressed by him. Henry Dumasse did not countenance embarrassment, whether accidental or not. He meant what he said when he'd disowned her.

Honey was ruined.

"I'll talk to him later," her soldier was saying. "I'll let him know it was all my fault. I'll let everyone know it was all my fault."

He was trying to come to her rescue again. She didn't want to tell him she was already doomed. What she wanted was to stay there on his lap while he stroked her back, crooned comforting delusions, and brushed her hair from her face.

But she couldn't. It was still entirely improper. She didn't even know his name.

"What's your name?"

"Ortega. Private Mark Ortega."

"Pleasure to meet you. I'm Honey. Honey Dumasse."

"Pleasure to meet you, too. In light of the circumstances."

The light of the circumstances? There was no light. Things were dark. Private Ortega clearly wasn't from this world. He didn't know how it operated.

It was the twenty-first century, but a girl's reputation was worth its weight in gold in her circles. Literally. Now that she was found with a stain on her person, thanks to the rip in her dress, she no longer held a place at the big table. Luckily, her soldier's lap was comfortable.

"I'm afraid you're mistaken about my father, Private Ortega."

"Please, call me Mark. I feel we know each other intimately now."

Heat rose to her cheeks. Honey stood, wobbly as she was still in only one heel. Then she clutched at the ruined fabric to cover herself.

"I'm sorry," he said, standing as well. "That was crass of me. I have a tendency to joke when things are serious."

"Things are serious. I've been humiliated in front of all of society. I've been disowned. I have nowhere to go."

Now that she was out of Mark's lap, the panic was starting to set in. Her fingers flew to her chest as her heart began to pound. She turned away from him, in the direction her father went. Then turned back when she realized she was still indecently exposed. She became breathless with indecision and lightheadedness threatened.

"Okay. Okay." Mark held up his hands like a tamer approaching a wild lioness. "I'm sure you're exaggerating."

Honey flashed her eyes at him like a cat at night.

"My bad." He stepped back, hands now raised in self-defense. "Did I mention that when things are serious, I say things that would make a woman cut me?"

"Duly noted."

Mark lowered his hands. "I just mean, your father couldn't really mean what he just said. Family doesn't cut each other off. They're, well, family."

"Not my family. Either you're perfect, and you abide by Sugar Daddy's rules, or you're out. I've embarrassed my father and made a spectacle, which makes me no longer perfect."

"I think you're perfect." His deep voice was soft, just barely above a whisper, as though he hadn't meant to say the words out loud. He turned away, his features contorted in a sheepish grimace.

Honey stood in a ruined dress, with one shoe on, black streaks streaming down her face, and her hair disheveled. He couldn't be serious. Yet he looked at her as though she were nectar, and he was a bee.

"Oh, Honey, my dear girl. There you are."

Honey looked up to find Mrs. Patel coming toward her with open arms. Honey let go of her dress and allowed the woman to enclose her in an embrace. She didn't feel the same safety as she'd felt inside of Mark's arms, but the hug was soothing nonetheless.

"Are you all right, my dear?" Mrs. Patel ran a hand down her face and then brought her into a second hug.

Belatedly, Honey realized that her backside was exposed to Mark. Before she could reach for the ruined fabric to shield herself, she felt cloth being draped around her shoulders.

Private Ortega had taken off his blue jacket and draped it around her shoulders. She was drowned in the coat and drowned in his dark roast smell. The weight of the coat and the masculine smell lessened her anxiety like a weighted blanket used for dogs during a thunderstorm.

"Mrs. Patel," said Mark. "I'm glad you're here. Can you sit with Ms. Dumasse while I go and find her father? I can let him know this is all my fault and his daughter is blameless."

Mrs. Patel squeezed Honey's shoulder. She participated in this world, but she was not immersed in it. She knew the score.

"I don't think that would be wise," said Mrs. Patel. "I'm afraid Mr. Dumasse is an impulsive man. He doesn't cool off quickly."

"So, he's just going to turn his child out in the meantime?" Mark's brows were raised in a mix of incredulity and disgust. Disgust won out and colored his handsome features. "What kind of man would do such a thing?"

Honey knew she should defend her father and his character, but she was too caught up in someone defending her. Besides, Mrs. Patel had the right of it. What she'd described was exactly the man that her father was.

"We will figure this out my darling," said Mrs. Patel. "We can call your sister."

"No," said Honey, a bit more vehemently than she'd intended. "She's on the road for her campaign."

"All right then. In the meantime, you'll stay with my family."

"I couldn't," said Honey. "It's nearing the holidays, and you'll have your entire family over. There won't be any space for me."

Truthfully, the Patels were her only option. She couldn't go running to Ginger, not when the two sisters had made such different decisions for their lives after their parents' divorce. Honey knew no one else in high society would offer her shelter.

"You could stay with me."

Both women turned to look at Mark.

"I have a spare bedroom at my cabin on the ranch," he continued. "This is all my fault. The least I can do is give you shelter until your father sees reason."

CHAPTER NINE

ark's pick-up truck crunched and sputtered over the paved gravel of the drive on his way up to the Dumasse estate. He hadn't seen Chase on his way out. The superior officer had already ducked out of the brunch by the time Mark had handed Honey into the loaner vehicle he sometimes used on the ranch.

He didn't have a car of his own. He'd never had his own vehicle. His entire family had shared the same clunker since he was in elementary school. The pickup truck was a step up as it had two working doors. But the seats were still a bit crummy.

Mark had done his best to wipe them down before he'd lifted Honey inside. They'd saved her shoe, though the heel had a few scuff marks from its cobblestone captivity. He'd laid down some napkins he'd scavenged from the glove box. The richest girl he'd ever known was now sitting on a McDonald's cushioned passenger seat.

The drive to her home was long and silent. Mark had turned on the radio. But when Tim McGraw's *My Little Girl* came across the wires, he turned the radio off. They sat in a comfortable silence for miles.

And then more miles after he entered the curlicue gates of the Dumasse estate. It felt like they were on the driveway for an hour. In reality, it was probably more like five minutes. But who had a driveway that took five minutes to maneuver?

Mark had known Honey was rich before he'd known her name.

She'd reeked of wealth. Literally. She smelled like a fine, delicate fragrance that was not present in nature; floral and sugar-coated with notes of sunshine.

He marveled at the lush, yet empty land they took to get to where she'd rested her head every night. Surely, she was a treasure that needed to be guarded. Maybe those guards were hiding in the rows of manicured shrubbery. But no one jumped out and halted Mark or his clunking vehicle.

And then the house loomed down on them. The mansion, or was it a castle, rose up into the skyline, making Mark feel even smaller and less than worthy. No one came out of the house as he pressed his foot, and the brakes squealed at the end of the driveway.

"You live here?" Mark asked.

"Not anymore," she said.

"But you did. How big is your family?"

"It was just me and my dad."

"Just the two of you in that big house?"

"Well, there are servants."

"I'm sure they outnumber you. It would seem it was their house."

Honey shrugged. Her gaze was on the steps that lead to the massive door. Her hand was on the door handle of the truck. But she made no move to get out.

Mark had only known this woman for an hour or so, but he knew she wasn't doing well. It was all a shock. He couldn't imagine his family disowning him, and for something so trivial. At least she wasn't crying any longer.

"It's probably best if you stay here," she said when he came around to hand her out of the truck.

"Afraid I'll break something else?"

"You couldn't make it any worse," she said as she stepped down. When she looked up into his face, her eyes went wide with sorrow. "I'm sorry, I didn't mean it that way."

"You don't have to explain. I'm clearly not from this world. I don't get all the rules." Her words had stung a bit. What soothed him was the fact that she hadn't let go of his hand. "I don't care what you say, no man could disown his child for something like this. Let's just give him the night to blow off steam. He'll call you in the morning."

The lift of her perfectly plucked eyebrow told him that she didn't believe his words. Mark still couldn't imagine it to be true. She was the man's little girl. All girls deserved protection.

Mark walked her up the steps, but he didn't accompany her into the house. Truth be told, he was scared to march inside that heavy door. He'd been out of his depth at the brunch. The majesty of this place was alien to him. Though he felt guilty for letting her go in there alone.

Forty minutes later, she emerged in a sundress and carrying a shoulder bag. But behind her were three servants carting luggage. Expensive-looking brown luggage with the gold crowns of a particular French designer. It was the large kind that would rack up charges on a commercial flight.

"I packed light," she said as she climbed back into the passenger seat.

Mark only nodded.

The servants gave him cool gazes as he closed the bed of the truck with the pricey luggage laying on hay. Mark climbed back into the driver's seat. It took three tries to restart the engine. When they were on their way, the truck moved slower under the weight of the luggage now in the back.

"You doing okay?" he ventured.

"I'm still numb. It hasn't sunk in. I guess I kinda figured this day would always come. I was walking on eggshells all my life around him, knowing anything could set him off."

"That's no way to live."

"That's why I wanted to find an escort at the Bachelor's Brunch. Escorts have been known to turn into husbands."

"So, you want to get married to get out from under your father's thumb?"

"It's the only way for a girl like me."

"The only way for a girl like you?" he parroted.

"I was raised in high society. I know, in some places, girls have many accomplishments and go to Ivy League schools. But in my family, if women aimed to achieve a career, it reflected badly on the male providers. It meant the men were lacking in some way."

That made no sense to Mark. His mother had worked every day of her life, rarely taking any day except Sundays off to go to church. And then, sometimes, she snuck in a shift after service.

"While other girls went to college, I was expected to attend dinner parties and organize charity events and talk with my father's guests. It was my on-the-job training, I suppose. And I'm good at it. I've been preparing for marriage my whole life."

Mark had learned about women's rights and women's liberation in the textbooks of school. But he'd lived the need for it in his everyday life. Every cent his mother and sister brought into the household counted, and it needed to count as much as each man's. In the Army, his life often depended on the training of the woman at his side. Equality wasn't a notion in his world, it was a necessity.

"Was there a particular bachelor you had your sights set on?" In the second after he asked the question, his stomach turned. The idea of Honey with some other man made his teeth clench. He gripped the wheel, squeezing the leather covering until a thread came loose.

"Yes," she said, her gaze fixed out the window. "He was there. He was standing next to my father when ..."

The toy soldier? Mark hadn't had any interaction with the man, but he knew the type. He was all training and no experience. A man like that wasn't equipped to take care of a woman like Honey.

But he was? Mark was the one who had ruined everything she'd worked for with a careless tug of his wrist.

"Now, he'll never have me."

"Good," Mark growled.

Honey turned to him. She tugged her bottom lip into her mouth. Her hands smoothed down the soft fabric of her intact dress.

"What I mean is, he's not good enough for you," said Mark.

"You don't even know him. You don't even know me."

"Oh, I know enough. Guys like him are not husband material."

"And guys like you are?"

"Yes. Eventually."

Honey tilted her head to the side and regarded him. Mark squirmed under her assessment, certain he wouldn't pass muster for a woman like her.

"Guys like me are good family men. We take care of our own, even if we struggle to do it our whole lives. Guys like me work hard for what we get. Guys like him are given it."

"That's the kind of girl I am. I was given everything. I've never had to work a day in my life. And like I said, I don't know how to."

Her hand went to her stomach. Her shoulder caved forward. She fidgeted in the worn seat as though she couldn't find a comfortable position.

"And here I am depending on another man," she continued. "A stranger at that. If you weren't around to take me in, I don't know what I'd do."

"You don't have anyone else? What about your mother?"

Her features darkened. "My mother passed away."

"I'm sorry."

She offered him a bland smile. He saw through it. He saw the pain she was trying to hide from him.

"Mrs. Patel mentioned your sister. Do you want to call her?"

"I ..." Honey didn't finish the sentence.

What kind of family was this? A father who could turn his back on his daughter. A sister who she hesitated to call when in need.

"This world you come from," he said, "it seems backward and not high at all. I would never turn my back on someone in need. And I'm as low class as they come."

"You're not low class." She sat forward, her gaze as fierce as her words. "You're an honorable man."

"Honor doesn't pay the bills. Your father isn't going to give us the land to open a recruitment center. That will ruin my career and my ability to earn money for myself and send home to my family."

Honey was quiet again. He left her to it, obviously having said and done enough for one day. But a few miles later, she turned to him. There was a spark of brightness in her blue eyes.

"I have a crazy idea," she said. "Maybe we can help each other."

CHAPTER TEN

"So, let me get this straight," Mark said as he cut the wheel for a hard right turn.

Honey gripped the seatbelt strap as Mark maneuvered through the winding roads of the Montana countryside. She'd never been in a car that had gone above the speed limit. None of her drivers would've dreamed of pressing the gas pedal so hard.

She had her driver's license because her father had bought her a Rolls Royce for her sweet sixteen. But she'd only driven it the once; on her sixteenth birthday for pictures and for the crowd of high-class society gathered celebrating with her.

That crowd had been mostly her father's associates and colleagues. It was all for show. Just as much of her life had been while left in her father's care. She'd played her part since her mother had left. She'd been the shiny trophy that he'd adorned and dressed to display his wealth. She'd gotten behind the wheel that day. All the while, she'd been so anxious that she might crash into something or, worse, someone.

She'd driven at the exact speed limit that day. It was what was expected. She'd smiled and waved for the photo ops. Mark drove like no one was watching, especially not police officers, intent on pulling over speeding drivers.

"You think you can find another location for the recruitment center," Mark continued, "and convince the owner to lease it to us?"

"Yes." Her response was strangled as he took another hairpin turn twenty miles over the posted limit.

"But the only way to do that is for us to pretend to be dating?"

"Yes."

The green of the trees blurred. Her life wasn't flashing before her eyes. She hadn't done enough with it for that. It was just a blur.

A blur of images of her smiling blandly while doing her father's bidding. Trying to be perfect and shiny and bright to please him. She knew he wouldn't be pleased with her new plan.

Honey couldn't believe she'd suggested that she and Mark take on the farce; to pretend they were a couple to restore her good standing and gain interest in his cause. But desperate times and all. If there was one thing she'd learned from her father, it was that she had to keep up appearances at all costs. Since she had no money, she had nothing to lose.

"By now everyone thinks that something happened between us," she said.

"I helped you out of a jam." Mark threw up his hands.

Honey gripped the edges of her seat. Another turn was on the horizon. With just the thumb of one hand, he took the turn with ease. She'd have been impressed if it wasn't her life in his hands. Or rather, his thumb.

"They won't see it that way," she said after filling her lungs with much-needed air. The windows of the pickup truck were cracked open since the AC wasn't in working order. "Even though it's true. It's more entertaining to think we did ... something else."

"And now you think we should do something else to make it real?" Mark's brows rose so high they reached his hairline. The truck slowed to normal speed.

"No!" Honey's cheeks heated. She let go of the seat and folded her hands primly in her lap. "I mean, we should pretend."

She took a deep breath and began again.

"We need to make them think we're together, that we're in love. That's a better story than you debauching me."

"Debauching? What is this, the eighteenth century? Honestly, if anyone did the debauching, it was you to me."

The breeze from the cracked window slapped her in the face. She had to blink a few times before she could turn around and face him. When she did, his dimples were deep with glee.

"Can you please be serious?" She turned to face forward, head held high. The breeze now slid past the smoothness of her forehead. "You said your livelihood was on the line. If this works, you get that back."

"And you?"

"I get welcomed back into the society I was born into."

"But you'll have to do with a low-class guy on your arm in the meantime."

The crease returned to her forehead. She turned to him again. He had an aristocratic nose, a chiseled chin. There was nothing low class about this man. She wanted to tell him that but she had no idea what was in his wallet or where his family line began.

"Why don't you approach the toy soldier?" said Mark. "It's him you want."

Honey thought about Quinn going after Beau, the man Honey had set her sights on. Honey didn't *want* Beau. She *needed* him to survive. By all accounts, he was a good man. By his account ledgers, he was well off. They would be perfect for each other. She could've been the sparkle on his arm, the shining centerpiece at his dinner parties. It was what she was meant to do in life.

"Beau and I hadn't been formally introduced yet. And then, when he saw me, my skirts were up. It wasn't my best look."

Mark scrubbed a hand over his face. Honey didn't like the remorse in his coffee dark gaze. His eyes were meant to be vibrant with life. She didn't want Mark to regret coming to her rescue. It was the most selfless thing anyone had ever done for her.

She knew her request was the height of selfishness. But it was all she could think of to get some semblance of her life back. She couldn't rely on Mark forever.

Despite what he'd said about taking care of her. They were from two different worlds. She had to get back to hers before it was too late and Quinn sank her claws into Beau.

"So, will you do it?" she said.

Mark slowed down as they approached the gates to a ranch. The Bellflower Ranch said the sign on the gate. But she knew it had been rechristened the Purple Heart Ranch by its inhabitants.

Honey had heard about this place for injured soldiers, but she'd never visited. They weren't on the charitable donations radar. It seemed the owner, one of the soldiers, was wealthy.

Sgt. Dylan Banks had never mixed in her high society circles. He would've been a sought after prize at last year's ball, but he'd married a local girl with no family. Honey had heard Sgt. Banks's wife had come from the foster care system.

"I just have to take you to this ball?" Mark asked as he pulled the truck up to a row of quaint cabins that looked like tiny, rustic pool houses.

The sun was setting, but people were about. An eclectic bunch walked toward a barn. Most were in paired couples. Men had their arms wrapped around women that they looked down upon as though the women were stars on Earth. Honey had never seen real men outside of a movie screen with such expressions on their faces. Were these a bunch of actors?

"And you'll have to pretend you adore me," Honey said as she gazed at the loving couples.

Mark turned to her. His gaze held her in place. Inside, her heart warmed as though a small flame had been given life.

"Yeah. I think I can do that." His gaze raked over her one last time, and then he turned away.

Honey felt bereft without him beside her. But he appeared in another second at her door.

Opening the door, Mark offered her his hand. She didn't know why she hesitated. Perhaps because she knew that once they began this farce, her life would take a new turn? Honey slipped her palm in his. Tingles ran down her spine as his strong hand clasped hers.

"Welcome to my humble abode," he said.

Honey looked over at the quaint little cabin. Up close, it was even smaller than a pool house. "It's … nice."

Mark chuckled. "You don't have to lie. It's probably smaller than your closet."

"I don't have a closet anymore."

His thumb rubbed circles below her knuckles. "I don't have much. But what's mine I'll happily share with you. I'd never turn family out."

"I'm not your family."

"No." He waggled his head, not committing to her denial or claiming the affirmative. "But you are my responsibility now. First thing's first. Let's get you fed. All I've had today were those finger foods, and I'm starved for a real meal."

CHAPTER ELEVEN

"You're dating Dumasse's daughter?"

Mark wasn't sure what irked him more. Chase's incredulity at the thought that he could pull a girl like Honey? Or … well, there was no or.

Chase was right. A guy like Mark could never pull a girl like Honey. Not without it being a trick.

"It's not real," Mark admitted. "Something happened after you left."

Mark filled Chase in on the good deed he tried to perform that had turned into a complete mess. Chase's eyes went wide, then wider, then they narrowed, and finally closed in utter disbelief.

"You're telling me she thinks she can make this right if you pretend to date?" Chase asked.

"If I pretend I adore her," Mark said.

He looked across the room to find Honey. She'd been surrounded by the wives of the ranch. The women all wore open, friendly smiles. But Mark wasn't fooled.

He knew the meddlesome matchmakers, who'd each been matched themselves, were pumping Honey for information about the status of her relationship with one of the few bachelors left on the ranch. Just as Mark and Chase looked to add numbers to the Army, the brides of the Purple Heart Ranch were always looking to add to their ranks on the ranch.

Honey smiled politely at the women. Her head turning right, left, and center as she addressed each woman as they fired question after question at her. Each woman watched her with genuine interest. But Honey's smile didn't reach her eyes.

Mark wanted her to like everyone here. He wanted Honey to experience what real family, friends, and fellowship was like. She wouldn't find any better folks than right there on the ranch.

He also wanted to go over and feed her. Honey had a paper plate balanced on her knees. On it, was a small salad with no dressing. But she hadn't taken more than one bite.

"This place," sighed Chase. "It got you, too."

"What? No." Mark shook his head violently. "I'm helping her out. Her father disowned her. Who does that?"

"Henry Dumasse, that's who."

Dylan Banks, the man who had made the whole ranch possible for Wounded Warriors to come and heal walked up with his pregnant wife on his arm. The man wore shorts that showcased his prosthetic leg, a souvenir from his time in the armed forces.

"Dumasse's wife wanted a divorce," said Maggie Banks. "But he demanded sole custody of their two girls. He made the girls choose which parent they would go to live with. Honey chose her dad. Her sister, Ginger, chose her mom. It was all over the papers years ago."

Mark couldn't fathom his parents apart. Much less making their children choose between them. It seemed to him the height of child abuse.

"That's not the worst of it," said Banks. He turned back to Maggie to complete the story. Maggie had lived there all her life and would know all the town secrets.

"He left his ex-wife and daughter near penniless," said Maggie. "He wanted to make them pay for leaving him and making him look bad."

"What judge would allow that?" asked Mark, outrage building in his chest.

"They didn't go to court," said Maggie. "I think Carletta Dumasse knew that her husband had many officials in his pocket. He owns so much land and businesses here. Ginger went from private schools to public schools. She's a couple of years older than me, but I remember her. She and her mom were always in church. They went from wearing designer clothes to secondhand, but they always looked happy to me. I only saw Honey in the papers. She has the same eye color as her mom, but she never had that same sparkle as Carletta. Her mother passed away before Ginger went off to college."

"I've had a couple of run-ins with Henry Dumasse," said Banks. "He makes Ebenezer Scrooge look like Glinda the Good Witch. I can't understand why any child would choose to stay with such a man."

"I can," said Maggie. "I understand that need for comfort and normalcy having grown up in foster care. After a time, you stop looking for love and settle for security."

Maggie looked down at her protruding belly. Bank's arms tightened around his wife. Mark's gaze went to Honey.

Maggie was right. Her eyes didn't sparkle. But some of the tension in her shoulders had seeped out. Now she was leaning slightly forward in the huddle of women instead of back.

Reegan's and Beth's gaze lifted and turned to Mark. Their lips tilted conspiratorially. The two women didn't hide the fact that they were discussing him.

When Honey met Mark's gaze, her smile spread slightly. There was a spark of something in her gaze. But before he could be sure, she looked away, her cheeks reddening.

"Wow," sighed Banks. "What is it about this place?"

Mark didn't bother to answer that rhetorical question. This ranch, where love sprouted quickly and unexpectedly, had not gotten to him. But if he were honest, that woman may have.

Honey had his protective instincts firing on all cylinders. He felt the urgent need to show her a different side of people after the childhood trauma she had gone through. Mark took a deep breath, then made his way into the den of lionesses. The women fairly purred at his approach.

He held out his hand to Honey. "It's a nice night," he said. "Want to go outside?"

Honey's lips parted. She nodded and slid her hand into his. There went those tiny pinpricks of sparks again.

"Ooh," the other women singsonged like they were in grade school.

Mark tried to hide his annoyance at their adolescent ways. But, on the other hand, he and Honey were pretending to be in love. They might as well get some rehearsal time in.

Before heading outside, Mark stopped by the spread on the table and filled up two plates with barbecued ribs, corncobs, and rolls.

"You have a healthy appetite," Honey said, eyeing the piles on the plates.

"These are for the both of us."

"I can't eat that. It's all sugar and carbs."

Mark scooped some green salad into the corner of one of the plates. He squirted some dressing on the top.

He led Honey back to his place. Instead of going inside, he indicated the plastic chairs on the deck. Honey smoothed her skirt and sat gingerly. Mark had a strong desire to muster up. But first, he wanted her fed.

He placed the food in her hands. She eyed the plate as though it were filled with worms.

"Not a fan of barbecue?" he asked.

"I've never had any."

"But you're from Montana."

"Eating ribs and corn on the cob were not covered in etiquette manners at finishing school."

"You're not in finishing school, or at brunch, or with that nose in the air society. Let your hair down and dig in, woman."

"Okay." She giggled, looking around. "Um … where's the knife and fork?"

"Right here." Mark held up his fingers and wiggled them before digging into the food.

Honey looked down at her plate. Her fingers hovered over the glazed meat. She had a couple of false starts, hands getting close and pulling back at the last second. Until finally, she picked up one rib.

She nibbled tentatively at the saucy slice of meat. A slow smile spread across her face. She took another bite, this time just a touch less dainty.

"This is really good," she said. "You guys should sell the stuff."

Mark didn't bother to tell her the sauce was store-bought. He felt far too satisfied watching her eat and smile and relax.

The night birds serenaded them. A gentle breeze brought the sweet smell of flowers from the garden. The moon shone down as their own personal nightlight. If this had been an actual date, the setting would've been perfect.

Mark set his half-eaten rib back on his plate. His belly felt full and content even though he had only had a few bites. He tipped his head back with a grimace of defeat, glad Chase and Banks weren't around to witness his realization.

Wow, this place. It had finally gotten to him.

CHAPTER TWELVE

*H*oney slept deeply. It was the most peaceful rest since the last time she'd laid tucked in her mother's arms. Her mom had crawled into her or Ginger's beds a lot when they were kids. Honey never knew why she didn't prefer the city-sized bed she'd shared with her dad. Honey loved those nights when she got to sleep inside her mom's hug.

Sleep was the only time she allowed herself to think about her mother. In the waking hours, if her father caught her staring off into space, he'd accuse her of wishing for her mom. As a child, he threatened to send her to live in the one-bedroom apartment that her mom shared with her sister.

The one time Honey had visited her mother there, she felt closed in by the small space. The walls were so thin, she could hear the neighbors. There was dust on the couch that had smudged her white dress.

Honey had panicked at the stain. Her father expected her to be perfect at all times. She would get in so much trouble for that.

Her mother had let out a weary sigh and then went to work scrubbing out the smudge. There had been sadness in her eyes when it came time for Honey to go. But for the short time Honey had been there with her mom and sister, they'd each looked happy, carefree. They walked around barefoot in faded shorts and T-shirts. Honey didn't own either garment in her closet.

Her mother's hair had been down, her face scrubbed clean of makeup. Honey remembered thinking how beautiful she looked. It was one of her last memories of her mom.

Honey had chosen her dad over her mom. To keep her dad's favor, she hadn't visited her mom often. And all too soon, her mother had gone to heaven.

Honey opened her eyes now. The first thing she recognized was that she wasn't in her own room. The space wasn't much bigger than her mom's apartment bedroom had been. This room was smaller than her en suite bathroom. The sheets were thin, the comforter scratchy. There was noise coming from the open window; laughter, conversation, animals. She was not at her father's home.

It all came back to her. The shoe. Her dress. Her father. Beau. Mark. Then more.

The group of women who'd flocked around her in the barn last night, whispering secrets about Mark like they wanted her in on all the private jokes. Mark pulling her away to be alone with him. The sweet tang of over-cooked meat dripping in sauce.

Honey still had the salty-sweet taste on her tongue. Her fingers still carried the spicy scent. Sucking at her teeth, she came across a kernel of corn stuck there.

If her father could see her now, he'd disown her all over again.

She didn't care.

It probably had something to do with the fullness in her belly. She'd finished off her meal last night leaving nothing behind. She'd slopped up the sweet sauce with not only her dinner roll but Mark's buttery roll as well. That's probably why she'd slept so well. She'd likely gained five pounds.

She didn't care.

That and the fact that Mark hadn't been satisfied until her plate was clean. No man had ever cared that she ate. Her father cared what she ate, only the finest and not too much so as to not put on any weight.

She put her bare feet on the floor. Her hair was down around her shoulders. She had on not a stitch of makeup. She felt … happy.

She should be in a panic about her future. But the sun shone into the windows. Wafting along the breeze was something that smelled good.

Honey gathered clothes from her case. She knew the bathroom was across the hall, having used it last night. Padding barefoot on the tiled floor, she reached for the door handle. It turned and opened on its own.

Honey was met with the tanned wall of man-chested muscle. Mark stood in the bathroom door, wearing only a towel.

"There she is," he said with a grin." You sleep well? Don't worry, I left enough hot water for you. You okay?"

No, she was not okay. She had no idea where to look. Not at his bare chest that glistened with water from the shower. Not down at the towel covering his private bits. Not at his bare feet with neatly clipped toenails. And definitely not up to his face in those dark roast eyes, dark enough to be reflective glass. She could just make out her reflection.

Her reflection. She wasn't wearing a lick of makeup, and her hair was a rat's nest. And she was in pajamas.

Honey covered her face with a yelp. "Don't look."

"What's wrong?"

"I'm a mess."

"Are you kidding?" He chuckled. "You're even more beautiful without all that makeup on your face. I know women don't believe guys when they say that, but it's the truth."

He slowly peeled her hands from her face. His smile was genuine as it had been every second she'd known him. Mark might like to joke, but he wasn't one for games.

"Hop in the shower and get dressed," he said. "Breakfast will be waiting for you when you get out."

Breakfast? Last night she'd eaten enough to keep her satisfied for days. But at the mention of food, her stomach grumbled.

Mark's dimples made a morning appearance. "I think that's your tummy telling me it wants some more real food; bacon, eggs, toast, hash browns with a side of fruit salad, of course."

All that food should not have sounded appetizing. But her belly grumbled again with what sounded like excitement. Mark chuckled, giving her arm a squeeze.

"Let's get dressed and get you fed," he said again. "I gotta get to work."

"Work?"

Was he leaving her? A sense of vulnerability washed over her. Honey had no idea what she would do today without him. She had no idea what her role would be there except as his pretend girlfriend.

"Yeah," he said. "I help with the JROTC program. Another soldier here started it, but he's off on his honeymoon now that his wife is on a break from college."

Mark's hand was still on her arm, squeezing gently. Honey's eyes dipped to his chest as he spoke. A droplet ran from his shoulder down his bicep. It was on a trajectory to slide down his fingers and land on her. But it evaporated before it finished the downward slope, as though it didn't want to leave his person. That totally made sense to Honey.

"Are you one of those girls who needs an hour to get ready?"

"I can be ready in twenty ..."

His gaze narrowed.

"Okay, thirty minutes." Especially if she went light on the makeup. "Don't leave me behind, okay?"

Mark's features sobered. "I would never."

The moment felt important. But also too large for either of them to manage. Especially since they weren't fully clothed. Or in a real relationship.

"I'll be out as quick as I can," Honey said.

She twisted from his hold and ducked inside the warm bathroom. Though she clutched her clothes to her chest, she felt somehow bared to her soul.

CHAPTER THIRTEEN

With the knowledge that Honey was watching his every move, Mark stood with his back straighter. His deep voice took on a bass note as he instructed his young troops. By some miracle, the kids did marginally better today.

Billy got his left and right foot straight. Mark was certain it had to do with the intact sole of the shoes on his feet. Janey even gave Billy a look of approval at his improved performance.

"Sir?"

Mark kept sneaking glances at Honey out of the side of his eye. She leaned against a white picket fence, watching him with a grin. He was too far away to tell if the grin was the polite, bland smile she often wore or something that was a bit more impressed. Before he could be sure, Honey turned away as Maggie waddled up with her pack of dogs.

"Sir?"

Mark turned back to his troops. They were at the end of the field, marching in place in front of a fence.

"Should we turn? Or about-face? Or just bust through the fence?" Eli Wilson asked.

"At ease," Mark said.

When he turned back, Honey was walking off with Maggie. She tossed him a wave over her shoulder. Mark raised his hand in response.

"Dismissed for the day, cadets."

Mark hadn't given that order. He turned to see Banks grinning at him. Chase walked behind the other sergeant, shaking his head at Mark as though his friend were a lost cause.

The kids peeled off, headed into the barn for their things. They gave each soldier a high five as they passed.

"Word on the street is that you're taking Honey to the Debutante Ball," said Banks. "Oh, man, I'm sorry for you. I was forced to live through those nightmares back in New York."

"I escaped them," said Chase. "Since they're always over the holidays, I always volunteered to plan the family vacations and made sure we were far away from society. Off on an island somewhere or on a ski resort."

"Smart man," said Banks.

Mark looked between the two men. Sometimes he forgot that Banks and Chase were from money. The two men looked and acted so, well, normal. Not at all like the stuck up men he'd met the other day at the brunch. And the two men would never leave a man or woman behind or kick them out of their unit the way Henry Dumasse had done his daughter.

"You'll need to get a top hat and tails," said Banks.

"Honey said I could wear my uniform to the ball," said Mark, nearly stopping in his tracks. His uniform was as fancy as he got. He was more a jeans and T-shirt kind of guy. He didn't even own a suit.

"Oh, there's more than the ball," said Chase.

"Yeah, there are rehearsals, and more brunches and luncheons."

"Luncheon? What's a luncheon?" said Mark

"And don't forget about all the networking and schmoozing that goes on," said Chase.

Mark groaned. He hated making small talk. It was all so fake.

"I had to take the daughter of a count to one of these things once," said Banks.

Now he had to learn how to bow? Honey didn't say anything about networking or royalty. He thought he'd simply escort her there, eat some snobby food, look at her with goo-goo eyes so others would get jealous and that would be it.

"You'll need a crash course in etiquette," said Banks.

"Etiquette?" Mark sounded out the big word slowly.

"Yeah," said Chase. "You know, which fork to use, which spoon."

"Wouldn't I use the one on the table next to my plate?" asked Mark.

Banks and Chase looked to one another. Their expressions were part pain as though their memories of their time in high society were painful. There was humor also etched in their expressions as though ready to live through and make fun of Mark vicariously.

"It would be easier if you just married her," said Banks. "Then her reputation would be restored, and she'd have someplace to live."

"Marry her?" Mark choked. He looked around, but Honey and Maggie were already stepping into Maggie's and Dylan's home.

"Yeah, I mean you've already seen what's up her skirts," said Chase.

"Hey!" Mark came to an abrupt stop. He glared at his superior, the man he respected above most others.

Chase held up his hands in mock surrender, but his humor wasn't gone.

Mark was surprised the man wasn't more upset. After all, Mark had lost them the perfect location for the recruitment center. But then again, Chase wasn't dependent on that income. The sergeant could afford to wait the time it would take the government to cut through enough red tape to set them up with a place on their own dime. Mark couldn't afford to wait that long. Which was why he had to make this work and soon.

But just the pretending to be in love part. He wasn't falling for Honey. He couldn't possibly take care of her. He liked providing for her with what little he had. He liked waking up with someone he looked forward to seeing. He liked that she'd seen him working. He did want to get married someday, but he had to be sure he could take care of his family. He certainly couldn't meet the needs of someone like Honey.

"There's food and then dancing," Banks was saying. "You do know how to waltz?"

Waltz?

Mark pinched the bridge of his nose. This was getting more and more complicated. Exactly what had he gotten himself into?

CHAPTER FOURTEEN

"*A*unt Maggie, Carlos took the pooper scooper from me. I haven't had a chance to use it."

Honey blinked twice, trying to ensure she heard the kid right. They were both of Hispanic descent. Honey didn't speak a lick of Spanish. She'd understood every word the little girl had said though. The words just didn't make sense.

"There are five dogs," Maggie Banks said. "Trust me, you'll get a chance to scoop some poop. Now go back outside, you two."

Maggie's tone had been patient and kind. Had it been her father, Henry Dumasse would've turned red at such an interruption. His bellows would've shaken the plaster of the attic walls.

The little girl huffed and stormed out mouthing under her breath. Those words Honey didn't comprehend. They'd had a definite Spanish lilt.

Maggie turned back to Honey, belly first. Honey hadn't had the occasion to be around many pregnant women. In the circles she walked in, most women were either looking for husbands or preparing to bury them.

"Sorry about that," Maggie said, lowering her body into a plush armchair. "I'm sitting them while their older sister is on her honeymoon."

"Is that Sarai?"

"No, you met Sarai earlier. Their sister is Eva. She's married to Fran. You'll meet those two soon. They'll be back next week."

Honey wasn't sure she'd be here that long. Although, even if her plan worked, there was no telling when she might move in with Beau. Or how long it would take him to propose. And then there would be the wedding planning.

She turned back to the woman who had welcomed her into her home. Maggie rubbed a hand over her round belly. Her gaze was soft and open, much like Honey's mother's had been. Everyone who she'd met here had the same look in their eyes.

Honey had already met a number of women on the ranch and a handful of the soldiers. Last night at dinner, the residents of the ranch walked in and out of each other's yards and houses without being announced. No one locked doors. Children and dogs and livestock were everywhere.

Honey brushed her hands over the fine fabric of her sundress. Maggie's home was neat and tidy. She needn't worry about smudges.

Dog drool? That was a different story. A dog sniffed at the toe of her heels. Then it laid its wet nose on her knees.

"Down, girl," said Maggie. "Sorry, are you not a dog person?"

Honey liked dogs. They just usually were the size that fit in her purse.

"I remember I used to see you at church during Sunday school when I was a kid," said Maggie.

"Oh, I loved Sunday school."

Honey had loved dressing up and sitting with the other kids while Mrs. Patel read them stories. Then they'd color and eat cookies. Her father hadn't approved. Too much riff raff, he'd said. And so he'd made their mother stop taking them. To Sunday school and church altogether.

"I don't get to church as often as I'd like," Honey said. "I have so many obligations now ..."

"I'd love for you to come with me this Sunday. Or, if you prefer more Bible study, Beth and Reece go on Wednesdays."

"Oh, I ..."

Why was she hesitating? She wasn't under her father's thumb any longer. She could spend every day at church.

Honey picked up the tiny dog and put him on her lap. Its paws smudged her dress. Honey rubbed at his back.

"That would be lovely," Honey said. "Thank you."

Honey looked out the window to see the two children who had been arguing were now playing together. The pooper scooper was forgotten in the grass. She and Ginger used to play like that, only quieter. And inside. But that was so long ago.

"Hey, Maggie."

A beautiful blonde came in with a baby on her hip and a baby bump on her belly. "Hey, your Mark's girl."

"Oh, I'm not his girl," Honey began but stopped.

Both Maggie and the new girl raised an eyebrow. Even the baby looked at her.

"We know the story," said Maggie.

"It's a good one," said the blonde. "The best one we've had so far."

"Right? It's like something out of a historical romance novel," said Maggie.

"What are you talking about?" said Honey.

The blonde and Maggie looked at each other again. Then look back at her.

"You don't know?" said the blonde. "I'm Cassie, by the way, Xavier's wife. Every marriage here starts out … as a means to an end."

A means to an end?

"Isn't that the definition of marriage?" said Honey.

"But here," said Maggie, "the means has a habit of turning into something true, in the end. Something deep, something long, and lasting."

"I give her two weeks, tops," said Cassie.

"To get married?" Honey sat up straight. The dog in her lap gave a yelp. "No, we're just pretending."

Cassie smirked. "We all were in the beginning."

"We could be wrong about you and Mark," said Maggie. "But we haven't been so far. Regardless, now that you're here, you're family."

"Can you take the baby for a second?" said Cassie, handing the baby to Honey. "His mom is on her way from work, and my back is killing me."

Honey made space for the chubby little boy on her lap beside the dog. "He's not yours?"

"I honestly can't keep track of who belongs to who," said Cassie as she plopped down on the sofa and kicked up her feet.

Honey had never put her feet up on a piece of furniture. But neither had she held a baby. Somehow, it all felt natural.

"See," said Maggie. "You're already one of us. Kids and dogs are the best judges of character."

The baby gazed up at her and let out a chortle of delight. The dog panted at her other side, dribbling onto her dress.

CHAPTER FIFTEEN

"The ball begins with a grand entrance of the debutantes. Each girl will walk in on the arm of her escort. In some balls, girls are assigned two escorts."

Mark raised his brows at that. "That's very liberal of them."

Honey sighed, looking tired and exasperated. Her eyelids pinched in. She crossed her arms over her chest.

Mark bit his lip to say no more. He didn't like the worry on her brow. He definitely didn't want to be the cause of any furrows there.

"An announcer will introduce us," she continued now that she had his full attention. "The audience will applaud politely."

"Like at a graduation ceremony? My family brought blow horns."

"Why?"

"To make a scene."

Honey's brows furrowed again. But he figured this time it was in incomprehension as to why anyone would shout at the rooftops at their kid's accomplishments. Wow, her family was not normal.

"I bet your school and your family followed the hold-your-applause-until-the-end rule?"

"Of course," she said, turning up her palms as though it was obvious.

"Of course."

They were in their dining area. It couldn't be called a dining room as it was an extension of the kitchen. Honey had set the table. But the table was overrun with dishes and silverware.

"After the grand entrance is the dinner," she continued.

Now, it was Mark's turn to sigh. Suddenly, he felt tired and exhausted. "You should know I'm more of a finger food kinda guy."

"Oh, excellent, there will be tons of bread served."

Mark hid his surprise that there would be carbs served around the debutantes. He decided not to make a joke of that. They had enough on their plate. He frowned again, looking down at the mass of cutlery.

Honey walked around the table to one of the two seats. Mark hurried after her. He did know enough to pull out her seat for her. Once she sat, she snapped open a napkin and laid it across her lap.

"The napkin goes on the lap when you start eating," she said. "Then it goes on the table when we're finished."

Mark took his seat, snapped open his own napkin, and then looked down at the daunting task before him.

There were ten pieces of silverware on the table, and they were all on his place setting. Honey had her own set of ten. She reached for the tiny pitchfork looking utensil with only three prongs instead of the normal four. Mark followed suit.

"Oyster fork." Honey held up the pitchfork.

"Oysters?" Mark blanched.

He wasn't a picky eater. He was just baffled at the rich folks. All the money in the world, and they dragged the bottom of the ocean for food.

"Salad fork. Salad knife."

She pointed to two utensils smaller than the oyster fork. But there was another set that looked normal sized to him.

"We can't use these two?" Mark asked, picking up the regular looking utensils.

"No, you can't." Honey pressed her hand to her chest. "You eat dinner with dinner forks. Dessert with dessert forks. And so on. Utensils are tools. Each one has a purpose."

"Like guns? You wouldn't take a handgun into the desert, would you?"

Honey looked at him blankly. She gave her head a shake and served some of the leftover ribs from the other night. Instead of using her fingers, she picked up the normal sized knife and fork and began carving into the dish.

Mark sliced the meat, keeping his knife in his left hand. The foot was nearly in his mouth when he paused. Honey stared at him again.

"What's wrong now?" he asked.

"It's customary to put your knife down after cutting a bite and placing it in your mouth," she said.

"Every time?"

She nodded.

Mark set both utensils down, leaving the meat untouched. "Maybe I'll be on a diet that night," he said with a grin.

Honey put down both her fork and knife. The creases in her forehead didn't make another appearance. Instead, she worried her hands. "I'm sorry. I know this is a lot. But if it is going to work …"

She picked up the salad fork and set it next to the dessert knife. Mark took the large fork and put it back in its place. Then he took her hands in his.

"Hey, I'm here for you. I'm just joking. I'll stop. I'll take it seriously."

Her blue gaze looked washed out, like the sea after a storm. "You think it's ridiculous, don't you?"

"I think it's important to you," he said. "So, it's important to me."

And just like that, the calm waters in her eyes settled, and a ray of sunshine broke through. "Why? You don't know me."

"I know you're a good person."

"Am I? I'm so worried about impressing other people that I'm forcing you to be someone you're not. You all do more good on this ranch in a day than I have done my whole life. Working directly with the children instead of putting money toward a cause to support them. Working with each other and supporting one another in the smallest things. To me, that's big."

"You're helping me."

"Only after you helped me first."

"I'm not keeping score. Tell me what's next. What happens after dinner?"

"There's dancing, but you don't have to do that."

"In for a penny, in for a pound."

Mark rose and extended his hand. He held his breath and let it out in a gush when she placed her hand in his. The tiny sparkles had upgraded into bona fide fireworks.

In for a pound? If someone else from the ranch could see him now, they'd say he was in for a band of gold.

CHAPTER SIXTEEN

"Do you know how to waltz?" she asked as she put her hand in his.

"I know how to salsa," Mark said, pulling her into his embrace. Left arm at a right angle, right hand at her low back.

"Those are two very different dances," she said, trying for some semblance of decorum. She was finding keeping cool and bland to be an impossible task around this man.

Sparks. They raced through her any time he touched her. But he had a magnetic personality. Mark was either making her laugh or frown. There was no bland smile for him.

"How so? You lead a lady around the dance floor. How hard can that be?"

His fingers curled around her palm, and she felt the heat. His palm burned into her back, but she didn't try to escape. She gave in, trapping herself to him. He'd held her before, during the most embarrassing moment of her life. Now, he was trying to help her through the most important moment of her life.

"Four steps in a circle?" he asked.

"Three. Three steps."

Honey began the counts. Mark was a quick study, and soon he took the lead. He smiled down at her, dimples blazing.

"Told you," he said. "I got it. Nothing to worry about."

For the first time in a long time, Honey wasn't worried about anything. Not whether there was a wrinkle in her outfit, or a hair out of place, or any emotion on her face. She relaxed in Mark's hold and let him sweep her away, just like when he carried her from prying eyes.

"I still can't thank you enough for everything you're doing for me," she said as they glided across the small space in his living room. "Everything you have done for me."

He shrugged those broad shoulders. "You'd do the same for me."

Would she? They didn't run in the same social circles. Would they have ever met if she hadn't gotten stuck in that pavement? She realized how perfect those shoes had truly been to hold her still in time enough for him to come to find her.

"I have a trust fund," she said. "It doesn't mature for another year when I'm twenty-one. But it's more than enough to build a recruitment center."

Mark halted mid-glide. Their bodies were bent slightly as he'd been about to turn her. Slowly, he straightened, but he didn't release his hold on her.

"I'm not taking your money."

"Technically, it's my father's money. You were going to do business with him before we met."

"That's is different."

"Because I'm a woman?"

"No. Because you're you."

The emphasis on his words made her heart flutter. But her brain needed clarification. "What does that mean?"

Mark took a deep breath, clearly searching for words. He let her go, and she felt bereft, unsteady on her feet. She wanted to sink down onto the cushions of the couch, but she held her ground.

"You said I was family," she said. She was embarrassed to hear a tremble in her voice. She was terrified that he hadn't meant what he'd said to her. What everyone on this ranch had insinuated; that she might belong.

"You are." His arms came back around her, but not in a dance partner's hold. This was a lover's embrace. Both arms wrapped around her torso. Both hands sealed at the small of her back.

"But still, my money isn't good enough?"

"No," he said. "Money is what you have, not who you are. I only want who you are." He shook himself as though he had said more than he meant to say. "So, yeah, if you just introduce me to people like you planned, that will work."

"We can work together," she suggested.

"I like that. I need you." He winced like those were more words that weren't meant for her ears. He cleared his throat and tried again. "Because I'm not good at schmoozing."

"Okay."

"Okay."

They were closer then prudent for a waltz or a salsa. They also weren't moving in counts of three. They were standing still. Still and close.

Honey tasted the sweet tang of barbecue on his breath. She could make out the fine lines on his lower lip that indicated he was thirsty. He looked beyond parched. He looked hungry.

She'd never been kissed before. She'd never danced salsa or the waltz in a man's small living room. So many new lessons. Now, she wanted a lesson from him in the art of kissing.

"Excuse me?"

They sprung apart. Honey knew people on the ranch didn't knock, but this person wasn't from the ranch.

"Ginger? What are you doing here?"

Ginger stood just inside the screen door. It tapped her backside as it closed, and she took another step inside.

"Mrs. Patel called me and told me what happened," said Ginger. "I was on the other side of the state, but I drove back as soon as I heard. Are you okay?"

Honey tried to pull on the bland smile. But her lips quivered. Ginger took the necessary steps to be nearer to her and pulled Honey into a hug.

"He's a low and vile creature." Ginger's voice was almost a hiss. "Why didn't you call me? You know you could've stayed with me. You always have a place with me."

No. Honey didn't know that. After she'd chosen to stay with her father, Honey had assumed battle lines had been drawn. Only Ginger kept coming back to check on her. Just as their mom had always called to check in on her even if Honey declined to take the calls to stay in her father's good graces.

Ginger squeezed Honey's hand. Honey squeezed her sister right back. When Ginger's hold loosened, Honey had to fight her arms to unlock.

"You're the soldier who rescued my sister?" Ginger asked, turning her attention to Mark.

Mark offered his hand. "Private Mark Ortega."

"Only a Private?" Ginger took Mark's hand. "I'm sure Sugar Daddy loved that."

"Ginger," said Honey in a warning tone.

"Don't worry," said Ginger. "I didn't inherit the snobbery gene in my family. And it looks like you're helping to disabuse my sister of the trait. So, I approve."

CHAPTER SEVENTEEN

He liked the sister. Ginger would've fit in in the military with her no-nonsense attitude and quick wit. The sisters spent the night together in Honey's room. He heard them chatting late into the night. They slept in for breakfast and were now in the Great Hall for lunch. Couples outnumbered the two remaining single men. So, of course, the brides of the Purple Heart Ranch sat Mark next to Honey and Chase across from Ginger.

"You misunderstand me, Sergeant Chase," said Ginger. "I think a recruitment center is a great idea for the community. I just feel that a college education should be the first push for our young people."

"Not every kid is meant for college," said Chase.

"That line of thinking short changes our youth. They need to be told they are smart enough for post-secondary education."

"You misunderstand me, Ms. Dumasse. It takes a great deal of intelligence to make it in the military."

"I wasn't attacking these young men's intelligence—"

"Young men and young women, Ms. Dumasse. We also have programs for those past their prime years. Today's militia is neither sexist or ageist."

Ginger Dumasse narrowed her gaze at the man known as the Terminator. Both spoke with cool detachment. The passion for their causes could only be seen in the spark of their gazes.

"I went to college," said Chase. "It was a waste of money that most of these kids don't have. Being in the military is a life of service. It will give these kids a purpose and a paycheck."

"So does a higher education," Ginger insisted. "I serve, as well. I'm a warrior for this nation here on the home front. I just do it without a gun."

"Problem with guns, Ms. Dumasse?"

"No, Sergeant Chase. I have perfect aim. I just know the pen is mightier than the rifle."

"Should we separate them?" asked Honey.

"Not a chance," said Maggie, who sat on the other side of Honey. "I hear wedding bells."

"Sorry," Mark said into Honey's ear. "You know how this place is."

He leaned into Honey and bumped her shoulder. He wanted to rest an arm at the back of her chair. Or better yet, around her shoulders.

But he was feeling self-conscious today. He'd almost kissed her last night. That hadn't been a part of their plan. But it was totally on his agenda now.

"Yeah," Honey said, her cheeks blazing. "I'm sorry. I know you're not that guy."

"Not what guy?" Mark leaned back so he could peer down into her face.

"You know," she said without any added clarification.

"No. I don't."

"Well, you're not the marrying type."

When had he said that? "Yes. Yes, I am."

"You are?"

"I want to get married."

"It's just, you said eventually."

"Yeah, eventually."

The silence in the hall caught Mark's attention. The debate between Chase and Ginger had gone mute. Many eyes were on them. Grins spread across smug faces.

"Someday," Mark said into the pregnant silence. "But not to get a ranch house. Even though I do love this place. I need to be in good financial standing before I take on a wife and family. It's the responsible thing to do."

Honey nodded, not meeting his gaze.

Those half dozen eyes around the table narrowed on him in disappointment. Wait? Was he missing something? Did she want a marriage of convenience? Well, that was a dumb question. She was angling for one with the debutante ball. Would she settle for him and the small cottage on this ranch?

But on what income? Even now, his extra pennies went to his family. He meant what he'd said about taking care of her so long as she was in need. He wouldn't leave her behind. His body was buzzing with the thought of providing for her.

No, actually that was his cell phone.

"Excuse me. It's my mom." Mark rose from his place beside Honey and went outside to take the call. *"Hola, Mami.* What's wrong?"

His mother was a no-nonsense kind of woman. She didn't believe in small talk. She was far too busy for that. Once a week she called to check on his health. But those were Sunday night calls. Today was Thursday. He knew if she was calling any other day, it was about money.

"We have an emergency," said his mother, confirming his assumption.

Mark pinched the bridge between his nose as he listened to his mother relay the injury her brother had sustained while helping out a neighbor. He wouldn't be able to work for at least a month, maybe two. That was crucial income his family would be missing.

"You said you were getting that new position with the recruitment center," said his mother. "Will you be able to give a little more this month?"

"Of course," Mark said. "I'll figure it out. Don't worry, I'll take care of it."

He didn't have the money. He had no idea where it would come from. But that never mattered before. Even if he picked up a part-time job, he would get it in time. What was he going to do?

CHAPTER EIGHTEEN

"Oh, Honey." Ginger breathed the words as she stepped into Honey's bedroom.

"You hate it." Honey looked at herself in the mirror. The dress that was meant to be her Cinderella transformation suddenly looked like she was smudged with soot.

Why did she let her sister help her? She knew Ginger hated all the society stuff. Honey remembered Ginger's come out ball. She'd been in a foul mood, but she looked beautiful in a dress that was much like Honey had had designed.

Their mother had already passed away by that time. Ginger was in her last year of college. She'd agreed to go to appease their father. But as Ginger stood in front of the mirror in her old bedroom, looking at herself in the mirror, she'd backed out.

Their father had nearly burst a blood vessel with how much he yelled about how his daughter's move affected him. It was always about him.

"You look beautiful." Ginger came and rested her hands on Honey's shoulders.

"You really think so?" said Honey. Her smile wobbled higher and wider until it killed her face.

"I wish Mom could see this."

Honey's smile faltered, shrinking in on itself. It began to fade into blandness.

"Oh, honey bunny, no. Don't go there. You don't have to shut down and put your show face on anytime her name is brought up."

"She's not here. She left."

Honey turned from the mirror. Because she no longer wanted to look at her face, which was so like her mother's? Or because she didn't want her sister to see the turmoil in her gaze? She wasn't sure which. Probably both.

"She didn't leave you, Honey. She ran from him. Our father is not a nice guy."

"Then why do you keep coming back?" Honey rounded on her sister, no longer caring about what she saw.

Ginger raised her shoulders in a helpless gesture. "He's still my dad. I keep hoping there's a kernel of good somewhere in him. But after this, after turning you out, I've lost all faith in him. Family doesn't do that."

Mark had said that to her. Now her sister, who'd never truly left, said it. But Honey had done that. She'd turned her back on her mother in fear of poverty.

"You were young, Honey," Ginger said as though she could read her mind. "We both were. We shouldn't have been forced to make that choice."

"I'm sorry, Ginger. You kept coming back for me. You and mom. But I was so intent on pleasing him. I understand why she ran now. I nearly buckled trying to live on his trophy pedestal. Luckily, my shoe got caught."

In the reflection of the mirror, Mrs. Patel's heart shaped necklace rested against her heart. The shoes that had brought her and Mark together were polished and again on her feet. They were her good luck charm. Honey giggled, tasting the salt of her own tears.

"You're going to mess up your makeup." Ginger sat Honey down at the small vanity. "I'll fix it."

Ginger set about doing just that. Honey closed her eyes and gave herself over to her sister's care. She had every confidence Ginger would make her pretty. But not as a trophy. As herself.

"So … you and the soldier?" said Ginger. "He's very *Officer and a Gentleman*. I heard he swept you off your feet at the Bachelors' Brunch. And now you're living with him."

"It's not like that."

"No? What's it like? I see the way he looks at you."

Honey's eyes slammed open, and she nearly caught an eyeball full of mascara. "How does he look at me?"

Ginger grinned. "The same way you look at him: with interest."

Honey closed her eyes, but she no longer bothered hiding. "He's handsome. He's kind. But he's not marriage material. He doesn't have a job or his own place."

"Isn't he opening a recruiting center? And this home is a pretty nice place. From what I understand about this ranch, it could all be yours with a simple I do."

Ginger said it with a smile. So, Honey knew she wasn't serious. Or at least she didn't think her sister was serious.

"I couldn't," said Honey. But her refusal was light-hearted. Was she actually considering a marriage of convenience to Mark?

She'd always known her life would come down to that? But she believed she'd marry a man in her social class. She'd always assumed she'd have a loveless arrangement. But every time she thought of Mark, her heart fluttered, her cheeks heated, her breath caught.

Mark had means of his own. It had only been a couple of days, but Honey felt warm and cozy in the little cabin. She could take care of it on her own, no need for servants. Or maybe two days a week for a cleaning service.

"I'm not saying you two need to get married. How about just dating?"

Dating Mark? Honey already knew she liked living with him, dancing with him, sharing meals with him. They'd almost kissed, and she knew for certain she would like that.

A knock sounded at the front door. Then it opened without their acknowledgment.

"Honey?" called Mark. "You decent?"

"It's him," said Honey.

Ginger brushed one last layer of color on Honey's cheeks. "You're ready."

They opened the door. Mark stood in his uniform, filling it out as no other man could. He grinned wide and then his mouth went slack when he saw her.

"I'm sorry," he said. "You just took my breath away."

Whatever color Ginger had put on Honey's cheeks was likely getting washed out by the heat that resulted from that compliment.

Mark offered Honey his arm, and they headed out for what she'd always thought would be the most important night of her life. Only now she realized it had nothing to do with the ball.

CHAPTER NINETEEN

e was a walking cliché.

There were butterflies in his stomach. Birds flying around his head. His heart beat fast and hard like a gong pumping out of his chest. He was every cartoon character's technicolor manifestation of a man falling hard.

"Where's your truck?" asked Honey.

They walked down the porch steps towards a dark sedan. Since all the soldiers here drove some version of a Ford or Chevy with a flatbed in the back.

"We couldn't show up to the ball in that. Besides, I wouldn't want to get your dress dirty. This is a rental."

He'd taken his grandfather's watch off as well and left it on his bedside table. He wasn't taking any chances tonight. It had to be perfect for her.

"Can you afford this?" The moment the words were out of her mouth, she grimaced. "I mean, I don't want you to go through any trouble for me."

Money was tight, but he wouldn't skimp on this night. He would show her the night of her life if it bankrupted him. Which this one-day rental had come close to doing.

"Woman, you are nothing but trouble."

He opened the car's door for her. Her body brushed his, and that spark between them ignited into a full-blown fire. Honey gasped, looking up at him with those doe eyes.

Mark resisted the urge to pull her to him and taste her lips. Though he had the right to. They were pretending to be dating. If the occasion called for it tonight, he'd certainly be willing to play that part.

But what about tomorrow?

He'd have to leave this place soon. With his brother laid up and the recruitment center on hold, he had to go back home and lend a hand to his family. Even though he knew his duty, he didn't want to leave Honey behind.

But he couldn't take her with him. Not to his family's two-bedroom apartment that currently housed four people. Mark would be sleeping on the couch when he went home. Where would he put Honey? In his dad's recliner?

No. Honey deserved better. Not because she came from wealth. Because she had a big heart. But the people in her world hadn't bothered to look past her designer labels to see it.

Mark did. So did her sister. So did the people on the ranch.

Maybe he could work out something with Banks where she could stay in Mark's cabin for the remaining time he had? Maybe she could go with her sister?

He wasn't sure what to do? Already, the pressure to help his family overwhelmed him. But the need to provide for her was right on the same level.

"You good?" she asked, parroting the expression the soldiers often used.

He smiled down at the beautiful creature who had been entrusted into his care. She wore a gown of the finest silk. Her jewels were likely worth every penny his family had ever earned in their lifetime —times two.

"Yeah, I'm good," he assured her. And it was true. "I'm great. I've got the easiest job in the world tonight; making you look good."

That's all he would focus on and not that he'd have to leave and go back home to help his family.

He would enjoy tonight with her. He would present her to the world. He would get her back into the graces of high society, the place she wanted to be. That way, at least he'd know she'd be financially taken care of.

He could never afford to care for a woman like Honey. His heart beat a stubborn rhythm of revolt. Mark ignored it and got behind the wheel.

Twenty minutes later, they pulled up to what could only be described as a castle. Mark handed Honey out of the car amidst a parade of limousines. He wrapped her hand in the crook of his arm, tossing the keys to the valet who looked suspect at his rental.

Entering the ballroom, Mark had another shock. It was even grander than he'd imagined. Silver and gold were everywhere. Ladies dressed in white moved like graceful dancers on a stage, though they were only walking around the room.

"Miss Honey Dumasse and Private Mark Oregon."

Mark shrugged off the mispronunciation of his name. This was about Honey and not him.

All eyes turned to gape as they came down the grand staircase. Mark clenched his elbow so tightly he felt Honey wriggle her fingers in his hold. People's gazes slid past him like he was invisible. He always would be invisible to these people. Their gazes focused on her, where they belonged.

"Oh, Honey. We were sure you wouldn't show."

A raven-haired beauty appeared at their side. On second thought, Mark decided to detract the description of *beautiful* from her. There was something dark and cold in the woman's eyes.

"Hello, Quinn." Honey smiled. Not the bland smile from when he'd first met her. Not the open one she'd adopted only a couple days at the ranch either. Honey's gaze was on Mark as she beamed brightly. "Why wouldn't I? I have been waiting for this day my whole life."

"After, you know …" Quinn slid her gaze to Mark.

"Have you met my escort? Private Ortega."

"Only a private?" Quinn, who was barely five feet tall, managed to look down her nose at Mark. "Are you advancing soon?"

"I'm retired," said Mark.

"Oh," sneered Quinn.

"Mark is going to serve the community by opening a recruitment center. Already he works with the youth, teaching them about opportunities in the military."

Mark didn't correct Honey. Not in front of her nemesis. They could discuss his departure after the night was over. Besides, he liked the pride in her voice.

"Have you met my escort, Lieutenant Bryant?" The toy soldier who'd stood by during Honey's fall from grace appeared at Quinn's side. "He outranks you, Private Ortega. Don't you have to salute?"

"No, he doesn't," said Lt. Bryant. The man offered Mark his hand. Then he turned to Honey. "I'm glad you're doing well, Ms. Dumasse. I inquired about you with your father. I'm glad to see you're in good health."

The man's glance slid over Honey before turning back to his date. It was clear to Mark that the lieutenant was interested in the woman on Mark's arm and not his own. His heart thudded to a stop when he realized Honey could still have that engagement.

"Thank you both for your concern," said Honey.

She gave Mark's arm a tug to lead them away. Mark stalled for a moment. Wasn't this what she wanted? This was her way back in.

Lt. Bryant's gaze was an open door back into her world. But instead, Honey clung to Mark's arm. Like a puppy on a string, Mark did her bidding.

"Honey, there you are."

They came to another halt. This time before the imposing figure of Henry Dumasse.

"Dad? What are you doing here?"

"I wouldn't miss my daughter's come out ball," he said. "I'll take it from here."

Dumasse gripped Honey's hand, peeling her fingers from the crook of Mark's elbow. Honey yanked her hand away from her father.

"Mark is my escort."

"Oh, yes, yes. Thank you for your service." Dumasse took out a crisp one-hundred dollar bill. "And thank you for your service."

Honey snatched the bill away and crumpled it in her hand. "You're being inappropriate and rude."

Her father frowned down at her, a pulsing vein appearing in his neck. "What's this? A couple of days living in squalor has done you some good. The humility will be a good look."

Honey's features iced over. Her jaw clenched so hard that Mark worried for her molars.

"I'll give you the location you want for your center and a sizable donation to get started," said Dumasse.

Mark was slow to drag his gaze from Honey. She was his first concern. It took him a moment to realize Dumasse was addressing him.

The center? A donation?

That would be the answer to all of Mark's prayers. He wouldn't have to leave. He could take care of his family. He could still see Honey.

"Why?" asked Honey, suspicion dripped from her tone.

"We don't need to discuss this in front of the help," said her father, indicating Mark.

"Oh, he's the help all right," said Honey. "He helped me when you turned your back on me."

"And now I'm helping him. Beau is interested in you. He came to talk to me after your … mishap. His father is on board with an engagement. A union between our families would be the merger of a generation. All you need to do is be a good girl and accept Beau's hand and everyone gets what they want."

CHAPTER TWENTY

*H*oney couldn't believe it. Here her father was again, forcing her to make another choice that was bound to hurt others while it raised his prospects. Her entire life flashed before her eyes as she gaped at him. What once was black and white was now filled with color. The color she mostly saw was red.

She remembered back to the time when she was a little girl, and her father had called her and Ginger in the room to make their choice. He'd stood in a corner, smug grin confident on his face. Her mother hadn't been looking at Honey. She'd been looking down at her hands crossed in her lap. Her mother had known then. She'd known that Honey wouldn't choose her.

Even knowing it, her mother had never made Honey feel bad for it. She had never stopped calling. She had never stopped visiting. She'd always held out hope that even if she wasn't Honey's choice, she could still get some time with her little girl.

But Honey hadn't been mature enough to make any choices. She'd had spent most of her life trying to make sure she was chosen. Chosen by her father. Chosen by the right friends. Chosen by the right man.

If she allowed her father to make this choice for her, if she allowed Beau to choose her without even asking, she would fail not only her mother again. Honey would fail herself.

Unfortunately, choices were never that simple. In this scenario that her father laid out, it wasn't a win-win for everyone involved. Like always, he'd tipped the scales to make sure he would come out ahead, looking the best.

Sure, her father would have a business deal solidified. He'd be able to brag that his daughter had made the social match of the season. Ha, maybe even the match of the decade.

Beau might think he was getting a trophy wife, but Honey had discovered that she was so much more than that. In just a matter of a few days on the ranch with Mark, she had seen that there were different sides to her, strengths she didn't know, abilities she wasn't aware of. She wanted to explore those.

Then there was Mark. That's where Honey got tripped up. If she agreed to her father's demands, Mark would have everything he needed for the life he wanted. He would get the location for the recruitment center he was so passionate about, along with start-up funds. And he'd get them now instead of a year later.

When Mark's needs entered the equation, it should've been a no brainer. It was a no brainer. The decision made sense. The problem was her heart.

Her heart wouldn't allow her to open her mouth and agree to her father's scheme. Everyone else would win, but she would lose. She would lose Mark.

Honey's heart beat faster as she looked up at Mark. There was clear outrage on his handsome face. He looked as though he wanted to punch her father in the nose. He needn't trouble himself. She was going to slap her dad; verbally, not physically.

But before she could say anything, Mark stepped up. He put himself between her and her father. Instead of raising his fist, he turned and spoke directly to her.

"You should do it," Mark said.

Honey gave her head a little shake. Surely, she couldn't have heard him right. The man who'd nearly kissed her the other day, the man who looked as though he'd wanted to kiss her earlier tonight, didn't just tell her to take a deal where she married a man she didn't love for money.

"This is what you wanted," Mark continued. "It's your way back into the place you belong."

The place she belonged? Here, in a room filled with dozens of people who didn't lift a finger during her time of need. Here with a father who cared more about his bottom line than his daughter's wellbeing. Here with a man who didn't know a single thing about her other than her last name.

"I told you I'd make sure you were taken care of," Mark was saying. "This is the only way that I can see that you will be cared for in the manner that you're accustomed to."

Honey's throat constricted. Her lungs burned as though a match was scrubbing them clean. At the same time, she felt like she was drowning. And then there was relief.

Cool, soft, spicy relief as Mark pulled her to him into a tight embrace. Honey felt his chest rise and fall. Their breaths came into synch as he held her. But this wasn't a comforting hold. It was a goodbye.

Mark took a deep breath, stealing her air. With his exhale, Honey felt all the fight go out of her. How could she fight for the two of them when they weren't even a couple?

His body went tense around hers. Perhaps he was changing his mind? As she pulled away, she saw that Mark's attention was no longer on her.

"I understand why you're doing this," Mark said to her father. "You want to be sure your daughter is taken care of. Any father would."

Mark got it wrong again. That's not what her father was doing. This wasn't about her. It was about him.

"You've raised a strong, resilient, kind-hearted daughter, Mr. Dumasse. Be proud of her. Do right by her. As any father would."

The vein in her father's neck worked. Honey took a step into Mark, certain that at any moment, her father would roar loud enough to shake the chandelier.

He didn't. They were out in public. He would never cause a scene around his peers.

Mark pressed a kiss to Honey's temple. He gazed down into her eyes with a smile that didn't reach his eyes or spread far enough to dig into his dimples. He opened his mouth. Then closed it. In the end, he pried her fingers from his and was gone.

"That's my girl," said her father when they stood alone in the crowded room.

His girl?

His girl?

She'd never been his girl. She'd only ever been a prize in his trophy case. Well, no more.

Honey rounded on him. "I won't do it. I won't be a pawn in your game anymore."

He stepped into her. The vein pulsing again, but his voice was quiet when he spoke. "Think about your words, little girl."

"I'm not a little girl. I'm a grown woman. And you can't treat people like this, especially not your family."

She hadn't known that before. She hadn't understood the rules of family having been raised by such a callous man. Back on the Purple Heart Ranch, she'd seen people taking care of those who weren't even their blood. They cooked, cleaned, babysat, and scooped poop for each other just because they cared.

"He's not of this world," said her father. "He could never take care of you the way you need to be cared for. Besides, he was only in it for the money. Why do you think he left so quickly?"

Honey opened her mouth. But then closed it. Much as Mark had done a moment ago. Her father had a point there. Not that she believed Mark had done it for the money. The kids he worked with, the kids he was trying to lead to a better way of life, they needed that recruitment center for their start.

Just as he'd promised to get her back to a life she deserved, he'd made the same promise to them. Mark was doing what he thought was right because that's what you did when you cared about someone you looked at as family.

"Come back to your world, Honey."

The problem was, this world no longer was right for her. It never had been. She'd had to sit silently in it, smile blandly, and never get a speck on her.

Well, no more.

She turned to see that the dinner had begun. Her father held out his arm for them to go in. Honey gave the man her back and walked into the room unescorted.

When she sat at her place, she tossed her napkin to the side. Ignoring the cutlery on the table, she picked up the piece of steak with her fingers and took a bite. Brown sauce dripped down onto her pristine dress as she smiled brightly at the aghast faces.

CHAPTER TWENTY-ONE

Mark folded his uniform in crisp, straight lines. He tucked the arms of his shirt in, then brought the collar to meet the shirt tales. Before placing the garment in his bag, he brought the fabric up to his nose and inhaled.

It was still there. Honey's scent. He was catching it everywhere that morning. In the bathroom, on the sofa, in the kitchen. She'd been in his life for such a short time, and she'd made a huge impact.

Honey hadn't come to retrieve her things last night. She'd probably forgotten about them and already replaced them with what she had back at her father's house. Or, maybe she'd gotten new things.

He'd refrained from going into the room she'd claimed to immerse himself in her fragrance. He wasn't that pathetic. He eyed the door. It was cracked open. At the last second, he turned back to the task at hand.

Mark shoved the last of his things in his duffel bag. There was plenty of room left in the belly of the bag. He hadn't had much to begin with.

He'd be on the night bus across the states in a short time. Headed back to his parents' two-bedroom apartment in a low-class neighborhood where he belonged.

He'd tried to make something more of his life with his stint in the military. But it hadn't worked out the way he'd wanted. Now, he had to return to the real world and be the man his family depended on.

Because that's what families did for each other. They made sure that everyone was taken care of. Sacrifices had to be made.

Although Mark's parents would've never asked him to sacrifice his happiness for their comfort. They wouldn't have to. Mark could never abide by seeing his family in dire straits. Not when he could do something about it.

They'd scrimped and saved so that he could go to the military. They'd made do with what he could provide on his government pay. And they'd been proud to do it.

As any family would, Mark's parents, his siblings, they all wanted to see him succeed. They wanted him to not only reach for but to grasp his dreams of being in the military. When he'd been medically discharged, they'd mourned the loss of that dream.

They'd been ready for him to come home and would've cared for him themselves if it hadn't been for the Purple Heart Ranch. This place had become a second home to him. The ranch and its inhabitants had given him a new life. But his time was up here.

There would come another time when he could give back to his country again. But for now, Mark was going home to contribute to his family's earnings.

He wouldn't take on the sole breadwinner role. They would all work together to lift each other up. That's what mattered at the end of the day. A man had to take care of his family.

He zipped up the bag. But the sound of the teeth closing his meager belongings in rattled him. He couldn't shake the feeling that he'd left something behind. But the room he'd lived in for the last two months was bare.

A knock sounded at the front door. He'd already said his goodbyes. The other three members of his unit had tried to pressure him to stay, even offering him the cash his family needed.

Just as he'd refused Honey's charity, he'd refused them. He worked for everything he earned.

Mark opened the door to find Banks standing on the other side. The man's prosthetic leg gleamed in the sunlight as he leaned against the door frame. His face was serious, like the sergeant he was.

"They said you were leaving?" said Banks.

"Yeah," said Mark. He hadn't wanted a send-off, and he'd knew that if word got out across the ranch, the wives would all insist on a big to do.

Banks shook his head. "But your job here is not done, soldier."

"Job? What job?"

"You took over the JROTC for Fran while he's been away."

Mark shrugged. "I was just helping out. Besides, that wasn't a job. It was a pleasure." Working with the kids had given him a new purpose while he'd awaited the fate of the recruitment center.

"Of course, you were helping out," said Banks. "That's what we do for each other. We're a unit; a family."

Mark bit at his top lip. In his mind, he was calculating days and bus schedules in his head. "I can stay a couple more days until Fran gets back."

It wouldn't make too much difference. He could spend his evenings calling around his hometown looking for work. Then he could hit the ground running as soon as he stepped off the bus a few days later.

His only hesitation was Honey. He didn't want to see her when she came to get her stuff; if she came to get her stuff. He definitely didn't want to hear any announcement of her marrying Lt. Bryant. That would gut him.

"I must not have told you that standing in for Fran came with pay," said Banks. "I assumed you knew."

Mark knew what the man was trying to do. He'd pulled this same trick earlier this week with Billy and the shoes. Just like the kid, Mark didn't want any handouts.

"I was talking with Fran this morning," Banks continued. "He said working with the JROTC and the Youth Program was too much. So, I'm looking for a permanent instructor for the JROTC program. I was hoping you might be interested. And when the recruitment center opens, you're free to do both and have a double salary."

Mark's mouth gaped open. He'd been set to protest this obvious ploy to keep him here and help out his family. The picture Banks painted was a pretty one, one he wanted to hang in his living room. But there was still one problem.

If he stayed there in town, he'd have to pay for living space. He couldn't afford that and send money home to his family.

"Listen," Mark began. "I appreciate what you're trying to do here. But I can't make it work. I only have another month on the ranch before the zoning regulations kick in."

"Oh, that," Banks waved his hand in the air as though he were brushing the nuisance of a thought away like an annoying gnat. "That can be handled."

"It can? How?"

"You know how."

Mark sucked in a breath. But when he did, his heart kicked into gear. It pounded a rhythm he could no longer ignore.

"I can't," he said. "She's going to marry someone else. Someone who's …"

Mark was about to say someone who was better for her, but the words wouldn't pass his throat. Was Beau better for Honey? Would the rich officer get a real smile out of her? Would he ever know the real Honey?

No. No, he wouldn't. Honey would be trapped behind her facade of fake smiles, fake family, and fake friends for the rest of her life if he didn't drop everything and go after her.

"I've gotta go and get her back," he said.

Mark dropped the duffle bag and rushed down the porch steps. It was time for him to go back and get what he'd almost left behind. Unfortunately, he didn't get far. His boot caught in a loose floor board of the steps. He tried to wiggle it free, but he was stuck.

"Can I give you a hand, sir?"

CHAPTER TWENTY-TWO

*H*oney stood off to the corner of the deck as she eyed her handiwork. She'd never held a hammer in her hand a day in her life. Luckily, Dylan had happened by and helped her with her plan to glass-slipper Mark. The sergeant had told her his plan while he'd helped her to enact hers. Mark had fallen for both. Literally.

"Honey? What are you doing here?"

Mark squinted as his torso turned to her, as though he couldn't believe she was actually there. Of course, she was there. This was exactly where she wanted to be. Exactly where she was meant to be. And now she had the man she wanted to start her life with right where she wanted him.

"I'm here for you. You didn't think I was going to let you get away that easy?"

Mark gave his foot a yank, but his leg wouldn't budge from its place on the floorboards. For a second, Honey worried he might actually hurt himself. She came toward him until she was standing on the step just above him.

"Like I said, this place gets to you." Dylan bounded down the steps and made himself scarce.

Mark slowly extricated his leg from the floorboards and came to stand on the level with Honey. "I was coming for you."

"I know." She rested her hands on his chest. She felt his heart beating through the fabric there. It matched the rhythm of her own heart. "But it was my turn to show up for you. That's what family does, right?"

Mark swallowed hard as he gazed down at her. His arms came around her in an unbreakable cage. "Yeah, that's what family does."

He bent down and captured her lips in a searing kiss, a claiming kiss. If she'd had any doubt before, she was certain now. Mark was her true end goal, and she'd just scored.

He brushed the loose hair from her face when he released her lips. "I was going to leave to go and help my family. But I don't have to anymore. I can stay here. I can be with you, which is what I truly wanted to do. Even if I had left, I would've come back for you. I could never have stayed away from you. Not with how I feel about you."

"I know," she said, resting her cheek in the palm of his hand. "I know how you feel because I feel the same way, too."

"You do? Because I'm pretty sure I've fallen in love with you."

"I love you, too."

Could a heart burst with joy? Honey was sure it could. Not only could she feel her heart pounding in her chest, but she could also feel the strong thump of Mark's heart from where her hand still lay on his chest. She'd never expected to have love in her life. Now that it was in her grasp, she didn't know how she could've ever lived without it.

"You said you'd take care of me," she said. "Now, I'm making the same promise to you."

"Honey, I'm not taking money from your trust fund."

She shushed him, placing a finger to his lips. He would be taking money from her trust fund in another year. Because if her new plan went right, they would be happily married by the time her trust fund matured. Then it would be their money, not hers. She'd wait to lay that on him until after the honeymoon.

Mark curled his fingers around hers, freeing his lips from her admonishment. "We're not taking your father's money either. No one here wants to be beholden to a man like that."

"You don't have to. I kept my end of the bargain."

She would've been here last night, but she had a bit of networking and fundraising to do. After the dinner, she paired up with Mrs. Patel. The two women had commitments from three donors and one organization to help house and fund the recruitment center.

Mark's brows shot into his hairline when she told him so. He pulled her closer, closing his eyes as though saying a prayer. It was Sunday. If they hurried, they might even make it to church service. Or better yet, they could listen in on Mrs. Patel's Sunday School class.

"This place," Mark said when he opened his eyes, staring around at the ranch. "Patel said that miracles happen here."

"He was right," said Honey. "You are my miracle. You are a work of divine intervention that was set in my path to make my life whole again."

"That, and there was not one but two Patels involved. Banks also warned me that those two have a direct line to the Big Guy."

Honey smiled at that. Mrs. Patel had always been a guiding light in her life, even when she couldn't see the woman. In fact, it was Mrs. Patel that had helped her choose the pair of shoes that had gotten Honey caught in the cracks awaiting her own Prince Charming. She'd also been the one to send Ginger when Honey needed her most, putting her family back together. The woman was truly her Fairy Godmother.

"So, I suppose you're staying with your sister?" asked Mark.

"I am," she said. "But I was hoping to find a new place in a couple of weeks. I heard there might be a vacancy here on the ranch. At this address, in fact."

"There is a vacancy." Mark scratched at his chin. "It can be ready for you in two weeks. There is one catch, though."

"What's that?"

His eyes shown down on her with more love than she thought her heart was capable of holding. "I'll ask you about it later. Just know it involves jewelry and a white dress."

"Sounds like my kind of party."

EPILOGUE

Colin Chase watched the newlyweds as they twirled around on the dance floor. He was thrilled that Ortega, Cartwright, and Lucas had found not only the healing their bodies needed, but the loves of their lives on this ranch.

Banks had warned him that there was something about this ranch. That something would skip over Colin. He'd already moved into his own apartment last week, just after his last day on the ranch was up.

The magic hadn't happened for him, and that was fine. He didn't need magic. Reality worked well enough for him.

He glanced again at his crew whirling and shaking their bodies out on the dance floor. The party wasn't even close to dying down. Single women from the town swarmed the reception, on the hunt for any remaining single men. Chase backed into the dark barn to avoid capture. He was well trained in evasive maneuvers.

"Ouch."

Colin turned around, arms reaching out for the interloper of his quiet space. The small shaft of light revealed a brunette with crystal blue eyes that brightened the dark room.

"Ginger?"

Ginger Dumasse brushed out her Maid of Honor Dress in a huff. He'd seen her around the town bumping elbows with the lower dregs of society. But like him, she was from the upper crust. Getting her hands, or her clothes, dirty didn't come naturally.

"I'm sorry, Ms. Dumasse," he said formally, releasing her to her own reconnaissance. Ginger also didn't take kindly to anything that she viewed as patronizing.

"It's not your fault," she sighed magnanimously. "You didn't know I was in here hiding."

"What are you hiding from?"

"Not hiding, just resting." She leaned against the door frame and tilted her head back.

Colin could help notice the elegant curve of her neck. Or how her dress displayed her collarbones. He knew her shoulders were strong. He watched her in the last local debate with her opponent where she'd held her own, seeming far more prepared than the incumbent state senator.

"I just have to be *on* all the time," she continued. "Say the right thing. Smile just enough, but not too bright. Eat the right foods or risk getting photographed eating a hot dog or a kabob. And I love hot dogs and kabobs."

"What's wrong with hot dogs and kabobs?"

"They'd make me look like a caveman. Not a good look for any politician, especially a woman."

Colin tilted his head, still not understanding. But she was straightening and reaching for the door handle.

"I have no idea why I just told you all of that," she said. She plastered on the bright, political smile. Her voice took on that affected tone of overly-cheerfulness he'd heard in the debates. It's not how she sounded when she was on the ranch talking with her sister. "I love what I do and believe my platform is the strongest for the people of Montana."

"Ginger," Colin reached out. "You don't have to put on a show for me."

She eyed him. There wasn't suspicion in her gaze. There was a kernel of hope, as though she wanted to believe his words. Perhaps she wanted another person besides Honey that she could truly let her hair down with. Was he that person?

"It's not like you'll get my vote," he continued.

And just like that, her walls went up and her eyes shuttered. "Because we're on different sides of the aisle."

"No," he said with a grin. "Because I'm not a resident of the state. I can't vote."

"But you still don't agree with my platform or policies?"

Ginger had a sharp wit, clear intelligence, and a mind that probed issues deeply. He had enjoyed his few debates with her. But he didn't want to get into this with her. He preferred the times when they were in a group and talking about philosophical matters. Or better yet, debating the top five movies or songs of all time.

When he didn't answer her immediately, she conjured the answer she expected from him. Before he could open his mouth to stop her, she turned the knob.

Flashes of light greeted them on the other side. Colin's instincts from years in the Army kicked in. He pulled Ginger to him, shielding her with his body. It took his brain a few seconds to register that the flashes of light weren't dangerous. At least not to him.

"Congresswoman Dumasse, is this your new beau?"

"How long have you and the sergeant been dating?"

"What? Beau? Dating?

Colin looked down at Ginger. She looked up at him. Another flash of light went off and the twin gazes of horror at this predicament were immortalized in polaroid for all the state to see.

———

Although these two are on opposing sides,
they're about to be stuck in the same party of two!
You won't want to miss
In His Good Hands
the ninth book in the Brides of the Purple Heart Ranch!

IN HIS GOOD HANDS

THE BRIDES OF PURPLE HEART RANCH
BOOK 9

CHAPTER ONE

"My grandfather was in the military."

"Mine, too." Corporal Colin Chase grinned down at the freckle-faced young man standing at his table. Good, thought Chase. This was an excellent start. Historically, kids with military members in their families were more likely to enlist.

"But not my dad," said the kid. He made a fan of the glossy pamphlets on the exhibit table and then shoved them all back into a single queue. "He thought military service was a waste of time and too dangerous. He decided to start a business instead."

Chase didn't repeat the *mine too* this time, even though this kid was narrating his life.

"But the business failed a couple of years ago," the kid continued, "and we had to move back in with my grandparents."

Chase winced. Not at the thought of living with his grandfather. Moving in with his grandfather would've been a delight for him as a kid. His grandfather had been his idol even after his death a few years ago. What was cringe-worthy was the idea of moving back in with his parents. It was absolutely unthinkable for Chase.

Luckily, Chase's grandfather had made sure he would never have to do that. General Charles Chase had left his grandson a healthy trust, which Chase had never needed to touch. What Chase had reached for instead was following in his grandfather's footsteps of serving his country in the Armed Forces.

"I've always thought about serving," the kid was saying. "But my mom wants me to go to college."

"No reason you can't do both," said Chase. "The Army offers excellent education benefits and job training."

"Yeah?" The young man's voice raised an octave as he scratched at the tiny hairs on his chin.

Chase couldn't hide his smile. He just knew the Army could make a man out of this boy. He was a perfect candidate. He hadn't made a single comparison to the military and video games, meaning he had some level of maturity. He hadn't asked Chase how many people he'd killed, meaning he wasn't a psychopath. And he'd wandered over to the table without being corralled.

Yes, here was an excellent prospect. Chase just needed to close the deal. He had never thought he'd be a salesman. That was his father's realm. But in this, recruiting for the service, Chase was selling something he believed in.

Even before his years in the Army, Chase could've sat on his rump and lived off his family's money. Instead, he'd wanted to do something important with his life. His years in the service had accomplished that.

Unfortunately, Chase was no longer able to go into combat with his injuries. But he didn't want to leave the service. This new job of recruiting young men and women into the service was the perfect new career for him. However, there were drawbacks.

"Timothy." An older woman yanked at the elbow of Chase's young prospect. "The recruiter from the university wants to talk to you."

"I'll be over in a minute, Mom," said Timothy.

Timothy's mother pinched her mouth in that universal language of mothers that said *do what I say before you get a spanking.* "He doesn't have much time. He'll be leaving soon. You should go now."

Timothy clearly read mom-speak. He huffed, but he obeyed his mom. "All right. I'm going."

Chase offered the young man his hand before he could step away. "Think about what I said, Timothy, and take my card."

His mother's hand snatched the card before Timothy's fingers could reach it. "Oh, I'll take that, honey. You go on now, the recruiter's waiting."

Timothy gave Chase a nod. The kid turned on his heel and headed over to the other side of the room, where the state college booths were set up.

Chase braced himself on the table. His palms touched down on the recruitment pamphlets, spreading them out into a fan, like a front line defense. He steeled himself for the attack to come.

Timothy's mother turned to him with a smile. It was genuine. They always were.

"Thank you for your service," said the woman. "But I'll thank you to keep your hands off my son."

With a glare that rivaled his own mother's, the woman turned and walked to her son, who was shaking the hand of the college recruiter.

A pulsing knot began at the base of Chase's skull. The headache was dull, but he got the feeling it would persist for the rest of the day.

Chase collected the pamphlets into a single queue. Not a single one of the glossy brochures had left the table today. He could understand parents being protective of their children. But, on the whole, the military wasn't any more dangerous than a college campus. In fact, he was sure there was more danger at a frat house or a college tailgate than at a base.

"Another one bites the dust?"

Chase turned to his partner in crime.

Mark Ortega's dimpled grin was grim as he eyed their empty table. His gaze lifted to the kids and parents meandering around the many college and trade school booths. "Looks like the college got him instead."

"I was so close to closing that kid," said Chase. "He's exactly what the service needs."

The kid leaned into the college recruiter. His mother patted him on the back encouragingly. The card Chase had given her slipped from her fingers as her kid shook the recruiter's hand.

Chase didn't begrudge the kid for getting an education. But couldn't his mother see that in the military he could do both and come out ahead? As a vet, Timothy would've come into the workforce with proven skills and leadership experience. And no debt.

"How many does that make for us today?" asked Ortega.

"A big fat goose egg," moaned Chase.

"And for the week?"

"Two."

The corners of Ortega's mouth lowered into a grimace. "Well, those stats at least put us on par with the national average."

Chase blew out a harsh breath. The national average for recruitment was down by the thousands. Chase was used to succeeding. He did not like to be anywhere but at the front of the pack, and now he was lagging behind.

"If we could just get into the schools again, we could get our numbers up." Chase dumped the pamphlets into a carrying container.

"Fat chance," said Ortega as he folded the table. "I can't get any guidance counselors to return my calls. And the one time we did go this year, students met with an anti-war protest."

Even now, they had been relegated to the back corner of the post-secondary fair. The only reason people had come to visit their table was for the raffle of a new pair of wireless earbuds. No one had actually stayed up to chat. They all thanked him for his service.

"Let's get out of here."

Chase was ready to go, but he wasn't giving up. The two men had spent half the day at this college and career fair sponsored by the city. They could head back to the recruitment center and make those phone calls. At some point, someone had to pick up.

In fact, Ortega was doing just that. The moment they stepped out of the doors, a blonde woman threw herself at Ortega. Mark dropped the table and scooped up his wife.

"Hey, Honey. What are you doing here?"

Honey Ortega's bright eyes lit as she gazed down at her husband. Chase would've sworn he saw red hearts coming out of her eyelids.

"I told you," said Honey, "my sister's speaking. Hey, Colin."

Chase forgot his manners. His ears perked at the mention of Honey's sister. Prickled was more like it. The last thing he wanted to do was to run into her. Ginger Dumasse was one of the reasons he was having trouble recruiting.

"Education, tech jobs, higher minimum wages, these are the wave of the future for our city."

Too late.

Her authoritative voice carried over the speakers set up in the courtyard. The woman didn't need the amplifier. Her very presence made everyone stand up and take notice.

Strawberry-blonde hair. A defiant chin. Square shoulders. Chase couldn't help but stare. How could someone so breathtakingly beautiful be so rigid?

Her gaze caught his. Did he imagine it, or did her breath catch in a gasp? Did he fantasize it, or did her nostrils flare? In the next blink of his eyes, wide blue eyes narrowed, and perfect lips pinched in distaste.

Ginger Dumasse leaned into the microphone and proclaimed, "College should be the first push for all youth."

Yup, it had been a figment of Chase's imagination. Ginger Dumasse clearly stood on the opposite side of the way from Chase on the issue of higher education versus military experience. Among other things.

Around him, parents nodded their heads in agreement with her.

"That's why I intend to invest in your children's future if elected. I'm a warrior for this state. I'll do it with nothing but my wits. I'm a sharpshooter, be it with a firearm or a pen."

The audience whooped and applauded at those choice words.

"My aim is perfect. And what I'm fighting for is to become your next state senator."

Applause boomed. He didn't agree with her, but her speech was rousing enough that his hands itched to add to the applause. Too bad his hands were full of his own interests. Chase hefted the container of pamphlets and turned to his car.

CHAPTER TWO

Ginger lived for this. She lived for the podium, for the talking points, for the questions, even for the defiance.

"What are you going to do about the C&C Factory moving jobs out of state?"

She had notes in front of her, but she didn't need them. Ginger spoke from her heart because that's where her ideas came from, that's where her platform had been built.

"That is a shell company from out of state. I know many in the community are employed there, but I'm a firm believer in investing in our community with neighbors who own businesses here. We can't expect others to do it. We must become self-reliant. That's why I have a plan to give tax incentives to local businesses and startups."

She watched as the man took a deep breath. His head tilted back, and his gaze squinted. She didn't have him yet. She knew why.

People didn't want talking points, they didn't want politics. They just wanted someone with a solid plan that reflected their needs. She had loads of those.

It wasn't an immediate solution. It would take time for her plan to work. But people needed relief now.

Ginger opened her mouth to win the voter over, but her heart skipped. She didn't shake. She never choked. But she did take a moment to swallow the excess saliva in her throat.

He was staring at her. Not the voter. Well, the voter was staring because he was waiting for her to continue on her stump. But behind him was a tall, thick-limbed, oak tree of a man.

Sergeant Colin Chase glared at her.

Did she imagine it, or was there a softness to his stern features? Did she fantasize it, or did his lips part? Dark brown eyes narrowed, and his kissable lips pinched in disapproval.

Yup, it had been a figment of her imagination.

Chase had thrown her off her game. And he saw that he had. He might have big muscles, chiseled cheekbones, and a gaze that pierced right through her. But she had the megaphone.

"What you all really want to know is why you should vote for me over an incumbent of twenty-five years. It's not because I'm younger with fresh ideas, although that's true. It's not because I'm a woman, and you want to show progress, although that's not a faulty idea since women are rising business owners and gaining more wealth."

For his part, Chase raised a brow and turned to leave. Her heart thudded again. This time it left behind an empty, hollow feeling. She didn't want him to leave. She wanted him to stay and fight, to argue with her. She ached to prove him wrong. But she couldn't do that if he was walking away from her.

Someone cleared their throat. Ginger turned to look at her campaign manager, Carla, who was also her best friend. Carla raised a perfectly trimmed brow with meaning.

Ginger turned back to the sea of faces waiting for her next bit of speech. She pulled on a smile. What was she supposed to say? It was all Chase's fault. He'd distracted her.

She pulled the cards from her pocket. She looked down at her notes. The documents were all out of order. No matter. She knew what was in her heart.

"You should vote for me because, at my core, I believe we should all live in a world that is fair and just. It should be that way in our families, in our work environment, and in our government. It doesn't matter what interest groups or red tape come at me. That's who I am at my core. If that's you, then I'm the candidate for you."

There was a moment of uncertainty. Then the crowd broke off in applause and whoops and cheers for *Dumasse.*

She'd done it. She'd won them over. Just a few more thousands to go.

"That wasn't in your speech," said Carla as Ginger came down off the podium.

"It was in my heart," insisted Ginger.

"Cute. Let's put that in your stump. It's playing well with the suburbanites and industry workers."

Ginger loved her bestie. Carla had majored in political science, where Ginger had majored in graphic design. A fat lot of good it did her.

A year out of college, Carla had talked Ginger into doing pro bono work for her first campaign. The client, a local mayoral candidate, had a message that captured both Ginger's imagination and her interest. Ginger designed posters for the candidate, only to realize she wanted to say the slogans she was designing.

She ran for local office the next election cycle and won a seat on the city council. Now she was ready for the big leagues. There was so much more she could do as a state senator.

"The polls are still showing you down amongst housewives and males," Carla said as she tapped on her tablet.

Argh. Ginger hated the polls. But if she wanted to win, she had to listen to them.

"Voters don't trust your unmarried status."

"Well, I'm not getting a husband just to win an election." Ginger shuddered.

She wanted a husband. Some day. But the qualifications for her partner were high. He'd need to be man enough to contend with a woman in power. And let's face it, there weren't many of those around.

"You don't need a husband, per se," said Carla. "You could just date until after the election."

Ginger stopped walking. They'd been down this road. She had no plans to take a single step in the direction her best friend was suggesting.

Carla shrugged, still tapping away at her handheld. "There was a lot of interest when you were linked with a certain sergeant"

Two months ago, Ginger had been photographed in the arms of Sergeant Colin Chase. It had been innocent. Not like he'd kissed her or anything. Even though he might have stared at her lips. But he didn't do anything about it.

"Isn't he here today?" Carla looked up finally.

"He's gone."

Ginger bit her lip when she realized her mistake. But it was too late. Carla was grinning the smug grin she'd worn when she'd gotten the highest score in the Psychology 101 class.

"What?" shrugged Ginger. "I saw him with Honey. I was checking on my little sister."

"Hmmm." That was the sound Carla had made when she'd gotten the highest grade in their Sociology 101 class.

"It would never work between us. We're on the opposite ends of … well, everything."

"Isn't that what your whole platform is about? Bringing two sides together."

Ginger rolled her eyes. "Don't we have real issues to talk about?"

And not the nonsense of dating a sergeant who couldn't even offer her a smile today. Or anytime they'd been breathing the same air.

It didn't matter. She didn't need his appreciation. She was a strong, confident, independent woman.

Even if when she'd been in his arms for that brief moment, her strong back had gone to goo.

CHAPTER THREE

"*E*llie Wilson," said the announcer.

The young man in question winced as he climbed the stairs of the stage. The announcer had butchered Eli's name, but his parents still applauded. Their applause was amplified by the two teams of soldiers, the soldiers' wives, and the ranch children taking up an entire wing of the audience in the gymnasium.

Of course, the soldiers of the Purple Heart Ranch were all here. Once anyone set foot on the ranch, they were treated as family. And the soldiers took care of their own, including becoming a cheering section for this year's senior graduates.

Chase's time on the ranch was up. He had moved out three weeks ago. But that didn't stop the guys from coming over to his place, the wives sending him off with food, and everyone still nosing in his business. Even though he lived in town now, he was on the ranch five days a week. Sometimes every day. It was as though nothing had changed.

"Billy Trent."

The soldiers hooted and hollered louder than the kid's blood family. Billy had come to them an uncoordinated mess. Now, he marched up the stairs to the stage with his back straight and his head high.

The same happened with Ayden Benson and Jordan Scott. The cadets of the JROTC program of the Purple Heart Ranch were each walking across the stage. Every one of them was decked out with academic and service honors.

Those two had been destined for factory work. Which was admirable. Chase knew many of their family members worked in the local C&C Factory. But there had been rumblings of late that the factory might close and move out of state. With their military career secured, the boys would be able to fill in the gaps for their families if they lost those long-held jobs.

"Janey Marsden," called the announcer.

Janey Marsden was a particular bright spot. Not only had she earned the highest honors in the training program, but she'd also earned the highest honors in the whole class. Every soldier beamed as she gave the Valedictorian speech.

Teachers had welcomed the soldiers the first time they showed up at the school a year ago. When the soldiers had offered to take on their troubled kids, the administration had leaped at the offer to give the kids more attention.

Eight out of the eleven kids the soldiers had taken under their wing were now going into the military. That success rate had given some pause.

The next class was only six students. Word of mouth was how they had gotten those few new students. No teachers, guidance counselors, or principals were returning their calls for another visit.

The ceremony concluded, and Chase joined the others in congratulating the kids and their parents. Off to the side, he spotted the school's principal. He made his way over to the slight young man. Chase didn't miss the wince when Principal Miller caught sight of him in his peripheral eye.

"Principal Miller, a word if you have a second?"

"It's a big day," said Miller, not meeting Chase's eyes. "Lots of families to congratulate and students to say goodbye to."

"I understand that, but you also have a lot of students still here awaiting their future. As you saw, the JROTC program helped a lot of them forge a solid path for their futures."

"Yes, including one of our best and brightest. Did you know Janey Marsden was offered a full scholarship to three Ivy League schools?"

Yes, Chase did know that. And she'd decided to use her bright mind in service to her country. He couldn't be more proud.

"But she's turned them all down to join the Army."

"I'm failing to see the problem," said Chase. "The military needs the best and brightest."

"Look, you can come after school to talk to the kids in detention. But coming into the classrooms again is just out of the question. Some of these kids have real potential."

"And the ones who get into trouble don't?"

The man sighed. "Look, I think the military is a viable path. But it shouldn't be the first road for some kids."

Chase's mouth opened, but only a choked sound came out. He was so shocked, he couldn't form words. He grit his teeth and clenched his fists as the man walked away.

A dull thud began just behind Chase's ear. He unclenched his fingers and rubbed at the spot. But it was useless. The migraine had dug in its tenterhooks.

Chase turned and faced the wall like a child in time out. He needed the solitude. After moments of deep breaths, he opened his eyes to find Dr. Patel beside him.

"You good?" the doctor asked. His wise eyes likely saw through Chase.

"I'm managing it."

Migraines were a common ailment. Not just to soldiers, but civilians alike. There was no immediate cure. Only management tactics. Quiet and darkness, sometimes a cold compress, was what worked for Chase.

"What brought that on?" asked Patel.

"Principal Miller thinks Janey's too good for the military. He won't let us speak to the full student body. He practically called us poachers. Can you believe that?"

Dr. Patel inhaled. "Once every family had someone in the military. That's not the case anymore. People today don't remember the honor it is to serve. That the military was the only viable path for some families."

"He can't bar us from the school," said Chase. "Can he?"

"No, but he can make it difficult. Want my advice?"

"Always."

Dr. Patel had been instrumental in Chase's healing. Chase had come to the ranch, mostly unscathed. His mind was intact, aside from the migraines. But he always enjoyed his talks with Patel and the advice the psychologist gave, but also the wise words of the man as pastor in the town's church. Chase rooted himself and prepared to take in Patel's wise gospel of scriptures and metaphors. He enjoyed working out puzzles and riddles, which Patel often spoke in.

"My advice," began Patel, "is to go speak to the school board."

Well, that was uncharacteristically straightforward and logical.

CHAPTER FOUR

"With all the work I've done for the school board, how can you not be prepared to give me your flat out endorsement?"

Ginger tried to keep her voice light, but it trilled into incredulity. As a female politician, she knew she could never be perceived as shrill. That led to emotional and hysterical. She had to appear cool, calm, and collected at all times. Even when she wanted to stomp her foot at the sheer ridiculousness of some people.

"We can't endorse this far out from the election," said Dawn Weber, the school district's Assistant Superintendent.

Ginger squinted her eyes. Her hands jerked off the desk. She wanted to spout off the facts that the School Board had endorsed early before.

"You know you have my vote. But Senator Norman Dean has a long history with the teacher's union."

"Dean hasn't kept a single one of his promises. I have a plan to-"

"Having a plan doesn't mean anything if you don't have any followers backing the plan."

"What's that supposed to mean?"

Dawn sighed. "Senator Dean has donors."

Ginger was staying away from the donor class. She didn't want to be beholden to anyone but her constituents. That's how government service should be.

"Money talks, Ginger. I don't make the rules."

"I have money."

Ginger was running her campaign with her own money, money from a trust fund she swore she'd never touch. But it wasn't for her. It was for the people. At least that's how she justified it. And she hadn't put a dent in the fund.

Plus, she knew that money could say cruel things. She was one to know. She'd come from cruel money. She had plans to make it say nice things.

"I have small donors," said Ginger. "Lots of parents."

"I know," said Dawn. "I've seen your social media campaign. It's clever."

She'd done the campaign herself. Put her graphic design degree to good use. There was the Oh, Snap slogan playing off her first name. And the Sugar and Spice slogan playing off her surname and the family sugar business.

"But not a lot of people here are on social media outside of Facebook groups of their families," said Dawn.

Ginger's glossy Instagram and Snapchat ads had gone viral. But to the wrong demographics.

"The truth is, you're young, untried, and unmarried."

"What does my marital status have to do with anything?" Ginger said.

"Don't be naive, Ginger. You talk about commitment and compromise, and you have no proof that you're capable of either."

"That's just insane." Her voice went shrill.

Dawn leaned back. "I don't make the rules."

No, the patriarchy did.

"Your best bet is to get an endorsement from a high society member. Like your father."

Ginger had no intention of seeking out her father. Not after the stunt, he pulled with Honey. All her life, she'd given him chance after chance. But the man was who he was.

It was clear Ginger wasn't going to forge a path here with Dawn, so she took her leave from the office. Outside the door, a reporter lay in wait. It was a school board meeting tonight, which was big news here in this small town.

"Can I get a quote, Ms. Dumasse?"

Ginger opened her mouth to give a canned sound bite, but her voice was drowned out by a deeper tenor.

"It's about having a plan. But not only having a plan. It's about learning how to make a plan, implement it, and evaluate it."

Ginger turned to the resonating sound of sanity and blanched.

"That's what the military taught me," said Sergeant Colin Chase.

He stood in his uniform before the school board. It was the second time she'd seen him decked out in all his patriotic glory. She still had dried dribble on her chin from the first time.

"I come from a wealthy family, but none of that mattered in the service. The Army was truly the great equalizer. There, I learned the value of compromise and commitment. The Purple Heart Ranch's JROTC program has taught that to many kids in the community who didn't have a plan, who didn't know what was in the future for them, who had odds stacked against them because of their birth, or their race, or their economic status. But they can rise in the service."

"No one here disagrees with you, Sergeant," said one of the board members. The man looked haggard and bored.

For most of the school board, this wasn't their day job. Many members were eager to get home and kick their shoes off after a long day at work and an evening hearing teacher and parent grievances and demands. They did not appreciate long speeches. Ginger had learned that the hard way.

"What is it you are here for, Sergeant?"

Chase cleared his throat. When he spoke, his voice sounded even more deep and resonate. "I'm having trouble gaining access to local schools for recruitment efforts."

"What kind of problems?"

"Some faculty and students protest."

"That is their right. We can grant you access to the school premises, but you'll have to change their minds about the military."

Chase's jaw tensed. He nodded and stepped away from the podium. The moment he did, his eyes caught hers. They were always catching her. Probably because she was always staring at him when he was near.

He had made a good sales pitch. But it was a hard sell in a world where tech jobs were the wave of the future, and the military base pay was less than the minimum wage of most states. Chase needed to find a way to emphasize other benefits if he had any hope of getting his foot in the schools.

But that wasn't her problem.

As Chase turned away from the board, a large figure blocked him from Ginger's sight. Norman Dean had his hand out to Chase. Ginger saw Chase's hand hesitate, but in the end, he took the proffered hand and shook.

That was all she needed to hear and see. She and Colin Chase were truly on opposite sides of everything. Ginger turned from the doorway and headed to the elevator.

CHAPTER FIVE

hase was used to giving orders. He was used to others following behind those orders or at least offering constructive feedback. So, when the school board dismissed his directive so easily, he balked.

He stood stunned for a moment, as though an explosive had gone off. The shock waves wore off quickly, though. He turned on his heel, but he knew he wouldn't be able to brush off the debris of this blowout. Before he could get out of the door, an icy palm clamped down on his shoulder.

"I think we may be able to help each other out, son."

Chase turned his head and met with Santa Claus. The man's body was a perfectly round ball in a straining white button-down. White tufts of hair protruded from his chin, his cheeks, and above his upper lip. But his head was bald. He wore a jolly smile, but it was his dark, beady eyes that told Chase this man only had access to the naughty list.

Chase could brush all the Bad Santa aside. There had been plenty of men promising sweets and delivering coal parading around his father's offices when he was a kid. What Chase couldn't abide was being called son. It was a power play. Even when his own father said it.

"Name's Norman Dean. I know your father."

Well, that explained the jolly old flashbacks. Mr. Dean stuck out his hand. Because Chase had been raised with manners, he accepted the cold shake.

"I'm running to keep my seat as state senator, which I've held for over two decades now."

So, this was Ginger's rival. The two couldn't be more opposite. Norman Dean was an older man promising candy cane dreams. While Ginger was a young woman and making plans to deal with the harsh realities of the day. Plans Chase didn't always agree with, but at least she was dealing with the truth of the matters.

"I can use an honorable man like you on my campaign," said Mr. Dean.

"As part of the military, we aim to stay out of politics, Senator Dean. As soldiers, we protect every citizen."

Dean threw back his head and laughed. It was a ho-ho-ho that made the spine tingle in the wrong direction. "Everyone has a political agenda, son."

"Not me." Chase gave a curt nod and turned. "If you'll excuse me."

"You'll change your mind," Dean said to his back. "When you do, give me a call."

Chase couldn't make it out of the room fast enough. Down the hall, the elevator doors were closing. He called out for the occupant to hold the doors but got no response. He made it just in time before the metal cage closed, slipping one hand between the two sides and forcing the doors back open. When they opened, the last person he wanted to see stood inside the elevator.

But if Ginger Dumasse was the last person he wanted to see, why did his heart kick out a few extra beats? Why did his lips part like they were ready to take a sip or a bite of something? Why did his hands itch as though they needed to reach out and touch?

Ginger's eyes flashed up at him. Those lush lips pursed. That regal nose lifted into the air. That proud chin jutted out. She would've been adorable if not for being, well, her.

For a split second, Chase contemplated the stairs. Before the thought could become action, his feet were moving. The doors of the elevator closed behind them before his mind figured out that he and Ginger were alone together. The last time they had been alone together, he'd almost kissed her.

"Ms. Dumasse."

"Sergeant Chase."

They retreated to their own corners as the elevator began to move. The school board was housed in an old building. The elevator had likely been the first of its kind installed. It creaked along, groaning and moving slowly with old age. There were only three floors. The board meeting had been on the top. The elevator's pace was such that Chase could've walked down the stairs and back up all before the elevator made it to the second floor.

After another long groan of their cage and a rattling shake, Ginger reached out for the wall to brace herself.

Chase opened his mouth to offer comfort. And then promptly closed it. She'd reminded him enough that she was an independent woman. He was sure she didn't need his reassurance.

"Saw you getting cozy with Senator Dean back there." She took her hand off the wall and wrapped it around her torso.

"Jealous?"

Why did he like the idea that she was jealous of anything he might do. Maybe because it meant she cared. But that was ridiculous. They had a mutual dislike for each other.

Well, no, he didn't dislike her. He just disagreed with her. She wasn't a bad person. She wasn't even mean. She was just opinionated. Very opinionated, and she thought her opinions were right. She'd have made a great drill sergeant if she had a positive view of the military. Which she didn't.

"Jealous of what?" Ginger scoffed. "That he made you a bunch of promises to get your vote. Promises that he won't keep."

"Isn't that the way politics works?"

"Not my kind of politics. I'm a woman of my word."

Chase hadn't had any reason to test her word. But he believed her. Ginger Dumasse was fiercely protective of her sister. And he knew some of her background. What he particularly respected was that after her parents' divorce, Ginger had chosen to live with her mother in near poverty rather than cow to her wealthy father's demands.

"They're right about you needing a better portrayal for your cause," she said. "You need to focus on the aspects that matter to people today."

A better portrayal for his cause? What did that mean? Make military service shiny and glossy? Sell it?

That was ridiculous. He was offering these kids a way out, a plan, a chance. That was the sale right there. Here's your opportunity at a future and a way to do it honorably.

Chase tried to hold his tongue as the elevator creaked along down from the second to the first floor. The silence ate at him. Especially when he was in the right.

"Honor and service are what the military is about," said Chase.

"This generation is more into public service, travel, adventure." She'd uncrossed her arms as if her guard was down. She snapped her fingers as though a brilliant idea occurred to her. "Maybe if you framed it as a gap year."

Her face lit up. For a moment, Chase was taken with the sheer beauty of her. Bright blue eyes. Her soft blonde hair could've been the rays of the sun. Too bad there was a cloud on the horizon. She'd gotten her facts wrong.

"It wouldn't be a gap year," he said, raining on her parade. "Service is at least two years."

Ginger shrugged, crossing her arms back over her body. It was like the sun had set on what had been a beautiful day. She didn't say anymore. Which was a pity? Her idea hadn't been bad. She just hadn't had all the facts.

"I just don't think it's right that kids are taught the military is a last resort," he said. "All I was asking for in there was an equal shot."

"You and me both," she muttered.

The elevator lurched again. Ginger took another deep breath. They should be on the first floor by now, but the snail's pace had slowed further.

"You okay over there?" Chase asked.

Ginger's spine straightened. "Fine."

The metal box lurched again as if trying to decide whether to be the tortoise or the hare. The jerky indecision caused both occupants to lurch. Chase caught Ginger in his arms before she crashed into one side of the wall. The lights went out, and the elevator came to a stop.

Ginger whimpered, burying her head in his chest. Chase wasn't afraid. He'd been trapped in worse conditions during his time in service. So, why was his heart beating twenty klicks a minute?

CHAPTER SIX

The world was dark and still inside the confining space of the steel box. But while she was suspended in midair inside the elevator, Ginger didn't know the metallic taste of fear. Because the elevator wasn't the hard cage she was focused on. Her senses were wrapped up in the fact that she was inside of Sergeant Colin Chase's arms, and she didn't want to leave.

Ginger was fine with confined spaces. She had gone from living in the lap of luxury in a mansion with more rooms than she could count to a two-bedroom apartment on the wrong side of town without skipping a beat. She liked tight spaces. She did not, however, like being trapped in a space where she didn't want to be.

That wasn't the case here. Being inside of Chase's hold reminded her of that space under a warm blanket on a cold night when she'd pull the four corners of the sheet in, tucking them under her toes and fingers. During those cold nights, she'd always tunnel into the mattress and burrow into the warmest spot. The warmest spot of Chase was just right of the center of his chest, where his heartbeat was strongest.

For the first time in a long time, Ginger's knees went weak. Her fingers dug into Chase's shirt. And she couldn't remember why she didn't have one of these male creatures on hand on a regular basis? This one sure beat the feel of the patchwork quilt she'd gotten from the department store last winter.

"You're safe," Chase soothed. "I've got you."

He brushed his fingers across her brow, placing a strand of hair behind her ear. Ginger's entire body shivered at the brush of his calloused fingertips. She'd been in Chase's arms before, during another moment of weakness. Why was she always going weak around him?

You're safe. I've got you.

Her body melted into his strong chest. She had never heard those words from a man in her whole life. Definitely not from her father. Surely, not from the two boyfriends she'd had in high school and college. They'd both been clueless. She took better care of herself than any man, and that included her father.

But in this moment of darkness, stillness, and warmth, Councilwoman Ginger Dumasse was happy to hand over the keys to her well-being to Sergeant Colin Chase. She knew with certainty that he could handle any situation he was thrust into.

The colors on his uniform became visible as the lights came back on. Now out of the darkness, those colors brought her to her senses. The sharp contrast between the dark colors of his uniform and the light colors of her business suit made her focus.

She and Chase were opposites. She disagreed with this man at every turn. Right?

But as he gazed down at her, Ginger couldn't remember a single thing she stood for. Was she for or against chin stubble, she wondered as she caught sight of Chase's five o clock shadow? What was her stance on kissing on the first date? Would she prefer a fall or summer wedding?

"I'll press the *help* button," he said.

His words snatched the edges of the warm blanket from her toes, letting the cold air hit her. She stepped back and out of his hold. "No, I've got it."

"You're wobbly," he said.

"I'm perfectly fine," she insisted.

Ginger stomped her foot down on the metal floor. But her right heel teetered on her pumps. The elevator lurched again, sending her back into Chase's arms.

She couldn't hide the wobbling or the teetering now. In fact, she was downright shaking. She was going to die in an elevator with Chase Collins. Senator Dean would run unopposed. Her issues, which she still couldn't quite remember, would never be brought to light. And the community she loved so dearly would continue to suffer without a clear vision and plan for the future.

But as she wobbled and teetered, she did it on firm ground with secure straps around her person. It was Chase. Her head was once again just off to the center of his chest.

"I'm going to get you out of here," said Chase.

His breathing was easy. His pulse steady. His demeanor one of total control, even though they were at the mercy of a rickety steel cage of death. But his heartbeat was racing too. It was the only thing that gave her any notice that he was human.

Meanwhile, Ginger was a quivering mess. Her limbs shook. She wasn't sure if she'd held back the cry that had lodged in her throat. And her heartbeat raced so hard she was concerned it might explode out of her chest.

No. This would not do at all for a woman who wanted to assume a leadership role. Ginger pushed off Chase and turned for the *help* button.

"I can get us out of here," she insisted as she depressed the button.

"You're not good at taking orders, are you?"

"You're not good at following behind a woman, are you?"

The red light above the *help* button turned on as if urging her to stop. She didn't. She never seemed to mind the boundaries when this man was involved.

"Your gender isn't an issue," said Chase. "I've had plenty of female superiors."

"So, what?" She cocked a hand on her hip. "You don't consider me a superior?"

Chase grinned. It was a devastating move. It turned his face from stern to handsome. "I think you're one of the smartest, most prepared persons that I've ever met."

Ginger came from a long line of pageant princesses. She'd rejected that lifestyle in her late teens. Hearing those words come out of Chase's mouth made her feel like she'd won the crown and the sash and the scepter. She wanted to preen under his compliments. But she sensed a *but* coming, so she tilted her head back as though to let any adornment slide off her head.

"But," continued Chase, "you can be too stubborn to do what's good for you. That's a mark against you."

Ginger pointed a finger at her chest. "*I'm* stubborn?"

Chase lifted a brow. The move made her dislike him more. The man had so much self-control that he could operate his facial features singly. It was unnatural and unfair.

"Because I offered to press a button?" she said.

"You didn't offer." He lowered his brow. "You demanded."

"Because I was in a better position."

"You were cowering in my arms."

"Cowering?" Both her brows rose to her hairline. "I do not cower."

"It's fine to be scared."

"I wasn't scared. I was startled." She pointed a finger at him. "And your heart was racing, too."

He didn't come back with an immediate retort. His throat worked like he was trying to gulp discreetly. Ha! So, soldier boy didn't have total control over his faculties. She'd gotten under his skin.

Ginger put her hands back on her hips. Her chest lifted in triumph. She wet her lips, preparing to go in for the kill.

Chase's nostrils flared. He let out a long, slow sigh as his gaze swept her body. Suddenly, Ginger's triumph felt like surrender.

He stepped toward her. Her fight or flight senses engaged. Her head told her to flee. Her heart told her to fly into his arms.

Now, it was Ginger who was trying to gulp discreetly. It didn't work. Chase's gaze latched onto her throat, and she would've killed for a glass of water.

He opened his mouth to speak. Before she was able to hear a single syllable, the ding of the door opening cut him off. They both turned to look out of the open doors.

They had arrived. They were on the ground floor. Outside the open doors stood the reporter who had badgered Ginger on the third floor.

Oh, no. If the newsman saw her and Chase together, they'd be paired again. The papers would label them a couple. Their names would be plastered all over the front page, linking them as involved with one another.

Which would be … a bad thing. Right?

Luckily, the reporter's back was turned to them.

Which was a … good thing. Right?

The last thing Ginger needed was to be linked to Sergeant Colin Chase for romantic or political reasons. And so she cleared her throat.

Fortunately, the reporter didn't turn around.

Ginger cleared her throat again. She coughed into her hands when the reporter continued staring down at his phone.

"Well, that's over," she said loudly.

"Yes," Chase agreed, his voice was too quiet to carry.

"Thank you for your service, Sergeant Chase."

At that announcement, the reporter hung up his phone. He slipped it in his pocket. And turned… toward the door.

Ginger let out a huff. The gust of air came loudly from between her lips. But the reporter was already at the door.

She looked up to find Chase quirking that single brow at her again. Ginger wanted to growl. But she kept it in. Instead, she turned on her heel and promptly caught a snag in the decades' old carpet.

Her momentum propelled her forward, but her heel held her back. She was on her way to crashing down and let out a yelp of helplessness. Instead of meeting the dingy carpet that had captured her foot, she was caught by Chase's strong arms and brought once more to his strong chest.

And that's when the camera flash went off.

CHAPTER SEVEN

"Oh, oh, oh! Here's another one."

Ortega unwrapped the newspaper like it was an oversized Christmas present. But there was no box. It was the wrapping that had the soldier in a holiday tizzy.

On the one-page spread was yet another glossy headline with a photo of Ginger in Chase's embrace. The image wasn't snapped from last night. The picture was from Ortega and Honey's wedding when Chase and Ginger had been caught together in the barn.

Not that they had been doing anything wrong. Though, in that picture, Ginger was gazing in his eyes like she wanted to do something. In that stolen moment, Chase had been staring at her lips. It had been easy to do at that moment; she had been quiet.

She had also been soft and vulnerable. Even after they'd been snapped by that photographer, and convention said they should break apart, Chase hadn't wanted to let her go. He'd felt the same way in the elevator last night when she'd been in his arms. She'd been even softer, quieter, with a touch more vulnerability. Her eyes had gone wide, her lips had parted, her nostrils had flared.

Or maybe that was just the way she looked when startled? They had been surprised by the cameraman at the wedding. The elevator getting stuck was also an unexpected occurrence. Maybe that was just her fight or flight responses he was seeing.

Why did he even care? He didn't want to kiss Ginger Dumasse. Did he?

"The headline reads the Soldier and the Senator." Corporal Brandon Lucas frowned at the thin sheet. "They didn't even get your rank right."

"I think they were going for alliteration," said Private Reece Cartwright. He was the youngest of their group, and the most well-read.

"Sergeant and Senator are alliterative," countered Lucas.

The four men stood in Ortega's small kitchen in his home on the ranch. The three men of Chase's unit all still lived on the ranch, at least for the time being. Brandon and his wife Reegan were rebuilding her family's home back in the heart of town. Reece and his wife Beth had learned not too long ago that they were expecting, so they were looking for a new home of their own in town. Mark's wife, Honey, was a former society miss. Chase caught sight of the young woman out the window with her hands in the mud, streaks of grass and grime were painted all over her shirt and pants. Honey loved the ranch and had no plans to return to high tea and ballrooms any time soon.

"It says she's only dating you to get her poll numbers up and to court the older voters who don't like her single status." Ortega frowned. "That's libel. Ginger is nothing like that."

Chase didn't say anything. Norman Dean had told him that an endorsement from a military man would lift his poll numbers. Chase wouldn't put it past Ginger. Politicians were all alike. His father had enough of them in his pocket for Chase to know.

But Ginger hadn't made Chase any offers. She hadn't tried to do any deals under the table with him. She hadn't even asked for his support. All she'd tried to do was convince him of her side of the issues. He didn't disagree with where she wanted to go, just how she planned to get there.

"What are you going to do about this?" Ortega demanded.

"Do?" asked Chase. "I'm not going to do anything."

"They printed lies," said Ortega, taking on his brother-in-law role. "About both of you. We can't let this stand."

Ortega put the paper down and focused on Chase. His eyes went over his face, left to right and back again as though he were reading Chase.

"Unless there is something going on between you two," said Ortega.

"Wait?" Lucas turned his back on Chase and faced Ortega. "I thought there was something going on between them."

"Yeah, me too," said Cartwright, also giving Chase his back. "And that they were just keeping it quiet."

"Is that true?" asked Ortega.

At least he had the decency to face Chase as he inquired about his private business. The other two men turned back around, giving Chase their full attention.

Outside the windows, leaves were falling off trees. A few brown and red blades aimed at the windows. They hit the glass with soundless thuds and dropped to the ground.

"There's nothing going on between me and Ginger Dumasse."

The three men traded knowing looks. Before any of them could voice their unwanted opinions, the back door exploded open, and a small army stormed in.

Maggie Banks came in with a baby in her arms and three dogs at her feet. "Oh, good, there you are, Chase. I was hoping you would invite Ginger to Sunday dinner."

The three stooges standing off to the side each wore wide grins. They knew their job in this battle was done. Reinforcements had arrived.

"Why don't you ask her sister?" Chase said. "Or call her yourself."

"I figured you'd see her sooner." Maggie switched the baby to her other hip.

Behind him, Chase heard snickering from the peanut gallery. The dogs all looked up at him, panting and drooling as they waited for his response.

"Ginger and I aren't dating."

"Yeah, right." Maggie snorted. "But can you ask her anyway? And let her know she's always welcome at our table. She's practically family."

Chase opened his mouth to … To what? There was no sense arguing with this bunch. Their minds were made up on this issue. It didn't matter that they were wrong.

"So, this is where the party is." Reegan came into the back door behind Maggie. "Oh, hey, Chase. Is Ginger coming to church this Sunday?"

"I don't know. We're not-"

"Make sure you guys pencil in couple's night out at Patel's restaurant, too."

Chase snapped his mouth shut. Why waste his breath?

"Welcome to the club." Lucas clapped Chase on his shoulder before going over and embracing his wife.

As plans for his life were being made, Chase escaped the madhouse through the front door. He made it all the way to the parking lot and into his truck without any more interruptions or invitations. The long drive back into town helped to clear his head. He loved his team. He loved the women on the ranch. But they had this mad idea that everyone should be in a relationship.

He wanted a family. Someday. But he had another passion to tend to first.

Thirty minutes later, Chase pulled into the recruitment center. It was tucked at the end of a shopping strip that featured a convenience store, a coin laundry, and a Chinese food takeout. Not the highest traffic. So, he was surprised to see someone waiting outside the door of the center.

When the man in shirt and tie saw Chase in his truck, he waved. So, it wasn't a mistake. He was waiting for Chase.

Chase climbed out of the vehicle and approached. As he got closer to the center's door, he heard a peculiar sound. It sounded like the phone was ringing inside the offices. It wouldn't be Ortega. The man had his cell phone number.

"You're Soldier Chase?" asked the man waiting in front of the door.

"Sergeant. Sergeant Chase."

"Right. I'm David Jacobs, the Assistant Principal at Charbury's Private Academy. We'd love for you to come and speak with our students."

"You would?"

"Yes."

"About the military?"

Mr. Jacobs waggled his head, neither up and down or left or right. "We're thrilled that Councilwoman Dumasse is taking an interest in the military."

"Well, I don't know if she is interested in the military."

"Her beau is an officer, so I have to assume she is. I'm hoping she might take an interest in a bill that deals with private school funding."

A bill? Private schools? Chase opened his mouth to correct the man, but the phone rang out again.

"Would you come in, Mr. Jacobs. I just need to get that."

Chase unlocked the door. He got to the phone before the call ended.

"Is this Sergeant Chase?" asked the caller. "The one dating Council-woman Dumasse?"

Chase let out a long breath as he slumped into his chair. "How can I help you?"

"This is AgriCo, we're a lobby group for Montana Farmers. I wonder if you might be interested in speaking at our annual meeting. Your girl-friend is invited too."

Chase bit his lip. He looked from the man in front of him to the phone receiver. He knew where both of these conversations were going. But just like with the issues with Ginger, just like with his friends back on the ranch, he might disagree with the tactics, but he didn't disagree with the end result. Perhaps he could walk this path on his terms.

"Well, do I have the right man or not?" said the man in the receiver. "Is this the sergeant dating the senatorial candidate?"

CHAPTER EIGHT

"Have you seen these polls?" Carla waved a stack of papers in front of her as she came into Ginger's office. "You're up amongst middle-aged women. And you're dominating college-educated women and career women. Not to mention, you've ticked up ten points with those in the military and military families."

"Hmmm." Nodded Ginger. She wasn't listening. She was too busy looking at the photograph on the society blog site.

It wasn't the image of her and Chase locked in an embrace in the barn back on the Purple Heart Ranch. No, that one was emblazoned in her mind. It was often the last thing she saw before she went to sleep each night … and then dreamed of what would've happened if the cameras hadn't caught them at that moment.

Nope. That image wasn't in her mind now. A different series lit up her cerebral cortex. There was a series of pictures of Chase in the spread of the gossip rag.

Chase as a young man. Chase in a suit. Oh, she couldn't take her eyes off Chase in a suit; dark blue that perfectly complimented his dark hair. Not that Chase in his uniform wasn't everything. But the sergeant in that suit was more. So much more.

"I'm so glad you took my advice on this." Carla plopped down in the seat opposite Ginger's desk and kicked off her expensive heels.

"Hmmm," said Ginger. Chase's middle name was Jefferson. Colin Jefferson Chase. How presidential.

"Just a few more snapshots of you two together, and we'll overtake Dean in many of the key categories where you're trailing."

"What?" Ginger lifted her gaze from Chase's profile. She had to blink a couple of times to bring her best friend into focus. All she saw was the calculating gaze of her campaign manager.

"Chase. Bring him to the county fair. Let people see you on his arm. I'll need to get you a softer outfit, maybe pastels. And we'll leave your hair down for that fresh, girl-in-love look."

"In love?"

"You can pretend," said Carla. "Though I doubt you'll need to."

"What? Wait, no. This story is completely fake news. We're not dating."

"You're faking it." Carla flitted her fingers, waving the notion away. "I get it. Just fake your way into a few more photos and appearances."

"I'm not not faking it with Chase."

"So, it's the real deal. Fan-freaking-tastic. It's about time you got you some."

"I'm not getting anything." Ginger's cheeks heated. The blush spread across her shoulders. Luckily, she was wearing a blazer today. "You know what I'm trying to say. Chase and I aren't real dating. We aren't fake dating. We aren't anything."

Carla lifted a single eyebrow. Ginger growled. Maybe if she got Botox, she'd be able to pull off that singular feat.

"We just got stuck in the elevator," said Ginger. "It was a disaster. We couldn't even work together to get out. We are two of the most incompatible people on this planet. The man is insufferable."

"Insufferable? Okay, Lizzie Bennet."

"Don't start with me." Ginger pointed a finger at her friend. "I told you I wouldn't play the fake game with my social life or my political career. I have principles."

So, why had she tried to get that reporter's attention last night? Why had she felt a sense of accomplishment when she'd finally succeeded? Why had a rush of adrenaline gone through her when she saw the flash of his camera? Why hadn't she slept last night as she waited for the first mention of the news of herself and Chase?

Because she was attracted to Chase. Because she wanted to date a guy like that; strong and principled—even if he was wrong—with a chiseled jaw that she wanted to see crack into a smile.

"I know that look," said Carla, leaning across the desk. "You like him."

"I do not." Ginger crossed her arms over her chest. Was the AC on in her office? It was suddenly hot on this fall day. "We have nothing in common."

Except, despite the fact that they pointed toward different directions, they both wanted to ensure kids had options for their futures. He was a planner like her, which she had to admit was kinda hot. But …

"We're on opposite ends of the political spectrum."

That was true. But they had both had similar upbringings where they came from wealth and forged a path on their own in spite of their family's money. And Chase was all for women in leadership. But …

"The Chase angle is a non-starter. We need to stick to the plan. This media hoopla," which she had been instrumental in starting, "will die down." As long as she steered clear of being alone with him in barns and elevators. "I don't care if I see him again."

There was a knock at the door.

"Ginger, there's a Sergeant Chase here to see you."

And now she'd need to steer clear of her campaign office too? No way. This was her turf.

What was he doing here? He probably thought the headlines were her idea. He was likely about to storm in her office and accuse her of using him for her political gain.

Great.

Ginger tugged her lip into her mouth. And then stopped. She didn't want to ruin her lipstick. Maybe she should apply more? Had she applied mascara? She'd rushed out this morning and stuffed her makeup in her bag, intent on doing her face at the office. Well, she was at the office, and she didn't remember applying any foundation or mascara.

Oh, for the love of all things!

She caught sight of herself in the window's reflection. Her blouse was a bit wrinkled. There was a scuff on her heel. And she'd missed her manicure appointment the other day. Maybe she could ask him to come back later when she was more put together?

"Can I show him in?"

"Yes," said her traitorous friend.

Carla grinned at Ginger as she rose. Unlike Ginger, Carla was perfectly made up and manicured. Unfortunately, Ginger couldn't murder her couture'd bestie. They had guests.

Chase appeared in the doorway. Thankfully, he wasn't in a suit or uniform. He was in jeans and a T-shirt, but he looked like a million bucks. His eyes landed not on her but on her campaign manager. Chase offered Carla a smile, and Ginger saw red.

"Nice to meet you, Sergeant Chase. I'm Carla Holt, Councilwoman Dumasse's campaign manager."

"Nice to meet you, Mrs. Holt."

"It's Miss." Carla was still holding onto Chase's hand. "But you don't need to concern yourself with that."

Ginger was too concerned with Carla's claws still being wrapped around Chase's hands. Finally, Carla released her prey. Chase shoved his hand in his pocket, and Ginger felt an acute sense of loss.

"Ginger, you don't have any appointments all morning," Carla said with a wink. She walked toward the door with a little too much of a sway in her hips. The door closed behind her with a quiet snick.

Ginger was left with Chase. The man's presence took up the small space of her office. He didn't offer her a smile. Instead, his brown gaze scrutinized her.

"Listen," she said, "before you say anything, I just want you to know I had nothing to do with it."

"I know."

"The press can be salacious. They have to sell papers. So, they print ridiculous things."

"I understand."

Ginger stopped talking. She took a few tentative steps around her desk to come and face him. He didn't look upset. His brows were down in one line as he gazed at her. His expression was thoughtful, calm.

"You do?" she asked.

"Yes." He nodded. "It's ridiculous."

"Ridiculous?" It was a feat, but Ginger held herself perfectly still as the whiplash of his statement struck her across the face. "You mean you and me?"

It was almost imperceptible. She only saw it because she watched him so closely. Chase's gaze dipped to her lips, then back up to her eyes.

"But everyone believes we're together," he said. "No matter how ridiculous it is."

His gaze dipped to the papers on her desk. The ones that showed them in an embrace. And the ones that showed her rise in the polls.

"Looks like you're reaping the benefits of the ridiculousness," he said.

"Sergeant—"

"Call me Chase."

Those brown eyes slid back to hers. She felt like she was being bathed in warm chocolate. Sweet and velvet and warm.

"Chase." His name felt like a Hershey's Kiss on her tongue. She had to swallow the richness of it down before she could continue. "I want you to know that that's not how I run my campaign. It's not how I live my life. I don't use people to get ahead. I shoot straight, and I play fair."

He smiled at her. When he'd aimed that missive at Carla, Ginger had seen red. Now that the brown of his gaze was trained on her, she was ready to drop her principles.

"Can I take you to lunch, Ginger?"

"Lunch? Why?"

"Because it's not using if we both agree to it."

CHAPTER NINE

"**O**rder whatever you want. I'm buying."

Chase expected an argument. Instead, Ginger opened up the laminated menu and began to peruse it. Her silent acquiesce unnerved Chase.

"No argument over the bill?"

She looked up over the menu. As they always did, her blue eyes struck him like a bolt of heat straight into the chest. But it was the smile that unmanned him. He'd seen her smile, just not at him.

Blue was the hottest part of a fire. But the red of her lips, which should've been the cool part, rang a four-alarm fire in his mind. All of a sudden, Chase was unsure of the plan he'd come up with. It was very likely that he was about to get burned. Even more probable that he would like the singe.

"No argument," she said. "I believe a man should pay for a woman's meal."

"I took you for a feminist."

"I am." She set the menu down, folding the two halves neatly in front of her. "I believe in equal rights and equal pay. Other than that, I'm pretty traditional. Men hunt. Women gather. God made it that way. So, I have no arguments there."

Chase knew there was a *but* coming. He leaned forward in anticipation. Not that he wanted to argue with this woman. Far from it. He simply liked engaging with her, and currently, arguing was the only means with which they did that.

"But," Ginger continued, "mankind made money, not the Lord. Since we created it, women should get their equal share. Regardless of whether they have to work inside or outside of the home."

Interesting. But Chase didn't say so. The pile of things they were on the same side of was growing alarmingly tall. If they kept agreeing, what would they have to argue about? Then what reason would they have to be around each other? Their entire relationship was predicated on disagreeing with one another.

"Do you disagree?" she asked.

"No," he said. "A man should provide for a woman."

"Are you saying a woman can't provide for a man?"

"Not at all. But the partnership will be weaker if he doesn't."

"What if she's a better earner, and he decides to stay home with the kids?"

"That's admirable. Personally, I plan to provide for my family, come home in time enough to raise my children, and pamper my wife after she gets home from a long day of work."

"Lucky woman."

They stared at one another. Neither blinked. But this time, her gaze wasn't a challenge.

Did he note a hint of interest? Chase didn't dare blink as he tried to discern what was flickering in that cool blue gaze. The waiter's arrival broke the trance, and they both looked away at the same time.

"I'll have the tuna salad sandwich, extra onions," said Ginger as she handed over the menu. She turned back to Chase and added, "What? It's not like I'm going to kiss you."

Chase bit his lip to keep from chuckling. "I'll take an Italian sub, extra garlic, please."

The waiter went to the back with their odorous orders. Chase lifted his gaze back to Ginger. That note of interest was still there. He decided not to wait and just go for it.

"So, here's my proposal."

Her brows lifted. He probably shouldn't have used the word *proposal*. This was a fake arrangement, a convenient arrangement. It wouldn't lead to anything permanent. Definitely not her coming home to him at night to be pampered after he put the kids to bed.

"My suggestion," he said, "is that we don't correct the papers or anyone when they say we're together."

"But … we're not together." Her voice was hesitant. The interest in her gaze was replaced with that touch of vulnerability.

"No," he agreed. "But no one believes us when we tell the truth."

Ginger rolled her eyes and nodded her head. Clearly, she had a peanut gallery of her own that she was dealing with if her campaign manager's behavior was any indication.

Chase continued on with his plan of attack. He'd thought this through at every angle, just like he would a battle plan. "So, we use it to our advantage."

"Our advantage?"

"You got a lift in the polls from being seen with a veteran."

She didn't nod. She didn't need to. They both knew how these things worked. He was gratified that she didn't try and orchestrate it.

"We're seen together at a few choice events," he continued. "I'll keep my mouth shut and smile adoringly at you."

Ginger's soft gaze turned to flint. "That won't be too hard for you?"

"What?" he grinned. "Smiling adoringly at you?"

"No, keeping your mouth shut."

He cracked a grin. Why had he thought this plan would be a hardship? Ginger Dumasse made every moment interesting.

"Why are you doing this again?" she asked.

"People are inviting me to speak at their events and organizations. That's all I want, a chance to make a case for joining the service. If I can just get people to hear me out, then maybe a few will actually listen, and I can change some young people's futures by bringing them into an organization that I believe in."

"This is fascinating." Ginger shook her head, her smile growing wider. But it wasn't a smile of joy. It looked annoyed. "For most of my political career—heck, for most of my life—I've been told I need to be on a man's arm to be taken seriously. Now, a man wants to use my arm so that he can be heard."

"So, you'll do it?" Chase asked.

"I have to." She shrugged. "Do you know how far ahead this will push the women's movement?"

Chase couldn't keep it in any longer. He threw back his head and laughed. After a second, Ginger joined him. Yes, she certainly made every moment interesting. Especially when she turned traditional conventions on their nose.

Soon, the laughter died down, and her shoulders drooped. "But there's one problem. You don't agree with anything I stand for."

"That's not true," he said.

"Oh, really? I believe education should be a kid's highest priority after graduation."

"I agree. I just believe education can be had in college, in trade, and even in the military."

She pursed her lips. Chase tried not to think about how they might taste. Where was that tuna sandwich?

"There's just one more issue we should discuss," she said. Her features went grave. "I believe that soccer is a far superior sport than football."

Chase picked up his napkin and threw it down on the table. "This relationship is over."

Ginger giggled. It was a delightful sound. A sound he could easily get used to.

The waiter brought out their smelly food, and they dug in. Unfortunately, the smell of fish and onions and garlic did nothing to tamp down his desire. He wasn't sure anything could stop his growing interest in this woman.

"I was serious about soccer, you know."

CHAPTER TEN

The screams of children and crank of wheels filled Ginger's ears. She turned her nose away from the saccharine smell of the cotton candy and funnel cakes only to be confronted with the greasy smell of fried meat, fried desserts, and was that a fried beverage? It was the county fair, and it was part of her duty as a candidate to attend.

She'd posed for pictures with her constituents. She'd shaken hands with the union leaders. She'd held screaming, smelly babies. It was all par for the course.

"Smile," demanded Carla.

"I am smiling," Ginger insisted.

"Smile for real. What's on your face looks tired and fake."

Because she was tired and fake. Ginger wanted nothing more than to kick off her heels, toss off this skirt, and kick her feet up on her couch for the rest of the evening.

And eat. Sheesh, did she want to eat.

Her stomach growled. Loudly. Chase looked over at her with concern on his normally stern brow.

He was keeping up his end of the bargain by being her escort today. He hadn't said much after joining them at her campaign headquarters and riding over. He'd been a silent observer as she'd done the rounds.

All the while, she felt his judging eyes. Why had she thought it was a good idea to put on this fake dating farce?

"Here," Chase said.

He presented her with a corn dog on a stick. It was golden brown and perfect. The scent of buttery goodness nearly made Ginger faint. She turned away before she had a moment of weakness.

"I can't eat that," she said.

"Don't tell me you're on a diet," he said. "I saw you put away a carb-loaded sandwich the other day."

"You did what?" said Carla.

Ginger shook her head like a child caught with their hand in the cookie jar. "It was whole wheat bread and low-fat mayo."

That didn't stop Carla's huffing. She insisted Ginger had to always look camera ready. Carbs put on pounds for the camera.

"She can't be seen eating," Carla said to Chase. "She can't risk being photographed. There are press and smartphones everywhere."

Chase turned to Ginger, corndog still in hand. "So?"

It took Ginger a second to take her eyes off the heaven on a stick and look at the man. "I risk looking very suggestive eating, well, that."

Chase looked at the meat on a stick. He wrapped his hand around the breaded hotdog and pulled it from the stick. "I can break it into pieces for you."

Though tempting as the idea was to have him handle her food and feed her, Ginger still had to decline. "I risk looking like a cavewoman taking a bite."

Chase held the two halves of the corndog in each hand. Now that the seal of the bread was broken, the buttery scent went straight to Ginger's head.

"So you starve?" he asked.

Ginger swallowed down her hunger. For the corn dog, as well as for the man trying to provide her with the sustenance she so desperately needed. Looking like she was in command was all part of the plan.

"I want to win," she said. More to herself than to him. And the corndog.

"Can you drink?" Chase asked.

"Alcohol? No, it would look like I'm a lush."

"I meant a milkshake. Fruit, milk, sugar. Unless sipping from a straw is uncomely."

Chase took the plastic container he'd placed between his arm and presented it to her. Ginger eyed the beverage. Again her stomach grumbled. She was about to give in. But it was showtime.

"Councilwoman Dumasse?"

She gave one last look at the shake and, by sheer force of will, turned to face the onslaught of curious voters. "Please, call me Ginger."

"Ginger, what's your position on upgrading farms to meet with today's demands?"

Ginger nodded sympathetically as she listened. She had a plan for that. "The world is changing. The way we receive food is different with delivery services. The way we grow food is changing, as well. Farms are becoming more and more technology-based. But that shouldn't scare those of us that work in fields."

She caught Carla's eye. Carla didn't look happy. The campaign manager didn't need to tell her. Ginger was stating too many facts and statistics. People wanted a story. Votes were emotional.

"I should know, I grew up on a farm. Sure, it was sprawling acres with a mansion. But I paid attention to what was going on in the fields. I understand what a hard day's work looks like. I also know that, increasingly, young people aren't going into farming. Machines can take some of the stress off the farming operations. But we'll need to invest in agricultural technology so that farms can thrive. I have a plan for that."

The man nodded, seeming impressed.

"What about healthcare?" said a woman off to the right. "My premiums are going up."

"I understand that, too. As many of you know, I was born with a silver spoon in my mouth. But that didn't last my whole life. My mother became sick, and we didn't always have the money to put food on the table and pay for her medicines. The state came to our aide, allowing us to keep our doctor and not pay exorbitant fees. I watched how they did that. I have a plan on how we can expand that program for all."

"That sounds all well and good," said another voter in the front of the crowd. "But taxes are rising, and jobs are few. What jobs there are available are computer-based. I don't have the skills to compete."

"That's where my education plan comes into play. I know many of our youth are leaving for the bigger cities. That's why we need to invest in job training for the young and old. These problems aren't insurmountable. Not when we focus on our commonalities and build from there. We are a community. We have lived together and thrived for hundreds of years because we hold true to the first tenet of American democracy, and that is an opportunity for all. That is the core of my being. That is who I am. That is what I have to offer you."

Heads nodded. There were murmurs of assent. Ginger was most gratified to see Chase watching her thoughtfully with a small smile on his face.

"That works well for civilians," called out someone from the back. "But what about veterans?"

Ginger turned to the newcomer. She opened her mouth, but nothing came out. Her mind reeled.

Veterans? She didn't have any notes or plans for veterans.

"There are problems with vet unemployment, housing, and mental healthcare," the man continued. "Do you have a plan for that, councilwoman?"

"I … um …" She didn't.

"I assume since you're now involved with a veteran," the man said, "you've at least thought about these issues."

Ginger looked to Chase and gulped. His features were impassive. He wasn't going to come to her rescue. This wasn't part of their deal.

But Chase stepped up, putting his hand at the small of her back. He gave her an encouraging smile as he did so. It bordered on affection.

For a moment, she forgot that they were in a crowd. She simply gazed into the eyes of a strong man, one who had never once cowed when she stepped up to take the lead or state her plan. Every time she pushed or prodded Sergeant Colin Chase, he held firm, or he pushed back. Now, he turned to the newcomer and spoke for her.

"As a veteran, I know that the problems we face are similar to those of everyday civilians. Many of Councilwoman Dumasse's plans will work for those in my situation. She has spent time at the Purple Heart Ranch listening to the issues today's soldiers face. But as you know, she is a thoughtful woman who likes to see the problem from all sides. She'll be presenting a full plan soon."

Chase gazed down at her. This time, affection was clear in his brown eyes. The silence lingered. Ginger knew she should say something, but her tongue was tied. Her stomach grumbled again, but not from physical hunger this time.

"Now, if you'll excuse us. The councilwoman and I have a lunch date."

CHAPTER ELEVEN

*C*hase broke the corn dog into four, even bites. Then, using a fork, he dunked the fried morsel into ketchup. He glanced up at Ginger before dunking it into the mustard as well. When she didn't object to the pairing, his own mouth watered. He was hungry, but not for the breaded hot dog.

Ginger eyed each of his movements greedily. He caught a flash of white teeth as she bit at her bottom lip. Then a sliver of pink tongue as she wet her upper lip.

"Open wide," he said.

Chase lifted the fork. In went the food. Her lips encircled the tines of the fork, lingering. Chase wished he'd used his fingers.

"Mmmm," she mumbled around a mouthful. "That is heaven right there."

He watched her chew, unable to take his eyes off her. They were in his car, having ditched her detail and the crowd of voters eager to pester her with more questions. Chase had her all to himself.

They weren't secluded in a barn this time. They didn't have the privacy of a stuck elevator. Still, he shielded her body from prying eyes as he fed her another bite of food. It wasn't that he cared about any prying eyes. He was simply enjoying having her all to himself.

Beyond that, Chase was thrilled that Ginger wasn't on a diet. Her figure was perfect. Too perfect if you asked him. If Ginger Dumasse had a flaw, it might help him to stop sneaking glances at her.

She slipped her shoes off with the third bite and turned her body fully to him. Her lips opened before he commanded, anticipating the last bite.

"Is that all?" she asked after swallowing the fourth piece down.

Her lips pressed together in a pout. Her perfectly arched brows slumped. Her fingers clenched into tiny fists.

Now, Chase was the one biting his tongue. She was adorable, like a disgruntled kitten. Man, if he didn't want to pet her and make her mewl.

Instead, he said, "I can get you another one."

Ginger twisted her lips in thought. She eyed the dollop of ketchup still on the fork tine. Chase put the utensil down. Neither of them needed to have that happen.

"No," she said finally. "That was enough."

"Are you ready to go in?" he asked.

"I am if you are."

Chase looked across the parking lot toward the private school. Charbury Private Academy, the pristine sign read. It could have been a replica of the private school he'd gone to as a kid.

No students lingered outside the front door before the bell. There were no school buses lined up as all of the kids had their own cars or drivers. Nor were there any flyers announcing bake sales or school fundraisers. There was no need. Tuition, endowments, and donations likely more than covered everything.

"It's been years since I've been in there," said Ginger. "I was glad to leave it."

"You went to public school?"

She nodded but didn't elaborate.

Chase's spidey senses tingled. It was the feeling he got in the desert when all was too quiet. He'd learned to listen to that sense. It was a harbinger that there was something else out there. The tingling sensation went to his belly when he realized what had to lay behind her silence.

"Your father wouldn't keep paying for you to go here after your parents' divorce?"

Ginger shrugged, but her gaze wasn't on him. It was out the window at the school. "I didn't want to go here. I never felt like I fit in with these kids. They didn't have any ambitions other than climbing the social ladder."

Chase understood that. It was the exact make up of his private school and his parents' social club. But he hadn't had a choice in changing schools. He would've made that choice if he could. By the way her nose turned up as she looked at the school, Chase got the sense that Ginger didn't regret having the choice thrust upon her.

Once again, he was stunned by how much they had in common. Maybe they could be friends after this?

"Community activist, councilwoman, and now state senatorial candidate." Chase ticked Ginger's accomplishments off on his fingers. "Seems like you've climbed pretty high up the social ladder."

She snorted. It was completely unladylike and entirely adorable. "Not if you ask my father. He couldn't be more disappointed in me."

That was a surprise to Chase. From what he knew of Henry Dumasse, the man coveted every advantage he could get. He'd even tried to marry off his youngest daughter for a profit.

"I take it, you two are on different sides of the issues?" asked Chase.

"Hardly. The side my father is on is the one that's the greenest." Ginger rubbed her index and thumb together in the universal sign for money. "He realized a long time ago that he couldn't buy me, and he's never forgiven me for it."

There went yet another tick in their similarity column.

"My father shares the same disappointment in me," said Chase. "He wanted me to join the family business. Instead, I joined the Army."

"Two community servants. What awful children we are."

Chase chuckled.

"I only accept small donations in my campaign. Absolutely no corporate sponsors. I pay my staff from my trust fund. I figure with all the wheeling and dealing my father's done that have hurt people in this community, it's the least I can do. I've barely put a dent in the monies, though."

"I used the inheritance my grandfather left me to secure the lease on the recruitment center."

Ginger took in a dramatic gasp and covered her mouth with her hand. "Why, Sergeant Chase, you naughty soldier. You used private funds to pay for a government enterprise?"

"They're still digging through the red tape. Meanwhile, I've helped a dozen men and women find a viable future for themselves and their families."

She gazed at him in silence for a long moment.

Chase held her gaze until his curiosity got the better of him. "What?"

Ginger shrugged one shoulder. "You're a better man than I imagined you to be."

Chase mimicked her movement, shrugging one of his shoulders. "You're okay, yourself."

She balled her fist and punched him in the still raised shoulder. Chase pretended to fall into the door from the impact of her assault. She had moved him, but more on the inside than the outside.

"Well, let's get this over with," she said, slipping her shoes back on. "I'm sure you want to finish up your obligation to me so you can get back to your real life."

"Yeah." Chase watched as her pink toes slipped into the high heels, disappearing from his sight. "Yes, you're right. No, wait. I'll get the door."

"Chase, I can open my own door."

"Ginger, it's my car door. I always open it for ladies."

Her hand rested on the handle. "You have a lot of ladies in this car?"

"No."

He held her gaze. The vein at her neck jump. Her throat worked as she swallowed. He had to stop wondering how the skin at the column of her throat tasted. He had to stop wanting to kiss her. They might have things in common, but they were still all wrong for each other.

Ginger released the door handle. She sat back in her seat with her hands folded primly on her lap. It took Chase a moment before his legs decided to work, and he could get out of the car.

She waited in her seat until he came around and handed her out. She hesitated before putting her hand in his offered one. But in the end, she relented and took his hand.

Big mistake.

A spark zinged up his arm. By the small gasp, he knew she'd felt it too. Chase rubbed her knuckles before releasing her hand. He wasn't sure if the move had been to comfort her or himself?

Assistant Principal Jacobs came out to the front office to greet them. "Sergeant Chase and Councilwoman Dumasse. Such a pleasure. Come in, the kids are waiting."

They started forward, but Jacobs wrapped a hand around Ginger's other arm and tugged.

"Councilwoman, while the Sergeant is talking with the students, I was hoping to tug your ear on a pressing matter."

Ginger's features shifted from relaxed to tense. The light that had been in her eye when she'd eaten the corndog dimmed. The smile she plastered on was fake and weary.

"I'm sorry, Mr. Jacobs," said Chase, wrapping an arm around Ginger, which broke Jacob's hold on her. "But Ms. Dumasse is here at my pleasure, not in any official capacity other than my girlfriend."

Chase felt the intake of breath as Ginger's shoulders straightened. He also felt a little kick to his gut once that single word left his lips. *Girlfriend.*

Not that it was true. But only they needed to know that. In any case, the ploy worked. Jacobs reluctantly let go of Ginger's arm, and they all proceeded down the hall.

Inside, Chase was confronted with a couple dozen kids in starched blue and white uniforms. The smell of trust funds mingled with a strong hint of entitlement. At least none held protest signs against the military. It was a good start.

"First, I want to thank you all for coming out to listen to me today. My name is Sergeant Chase. I served with the United States Army for six years. They were the best years of my life. I learned leadership, made lifelong friends, and was able to serve my country. I believe that the military is a viable career path, especially for bright minds like yours."

A hand went up. Chase pointed to a young man with gelled hair pushed back with Aviator sunglasses.

"I wanted to be a pilot when I was a kid, but I got into Harvard. No way are my parents going to let me give that up."

And here is where the problems started.

"You could think of it as a gap year."

That idea hadn't come from Chase. Ginger stepped up beside him. All heads swiveled to her.

"The minimum commitment to the military is two years." She turned to Chase for confirmation. After he nodded, she continued. "And I think you can serve on the weekends, once a month?"

"That's right," said Chase. "In the Reserves."

"I was thinking of joining the Peace Corps," said another student, a young woman this time.

"The Peace Corps is a great option," said Ginger. "But in the military, you would serve your flag, your home country."

"My parents want me to take a gap year," said a kid in a wrinkled shirt that was one size too small and a few scuffs at the knees of his pants.

"Do it while serving your country," said Chase. "You get to travel in the service. You'll be in the best shape of your life, too. There's adventure and public service. What more could you ask for?"

It looked as though a handful of the kids were actually considering it. Chase looked over to the woman standing beside him. She didn't know it, but this was a win. And he wouldn't have thought of any of those spins without her.

"I have a question, Sergeant," said the wrinkled shirt kid. "How's the food?"

And now he was back to square one. But at least he still had their attention.

# CHAPTER TWELVE

"You guys make such a cute couple."

Ginger didn't respond to Eva Lopez's query. She didn't want to be rude, but she didn't know the woman well enough to answer such a personal question. The two women had gone to high school together, but they hadn't run in the same circles.

Ginger had been active in clubs, but Eva never stayed after school. She'd had too many responsibilities. First, her sick parents, and then her two younger siblings to take care of. Now, Eva was nearing the completion of a college degree.

She still had her two siblings to care for, but she also had a husband. Eva—well, she supposed she was Eva DeMonti now—had married one of the soldiers who came to convalesce on the Purple Heart Ranch. Fran DeMonti had come to Montana with shrapnel in his heart. But when he met Eva, a miracle happened. The shards that could've pierced his heart moved aside to allow love in his life.

It was an amazing love story. One for the books, for sure. But Ginger didn't have time to read romance novels. She was too busy solving the world's real problems.

So, she pretended not to hear Eva's statement about her and Chase because Ginger knew there was a hidden question mark in there. A question mark that Ginger wasn't sure of the answer to.

Chase had called her his girlfriend back at the private school. But it had been part of the act. Hadn't it?

What hadn't been an act was the way her heart had flipped. The way her fingernails had dug into her palms with want. The way her body had melted and molded into Chase's as he'd put his arm around her.

"I knew there was something between them after that dinner," Maggie Banks was saying.

Ginger knew Maggie from high school, as well. Maggie had mostly kept to herself back then. Or she'd engaged whatever animal was about. Even now, the veterinarian had two dogs at her feet and a beautiful baby bouncing on her lap. Across the table, Maggie's husband, Dylan, sipped his sweet tea while gazing adoringly at his family.

Eva's husband Fran told knock-knock jokes with her little brother while her little sister rested against Fran's healed chest.

Reece Cartwright and his wife Beth, who was the daughter of the town's pastor, held their own private conversation while his hand rested on her growing belly. Beside them, Reece's twin sister Reegan laughed at something her husband, Brandon Lucas, said.

Ginger was surrounded by happy brides and adoring husbands. The group included her newlywed sister. Mark Ortega hung on Honey's every word as she went on and on about the little projects she was taking up around the ranch. Ginger still couldn't believe that her sister, who had never gotten a single speck of dirt on her her entire life, had happily taken to ranch life like she'd been born to it.

"Chase is the last of his team that's single, you know?"

Oh, Ginger knew all right. She was made aware of that little fact any and every time she came and visited the ranch these past three months. Also, the hint was dropped each time she was in town and ran into one of the Purple Heart Brides as the townsfolk liked to call the women who lived on the ranch.

"I was sure you two would get together before his three months were up," Maggie was saying.

Ginger also knew all about the zoning issue that said anyone who lived on the ranch had to be married. The red tape read that soldiers only had three months to live in the housing on the ranch, or they had to get out. As a city representative, Ginger knew the clause could be easily fought and defeated in a court of law. But no one from the ranch had launched a complaint. Instead, they all complied.

Chase's other team members had all gotten married within the window. First Brandon and Reegan. Then Reece and Beth. And last month her sister had walked down the aisle with Mark. But Chase had stayed single the whole time. In fact, he'd moved off the ranch right at the three-month mark.

"I lost a bet because of you two," said Eva.

"The new bet is how long it'll take you two to get engaged," Reegan chimed in. "My money is on a month."

"I've got a week," said Maggie.

This was insane. Ginger had to come clean. Even though these women were pains in the neck about her relationship status, she did actually want to be friends with them. She wanted to belong in this tight-knit community that had embraced her sister. She missed having a family looking out for her.

And so she took a deep breath and let the truth out. "Guys, it's not real. It's fake."

Instead of having gazes narrowing at her in anger; rather than chins raising high in indignation; every woman's eyes went wide with joy.

"I'm changing my bet," said Maggie. "I give it a few days."

"I give it until the weekend," said Eva.

Bewildered, Ginger turned to her sister.

Honey shrugged. "Apparently, that's how it all begins. If you pretend to date or masquerade as a couple, the real thing follows."

Ginger knew Honey had done that with Mark during her debutante ball. Within a week, the two were in love and engaged. She'd heard a little about Maggie and Dylan's story where he'd proposed to save the ranch, and she'd said *I do* to save her animals. She knew Brandon had proposed to Reegan after her house had burned down. And Reece had believed he was already engaged to Beth when he'd experienced temporary amnesia.

Wow, this ranch was a haven for cheap romance novels.

Well, it wasn't happening to her and Chase. They weren't compatible. Even though he'd come to her rescue earlier, and she'd come to his. Even though his hand at the small of her back was the best thing she'd felt in a long time.

She felt it again now. A warm weight settling right between her shoulder blades. If she weren't sitting upright, Ginger would've sunk down into the cushion of that palm.

"Had enough?" Chase said into her ear.

She turned to find him grinning at her. The look in his gaze was knowing, as though he'd been privy to a similar conversation with the guys.

"You want to get out of here?" he asked.

"Yes."

Ginger threw down her white napkin, signaling her surrender to the crazy conversation and betting still going on around her. As she headed to the door, there was the distinct sound of kissing noises. But when they turned, everyone at the table looked away innocently.

CHAPTER THIRTEEN

Chase couldn't keep his hands to himself. They'd rested on Ginger's shoulder blades as they walked out of the ranch's dining hall. He'd toyed with a strand of her hair as they made their way down the stairs. His fingers had brushed her ear lobe as they crossed the fields. She'd shuddered, but he'd been the one to get a shock.

All throughout dinner, he hadn't been able to take his eyes off her. Not for long anyway. He'd lost threads of conversations as he spoke with the other males around him. He answered in monosyllabic words when asked his opinion.

Each time he was able to tear his gaze from Ginger and back to his dinner companions, the men all wore goofy grins. At one point, Reed Cannon simply called him out.

"We're obviously not holding your attention," the Specialist had said. "Go talk to her. Sooner rather than later so I can win this bet."

"What bet?" Chase had demanded.

"Doesn't matter," chimed in Sean Jeffries with a rare smile on his scarred face. "Just get a move on before the weekend."

Something was afoot, but Chase couldn't spare a care. He was more than happy to leave the guys and move in on his true target. Ginger Dumasse had gotten under his skin. Not just under his skin. In his very fingertips. In the palm of his hand, which he now rested at the small of her back. She'd gotten into his mind through his nostrils, which flared to take in more of her spiced-sugar scent.

"That roast at dinner was really great," she said as they walked the graveled path.

"Yup," Chase agreed. "Tender and sweet."

"There was a bit of toughness to it."

"Just a bit around the edges," he agreed. "But it was well done in the center, where it counts."

"You think?"

Ginger stopped walking and turned to face him. Her eyes were bright stars in the moonlight. Her parted lips glistened, begging to be kissed.

What were they talking about again?

Chase took a deep breath to try and clear his head. He let the air out slowly. Tilting his head up, he looked to the sky.

Nope, those stars had nothing on the woman before him. Their shine was dim compared to the light within her. The light shining bright, warming him from the outside in. How had he ever thought her rigid?

"You wanna go for a ride?" he asked.

"You're ready to take me back home?" The disappointment in her town was clear in the darkness.

"No." Being parted from her was the last thing he wanted right now. "Not a car ride, a horseback ride."

"Now?"

Chase tugged Ginger along to the stables. The strong smell of horse manure brought some sense back to him. But not enough to turn back around.

He wasn't entirely sure what he was doing here, alone in the dark with this woman. He simply knew he didn't want to be anywhere else.

He lifted a saddle from the wall and opened one of the horse's stalls. "You know how to ride?"

Ginger grabbed hold of the straps and began buckling them. "Of course, I know how to ride. I'm from Montana."

Of course, she knew how to ride. She could probably run this ranch single-handedly. Was there anything this woman couldn't do? Nothing she couldn't plan for?

"Do *you* know how to ride, city boy?" she chided.

"I guess you're about to see."

Chase swung himself up on the horse. Then he extended his hand down to her. Ginger took it with a smile and saddled up behind him.

Chase knew it was a mistake the moment her arms wrapped around his waist. He recognized the miscalculation when her front pressed into his back. He sensed his misjudgment as her breath tickled the bottom of his earlobe. He may have made a mistake, but he knew this underestimation would pay out in huge gains.

And so he didn't back down. He didn't stop and step down from the horse that was ready to carry them into the night. He didn't turn around and admit to this error. He no longer wanted to run from what was clearly between them. With a slap to the horse's hide, they took off into the night.

The ranch by moonlight was a vision. The tall trees resembled fluffy clouds touching the sky. The stars were pinpricks in a dark blue comforter. Along with the moon, those pricks of light provided ample illumination to guide them along the path.

When he'd lived here, Chase had often gone riding alone at night. There was a peace in galloping over the green fields in the dark of night. With Ginger resting her chin on his shoulder, he felt like he could conquer the world.

They didn't speak. They didn't need to. He felt her every move; the brush of her fingers, the twitch of her thigh.

He was completely tuned into this woman. Probably had always been since the first time they'd argued with one another. How could he disagree with someone, but be in complete accord at the same time?

He knew how. Their differences didn't separate them. Their differences, and the stark boundary lines between them, simply outlined more clearly who they were.

The horse slowed to a canter as they headed back to the stalls. Chase dismounted first. Then he reached up to hand her down.

Ginger wasn't a slight girl. She was a healthy woman. He brought her body to his to brace her weight. Soft curves met hard muscle. They both gulped at the intimate contact as she slid down his body.

Chase watched intently as she slid down his chest, coming closer and closer. When her lips were just a couple of inches away, he knew that he would kiss her. He knew it was inevitable, had been since she'd given him his first tongue lashing over higher education versus military service.

Well, now she was about to learn something new. And he would be the one providing the service. His lips were less than an inch when it happened.

The pain was sudden and acute. He gripped Ginger to him instead of grabbing at his aching skull. It didn't matter. The stabbing migraine turned the dark night completely black.

Before he became completely incapacitated, Chase set Ginger on her feet and turned away to deal with the torment.

CHAPTER FOURTEEN

Chase was a big guy; a big, healthy, powerful guy. So, to watch his body convulse in pain was a shock to Ginger's system.

For the first time in a long time, she didn't know what to do. No steps formed in her mind. No process or procedure became clear. The only thing she knew she wanted to do was to make whatever was hurting him stop.

Chase's hands, those same palms that had spread warmth through her, cradled his head. Ginger turned her focus there. She put her hands over his. Her fingers aligned with his as he pressed against his temples.

She didn't know if it was enough. But it seemed to comfort him. His ragged breaths slowed. He stopped panting and began to take full, slow, deep breaths.

That was a start. But he still didn't pull his hands away. His brow was still crinkled in agony.

Was this a PTSD episode? She knew that many soldiers, more than were reported, re-experienced the trauma they saw and lived through when they came back into civilian life. Was Chase having a flashback? Was he remembering something horrible from his time in a combat zone?

Part of her brain flared a red warning sign. Ginger realized she should probably step back from him. She should put a safe distance between herself and him until she had more information as to what was happening. What if he didn't recognize her and lashed out at her?

No sooner than the thought rang in her mind did she dismiss it. This was Chase. Though he was big and often stern, every bone, every muscle in his body had shown her nothing but gentleness. Even when he disagreed with her, his tone had never been harsh.

He'd even placed her away from him when the episode began. He'd been thinking of her care and comfort even as he was experiencing pain. For that, but also for so much more, she would not leave him, whatever the consequences.

His hands still covered his face, like he was hiding from her. Ginger slid her fingers in between Chase's fingers to press directly against his skin. She knew she'd done the right thing when he sighed against her palm.

Soon, he let her have his head. His hands fell away, leaving only hers. Ginger worked hard to earn the trust he'd just given her. She kneaded in tight circles. Then in smaller circles.

The plan was working. Chase kept his eyes closed. His breath steadied, going from ragged gulps to easy inhales and even exhales.

Ginger didn't speak as she cared for him. She somehow knew that sound would not be welcomed. She waited for him to initiate conversation.

He didn't. He remained quiet, reverent almost as she rubbed at his sore spots.

At some point in her maneuvering, her fingers moved away from his temples. They traced his jawline. She felt the prickly stubble there that had begun around five o'clock this evening.

As she came closer to his mouth, Chase's chin lifted. His eyes opened to reveal the dark pools of brown. And, finally, his lips moved.

"I have a headache," he said.

"Isn't that supposed to be my line." She grinned.

Chase didn't return her smile. He didn't lean in to taste her lips. His head was still in her hands. But, slowly, he was taking the weight of it from her.

"This is for the best," he said as he leaned back.

What did that mean? What was for the best?

"I'll give you a ride home," he said.

"I drove," she said.

"I'll walk you to your car, then."

The softness was gone from his voice. She could hear the residual pain laced in his tone. Was he pulling the guy thing? She'd seen him vulnerable, and now he had to macho up? Was that what was going on?

As if she hadn't just spent the last ten minutes tending to him, giving him comfort, letting him know that she wouldn't hurt him, that she could, in fact, help take away the pain. All that, and he was now shutting her out. Well, screw that, and the horse he came in on!

"Don't bother," she said. "I can do it myself."

Ginger whirled around. She pumped her legs hard as she made her way back up the path. She couldn't get to her car and away from Sergeant Chase fast enough.

The moment she heard his footsteps, she whirled around to face him. "You know, I don't need you to be my knight in shining armor."

"I wasn't trying to be," he said.

"Yet, the moment you show a sign of weakness, you run."

"I didn't run. I was on my knees with my head in your hands."

"And what? That scared you? Being vulnerable in front of a woman."

"I'm not scared."

"Oh, yeah?" She squared off against him and poked him in the chest. "Then why are you sending me away? Why put distance between us if you're not scared?"

"Because I don't want this." His voice was raised as he motioned his hands between the two of them.

Ginger reared back as if he'd slapped her. His words certainly did. He didn't want her?

Chase put his hands back to his temples and closed his eyes. "I don't want to think about you every day. I don't want to wonder what you're thinking about every second of the day. I don't want to wonder what your opinion is on a particular topic and wonder if we'll disagree and how you'll try to change my mind."

He let go of his temple and paced the grass. He marched in a perfect line, back erect, head up high. The perfect soldier.

"I don't want to think about kissing you every second. I don't want to actually kiss you because then I'll know. I'll know, and I'll want to do it again and again."

He stopped marching and about-faced, which brought him right to her. He glared down at her, brown eyes accusing. But his voice softened.

"I don't want to want you because you're the kind of girl that a man doesn't stop wanting once he's caught her."

Ginger ran her hands through her hair. She pressed at the throb in her temple. "I'm so confused."

Chase let out a soft chuckle. "Well, I'll bet that's a first."

He grinned down at her. Which only served to make her even more confused. Was he telling her he wanted her? Or that he didn't? There were so many double negatives in his statement she had no idea where she stood. She was completely lost.

Chase looked lost too. He raised his hand and rubbed at his forehead. Ginger reached for him, placing her fingers over his.

"Is it back?" she asked. "Are you feeling okay?"

Chase let his hand drop but not to his side. His palm cupped her face. The moment his skin touched hers, that delicious warmth that seemed to come from somewhere deep in him spread all through her.

"No," he said. "I'm not okay. I am so far gone."

His lips brushed hers. Lightly at first. Just a taste. Then, just as he predicted, he took another and then another kiss.

And so it went until the crickets began to chirp, and the other night creatures crawled out of their hovels and announced their presence. Ginger and Chase ignored them all as they clung to one another. When they finally broke apart, they both were very clear on where they stood.

But they decided not to let any of the other residents of the ranch know that the two of them were now a sure bet.

CHAPTER FIFTEEN

"Ladies and gentlemen, please welcome your next state senator, Ginger Dumasse."

The crowd's applause thundered in Chase's ears. He ignored it in favor of the sweetness on his lips. The voters gathered in the union hall whooped and hollered for Ginger. They could yell, shout, and clap for her to come on stage all they wanted. Backstage, Chase had her in his arms and was not letting her go any time soon.

His palm cradled the nape of Ginger's neck. He used his thumb to tilt her chin up for better access to her perfect lips. He tried to only sip, to pace himself.

That plan failed. Chase took healthy gulps of her. He couldn't get enough. He knew he'd never be able to get enough of the spicy-sweet taste of this woman.

"I know she's back there," said Carla from the stage. There was a tinge of annoyance in her voice. "Maybe a bit more applause will get her out here. Let's show Councilwoman Dumasse that we believe she will be our next senator. Put your hands together, people!"

Chase latched his hands onto Ginger. He laced their fingers as he continued to take from her lips. But the louder applause got to Ginger. She squirmed in Chase's hold as duty called her.

With great effort, Chase tore his lips from hers. His mouth obeyed, but his hands refused to cooperate. One by one, he peeled his fingers off her. But as his pinky left her, he dipped down for another kiss.

"You two, get a room," Carla hissed from the curtain separating the stage from the back of the platform.

Chase finally let Ginger go. He did it with a cheeky grin that said he would do it again if he got a chance. Ginger showed no remorse either.

"Or," Carla grinned, her gaze going shrewd, "he could put a ring on it. Everyone loves an engagement."

"We're not getting married," said Ginger. "We've only just started dating."

She said the words adamantly, even crossing her arms over her chest. Something about the phrase didn't sit well with Chase. The statement simply didn't sound true.

Ginger looked up at him. There was a hint of doubt in her clear blue eyes. "We *are* dating, aren't we?"

In response, Chase leaned down and stole one more kiss. "Dinner tonight?"

She nodded. The doubt was gone from her gaze, replaced with a dreamy look.

"Come on." Carla yanked her away. "You've got a job to do."

Ginger went with her campaign manager, but grudgingly. Her gaze was still on Chase. "Wait for me?"

Chase couldn't form words. Well, he could. He just wasn't ready for her to hear them. Or perhaps he wasn't ready to admit them to himself.

At that moment, Chase knew he'd wait forever for this woman. He realized he had been waiting a lifetime for her. He knew for certain that he would spend a lifetime with her.

He didn't say any of that. He simply nodded at her. Her smile broke open his heart.

Chase was so totally marrying Ginger Dumasse.

Most of her speech brushed over him. He leaned against the wall backstage and took her in. He took in her passion, her conviction, her drive.

A few words of her platform penetrated his mind. His first instinct was to argue with her health care plan. To rebut her proposal on tax reform. To reject her course of action on interstate trade deals. In the end, he realized the strategies didn't matter. What did was that she wanted the best for the people of this state, and she was prepared to work hard to make their lives better.

Wow, he was completely head over heels for that woman.

Ten minutes after her speech was over, hands were shaken, and pictures taken, she was back in his arms where she belonged. They had pulled up outside her campaign headquarters. The sun lit her face. A small smile played at her lips. Chase could've stared at her all day.

"You did really well back there," he said.

She preened at his compliment, snuggling into his hold as she leaned into him from the passenger seat. "They believed me."

"Because you told the truth. You're a novelty; a politician that speaks truth to power."

She turned her head into his chest, so he couldn't see her features, but he felt her mouth spread into a grin. "I just hope it's enough to win."

"You're gonna win."

"How do you know that?" She tilted her head back and gazed up at him.

Chase ran his index finger down the side of her face. "Politics isn't about the issues. It's about the people. Even when you disagree with people, you've proven that you'll listen. That's really what they want; someone who listens to them."

"Are you speaking for yourself, Sergeant?"

"I think I know the will of the people."

Ginger tugged her lower lip in her mouth. Chase had to grit his teeth. If he started kissing her now, he wouldn't stop. They were parked on the street. Even now, someone might be snapping a picture for tomorrow's headlines.

"You should go to work before I'm charged with abducting a government employee," he said. "That would not look good on my rap sheet."

Ginger brought his hand to her lips and kissed his knuckles. "Thank you."

"What for?"

"For supporting me, even when you don't agree with me."

"We have a lot more in common than we differ."

"I'm coming to see that."

Ginger smiled again. Something squeezed in Chase's chest, likely the very last objection to spending forever with this woman. She was going to be late for her next appointment. They both were. Chase threw caution to the wind and captured her lips.

Just as he was about to deepen the kiss and make them both even more late, a knock sounded at the passenger side window.

"You two should know you have an audience," said Carla.

Chase looked over to see photographers snapping away. He shrugged and gave Ginger one more kiss before letting her get out of the car. They were together, and he wanted everyone to know it.

He watched her walk up the steps, making sure she got inside the building before starting his engine. Though his engines were already raring to go. His head was clear, and his heart was full, and he could not remember how he'd gone from happily single to enthusiastically in a committed relationship in what? Two days? That had to be a Purple Heart Ranch record. He doubted anyone of the soldiers or wives had bet on those odds.

Pulling into the recruitment center, Chase saw a luxury car parked out front. Standing at the front of the car was a large man smoking an expensive cigar. Ice cold washed over the warm feeling in his body. Chase knew the man.

"Mr. Dumasse," Chase said as he came out of the car.

The man didn't bother with a preamble. "We need to talk about you dating my daughter."

He hadn't expected this. From what he'd seen with Henry Dumasse's treatment of his youngest daughter, Honey, and what Ginger had told him about her father, Chase doubted the man would care what his eldest daughter got up to.

But it looked like he was wrong. Maybe Dumasse had a change of heart. Still, what was happening between Chase and Ginger was not the man's business.

"Ginger is a grown woman," said Chase. "She can determine who she dates."

"This has nothing to do with dating," said Dumasse. "It's about the campaign, and what my endorsement will do for Ginger. That is if you play ball."

CHAPTER SIXTEEN

"Ginger, David Jacobs from Charbury Academy is calling, should I take a message?"

"Yeah," said Ginger automatically.

She'd been operating on autopilot since Chase handed her out of his car. She'd never felt more alive than when she was in his arms, and he was holding her, kissing her. Agreeing with her that she would make an amazing leader because she listened.

"You know what?" Ginger said as her assistant was nearly out of the door. "I should invite Mr. Jacobs to lunch."

Her assistant blinked. She gave her head a waggle, like a dog who was uncertain of its human's command. "All right … I guess I'll find time in your schedule?"

"You do that," said Ginger. "He and I should meet face to face and work our issues out."

Ginger's door was wide open. The campaign office was usually filled with chatter. People working the phones and talking to constituents to get votes. People typing away on keyboards, posting to social media. People chatting with each other, discussing the latest issue and how to solve the problems of the world.

If it hadn't been for the abrupt and total silence, Ginger may not have ever noticed something was the matter.

Phones dangled from earlobes like loosened earrings. Fingers were held suspended in the air over keyboards. Mouths gaped open, hanging mutely in mid-sentence. All gazes were wide as they focused on her.

"What did I say?" Ginger asked no one in particular.

Carla ushered her assistant out and came into the office. She closed the door and turned to face Ginger. "What has gotten into you, girl? Or rather, should I say who?"

"Don't be crass, Carla." Ginger rounded her desk and plopped into her seat. She didn't face Carla. She swiveled her chair until it faced the window. The clouds were particularly fluffy today, with swirls and swoops like a pillow. She'd bet they'd be just as soft, like a lover's kiss. "We've only just started dating."

She was dating Chase. He'd said as much. What was she going to wear tonight for dinner? Maybe she should go and buy a new outfit? First, she needed to clean her apartment. It was a mess. Not that he'd be staying over or anything. They were only dating.

"Gin, I'm happy that you finally have someone in your life because goodness knows, you needed a man."

"Hey." Ginger swiveled back around to face her friend.

"The soldier has my approval. But," Carla held up a finger, "not if he's going to change everything you stand for."

"He hasn't. He can't. Chase isn't like that."

"You just agreed to a sit down with the assistant principal of a private school who is diametrically opposed to your platform on public education."

"Because that's the adult thing to do. The two of us have an issue. We should sit down face to face and talk it out like mature, grown people."

Carla reared back as if Ginger's words were throwing daggers. "In what world would that work?"

"In the real world," Ginger insisted. "Not this hyper-polarized world we all are imagining is the real thing. Nothing is working with everyone in their own corners. We need to come to the middle and actually meet."

"Huh." Carla pursed her lips. Then she took out her phone and began tapping away.

"Who are you texting?" asked Ginger.

"I'm not texting. I'm writing all that down. It's going to go great in your next speech."

Ginger sighed, but then she rose and rounded the desk. She sat on the edge and hugged her friend.

"Really?" asked Carla. "Is the soldier's loving that good?"

"Yeah," Ginger grinned.

Not that Chase had made any declarations of love to her. It was way too soon for that. Too soon for her to even feel anything close to love. Definitely too early to be planning the cut of her wedding dress, or where they might live, or what their children's names would be.

Just tell all that to her overactive heart. The thing pounded just at the mention of his name. Yes, she did have it bad …and it was so good.

Chase had shown her another side of himself last night on the ranch. He'd shown his vulnerable side. It had been painful to watch him suffer, but that episode had broken down the remaining walls between them. It was clear he trusted her enough to let her hold him during his time of need.

"I don't have to change who I am just because I'm with someone who is on a different side of an issue than me. I think just being with Chase has made me stronger. You know the saying; iron sharpens iron. Right?"

"I have no idea," said Carla. "I use a service to sharpen my kitchen knives. I have no idea how they do it."

"Trust me, that's how they do it," said Ginger. "If all we ever do is try to get strong in a group of like-minded people, we won't get any stronger. It all would get dull soon."

"So, you're changing your platform?"

"I'm not changing the platform." Ginger took a deep breath as she realized the truth. "I've changed. I'm open to listening to others and making the platform stronger by running it up against ideas that aren't wholly mine. We'd leave a whole section of the community out if I got one-hundred percent of what I wanted. There's enough room for some give. With the give as well as the take, everyone gets some of what they want. It'll make the platform stronger if more people are included."

Carla took a deep breath herself. Ginger waited, her own breath baited. Luckily, her friend and campaign manager bit.

"Okay," said Carla. "I'm with you."

Once again, the two friends hugged it out.

"What's going on up at that ranch?" said Carla. "Maybe I need to pay them a visit, get a soldier of my own."

Before Ginger could respond, a knock sounded at the door. Her assistant poked her head in.

"Ginger, there's a Mr. Chase to see you."

And there her heart went again. They hadn't been apart for ten minutes, and he was already coming back for more. But when her assistant moved aside, it was a gray-haired man that darkened the doorway. He had Chase's face but under a number of wrinkles. And the smile was wrong. It was predatory.

"Ms. Dumasse, I'm Lloyd Chase. I believe you are acquainted with my son."

CHAPTER SEVENTEEN

"It's simple, son," said Henry Dumasse, the man also known as the Sugar Daddy due to his family's sugar plantation.

Dumasse moved his large frame around Chase's office, neither sitting or standing still. He sprinkled his presence all over the room, touching surfaces and glaring at the furniture. He was the sugary sprinkles on top of a healthy fruit salad, completely out of place.

None of that chafed as much as the last word Dumasse had uttered. Chase did not like being called son. Not by this man. Not even by his own father. It had even rankled when drill sergeants had said the word.

Chase never used it when he was doling out orders to his own soldiers. He gave them more respect than that. If you survived boot camp, you were a full-fledged man or woman. Not a child.

"My daughter is not going to win this race," said Dumasse.

Chase grit his teeth. Wasn't there a rule that parents had to support their kids? Not just financially but spiritually, socially, in their dreams. The other men in his squad had come from excellent homes where their parents cheered them on.

But not Dylan Banks. Dylan's parents, who were New York socialites, hadn't spoken to him since he lost his leg in combat. Maybe it was rich people's problems?

"Norman Dean has too many endorsements for her to have any real impact," her father was saying.

Maybe that was it? Maybe money was the corrupting factor? Chase and Ginger came from wealth, but they were both good people. They'd also both walked away from that wealth and struck out on their own.

"Meanwhile, my daughter has cornered the youth and mommy blogger vote."

It was a shame. Chase's own parents hadn't believed in him. They hadn't been in support of the way he wanted to live his life in service to his country rather than to the family business. They couldn't see that service to his country was serving his family.

"Dean is too well connected in this community," Dumasse continued his disparaging tirade against his daughter's chances at success in the race.

Chase begged to differ with that last statement. He hadn't seen Norman Dean out in the community, other than his face on a glossy poster at a bus stop. Chase had seen pictures of Dean at fancy dinners in newspapers and in negative television ads.

The man had never gotten his hands dirty in the trenches like Ginger. Dean hadn't visited the schools and seen the plight of teachers. He hadn't been on ranches and farms and seen the conditions of the laborers. He hadn't been to factories and seen the conditions of those workers.

But Ginger had. Not only that, but she had a plan to help each person in this community find their next level of success. True, Chase didn't believe in every one of those plans. But he'd stand behind her and hold her up while she tried to make her vision work. Because he believed in *her*.

"She needs a high-level endorsement if she has any hope of beating him," said Dumasse.

"Well, seeing as she already has her father's endorsement, I'm not sure how much higher she could get."

Chase was surprised he got the statement out with a straight face. He held his features still while he waited for Dumasse's reaction. Ginger's father glared at him.

Chase glared right back. He had no idea what was about to come out of the man's mouth, but he knew he wouldn't like it. He also knew he wouldn't stand here and listen to much more of this vitriol about the woman he believed in, the woman who was the right choice to lead this community, the woman he loved.

"My daughter and I have never seen eye to eye," said Dumasse. "We are on the opposite sides of most issues. I have every reason to believe the two of you are opposites in most respects, as well."

Again, Chase held his tongue still and kept his face blank. He would give nothing away to this man. But in the end, he had to know. "What do you want, Mr. Dumasse?"

"Let me make myself plain, son. I'll support my daughter's candidacy if you broker a deal with your father."

Chase's blank expression turned fierce. Was that what this was about? A business deal? Dumasse was going to sell his daughter out over money. Too bad he had the wrong Chase.

"I have no say in my father's business," said Chase.

"You're his son."

"She's your daughter," Chase countered. "See how that works."

Dumasse took a deep inhale. He was clearly trying for patience. Chase bet the man wasn't used to hearing the word no.

"Your father has always thought he was too good to do business with me. Industry folk have always thought themselves too good to get their hands dirty with agriculture. But my money is just as old as his."

Chase didn't bother to engage in this age-old debate. Money was money. It wasn't good or bad. It wasn't even old or new. It was just an indication of how much an individual or group hoarded their part of the pie. Chase had learned in the Army that it wasn't every man for himself. If he didn't have his brothers' back, they'd all fall.

"She's down in the polls," said Dumasse.

"Not anymore. She's rising."

"For how long? There's one point I agree with my daughter on; at the end of the day, this community is about family. What does it look like that her own father won't endorse her?"

Chase had some choice words of what that looked like.

"Think of it like this," Dumasse continued, completely oblivious to Chase's rising ire, "you'll be bringing two families back together."

That was just it. Chase wanted nothing to do with his father. He wanted nothing to do with Ginger's father, either.

But he did want her to win.

"It's just a phone call," said Dumasse.

But that was it. It wasn't just a phone call. Anyone dealing with his father would get up with the short end of the stick. It was the way the man worked.

CHAPTER EIGHTEEN

"You're pretty, at least."

The man before her looked her up and down like she was a car he was considering purchasing. Ginger fought the urge to cross her arms over her chest. Had Ginger heard Mr. Chase right? Her head must still be full from thinking about Chase's kisses. That couldn't have been what Chase's dad just said to her.

"I beg your pardon?" she said, hoping in vain for some clarification.

"Good figure." Mr. Chase tilted his head and regarded her from a different angle. "Nice enough face. You'll do."

Ginger Dumasse was rarely at a loss for words. But as she ran his over and over again in her head, she couldn't get past them. He wasn't hitting on her, thank goodness. He was evaluating her, assessing her quality like some piece of meat. It was so much worse.

"If my family is going to shift political parties for the woman my son is going to be with," Mr. Chase continued, "she at least better be pretty. Politics are changeable. Ugly grandbabies are not an option."

Bile rose in her mouth. Ice shivered down to the base of her spine. Her fingertips went numb.

Ginger wanted to protest that she wouldn't be having Lloyd Chase's grandbabies. More important, that if she did, they would be the most beautiful babies on the planet because they would be a part of Chase and not this ugly man that stood in front of her.

The truth was, Ginger knew she was going to have Lloyd Chase's grandbabies. She'd already had the daydreams. She'd already picked out the names. She'd already planned the ceremony for the day that she would become Mrs. Colin Chase.

No, scratch that. Mrs. Ginger Dumasse-Chase.

But all she said to the despicable man darkening her doorway was, "Chase isn't here. And knowing that he has no relationship with you, I have no intention of telling you where he is."

Chase hadn't spoken much about his parents. Just enough to let her know that they shared the same disdain for the men who had donated half the spark that brought about their existence. Meeting Lloyd Chase in person, Ginger wondered if she was being too harsh on her own father.

"Oh, I know where my boy is," said Mr. Chase. "He's either on that charity ranch for cripples or at the ridiculous center of his to recruit more lambs to the slaughter. It's you, I'm here to see."

"I have nothing to say to you."

Ginger was so disgusted by this man that she stepped around him and reached for the door. She didn't want to spend any more time in his presence than necessary. She might be the new girlfriend, but making a good impression on such a bad man was not in the cards. Besides, she doubted Chase would disapprove.

"Good," said Mr. Chase, ignoring the open door. "I'm not interested in what you have to say. Only what you can do for me."

"I'm not doing anything for you. Do you really believe I would after you come into my office and insult me?"

Mr. Chase looked bored. "Are you quite done? I have to be back on my private jet in an hour to make a business meeting."

She was not. She balled her hand into a fist and wished she was a man. If she were, she could sock him in his arrogant nose.

Wait? Did her gender matter here? She did stand on a platform of gender equality. So, maybe she could sock him in the nose ...

"I can't stand a woman who has too many opinions," said Mr. Chase. "But, having you come into the family will soften that image of me, which is good for business. Too bad your family line is one of field workers."

This guy couldn't be for real. He was the live caricature of every misogynist screen or book villain come to life. How had Chase come from this?

"You're not going to win this race," said Mr. Chase.

The absolute audacity.

Ginger slammed her door shut. She didn't want any of her staff to witness the act of violence she was about to perform. Before she could ball her hand into a fist, Mr. Chase continued.

"Norman Dean is up in the polls. He has more money, more endorsements, more testosterone."

Ginger truly doubted that last one but whatever. "In case you haven't noticed, my poll numbers are up and rising."

"Not fast enough. It's simple math, sweetie."

Yup, she was socking him in the nose. The assault charges would be worth it. The women's liberation movement simply demanded this act of civil disobedience.

"I'll endorse your campaign," said Mr. Chase.

"Thank you. But, no thank you. Your vote doesn't count, seeing as you don't even live in this state."

"No, but I have tons of workers who do live here. They could make a dent in your campaign numbers. I own the C&C Factory."

The C&C Factory? The one that was in danger of moving out of state. Lloyd Chase was the out of state shell company. It all made sense now.

Be that as it may, there was still a more important matter on her agenda. "I don't buy votes."

"No, but I'm sure you want your constituents to all still have a job after your election. I can close that plant if I don't get my way."

Now, the ice down her back turned to a blazing fire. "You wouldn't."

"Try me." Lloyd Chase crossed his arms over his chest. He looked absolutely nothing like his son. Both his brows were lowered. His lips were pursed, not in a stern manner. In a devil may care manner.

Ginger was sure this devil didn't care about anyone but himself.

"All I want is for you to work your feminine wiles to get my son to come back to the company."

"You want Chase to come and work for you?"

"You're not the brightest bulb, are you? Yes, that's what I said. This military career looked good when he was young. But now, my shareholders are starting to question the viability of my business. All sons come back to work for their father's company. If Chase doesn't, people will think something is wrong, and my stocks will drop."

This was ludicrous. He wanted her to convince Chase to give up something he loved and come work for a man he didn't even like. Even if she wanted to, they'd only just started dating today. She didn't have that kind of sway with him. She couldn't even get him to change his mind on sports.

"The clock is ticking, Ms. Dumasse. If my son isn't on the company payroll by the election, then I see no reason to keep C&C Factory in Montana."

CHAPTER NINETEEN

hase peered down at the limp noodles on his plate. He separated the vegetables, lining up the broccoli on one side and the carrots on the other. It would be a weak assault for either side. The diced carrots began at a disadvantage being chopped in circular discs and halved into tiny triangles. The broccoli florets were drooping in the marinara.

"How's the pasta?"

Chase lifted his gaze, and all the fight went out of him. When he saw the beautiful woman seated across from him, he put down his knife and fork. All the days' stresses and strains washed away with just a single glance of Ginger.

"The pasta is perfectly cooked," he said. Not that he had first-hand experience. He hadn't taken a single bite. "How's the steak?"

The thick slab of meat sat untouched on her plate. Like his, her hands were bare of utensils. Her arms were crossed over her chest, her fingers worried the sleeve of her shirt.

"It smells delicious," she said.

Ginger picked up her knife and fork. She sliced a piece. The meat gave easily, and the brown char gave way to a pink interior. She popped the bloody morsel into her mouth. Chase couldn't tear his gaze from her lips as she chewed. He would trade places with that cow in a heartbeat.

"Perfectly medium-rare," she said.

"Really? It still looks like it's mooing to me."

"That's how I like my meat. You want a salad with that pasta, lightweight?"

Chase chuckled. He loved how she always flipped the script on him. Here he was eating a dainty pasta dish while she threw down with meat and potatoes. Life would never be dull with Ginger Dumasse. And Chase planned to spend as much of his life with her as possible.

He just had to figure out how to do it with her slime bag of a father out of the picture.

There was no way Chase was selling Ginger out. He may not be in line behind all of her positions. But his main position was firm; he would always stand behind Ginger. He'd stand beside her when she needed support. He'd stand in front of her when she needed protection.

He vowed here and now that he would always be there for her regardless of where they stood on an issue. Because even when she had it wrong, her heart always was in the right place. He could not say the same for Henry Dumasse.

Chase rubbed at his head. The nagging of a headache was at the crown of his temple. Before it could creep around his skull, something cool and soothing touched his forehead.

Ginger.

With the pads of her fingers, she began a wiping motion. Her gentle care was too much artillery for the migraine. With each brush, with each press, with each caress, the dull ache receded.

Chase wanted to rest his whole head in her hands. Not just his head, his heart, his very soul. But he couldn't. They were out in public.

From his peripheral vision, he saw people staring at them. There were no flashes of bulbs. No whispers from behind cupped hands. No, instead, the other diners smiled at them. Clearly, they had this crowd's approval.

Chase lifted his head. He took Ginger's fingers in his hand. One by one, he kissed each one of her fingertips, then her knuckles.

"Is your headache back?" she asked.

"They're migraines," he admitted. "I get them from time to time."

"I hear they come when someone is stressed."

Chase turned Ginger's hands over and pressed his lips into first her right palm and then her left. "It was stressful in combat zones."

"You're not in a combat zone any longer," she said.

"I'm not?" He looked up at her with a grin.

Ginger returned his grin. She still held his face in her hands. Her thumbs brushed his lips. Not in a way that he felt silenced. In a way, he felt acknowledged, understood, accepted.

Her gaze was so full of compassion and care that Chase felt undone, unmanned. All of his defenses came crashing down at the words of this woman. Had they been adversaries only a couple of days ago?

"Is there something else going on?" she asked. "Something stressing you out."

Chase wrapped his fingers around hers, taking over the caretaker role. He was the one who was supposed to protect her. And that's exactly what he intended to do.

"I just had a trying day," he said.

"Do you want to talk about it?"

No. He would not concern her with what a degenerate her father was. He'd figure out a way to fix this.

If he was honest with himself, he had an idea of how to fix it. That's what was bringing on the migraine. The stress he was about to endure with his plan.

"I'd rather talk about your day," he said. "Anything interesting happened after I left the campaign offices?"

"No." Ginger slid her fingers from his hands. She picked up her knife and fork and sawed into her steak. "Nothing interesting. Just the same old politics."

Something crossed her features. Her blue eyes churned, like the sea in a storm. But her smile was cool, calm, like the eye of a hurricane. He could see the wheels turning in her mind. He just had no idea where they were blowing.

Her gaze met his again. There was something that looked like need in her eyes. Impulsively, he reached for her again, needing her to know that he was there for her.

She let him take her hand. He pressed their palms together, needing to feel the center of her. She squeezed back.

"We're on the same side now," she said. "Well, not with political, social, or economic issues."

"No," Chase chuckled. "Not with any of those. But I always have your back. I want you to know that."

"And I've got yours."

CHAPTER TWENTY

"You sure you want to do this, Gin?"

Ginger sat back in the passenger seat of Honey's truck. Her little sister used to drive a luxury car. No, scratch that. Her little sister used to be driven around town in luxury cars. Now, she was behind the wheel of a rusty pickup truck.

The air conditioner didn't work, so they'd rolled the windows down. Honey's normally coiffed hair was pulled back in a ponytail. Loose strands flew around her bare face. She wasn't wearing a stitch of makeup, except maybe Chapstick. And she was dressed in worn jeans, with mud on the knees, and dingy work boots.

Out of designer heels and tailored cocktail dresses, Honey was thriving. She'd married a man who showed her the love she deserved. She was surrounded by a tribe of people who nurtured and looked out for her. And yet, they were parked outside of the loneliest, most soul-crushing place on earth.

The Dumasse estate.

"Yes," said Ginger. "I have to do this."

However, Ginger's hand hesitated on the door handle. Instead, she reached over and swallowed her sister in a hug. They both had survived this place and come out the other end awesome individuals. It proved that where you came from didn't have to determine the rest of your life.

People failed and succeeded based on their will and perseverance, not their circumstances.

Honey reached for the door handle when Ginger released her.

"No," said Ginger. "You stay here. If I'm not out in twenty minutes, then you can charge through the door."

"You don't have to tell me twice." Honey twisted her watch to face her. She clicked a few dials. "Clock's ticking."

Ginger giggled at the fierce look in her sister's gaze, a gaze so much like their mother's. The two had been estranged for most of Honey's life when Honey chose to stay with their father in the divorce instead of coming to live with Ginger and their mom in a downsized apartment on the fringe of the middle class. But neither Ginger or their mom had ever stopped reaching out for Honey. She only wished their mom was here to see Honey blossom into the strong, confident, and capable woman she'd become.

Ginger climbed out of the truck and made her way up the steps to her ancestral home. The doors to the manse opened for her automatically. She had wondered if she would be welcomed back after her last run-in with her father when she told him she never wanted to see him again.

She'd meant it at the time. He'd tried to sell Honey's hand in marriage off to profit his business. It was despicable.

Luckily, it was the worst thing he could do. He couldn't slip any lower. The plan she'd formulated to counter Lloyd Chase's request would be the last chance her own father had at redemption. If he didn't rise to this occasion, she would not be coming back again.

Ginger walked the halls of the house to his office. She knew that's where he'd be. That's where he always was. When she had a school performance. When they were having family dinner. When she had a nightmare. This was where he always was.

Like every time before when she'd needed him, and he wasn't there, she found him here. Henry Dumasse sat behind his desk. There was a mountain of papers piled high. Unlike his contemporaries, the Sugar Daddy preferred paper to digital.

"Dad?"

He looked up, confusion on his brow. Perhaps at the title, she'd called him? Or at the interruption in general? She would never be sure. It wasn't what she was here to ask him.

"Hi," she said.

Her father frowned. He didn't put down the stack of papers in his hand. Of course, he didn't. Like when she was a girl, her interruptions, her seeking of his affections, was not welcome. She might as well get to the point.

Ginger took a few steps into the room. She didn't invite herself to sit down. She stood before him and presented her platform like she would any other person whose vote she wanted.

"I have a proposition for you," she said.

Wonder upon wonder, he sat his papers down. But not his pen. That, he kept in his hand, clicking the balled point out, then in. Ginger decided to take the small victory. Her father leaned back and regarded her with something that looked like interest.

"You know the company C&C Factory?" It wasn't really a question. She knew he knew of it. He knew of every business in this town that wasn't his. "I happen to know that it's going to be up for sale soon. I have it on good authority that the shareholders are going to get antsy over some poor dynamics between the owner and his son."

Lloyd Chase was certainly not going to like the dynamic of Ginger ignoring his request to get Chase to work for him. Chase's happiness was far too important to her to put him in a miserable situation as working for that man. But she still needed to save the jobs of the people in this community. She just hoped this plan would work. It should. It appealed to her father's greed.

"I've run the numbers," she continued, "and the profit margin is good. I think you should consider buying it and taking it over."

"So, he came and talked to you, did he?"

Her father's grin was predatory. It was the look she'd seen him give the rare times he'd discussed business at the dinner table. He was most happy when he was preparing to take a business down. It was the same look on his face during the divorce trial.

Ginger got a bad feeling in her stomach. Her father knew Lloyd Chase had come to her? Did he know about the estrangement between Chase and his father? If her father did know, he'd likely side with the elder Chase. Henry Dumasse had never forgiven Ginger for what he considered abandoning the family. All the more reason to keep Chase out of business with these two men and pit them against one another.

"So, you and Mr. Chase discussed this already?" asked Ginger.

"*Mister* Chase? Not the father, the son. Chase, the boy. The soldier."

Wait? What? "Sergeant Chase? You spoke to Chase?"

What had her father been doing speaking to Chase? More importantly, why hadn't Chase come to her and tell her about it?

"I told the boy I wanted him to put me in touch with his father. That pompous man hasn't returned any of my calls. I've been trying to work a deal with him for months now. But you say there's a weak spot in one of his businesses?"

Her father picked up a blank sheet of paper. He began scribbling on it in his unintelligible chicken scratch. But Ginger didn't need to read his words to know that he was planning a takeover.

What had she done? Her mind went back to the people at her rally, those who worked in the factory. They were about to be at the mercy of one or the other of these men who didn't care enough about their own families. They certainly weren't going to give a care to people they didn't know.

This had been a mistake. In her bid to protect Chase, she'd only traded one devil for the other. But why hadn't Chase told her about her father's talk with him?

Probably for the same reason she hadn't told Chase about his father coming to her. They were trying to protect each other.

The door to her father's office burst open, and a blonde tornado darkened the doorway.

"It's been twenty minutes," Honey said as she glared at their father. "I'm here to rescue you."

Of course, she was. Because that's what real family and friends did. That's what community did. Regardless of where they stood, they all protected one another. Ginger quickly formulated a new plan to do the same.

CHAPTER TWENTY-ONE

ontana mountains gave way to Spokane rain. It had been a long time since Chase had been back home to Washington state. The long drive helped to clear his head and get his mind straight. Still, the blue clouds in the sky reminded him of a certain blonde's gaze when she was on a stage and owning a crowd.

Ginger was never far from Chase's mind these days. Last night, after dinner, he'd left her at her door. It wasn't the marinara that had been on his tongue as he'd gone to sleep. It had been that sweet-spicy taste of her.

She'd invaded his dreams and was working her way into each chamber of his heart. He was determined to protect her from her villain of a father. Hence, the need to leave the state.

Chase pushed his foot down on the gas pedal. He could've flown and made the trip home faster. But he needed the time and space away from Ginger. His instincts to protect her were growing stronger each day. He hated that he wasn't telling her the whole truth, aka lying to her. She had enough on her plate. This was a burden he could handle.

Five hours later, on a road trip that should've taken nearly eight hours, he parked in the driveway of his parents' house. He let loose the seatbelt and waited for the migraine to take him.

But his head was steady. He was doing the right thing. And when he was done righting this wrong, he got to go back and be with the woman he was falling in love with.

Ginger had a campaign rally later tonight. Chase was determined to be there for her. To show everyone that she had his support, even if they didn't see eye to eye. She was the best man for the job.

"You want me to come in with you?" Ortega asked from the passenger seat.

"No," said Chase. "You don't need to witness this. But if I'm not out in twenty minutes, call for reinforcements."

He gave his friend a complicated handshake and then climbed out of the car. It had been years since he'd climbed the steps to his parents' front door. The military had provided an excellent excuse to stay away. Now that his service was over, and he lived just one state away, he had no excuse not to come home every once in a while.

The door opened, and his mother stood on the other side. "Colin, darling. What are you doing with your hair?"

Chase ran a hand over his short-cropped cut. It was habit. His mother was all about keeping up appearances.

"I thought you'd let it grow back now that you're out of the Navy."

"Army, Mother. And I still work for the military. I'm a recruiter."

"Are you sure, darling?" Annabelle Chase's brows pinched in distaste as she looked everywhere but in her son's eyes. "Your father told me you were coming back to the family business."

Back? Chase had never been in the family business. But his mother rarely concerned herself with the facts of his life.

"I hear you're dating? The girl is from a wealthy family? But it's farming, I hear?"

Chase balled his hands into fists so that he wouldn't pinch the bridge of his nose. He was surprised he hadn't inherited his mother's snobbishness. It was likely because she'd never held him as a baby. She'd left that to nannies.

"But I don't know about her character. She takes on things outside her gender. How will I know she can take care of you the way you need, darling?"

Seemed they were getting the gossip rags from Montana here in Washington.

"Mother, Ginger is an amazing woman. She makes me a stronger man. She challenges me, and pushes me hard to do better, be better. She makes me the best version of myself. How could you want more for your son?"

His mother frowned at him as though he'd just spoken another language. Chase knew it was a waste of time. His mother had only ever aspired to be a trophy on a rich man's arm. Chase had always aspired to be in the heart of a woman with an indomitable spirit. Both their wishes had come true. Though Chase appeared to be the only one of them happy about the turn of events.

"Colin, there you are, my boy."

The vein in Chase's temple popped. But still, there was no aching pain starting in his skull. He turned to face his father.

Lloyd Chase was not aging well. His cheeks looked hallow but bright. Not a healthy bright. More like a plastic kind of bright. He wondered if his father had traveled south to the surgeons of California?

"It's about time you got here. Your first order of business will be to help me unravel this mess."

"What mess is that?"

"The mess with the Dumasses."

His father slumped into a chair. Chase remained standing. This conversation wasn't starting the way he'd planned.

His father thought he was coming to work for him? There was a conflict with the Dumasses? And not one, but two of them? He knew his father wasn't talking about Honey. Mark's wife was happily up to her knees in dirt back on the ranch.

"When I went and spoke to that girl of yours, I thought I made myself clear," his father was saying.

"You went to see Ginger?" Chase felt a prickle at the back of his knees. The prickle urged him to sit down for what was to come. He didn't dare get too close to his father. He wasn't entirely sure patricide wasn't on the table.

"Of course, I did," said the old man. "How else would she know about the C&C Factory?"

The C&C Factory? Chase didn't keep abreast of his family's holdings. The Chase family holdings were a massive empire that spanned many states. It was likely that his father owned the factory back in Montana. The picture was still a blur, but the edges were slowly sharpening.

"Now her ape, who thinks he's a sugar baron, is trying to buy me out."

"You're selling a factory in Montana?"

"No," his father huffed, eying Chase like he was an idiot. A look Chase had become used to in his childhood. "I was never going to sell. Downsize, sure. But the deal I made with that girl of yours was just to get your attention, to get you back into the fold."

Everything was becoming clear. Still, Chase's vision blurred nonetheless. His father had tried to use Ginger to get him to come into the business.

Chase wasn't angry.

He was numb.

Here, he'd come to warn his father that Henry Dumasse might have something up his sleeve. Chase had still harbored some loyalty to his family to try and protect them. Meanwhile, his father was trying to blackmail the woman he loved.

But with what?

The moment the question formed in his mind, Chase knew the sickening answer. C&C Factory. The workers had come to Ginger at a rally earlier in the week, asking what she as a candidate could do to protect their jobs. And his father had used that as blackmail.

That's what he'd seen in her eyes the other night. She'd been hiding her knowledge of what a lowbred his father was. Just as he'd been hiding the same knowledge of her father from her.

The two men deserved each other. But the workers didn't deserve either of them. People weren't pawns.

Chase didn't waste his breath on his father. The man wouldn't understand. He was already back-stepping out of the room. He needed to put as much distance between himself and this excuse of a man as possible.

"Wait? Where are you going? If the board doesn't see that you've finally taken your place in the company, they'll think there's something wrong."

"Oh, there's something wrong, all right."

And now, Chase was formulating a plan to right that wrong. He just hoped he could make his bid for change before Henry Dumasse ruined things.

"If you walk out that door, you'll be abandoning your family."

"Nope," said Chase as he crossed the threshold. "I'm going home to my family."

CHAPTER TWENTY-TWO

Ginger looked out in the crowd. It was a full house. But she didn't see the one person she wanted to see. Where was he?

"Ginger," called Carla from the side of the stage. "It's time."

Yes, it was time. Time for her to walk her talk. Time for her to put her money where her mouth was. And every other cliché that meant she had to stand firm in her beliefs.

Ginger had been a strong, independent woman before she was of legal age. But today, she wanted to lean on the shoulder of one particular man. She wanted Chase's blessing on this particular plan. She wanted his acknowledgment on what she was about to do. She wanted his support.

But he wasn't here.

She was certain he'd be on her side. At least she hoped he would. Her actions would severely tick off his father.

"Gin?"

Unfortunately, Ginger couldn't stall any longer. She stepped onto the makeshift stage inside the C&C Factory. They'd moved their campaign rally here at the last minute. The workers here needed to hear what she had to say as they were about to be impacted by her announcement.

Applause greeted her as she looked out at the crowd. There was a mix of people. Most of the crowd were workers in their blue overalls.

There were also moms with babies on their hips or toddlers in hand. A large group of coeds held up snazzy signs. There was even a nice sized group of men and women in business suits leaning against one of the walls. Standing at the front, where she could see them, was a large party from the Purple Heart Ranch.

From the cradle of her husband's embrace, Maggie winked at her. Eva and Reegan both gave her the thumbs up. Honey and Mark whooped and hollered the loudest.

Ginger couldn't help but feel a sense of pride well in her chest. This was the coalition she'd wanted to build. These were the people of the town, her community.

"I've got some good news and bad news," she began. "The bad news is that the plant is changing ownership."

A ripple of surprise went through the crowd like a heatwave. Just as soon as the room heated up, a cold wind of reality breezed over everyone. Ginger could feel despair settling in like dark clouds. She rushed on to show everyone that the sun was on the horizon. Or at least it would be. Once she enacted her plan.

"The good news is that I've decided to purchase the factory with the remaining monies of my inheritance."

Another ripple went through the crowd. This time it was as though night turned to day. Heads that had bowed in expectation of dark times lifted, a new ray of hope dawned in their eyes.

Ginger had spent the morning on the phones with a financial planner and lawyer. They had already started negotiations with C&C Factory's board of directors. There was only one snag. There was another buyer in the mix, but Ginger was prepared to raise her offer. That other buyer didn't know who they were messing with. She wasn't about to let another shell company, which was nothing but an absentee parent, move into her community and wreak havoc. They'd all had enough uncertainty.

"I've been a part of this community all my life," she said. "It's invested in me. From the teachers in the public school system to the pastors in church, to the leaders in the recreational centers. I would not be here today if it wasn't for my neighbors. Win or lose in this election, I plan to be my neighbor's keeper."

A slow golf clap began in the audience. It picked up speed rapidly until the room thundered with applause. But Ginger's eyes had found the epicenter of the beginnings of the growing praise.

Chase.

He stood in the middle of the room. Clapping his capable hands. Smiling that devastating grin. Walking slowly toward her. And then he was there. Standing at the edge of the platform. He stood in front of her, his support of her clear in his warm, brown gaze.

The room had gone silent as the community members looked between the two of them. If people didn't know there was something between her and Chase, they wouldn't be able to mistake it now. The heat coming off them was hotter than a summer day under the Montana sky.

With great difficulty, Ginger tore her gaze away from Chase and faced her constituents. Her job wasn't done. She still had to actually purchase the factory.

"I promise to do everything in my power to win the bid and buy out this company—"

"The factory was sold earlier this afternoon." Chase's deep voice easily carried over her amplified words.

Ginger looked down to Chase. Was she too late? Had their fathers made some under-the-table deal?

Chase climbed onto the stage. He leaned into the mic to speak to the people, but his gaze never left her. "The shell company that owned this factory belonged to my family. Being that I had an interest, and thanks to a bit of nepotism, I was able to take ownership of this factory."

"Chase, you didn't." Ginger placed her hand on his heart. This was the last thing she wanted. She knew Chase didn't want to be in business with his father. All her efforts had been for naught.

"I didn't go into business with my father if that's what you're worried about. I went to the board of directors and purchased the factory directly, using my inheritance."

Ginger reared back. She snatched her hand from his chest. Then she balled her fist and punched him in the shoulder.

"I was going to do that with my inheritance."

Chase chuckled as he caught her fist. He pressed her knuckles to his lips for a sweet kiss. "I'd offer to sell it to you, but seeing as I'm going to make you another offer in the near future—one that would entitle you to fifty percent of everything I own, and one hundred percent of my heart and devotion—I figured it would be a moot point."

For the second time in her life, Ginger was speechless. She stood on the stage, in the embrace of the strongest, most capable man she knew, and she had no idea, no plan of how to deal with him. For the first time in her life, she was content to simply follow.

"So, we'll be working for both of you?" someone called from the crowd.

"Yes," answered Chase.

"But you two are on opposite sides of most of the issues."

"Not when it comes to family," said Chase. "For both of us, this community, and its people, are family."

"I agree," said Ginger. "It was never about donors, or endorsements, or deals for me. It was always about you. Whether you agree or disagree with me, I'm always going to have your back. I'm always going to fight for you. Because that's what you do for the people you care about, for the people you love."

"I don't know about you," said Chase. "But this woman's certainly got my vote. And my heart."

"Then," she said, "I'm a winner."

Chase brushed his lips against hers. Ginger tilted her head back and accepted his claim. She knew that in the near future, she would accept his ring. She would accept everything about this man. And work her hardest to convert him into a soccer fan.

But that would be for another day.

EPILOGUE

"Oh, oh, oh! Here's another one."

Ortega had the television remote in his hand. He was clicking through the various local and national news channels for updates on the race. Due to the combined stories of Chase's takeover of the factory his father had owned, and the love story between himself and Ginger, the media outlets had all picked up the story and ran with it.

Good thing too because the story had ticked up Ginger's poll numbers so high that she'd overtaken Norman Dean in the race. They couldn't have planned it better. There were some factions that believed that the two of them had connived their whole affair. Those stories had been put out by the Dean campaign.

But the ring on Ginger's finger, the announcements that had gone out in the mail last week, and their impending nuptials all put a damper on those conspiracy stories. Anyone looking at Chase or Ginger could easily tell that they were madly, deeply, head-over-combat-boots in love.

"She's ahead in the Stokes Poll," said Ortega.

The barn filled with cheers, so loud the rafters shook a bit. The four corners of the room were filled with people from Ginger's campaign, supporters from town, and of course, their family at the Purple Heart Ranch.

Every man, woman, child, and dog had gone to work over the last couple of months for Ginger's campaign. They'd knocked on doors. They'd manned the phones. They'd shouted from the rooftops. And their voices weren't alone.

Ginger's support in the neighboring towns of the district had also risen. So too had Chase's invitations to come and speak at schools and churches and recreational centers about recruitment into the Armed Forces.

It just went to prove that all it took was sincerity, an open mind, and a good heart to get people to listen and have your back.

"Oh, oh, oh," shouted Ortega. "Channel Two is calling it for Dumasse."

The room went insane with applause and whoops. Chase ignored them all as he made his way through the bodies in search of one person in particular.

"Looks like I'm going to win this bet, too," Maggie Banks was saying to Ginger.

Chase had found the two women in the corner of the room. Ginger was surrounded by the brides of Purple Heart Ranch. Even though they hadn't said their *I do's* just yet, she had been inducted into this ever-growing sisterhood. Just as Chase had been drafted into the brotherhood of the males that had started this whole operation.

Surrounding the women in a loose formation were the men of his team. Reece and Brandon sipped from beer bottles as they both gazed at their wives. Dylan and Fran were on the floor, rolling around with the kids and the dogs.

The soldiers and the brides made way for Chase as he marched to Ginger. He swept her in his arms and stole a kiss. As there had been for the last few months of their courtship, there were catcalls and *ahhhs* behind them.

Chase didn't bother turning around to see who was making the ruckus. He knew that his little community here had his back. They were his family as much as the woman in his arms was.

"Nervous?" Chase asked Ginger.

"About what?"

"Looks like you're about to win a state senate seat. That's going to be a lot of responsibility."

Ginger shrugged, her blue eyes bright and filled with love as she gazed up at him. "I have all the support I need right here."

"And the winner is …"

Neither of them looked to the television screen as the race was called. Chase pulled Ginger's body into a tighter embrace. As the community cheered around them, Chase and Ginger leaned into each other and shared a kiss that promised commitment and compromise for the rest of their days.

———

Get ready for more stories from the Purple Heart Ranch. Be sure and check out
Light Up His Life
the tenth book in The Brides of Purple Heart Ranch series!

LIGHT UP HIS LIFE

THE BRIDES OF PURPLE HEART RANCH
BOOK 10

CHAPTER ONE

"Slow down, Luke. This isn't the Millennium Falcon."

In his peripheral vision, Luke Jackson saw that the green of the trees whizzed by in a blur, much like the end of a *Star Wars* scroll. He lifted his right foot from the gas. Moving it over to the brake pedal, he stomped down. The leaves on the trees became visible as though they'd just shot out of hyperspace.

"Oof."

"You okay?" Luke reached his arm out to brace his friend Paul Hanson. Paul rubbed at the back of his forehead. His head had slammed forward but missed the dashboard. When it slammed back, the back of his head collided with the cushions of the headrest.

"Man, I'm sorry," said Luke, as he pulled over to the side of this road. "I didn't mean to."

Luckily, there weren't many vehicles on the road early this morning. He doubted there were many vehicles on the road at any one time. They were traveling the backroads of Montana. There was nothing but fields and mountains as far as the eyes could see. The countryside was a welcome change from the harsh desert they'd come from.

Afghanistan looked very much like Tatooine, the fictional planet of his namesake Luke Skywalker. Luke's father had named his only son after his favorite science fiction character. No wonder Luke had gone on to be a pilot in the United States Air Force. But that life was over for him now.

Luke had retired from service. He was now ready to start his civilian life in full. He just had one more mission to complete.

"Calm down, buddy." Paul chuckled. "I get that you're used to speed and no one being on your rear in the clouds. But down here on the roads, there is an actual speed limit."

Luke looked up at the white sign on the road. There were only two numbers in black on the sign where Luke was used to doing at least triple digits in the air. He'd performed many a death-defying stunt in his time in the air force. He'd saved many lives in his mission. When he was in the air. The one time his mission put him on the ground, his best friend got seriously wounded.

"You think you might have a concussion?" asked Luke. He put the back of his hand to Paul's head.

"What?" said Paul. "No. I'm fine." Paul slapped at his friend's hand like an annoyed adolescent swatting away a parent who was babying them. He brought his hand from his neck and down lower to rub at his back.

"Is your back bothering you?"

"Luke—"

"Do you need to get out and stretch your legs? We've been driving for more than thirty minutes." Luke reached for the door handle, but Paul reached over and stayed his hand.

"Luke, I'm good."

Those were the same words Paul had said after the explosion rang through their ears. Paul hadn't been good then. He wasn't good now. Luke had walked away from the explosion with only a scratch on his knee from where he'd impacted the ground.

"Look," sighed Paul, "if you must know, I'm just not in a hurry to get to this place."

"Everyone has said it's the best place for an injury like yours."

Paul shook his head, but he didn't argue. That was the problem. Paul had an opinion on everything. But these days, he wasn't arguing much. He hadn't so much given up as he had given in to his injury.

"Three months, that's all I'm asking," said Luke.

"Why three months?"

Luke shrugged. That's what the pamphlet for the Purple Heart Ranch read. *Give us three months to change your life.* Luke didn't need anything in his life changed. He was the luckiest man he knew. He'd survived three tours and only walked away with a scratch. But he'd lost many of his friends. He'd nearly lost his best friend. But he'd managed to save Paul's life.

Paul had limped away with all his limbs attached. But he was in chronic pain every day. Pain changed a man. It took a lot for Paul to laugh and find joy these days. It took a lot for him to want to try to live his life to the fullest.

Paul had been honorably discharged for his injuries. Luke had had a year left in the service at that time. He'd gone to see Paul every time he could. Each time, his friend was more and more a shell of his former self.

"You don't have to stay and babysit me," said Paul.

"Yeah, I think I do. With all the trouble you'll get yourself in if I'm not around."

There was a flicker of amusement in Paul's light gaze. But only a flicker.

Guilt washed over Luke. If he hadn't been there to dive on Paul, his friend might not have made it out unscathed. Might. There was a chance that he could've walked away whole. But because Luke had hefted his bulk and thrown his friend to the ground, Paul had landed on a pipe that caused damage that wouldn't let up on the pain.

"We're here," Luke announced, pulling up to a gate.

"Are you sure?" asked Paul.

There was a curly flower on the gate. The name read The Bellflower Ranch. The purple flower looked much like a heart.

"This is the right address," said Luke.

They'd drove through the gates and realized that they were indeed in the right place. A JROTC regiment practiced drills in the field. Men and women walked with rifles slung over shoulders toward a shooting range. A few men were on horseback. Their buzz cuts and rigid shoulders couldn't hide the fact that they were all military. Neither could the prosthetic limbs many sported.

This was the Purple Heart Ranch. A place for wounded soldiers to convalesce and get their lives back. Hopefully, they could help Paul get back to a good place.

Luke parked the car. He stopped himself from hurrying around to the other side to let Paul out. He knew it wouldn't be appreciated. It also was an unmanly thing to do, and Paul would ridicule him ... for longer the second time.

"You must be Major Solo."

A blond-haired soldier marched up to him. His gait was off. Luke looked down to see why. His right leg was a prosthetic. Beside him was an older man with golden-honey skin and a serene smile like a Buddha statue.

"Oh, I get it. Luke and Han. *Star Wars.*" The young blond soldier turned to the older man who clearly didn't get it.

That was a running joke in the service. And the monikers were true to characters. Luke had been the golden boy who could pull off impossible missions. Han had the swagger and got all the girls. Or at least he used to. But his swagger was off with his chronic back and hip pains.

"I'm Sergeant Dylan Banks."

"You're the one in charge?" asked Luke after shaking the man's hand.

Banks shrugged. "As much as anyone could be in charge of a herd of wildcats."

"This is Dr. Patel, the ranch therapist. He works with your internal wounds."

The old man had a friendly grin and kind eyes. But they were focused on Luke instead of Paul, the actual patient.

"Welcome," said the doctor. "We're glad the two of you will be staying with us."

"Oh, I'm not staying," said Luke. "I've found a place off the ranch in town."

"Nonsense," said Banks. "Each unit has two bedrooms. The second room is unoccupied. You're welcome to it."

That hadn't been part of the plan. Luke had work of his own to do while his friend healed. But if he stayed, he could low-key spy on Paul's progress. Paul shook his head like he saw Luke's plan clearly.

"You're welcome to take part in the activities as well," said Dr. Patel, his serene gaze still fixated on Luke instead of Paul.

"Absolutely," said Banks. He addressed the one of them with the actual problem. "We have physical activities, such as horseback riding, which I think will help with your hip and back. It certainly helped with me."

Banks indicated his prosthetic leg. The idea of riding horses did intrigue Luke.

"We also have mental health activities, which Dr. Patel leads."

"Oh, I don't think I'll be needing that," Luke said.

Both men raised their brows at Luke, as though he was an addict holding a bottle of whiskey in his hand while denying his problem.

"I'm not injured," Luke said. "I'm here to support Paul. And to finish my latest book."

"Wait, you're the pilot that writes the Military Science Fiction under the name Walker Skye."

"Yeah, that's me."

It was still strange for him when people praised his books. Mainly because he'd had to keep his literary activities quiet while he was active.

Luke's stories took place in another time and dimension, but war was a universal language. He had to avoid the appearance that he was disparaging his superiors in divulging secrets. Hence, the pen name.

"I love your books," said Banks. "So do a lot of the kids in the JROTC program. Will you talk to them?"

"I wonder if you would be willing to do a talk at the local library?" asked Patel. "It's difficult for kids to get out here. I think a lot of young people and older men would love to meet you and have a reading."

Luke hadn't done a talk before. He hadn't gone out as his pen name. Now that he was a full-time author, this would be expected of him. What better place to practice than here?

CHAPTER TWO

There was nothing like the smell of old books. Musty, like something aged and left under a protective sheet for years, with a bit of manured earth and a touch of human sweat. Elaine reveled in it.

That combination could only be found in a library. There wasn't the old smell there as most bookstores featured newly printed materials that were on some bestselling lists curated by people who only cared about what was popular at the moment. Those people didn't take into account what had been popular a hundred years ago. Or what had stayed the test of time.

Elaine clicked on the lights of the library. The stacks illuminated one by one. Dust mites swirled as she turned on the air conditioner. She sneezed into her hand at the gathering dander and smiled.

No, there were no new books in this section. These weren't the books that were pristine and purchased by one person to covet. Every volume had been through the trenches. Shared, paged through, returned, only to be picked up by someone new to experience what was between the pages.

Well, some of the books had taken that journey. Many of the cards at the backs of the books of the classics had only a handful of checkouts. Or none.

But they would always have a home in the library. That's what libraries were for. Homes for books, where people showed up to take them out and were fined if they forgot to bring them back. If only it were that way during her parents' divorce. Then their remarriage. And then their second divorce.

Elaine walked to the front door of the town library and flicked open the lock. There was no line waiting outside to come in and snatch up a book. It was nine in the morning.

At noon, she was still the only person in the library. The shelves had been dusted. Book jackets stood straight with no slouching at the ends. Reading list books stood faced out waiting to be picked up. But no readers had arrived yet. Elaine sat behind the circulation desk, arranging and rearranging pens. She tugged at her cardigan, smoothing the warm fabric around her shoulders to find warmth in the chilly atmosphere.

"I have great news."

Elaine nearly fell out of her chair at the voice that came from behind her. Mary was the head librarian here. She'd gotten the job right out of college. Mainly because the last head librarian had been her aunt. Nepotism ran rampant in this small town.

"I just got a call from Pastor Patel," Mary continued, not noticing Elaine's heart attack. "He said Walker Skye is in town, and he's open to coming and doing a reading here."

"Walker Skye?"

The name did not ring a bell.

"You know who he is. He writes military science fiction. He hit the bestseller's list earlier this year."

Elaine still didn't know who this person was, but she knew of that genre. She wasn't a total literary snob. She enjoyed speculative fiction. But space wars? Really? What kind of value did that add to literature? None.

"I don't think he's ever done a reading or a signing," said Mary. "This is going to be so popular with the younger group. For the last year, we can't keep his books on the shelf."

Mary walked over to the bestselling books section, a section Elaine always neglected. She could see one of the offending books from here. Very few of those books had been turned faced out this morning. Mary frowned, turning one particular cover outward-facing.

A big old space ship was on the front cover. Vibrant colors splashed the jacket. The bold colors hurt Elaine's eyes.

"Looks like someone neglected her shelving duties this morning," said Mary.

Someone hadn't. Someone had spent time on the books that mattered, the books that shaped human thought, the books that changed lives. Though most people in this town preferred things the way they always were.

Elaine pinched her lips. "If we don't showcase the classics like we do the bestsellers, how can we expect people to pick them up?"

"Elaine, honey, you have to remember; the classics make kids think of school and homework. The bestsellers like Walker Skye make them think of downtime, relaxation, and entertainment. Which would you grab for after a long day of work?"

Elaine opened her mouth, but Mary stopped her.

"Don't tell me. I already know what you're going to say. Something by Hardy or Eliot or Austen."

Contrary to popular convention, Elaine was not an Austen fan. Sure, *Pride and Prejudice* and *Emma* were classics. But the stories were wholly unrealistic. The one where the wealthy guy fell for the plain, poor girl. Or the other one where the wealthy guy falls for the penniless girl. Like any of them would stay together. But Elaine held that unpopular opinion to herself.

"Not everyone is like you, Elaine. Not everyone finds joy in five hundred page literary tomes that aren't *Harry Potter*."

Elaine rolled her eyes again. She never got the *Harry Potter* draw. It was just *The Lord of the Rings*. But written for children.

They were walking by the romance section. Mary's favorite section. Elaine avoided this section like the plague. The short books were even more unrealistic than Austen or Rowling. Love that happened in just a couple hundred pages was doomed to fail after the last page. A book could end with a happily ever after. But no books ever showed what happened after the happily ever after began. After the last page was where the hard work started, and that's where the fairytale fell apart.

"Look, I know I'm not going to convince you of this," said Mary. "But we need this kind of attention. Attendance is down here. If we can't increase circulation, then the county will target staff for upcoming budget cuts."

Elaine still had objections. But she couldn't argue that one. Either get the *Star Wars* author in here or risk losing her job. She would simply have to practice holding her tongue while the old guy espoused the virtues of space warfare.

"Why don't you take your lunch break," said Mary. "It's taco Tuesday, your favorite."

Elaine was nothing if she wasn't a creature of habit. She liked her routines, just like she liked knowing the end of the stories she was reading.

"No, it's *your* favorite," Elaine countered.

"That's right." Mary grinned, reaching in her pure for cash. "Could you bring me back a chicken taco with extra guac?"

"Sure, Mary."

CHAPTER THREE

S o this was small-town America. The convenience stores were named for a family instead of the normal chain stores that broadcast commercials during morning television. The diners and restaurants also had family names; O'Malley's Pub, Castro's Mexican Cuisine, Patel's Family Restaurant.

Walking down the main street of the town, Luke was greeted with delectable smells, friendly smiles, and welcoming mats at every turn. After years in hostile territory, he could get used to this.

He wandered into the town's only bookstore. It too wasn't a chain, not that there were many bookstore chains left now that much of human literature and entertainment could be held in the palm of the hand. Still, the internet age was alive and well in this quaint town.

Satellites outnumbered the phone lines up above. A couple of phone carrier outlets were tucked into the two gas stations and smaller corner stores he'd passed by on his walk. Cell phones were in the hands of the young and the old. Unfortunately, he didn't see anyone walking the sidewalks carrying a paperback.

There was a book in the hands of the woman across the street at a diner. She held a hardback book to her nose. He could tell by the title on the cover that it was classic British Literature straight out of Advanced English class.

Luke had never liked those books in school. They never ended happily. Usually, it was the heroine who suffered some moral punishment that was all the hero's fault.

The woman with her nose in the book was quite pretty. Brown hair pulled back in a bun. A pert nose. Glasses covering her brown eyes. She looked like a stereotypical librarian. Not a real one, more like a young woman who was trying to dress the part, complete with a pastel cardigan. Only she was more pretty than bookish.

There had been a ton of librarians back in Luke's hometown. His upscale neighborhood in Northern Virginia had had a library within every five miles. All the librarians there looked the same. Like doting grandmothers or spinster aunts pushing books into the hands of impressionable youths.

The grandma-librarian types were thrilled that kids were reading and didn't try to censor the titles. They'd push dragon books, science fiction books, war books, anything that the kid was guaranteed to open.

The spinster-aunt looking ones were a different case. They often hid the bestselling titles. They shamed teenage girls from reaching for the romance novels. They tsked at the young men who reached for covers with spaceships and guns.

Luke's days were planned around the librarian's shifts. He knew when the grandmas were there behind the circulation desk and when the aunts patrolled the stacks.

The woman in the dining window turned the page. She reached for a napkin and placed it between the pages before setting the book down and taking a bite of her taco. The innards of the taco spilled down on the plate and her dress, which she'd covered with a napkin.

So, not only was she pretty, she was careful with the book. She'd taken great pains to separate the taco. And she wasn't a dog-earring reader. She wouldn't appreciate Luke. Dog ears helped him not only remember his place, but it also helped him remember the best parts of the book. When he saw that crease, he could go back and reread the best parts.

Though the bibliophile fascinated him, Luke turned away from the diner and the window. A relationship was not in his cards. He had work to do and a friend to look after.

He knew survivor's guilt was a form of PTSD. And he was doing something about it. He was getting his friend the help he needed. Once

Paul was situated, then Luke would start to date again. Maybe he'd set his sights on the library. He'd be sure to bypass the town's spinster aunties and ask the kind-looking grannies for their granddaughters' phone numbers. Surely they would have taught their young ones the beauty of the written word.

The town's library was quite small compared to all the libraries in his home town. It was the size of a small house where the libraries back in Northern Virginia had been as big as department stores, often with two floors. Walls and walls of books, CDs, movies, video games, magazines, even toys that kids could check out.

This library was one room. Wall to wall shelves covered each corner. And there were five stacks in the middle of the room. A row of tables sat off to the side. Two young people sat at one with iPads out.

Well, the young woman had her iPad out and was tapping away. The young man had a book with the rear of a spaceship and its thrusters glowing brightly on the cover.

"Would you put that down?" said the young woman. "We have serious literature to do a project on. I don't want you talking about photon guns when we're supposed to talk about morality and feminism in the Victorian era."

The young man peaked over the cover of the book. "This book is actually filled with feminism. Did you know the captain of the ship is a woman? And the sexes are equal in this future. In the military, men and women even share the same bunks and bathrooms."

Luke took a closer look and saw that the young man was reading his first book. Although the military wasn't that advanced, Luke had served with many women in the service who were his betters. The creation of his heroine was dedicated to the female pilot who'd taught him everything he knew.

The book had been a hit, and he'd gotten a four-book deal. It was the third book that he was supposed to be writing now. But it had stalled during Paul's recovery.

"Can I help you find something?"

Luke turned to the circulation desk. There wasn't a gray-haired, rosy-cheeked granny sitting there. Neither was this woman quite the spinster auntie type.

She would definitely be classified as young and beautiful. She didn't dog-ear the pages of the book she'd been reading. She didn't stuff a napkin or bookmark to hold her place either. This librarian laid her book down with the covers open and the pages pressed into the desk. The book was clearly a women's fiction book.

"Yes," said Luke. "Dr. Patel sent me. About doing a reading."

Her eyes remained blank. And then they lit up. "You're Walker Skye?"

Luke nodded.

Behind him, the young man reading his book turned and gaped.

Luke hated this part. He didn't like to be the center of attention. He preferred to have his characters do that. Why had he agreed to this?

"I'm Mary, the head librarian here. We are so thrilled to have you."

Luke mustered a smile. He'd never been a charmer when it came to ladies. Probably because he never looked at them as objects of desire. Having been around military families his whole life, women were either caretakers in the home or defenders on the battlefield, often both. Asking women to cover his back was no problem. Asking one on a date had always been a challenge for him.

Mary, the librarian, was looking at him with interest. But he didn't feel the same pull toward her. Not like the taco-eating, classic book reading woman back at the restaurant. Luke wasn't sure what drew him to her? By their reading tastes and place holding habits, they had nothing in common. Though he did like Mexican food.

"Mr. Skye?"

Luke blinked to find the young man with his book, and a pen extended to him.

"I'm so sorry for bothering you."

"It's no bother at all," said Luke.

He beamed. "Could I get your autograph?"

"That's a library book, Daniel," said Mary, the librarian.

Daniel's face fell.

"Tell you what," said Luke. "I'm giving a reading here in a couple of days. You come to the reading, and I'll bring you an autographed copy."

Daniel's face lit up.

Luke made the arrangement for his reading. Mary made advances that he dodged like he was in a fighter jet. They exchanged numbers, but he only had the intention of using hers for business purposes if the need arose. He doubted it would.

With a wave to the young man who still wasn't typing on his iPad along with his classmate, Luke exited the library. He needed to get some writing done. He suddenly had a hankering for tacos. He hurried down the street, back toward the Mexican restaurant. But he stopped in the bookstore first. He figured he'd support the local economy and buy his book there to autograph instead of going into his personal stash. He was already feeling like a part of the community.

CHAPTER FOUR

$\mathcal{E}$laine brushed the salsa from her blouse. This was why she always wore dark colors. Food, drinks, pen markings inevitably ended up on her clothing. It was also why she always kept a cardigan handy to wrap around her shoulders and cover the evidence.

She wasn't clumsy. She just was careless with anything that wasn't parchment. Fabrics shuddered when she pulled them onto her body. Each article of clothing knew their time in her closet would be short-lived.

But the books on her shelves got the utmost care. Weekly dusting. A heavy curtain over the window to protect them from light. Thick comforters on her bed, so that the books didn't suffer the dreaded AC unit being on for too long or at all.

A side of chips and guacamole appeared before her on Elaine's table. She looked up to see Juan Castro grinning down at her.

"On the house," said Juan.

Elaine pushed the salty treat back toward him. "No *gracias*."

"Oh, come on, Elaine. It's not an engagement ring."

Elaine shuddered and slipped her cardigan over her shoulders. It might as well be. That's how most animal mating rituals began. The male would offer the female the choicest morsels of food. And then he would pounce.

Elaine had no interest in being pounced on. Her belly was full of tacos, which she'd paid for herself. No matter that a good portion of it was on her shirt.

"I'm not even asking for a dinner date, just lunch," said Juan.

"Juan, you know I don't date."

"No woman doesn't date."

"This woman does." Elaine paused, examining her sentence structure. "Doesn't. Whatever. We've been through this before."

Elaine gathered her book. She removed the napkin from her book and pressed a cloth bookmark between the pages to hold her space. Not that she needed the reminder. She'd read *Tess of the d'Urbervilles* from cover to cover more times than she could count. And the book looked as pristine as the day she'd bought it.

Placing the book carefully in her bag, Elaine scooted out of the booth and around Juan. The man was unrelenting. But she came here every Tuesday for the last four years because the tacos were to die for. She grabbed the to-go bag for Mary, making a mental note that next time it would be Mary's turn to come out for Taco Tuesday to-go.

Mary easily dealt with male attention. Because Mary wanted male attention. Elaine did not.

"I don't think you've dated anyone since high school," said Juan.

He was wrong. Elaine hadn't dated anyone in high school. She hadn't dated anyone in college either. What was the point? More than fifty percent of all marriages ended in divorce. And those that didn't held the two participants trapped in a cycle of unhappiness.

Why bother? All Elaine needed was her books to keep her warm at night. She was happy getting lost in a story where she knew how it ended. And most stories she read ended in tragedy, thus confirming that true love was a made-up concept by the Hallmark Channel.

"Just a coffee," Juan said.

"See you next Taco Tuesday, Juan." Elaine left a tip on the counter and headed out the exit.

The fall air was brisk. She cradled her book to her chest. Her cell phone buzzed in her pocket. Elaine backed up off the sidewalk and under an awning to answer it. She wasn't one to walk and talk, or worse, walk and text. Safety first, especially since she was often carrying one of her precious books in her bag.

Elaine pulled her phone out of her bag to see that it was a text from Mary. "Hurry back," it read. "Exciting news."

Elaine could use some exciting news. Jobs as a librarian were hard to come by in today's world. Many circulation desks were turning digital. Like the science fiction novels she detested, artificial intelligence was taking over her world. If they didn't figure out something to increase circulation at the library and get more bodies into the building, Elaine's job might be in jeopardy in the near future.

"On my way," she texted back. Then put her phone back into her bag.

Elaine waved to a few people she knew as she headed back down the main street. She'd lived in this town her whole life, deciding to stay after her parents' latest divorce. Elaine had gotten the house in the second divorce. It had always been the one constant in her life, and so she'd decided to stick close to it. Her parents were long gone; this town had always felt like home to Elaine. So, she'd staked her roots.

She liked the predictability of small-town living. She liked knowing all of her neighbors. She liked that change moved at a slow progress. Slow she could handle. Fast and unpredictable, she didn't like.

A man was moving slowly across the street. Elaine noted that he was tall, well-built. He walked with his shoulders straight like he had a purpose. His stride was long, sure. But his head was down, so she couldn't see his eyes.

He wasn't looking down at his phone. He was looking down at a book. More than wanting to see what color his eyes were, she wanted to know what he was reading.

A car rounded the corner. The reader was almost out of the crosswalk and to her side of the street. But he wasn't looking up, so he didn't see the car.

It took Elaine a second to make her decision. She dropped her bag to the ground. Then she dashed out into the street.

Her hands wrapped around his wrists, making sure to cradle the book he held. And then she gave the big man a tug.

They tumbled to the ground. Elaine felt the impact on her shoulders and bottom. She was going to be bruised in the morning. But what hurt most was her head. Her good deed for the day would leave her with a headache for the rest of the afternoon.

Brown. His eyes were brown. That was the last thing she remembered.

That and the title of his book. It was a science fiction book. One where the AI's take over the planet. Fitting.

And then everything went black.

CHAPTER FIVE

*L*uke paced the linoleum floors of the emergency room. The soles of his shoes peeled off the floor with something sticky each time, trying to hold him in place. He hadn't held still since they'd wheeled her in here.

Elaine was her name. He'd learned that when he'd grabbed her purse from the ground. He'd left behind the taco take-out bag as it was a casualty, and the ants were already on it. Her state ID had slipped from her purse, and he'd seen her name.

He wasn't the only one who knew her name. One of the EMT drivers had known her name, as well. It was a small town. Of course, everyone knew everyone else. He'd given Luke the side-eye. It was the first unwelcome gesture he'd been presented in this town.

He couldn't blame them. It was his fault. He was surprised more people weren't glaring at him from the sidewalk.

The accident had happened after the end of the lunch rush, so not many people had been out. He'd been able to whisk her to a bench and out of the road. The car that had been driving by had out of state plates, which was likely why they hadn't stopped. No ties to this community.

It hadn't been the driver's fault. It had been Luke's fault. He hadn't been paying attention, and she'd tried to save him. Then everything had gone in slow motion.

He'd felt the tug on his wrists. He'd turned, and there she was. She was backlit by the sun. Her hair wasn't all brown. There were golden highlights amongst the strands, and they sparked in the sun's spotlight.

The same golden flecks were in her brown eyes. Like twinkling stars in a hazel galaxy. Luke felt himself being pulled into warp speed. Everything around him went fuzzy, except her clear, sparkling eyes.

Her clear, sparkling eyes that were filled with alarm. Why was she alarmed? Was she feeling the pull too? She certainly was pulling him toward her.

Only her gaze wasn't filled with passion. It was filled with worry. No, that was fear. Actually, it looked more like terror.

Luke spotted the danger in his peripheral vision. A car was headed straight toward them. She was trying to save him.

Instincts took over. He swung their bodies around so that he was closest to the danger. But in doing so, she landed on her side. His body wasn't able to cushion her blow. The sparkles in her eyes dimmed, then went out as she closed them and lay unconscious.

He just wished it had been him unconscious on the street and not her.

She was still unconscious when the ambulance arrived. She was unconscious the whole ride. Though they'd let Luke ride with them.

"Mr. Jackson, your girlfriend has been moved to a room."

There was also that. In order to ride with Elaine in the ambulance, he'd had to tell a bit of a lie. Luke didn't hesitate to mislead the paramedic. He had no intention of letting Elaine out of his sight now that he was paying attention.

"Is she all right?" he asked as he followed the nurse.

"It just looks like a concussion. Nothing is broken. She should wake up soon."

Luke exhaled. But not fully. He wouldn't let go of his full breath until she walked out of the hospital on her own two feet. He didn't plan to leave until then.

The nurse led him into a room. There were two beds separated by a thin curtain. On one side of the curtain lay an older woman, snoring lightly. And then Luke saw her, Elaine.

She looked peaceful with her eyes closed. Like an angel dressed in blue and white polka dots. She made the hospital gown look like the height of fashion.

On the table sat her belongings. There was the bag with her book poking out. Luke tore his gaze away from her face and picked up the book.

Thomas Hardy's *Tess of the d'Urbervilles* was not one of Luke's favorites. He didn't like books where the decks were stacked against the protagonists. True, he wrote books about the underdog. But in his books, the protagonists eventually won and defeated the evil empire. Hardy didn't always play by those rules.

But it would seem those rules followed Luke around. This wasn't the first time someone else had suffered because of him. First, his mother. Then Paul. And now her.

A soft moan escaped Elaine. Luke went to her immediately. He held his breath while her eyes fluttered and then opened.

She stared at him. He stared at her. He held still as her gaze flicked over him, and he waited for recognition. And finally, there was a sparkle in her eye.

Luke's heart skipped a beat gazing into those coffee-colored supernovas. It was like a shot of adrenaline right into his chest. Her lips parted, and he forgot how to breathe. Her hand lifted off the bed, and he felt like he should take a knee, like a knight pledging fealty. Shakespeare rang in his ears, *what satisfaction canst though have tonight?*

"My book," she said.

Luke blinked. She wanted a book. No, he wanted her book. Her *Tess* book. Luke presented it to her like it was the flag from an opponent he'd just bested in a joust.

Elaine examined the book, brushing her fingers over the cover. She sighed as she cradled the book to her chest. Luke felt intensely happy as if he'd just given her the world.

"You saved my book," she said.

"You saved my life. We're even. But I'm afraid your taco didn't survive."

"Oh, Mary—ouch."

Elaine had tried to rise from the bed. But winced the moment her head came off the pillow.

Luke flew into action. At least he would have if he knew what to do. "Should I call the nurse? Do you need medication? Another pillow?"

Elaine rubbed tenderly at the back of her head. "No, no. There's just a bump here."

"I'll get the doctor," he said. "They should run more tests."

"For a bump on the head? I'm sure I'm fine."

Luke wasn't so sure. Before he could reach for the door, an older gentleman came in.

"Hello, Elaine. Pretending to be a superhero, I hear?"

"Just doing my civic duty, Dr. Brady," she said.

"It was my fault," said Luke. "I was looking down at—"

"Your cell phone?"

"No," both Luke and Elaine said at the same time.

"He was looking down at a book," said Elaine.

"Sounds like something you would do," the doctor said to Elaine. "I've brought your discharge papers. And one of the nurses let Mary know you're here and that you're fine. She said to take the rest of the day off, obviously. You're free to go when you feel up to it."

"Free to go?" said Luke. "Have you done a cat scan? X-rays?"

"There's no medical need for any of those things," said Dr. Brady. "It was just a bump on the head."

Paul's injury started as just a bruise on his back, and now he had chronic pains. Paul just had a twinge in his back before they discovered it was more. Luke's mother had had a few cramps and dizzy spells before she'd been taken by her ailment. There could always be something more lurking beneath the surface.

"Just take a few aspirins, and you'll be right as rain in the morning," said the doctor.

'Thank you, Dr. Brady."

"Shouldn't she at least be under observation?" asked Luke.

"You look after her tonight then," said the doctor. "You're qualified as her boyfriend."

And with that, he ducked out into the hall. The older woman on the other side of the curtain continued snoring lightly. Luke turned to face Elaine slowly. He sensed he was turning to face a firing squad. He was right.

Her narrowed gaze and pinched expression confirmed his suspicions. "Did he say you're my boyfriend?"

CHAPTER SIX

Elaine's head throbbed. Her mouth was a bit fuzzy, and the words didn't feel right on her tongue. They also didn't sound completely coherent to her ears.

She'd been dreaming of dancing at a May fair. Tess had met the man she would fall in love with at the fair. In the book, Tess had made eyes with Angel Clare across a bonfire. Elaine was making eyes with a man in her dream. Only instead of across a bonfire, he'd been standing across a street. And there was no one else there dancing. There were just cars between them as they flirt-gazed at one another.

She'd opened her eyes to see the man she'd been flirting with in her dreams standing over her. His gaze wasn't saying come hither. It was filled with compassion and care. She might be delirious, but there looked like a hint of devotion. Which was madness. She didn't know this man. But she did know that any man looking at a woman he did not truly know with devotion would only spell her doom. It said so in her favorite book, which he was holding.

And then it all came back to her. But what she was still having trouble understanding was why anyone would think he was her boyfriend.

She did not date. She had no plans to ever date or marry or lose her heart to the madness of love. But Dr. Brady was already gone, and she was left with him.

"Elaine …"

And he knew her name. This man who people thought was her boyfriend. Which he clearly was not. She didn't date. She didn't even know his name.

"Let me explain."

He came closer to the bed. She should scoot away. She should call for the doctor. But his gaze held her in place. The only thing between them was the massive tome of *Tess*.

"They would only let me ride in the ambulance if I was in some way related to you. So, I told them I was your boyfriend."

Okay, well, that was logical. She had saved his life and his book from flattening. It made sense that he'd want to accompany her to ensure she was well. He was showing signs of Angel Clare, the hero of *Tess of the d'Urbervilles* who'd decided to become a farmer to preserve his intellectual freedom outside his family of clergymen. The man looming over her looked like he could be a farmer with his strong arms and broad shoulders. And he'd brought her book along with them to the hospital, so he couldn't be that bad.

"I couldn't let you go by yourself, not when your fall was my fault …"

Logical and responsible. Not at all like Alec d'Urberville, the villainous, manipulative wealthy son who becomes obsessed with Tess. Though Tess rebukes Alec at every turn, he manages to ruin her body and soul. No, this man was no Alec. He looked far too capable and authoritative.

"Not until I knew you were okay."

"I'm okay," Elaine said. There had been an ache at the back of her skull. But since she'd begun listening to his dulcet voice, the pain had ebbed away. She couldn't let him know that. It was entirely logical that a stranger's voice could make her feel better. "Dr. Brady said so."

"Be that as it may, I would feel much better if you stayed in the hospital overnight." He pulled up a chair and sat at her right side. His eyes now on level with hers. "I would stay with you."

That should not have sent a shiver of warmth through her body. Mainly because one did not shiver when they were warm. But shiver she did as the toasty feeling reached down to her toes.

"Are you cold?" He reached for the blanket at the edge of the bed.

Elaine had the absurd notion to snuggle down into the uncomfortable mattress and await this man, this stranger, to tug up the threadbare hospital sheet and tuck her in. She couldn't remember the last time she'd been tucked in. Certainly not by her parents, who were more interested in arguing with one another than paying her any attention.

"I'm not sleeping in a hospital." Elaine sat up and immediately regretted the action. She winced as the pain from her head returned. She winced again when she realized she was wearing only a thin hospital gown, and her legs were bare.

The stranger in the seat rose and confirmed he was far more Angel than Alec when he turned his back. So, he was a caretaker, a gentleman, as well as a book-lover.

"What's your name?" Elaine asked as she slipped on her skirt under the bedsheets.

The man hesitated.

"You don't want to tell me your name?"

"No," he said. "I mean, yes." His shoulders bunched, and he let out a breath. "I just… It's Luke, like the Jedi."

"What's a Jedi?"

His head swiveled around, reminding Elaine of an owl. His eyes were even as wide as the winged creature. She was dressed now, so she knew he wasn't peering at her body as she straightened her blouse.

"Luke Skywalker," he said.

"Oh," said Elaine as she stepped into her shoes. "That's a *Star Trek* character, right?"

Luke made a choking sound. The rest of his body uncoiled until he stood facing her once more.

Elaine got the notion that she'd gotten that answer wrong. "Sorry," she shrugged. "I don't watch much television."

His grimace was slow to melt away. Elaine watched transfixed as it turned from incredulity to amazement. Then he gave her a sheepish smile.

"It doesn't matter," he said. "It's not important. What is important is your health."

She picked up the discharge papers and waved them in front of his nose. "I've got a clean bill of health. Says so right here."

And with that, she stood up. And nearly fell back onto the bed. Luke's arms were around her before her body touched the mattress.

There went that shiver again. Like a warm cup of tea while she was curled up in a window seat reading her favorite book. That's what it was like to be in this man's embrace.

"Where do you think you're going?" he asked.

Elaine gazed into Luke's eyes. They were brown, like hers. But there were small twinkles in them, like stars. She'd read the flowery language of eyes twinkling in the more romantic sections of books. But the twinkle always faded away by the third act. Elaine stepped out of his embrace, and he let her go but continued to stand too close to her.

"Home," she said. "It's been a long day. I want to take that aspirin and go back to sleep."

"Back to sleep after a concussion?"

"Look Skywalker—"

"It's Luke."

"Luke. It was just a bump. It could've been much worse. I'm lucky I live in the twenty-first century. Back in the Victorian age, a scratch could mean certain death."

"A bump could be something different beneath the surface," said Luke.

"But it's not. I'm fine. And I'm glad you're fine. I'd say keep your head out of those dangerous books while you're walking, but then ..." Elaine held up her own book. "I'm guilty of that, too."

Elaine stepped around him, but he reached for her. He only rested his fingertips on her forearm. But the light touch was enough to stop her in her tracks.

"I ruined your lunch," he said. "Let me take you to dinner."

"I've got food at home."

"Let me take you home."

"It's within walking distance."

"Let me walk you."

Elaine took a deep breath. If she'd known that when she'd saved this man's life that he'd attach himself to her, then she would have ... well, she still would've done it. The best thing for her to do was to set the record straight.

"Luke, you know you're not really my boyfriend, right?"

Something passed over his features. Something that made Elaine take in a tiny inhale of breath and hold it. His gleaming brown gaze flicked over her, going from the top of her head, down to her toes, and back up again until their gazes connected. Once again, Elaine felt that heat. But it wasn't a shiver this time. It felt like tiny bursts of fire sparking all over her skin, like Fourth of July sparklers.

"You should also know that I don't want a boyfriend," she said when she found her voice. "I don't date."

Luke frowned. "You don't date?"

"Nope. I philosophically disagree with it."

His grin wasn't predatory. It was curious. But Elaine felt like she was caught, even though she was the one closest to the door.

"Like ever?" he asked.

"Like never," she confirmed.

"Well, that's perfect," he said. "Because I'm awful at dating."

His smile was genuine. So, why did Elaine feel a sense of disappointment that he wasn't pushing the issue? He looked perfectly happy to not date her.

"I still want to take you out," he said. "As friends. A thank-you-for-saving-my-life dinner. You can't say no. I owe you my life."

"You said we were even."

"I forgot to add on the tip."

CHAPTER SEVEN

"You have a date?"

"It's not a date," Luke said to Paul when he got home later that night.

The walk to Elaine's home was uneventful, mainly because he kept his mouth mostly shut. He wasn't sure if the silence was awkward or companionable. He was far too busy watching for any signs of stress or strain from her. But her gait was steady. She didn't wobble or miss a step.

She wouldn't let him call an Uber. Apparently, there weren't any in this small town. There weren't taxis either. Either you walked, or you called someone for a ride. Most people didn't need a ride unless they were going out of the town to one of the farms or ranches.

So, they'd walked.

Elaine had winced when she'd climbed the steps to her small brownstone. Luke had balled his hands into fists so that he wouldn't reach out to her. He'd been around enough wounded soldiers to know the high price of pride. But he had stayed one step behind her in case he needed to catch her.

Was it wrong that part of him had wanted her to fall back into his arms so that he could hold her again?

"It's not a date," Luke repeated, but to himself this time. "It's a thank-you dinner."

"Because she saved your life?" said Paul.

"Yeah."

"From a book?"

"I was reading a book while walking into the street."

"What book?" Maggie Banks, Dylan's wife, spoke up from the kitchen counter. She was lifting food out of Tupperware and placing it onto plates. Paul's fridge was stocked with foods for days after a few of the wives, and their husbands, had stopped by to introduce themselves. Maggie's offering was hot dogs and chicken nuggets.

"It was my book," said Luke. "I'd grabbed a copy from the local bookstore to sign for a young man I met at the library."

"Dylan got me to read your first book," said Maggie as she pulled out ketchup and mustard. "I was surprised I liked it. I'm not usually one for space wars, but I loved the underdog story."

Of course, she did. There were dogs running all under her feet.

"I only wished there was a love story," Maggie said.

"There is a love story," said Luke.

"Her true love died before the story starts," Maggie protested. "It's been two books. I think she should fall in love again. Don't you?"

Luke pursed his lips. Every female reader he came across had this same complaint. It wasn't enough that a female heroine led a ragtag army to victory in two books. They weren't satisfied until someone's heart was on the line.

"Well, Luke only writes what he knows," said Paul, "and he's never been in love."

"You've never been in love?" asked Maggie.

"No, I haven't," said Luke, glaring over Maggie's head at Paul. "But I know what it looks like."

That sobered his friend up. Paul knew the love story of Luke's parents, along with its tragic ending.

"Your father was a widow?" said Maggie.

Luke nodded.

"He never found love again after your mother passed?"

"He didn't see a need to. Some kinds of love only happen once, especially that kind that hits you square in the eyes and knocks you off your feet. When that happens, it's typically just the one time."

"Sounds like this woman knocked you off your feet," said Maggie.

She certainly had. Quite literally. Elaine was a small thing, too. It was a wonder she'd managed it.

But Luke knew he wasn't in love. This was simply an attraction. Possibly gratitude.

No, it was definitely an attraction. He'd felt a tug of something when he'd seen Elaine earlier in the day, sitting in the restaurant reading that tragic book. He'd felt it when she'd tugged him out of harm's way, and the sun spotlighted her beauty. He saw it again when she woke in the hospital.

"He knocked me square off my feet," said Paul, "and I'm not in love with him."

Luke shot Paul a dirty look. Paul leaned back in his chair with a cheeky grin.

"What's her name?" asked Maggie.

"Elaine. Elaine Reynolds."

"Ohhh," Maggie grimaced.

"What?" asked Luke. "Why, ohhh?"

"Well, the thing about Elaine—"

Maggie didn't get to finish telling him the thing about Elaine. The dogs began to bark as two other women came into the back door. Luke had learned quickly that knocking on doors was not a habit on the ranch. Neither was locking doors.

Two other wives entered the back door carrying plastic containers. Luke was momentarily diverted by the smell of curried spices as Ruhi Jeffries, another wife here but also the daughter of Dr. Patel, came into the back door. At her back was Ginger Collins, another wife, but also the state senate representative.

The conversation halted for five whole minutes as the women shuffled around the kitchen, making their own pleasant conversation, fussed over Paul, and piled more food into the refrigerator.

"What's the thing about Elaine Reynolds?" Luke prompted Maggie at the first lull in the friendly banter.

"Elaine Reynolds?" asked Ginger. "I remember her from high school. I haven't seen her in forever."

"She's still working at the library," said Ruhi. "I see her when I take the kids in to study. It's the quietest place in town."

"I remember she always used to have her head in a book," said Ginger

"But only the tragedy books," said Ruhi. "Like the ones we had to read as part of English class, she'd read them for fun. More than once."

Was that it? Was that the thing about Elaine? She was a lover of classic literature?

"Is she still not dating?" asked Ginger.

"I don't think so," said Ruhi. "I know Juan has been after her since she got back from college, and she always turns him down."

"Well, Luke here has a date with her," said Maggie.

"It's not a date," said Luke.

"Which is a good thing because Luke is terrible on dates," said Paul.

"Why is he terrible?" asked Ginger.

Before Luke could defend himself, his best friend, who was taking way too much pleasure out of this, continued. "His palms sweat for one. He always winds up spilling something on himself, or on the date. And he can never close the kiss. He can't read signals."

Luke opened his mouth. But he had nothing. All of that was true. Paul smirked, knowing he'd spoken nothing but facts that Luke couldn't dispute. Luke always felt like it was his first time in the cockpit when he was around a woman he liked. And the flight always ended with him crashing and burning. Whereas Paul Hanson could swagger onto the scene with confidence, brandishing his blaster pistol, and having the women fall at his boots.

"We can help," said Maggie.

"Maggie, you've never been on a first date in your life," said Ruhi. "The first time you met Dylan, he proposed a marriage of convenience."

"And look where I am now," said Maggie, brandishing the rock on her left hand. "Besides, the same thing happened between you and Sean, and look at the two of you."

"I've had plenty of bad first dates," said Ginger. "I can help."

"It's not … I'm not …" But the women were all talking over Luke, planning out his first date with Elaine. He had to wait for another lull in the banter before he could ask the question that plagued him. "So, why doesn't she date?"

Maggie shrugged. "I remember that her parents went through a really nasty divorce. When she was a kid, Elaine was at the library every day until they closed."

"Then she would come to the church until late," said Ruhi. "She'd be reading in the pews during evening service. That probably had something to do with it."

"But she's really smart," said Ginger.

"And really pretty," said Ruhi.

"She loves books," said Maggie. "And you write books. This is a match made in heaven."

"Wait," said Luke. "Slow down. The woman doesn't want to date, but you all are trying to match us like we're going to get married."

Not a single one of the wives denied the statement. They were all sizing him, as though they were taking his measurements for his wedding tuxedo.

Luke looked around for Paul and realized his friend had already made it out the back door, moving faster than his injured hip should allow. He was stuck in a room full of female matchmakers on a ranch where soldiers were known to tie the knot within three months. He was in trouble.

But, for some reason, he didn't run.

CHAPTER EIGHT

Despite being extremely tired after the day's events, Elaine couldn't sleep that night. She couldn't shake the feeling that she was being watched. Hazel brown eyes peered back at her. The eyes reminded her of the browning of a first edition book. There were stories in those eyes. They whispered to Elaine to open the covers, crack the spine, and get comfortable in her favorite reading chair.

The watchful gaze wasn't threatening. It was welcoming. So, why couldn't she sleep?

Probably because she did want to know the story within Lieutenant Luke Jackson's sparkling brown eyes.

Elaine threw the covers off and got out of bed. The dull ache in her skull didn't allow her to get too far. What if he was right? What if there was more damage than the doctor's saw? There had to be if she was thinking about Lieutenant Jackson and feeling something close to anticipation for their thank-you dinner in twelve hours.

Twelve hours? How was she going to pass the time? Mary had insisted she take the day off to rest and recover. So, Elaine did what she did at nights and on the weekends, she pulled open an old book.

Lieutenant Jackson had saved her copy of *Tess of the d'Urbervilles*. Elaine was still a little surprised that she'd risked her treasured book to save his life. But only a little.

Elaine opened the book. She was just at the part of the story where

Tess met the man she would marry. Elaine settled down to read the slow burn love develop between Tess and Angel Clare while the two worked on a dairy farm. Elaine turned the page, knowing that at the end of this chapter. Angel would propose to Tess. Elaine also knew that Tess would hesitate to accept Angel's offer because of the dark secrets of her past that involved the villain Alec d'Urberville.

There were always dark secrets in people's past. Those secrets were what come back to wreak havoc. In any love story. Her parents had tons of secrets; secret affairs, secret bank accounts, secret trips, secret secrets.

At this point in Tess's story, Elaine always had to push herself forward. Hardy rarely wrote happily-ever-afters. He spoke about real life. That's why Elaine enjoyed his tales.

They spoke of the harshness of class and society, the futility of relationships and love. It didn't matter that Tess's shame wasn't her fault. Human beings did wretched things in the name of love. That's why Elaine avoided the institution at all costs, starting with dating.

Dating was the gateway drug to love. So, Elaine always just said no.

A knock sounded at her front door just as Angel and Tess were confessing their secrets after their wedding. Angel has told Tess about an affair he had with a woman in his youth. Tess has accepted this and then tells her dark secret; that she was assaulted by Alec and delivered his stillborn baby. Elaine placed her bookmark at the passage where Angel says he can't get past Tess's shame, and their love begins to crumble. Elaine decided to let the lovers linger in the possibility that their love would last for a few minutes and went to open the door.

The sun was low in the sky as she pulled open the door. The day was nearly over. She had gotten so lost in the story.

"How are you feeling?" Mary stood on the stoop.

"Fine," said Elaine. And she did feel fine. That's what a good book with big words and a thought-provoking theme did to the brain.

"They said you saved someone in a car accident?" Mary pushed past Elaine, coming into the house.

"No, I saved a pedestrian from a car accident. He was reading while walking."

"Sounds like a crime you would commit."

Elaine blew a harsh breath. "I would never put my books in danger."

Mary plopped down on the couch. "Who was this pedestrian?"

"A soldier," said Elaine.

"A soldier?" Mary parroted.

"A lieutenant."

"A lieutenant?

Elaine knew what was coming next, and she blamed all those Harlequins Mary inhaled in-between the stacks. Sometimes three a day. Those slim, lightweight novelettes rotted the brain.

"From the Purple Heart Ranch?" asked Mary. "One of the taken ones? Or a new one?"

"I think he's new."

Mary bounced up on her toes and squealed, which hurt Elaine's head. "This is it. Fate has found you. You know what happens on that ranch."

Elaine had heard the tales of love at first sight and marriages of convenience turning into the real deal up on that plot of land. There were even enemies-to-lovers relationships that had happened recently between a soldier and the new state senator. It all sounded like fairytales. Elaine never read any fairytales.

"I'm not going to the ranch," said Elaine.

"But you're going to see him again. You saved his life."

"He's taking me out to a thank-you dinner."

"A date."

"A dinner."

"What are you going to wear?"

"I hadn't thought about it."

Mary went straight for her closet. She tugged Elaine's cardigans off hangers and tossed them to the ground along with any buttoned-up blouses. Finally, Mary pulled out a summer dress that would show of Elaine's shoulders and bust line.

Elaine backed out of the closet, arms up to ward off her friend and boss. But Mary advanced.

"It's not a date," Elaine insisted. "I don't date, remember."

"Elaine, you can't be alone for the rest of your life."

"I'm not alone. I have my books."

Elaine waved her hand at the tomes taking up half of her closet. She had far more books than she did articles of clothing. Clothes changed with the seasons. They went into and out of style. They needed to be altered or replacements purchased as the body changed.

"I know your parents' divorce was ugly…"

Elaine turned from her friend and began straightening the books on her closet shelves. Unlike clothing, books were evergreen. The stories inside never changed. They always remained the same. And right where she'd left them.

"… but not all relationships are like that."

"What? You mean not ripping out each other's hearts only to use jumper cables so you can feel that euphoria of endorphins over and over again?"

Elaine's parents had gotten engaged ten times before finally marrying. They got divorced three times and were now planning a vow renewal for their fourth marriage. Her parents were addicted to that feeling of love, the racing heart, the rush of adrenaline, that feeling of falling. Elaine had always preferred two feet on the ground and a clear head. She saw from a tender age that her parents were alternately painfully cruel and lovingly suffocating toward each other. What they called it was love. She never wanted any part of that freak show.

"And my life is full," she said. "Just look at my TBR pile."

The pile Elaine indicated was massive tomes that rivaled *War and Peace*. She preferred the Shelly sisters to Austen. *Frankenstein* was her kind of happy ending, the monster crying over his creator's dead body. That was a better approximation of true love in Elaine's eyes.

"And I have my work at the library," she continued. "We need to do all we can to get more circulation."

"Speaking of that, I met Walker Skye the other day. He's going to do a reading and a signing at the library. People are already signing up. Don't roll your eyes!"

Too late. Elaine's eyes had rolled all the way back in her head. She just couldn't understand the draw of space wars. Oh, wait. *Star Wars.* That's what Lieutenant Jackson had meant. The one with Luke Skywalker. She only knew that because the actor who had played the part had voiced a number of middle-grade books that were shelved at the library.

"Promise me you'll be on your best behavior when you meet him," said Mary.

"What do you think I'll do? Spit on him?"

Mary gave her a knowing look.

"I will use my best manners." Elaine held up her right hand like when she and Mary were in Girl Scouts. But she didn't tuck in her thumb and pinky finger as was custom.

"And smile."

Elaine frowned.

"And make polite conversation."

Elaine grimaced.

"And don't put down his books."

"I can't do that. I haven't ever picked them up. And I doubt I ever will."

CHAPTER NINE

Luke arrived at her place five minutes before the appointed time. He was chronically five minutes early, a leftover from his time in the service. If you weren't early, you were late. He was usually fifteen minutes early, but he didn't want to look like a creeper. That was one of the rules the brides of the Purple Heart Ranch instilled in him during their coaching session; be eager, but play it cool. Women can tell the difference.

He'd been sure to wear dark clothing in case he did spill something on himself. He'd been sure to avoid liquids on the drive over. A puddle of mud was in the crack of Elaine's walkway. Luke managed to step over it without incident.

All signs were pointing to good.

He took the stairs, one at a time, to avoid the possibility of tripping over his own feet. Once at her door, he knocked three times. His palms were dry, another good sign.

He knew that technically, this wasn't a date. And that was fine. He really shouldn't be trying to date someone when he had no firm plans of where his life would take him next. His new job of full-time author didn't require him to live in any one place. His main concern was getting Paul back in a good place, whether his friend liked it or not. So, no, Luke didn't need to get into a serious relationship right now.

The door opened, and all his best-laid plans vanished from his mind.

Elaine stood in dark jeans and a simple t-shirt. She was dressed far too casually for their outing to be considered a date. Still, she looked like a knockout nonetheless.

Her hair was pulled back in a messy bun, the way women fixed it when they wanted it to appear they weren't trying too hard, but it was evident that they had. Her makeup was slight as though to look like it wasn't there. Though her lashes were long enough to be wingtips, he could see the outline of the eyeliner there. There was a touch of gloss on her rosy lips, even though her tongue struck out to lick at her lower lip.

This was a good sign, right? When a woman looked as though she hadn't tried real hard, it usually meant she'd had. At least that's what the brides had told him.

Luke's eyes caught and held on Elaine's lip. He watched as it moved, stretching wide and then forming an O and finally pressing closed.

Oh, wait. She had been forming words. She had been speaking to him. What had she just said?

"You look amazing," he said. A compliment was always a perfect response.

"Thanks," she said. "I was going for a comfortable night out with my potential new friend."

"So, I have potential?" Luke waggled his brows, which he hoped looked cute and endearing.

Elaine's brows pulled together, and she leaned back a bit. She reached behind and pulled the door closed. Great, he was already off to the wrong foot with her.

Luke went to follow Elaine down the steps. Unfortunately, he misstepped, and his foot stepped into one of the potted plants.

The brown guts spilled and exposed the plant's roots. Luke bent to save the plant, just as Elaine bent down as well. Their heads collided.

Elaine's hand went to her forehead. Luke's hands went there, as well. Their fingers intertwined. Their gazes locked.

The wince she'd worn fell away. The sparkle returned to her brown gaze in the pale moonlight. Luke brushed his thumb across her forehead in a windshield wiping motion.

"We've gotta stop bumping into each other," she said.

That was the last thing he wanted to do. Though he didn't relish the small hurt he'd given her. Her skin was satin in his hands. There was no bruise forming on her forehead. He should give her her head back, but he liked the feeling of her in the palm of his hand. It felt right.

Elaine blinked, snuffing out the sparkles. She turned her head. When she did, she broke his hold on her. She reached for and repotted the plant. Luke brushed the dirt off his shoe. The dry dirt turned to mud in his sweaty hands.

"This is a nice looking house," said Luke when they were down the steps and on a level playing field. "Do you have roommates?"

"No, it's my house. It's been mine since I was twelve. After my parents' second divorce, they tried for split custody. But, instead of me going to my dad's apartment every other day and living out of a suitcase and backpack, the judge made it so that they would take turns and come stay at the house so that I could stay put."

"That was very responsible of them."

Her gaze tracked up to his. "It was my idea. I hated living out of a suitcase, especially when there were mostly books in my suitcase instead of clothes. It was pretty heavy."

"Divorce is hard. Are they remarried?"

"Yes, they are. To each other. This is their fourth time getting remarried. This last one was a destination wedding. I stayed home. I'm a little too old to be a flower girl, don't you think."

The words were flippant, but Luke saw the crinkle at the edge of her eyes. He saw the tug at the corner of her forced smile. Her lashes fluttered, like a wounded bird's.

Elaine hugged her arms around herself in the breezeless night. Luke noted that she alternately scratched at her chest or balled her hands into fists as she talked about her parents.

"What about your parents?" she asked.

"My mother died when I was very young."

"I'm sorry."

Luke shrugged, scratching at his own chest. "I was too young to remember her." He balled his hand into a fist. "She died from complications due to pregnancy."

Elaine's face contorted into horror.

Luke shook his head, hoping to clear the horror. He hoped she didn't ask. He didn't like to talk about it. But he knew that if Elaine asked, he would tell her.

He would tell her how the pregnancy was high risk, but his mother decided it was worth it. He was worth it. He'd tell Elaine how his mother had nearly died delivering him. That she only survived his first year before she succumbed to the ravages of her body.

But Elaine didn't ask.

"And your father?"

Luke scratched at his chest with his balled fist. "He never remarried. He said she was the one. You'd think he'd be bitter that he lost her. But he's not. He says every day that he was blessed to find her. Not everyone finds their true love."

Elaine snorted. Then covered her mouth. "I'm sorry. That was insensitive."

Luke quirked an eyebrow. "Right. You don't believe in love."

Elaine waggled her head. "I believe that people can care deeply for one another. But the concept of love ..." She shook her head instead of completing the sentence. "No, not love. Passion. Passion like that is dangerous. It's a chemical reaction, a rush of endorphins that increases your blood flow and makes your heart race and your breath catch. That's medically dangerous. Who wants to live in that state all their lives?"

Elaine lifted a brow at him. Luke felt a rush of endorphins when their gazes connected. His heart didn't skip a beat, but it did speed up. His breath didn't catch, but he felt light-headed all the same.

"It might start that way," he said. "That's your body's fight or flight response. But you can choose to run away from it or stick around. When you stick around, the body will find a plateau because that's its natural state. It wants stasis, so that person that initiated those feelings if you both stick around, the feeling will change to something normal."

She'd been eying him skeptically, but there was a slight twitch of her cheek. The twitch pulled down the doubtful brow. It lifted the slight frown. Did part of her want to believe him? Because all of him wanted her to.

"Where are we headed?" she asked.

"I figured since I ruined your taco, I owe you one."

"It wasn't my taco. It was my boss, Mary's taco."

"Your boss? What exactly is it that you do?"

"I work at the library."

Mary? The library? Where he was speaking tomorrow.

Did Elaine know who he was? No, he didn't think she did. Especially not with how she had reacted to him since their first meeting. He didn't have any pictures on his author profile. At first, because he needed to keep his anonymity as he was still in the service. But now that he was out, his publishers were pushing him to do more signings.

"We have a big day there tomorrow," Elaine continued. "Some hack author is coming to do signings."

CHAPTER TEN

He was making a good argument. But he wasn't raising his voice. So, was it an actual argument? What Luke had described between his parents sounded far different than what she'd experienced with her parents.

Gentleness. Kindness. Consideration.

Elaine preferred her parents apart than together. Their simpering anger was better than their wild passion. In any case, she didn't want to talk about love or passion anymore.

Luke had been guiding her, walking on the outside of the street. Actually, crossing over to the outside of the street each time they turned a corner. Seems he was determined if a car should hop the curb, it would hit him first. He was taking this hero thing a little too far. But she didn't say anything about it. She kept in step with him between her neighbor's picket fences and his strong shoulders.

He'd gone silent as they came up to the restaurant. He pulled the door of Castro's Mexican Cuisine open. Juan stopped in his tracks when he saw them.

"It's not a date," Elaine said as Juan tossed their menus on the table. "He's thanking me for saving his life."

Juan still gave Luke the stank eye as he took his order. Elaine winced when Luke asked for a substitution. Juan was usually annoyed at any alteration to his menu.

"I'm worried there might be a sneeze in your burrito," said Elaine, trying for the brevity they'd shared on the way here. But Luke seemed distracted. "Juan and I have never dated, in case you're wondering."

Luke turned back to her. She noted his body posture was rigid. He was sucking in his cheeks, as though he was trying to hold his tongue. His body was turned at an angle, as though he were shielding himself from her. Elaine realized she preferred his open chest from when he walked on the outside of the sidewalk.

"I've never dated anyone," she clarified. "Not that I wasn't asked. I just—"

"You don't believe in love."

Elaine nodded, but her head felt light like it was disconnected from her neck. Her hands fidgeted, and she wished she was holding a book. But she hadn't brought one with her tonight.

"You also don't appear to appreciate any literature that was written in the twenty-first century." He speared a tortilla chip into the bowl of salsa.

"What's that supposed to mean? I'm a librarian. Of course, I love books. You have something against libraries?"

"No, they are one of my favorite places in the world."

"Mine, too. I spent many an after school day there."

"Because of your parents?"

Why had she told him about her parents? Now, he'd think of her as some wounded animal. Which she was not.

She decided to change the subject. "Hey, what book were you reading when I saved your life?"

"The first Walker Skye book."

"Oh," she sighed. Her heart rate slowed. Her blood flow evened out until it was closer to still waters. Had he said a classic, any classic, it might have skipped a beat.

"Oh?" He leaned forward. Not quite crowding her space, but definitely crossing the line.

Elaine shrugged, not wanting to disparage the author like she promised Mary. Here was one of his fans, and Mr. Skye was coming to the library to talk. She might as well invite Luke to meet him. "He's doing a signing at the library tomorrow. You should come to meet him."

"I think I will come," he said. "But you don't seem excited to meet him."

"Military Science Fiction is not my cup of tea."

"Right, you're a Hardy girl."

"Hardy wrote important works about struggle and morality and the futility of love." She didn't mean to jump back on that subject. But here they were again.

"Futile is definitely a word I'd use to describe those books," said Luke. "There's no justice for Tess. She pays a hefty price because of what others did to her."

Now Elaine leaned forward, stepping over into Luke's territory. "No, it shows that if you succumb to passion, you will suffer."

"I think we read two entirely different books. I read a book where an abused woman finds love. But that love casts her off because of what someone else did to her. If you love someone, you're there through thick and thin. It says so in the vows."

"Not everyone keeps their promises." Elaine broke a tortilla chip in half and crumpled the pieces into the salsa bowl.

"That's a very sad fact. But it doesn't apply to all people." Luke scooped up the broken bits with a whole chip and plopped it all into his mouth.

She wouldn't hold his gaze. "You think Walker Skye's space war books are better. Those books are entirely unrealistic."

"Again, I disagree," Luke said after a sip of water. "They show the triumph of the human spirit. They show that an underdog can win, especially if he or she is backed by a support system. It shows that every person has value. At least that's what I get out of them."

"You're very passionate about these books."

"I read *Tess of the d'Ubervilles* and am making an informed comparison. I think you should give Walker Skye a try. To be fair."

Elaine brushed the crumbs and residual oil of the chips off her hands. "I suppose I should read a few chapters since the author is coming to my place of business."

Juan arrived then with their burritos. Luke offered the cook a smile, which was not returned. They ate in companionable silence. Luke steered the conversation away from love and books. He told her instead about his time in the military. He asked her questions about the town and its people. He listened more than he talked. He leaned forward, asking for details. If the military didn't work out, he might have a career in small-town journalism or detective work with the way he paid attention.

When the check came, Elaine reached for it. He held up his hands as if in defeat. His grin caught her off guard.

"No argument?" she said.

"I'm secure enough in my masculinity to have a woman pay for a five-dollar burrito." Luke waggled his eyebrows.

Elaine had to fight back a smile at the facial expression. She was finding it endearing.

"It was actually seven because you got extra guacamole." She counted out the cash, including a sizable tip for Juan for showing a modicum of civility.

"Looks like I'm a cheap date." Luke held up his hands. "Oops, sorry. Not a date."

"Right." But the word felt thick as guacamole on Elaine's tongue.

Luke offered her his arm as they walked out. "This is a gentlemanly gesture," he said when she hesitated. "It was very popular in the Victorian age."

Instead of arguing, Elaine found herself taking Luke's arm. They walked in silence for a few moments; bellies full, safe topics exhausted. The silence was easy. She liked the warmth of his body. The strength of his forearm. The certainty of his stride. And then she was being crushed against his body.

The dinging bell of a cyclist whizzed in her ear. Her nose was crushed into the side of Luke's neck. She got a strong whiff of after-shave, cilantro, and male. Her belly grumbled as though it was nowhere near full and was hankering for a large helping of dessert.

"I saved your life that time," he said.

"So, we're even?" she asked, her voice breathy as she gazed up at him.

The way he smiled at her made her take another whiff of him. She felt her blood flow increase and pool in her fingertips and cheeks. Her heart didn't skip a beat, but she became acutely aware of its pounding.

"Yes," he said.

His gaze was on her lips. His hands held her elbows. There was an inch between them, but she could still feel his heart.

"We're even," he said.

Disappointment washed through her, causing her to shiver. What reason would they have to see each other again now?

"You cold?" Luke pulled his jacket off.

Elaine ducked away from the romantic gesture. The last thing she needed was to have his scent embedded in her clothes. "Just tired. I think I need to lie down."

"Of course." Concern shone through his gaze. "Let's get you home."

He slipped back into his jacket and wrapped an arm around her waist. She knew the arm was to support her, though she didn't need it. Still, she didn't shrug it off.

Elaine couldn't remember the last time she'd been held, hugged. She felt Luke's pulse thrumming as his hand rested on her hip. She felt his heart beating where her shoulder met his chest. For a moment, her world tuned to the sounds of another.

She walked to his rhythm all the way to her house, her safe haven. They climbed the steps together. There was still some dirt from the spilled pot. But the plant was fine, not wilting at all.

Elaine turned to Luke at the top of the stair. He had stepped down a rung. So they were eye level.

"Tonight was fun," he said.

"You argue literature with all your friends?"

"No, most of my friends prefer hack military science fiction to literature," he said the word *literature* with a snotty accent.

Elaine felt like a snob. She wished she'd behaved better. That she'd kept some of her opinions to herself. She didn't want him thinking badly about her.

Because they were going to be friends.

Should she invite him inside for coffee? No, that's what someone on a date would do. What would a friend do?

"I'll see you tomorrow," Luke said, stepping down one stair.

"Tomorrow?"

"For the signing with the hack author." There was a bite behind his smile.

"He's probably not a hack," Elaine admitted.

"Hang on a second." Luke ran to his truck. He was back in a moment with a book. "See for yourself."

It was a copy of Walker Skye's first book. "So, now I have homework."

"That's how dinner with friends ends. Had this been a date, there might have been a kiss."

She held his gaze this time. Sweat collected in the palm of her hands. Her fingertips tingled with the need to touch. And then his hand was between them.

"Goodnight, Elaine."

Elaine put her hand in his. Her palms were clammy. His were damp too. But there was heat between them. That heat evaporated the droplets.

Luke took the last few steps down the stairs and hopped in his truck. Elaine stayed for a few moments on the front steps, holding the book to her chest. Then she cracked open the cover.

CHAPTER ELEVEN

"You know that was a sign, right?"

Luke turned to Paul, but only for a second. He had to keep his eyes on the road. Not only did he need to worry about other cars, but he also needed to worry about pedestrians. Most were looking down at their phones and not flipping through a book.

"What are you talking about?" said Luke.

"That lingering handshake? Totally a sign that she wanted you to kiss her."

"It was not." Was it? "She did not." Did she? "It wasn't a date. Therefore, there were no signs."

Except maybe there were signs. When Luke had thought Elaine was cold and he'd gone to do the gentlemanly thing with his jacket, she'd stepped back. But she hadn't shrugged him off when he put his arm around her as they walked. In fact, she kinda burrowed herself into his side like he was a favorite pillow.

They had been silent as they walked. But it wasn't uncomfortable. It was pleasant. They'd said everything they had to say back at the restaurant, and man had they said a lot.

Then there was that handshake. Luke had certainly felt sparks. Perhaps, she had too. He'd heard her gasp, only because he'd been paying such close attention to everything about her.

Her lips had parted. Her gaze had dipped. Had they dipped to his lips? He wasn't sure. He couldn't take his eyes off her at the time to determine where she was looking.

Had it been a sign?

Luke was normally a good read of people. He had to be in his former line of work in the armed services. But it truly served him in his current line of work as a novelist.

Writing wasn't just about plot. It was about character growth and development. That's what truly got his readers hooked; that he could get to the heart of what his heroine, and even the villain, wanted. What motivated them to go after a goal. Which conflicts he could put in their path to test them and get them to grow. That's what got him five-star reviews.

But Luke couldn't read Elaine. She was a walking, talking, reading contradiction. He knew he'd scare her off if he pushed. But man did he want to push. He just didn't want her running scared before he could pull her in.

"You might be right," Luke admitted.

"I know I'm right," snorted Paul. "I know women."

"Not this one. She's afraid of emotions. Her parents' love story sounded warped."

Luke told Paul what Elaine had told him about her parents' divorces and remarriages. He could fill in the blanks that the Reynolds's passion was destructive. He'd seen the end product in their daughter.

"That's interesting," said Paul. "Your parents' love story is on the other end of that spectrum."

"What am I gonna do?"

"Why do you even like this girl?" asked Paul.

Good question. "She's beautiful. She's smart."

All surface-level observations.

"She's opinionated," he went on.

Which might turn off another man, but he liked the challenge.

"She's a strong woman," he continued.

She had to be after what her parents had put her through as a child. She'd come through the other end scarred, wounded. Like a soldier after a war. But like Luke, Elaine didn't have a visible scratch on her. All her hurts were on the inside.

"There's a softness to her. Something in her eyes that tells me she needs to be held."

"Another rescue," sighed Paul.

"What are you talking about?"

"It's clear as the plot of one of your books," said his friend. "You feel like you need to rescue everyone."

Luke opened his mouth to argue. Then closed it. Most of his relationships had been with women in the service. There were no wilting flowers there.

He had fallen for Jessica Kilmeade while she was in the infirmary. He'd started dating Tonya Horwitz after she was medically discharged, but that only lasted until she was on the mend.

He'd noticed Elaine when she was reading while eating a taco. But he'd felt that spark of something when she'd been lying unconscious in a hospital bed. Was he a rescue romantic?

"Wait?" said Paul. "You said she works at the library?"

"Yes," Luke said, parking in a visitor spot at said library. It was one of the last. When he'd come here the other day, he'd had his pick of spots.

"Did you tell her who you are?"

"Nope. She called Walker Skye a hack. Even though she's never read my books. I gave her a copy last night."

"This is gonna be good." Paul chuckled. "Better than watching a telenovela."

"I don't understand why you watch those. You don't even speak Spanish."

"Drama is clear in every language."

Paul hopped out of the car and winced. Luke held his tongue as his friend massaged his low back. He knew better than to notice Paul's pain.

The familiar pang of guilt washed over him. Then the guilt washed out of him when he spotted Elaine. She was behind the circulation desk. His book was in her hands. Anxiety took up the space where guilt fled.

"That her?" asked Paul.

Luke couldn't answer. He was too busy watching as Elaine's eyes scanned across the pages. She wasn't smiling. She wasn't frowning. Was that a thoughtful look? Did she hate it? Had she found a grammatical error? A plot hole?

"You said her favorite book is *Tess of the d'Urbervilles*?" asked Paul.

Luke wanted to shush the man like they were in a movie theater, and the opening credits were through. Paul was talking at the opening, pivotal scene that would set up the whole story. "I don't know if it's her favorite."

"A book where secrets destroy the life of the heroine?"

Luke had never noticed that theme. But, then again, he hadn't thought about the book much since the one time he'd had to read and write a paper about it in school.

"You are doomed, my friend," Paul said with glee, clapping Luke on the shoulder.

"Mr. Skye, we're so happy you're here." Mary, the librarian, was dressed more like a naughty librarian today. Her skirt was so tight her knees stayed pressed together as she walked. Her blouse had one too many buttons undone. Her make up could be seen from miles away.

"You have a full house awaiting your reading," said Mary. "We'll be ready in just a moment."

"Thank you, Ms. Charles. Everything looks great."

"Oh, no need to be so formal," she leaned in. "Please, call me Mary. I thought we might grab dinner afterward to celebrate—"

"Would you excuse me for just one moment?" asked Luke.

He walked away from the head librarian to the assistant at the circulation desk. Elaine didn't look up at his approach. Her nose was buried in his book. Was that a good sign? Maybe she was enjoying it. He had to find out.

"What do you think?" he asked.

Elaine looked up. It took a second before recognition dawned. Her expression changed from pensive to pleased. Luke felt something turn over inside him.

Elaine offered him a little smile as she reached for a cloth bookmark and put it in-between the pages. Luke felt a bit disappointed that she didn't dog-ear the page and leave a permanent imprint on his work.

"It's not bad," she said. "It's not Pulitzer material either. The writing flows. The descriptions aren't flowery, but they're evocative."

Luke's chest puffed up at all the compliments. He was ready to come clean that it was his pen that had written those flowing, evocative words.

"It's just that the relationships are unbelievable. I can't believe that these people would get behind an untried leader so quickly and believe in her so thoroughly."

It wasn't quite a slap in the face. It did shake off the puffy feelings in his chest.

"That's what happens when someone saves your life," Paul spoke from behind Luke. "In the book, the captain saved their lives, and now she feels a sense of loyalty to them and they to her. You ever notice that?"

Paul looked pointedly at Luke. Luke glanced at Paul. Elaine glanced between the two, clearly waiting patiently for an introduction to the newcomer.

"This is my friend, Major Paul Hanson," said Luke.

"Did you save Lieutenant Jackson's life, Major Hanson?"

"Not me," said Paul. "The lieutenant here is the hero. He threw his body on mine to protect me from a grenade," said Paul.

"That happen a lot around you?" Elaine asked Luke. "What is it? Do you attract danger?"

"No, I'm a regular guy," said Luke.

"Excuse me, Mr. Skye?"

Luke had heard many an explosion go off in his career in the military. Those four words were louder than a bomb.

"Can I get your autograph?" The woman held his two books to her ample bosom. Luke wasn't sure where to reach. Especially when the only thing he wanted to reach out to was Elaine.

Elaine's brow crinkled. Then realization dawned. He only saw it because he watched her so closely, but he was sure he saw her gaze shutter closed.

CHAPTER TWELVE

It always came down to secrets.

Elaine looked from the man she thought she was getting to know and down to the cover of the book she had been getting into. She was surprised she had been enjoying the bit of pulp fiction. There were thousands of words written on the page. But Luke had forgotten to tell her the most important ones. There were only two that mattered; that he was Walker Skye.

With one final glance at her, Luke took his place at the lectern. He'd lied to her.

Well, he hadn't stood in front of her and told her a bald-faced lie. But omission was just as strong. That's what her parents' fights had taught her.

Elaine wasn't sure if the two of them had ever cheated on one another. She doubted it. Who else would put up with the madness they inflicted on each other. She was their daughter, and she didn't want to deal with it.

But they'd kept secrets. They'd said hurtful things. Then the next hour, the next day, the next week, they'd take it back. Only to repeat the cycle the next month.

They never tired of fussing and fighting. They could cut each other so deep, not recognizing the collateral damage it did to those around them. Because just as much as they salted the wounds, they were also the salve. It was a sickness Elaine did not want to allow into her system.

Luke looked away from her. Before he turned, Elaine saw remorse was clear on his face. He hadn't tried to make amends with her. He hadn't tried to explain. He'd taken the buxom woman's book and signed; Walker Skye. There was a flourish with the Y in his last name. Or his fake last name.

Or maybe that was his real name. Elaine had no clue.

He walked up to the lectern, where his books were placed on display. It was a packed house, more people than had visited the library all week. He didn't glance at her when he spoke. His gaze remained cast down.

"I'm supposed to do a reading from my book, but I'd like to tell you a story you might not know instead."

Luke looked up then and found her gaze across the crowded room. But Elaine couldn't hold his gaze. How could she when she could no longer trust his words; the ones he spoke as well as what he'd written.

"I felt powerless as a child," he said. "My mother died because of me."

Gasps went around the audience. The audience was a good mix of men and women. But where the men were dressed in casual slacks and jeans, all of the women wore tight clothes and a pound of makeup.

Elaine had never seen half of them in the library. They were all here for the famous Walker Skye. The man who wrote strong female protagonists that led armies to defeat evil empires. Yet, here, her creator was peddling lies.

But wait? Hadn't he told her this the other night?

"My father always told me that it wasn't my fault. I even have letters where my mother tells me that her death wasn't my fault. She knew the risks going into the pregnancy. But she wanted to take the chance. In her letters, she told me I was worth it."

Every person was riveted to his words. Including Elaine. Something in her told her he was telling the truth.

"Every heroine I write is my mother. The woman I met in the letters. The woman that believes that everyone deserves a chance, even if it means that she doesn't make it in the end."

Elaine's anger was dying down. She had the urge to reach out to him. To grab his wrist and tug him out of danger. To take off her cardigan and wrap it around his shoulders.

Last night, Luke hadn't told her this part of the story. But why would he? She had disparaged his books before he could even say anything.

"I joined the military not only to do my part for this country that has provided so many opportunities. I did it because, well, I wanted to be someone's hero."

He wasn't looking at her, but Elaine felt his attention on her. She knew this information was more for her ears than his fans. Was this his apology?

"The reality of war is a harsh one. Both at home and on the war front. It's not always clean boots and pristine outfits. There's sweat. There's dirt. There's blood. Writing these stories was how I escaped, but it's also how I planned to make the world better. The military is how societies protect themselves. Science is how we try to understand the world. Fiction is how we dream the world could be."

He did look at her then. This time, Elaine met Luke's gaze. Everyone else in the room disappeared. Gone was the salt she'd felt at his betrayal. His words were more than an apology. They were a salve.

"I put all those together in my books to bring forth a vision of how the world could be a better place. I've seen destruction and death. Military science fiction is more than politics in space. It's also literature that investigates our morality. It forces us to soul search in unfamiliar territory. And hopefully, come out the other end a better species."

There was loud booming applause. Elaine took a moment of refuge in the crowd's boisterous praise. She took a deep breath. She hadn't realized she'd been holding her breath as Luke spoke. She'd hung on his every word. Much like she'd hung on every word of his book, so far.

True, Elaine didn't suspend her disbelief at the character of the captain and her plight. But Elaine had wanted to believe in her.

"Samuel Langhorne Clemens."

Elaine turned back to Major Hanson. "I beg your pardon?

"Mark Twain's pen name," he clarified. "Mary Ann Evans was better known as George Eliot. Charles Lutwidge Dodgson is known to most as Lewis Carroll. And we can't forget Eric Arthur Blair, better known as George Orwell. They all had pen names for various reasons. Luke started writing while we were still in the service. Some plots hit close to the battlefield, and he would've gotten in serious trouble if our superiors knew what he was doing. He's retired now and coming out of the pen box for the first time."

Elaine plopped down in the chair behind the circulation desk. Her legs felt worn out like she'd ran a marathon. Her arms felt sore like she'd been on both sides of the rope in a tug of war.

"He likes you," said Major Hanson. "More than friends. I know because the pen keeps slipping from his hands up there. His palms sweat when he likes a woman."

Elaine looked up as Luke was listening to someone ask a question. Sure enough, the pen he held slipped from his fingers. His palms had been sweaty the other night when they'd said their goodbyes. So had hers.

Instead of admitting that, or addressing any of the facts Major Hanson stated, Elaine said, "That's a long line of women there."

"They're here for Walker Skye. You came for Luke Jackson."

"We're just friends," Elaine insisted.

"I don't think so."

Major Hanson's shoulders were back, his chest out, and his chin high. His confidence irked Elaine.

"Walker?" called a woman from the audience. Her lipstick was so red, Elaine wondered if she wasn't bleeding. "Your heroine is such a strong character. Will she never find love?"

The pen slipped through Luke's fingers again. He left it on the lectern this time. "My parents had the greatest love story I know. So, I've only seen a man loving a ghost."

"I have a follow-up," said the blood-lipped woman. "What do you look for in a woman?"

Luke swallowed before he answered. He reached for the pen, then must've thought better of it because he put his hand behind his back. "Well-read. Open-minded. Believes in love."

Two out of three. Or maybe one out of three. Well, that wasn't Elaine. Which proved he wasn't truly interested in her. Not that it mattered. They were just friends.

Luke stepped down from the lectern and was immediately mobbed by the women. But he moved for the younger people with books to sign.

"He is even yummier in person," said Mary. "I thought he would be the broody type. Collecting numbers and waxing poetic about his time in the service to get the women to swoon over him."

"He's not like that at all," said Elaine.

"How would you know?" said Mary.

"They went on a date last night," said Major Hanson.

"It was not a date," said Elaine.

"Him?" said Mary. "That was your soldier?"

"He's not my soldier," said Elaine.

"Elaine, why didn't you call dibs?" Mary threw up her hands. "I wore my best bra for him today. This thing pinches … "

"He's fair game," Elaine insisted. "You know I don't date."

"Right," said Mary, glancing between Elaine and Luke. "You're clearly not interested in him. And he's clearly not interested in you."

Luke glanced up at her every other book he signed. As she moved through the library, she felt his gaze on her. She watched as every single woman came up to him. It was clear they were flirting. But, time after time, he shook his head or turned down a card or written note. And then his gaze would find her again.

Elaine felt the butterflies in her stomach. She could hear her pulse thumping. Despite many deep breaths, she couldn't help her heart racing and her mind wondering.

Everyone in the room knew his stories. But Luke had given her the truth of himself, of his private pain.

"I'm no Angel," Luke said ninety minutes later after the crowd dispersed, and the doors to the library were closed.

The reference to *Tess* was so unexpected that Elaine laughed. Look at her. Laughing at a tragedy.

"Let me explain?" he said.

"You don't have to," said Elaine. "Paul explained. You were protecting yourself. I get it."

Did she? Something like this would've sent her parents into a tizzy. Surprise was evident on Luke's face. The sparkles danced in his brown eyes.

"So, we can still be friends?" he asked.

Friends. That word felt like a lie

"Yeah." She offered her hand. "Friends."

And there it was again; the tingle.

CHAPTER THIRTEEN

Luke's fingers flew across the keyboard. His heroine had just finished a moving speech. It was right before a pivotal battle scene. His heroine excelled at these because they were her creator's favorite thing to write.

Luke loved movies where the coach rallied the team before the homecoming game. He loved the war movie where the commander gave a moving speech before the big battle.

That swell of emotions. That charge to advance forward and conquer. Luke couldn't get enough of it.

He wasn't at the end of the book. Not yet. In this part of the plot, the Captain and her ragtag team were going to make a small advance on the enemy. Her troops were rallied and ready. She'd thought of every eventuality, and Luke had put each event down on the page as an inner monologue.

All except one. The one eventuality that he'd laid as a trap to trip her up right before the climax of the book. He knew his readers would be flying over the pages at this part of the story. Their anxiety high and their anticipation at an edge.

He'd finished the captain's moving speech. It was one of his best so far. He knew it would move readers. But now, he was stuck.

Luke knew he couldn't have the troops rush directly into battle immediately after the speech. The readers needed a breather scene, a bit of space to digest what was just said, to build the anticipation of what was to come. But what plot device could he use to fill the next few pages before the deciding battle?

Even as he asked himself the question, his fingers began typing. Her second in command, who was a hero in his own right, came into her makeshift office. The man she'd trusted most, the man who knew her best, had a bone to pick with her about her speech.

On one page, they were arguing about the battle plan. On the next page, he had pulled her into his arms and was professing his long-held feelings for her.

Luke's hands froze over the keyboard. His fingers curled away from the keys. The captain remained trapped at the cursor in her best friend's arms. Both his heroine and her author were stunned at this new revelation.

Luke had never intended to go in this direction. He wasn't a romance author. Love stories were not his forte as an author. Or even as a man. He never thought he'd live up to his parents' epic love story. So, he never attempted to write one for himself. Yet, here, love was showing up on the page.

He fought a war with his fingers as they flexed and relaxed. His index fingers twitched to get back to the keys. But his thumbs rested on the space bar. In the end, Luke left the tug of war at a stalemate and backed away from the computer.

He needed some space to work out this particular plot point. Did he want to go down this road with these two? He wasn't sure? He wasn't sure about anything. He needed to take a walk to clear his head.

The good thing about staying on a ranch was there was plenty of space for him to clear his head. And he didn't have to do it on his own two feet.

Luke made it to the stables when the sun was the highest in the sky. He mounted a horse and took off. Horseback riding was like flying. But in this case, he felt both the wind and the power of the ground at the same time.

His head felt clear when he came back to the stables. But he still didn't have an answer to his plot problems.

"Writer's block?"

He turned to find Dr. Patel.

"No," Luke confessed, "the opposite. The book wants to go in a new direction."

"And you don't want it to go that way?"

The man's voice and smile reminded Luke of his own father. So, he couldn't help spilling his guts about his literary problems.

"I'm not sure what I want. My heroine is fearless in battle because she's used to fighting for others. But she's never fought for herself. I don't know how to make her see that she's worthy of love. That having love in her life might add to her life. That it might strengthen her to stand beside someone instead of in front of them. That love isn't a weakness."

Luke looked into the doctor's bright gaze. Patel's gaze was so clear that Luke felt he was looking into a mirror at his own reflection. But all the psychologist did was nod.

"Why does your heroine believe that love is a weakness?"

Good question. "I've kept her backstory vague." Luke paused. His mind turned back to the other night for an answer. "But, what if she came from divorce, her parents' divorced, I mean?"

Patel looked at him as though he knew where this new story was coming from.

"Parents teach kids how to love. Children of divorce have seen both sides of love and know that love can hurt and make people vulnerable. They have seen that love is a risk."

"I'd never hurt her," said Luke. He cleared his throat and began again. "My character, I mean. How do I get her to see that? In dialogue, of course. What could the love interest say to her?"

Dr. Patel nodded. "He—your hero—would have to know that communication is key. He should strive to be honest and open with her. Those two things are paramount."

Well, there went strikes one and two. Luke hadn't given Elaine the whole truth when they'd met. But she'd said it was fine back in the library.

"For dialogue, if your heroine gives short answers like *I'm fine*, you will know she isn't telling the truth. That is not good communication."

"She said that." Luke sighed, rubbing a hand across his forehead.

"Your character?"

Luke bit his lip. He didn't feel the need to answer. He knew his motives were transparent. But Patel kept up the farce, likely for Luke to save face.

"She's not fine," said Patel. "But, you can use that as subtext in your book."

"What can he—the male love interest—do to win her trust?"

"He can show her support. She'll likely have high expectations due to her need for stability and routine. She'll have a fear of abandonment and will need constant reassurances. For her, love is associated with pain. It'll take time for her to believe it otherwise. How long is this book?"

"I'm willing to make it as long as it needs to be for her to believe it."

Patel patted Luke on his shoulder as they walked away from the stables. "I have a feeling it's going to be a bestseller."

CHAPTER FOURTEEN

*E*laine pinched the top of the last page of the book. Her gaze struggled not to skip ahead a few paragraphs to the end. She wanted to savor every last syllable.

She loved this part of the book. The part when she was not quite done and still in the thick of it. It was like that few moments before the morning alarm went off, and she got to snuggle deeper in bed before the day started.

Walker Skye's book had started slow, even though it was fast-paced. Space battles weren't Elaine's thing. Though that was part of the plot, the book had deeper themes. Morality, acceptance, friendship, family.

The book had begun in medias res with the heroine already having a following of troops. But as Elaine read on, she found out why these people followed her. Elaine read the struggles, the triumphs, the setbacks, and small victories that won the captain her loyalty.

There were times Elaine had cheered and clenched her fist as the book's heroine advanced. At other times, Elaine's palms pressed to her heart when danger lasted for pages. Luke's words were all for the heart and not the head. Always by the captain's side was her second in command. Elaine had read on as his quiet doubt turned to vocal support for the captain. The stoic soldier never pressed his suit, but it was clear that something was bubbling between the two. Luke had said there was no romance at the reading. Still, Elaine saw it.

By the end of the book, the second in command stood by the captain and pledged his loyalty, his fealty. Elaine realized she'd been hoping the soldier would embrace his leader. But that wasn't this kind of story. On the last page, the story ended on a note of hope and anticipation.

Elaine closed the covers and felt a deep sense of satisfaction. The good guys had triumphed and came out stronger. A semblance of balance was restored, and a greater challenge was on the horizon. But the captain, who had been abandoned on the first page of the story, was no longer alone.

Elaine stared at the last three words. She was used to books ending with two words; The End. This book said; To Be Continued …

Elaine couldn't take her gaze off the ellipsis. There was more to this story. She could find out what happened next.

If she wanted to.

She'd never been a fan of series. Standalones were her thing; one and done. But now …

Elaine jerked back as her phone beeped. She dropped the book as though guilty that the caller could read her intentions. She looked over to see Luke's name on the caller ID. She'd given him her cell phone number the other day.

Thank you for inviting me into your world.

Inviting him into her world? It was his book she had devoured.

I had a great time at the library and speaking to your patrons.

Oh. Now she understood. What should she text him back? Should she text him back? Looking down at her phone, she saw the ellipsis was bubbling on his end. He wasn't done. There was more he had to say.

I look forward to Sunday dinner at the ranch.

The ellipsis stopped, and the ball, or rather the cursor, was in her court. But she still didn't know what to say. She didn't like text conversations, not even with Mary. Elaine preferred to speak in person. So, she decided, she'd just wait for that time to speak to Luke.

Elaine began her routine. She dressed for work. She walked to the library. She unlocked the door and turned on the lights and computers.

The display of classic books and literature was at the front of the room. But in a stand next to it were Walker Skye's Book One and Book Two.

Elaine reached for Book Two. She looked around the empty library before opening the cover. She read the first passage, intending only to see where the book was headed. She was immediately sucked into the continuing tale. So much so, that she didn't hear the door open.

"Just friends, huh?" Elaine looked up to see Mary standing over her with a raised brow, a smug grin, and three Harlequins in hand.

"It's a professional courtesy that I read his book," said Elaine.

"That's book two, meaning you finished book one last night. And you must've liked it."

"He's really good," Elaine admitted. "He makes you want to believe in … possibilities.

Mary set the Harlequins down. She reached across the desk and grabbed Elaine's hands in her own. "You deserve a possibility, Elaine."

Elaine's fingers trembled as Mary squeezed. But she didn't pull away. She held on.

"That man had half the eligible women in the town fawning over him," Mary continued. "He only had eyes for you."

Before Elaine could respond, the bell dinged over the library announcing new patrons. In walked their two regulars for the last few weeks. Two college students from the local university who had been paired as partners for a literary project.

"We are not putting that in our paper," said the female in a knee-length skirt and cardigan. The girl could've come straight out of Elaine's closet. "It has nothing to do with *Tess of the d'Urbervilles.*"

And Elaine's bookshelf, apparently.

The young man behind her was dressed in rugged jeans and a button-up. His hair was buzz-cut as though he'd been in the military, though he looked too young.

"In Tess, Hardy says your history determines your future, and you don't have control over it. But Skye's heroine took control and overcame her past, instead of continuing to suffer. She doesn't run away. She faces her demons and wins."

"Against aliens in space," countered Elaine's double.

If Elaine hadn't been certain before, there was confirmation they were talking about Luke's books.

"It's not about the space battle," said the young man. "Just like Tess isn't about the d'Urberville name. It's internally who you are and how you present yourself to the world."

"He's right," said Elaine. All gazes turned to her. She would've turned a shocked glance on herself had she been anyone but herself. "You can't let how others behaved in the past rewrite your whole life. Tess should've fought back. She should've fought Alec. She should've spoken up to Angel."

"Now you're talking," said Mary.

She was talking. And she didn't want to stop talking. She pulled out her phone but knew a text message wouldn't do.

"I have to go," said Elaine.

"Don't you dare come back without a Jedi Knight," Mary called after her.

Elaine grabbed her cardigan and the book.

"Wait," said Mary. "You do have to check out that book before you take it. We're librarians, not heathens."

CHAPTER FIFTEEN

"How's it going with the librarian?" asked Maggie.

She sat in a rocking chair on someone's porch. Luke was fairly certain it wasn't her house. But that's how people came and went on this ranch.

Luke and Paul had been headed back to their place. Luke had waited outside the doctor's offices where Paul got results from his tests. He'd had been waiting patiently for his friend to tell him what the doctor said, but Paul kept skirting the subject. Now, they were on a subject Luke wanted to skirt.

Luke tried not to sigh, but with another glance of his phone and his unanswered text message, the weary gush of air came out. "She said she's coming over for Sunday dinner."

Well, she had said that when he'd seen her last. She hadn't responded to any of his texts today. Luke's fingers itched to text again, but he knew he was pushing it.

"You're at the meet the family stage already?" Maggie cuddled the baby, who slept on her chest. Again, Luke didn't think this was her child. But again, that's how the people and kids on this ranch came and went. "That's progressing nicely."

"I expect a proposal in less than a month," said another of the brides. Cassie Ramos poked her head out of the screen door. Luke thought she might be the child's mother?

"It's not like that between me and Elaine," said Luke. "We're still just friends."

"Yeah," said Maggie. "The way you said that isn't believable."

Luke sighed again. "She spooks easy. I need to take it slow. Get her comfortable."

"You make her sound like a new colt," said Cassie.

She was. Elaine hadn't responded to any of his text messages. Maybe Dr. Patel had it wrong. Maybe he was coming on too strong and scaring her off?

"These women will have you married by three months if you're not careful," said Paul.

That didn't sound so bad to Luke. He could see himself discussing books with Elaine over tacos on Tuesdays for weeks, months, to come. Maybe even years.

"Wow? Really?" said Paul as he eyed his best friend. "What do you even know about this girl?"

"That's just it," said Luke. "I'm trying to get to know her."

"What you're trying to do is save her," said Paul.

"She saved me," Luke insisted.

"I've seen her. She's a wounded bird. She's hurt on the inside. You told me her parents made a mess of the nest and flew the coop. Now, here you come to save her. Not every wound is your fault. Not every scrape needs healing."

The longer Paul spoke, the touchier his tone got. Luke knew his friend, and he wasn't taking the bait. This wasn't about him and Elaine. "What did the doctor say?"

Paul looked away from Luke. Over in the neighboring yard, a few of the men played football. "I'm not getting surgery. I'm fine. I'm leaving here and going back home at the end of the week."

"Paul—"

"You can stay and court the librarian if you want, but don't use me as an excuse."

"If the doctor—"

"It's my life. It's my decision. My condition is a manageable one. This is how I choose to manage it."

The football landed between them as though to punctuate the end of the argument. Paul picked up the pigskin and tossed it back. He winced with the throw.

"Good arm," called Xavier Ramos.

"It's been a minute," said Paul

"Come play," Ramos invited.

Paul hesitated for a second before joining the other guys. Luke held back. Instead of joining in the game, he took the opportunity to watch his friend. He searched for any other signs of pain and discomfort. After fifteen minutes, he didn't see any. He only saw joy on Paul's face at the normal interaction between other fit men. Maybe his friend was okay?

The crunch of gravel turned Luke's attention from the game and to the road. A car pulled up. When the vehicle came to a stop, Elaine hopped out. She was holding Luke's book in her hand. Luke rose from his chair. As she approached, he saw that it wasn't the book he'd given her. It was the second one.

"I finished the first and started the second," she said, her voice breathless, her words were stilted as though she had difficulty forming them. "I really like it."

A slow grin spread across Luke's face. "You sound surprised."

"Because I didn't expect to. I prejudged the book and the author. But last night, I gave the story a try." She hesitated. Her brow pinching. Her lips contorting. "And I really liked it."

"I'm glad you like it. I'm partial to it myself."

"Maybe we could discuss it … over tacos?"

"I'd like that."

Elaine bit her lip, as though chewing on her next words. "Maybe not as friends. Maybe as two people who…like each other."

Luke knew he should take it slow. He knew she was spookable. But he had no trouble getting his words out. "Do you mean a date?"

Elaine nodded.

"I'd really like that."

Behind them were a few girlish squeals of delight. They turned to see Maggie and Cassie applauding the scene that he'd just played out.

"I love this place," sighed Maggie as the baby in her arms burped and deposited a little gift on her pristine blouse.

CHAPTER SIXTEEN

"So, how did you two meet again?"

Elaine sat in the dining room of Beth Barrett's house. Although she supposed she was Beth Cartwright now having married Reece Cartwright.

Elaine was surrounded by other familiar faces from her past. She'd gone to school with Maggie Banks, Eva DeMonti, and Ginger Chase as well. Though none of them had run in the same circles. Elaine hadn't had a circle. Her nose was always in a book.

But she'd had classes with Maggie. She'd seen Beth in church. And she'd been lab partners with Eva once. Now, these girls were all one big clique. It boggled the mind.

"Luke was about to get hit by a car," said Elaine. "And I kinda saved him."

"Well, that's one for the books," said Eva.

Elaine looked about the room at the nods of approval. "One what?"

"Meet cute," said Ginger.

"What's a meet-cute?" asked Elaine.

Maggie set a glass of homemade lemonade down on the table in front of Elaine. "It's a romance novel term for when the two love interests meet."

Love interests? Elaine should've shuddered at that. But she didn't.

"Beth and Reece re-met when Reece lost his memory," Maggie continued. "Amnesia trope. Brandon heard Reegan sing, and he fell in love. Fran rescued Eva from prepubescent gangsters. And my dogs brought Dylan and me together."

Elaine's head spun at the many and varied and unbelievable pairings.

"But, I think you're our first actual heroine to save the soldier," said Maggie.

"Oh," said Elaine, holding up her hands. "This isn't the start of a …"

The three women all looked at her with raised eyebrows. Their triplet smiles stopped Elaine's mouth from moving. Leaving her sentence hanging on an ellipsis to be continued.

Was she ready for an ellipsis? Would she continue this story with a romance? Elaine gulped when she realized her answer.

"It's gonna be my first date," Elaine admitted.

The women clapped and cooed. Elaine did not feel elated. Panic set in.

Should she even start this? What if it didn't turn out well? What if it turned into something more? Was he even here permanently?Would he move in? Would he expect her to move out? What if he wanted to mix their bookshelves?

"Leave her alone," said Dylan Banks as he walked into the door with his toddler in hand. "Not every date needs to end in marriage."

Maggie rounded on her husband. "Says the man who asked me to marry him the day we met."

Dylan ignored his wife's fact and handed over the child. "Can you take him? I'm gonna go play ball with the guys."

"I'm having girl-time here," Maggie countered.

Dylan looked around the room. "It looks to me like you're pressuring someone to join your squad."

"My squad?"

Elaine's shoulders hunched as Maggie's brows rose. Like a bloodhound, Elaine smelled a fight brewing. With that knowledge, panic left her, and anxiety settled in. She wanted to be anywhere but here with two parents fighting.

Elaine looked at the little boy. He looked back and forth between his parents. But instead of crying or even frowning, the child was giggling.

Elaine hated that his innocence would soon be lost when he came to understand the insults and the hurts being flung over his head by the people who were supposed to care about him the most. But the child was still oblivious. For now.

Elaine turned away from the couple to Beth, Ginger, and Eva. The other women didn't look away from the fight. They leaned in, shoveling snacks into their mouths and sipping their lemonade.

"Yeah," said Dylan. "Squad. I know I use that word right. I heard the kids say it."

"We are totally a squad," said Maggie, poking a finger into her husband's chest. "And we have squad goals. We aim to increase our ranks until every woman in Montana is as deliriously happy as we all are."

Maggie tilted her head back. Dylan ducked down and kissed her. Their son giggled. Elaine stared between the three.

"But you're keeping the kid for another thirty minutes," said Maggie when she pulled away from the kiss.

Dylan groaned. But there was no bite to it. He didn't even look put out that he'd lost the fight. He lifted his son into his arms like he was a football. "Fine. I'll catch the ball one-handed."

"Dylan Banks, my son better not come back with any dents."

"I make no promises." Dylan shifted his son into the other arm. The kid dissolved into a fit of giggles. The door closed quietly behind him.

Elaine blinked a couple of times, still unable to accept what she'd just witnessed.

"He's right," said Maggie. "I'm sorry, Elaine. I know not all women want to get married. I just—"

"How did you do that?" said Elaine.

"Do what?"

"You two just fought. And then you made up. Quickly. With no broken dishes. No slammed doors. You barely raised your voices."

"Oh, honey, that wasn't a fight," said Maggie.

She had that right. No one was crying or cursing or packing an overnight bag.

"Marriage isn't always easy," Maggie continued. "Communication is key."

"Preach sister," said Beth. "Add patience and forgiveness to that."

Ginger held up her hand. "I'll toss in humility and trust."

"Top that off with love and commitment," said Eva.

"If you build that in a dating relationship," said Maggie, "you have a good chance of making a good marriage."

Elaine wasn't so sure. Instead of arguing, like she'd been taught by her parents to do, she sat back, sipped her tea, and observed these happily married unicorns and their strange customs.

CHAPTER SEVENTEEN

*L*uke caught the pass and ran it into the makeshift end zone. He threw up his hands in celebration. The men on his team whooped. The dogs running around their feet yipped. But Luke only had eyes for Elaine.

She sat on the porch with the wives and the small children of the ranch. Elaine looked out of place in her cardigan and plaid skirt while the other women were in jeans or sundresses. The wives of the Purple Heart Ranch had their hair loose, flowing freely around their shoulders. Scuffs and dirt were a part of their wardrobe, just like their wedding bands.

They surrounded Elaine. More like ants scenting a sweet treat than anything else. Pretty soon, they'd cart her off through their collective effort and bring them back to their queen. Maggie stood in the doorway, waiting for the addition to her ranks.

Instead of rooting for his touchdown, Luke wanted to root for the hive surrounding Elaine. Slowly, she was loosening up. She didn't look like she belonged here. But she was clearly becoming more comfortable the longer she stayed.

"Eyes on the ball, Romeo."

Luke frowned at Paul. He was more annoyed with the analogy his friend had used than being called out. "Romeo and Juliet ended in tragedy."

Luke certainly did not want his story with Elaine to end in a murder-suicide.

"A tragedy?" said Paul. "Sounds like the exact ending your team is about to experience."

Luke laughed at that. It was good to play and joke with Paul. It was good to see the man's cheeks flush with exertion.

Paul had been cooped up for the last two years. In and out of doctor's visits. On and off bed rest.

Luke didn't miss the winces and grimaces that had become a part of his friend's everyday struggles. Luke had to admit that he was experiencing a few winces and grimaces himself as he played with the other men. He was severely out of practice on the football field for all the writing he'd been doing the last two years.

The soldiers of the Purple Heart Ranch had their fair share of internal and external injuries. But not a single one of them let his injuries keep him down. Reed was a master blocker with his prosthetic arm. Dylan kept pace with all the men with his prosthetic leg.

Their injuries weren't the end of any of them. Luke knew that finding love had played the biggest part in each of their healing. He wondered if he could be so lucky having found Elaine when he wasn't injured.

Not that he was in love with her.

He just liked her.

A lot.

Paul had been wrong about Luke's tendencies with women. There Elaine sat, fit and fine. The bump on her head was gone. She had no bruises, save the ones her parents had left behind. And she was working to heal those wounds. All signs proving that Luke did not have a thing for wounded women.

"Heads up, Jackson."

Luke lifted his head in time to see the ball. It came straight for his nose. He had no time to duck out of its path before it touched down. Right in his face. He went crashing down to the ground.

"I told you, Romeo," came Paul's voice. "Such a tragedy."

Luke rubbed at his nose. He didn't come away with any blood. Just a bruised ego.

"Are you okay?" Elaine was over him.

Luke would've sworn he saw birds flying around her head. Man, he had it bad for this woman. "Yeah, I'm good."

"Are you sure you're okay?"

Elaine's hand cupped Luke's cheek. Her warm touch spread across the entire surface area of his skin. He wasn't okay. He was in desperate need, in desperate need of his lips on hers.

"You tackled me harder than that ball," he said.

There was a double meaning in his words. He was sure Elaine got them by the blush on her cheek.

"Why don't you go walk it off," said Dylan.

Luke came to his feet. Elaine kept a hand around his forearm like he'd done to her the night of their thank-you dinner. Like she was the gentleman in Victorian England. He didn't need her assistance, but he liked having it. He liked having her on his arm.

They walked away from the game. Away from the prying eyes of the soldiers and the busybody-ness of their wives.

Luke took Elaine over to the house he shared with Paul. The place wasn't much lived in. Which reminded him, if Paul was going to leave, then Luke didn't have much reason to stay. Except he had every reason to stay.

Elaine grabbed an ice cube from the tray in the freezer. Then, turning back to him, she pressed the cube to his cheek. The solid quickly turned to liquid with the heat between them.

"Paul's treatment is going to be up sooner than we thought."

The cube slipped from Elaine's hand. What was left of it clattered to the floor between his sneakers and her penny loafers.

"He's thinking of leaving next week."

Luke watched Elaine's features crumple into disappointment. He was a sick man to get pleasure from her sorrow. But that sorrow was because she thought he was leaving. It meant that she cared.

"The good news is," he continued, "with my job as a writer, I can work from anywhere. Including here."

The sadness didn't immediately melt away. It was replaced with wariness. The same wariness from when she'd awakened to find him in her hospital room.

"I'm working on my third book. I thought if you had the time, and since you finished the second book, you might look at the third book's draft to give me some feedback."

"I can do that," she said. She reached into the freezer for another ice cube. "You know, I thought you were going to introduce a love story by the way the second story ended."

"That's funny because I've been thinking about just that."

"The captain has been through a lot."

"I know she has."

"Her second in command has been so patient with her."

"Well," said Luke, ignoring the cold trickle of the melting ice between them, "he believes in her and would do anything to protect her."

"Yeah," said Elaine. "I got that as I was reading their story."

"Then you know he would never do anything to hurt her."

"I think I believe that," she said, her gaze locked on his. "But, still, I think you should probably take it slow. In the draft, I mean. You don't want the readers to get upset that there's now a love story where they hadn't expected one."

"You're right," said Luke. "We should take it slow."

Elaine parted her lips to respond. But before she could draw in the breath to get any words out, Luke's lips crashed into hers. The honey of her lips was sweeter than anything he'd ever tasted. Which was why it was pure agony to pull away from her as he winced in pain.

"Did I hurt you?" she said.

"Yeah," he grinned, brushing at the bruise from the football. "But, I'm fine."

He wasn't going to let a small injury like that keep him from what he wanted most in the world. Luke touched his lips to Elaine's again. Lightly this time.

He sipped at her, like a treat that had a hard exterior. Yet he knew that once he wore the outer shell down, the center was nothing but ooey-gooey goodness. And he was right.

Elaine was pure nectar at her center. It only took a few strokes of his bottom lip to wear her down. And then she melted into his arms.

Luke held her for long moments after their kisses. She hid her face in his chest for a while. He allowed her to compose herself.

When she straightened, her smile was shy. "Walk me to my car?"

Luke did so, keeping her wrapped up in his arms. Wishing for the day when he would never have to let her go.

"About Sunday," she said.

Luke's heart stopped and then fumbled around in his chest. "Yeah?"

"I think I've had enough of ranch life today," she said. "Can it just be the two of us? Will you come to my place tomorrow?"

Luke chuckled, dipping his nose into her hair. This ranch was a lot to take in for a woman who preferred the quiet of the library stacks. "I'll be there."

"Dinner is at five o'clock sharp."

"I'll be there five minutes early."

Luke handed Elaine into her car. He waited until she was buckled in before he shut the door. With a small wave, she turned the engine on and pulled out.

He was on cloud nine as he walked back into the house. As he returned to the kitchen, aiming to clean up the two ice cubes that had turned to a small puddle of water on the floor, he noticed that the back door was open.

Luke closed the door and went in search of his guest. He assumed it had to be Paul. He found Paul in the bathroom. His broad body was bent over the toilet. His chest caved in as he heaved. Luke smelled the metallic tint before he saw the blood.

"I may have pushed it a little too hard," Paul said before his eyes rolled back in his head, and he passed out cold.

CHAPTER EIGHTEEN

"You can't make him a steak." Mary jerked back from the glass display as though there was a live cow mooing from the other side.

"Why not?" Elaine asked.

"Because any woman would make him a steak. That would show you are basic and not trying at all. The hard part of making a steak is picking the best cut from the butcher. So. if he wants to date the butcher, it's a go. No one can screw up a steak. We want to show some effort."

Elaine pushed her cart away from the red meat and came to the seafood section. "Scallops?"

"Oh, my gosh, no." Mary slapped her forehead. "Do you want to have fish breath when he kisses you?"

No. Elaine definitely did not want fish breath. That would make him pull away from her, and she wanted Luke to pull her closer. She had been breathless after their first kiss. Heck, she'd been breathless during it.

She'd found herself collapsing into his chest and seeking refuge there. He'd held her to him. She'd never felt so safe, so secure. She wanted more of that.

What was happening between her and Luke, what was happening

inside her, was scary. She'd seen scary when her parents fought. She'd seen warm when they were lovey-dovey.

Elaine didn't want scary. She wanted warm and lovey-dovey. So, she put the scallops back.

"And nothing with garlic." Mary smacked the back of Elaine's hand, forcing her to drop the bulb of garlic back into its display basket.

"I like garlic," Elaine said, cradling her hand. "I can't believe there are this many rules to a dinner date. Why don't I just text him what he wants."

Mary slapped the cell phone out of Elaine's hand. It clattered into the empty grocery cart. "Do not text him first. Do you want to seem eager?"

"I'm so confused?" Now Elaine cradled both of her hands to her chest, afraid of another rebuke from her friend. "I don't want to seem that I'm trying hard, but I actually want to try. I don't want to appear eager, even though I want him to kiss me again?"

"Yes," sighed Mary, as though she'd just experienced a breakthrough with a dunce of a student. "Now, you're getting it."

Wow, dating was hard. No wonder Elaine had never bothered.

"Duck," said Mary.

Elaine prepared to bend down and take cover. Then she saw the choice of meat in Mary's hands. "You want me to make him a duck dish?"

"With rosemary potatoes and buttered green beans. It shows a bit of effort, that you like fine things, and aren't cheap. But it also has a dash of homey and healthy baked in."

"This is so complicated," Elaine said, taking the duck and placing it into the basket.

"This is dating in the twenty-first century, honey."

"You're dating?" They looked up to find Juan. He wheeled a cart of mangos and avocados to a stop in front of them. "I've known you since we were kids. This guy has known you less than a week. Now, you're going on a date with him?"

"Well … He knows me differently," was all Elaine could manage to say. "He's the first guy to make me want more than a friendship."

She wanted the warm and safe, but she was willing to go through a bit of scary to get to it. She was willing to break her routine. But not who she was.

Elaine picked up the garlic bulb and tossed it into the cart in the face of Mary's ire. Luke had been patient with her. He'd accepted her with all her quirks. So, she was not going to hide the fact that she liked garlic. Besides, two garlic mouths canceled each other out. Right?

After leaving a dejected Juan, and a scowling Mary, Elaine went home and began cooking the garlic and rosemary duck dish. She also broke Mary's rule and texted Luke.

He didn't respond immediately. But she supposed he was driving. That was a good sign, he didn't text and drive.

The duck came out perfectly. She set the table with a set of mismatched dishes. Over the years, her mom had broken each set her dad brought home.

Elaine dimmed the lights. She had just enough time to change and touch her makeup up. Pulling open the bathroom door, she noted the crack in the wood from a time when her mother slammed it in her father's face and refused to come out all day.

Elaine stared at herself in the bathroom mirror. She had her mother's eyes, her father's nose. But everything else was all her. She was her own person. She had let them keep her cooped up in this house all her life. She had never invited a man over because she was too afraid of the damage he might cause. That was changing tonight.

Walking out of the bathroom and into her bedroom, she saw *Tess of the d'Urbervilles* lying on her nightstand. Elaine had stopped reading the story after Angel had abandoned Tess when she told her deepest shame. Angel hadn't been able to deal, and he'd sailed away and out of her life, leaving his wife, the woman he'd promised to love and care for, practically destitute.

Elaine picked up *Tess*. She pulled out the bookmark, letting the pages shut without a marker. Turning to her closet, she put the book back on the shelf.

She knew how that story ended. She was looking forward to experiencing a different ending with her own love story. One where no secrets were kept. One where she and her Angel talked out any differences and tried to accept each other for who they were.

Elaine went downstairs to wait for Luke. Looking at the clock, she saw that he was five minutes late. She didn't panic. She thumbed her phone.

At fifteen minutes late, she put the duck back in the oven.

At thirty minutes late, she put the dishes in the fridge.

After an hour, she turned off the porch lights, scrubbed off her makeup, and climbed into bed.

CHAPTER NINETEEN

Luke woke with a start. Like he'd been pulled from a nightmare. It was dark, but he heard crashes and explosions in his head.

He looked around the room, trying to get his bearings. He wasn't in a war zone. It was light outside. Not an afternoon kind of light. More like the light of day. A new day.

He must have slept through the night. His body creaked and groaned from the awkward position he'd curled into in the night. He was in a hospital room. His large body folded into a small, uncomfortable chair.

Paul lay in the bed. There were wires and tubes going into his body. His heart monitor showed a steady beat. His chest rose and fell in a normal rhythm.

It was a normal scene. But it was one Luke had hoped he wouldn't have to witness ever again with his friend. The door opened, and the white-haired doctor walked in. His features were grim.

Luke swallowed. He inhaled through his nose, forcing the air to steel his insides before he heard the news. On the bed, Paul remained asleep. The man didn't have any remaining family. He'd long ago signed documents that Luke could hear details of his prognosis, but not make any decisions for him.

"Major Hanson is going to need surgery," said the doctor. "But he knows that."

Luke had suspected as much.

"It's going to take a lot of hard work, but I have every confidence that he'll make a full recovery if he elects to have the surgery. Otherwise, we might wind up back here in a few weeks or a few months."

"How long will the recovery take?" Luke asked. "If he does elect to do the surgery?"

"A year, at least."

When the doctor left the room, Luke let out the breath he'd used to steel himself. His body caved in on itself as he did so. He looked down at his friend. Now that the doctor was no longer in the room, Paul's eyes were wide open.

Paul's gaze connected with Luke's and held. Luke wanted to look away. But his friend wouldn't let him. He knew where this conversation was about to go.

"Not your fault," said Paul.

"I know," Luke said. "That interception you caught was a foul, and you know it."

Paul let out a chuckle. That turned into a laugh. That turned into a guffaw. And then he winced.

Luke didn't go to him. He didn't reach out to his friend. He couldn't make any of this better for Paul. Paul had to make it better from himself.

That day in the war zone, Luke had done what he could to save his friend. He knew with perfect certainty had the roles been reversed that Paul would've done the same. In a heartbeat.

But Luke also knew that had the roles been reversed, he'd have gotten the necessary surgeries and done what was necessary to regain as much of his health as possible. Luke didn't understand Paul's hesitancy. He might never understand it. That didn't mean he was giving up on Paul.

"You're my family," said Luke. "You would've done the same for me. But you'd get on my nerves worse if I got injured."

"Debatable."

"I'm staying here, and so are you." Luke sat back down in the uncomfortable chair.

Paul twisted his lips before he spoke. "You're using me as an excuse to go to the town library."

Luke knew that was as close to an admission as he would ever get from his friend. Luke grinned. Then he frowned. Then he groaned. "Oh, no. I gotta go."

He'd not only missed their date. He'd missed an entire day as he waited for Paul to come out of the emergency room.

Luke floored it into town. He swung into an empty space at the library. Bursting into the front doors, he didn't see a cardigan-wearing bunhead behind the circulation desk.

"I rooted for you," said Mary, looking every bit the stern, banned-books type of librarian from his youth.

"There was an emergency," said Luke.

"It couldn't have been life or death."

"It was."

The stern look on Mary's face fell. "She's not here. She took the day off today. She never takes the day off."

That was all Luke needed to hear. He raced to Elaine's home on foot, not wanting to deal with the traffic stops. Racing up the steps to her porch, he knocked.

He was about to knock a second time when the door opened, and there she was. Her hair was down. She wore a t-shirt with no cardigan. Elaine's face was impassive as she regarded him like she barely knew him.

"Let me explain," he said.

The smile that tugged at the corner of her mouth was not a pretty affair. "That's what my dad always said."

"Paul got hurt—"

"It doesn't matter."

"It does," Luke insisted. "I didn't mean to hurt you."

"But it did hurt," Elaine said. "Just like I thought it would. Imagine if I'd actually fallen in love with you."

That hit him straight in the heart. Because he was falling in love with her. He wanted to spend his days loving on her. He wanted to spend his time showing her what love could really be like. But more importantly, Luke wanted Elaine to not be afraid to fall in love with him.

"Don't back away from this," he said.

But she was shaking her head and backing away from the door. "It's not your fault. I'm just not built for this."

Luke could see the pain in her eyes. Once again, he'd hurt the one he cared about. He needed to regroup. He stepped to the side and heard a crash.

The pot he'd stepped into on their first night, the one that had spilled its innards, it was now broken into large pieces. The flower's leaves and bulbs crashed down onto the ground. The soil that had protected it was now slipping through the cracks of the porch and showing the plant's roots.

"I can fix it," he said.

"It doesn't matter. The cracks were already there."

Luke looked back to her. It was as though the life had gone out of her eyes, out of her very being. He wanted to reach out to her, to grab hold of her and pull her close, but she was too far away.

"Elaine, relationships aren't perfect. People make mistakes. I make mistakes. I use my body as cover to save the ones I care about. I don't always look before I cross the street."

She wouldn't meet his gaze. She looked suddenly weary and tired. Luke went to her, but she backed up behind the door. Her body stood rooted on the threshold, not letting him pass into her inner sanctuary.

"Let me try and fix this," he begged.

Elaine looked into his eyes. There was a tiny spark of hope. But mostly there was fear. And the fear won out.

"There are just too many cracks. It's not your fault." She shook her head, stepping back behind the door and closing it with a quiet snick.

But Luke wasn't giving up. Not on her. Not on them.

He picked up the pieces of the broken pot and backed down the steps.

CHAPTER TWENTY

She'd made a good decision with the duck. And the garlic, with its pungent and aromatic spiciness, was the perfect added touch to the leftovers of the dish. Elaine let out a sigh. The fiery kick from the bulbous onion on her breath knocked her back down on her pillow.

She checked her phone, but like the last two days, it was silent. He hadn't texted, or called, or come by again. Elaine realized she was a hypocrite because she desperately wanted him to. The silence that resulted from Luke's lack of presence in her life was driving her crazy.

Elaine used to crave the quiet when her parents fought. To tune them out while they went at it, she'd lose herself in a book. Most of the time, she got lost in a story where she already knew the ending, finding safety and security in the familiarity of the pages.

Right now, Elaine wanted to hear Luke's voice. Even if he yelled, which he'd never done. She wanted to sit at dinner with him. Even if he hated her cooking, which her full belly and garlic coated tongue reminded her was excellent. She wanted him to come through the door. Even if he slammed it behind him, which he hadn't done. He'd stepped back as she quietly closed the door in his face.

Because Luke wouldn't do any of those things. From the very first moment, since she'd opened her eyes and found him sitting beside her in the hospital room, he'd listened to her. Even when he disagreed with her decisions, he still respected her wishes. He'd thought of her safety first, but her comfort had been paramount.

Except for the one time when he'd let her down for dinner.

But he'd come to her. He'd apologized to her. He'd wanted to make it right with her. She was the one who had turned him away.

It had to have been something big that had kept him away from their date. He'd looked tired when he'd come to her. Worn out. Weary. Like he hadn't slept the night before.

He'd said that Paul had gotten hurt. Where had they been? What had happened to put those bags under his eyes? What could she do to take his stress away?

Elaine didn't have the answers. And if her silent phone had anything to say about it, she wasn't going to get the answers anytime soon. She'd shoved Luke out of her life, and like the considerate person he was, he was going to respect her wishes.

Elaine wanted to make another wish. But what would she wish for? That he'd come to her again last night? That he was perfect and wouldn't make any mistakes in the future? That he had never hurt her?

It was an impossible feat. Relationships were messy. But Luke hadn't made anywhere near a mess like her parents had.

Needing some sort of action in her indecision, Elaine got out of bed. The sun shone into her bedroom window, announcing a new day. She reached for the curtains, intent on closing out the happy star when she saw something on her porch.

Leaving the curtains wide open, Elaine raced down the stairs. She flung the door open and had to immediately throw her arms up over her face. The sun's rays tackled her with their warmth, and her eyes weren't ready for it.

It didn't matter. When she managed to pull her hands away from shielding her eyes, she saw that he wasn't there. What was there was her potted plant. The one he'd accidentally broken. It looked whole again.

Picking up the pot, she saw that it wasn't entirely intact. There were still cracks in the ceramic. But he'd done his best to piece the broken parts back together. Inside the pot, the flower stood strong. It's leaves outstretched as though it were offering her a hug. The bud was opened, showing its petals, offering its most vulnerable part to her, as though it had never realized it had been through a battle.

Elaine's father would've replaced the pot. Her mother would've pretended it had never happened. Not Luke. He'd fixed it. Because that's the kind of man he was. He fixed what was broken.

Elaine looked down to see that the fixed pot wasn't the only thing Luke had left for her. A thick envelope lay on the welcome mat at her doorstep. By the heft and size of it, she knew there was a ream of paper inside.

Opening the package, she found the manuscript for Walker Skye's third book.

Elaine put the pot down. She dusted the nonexistent specs of dirt from her hands. Then she lifted the title page and carefully turned to the next page.

She'd expected to see Chapter One. That wasn't what was on the page. The Dedication made her heart stop, restart, and then fall.

For Elaine, it read, *who is worth fighting for.*

She stared at the words for a long time. Then she looked up. When she did, she could feel the hope in her eyes. But gazing up and down the streets, she saw that they were still empty.

Elaine had read hundreds of books. She'd gotten lost in countless stories. She'd imagined herself as dozens of heroines, even a few villains. This was the first time she was actually on a printed page.

Turning to the next page, she was immediately sucked into the story. By the end of the first page, she was well and truly hooked. By the end of the first act, she could no longer deny it.

Just like the heroine in the book, Elaine was truly, deeply in love with the commander of her heart. The second in command in the book had just put himself in the line of fire for the captain. The question was, were both the captain and Elaine brave enough to go into the battlefield to get the love they both wanted.

Elaine didn't turn to the page to find out. She set the book down, without a bookmark, and headed out of the door.

CHAPTER TWENTY-ONE

*L*uke looked down at his phone. There were new messages there, but they were from his agent asking about the manuscript. For the third time this week, Luke put the agent off. He wasn't prepared to show anyone the book, not until he learned what Elaine thought of the ending.

He'd left the book on her porch the other day. He hadn't heard anything back from her. But he'd already decided he wasn't giving up. Not on her. Not on what they could be.

"It's good," said Paul.

The man lay in the hospital bed. He was immobile after his surgery. Surprisingly, he was in good spirits. But that's what relieving chronic pain tended to do.

Luke kept his mouth shut on that opinion. The doctors expected Paul to make a full recovery. In time.

Luke had sent the first draft of the book to Elaine. But he'd also left a copy for Paul. His best friend had always been his first reader. Paul's vote of confidence was up there with Elaine's. Although his and Paul's future relationship wasn't hanging in the balance.

"Really?" said Luke. "You liked it?"

Paul nodded.

"Even though the hero doesn't get the girl?"

"It true to the character's growth," said Paul. "The two of them are just at the beginning of things. They both have a lot of scars that need to heal."

The second in command had offered himself up as a sacrifice for the captain. But she'd come to his rescue, blasting the enemy with her phaser. Her most trusted soldier had raced to her, swaggered was how Luke had described it on the page.

After he'd kissed her, she'd pushed him away. Both the captain and her creator knew she wasn't ready to receive love. Not yet. But it had awakened something in her, something she wanted to fight for.

Just like the captain did with every battle, she would be methodical about it. She would be thoughtful. She would work on her plan.

The plan was to help her new love interest heal the wounds he'd sustained in battle, the wounds she'd tried to protect him from. She'd learned that she couldn't protect the people she loved from hardships. All she could do was stand by them, help them heal.

"You realize I'm in the recovery wing of the hospital," said Paul. "I'm in the healing process. Your librarian is still out there on the battlefield."

Luke scrubbed a hand over his face. He wanted nothing more than to charge back into the minefield that was Elaine's past and slay all her demons. It had killed him to leave her at the door the other day. She'd looked so lost and in need. But he knew she wouldn't reach out to him. She was still too wounded to even lift her hand.

"I'm going to have to be patient with her," Luke said. Just like the heroine he penned, the female main character in his real-life wasn't ready to receive love. But he was certain something had awakened inside her. He needed to be methodical about his next move. "I have a plan. I need to show her I'm not going anywhere."

Paul made a sound of disbelief. "You crowded me when I got injured. You bullied me into this treatment. You've been nothing short of a helicopter parent. But she gets space to make her own decisions?"

"Yeah." Luke shrugged. "You can't outrun me. I don't want to scare her off."

Paul tossed a pillow at Luke's head. Luke easily dodged. When he straightened, both men chuckled.

When Paul sobered, he stared his best friend straight into the eye and asked the million-dollar question. "What are you doing here babysitting me? Go annoy her into submission."

That wasn't part of the plan. He needed to give her time. He knew

Elaine was it for him. He knew it in his bones. Just as he'd known that he and Paul would be more than military brothers.

"It's been two days," said Paul. "She could use a little nudge. Plus, I need to get my beauty sleep."

Maybe Paul was right. Maybe Luke could just stop by her house and check on her? Or stroll by the library. It was Taco Tuesday and getting close to noon. He knew where she'd be.

"And then get to work on the final book so that captain and her boy toy can finally get together."

Yeah. Luke was eager to write that book. But before that, he needed to pen his own final chapter. He was ready for his own happily ever after. He was ready for the battle to be over.

He headed out of the hospital and down the main street. He pulled out his phone and pulled up Elaine's number. Before hitting her contact, he made sure to look both ways at the intersection. And there she was.

Elaine stood on the other side of the street, looking down at her phone. Her fingers worked furiously. Luke watched as she took a deep breath and then hit one final key.

A second later, he startled as his phone chimed. Her fingers had moved so fast, so furious, for a long stretch. But her message was simple.

I made a mistake. Will you give me another chance?

Instead of replying, Luke looked up from his phone. He'd hoped to catch her gaze, but she was looking down at her phone. Her gaze was intent as she waited. She cradled the device in both her hands, as though afraid she'd drop it.

Luke took a step into the street, only to jerk his foot back when the screech of a honking horn demanded his attention.

Elaine looked up then. She caught his gaze. Her features broke into a beautiful smile, brighter than the sun.

She stepped a foot into the street, only to jerk back when another vehicle honked at her.

Looking up to the street lights, Luke saw the white walking man flashing on the opposite street. The orange numbers counted down, telling him that he only needed to wait another twenty seconds before he could get to her.

It was too long.

Luke held out his hand, strong-arming the cars on the road to stop for him. He was able to make it safely across to her in under five seconds.

He had a carefully calculated plan. It all went out the window the moment he was standing at her feet. Without waiting for a protest, he brought his lips to hers.

Just like she had the first time he'd kissed her, Elaine melted into his arms. She opened to him. She opened for him. Without any words between them, Luke knew that the healing process had begun. Not just for her, but for him as well.

"I'm sorry," she said when he let her up for air. "I don't know how to do this. I said I'd never do this. And now that I'm here, I'm just so scared."

"I've got you," he said, pulling her closer to him. "I'm not going to leave you. I'm never going to leave you. Even if you want to read Hardy to me every night, I'll still be here in the morning."

That got a small smile out of her. Then she gulped. "So, we're going to do this? We're going to date?"

"Date?" Luke grinned, biting his tongue and the proposal that was right at the tip of it. "Yes, we're going to date. How about I buy you a taco?"

"I'd like that."

Luke offered Elaine his arm. Just like something out of the Victorian era books that she liked. When she took it, he swaggered into the restaurant, just like the heroes of the military science fiction books and movies that he liked.

From behind the counter, Juan glared at the two of them. Luke let it slide. He had time to win the chef over. As long as the man realized the battle for Elaine had been fought and won. Because like he said, he wasn't going anywhere.

HIS STRENGTH TO STAND

THE BRIDES OF PURPLE HEART RANCH
BOOK 11

CHAPTER ONE

a cool breeze blew into the window. The tendrils of fresh valley air brushed through the room, ruffling the pages of a calendar that hung on the wall. When the pages settled down, the fourth day on the calendar was circled with a big, red O.

May the Fourth. The fourth—or rather, the force—certainly was with Paul Hanson today, his favorite day of the year. Paul loved everything Star Wars, including the franchise's true hero—his namesake Han Solo.

It wasn't Luke who got the girl in the end. It was Han who scored the beautiful and highly capable Leia. Luke had been born a hero. Meanwhile, Han's character arced from outlaw to rebel alliance. So really, who took an actual hero's journey?

Outside the window, Paul saw his best friend Luke Jackson—and no, the irony wasn't lost on either of them that they had become best friends in spite of their names. Luke had his wife wrapped up in a tight embrace and was going in for the kiss.

Paul played voyeur for perhaps a second longer than was proper. Finding a love of his own was next on his agenda, now that he had his health in order. He'd had faith that his body would heal, and it had. The same faith told him that love was just around the corner for him.

Turning back to the calendar, Paul noted that the circle he'd drawn wasn't a perfect O. The ending point didn't touch the starting point. It more so overlapped it. Also, the bottom half of the O was heavier than the top, as though the ink had gotten tired halfway into its journey.

Still, the shape did its duty. It marked the important date. His final day here at the Purple Heart Ranch.

The rehabilitation ranch for wounded soldiers had been a haven for Paul. He'd come to the ranch with reluctance. But one look at the wide-open spaces, and Paul had felt like he'd come home.

True, Montana was as far away from home as he could get. He was a Florida boy, born and bred. Being landlocked in the middle of the country without the ocean in sight should've made him feel claustrophobic. Instead, it had the opposite effect on him. He'd felt free.

The horseback riding had been his favorite. When he sat atop a horse, not a single pain from his battle injuries bothered him. He and the horse became one, and Paul could fly again.

He'd fallen so in love with the horses that he'd signed on to be a ranch hand at the Vance Ranch next door. Which meant this move would be over and done with in an hour, and he could get on with the rest of his life tending to the small stable of horses at the cattle ranch.

It was the perfect job for him. He could be out of doors. He could work with horses. And he could be independent. Bonus, there was even a creek that bordered the property. So, if he pretended really hard, he could almost, kinda, sorta imagine he was back home on the Florida coast.

The horses next door needed him. Most of the people on that ranch were focused on the cattle, which was how the ranch made its money. But Paul would be there solely for the horses. It was going to feel good to be needed. To be a leader again.

Paul bent down to pick up a moving box. He hadn't come here with much, so it was only filled with a few game boards. Board games were his second favorite pastime.

"Hey! Drop it."

With a sigh, Paul straightened and held up his hands. He turned with his hands up and his mouth turned down. Luke stood in the doorway like a hovering mother.

"It's only three months after your surgery," Luke henpecked. "You're not supposed to lift heavy objects."

"I've been cleared for weeks," Paul said, trying to rein in his patience. He knew his best friend meant well, but the man could nag worse than his mother. "It's a ten-pound box."

"This is at least twenty-five pounds," Luke said, easily hefting the box filled with cardboard and plastic game pieces. "The other guys are coming to get the rest."

Paul opened his mouth to argue, but the room filled with other soldiers from the ranch. It was too many against one, so he clammed up. At least on Vance Ranch, he wouldn't be treated with kid gloves. They only knew the basics of his injury and had only known him since his recovery.

"You sure you don't want to stay?" asked Dylan Banks, the founder of the Purple Heart ranch and one of its permanent residents.

"I can't pay the price tag," said Paul.

The other guys laughed. Any veteran's stay at the rehabilitation ranch was free. At least for the first three months. After that, the price tag to stay at the ranch wasn't monetary. It was matrimonial.

Paul liked the ladies. And they liked him back. But he had yet to meet his Leia.

Dating hadn't been at the top of his daily to-do lists. Not with the chronic pain from his injuries. Paul had had every intention of powering through the daily pain until the day he literally could take it no more. That day three months ago, the pain had hit him so hard that he'd passed out cold.

When he'd woken up, the doctors and his best friend insisted the damage wasn't something a horse ride or prayer could fix. Surgery was his only option.

Three months post-op and the pain had lessened. But in truth, it was still there most days. It was manageable if he popped a couple of aspirin in the morning. And sometimes again in the late afternoon. At night, he often cheated on NyQuil with a steaming mug of chamomile tea, but Paul suspected they knew about each other and talked while he slept peacefully. Well, mostly peacefully. Except when he woke up in the middle of the night with twinges of pain.

"You could always come and stay with me and Elaine," said Luke.

"Nah, I'm good."

Paul had said those words after Luke had rescued him from an explosion. He'd said them a few times after that life-altering incident. Each time he'd uttered the words, they'd been a lie.

Luke had already packed and moved out a week ago, when he'd married Elaine Reynolds, the town librarian, after only two months of dating. The couple had offered Paul a place in their brownstone in town. Paul had declined. It was a step shy of moving back in with his parents.

"I don't know if you realized this or not, but I am a grown man," Paul said. "I don't need you to babysit me, buddy."

Luke had probably saved Paul's life back in the military. Right before the explosion detonated, Luke had thrown his body over Paul's. The problem was, there had been a metal pipe on the ground that had made contact with Paul's low back. That's when the pain had started. It's also when Luke morphed into a helicopter mom, hovering over Paul like he was taking the SATs.

His friends had his cabin on the ranch cleared out in twenty minutes. That's how long it took to pack up his life. Paul took a step to the door. His hands were empty, but there was a sensation growing in his low back.

The twinge was a familiar sensation. He knew that the pain would pass if he gave it a moment. It always did.

Except this time, it didn't.

With all the contents of his medicine cabinet packed into one of the boxes, Paul realized he wouldn't be able to get to a couple of aspirin in time to tame the pain. As though it knew it wouldn't meet any resistance, the ache grew into agony. The agony burst into a burn.

And then it all went away.

Surprised at the quick surrender, Paul tried to take a second step forward. But it felt as though his legs had gone out under him.

They hadn't. But all the feeling had.

The next thing Paul knew, he was crashing to the ground. He heard shouts coming toward him. Luke's voice boomed over him the same way it had when the bomb went off back in the war zone. And then everything went black.

CHAPTER TWO

*M*adison Gray's Manolo Blahnicks smacked down against the pavement. The pavement smacked back. A cloud of dirt à la Pig Pen from the Charlie Brown comic strip swirled up, fairly licking at her expensive shoes. Madison hopped away from the cloud, but she wasn't quick enough. The dark dirt settled on her pastel pumps.

"You gotta pay your fare, ma'am," called the taxi driver from the front of the orange sedan.

Madison balked at the three-digit number on the meter. It cost half that to go from JFK to anywhere in New York City. But she wasn't in the Big Apple any longer. She had flown from JFK out into the middle of nowhere. She'd known that leaving would come at a cost, and she would have to pay it.

The driver frowned at the piece of plastic she handed him. "Cash only."

Cash? As in dollar bills? Who carried actual currency around these days?

Actually, she did. She'd grabbed a few hundred from the ATM before she'd boarded the plane. She'd pocketed the money for such emergencies as tipping porters at the airport, tipping handlers at the hotel she would be staying at, and tipping drivers to give her lifts until she got a car of her own. Madison handed over the entire wad of cash. She was sure there was an ATM inside the hospital.

The taxi pulled off in another plume of Pig Pen dirt tornado. Madison hopped out of the way, tugging her purse behind her back so that it wouldn't collect any dust in its now empty confines. When the soil and sediment settled, she turned and looked at her new place of business; Mercy General Hospital out in the middle of nowhere, Montana.

It was a long way away from the emergency rooms of New York City, where she'd cut her teeth on elite clientele, state-of-the-art technology, and cases worthy of medical journals. Mercy was also a VA Hospital, so there wasn't the latest tech available. Which was a shame. The government should be funneling in as many tax dollars as possible to care for the men and women who served this country.

Well, today, at least, they were getting the best orthopedic surgeon on staff.

Madison walked up to the reception area. She offered the haggard-looking nurse her most winning smile. Which the woman didn't see as she cradled two phones in one hand and scribbled on a pad with the other.

Madison waited patiently while she looked around. There was a woman who sat in a wheelchair. Both her legs were lost, but there was no frown on her face. She looked out the window at the flower patch bordering the walkway.

Across from her sat a man. He had all his limbs. But his features contorted in a grimace of chronic pain. Beside him sat a child who clutched at a stuffed animal.

Madison's gaze held on the child. Pain she knew how to mitigate. Loneliness and abandonment whether a parent was there or far away, she had no cure for. Solitude had been a constant friend of hers growing up with a four-star general for a father. Tutors and private schools and, finally, boarding schools did not fill that void.

"Yes, can I help you?"

Madison turned back to the nurse. She inhaled, pulling her winning smile back on, the smile that she was Doctor Madison Gray, and nothing fazed her. "I'm Dr. Madison Gray and—"

"Right." The nurse turned from her, shifting the phones into the opposite hand. She grabbed a manilla envelope and shoved it toward Madison. "The chief said you'd be coming today. He's in a meeting with another candidate for Chief of Orthopedics."

Another candidate for Chief of Orthopedics? There was no other candidate for Chief of Orthopedics. She was *the* candidate for Chief of Orthopedics.

"There must be a mistake," Madison started. "You see, I'm Madison Gray-"

"If you'll just take a seat, Dr. Gray, I'll call you when he's ready for you."

The nurse placed one of the phones to her ear and began another conversation, summarily dismissing Madison. Though Madison stood bewildered long enough for the nurse to place the other phone to her ear and embark on yet another conversation.

Finally, Madison was able to regain her wits. She turned to the chairs in the waiting room. The father and son had vacated the chairs. Madison walked over and took the kid's empty seat.

What was going on?

She felt like she did when she'd earned the Valedictorian spot at her boarding school, and her father had failed to show to hear her speech. Or the time when she'd earned the Valedictorian spot after her bachelor's and her father had failed to show to see her walk across the stage. No, no, this was definitely more like that time she'd earned the Valedictorian spot in medical school, and her father had shown, but he'd spent the time on his cell phone talking to the Pentagon.

Steve Pena was the Chief of Medicine at Mercy. He'd been her teacher in med school. She'd been his star student. Only ever falling second a couple of times to He Who Shall Not Be Named. Pena had fairly groomed her for this job. And yet, she wasn't his first pick. She wasn't even his only pick.

Who could it possibly be? Likely some hometown boy who'd moved up the ranks of Mercy General.

The sound of two men laughing filled Madison's ears. Both laughs were familiar to her. One was the chief. The other she wouldn't name.

The man whose name she wanted to forget came around the corner first. Doug Lamb's golden locks shone brighter than the sun. But his blond was harsh and hard for her to look at. He still had those sharp blue eyes that pierced into any woman's soul.

That was the problem. Doug's clear blue gaze wasn't discriminating. It would latch onto any woman in the vicinity, regardless of whether it was his girlfriend or not.

Those blue eyes latched onto Madison now. That grin grew impossibly bigger, brighter. *All the more to eat you with, my pretty.* But Madison was no longer naïve enough to follow a wolf into the woods.

"Madison, you made it," said Pena.

Madison rose to greet him, allowing him to kiss both her cheeks. The country seemed to be doing the old man well. He'd lost the pudgy belly he'd had back during his tenure in medical school. He looked lean and happy and at least ten years younger.

"Give me one second to check my messages, and then we'll chat," he said, turning to talk to the nurse behind the reception desk.

When Doug came in for a kiss, Madison took a step back. She'd sworn he would never kiss her again, and Madison was a woman of her word. Unlike him.

Doug's grin didn't falter. "You look surprised I'm here, Madison."

"I was looking forward to never seeing you again, actually," she said brightly, with a harsh glare in her eyes.

"Sorry to disappoint," said Doug. He wasn't.

"Aren't you supposed to be in California moving your way up the ranks of some Beverly Hills boutique hospital?"

"California has a lot of great doctors. But I couldn't pass up the opportunity to work with Doctor Pena again. Besides, you don't mind a little friendly competition?"

Friendly? She was going to tell him what he could do with his friendliness when the doors to the front entrance swung open with a gust of hot air. The sound of boots on the ground reminded Madison of standing beside her dad during a military demonstration. Looking up, she was sure those men marching into the door were all soldiers. So was the man they carried in as though he was a warrior fallen in some great battle.

"We need help," one of the soldiers barked out the order.

Madison didn't think. She jolted into action, grabbing a wheelchair. She pushed it over to the man. But once she got close, Doug tugged it from her grasp.

Was he serious right now? He was already trying to poach her job. Now he was going to poach this patient. Not today, Satan.

Madison didn't loosen her grip on the wheelchair. Doug didn't let go. A small tug of war ensued as the patient's eyes opened.

"I'll let you two fight it out," said the man. "I can just crawl to the intake desk."

CHAPTER THREE

It was a lie. Paul couldn't crawl. He'd need the use of his knees to crawl. There was no feeling in his left leg at all. The right one felt like a million little pins and needles were stabbing into it all at the same time.

Man, was this the perfect time to look like an invalid or what? He'd dreamed this moment. Where most people had the dream of walking into class naked and there being a test, Paul had nightmares of being helpless in front of a beautiful woman.

And, man, was this woman beautiful. Skin the color of caramel macchiato, as though there were both rich dark chocolate and heavy cream in her lineage. Hazel eyes that were bright and intelligent. A set of full lips that looked ripe for kissing.

He'd never wanted to kiss someone so much in his life. Except he couldn't stand to get close to her mouth. He was useless in his friends' hold, as Luke commandeered the wheelchair from the warring medical professionals.

As always, Luke swept in to save the day. Meanwhile, Paul was Han Solo frozen in carbonate while Leia duked it out with Jaba the Hut.

"It's fine, nurse," Paul began as he used his upper arm strength to shove himself into the wheelchair. "Not all of me is down."

He grinned up at her. But then those hazel eyes shot a dagger at him.

"It's *Doctor* Gray," she enunciated each word.

And, now, not only was Paul naked, unprepared for the quiz, and incapacitated, he had just proven himself a chauvinist pig. What he wouldn't give to be an unintelligible Wookie right now. The groan that escaped him might've gotten him the role.

"What are the symptoms?" asked the guy she'd battled with. There was a raspy quality to his voice, which reminded Paul of Darth Vader.

The Vader guy looked every bit a doctor. From his black, polished wingtip shoes that had likely never seen a day on a battlefield to his pristine collared shirt, which blood wouldn't dare sully.

Paul decided he hated the man. That seemed like the right call when Dr. Gray's hazel eyes turned their daggers on Dr. Darth, giving Paul a relief. Good, the enemy of my enemy might make the cute doctor my friend. Paul turned back to Dr. Gray. But before he could open his mouth, his mom spoke up.

"He was in three months ago for a microdiscectomy," said Luke. "He's been doing PT and making progress. But I suspect he's been over-doing it. We were packing today, and he just collapsed."

"I didn't collapse, Mom," said Paul, huffing like a middle schooler whose mother insisted on walking him to his first day of class. "My leg just went numb."

"Which leg?" asked Dr. Gray.

"The left one."

Long, slender fingers reached down to prod his leg. Paul wanted to curse anything holy that he couldn't feel this angel's touch. Then she reached for his right leg.

"Does this one tingle?"

Paul sighed, unable to answer in the affirmative. Not because his leg had stopped tingling. The pins and needles he'd felt for the last hour turned to a herd of bees stinging him. Except in his mind's eye, he saw butterfly wings surrounding each stinger.

Dr. Gray's gaze connected with his. Her eyes were perfectly symmetrical. The corners of her long lashes swooped into a curve, just like a butterfly would.

"Any pain when you try to lift something?" Dr. Vader's raspy voice made them both wince.

"I didn't lift anything," Paul answered, wishing he had a light saber to be done with the fallen Jedi. But he was the outlaw with a pistol. So, of course, the man who thought he was a living, breathing Jedi knight had to step in.

"He lifted a twenty-five-pound box right before this happened," Luke said to Vader.

"It was maybe five pounds at the most," Paul said to Dr. Gray.

But she wasn't looking at him. She glared at Vader. Which was totally a Leia thing to do. Except the glare wasn't paternal. It looked like there was a different kind of relationship going on there.

"I'm his doctor," Dr. Gray hissed to Vader.

"You don't have privileges here yet, Madison. You haven't signed the paperwork."

"So, now you're not only a cheat with other women, you're going to start poaching my patients as well?"

Yup, definitely not a paternal thing happening. Looked like Vader had been seduced by the dark side. Paul couldn't imagine anything calling him away from a force as bright as Madison Gray.

"I do have other symptoms, Dr. Gray," Paul cut in, wanting her attention focused solely on him. It was only fair since he was caught in her gravitational pull.

She turned back to him with a grateful tilt to her perfectly arched brows. "What are they, Mr. ….?"

"Paul, you can call me Paul." He grinned at her then. It was the grin that stopped women walking on the street. It was the grin that got him out of a speeding ticket, a parking ticket, and detention in high school.

But Madison Gray wasn't looking at his mouth. She wasn't even looking at his face. She was peering down at his legs.

"Symptoms?" she prompted.

"Racing heart," said Paul.

She reached into what looked like a pricey designer handbag. Paul only knew because he'd seen many a senator or diplomat's wife or daughter with the large, busy patterned bag. They had cosmetics in there. Dr. Gray pulled out a pink stethoscope.

She breathed on the metal part, warming it up before placing the device on his heart. The spiraling curls of her hair tickled his nose as she leaned close. Paul inhaled. She smelled of the sweetest ripe apples.

"There are also little birds chirping," he said. "And hearts floating around."

Dr. Gray straightened. She peered at him. "Maybe we'll need a psych consult as well."

"Why?" grinned Paul. "You think a man falling in love is crazy?"

She blinked once, twice. But Paul caught it. There was the tiniest tug at the corner of her mouth. He hoped that was amusement and not a clinical assessment.

They stared each other off. She was Leia rebuffing Han's advances. She looked every bit the pampered princess. Paul felt like an unworthy space rat.

"What I think," she said, "is that you have a pinched nerve causing spinal degeneration. I think you're going to need another surgery, either artificial disc replacement or spinal fusion."

Paul turned her words over in his head. He met Luke's gaze first. The man ran his hands through his hair to expose his worry lines. Paul's gaze swept past to Dr. Vader. The man's hands were clenched into fists as though he wanted to put someone in a telekinetic choke hold

Finally, Paul turned back to Dr. Gray. "I want a second opinion."

CHAPTER FOUR

adison knew she was attractive. But only because her mother had been beautiful. Lois Gray had been second runner-up in a Miss America pageant before she'd gotten married. When looking at old photographs of her mother, Madison saw shades of her own profile. Artfully applied makeup and tailored clothing helped color in the lines to round out her appearance.

So Madison was used to being hit on. By construction workers as she walked down the streets of New York City. By businessmen as she lunched at exclusive restaurants and artists as she tried out little-known hole in the wall dives. In the halls of the hospitals, attendings often tried to play doctor with her. She'd even had a few of the male nurses and technicians shoot their shot. Too bad for them that her dad was a general, and she expertly shot each one down.

The soldier's come on had been cute. Unexpected. And just a little charming.

Madison couldn't decide if it was bravado that ushered the words out of his mouth? The man had come into the doors helpless, having to be carried by his friends. But the grin on his face seemed undaunted.

It had to be an act to cover his fears of his condition.

Or a delusion.

Whichever it was, it was out of her department. Though she hadn't called psych. Yet. Madison was far more interested in getting a crack at Major Paul Hanson's back first.

"He's showing clear signs of degenerative disc disease," she said, pointing to Major Hanson's medical chart. "See here, the bone where the initial injury occurred is unstable."

"But he's already had a discectomy," Doug interjected. "His body is still adjusting. Give it time to restabilize, and the injured segment will likely resolve on its own with no need for further surgery."

"Or it could get worse and lead to permanent damage," Madison said through gritted teeth.

"Or you just want to cut into a patient unnecessarily."

"I'm a surgeon."

"Exactly. You see a problem, and you want to cut it."

Was that hurt in his voice? Not possible. Madison rounded on him. And yes, there it was. Doug wore his pouty face, the one where she wanted to grab a slice of pizza from the street vendor around the corner, but he wanted sushi from the newest high-end restaurant. Back when they were dating, she'd always cave, get dressed up, wait for a taxi to take them across town, and then eat unsatisfying blobs of rice and barely cooked fish.

Well, not today. She was having greasy pizza, and she didn't care how low his lip drooped.

"Are you two going to be able to work together?" Chief Pena rubbed at the salt and pepper stubble on his chin as he regarded the two of them. "You've never let your personal life interfere in your professional life before."

That's because Madison had always thought they were on the same side, even when they were each other's competition. They'd alternated first and second place in school and then jockeyed for position at the hospital where they were interns. But like a dummy, she'd mistaken their fierce competitiveness for love. She didn't realize until it was too late that Doug was more interested in being at the top of everyone's mind, not necessarily the best at what he did. And that included having the attention of other women because he certainly hadn't been the best boyfriend.

But that was over. So very, very over. This wasn't a popularity contest. This job was all about skill. And they all knew that Doug was the best at getting noticed, but she was the best at getting it done. He didn't stand a chance at the Chief of Orthopedic Surgery position.

"Just a passionate discussion over a case," Madison said with her winning smile. "You've seen worse between us in your classroom."

A smile full of nostalgia crossed Chief Pena's face as he nodded. Then he picked up the paperwork and frowned. "Major Hanson was under our care just a few months ago. He was seen by the last Chief of Ortho. It looks like we missed something. If I remember correctly, Major Hanson was against surgery then. I doubt he's changed his mind now."

"Well, that's my job as his doctor," said Madison. "To present him with all the data and advice so that he can make the best choice and course of action."

"Not so fast, Madison," said Doug. "The patient asked me for my opinion. And I say we need more details. Let's start with an MRI."

"Doug's right," said Pena.

Madison dug her nails into her palm to keep from shouting.

"We do need more information to help the patient make the best decision," the chief continued. "Not all soldiers want surgery. And in this case, if we've made a surgical error, it's going to be bad for us. We need to handle this case with the utmost care."

Madison understood that sentiment. When her father had been injured in the line of duty, he'd resisted any medical intervention, insisting that he could walk it off. He'd been wrong. That bravado had cost him his life, where a simple surgery might have prolonged it.

"We need to go in and do our due diligence on this one. Look at every x-ray twice. Triple check each chart."

"Yes, chief," said Doug, but his gaze was on her.

"Understood," said Madison, holding Doug's blue stare.

The smile on both their faces was the same one when they wished one another luck on an exam, knowing full well they hoped the other got an answer wrong. But Madison was going to ace this exam. She was going to get the top grade.

"And chief," Madison went on, "what about filling the Chief of Orthopedic Surgery position?"

Chief Pena's fingers went back to stroking the gray hairs on his chin. He looked between the two of them again. "I had originally been ready to offer you the job, Madison. But when Doug showed interest, I couldn't pass up the opportunity to have two of my best students on staff."

Doug nodded his head as though he actually agreed with Pena. But

Madison saw right through it. He wasn't here for the job. He was here to take it from her.

Be it a misguided attempt to win her back? Or a final sucker punch after his infidelity? She wasn't sure which, and she didn't care. Because she actually wanted this job.

A chance to work with veterans. To do the work for the men and women of this country who really needed her expertise. To perform the surgeries that would've saved her father's life, that's why she was here. Not for some silly rivalry with her ex-boyfriend.

Doug turned to her with a smile that used to make her heart fluttery like butterfly wings. But instead of seeing birdies and hearts floating around her head, she saw arrows aimed at a goal.

"May the best man win," said Doug.

Her GPA was one-tenth of a point higher than his. The recommendations he'd gotten had said that he was *great*. Her recommendations from the same faculty had said *stellar.*

So Madison didn't doubt the best man would win. And it would be her. She just needed to convince a scalpel-shy soldier to let her cut him open. Easy.

CHAPTER FIVE

The sound of boots impacting the ground brought Paul awake. He knew he wasn't overseas on the battlefield. There was no smell of burnt carbon from gunfire, or sulfur from explosives, or iron from fresh blood. The place he was in smelled of antiseptic cleaners. Because he was in a hospital room. The last place in the world he wanted to be.

His immediate response was to hit the ground and run. But he couldn't. He couldn't even lift his legs to move from the bed. The pins and needles pain was gone. Laying in the bed, Paul felt nothing below his waist.

He didn't open his eyes. He wasn't ready to face the possibility that he might never walk again. The very notion felt like a lie to him.

Something in his heart told him he would walk. That he would walk right past this trial. It was his faith.

Paul had felt that same calling to serve in the military. Yes, he went to fight for his country. But he also went to lend his strength to those souls who couldn't defend themselves. Paul had felt a niggling that his work was nearing completion just before the bomb that ended his time in service went off.

He'd known in that deep well inside of himself that that door was closed for him. He also felt a nagging that another was opening. He felt certain of his new path the first time he climbed on a horse. He knew with the same certainty that he would ride again. He just had to get out of this hospital first.

The thumping of soles on the ground continued. *Thump, thump, thump, squeak.* And then again, and again. The incessant noise finally forced Paul's eyes open to Luke, pacing the length of the small hospital room. The man reached one wall, then turned on his heel to march back to the other side.

"Will you sit down? You're making me dizzy," said Paul.

That wasn't the truth. Paul was lying prone, and he didn't feel anything. He should be the one panicking. But Luke was doing it well enough for the both of them.

"The doctors haven't been by here yet," said Luke. "The nurse said they'd be by this morning. It's almost afternoon."

The nurse had informed them that the doctors were reviewing his charts. Dr. Madison Gray and… Paul hadn't bothered remembering who the second one was. He regretted that he'd asked for that second opinion. Especially if it meant that he wouldn't get to see Madison Gray again.

She was the bright spot in all of this. He needed a little brightness now. The sky outside offered him none. There were too many clouds in the way of the star out there.

"Maybe I should go and find the nurse?" said Luke. "To see what the holdup is?"

The man had stopped his pacing and was now sitting in the lone chair in the room. Luke's long body folded awkwardly on the four-legged apparatus. He tried straightening his legs, but they hit the edge of Paul's bed. He folded them, but his knees bumped a tray.

There was a part of Paul that wanted to revel in his best friend's discomfort. Maybe that would get him to leave the room. But Paul knew better. Luke would stay with him, no matter what. This behavior went beyond what a best friend would do. Luke did it because he and Paul were family.

Paul knew Luke still felt responsible for his injury. But at the end of the day, Luke had saved his life. Nearly at the expense of his own. Just a few more meters and Luke would've been in the blast zone, blown to bits and no longer hovering over Paul.

"It'll likely be another surgery," said Luke.

Paul barely kept in his groan. Truth be told, he'd rather face another bomb or pipe to the back than a surgery. He'd gone under the knife once. He did not want to go back down that road.

His body apparently agreed with him. At the mention of the word *surgery*, the tingles returned to both his legs. The return of the feeling in his lower extremities gave credence to Paul's belief that this paralysis was just a temporary setback. Likely his body working out the kinks of the injury. It would pass, just as all pain did. There was no need to cut him open. He just needed time.

What he did know was that whatever was going wrong with his body now, it would derail all of his plans if it didn't resolve soon. He wouldn't be able to work at the Vance Ranch now, not when he couldn't be relied on to stand.

Neither could he go back to the Purple Heart Ranch. His time there had run out. Unless he got married.

But that was a no-go. Not because Paul had no desire to marry. Despite all his flirting, he wanted a wife and family of his own. But not until he knew for certain he could perform as a husband and father should.

He should be able to sweep a woman off her feet if he wanted to make her a wife. He should be able to carry her over the threshold of their home. He should be able to chase after any tykes he brought into this world.

A knock sounded at the door. Paul's heart jumped. But when the door opened, he didn't see a dark-haired bun with spirals trying to escape the hold. He saw slicked-back blond hair.

"Mr. Hanson," said Dr. Vader.

"It's Major," Paul corrected. The doctor worked in a hospital that catered to vets. and he didn't bother to use their rank? That was strike one against him.

"Right, Major." Then the man mock saluted with a grin. "I've been looking at your chart, and it tells me it's possible you don't need surgery."

Paul perked up at that. He could get out of here, likely sooner rather than later.

"This is all possibly your body still working out issues from your initial injury and the first surgery."

Huh? Paul's estimation of this doctor was growing. But he knew better than to be easily led by the dark side of the force.

"Still, I want to run some more tests to be sure."

Tests would mean sticking around. Sticking around would mean he'd likely bump into the pretty surgeon again. Dr. Vader droned on, using big words that Paul didn't understand while wearing a smirk that said he knew he was the smartest person in the room.

Paul wasn't interested in that particular measuring contest. He leaned to the side to peer over Vader's shoulder. But he didn't catch sight of Madison Gray.

"… I think that would be the best course of action."

Paul blinked his attention back to the male doctor before him. He hadn't heard a word the man said. Didn't matter. "Thanks for your opinion, doc. I'll talk it over with my actual doctor."

"I am your doctor."

Paul only just held in his snort. The way the man said that sounded way too much like Vader telling Luke that he was his father.

"No, you gave me a second opinion. Dr. Gray is my doctor. I'd like her opinion on your opinion. Where is she?"

CHAPTER SIX

esterday had been a long day of travel. The four-star hotel had had a two-star mattress. And she was still waiting on the bulk of her wardrobe to arrive. And, now, the day was stretching into forever as Madison tried to dig herself out of all the case files she'd just been assigned.

There was a backlog. Patient wait times for simple procedures were simply unacceptable. But that was nothing compared to a mile-long list of patients who needed more sophisticated procedures, which simply weren't possible at this facility that was over fifty years old.

Still, Madison dug into the problem like the documents were a sickness that she was going to root out. By the time lunch hit, she had only come away with a series of paper cuts. But she was undaunted. There was a solution in there. She just needed more time to solve it.

Mercy General just needed better organization and a little less red tape. Too bad red was the favored color of the government. Madison had grown up playing with red tape. She knew where to cut and when. She knew ways around, above, and through. She could be of use here. She knew it.

Alongside notes on patient charts, she drafted a proposal for a new intake system and chart management. She looked over the budget and saw places to cut and expand.

By the time she was done, the sun had set. She hadn't seen a single patient, but she felt like she had touched them all. Her eyes were bleary from going over all that ink, and her mind was full of numbers. She needed a break, preferably an eight-hour break. Her two-star mattress back at the hotel was looking good right about now.

"Dr. Gray?" one of the nurses called to her on her way out. "Major Hanson was asking for you."

"Major Hanson?"

The moment Madison said his name, the image of his handsome face bloomed in her mind, shoving away all the numbers and other names. Which was odd for her because she always remembered a patient's chart before she could recall their faces. That was what was most important; the data about what was happening inside, not their outside appearance.

Maybe she was just remembering this patient's face because of the importance he meant to her career. If she could convince him to get the surgery that she was certain he needed, that would hold a lot of sway with Chief Pena and her winning the Chief of Orthopedic Surgery position that she'd come here for in the first place.

Madison took the chart the nurse handed her and went down to his floor. When she came up to Major Hanson's room, she noted a group of people walking away from the door. They were a colorful and eclectic bunch, reminding her of her friends back in New York.

Not that she got to seen her friends a lot during her five-year surgical internship. She'd seen even less of them during her two-year residency. In fact, she wasn't sure she had most of their numbers any longer since many had gotten married or moved. She hadn't even had a going away party when she's left New York, just a few social media posts that were met with hearts and confetti emojis.

The group in Major Hanson's doorway looked like they were as thick as thieves and stuck together like glue. They probably left words on social media posts and not just a series of emojis. In fact, not a single phone was out. They blew kisses with fingers against lips, said goodbye with their actual mouths and waves of hands. With that much hand action, Madison doubted they would ever lose touch.

"Dr. Gray, you're finally here."

Madison recognized the brown-eyed man from earlier. He'd been the one to give the initial run down on Major Hanson's condition. His expression was pinched as he looked down his nose at her, as though he was the parent of a child she'd just given a bad grade to.

"Dr. Lamb was here earlier. He said he didn't think Paul needed surgery, but he wanted to run more tests."

Madison pursed her lips at the mention of Doug. He said he would play fair, but here he was already overstepping his bounds. They'd agreed to run more tests and then present their findings to Pena. But, of course, Doug ignored the rules so he could get himself front and center.

Seriously, what had she ever seen in the man?

"Paul says he wanted to hear from you before making any decisions since you are his doctor. But I think he's just stalling. He's not a fan of surgery. The first one… and now this. Do you really think he needs surgery?"

"I can't discuss that with you," said Madison.

"I have power of attorney."

Madison looked the man over again. Had she misread Major Hanson's flirting the other day? This guy had been hovering over him like a nagging wife. And then she remembered Major Hanson's eye-rolling retort from the other day.

"Oh? Now I get why he called you mom," said Madison.

A bark of laughter came from the room. It was full and deep-bellied. The sound wrapped around her, inviting her to come inside and play.

"Marry me," Major Hanson said when she went inside the room. "But, first, shut the door, so mom won't walk in on us."

Madison did as her patient asked. She shut out the male helicopter mom, who did not look at all amused. Well, there was no need for a power of attorney, as the patient was in possession of his full mental faculties. Though that impromptu marriage proposal gave Madison pause.

"Any woman—aside from his wife—who can shut Luke down like that deserves my undying devotion."

"He cares about you," she said. She watched as Luke's friends tugged him down the hall toward the exit. Most people would've been thrilled to have such a large group of people surrounding and cheering for their recovery.

"He blames himself for this." Major Hanson waved his hand up and down his prone body.

Madison looked Major Paul Hanson up and down. He looked every bit a virile man. A handsome, virile man. A handsome, virile man who knew it. As evidenced by the smirk on his face.

"You wanted to talk about your condition, Major Hanson?"

"Call me Paul."

"You didn't like your second opinion, *Major Hanson?*"

"That guy seems like an idiot."

A litany of every wrong Doug had committed against her during their relationship came to mind. But then, so did the truth. "No," she huffed the word. "He's not an idiot. He's brilliant, actually."

"Any man who would let a woman like you slip through his fingers is an idiot."

For the first time in her life as a medical professional, Madison blushed. She was alone in a room with a man reclining on a bed in nothing more than a slip of thin fabric. Major Hanson did not look like an invalid. He looked like a warrior having a rest before he went back to the business of conquering.

Madison gave her head a shake and looked down at his chart. "Your condition is serious, Major. My instinct tells me it may be a pinched nerve, but I need to do more tests."

"You trust your instincts?"

"After I back them up with data, always."

"I don't believe that." He shook his head. "I think your gut tells you the right answer. The data is so that other people will believe you."

"Do you want me to just cut you open blind and poke around to feel for the right answer?"

He grinned like a lion toying with a mouse. He was mistaken to think of her as something so small. At the least, Madison was a gazelle, and she was going to outrun this predator.

She opened her mouth to cut him down to size. Only she didn't feel in the least threatened by him. She didn't feel leered at or patronized. Major Hanson's gaze stayed strictly north, right on her eyes. Like he liked sparring with her, talking to her, seeing what she'd say next.

He'd asked her to marry him a moment ago. Sure, it had been a joke. But still, it had made her tingle.

"Let me help you, Paul."

His breath caught at the use of his name. His gaze dipped then. Down to his legs, not hers.

"My gut says you need surgery. I want to be sure exactly what kind so that I give you exactly what you need."

His gaze lifted and met hers. Madison had to resist the urge to gulp. His eyes were so wide, so open that she would've sworn she could see right into the heart of him.

Which was impossible. If she saw right into his eyes, she'd see first his ocular nerve, followed by brain matter. Not his heart.

"I'll let you run some tests," he said finally. "But I'm not agreeing to another surgery. Not yet."

"Deal." She held out her hand.

He took it. And when he did, electricity sparked across her wrist. Madison's breath caught then. She couldn't catch it in time to silence it.

That lion-like smile spread even wider across his handsome face. She'd thought she was fast, but she was a gazelle caught inside a lion's paw. And then he let her go.

Madison felt her legs wobble as she turned on her heel. Even when she walked out of the room, she felt as though he was following her. Which was impossible, as he was confined to the bed.

CHAPTER SEVEN

There was a chill in the air of the exam room. Off and on, Paul felt something nip at his toes. Those sensations were there and gone before he could be sure. Playing peekaboo like the rest of him was a child. But unlike a baby, Paul was never surprised when the feeling came back to his legs. He knew that each time his nerves hid his sense of touch away that it would always come back to reveal itself.

He was happy to wait awhile longer for the sensations to come home and stay for good so long as he was able to keep looking at Madison Gray. The gorgeous doctor kept hiding behind the clipboard with his medical records or dipping behind the machine. Each time she returned, Paul felt a giddy bubble of joy in his chest, like a baby seeing the magic of what was once lost unveiled again.

Paul wanted to turn and twist his body so that she was always within view. But he lay prone at the mouth of an MRI machine. The large oven-looking machine waited to eat his body whole.

"Now, you just relax, Major," said the nurse as she patted his leg.

Paul couldn't feel her tapping. He could only see the actions. Her smile was comforting, like his grandmother's. Her midwestern twang was oddly maternal.

"This is why I keep coming back here," he said. "The hospitality is better than a five-star hotel."

The nurse—Reeves was her surname. Nurse Reeves giggled, just like his grandmother.

A throat cleared on the far side of the room. "If you two are done flirting, we need to get this procedure started."

Dr. Madison Gray spoke with pursed lips. Her hazel gaze was on the clipboard in her hand, not on either Paul or Nurse Reeves. Madison thought they were flirting? As though Paul could pay attention to anyone else when she was in the room.

Paul couldn't tell if the doctor was joking or not? He expected not with the pinch to her beautiful features. Just the fact that she'd used the term flirting made Paul wonder if she was in any way jealous. Which then made him wonder if maybe he had a real shot at taking her out on a date?

"I'll leave you in Dr. Gray's hands," said the nurse as she headed for the door to the lab.

"I couldn't ask for better in my wildest dreams," said Paul.

Madison looked up from the clipboard then. There was surprise on her beautiful face. Her long lashes fluttered like they were butterfly wings. Her heart-shaped lips rounded into a soft O.

At that moment, Paul would've given up the use of his legs to pull her close. He didn't need his feet or his knees to taste that letter of the alphabet on her lips. Just his hands and mouth. Anything else was dead weight.

But she turned away from him, hiding her features. By the time she turned back around, the O was gone, and her gaze was narrowed.

"So, Major Hanson, the MRI machine is basically a big, 3-D x-ray machine. It will draw images of the deep tissue and skeletal system of your body, which will allow me to get a clearer picture of what's gone wrong with you."

"I know the drill, Maddie. It's not my first rodeo. And there's nothing wrong with me. Just a setback."

Her head whipped to him. Hazel eyes burning bright. For a moment, Paul was mesmerized. Whatever just happened to bring that look onto her face, he wanted to do it again.

"What did you just say?"

Paul couldn't remember what he'd said? He couldn't see anything past that golden spark in her eyes. He'd said something about a drill and a rodeo. That was all.

Oh, wait? Maddie. He'd called her Maddie.

"Did I overstep?" he asked.

Madison swallowed. "My mother used to call me Maddie."

She said it with that far-off look that let him know that her mother was in heaven and not here with them.

"It suits you," he said. "Part girly. Part fierce warrior."

"I'm neither girly nor a warrior." She snorted. Then caught herself, and the professional look was back.

"I think those shoes would beg to differ."

Today, she wore a pair of six-inch heels. They did wonders to accentuate her lean calf muscles.

"They were my mother's shoes. She was a beauty queen. She left me all her clothes, shoes, and handbags."

A soft expression came across her face. Paul said nothing as she got lost in her memories. It gave him a reason to bask in the beauty of her. He could imagine Madison being from pageantry stock.

"Anyway," she said, clearing her throat and looking back at her clipboard. "We should get you started. The sooner we find answers, the sooner I'll know how to fix you."

"I already told you, Dr. Gray, there's nothing wrong with me."

She studied him then. Really peering down at him with those bright eyes. "A man like you should be on his feet and not on his back."

"I don't mind so much when I have this view of looking up at you."

She inhaled. Not in the quick way of someone who was shocked. Her intake of breath was slow and controlled, as though she was tempering the words she was about to say.

"You're going to have to stop with this flirting. I'm your doctor, and your condition is serious."

"Dr. Vader doesn't think I need surgery at all."

"Dr. Vader?"

"The idiot you dumped. He's clearly been seduced by the dark side of the force."

Madison snorted. A full opened mouth snort where her nostrils flared and the sound caught in her throat. Paul found it delightful.

"So what? You're Han Solo. Your helicopter mom is Luke Skywalker. Doug is Darth Vader. And I'm …" She raised those brows at him. The O reforming on her lips. "Am I Princess Leia?"

"You seemed too serious to be a princess. You know Leia grew up to become a general. I think that suits you."

"Stop flirting with me." But she was struggling to hide a grin as she said it.

"I can't help it. Not now when Nurse Reeves has left me."

Madison tried to stop the smile from coming to her lips. She failed.

"You can always run away if you don't like it, Maddie."

"What I'm going to do is make your legs better so that you can return to soldiering for the Rebel Alliance."

That elicited a laugh from Paul. Women didn't always get his Star Wars references. Just another sign that Madison was different.

"I'm very good at what I do, Paul. Trust me."

Madison placed her hand on his knee. When she did, the grin fell from Paul's face. He could feel her hand. He could feel his toes. He wiggled the toes of one foot. Then the other. He bent his knee up, which displaced her hand.

Madison looked down at his legs in shock. She stepped back in disbelief when Paul sat up and swung his legs around and off the table.

"Wait," said Madison. "I don't think you should-"

But Paul was already doing it. He was standing. Standing tall, without any pain in either of his legs.

CHAPTER EIGHT

Madison's clipboard clattered to the floor. She didn't bother to reach for it. She was prepared to catch Paul if he fell.

Though how she would manage that, she had no idea. She'd only seen the man sitting or lying prone in a bed. She had no idea just how tall he was. He stood well over six feet, towering over her even in her high heels.

Neither had she been prepared for just how broad he was. Unlike the hotel bed she'd slept in last night, she could fit her whole body against Major Paul Hanson's chest and still have room to toss and turn. The man was a California king size bed. Which meant that if he did fall, her twin-sized body would be crushed.

So why didn't that thought make her move out of his way?

Maybe because she had never felt both dwarfed by and secure in front of a man before? Maybe because she had been wanting to take a break and curl up on his form even when he'd been laying prone in the hospital bed? Maybe because she got the sense that he wasn't the one that was falling. It was her.

But Major Paul Hanson didn't fall. He stood on strong, sturdy legs. His bare toes rooted into the ground to allow the rest o him to spring up and tower over the MRI machine.

It should not be possible for him to stand in his condition. And yet, there he was. Standing tall with the proudest, cheekiest grin on that handsome face of his. He didn't wobble. He didn't falter.

Paul Hanson stood like a mountain that Madison could take shelter in. Which was funny, because Madison had never been the kind of woman to seek shelter from a man. She was the kind of woman who booked the poshest cabin at the top of the mountain and glamped in warmth and luxury.

Just looking at Paul standing tall before her and she knew he was the kind of man who could build her that cabin. He was the kind of man who would carry her up to it. He was the kind of man who would keep her warm for the rest of the days.

Madison gave her head a shake. What was she thinking? This was a patient. A patient who just might be a medical miracle.

If she was smart, and she had been at the top of her class, she would be documenting this; a man who presented with degenerative spinal disease but was now standing. She should be looking at the chart, taking notes, asking questions.

Instead, she said, "You need to sit down."

"I've been sitting for two days," said Paul, still towering over her like a mighty lion.

Only now that he was on two legs, he made her think of a bear. Though there was still a rumbly purr to his voice. But deeper. Almost like a growl. Had his voice grown deeper? Or was it just that his words were now sailing down toward her instead of rising up?

"It feels good to stretch my legs," he said, straightening his spine to rise another inch. He put his shoulders back and blocked out the rest of the room.

Madison gazed up at him. He grinned down at her.

Her hand rose to his chest. She felt his strong heartbeat beneath her fingers. Her hand had had a purpose in rising to his chest. What had it been?

Oh, right. She had meant to give him a push to get him sitting again. But it seemed there was a magnet inside his chest. Once her fingers brushed the thin cotton there, she couldn't seem to let go. That drum beat of his heart reverberated all through her.

"This shouldn't be possible," she said.

She wasn't sure if she was referring to him standing? Or if she was referring to the powerful attraction that had sprung up between them.

"Why not? You said you have magic hands." Paul's hand covered hers. "Maybe that's what healed me."

"You're not healed."

But was he? Had she been wrong about his diagnosis? It was possible that his body might work out the kinks of his initial injury. But she hadn't been prepared to bet on those chances. Mainly because Madison wasn't a betting woman. She preferred facts over odds.

Paul's hand reached up to cover his large paw with hers. Again, she had never felt so delicate with another living soul. That desire to snuggle into the center of his chest came over again. He was just a few inches away. She could rest there and regain her senses. It looked like he wouldn't mind. Not with how he was smiling down at her like she was a flower filled with honey.

His thumb reached up and brushed the bottom of her chin. A shiver went through Madison. That sensation was followed by a liquid warmth that spread up her elbows and across her shoulder blades, like golden honey running all the way through her.

Yeah. She could take just a moment to rest there. Just sit back and relax in the hold of this big bear of a man who would likely growl at anything that came near his stash of honey. And she was the honey.

"What's going on here?"

The sound of Doug's voice was like a nightmare in the middle of a dream. Madison peered around Paul's massive shoulders to see her ex standing in the lab's open door. Doug's gaze was locked on Madison's hand, which was still against Paul's pounding heart.

Madison noted that she was staring Doug right in his eyes. Because he never towered over her. He was on her level. She had an inch on him when she wore her heels, which she'd stopped doing as much when they'd dated. Which was a shame since flats simply didn't become her long legs. She'd started wearing them again after they'd broken up.

However, her shoes weren't the issue at the moment. The issue was that she was standing in the embrace of a patient.

No. No, that wasn't exactly the problem. The problem was that she was melting into the embrace of a patient.

Yes, that was it. Because if Paul had simply made a pass at her, she could've handled it herself. Paul had made a pass, and Madison was standing firm inside his catch.

Or she had been. Paul was shrinking down to her size. No, he wasn't shrinking. He was collapsing.

"Major Hanson? Paul!"

His features contorted into horror as his massive chest caved in. He released his gentle hold on her face and grasped for the bed, but not quickly enough. With his legs slowly giving out, there was nothing for him to balance on. Madison was not strong enough to hold all of his weight. Just as she had predicted, his large bulk was going to crush her.

CHAPTER NINE

One moment Paul had been standing tall in front of Madison. He'd felt the urge to pick her up, sweep her off her feet, and carry her away from this hospital to a field of flowers, just like in some sappy romance movie. The next, he was falling into her, his own legs knocked out from under him.

He'd like to say his pride had been hurt from that fall. The truth was that Paul felt nothing as his body came crashing down around Madison. At least he'd had the presence of mind to twist his torso to avoid direct impact.

It was just too bad that Dr. Lamb hadn't made it over in time. Paul would've happily crash-landed on top of the man. But no, Lamb had stood dumbfounded in the doorway, not moving until after Madison was tugging at Paul's forearms in vain.

It had taken Madison and the MRI technician to get him back onto the table. In the end, the medical professionals decided it was best to have him go into the machine to get the details that they needed to figure out what was going on with his body.

Paul was thankful for the solitude inside the machine. The machine clanked loudly, making him feel he was inside a clock tower with rusty gears. He was even more thankful that he had no choice but to keep still as the machine began its detective work to figure out what was wrong with him.

Paul knew exactly what was wrong with him. He'd gotten cocky. And just like the mighty Sampson, who allowed his vanity to get the better of him, he'd allowed his growing feelings for a woman to weaken him. Well, at least Paul still had his hair. So there was a bright side.

"Just a few minutes more, Major Hanson."

The sound of Madison's sweet voice filled with professionalism grated on Paul's nerves. She'd called him Paul twenty minutes ago. He'd been getting under her skin. He'd been close enough to kiss her. When he'd stood over her, she hadn't pulled away. She'd tilted up her head like an invitation.

Paul hated that he'd had to decline. He wanted a rain check, and he wanted it now. The only place he'd get to taste the sweetness of her lips was in his dreams. Paul closed his eyes and tuned out the world.

Even behind his closed lids, he was seeing a dream. He saw a woman walking to him, barefoot in a field. Her golden-brown skin in stark contrast to the green blades of grass. In his mind, his gaze panned up to a pastel-colored dress covering a round belly filled with a child, his child.

"Major Hanson?"

Paul had to get to the woman of his dreams. But he was encased inside a tomb. The truth was, the real tomb was his body. One day it would work and the next it wouldn't. If he didn't get answers, he would not only be out of a job, he had no idea how he'd live his life.

"Paul?"

Paul opened his eyes. The fluorescent lights overhead urged his lids to close, but he couldn't. He didn't dare. His dream come true stood over him.

"I'm going to marry you," he said.

Madison's lips parted. He watched her try and fail and then try again to swallow. She tried to pull the professional veneer back over herself. It was a joy to watch. But he wasn't fooled. He saw right through her.

"I had a vision," he said.

"Oh?" She frowned. "You had a vision while inside an MRI machine?"

"Clear as day. Though you were smiling in my vision. Made you look a lot prettier."

"I think maybe we need that psych consult after all." But there was a smile in her words that didn't quite stretch across her mouth.

"That might be for the best since I see those little hearts and tweety birds floating around again."

That was a definite smile on her face. "I'll schedule an optometry consult as well."

"You should probably add cardiology onto that, too. My heart keeps skipping beats when you're near."

The war between professional and woman was lost. Madison grinned like a schoolgirl at the after-school dance. And even though he lay prone on a medical table, Paul felt like he could take on the world for this woman.

A throat cleared behind them. The sound was louder than the churning gears of the MRI machine. Madison looked over her shoulder, and the gates of her features clanged down in place.

"If the two of you are done flirting," said Dr. Lamb, "we have results to look at."

Madison pulled her clipboard to her chest like it was armor. Paul noted she had an inch over Dr. Lamb. It appeared Dr. Lamb noted it as well. He looked down at Madison's heels with irritation.

Paul used his forearms to push himself up to a sitting position. His legs were still number and useless. But from his seated position, Paul was eye to eye with the other man.

"The tech will help you back to your room, Mr. Hanson," said Dr. Lamb.

"It's *Major* Hanson," Madison corrected.

Lamb ignored her. "While Dr. Gray and I discuss your results and consult with you later."

It was clear Lamb meant his terse words to be a dismissal. He turned on his heel, his over-polished shoes squeaking on the linoleum. He paused when he got to the door, turning back for Madison.

"I'll be there in a second," she said.

Lamb glared at her. His eyes shouting protests that even Paul could hear. With a slight raise of Madison's brow, Lamb lost the staring contest. He huffed out a breath and walked out the door.

Madison turned back to Paul. There was worry in the crease of her brow. Paul wanted to reach up and smooth it away. Instead, he kept his hands to himself.

"You've seen the results?" he said.

She canted her head to the side like a bird. She scratched at her chest with the other hand not holding the clipboard. All while avoiding his gaze.

"It's bad?"

"I want to take a closer look before I make any determinations."

She wasn't telling him everything. She wasn't telling him anything. Instead of fear or trepidation, Paul felt calm and certainty. Just as he knew he would heal and walk again, he knew that the vision he'd seen of Madison in the field was true.

Call it faith. Call it crazy. It was going to happen.

"Promise me something?" he said.

Madison shuffled uncomfortably.

"If it's surgery, I want you to do it."

Her gaze did meet his then. Her palm flattened on her chest. She took a step closer to him.

"And if it's a success, you'll go on a date with me after."

She took a step back. "I cannot promise that. It's against ethics."

"For you to heal me? Didn't you take an oath? Or are you a hypocrite?"

That earned another crack of a smile from her. "It's a Hippocratic Oath. The doctor dating a patient thing is against hospital policy."

"I respect that. But after the surgery, you won't be my doctor anymore, so that won't be a problem. Unless you don't think you can actually heal me."

"You're incorrigible, you know that."

"A man won't get far without a little courage."

Madison took two steps toward him. She was standing so close that the fabric of her white coat brushed up against his knees. Even though he couldn't feel anything below his waist, he still felt warmth flood his chest.

"Paul, I promise you one thing, I'm going to do everything I can to get you back on your feet. Mainly, because it's the only way I'll get you out of my hair."

And with that last quip, she turned and sauntered out of the room. Paul felt a tingle in his toes, watching her depart.

CHAPTER TEN

he door to the MRI lab room shut behind Madison with a quiet snick. Inside her head, there was a loud whoosh, like water cascading down from a waterfall. Or the beads of a hot shower falling down her back because Madison felt like she'd stepped under a warm spray after Paul's words.

Little read hearts? Tweety birds? Skipped beats.

Madison grinned at the memory. She tugged at her bottom lip with her teeth, trying to hold back the grin spreading there. She brushed a tendril of hair out of her face like she was at a bar and trying to signal the cute guy to come over and buy her a drink.

How did that man have this kind of effect on her?

He certainly wasn't the first patient to ever hit on her. But Madison had always easily shut the others down. The problem was, she liked sparring with Paul Hanson.

It never felt like he was coming on to her. Each time he flirted with her, by the time he'd stopped talking and it was her turn to respond with a witty quip, he had already snuck past her defenses. And Madison liked having him in enemy territory.

She'd worried he wouldn't try to sneak over her boundary line again after he'd collapsed at her feet. He'd shut down when he'd gone into the MRI machine. But he rallied shortly after coming out and had her smiling again. She'd almost giggled at his last advances like a smitten schoolgirl.

It was insane to think about going on a date with him. But in her head, she was already picking out her best outfit and a matching pair of stilettos because—if she had anything to do with it—Major Paul Hanson was going to stand tall again.

At least, she hoped he would. The initial results from the MRI did not look good. But Madison had been faced with worse charts. She was determined to figure out what was happening to his body and fix it.

"Exactly what do you think you're doing?"

The sound of Doug's voice wiped the smile from Madison's face. He stood at the edge of the hall. His feet planted in a wide stance. His fists balled and resting on his hips. His features pinched as though he'd just taken a whiff of antiseptic.

"I don't know what you're talking about," said Madison.

"You know exactly what I'm talking about. Wanna know how I know? You got an A in ethics class."

"While you got a B."

"That's exactly my point."

Madison planted her feet in a wide stance, mirroring Doug's posture. Instead of balling her fists and resting them on her hips, she crossed her arms over her chest and waited for his next missive.

"Are you trying to convince that patient to let you do the surgery over me?"

"What?" Madison dropped her arms to her sides. "Are you serious?"

"You've never used your feminine wiles before to get ahead."

"My feminine what!"

"You've always used your brain."

Madison wondered if she needed to go see psych or the eye doctor for herself. Those hearts that Paul had said he'd seen all around her burst now as she glared at her ex-boyfriend. All she could see was red.

"If you're trying to make me jealous, Madison, this isn't the way."

"Jealous? Why would I care about your feelings when there is no us?"

Doug's arms came to his sides, but his hands remained balled into fists. They stood eye to eye. But when Madison straightened her shoulders, she had an inch on him. She realized she'd always hunched a bit when they were dating. She put her shoulders back now and reveled in that breadth of height she had over him.

"You saw the scan. You know what it means."

Madison's shoulders slumped. She had seen the preliminary results. But she wasn't ready to admit the prognosis.

"He's failed all conservative non-surgical treatments," Doug began to list off Paul's issues. "His microdiscectomy failed. And the MRI showed that the impacted disc is severely degenerated with endplate erosion."

Madison wanted to close her eyes to all the evidence that had been in black and white. What it all meant was surgery. A very serious procedure that she would've been chomping at the bit to dig her scalpel into on any other day, in any other patient.

"I get it. You're just pitying him," said Doug.

"Pity? There's nothing about that man to pity. He's a hero."

"He's a broken soldier, Madison. We're going to see a lot of them while here. We won't be able to fix all of them. He might be one of the unfixable."

Madison looked at Doug anew. She didn't believe for a second that Paul was unfixable, not with the strength he displayed while laying prone in a bed. The man who was unfixable, unsalvageable, was the one facing her.

"Doug, what exactly are you doing here if you don't think we can help these patients?"

He shrugged as though the question was inane. "This is just part of the overall plan. It's going to look great on my resume that I worked for a VA hospital when we finally move back to the city. It won't matter which one of us gets the chief position, not when we're a power surgical team. Any major hospital will be salivating to have us."

The red drained from her vision, and she saw Doug clearly. He was still playing the game. Still competing with her like they'd done all throughout their studies. But Madison wasn't in school anymore. This was her real life.

"You're right, Doug. This was always my plan. But what you don't understand is that this is my end goal. Working at a veterans' hospital isn't some jumping-off point for me. It's where I want to be."

Doug huffed an annoyed breath. "Fine, we can stay for a couple of years. But we're going back to civilization when we start our family."

"For the last time, there is no us."

"You know those other women meant nothing, Madison. I have plans to spend my life with you."

Madison could only shake her head as she regarded this man she wasted so much time on.

"Look, I won't tell the chief about your little indiscretion with a patient."

In her mind, Madison heard shots fired. She felt the enemy encroaching on her territory. She sucked in a slow, deep breath, pulling on her armor.

"There's nothing to tell," she said.

"Then have dinner with me."

Proximity alarms blared all around her. Danger and warning signs flashed yellow and red. "No. Because I don't want to. Not as your girl-friend. Not as your colleague. I'm not even sure I want to be your friend right now."

And with that, she walked off down the hall. Heels clacking like boots in a forward march. Thankfully, she didn't hear the squeak of Doug's expensive shoes following her.

CHAPTER ELEVEN

*P*aul was still reeling from Dr. Lamb's interruption. It was the second time he'd been in kissing distance of Madison, and the man had stepped in and blocked him. The dark side of the force was really trying to get at him today.

Interestingly enough, Paul had been virtually helpless each time he was near enough to Madison to steal a kiss. But somehow, helpless was the last thing he felt when he was close to that woman.

Madison's touch brought Paul back to life. Her smile made him feel as though he could conquer an advancing army of insurgents. What was wrong with him—whatever it was—he knew it was temporary. Just an annoying blip on his way to a life with Madison Gray.

One day soon, he'd stand tall and sweep her off her feet. He felt it in his bones. His toes tingled with certainty.

Except now, he was rolling away from her. Leaving her behind with that Vader in designer suit clothing.

"You look like a soldier preparing for battle."

Paul glanced up to see Dr. Patel coming down the hall. The Purple Heart Ranch's resident psychologist wore his usual amused grin. Paul hadn't put much stock in psychology. But when the doctor, who was also a pastor, mixed in scripture with his head shrinking, Paul became a convert of Patel's ways. He was the first person to suggest that Paul take up riding when he came to the ranch.

Dr. Patel had been right in his assessment. It was the horses that had begun the process of putting Paul back together again. Paul itched to mount one of the majestic beasts and ride away from there. Preferably with a pretty surgeon in tow.

"I'll take over from here," Dr. Patel said to the technician who had been wheeling Paul back to his room. The tech happily released Paul into Patel's hold.

"Did Luke send you to check on me?" Paul asked as they began to roll down the hall toward his room.

"I was on rounds here at the hospital. I work with many of the soldiers here as well as on the ranch."

Paul frowned, wondering what Patel would prescribe for a soldier here at Mercy General? There wasn't a stable out back. Then Paul remembered Madison's threat to get him a psych evaluation.

"Was it Madison who sent you?"

"Madison? You mean the new surgeon, Dr. Gray?"

"Yes, her."

Paul couldn't see Dr. Patel's face, but he was sure the old man was grinning. From what he'd been told when he'd come to Purple Heart Ranch, Dr. Patel had had a hand in matchmaking most of the couples there. Marriages of convenience were another of the man's specialties.

"Madison—Dr. Gray—has been joking about me being crazy."

"Joking?" asked Patel.

"Because I told her I see stars and hearts and baby birds flying around when she's near."

It was the truth. But a truth from his imagination. He didn't actually see those things. What if she did think he was crazy? He'd have to set her straight. But what would he tell her instead? That he felt in his soul that they were meant to be together. Just as he felt it deep in his gut that he would stand on his own two feet again.

"Strong emotions can sometimes manifest as realistic visions," Dr. Patel was saying.

Paul should've known Dr. Patel wouldn't have chided him. He might be a doctor of the mind, but he was also a man of God. That meant he knew that sometimes truth wasn't always tangible.

"She's the one," Paul admitted. "I feel it in my bones all the way down to my toes."

"You do?" asked Dr. Patel. "Does that mean you'll get the surgery?"

Paul took a deep breath. When he'd first been injured, he knew that it was by divine mercy and a hovering best friend that he'd survived. With his faith and his strong body, he'd decided to leave his healing in the hands of a higher power.

Exercise, a good diet, and prayer had worked for months. Until the tingles and loss of sensation began. Then he'd succumbed to the demand for surgery.

And here he was doing worse than before. Except when Madison was around. When she was with him, Paul felt more than he'd ever felt in his life. The problem was she wanted to cut him open and rearrange him from the inside out.

"I've never understood how you, a man of God, can coexist in the world of science," said Paul.

"God gave his children the ability to learn to heal our bodies and the science of modern medicine."

"I was taught that faith heals."

"You have a picture in your mind of what your healing looks like. I believe this frustration comes when your plan of healing is different from His."

Paul was not a man who wrestled with his faith. He knew he was here for a purpose. He had felt called to serve his country in the military. After his injury, he felt a kinship with the horses who aided in his healing. Now, his heart cried out for a certain doctor whose hands felt like magic to his frayed nerves.

"Dr. Gray is at the top of her field," said Dr. Patel. "I believe your health is in good hands with her."

It wasn't his health that Paul was worried about. It was his heart. Another surgery could heal him or leave him worse off than he was now. But a man wasn't a man without his heart, and Paul's heart was ready to jump the ship of his chest to be with Madison.

What if she wasn't prepared to catch it? What if she healed his back and then had no further interest in him?

No. No, he didn't believe that was true. He'd seen the way she'd looked up at him in the MRI lab. She'd wanted him. She just didn't want to want him.

Maybe it was that Hippocratic oath. If she allowed herself to feel anything for him more than as a patient, it would make her work difficult. But just as Paul couldn't make his legs work at will right now, he couldn't tell his heart who to latch onto.

When they arrived at his hospital room, Paul saw the figure of a woman moving about inside. His heart leaped that it might be Madison. A pale-skinned woman with coffee-colored eyes turned and smiled at him.

"Yes, Luke sent me. No, he's not here. But I brought entertainment."

Paul's heart thudded to the bottom of his chest. But it quickly rallied when Elaine held up his box of board games. He'd been bored to tears during his stay, with nothing to do but wait for glimpses of Madison.

"I'm glad you're here, Elaine. If my best friend hadn't scooped you up, I would've married you."

"So you propose to women a lot, I see," Madison said as she walked toward him. Those hazel eyes sparkling like the sun's rays touching down on sand.

Paul heard the chirp of a bird outside. His gaze fixed on the red of her lips. And his heart skipped over its ventricles, and it shoved at the front of his chest to get to her.

CHAPTER TWELVE

"Is this her?" said the pretty woman with her hand on Paul's shoulder.

She wasn't the type Madison would've thought Paul would choose. She looked like a librarian with her pastel cardigan and white blouse. But she had a warm smile, like that guy on public television who invited kids to take a look in a book and go on a reading rainbow.

Paul wasn't looking at the woman or her smile. He was gazing at Madison with a goofy look on his face that reminded Madison of—well, Goofy, the cartoon dog when he saw Clarabelle, the cow. The same goofy look from the first time they'd met when he'd threatened to crawl to the intake desk. The same goofy look when he'd asked her to marry him.

Just like he'd asked this woman to marry him.

"Don't let me interrupt your second proposal of the day," said Madison.

There was a chuckle that came from the corner of the room. Madison looked over to see one of the psychologists on staff. She'd only met Dr. Patel once, but she'd liked him instantly. He winked at her as he turned and walked out of the room.

So it looked like Paul had had the psych consult. Maybe this was his condition. He chronically asked women to marry him.

"This is her," Paul was saying to the other woman. He leaned in close to her, stage-whispering in her ear. "This is my future wife, Dr. Madison Gray."

How could Paul be referring to Madison as his future wife in front of the woman he was currently proposing to?

"She's pretty," said his other future wife.

"No, she's not. She's breathtaking. She swept me right off my feet. Literally, made my legs go out from under me when I looked into her eyes."

Warning signs were flaring up all around Madison. Not the black and yellow danger signs. These were the blaring red lights of a proximity alert. The problem was that the intruder was already in the house.

Here again, Paul had slipped past her defenses before she'd even known she was under attack. Madison didn't feel the need to slip on any armor. In fact, she wanted out of her white coat and heels. She wanted to curl up beside Paul and let all her worries melt away in his strong hold.

"If she can get you back on your feet, then Luke will approve," said the other woman.

"She's right, Maddie." Paul sighed. "We can't get married without Luke's approval."

"Who's Luke?" asked Madison.

"My mom," said Paul.

"My husband," said the woman, giving Paul a slap on the shoulder. She slapped Paul with her left hand, where a diamond sparkled on her fourth finger.

"Ouch, Elaine. I'm a wounded man in his sickbed."

"Hi, Dr. Gray. I'm Elaine. I work at the town library. Have you gotten your library card yet?"

"I... no," said Madison, looking between the two. "I haven't even found a place to live yet. I'm still in a hotel."

So Elaine wasn't going to marry Paul. Not that Madison cared. She wasn't going to marry Paul, either.

"This works perfect," said Paul. "I just got a new place. You can move in with me. After we're married, of course."

"Right," said Madison, her head spinning from the onslaught that was Major Paul Hanson. His offensives were coming from every direction and making her dizzy. "Elaine, can I talk to my fiancé—I mean my patient—alone?"

Paul's goofy grin spread impossibly wider. But after Elaine left, he took one look at Madison's grim expression, and he sobered.

"You have my MRI results," said Paul.

Madison nodded.

"You don't like what you found."

"You're going to need surgery," Madison said.

Paul hefted himself out of the wheelchair and onto the bed as Madison went over his test results and her diagnosis. "Spinal fusion," he repeated the type of surgery she'd said he'd need.

Madison came to stand beside him. She wanted to reach out to touch him, partly to reassure him but somewhat to reassure herself as well. "I'm good at what I do, Paul. I'm the best."

"I believe you," he said.

He said it simply. Not a flinch. Not a hesitation.

He said it with a certainty she didn't know was possible. When he said it, she knew it was the truth. She was going to heal this man. He would stand again. But his belief in her ability wasn't a yes to the surgery.

"Is that a yes?" she asked.

Paul grinned. Not the wide, goofy grin. This one was more subdued, a little tired. "I'll tell you what, I'll play you for it."

He reached off to the side of the bed and into a packing box. Out of the box, he pulled a child's game.

"This is your health. Your life. It's not some game."

"What? You think you'll lose?"

Madison blew a gust of air out of her nose. How did this man tweak her confidence and her competitiveness at the same time?

"What I want, Dr. Gray, is a few moments with you while I'm whole and conscious before you have me on my back."

"It's back surgery. You'd be laying on your front."

His grin spread wider, nearing goofy size. "Are you so eager to cut me open?"

"I make beautiful scars, you know." Madison pulled up a chair to the edge of his bead. "I'm going to kick your butt in this game."

"I believe that too," said Paul. "But here's the thing; if you win this game, you get your surgery. If you get your surgery, you'll heal me. If I'm healed, I get a date. So there's no way I can lose."

CHAPTER THIRTEEN

After winning the first game and losing the second, Paul knew three things about Dr. Madison Gray.

The first thing Paul knew about the woman was that she bit her lip when she was deep in thought. She nibbled at the left side when she was uncertain and was still working through her thoughts. She clamped down on the right side of her lip when she'd solved the problem and was sure she'd backed her opponent into a corner.

Paul settled back against the pillows on his hospital bed. He crossed his arms over his chest and watched the show at play on Madison's mouth. Her lips were pursed together now as she studied the game board.

But, no, wait. Just there. He saw it.

The pearly white of her left incisor snuck out. The sharp point bit down into the plump flesh on the left side of her mouth in uncertainty. Everything in Paul ached to reach his thumb out and tug at her lower lip, to wipe away the uncertainty and replace it with a kiss.

The flash of white disappeared. Madison retracted her left tooth, but it left a dent. A grin split her beautiful face, and her right incisor bit down on the right side of her mouth.

So she thought she had him. She was right. Madison had Paul completely at her mercy.

The grooves of the ridged game pieces made a grinding noise as Madison pressed them together in a windshield-wiping motion between her thumb and forefinger. It should've grated on Paul's nerves. But, like everything about this woman, he found the sound delightful.

Madison reached out and dropped a red game piece into a slot at the top of the yellow chute. The plastic slid down the grid and landed with a thud on top of one of his black pieces that had gone down the chute a few moments ago.

"Your move, Major."

Paul didn't bother looking down at the standing game board. He simply raised his hands and let one of his black pieces drop down the chute and land where it may. The move elicited the exact response he'd been after.

"What? Are you insane?" Madison huffed. "Why would you make that move when you could've blocked me?"

Paul tore his gaze from the cute scrunch of Madison's face to look down at the game. He hadn't played Connect Four since he was a kid. But that was the game at the top of the box. It could've been Candy Land for all he cared. Because it wasn't about the game. It was simply about playing. That might have been what was happening with him. It was a different story with Madison.

The second thing Paul knew about Madison was that she was competitive. She went into the arena expecting to win. And she did not like to lose.

Even in something as trivial as a kid's game, Madison had gone in with a strategy. The first round of the game, she had played the middle column, aiming to gain a strategic advantage and push him to the edge. She was pushing him to the edge, all right. Little did she know that Paul was one to push back, but she was about to find out.

As Madison became focused on taking control, Paul easily snuck past her defenses and built a solid diagonal line that she'd missed. Her lovely face had contorted in disbelief as she counted and then recounted the four black pieces that connected to give him the victory.

"Let's play again," she had demanded.

Paul had agreed. The second time they'd played, she'd won. Because the second time, Paul had been focused on learning and memorizing her facial features as she played. Which led him to the lip-biting discovery. His attentiveness to the lip-biting had led to his loss.

As a soldier, he knew that sometimes a battle had to be lost in order to make an advance. He'd gathered valuable intel with that loss. Even more valuable intel than when he'd watched her win.

The third and final thing Paul knew about Madison—and this he knew for certain—was that he was definitely going to win. Not the third game in the tiebreaker of their Connect Four bout. It didn't matter which of them connected four game pieces first. Paul was going to win at connecting the two of them together. Because unlike Madison, who was playing simply to win, Paul was playing for keeps.

Except when he looked down to make a new move in the children's game, he realized he didn't have any pieces left. Neither did Madison. They'd packed the game board without making the appropriate amount of connections with their game pieces.

"A tie?" said Madison in utter disbelief. "I didn't even know that was possible in this game."

"Maybe you've finally met your match, Dr. Gray."

Madison bit at her lip. First, she nibbled at the left side with uncertainty. A second later, she tugged at the right. Finally, she tugged at the center to pull her whole bottom lip inside her mouth.

What did that mean?

"What does this mean?" she asked. "Does this mean you're going to let me perform the surgery?"

Oh, right. They were back to that. The game of life. His life.

Speaking of his life, Paul felt a twinge in his toes. He looked down at his leg. His torso was covered by a blanket, but he saw the twitch at the bottom edge of the covers.

Madison looked down as well. "You feel something?"

Once again with the loaded questions. "Yes. Yes, I do feel something."

Her gaze shifted from his legs to his face. Her hand was on his knee, but she was leaning in to him. It would just take a few inches, and Paul would have that kiss he so desperately wanted.

He leaned forward.

Madison didn't retreat. She bit at the left side of her lip. Paul had every intention of placing his lips first on the left side of her mouth. He was going to wipe away any trace of uncertainty in this woman.

"Ahem." A throat cleared behind them.

The tingling in Paul's legs grew, letting him know that he had enough strength to stand. He was going to march over to the door and slam it in Dr. Vader's face.

"Chief!"

Before he could swing his legs off the bed, Madison leaped to standing. Her motion nearly sent the entire game board and its pieces scattering to the floor. But Paul caught it at the last second.

CHAPTER FOURTEEN

Madison had had only one scolding in her entire life. The one and only time was from her father. Madison had gone to stay with her father's sister while he was away at an overnight event in Washington, DC. She'd begged him to go, promising she'd be on her best behavior. The General had been unmoved by her pleas, and Madison had been shipped off to Aunt Bess.

Aunt Bess was a tyrant who wouldn't let Madison do anything but sit still and keep quiet. When Madison decided she'd had enough of Aunt Bess's hospitality—which had been all of two hours into her stay—she decided she'd walk home. Over fifteen miles away. At the age of seven.

She'd been found three miles from Aunt Bess's, walking on the side of the road. When her father had found out, he had been quiet at first. But after he had his daughter safe in her bedroom, he yelled so loud that the ceiling fan spun around even though the power switch was off.

Madison had sat quietly through the tirade. Though she'd been scared of her father's anger, she didn't budge from her belief that she'd been right in running away. Aunt Bess was the Wicked Witch come to life, and no child should be subjected to that. She'd never gone to spend the night again.

Madison sat in Chief Pena's office now. The man who had been her teacher, her mentor, and was now her boss sat quietly in his wingback chair. He was not even looking at her. He rubbed at the bridge of his nose. A red mark formed there from where his glasses sat all day. He took them off now and looked at her.

"Madison, you got an A on ethics," he began. "Though I wasn't your teacher, I know that to be true because you never got anything less than an A."

That wasn't true. There had been that B in Art History. She just couldn't bring herself to take Jackson Pollock seriously.

"There's nothing romantic going on between me and Major Hanson," said Madison.

The lie burned on Madison's tongue. Just a few moments ago, Madison had had the burning desire to press her lips against Paul's. There was absolutely no medical reason for her to do that.

"Romantic?" Chief Pena put his glasses back on. "I didn't say there was."

Madison pressed her back against the chair. Her chair didn't have a winged back, so there was no support for her shoulders. She wasn't sure which way this conversation was going? Part of her back was up because she thought she was being accused of inappropriate behavior with a patient, which there might be a smidge of truth to. The other part of her back was up because the chief hadn't seen anything romantic when he'd walked into the room.

Paul had wanted to kiss her. She was sure of it. He'd been staring at her lips all through the game. That's how he lost the first time. She had no idea how he'd won the second game. Or how they'd come to a stalemate in the third. What she did know was that she wanted a rematch. Not so much because she wanted to beat him. She just needed to know where she stood with him.

"I know that you know better than to get attached to your patients," the chief was saying. "You've never had that trouble before."

He was right. Madison had always looked at her patients as symptoms on a chart, a puzzle that she was going to solve. That's all Paul Hanson was. He was a scattered puzzle of symptoms. All of which were clues to help her to arrive at the right diagnosis and win this game.

"But you're clearly trying to one-up Doug so that you can get the Chief of Orthopedic Surgery position."

The position? Is that what he thought this was about?

Well, wasn't it about that?

Madison wanted the position. It's why she'd uprooted her whole life and moved out to the middle of nowhere. She wanted to help veterans like Paul. She wanted to solve their problems. The important problems of the women and men who gave so much to this country but often got the poorest health care.

"It looks like Major Hanson has agreed to do the surgery," said the chief.

He had? When? She'd only left him twenty minutes ago.

"I'll be the one deciding who is doing his surgery," said the chief.

Madison wanted to argue that point. She had more surgeries under her belt than Doug. But only by a handful of operations.

Doug hadn't believed Paul even needed the surgery. He certainly wouldn't give Paul the care and detail to attention that she would. Madison would go in and find every little issue and solve it. She wouldn't cut corners like Doug had a tendency to do.

"No more trying to get Major Hanson to pick you to do the surgery," said the chief.

Madison pursed her lips together. She nodded. But she only agreed with the chief because Paul had agreed to the surgery only because of Madison. He'd been the one to pick her. Surely he would insist on Madison being his doctor. Just as he'd insisted on taking her out on a date after he was well. Just as he'd asked her to marry him more than once now. Madison realized she hadn't said no to either proposal.

She thought back to the time in the MRI room when he'd stood towering over her. She'd liked the feeling of him standing over her. She'd wanted to step into his broad chest, rest her head against his heart, and let all of her worries fall away.

She'd felt the same draw when they'd tied in Connect Four. Madison hated losing. Hated unclear outcomes even more. She wanted to go back to Paul's room and strike up another game. It didn't matter if she won or loss. She just wanted to play the game again. Or any game. With him.

Uh oh. This was bad.

Madison left the chief's office. She walked past the patient wing of the hospital. She itched to go back inside Paul's room. Not to talk about his back or her nerves. She didn't want to talk at all. She just wanted to kick her feet up on the bed and sit quietly beside him. She'd never had that feeling before. It was the opposite of non-attached. It was a feeling she couldn't afford.

Like when she was a child, Madison couldn't sit still or be quiet any longer. She had to get out of there. Running away was the only answer. And so she left the hospital to head back to her hotel room. This time, no one came after her with a scolding.

CHAPTER FIFTEEN

The late afternoon sun streamed into the hospital room. Paul eyed the Connect Four game board sitting on the bedside table. The black and red pieces filled the entire chute. The stalemate from last night stood.

Madison hadn't returned last night. She hadn't come in this morning during rounds. He listened hard for the clacking of her heels on the linoleum floor. But he was greeted at each turn with the squeaking protests of visitors' soled sneakers, the tapping superiority of doctor's loafers, and the quiet calm of nurses' mules.

When two sets of loafers stopped outside his door, Paul slumped down in the bed. He slumped even further when Chief Pena and Dr. Lamb came inside.

"How are you feeling today, Major Hanson?" asked the chief.

"Like I could dance the merengue."

The chief chuckled. Dr. Lamb's lips spread when the chief turned to include him in on the joke. But the moment the chief's back was turned, Lamb's fake grin turned into a real scowl.

"We hope to get you out of here soon," the chief was saying. "I believe Dr. Gray explained the parameters of the spinal fusion surgery."

"She did."

"I just want to make sure you understand all the particulars before you make a final decision."

The older man went into a litany of processes and contraindications that Madison had already gone over. Paul didn't hear much of what Chief Pena said. He was too busy looking over his shoulder for any sign of Madison. When it was clear she wasn't coming, Paul started listening out for any censure for what the chief had walked in on last night. He couldn't detect a single note of reproach there either.

"And if I don't want surgery?" said Paul after the chief paused to see if he had any questions.

That perked up Lamb. The other man inhaled loudly, reminding Paul once again that he could be a minion of Darth Vader.

"These sensations and numbness, they come and go," said Paul. "There's the possibility that one day it'll just stay gone without me going under the knife again."

"There is that possibility," said the chief. "But I don't like the odds."

"Dr. Lamb initially thought it might be a possibility," said Paul.

Lamb sniffed loudly again, a wheezing sound that was definitely like Darth Vader. "That was before we ran all the tests."

"You mean the tests Dr. Gray insisted on?" asked Paul.

"The tests we both needed to make an informed decision."

"Dr. Gray seemed to have the right answer even before the test results."

Lamb narrowed his gaze at Paul. Paul was certain that if the man had any access to the force, he'd be using it to choke Paul right now.

"The good news," said Chief Pena, "is that you have two of the best doctors on staff available to perform your surgery. You couldn't be in better hands."

The thought of going under and having Lamb operate on him did not appeal to Paul. The thought of being in Madison's care warmed him through. Just the thought of it made his toes tingle.

A pager went off. Chief Pena looked down at the device on his hip. "I'm sorry. I have to get this. Dr. Lamb, will you stay behind and answer any of Major Hanson's questions?"

The chief didn't wait for a response. He turned on his loafer'd heel. With a couple of barely audible squeaks, he was out of the door.

Paul looked up at Lamb. Lamb looked down at him. The man straightened his back in a move likely meant to show dominance. Paul didn't feel in the least cowed. If this were a fistfight, Paul would win with one hand tied behind his back and his legs still incapacitated. Lamb stepped back toward the door as though he sensed the odds.

"You should know I have extensive experience with this surgery," said Lamb. "You'll be in the best hands with me on this operation."

"Madison's doing my surgery. And that's only if I decide to go through with it."

Paul hadn't decided to go through with it yet. He'd only told the nurse last night that he was leaning toward it. And that had only been when he thought it would bring him closer to Madison.

He knew he was a bit touched in the head to make such a monumental decision based on what was going on in his heart. But if he couldn't trust the woman he was falling for with his life, then he didn't know what the point of it all was.

"You might not go through with it?" Lamb looked as though Paul had just spoken Mandarin. Then he looked back to the door. "Wait? Is that why she's not here?"

"Who?"

"Madison." Lamb looked down at the chart as though he was speaking to it and not Paul. "If she knows you're not going through with this surgery, then she's probably off to find another. I should've known it."

Lamb balled his hands into fists. Paul was surprised that the man didn't stomp his foot like a child who was told he had to share his favorite toy.

"This has just been a waste of my time." Lamb rubbed one of his fists at his temple as he laughed to himself. "And to think I thought there was actually something between you two."

Paul knew he should lend credence to the denial that anything was going on between him and Madison. He knew that any impropriety could cost her her job. But he couldn't make his mouth work because his heart knew there was something between them. His gaze went back to the Connect Four game. Lamb's eyes went there too.

"Did you play that game with her?" asked Lamb, his features screwing into uncertainty again. "She never loses."

"She didn't lose," said Paul. "It's a stalemate."

"Madison doesn't do stalemates," said Lamb. "She doesn't do shades of gray. She wins. And if she loses, she'll come back harder. She's not going to stop until she gets this promotion."

Paul didn't ask what promotion, which seemed to tick Lamb off more. But Paul wasn't an idiot. He'd figured from that first day when Madison and Lamb fought over his wheelchair, they were in a battle over something bigger. Paul was just thankful it was a job and not a relationship between them.

"You should know this job is just a stepping stone for her. She's a city girl. She'll leave in a few years."

Now that was something Paul worried over. He saw himself walking toward Madison. He saw himself sweeping her off her feet. He saw her swollen belly with his child. He saw them living happily ever after here on a ranch surrounded by horses and friends and their children.

He wanted to deny Lamb's prediction of how this would all end. But when he looked up, Lamb was already halfway out the door. The door closed with a quiet snick as his loafers squeaked down the hall.

CHAPTER SIXTEEN

Madison was tired. She was tired of the firm hotel mattress. She was tired of the continental breakfast. She was tired of the tiny soaps and shampoos.

She wanted to walk out the door to her own yard. She wanted to drown in shampoo. She wanted to sleep on memory foam that only knew her body. She wanted to be held by the tall, broad form of the man in her dreams.

Except she was awake. She was awake, but she clearly saw the form of the man she wanted her mattress to remember in her mind's eye.

She punched at her pillows. Unfortunately, that move did nothing to make her more comfortable. Nor did it shake the vision of Paul Hanson from her head.

What would make her feel better was to get a scalpel in her hand and slip into an OR. There were other patient charts piling up on her desk. She should be focused on one of them and not one who could cost her everything she was working for.

Slipping into a pair of her mother's heels, Madison headed out to start her day. When she walked into the hospital, all seemed quiet. Which was never a good sign at a hospital.

She walked straight to her office, avoiding the patient ward. When she'd left the other day, she'd left with a clear desk. All of her files had been neatly organized and put away. Now there was a new stack on her desk. Papers spilled out from the manilla folders.

Madison gave a happy sigh. This was exactly what she needed. A stack of someone else's problems to solve. She pulled out her desk chair and prepared to dig in.

"I'm surprised to find you here."

Madison didn't look up at the sound of Doug's voice. She was not in the mood to deal with him today. But the sound of his loafers pacing against the floor grated her nerves and broke her concentration.

She did look up then, and she was confronted with a stranger. Doug looked like an irate child with his pinched expression, a child who had everything handed to him on a platter. He had a superior air to him. Most of it earned.

Doug was brilliant. She couldn't deny it. But had there been anything else that had attracted her to him?

Madison couldn't think of a single thing. All she could remember was how the two of them would compete. Had that been it? Had she just wanted a good fight?

She didn't fight with Paul, not really. And it wasn't really a competition. Not when each time she came at him, he completely disarmed her. With a grin, or a joke, or a few words that caught her totally off guard. It felt nice to be off guard and not itching for a fight.

"So, you won the surgery," said Doug.

"What surgery?"

"Don't play coy. The Hanson surgery. He as much as said so."

"He did?" Madison stood. "He said he'd do it."

Joy infused her. She wanted to twirl around. Paul was going to do the surgery. She promptly forgot that she was trying to stay away from him and rushed to the door to get to his floor. But there was a Doug-sized obstruction blocking her way.

"This isn't over, Madison. I've racked up two other surgeries while you've been playing footsie. I'm still in the running."

In the running? Oh, he meant for the Chief of Orthopedic Surgery position. Which was what she'd come here for. But right now, she just wanted to double-check that Paul actually said he'd do the surgery.

"Good for you, Doug." Madison slipped around him and headed to the patient wing.

When she got to Paul's room, he had a packed house. His friends were all around him. It wasn't hard to find him, though. Not because he was the one on the bed. Because he was the only one whose smile didn't reach his eyes.

Paul looked tired. He looked weary. He looked a little sad.

"Paul?"

His gaze found hers. There was a spark that flared, but it didn't ignite like it had before when he looked at her.

"Can you all clear the room," Madison said to the people gathered. "I need to check on my patient."

There was a chorus of yeses and thank you docs. Madison ignored them all. Her gaze fixed on Paul, who had turned to look at the Connect Four game board, which was still in the stalemate they'd left it in the night before.

"How are you feeling?" she said.

Paul's gaze made its way back to her. There was an accusation in his eyes. She had no idea what it was for? What had she done?

"I hear I'm going on a date soon," Madison tried.

"Yeah? You and Dr. Lamb rekindling the old magic?"

"With Doug? Ew, no."

Paul quirked an eyebrow. A smile touched the corner of his mouth. But again, it didn't reach his eyes.

Madison took another step toward him. She knew she was walking a fine line, but she couldn't stop the forward motion. "There's this guy who said he'd take me on a date if I did his surgery."

"Yeah?" Paul cocked his head to the side. "I think I know that guy. You should stay away from him because he plays for keeps."

"I think he's getting the short end of the stick because he has no idea how much I can throw down in a restaurant."

Paul snorted. When he took a clearing breath, his smile touched his eyes. "So, you're not one of those dainty salad eaters, I take it."

"I like a salad. On the side of my steak."

She was standing within touching distance of him. She could touch him. Maybe use her stethoscope to listen to his heartbeat. That's what his doctor would do. Except she wasn't wearing a stethoscope. She had not a single medical apparatus with her. She didn't even have his chart in her hands for cover.

"You scared?" she asked.

"Yeah," he said.

"I'm the best, Paul. And I promise I'm going to do my very best with you."

He took her hand and tugged her closer until she was sitting on the bed. "I believe you're the very best, Maddie. I'm not scared of the surgery. I'm scared of after the surgery."

"Fine, I'll order the chicken instead."

He chuckled, and his gaze lit up. Madison finally felt a sense of relief, a sense of rightness. But the light in his eyes flickered, and his smile dimmed.

"This will earn you that promotion?" he said. "Winning my surgery over Lamb?"

Oh, that's why Paul was upset. Probably why Doug was upset. Doug could never keep anything to himself. Not his words, not his kisses, not his promises.

"I can see by the look in your eyes that it's true," said Paul.

Madison scooted closer so that this man could see into the heart of her. "I'm going to earn that promotion because I'm the best at what I do."

"And then you'll leave. Because working here at Mercy General is just a stepping stone?"

"Who said that? Doug? That jerk." Madison rubbed at her forehead as though she could wipe Doug out of her consciousness. "This is where my dad's from. He and my mom left me their place in New York, but it never felt like home. I thought maybe this might feel like home. It feels like a place where I can make a difference."

Paul pulled her close. Madison knew she should resist. But it felt like she'd been there before. It felt like a memory. It felt like home.

"You can have the steak on our date," Paul said. "Lobster, too. I think that will cover the cost of my surgery."

He rested his forehead against hers. They were so very close to each other. If she tilted her head, she could kiss him.

Memories were often the past repeating itself. So it didn't surprise Madison that in this moment, just like it had happened before, that there was the sound of a throat clearing at the door.

CHAPTER SEVENTEEN

*P*aul watched as Madison shut her eyes and clenched her fingers. The pain etched there made his heart ache. It made his gut wrench. It made his toes twitch.

He ignored the sensation in his limbs and reached for her. He took her hand in his and unfurled her fingers. He reached his other hand to her brow and smoothed out the creases he found there.

Madison opened her eyes and looked at him. For one perfect moment, no one else in the world existed but the two of them. In that perfect moment, Paul saw his life flash before him.

Not the events of the past that those near death saw as they were near dying. No, Paul saw his future as it was going to be because he was going to live. He was going to live the rest of his days with this woman.

He saw her kicking those heels off after a long day of surgery and running to him. He'd catch her in his arms and twirl her around in a field of green. A stable of horses would whinny their approval as their trainer sipped from the lips of the woman he adored, the woman he loved.

He loved her.

The hard facts of that singular truth knocked the breath out of him. He'd always known that when he fell in love, it would be hard. The landing into this reality smarted but in the best way possible.

A chuckle escaped his lips. Madison's lips parted as she gazed up at him. He'd been so near to kissing her just a second ago before they were interrupted.

In Paul's mind, a scene from the end of *The Return of the Jedi* played in bright technicolor. It was the scene where Leia and Han were trapped on Tatooine. There were stormtroopers at Han's back, and it looked like all was lost. Until Leia revealed that she had a blaster.

"I love you," Paul said, just as the anti-hero of the film had said to the princess when danger was at their backs.

Madison didn't repeat Leia's line. But she had to know. Even though they'd been caught, he had to make his feelings known.

Instead of a blaster to take down the intruders in the doorway, Paul pulled Madison to her and stole a kiss. She might as well have had a blaster because the moment his lips impacted hers, everything inside him was blown apart.

Paul's heart raced when Madison pressed into him. Her pulse raced at the base of her neck, where he held her. It matched the quickened pace of his own heart. If he hadn't already been laying prone, his knees would've gone weak.

"Dr. Gray, may I see you?"

Breaking apart from Madison was the hardest thing Paul ever had to do in his life. And he'd seen three tours and come far too close to an explosive. But nothing matched the tingling jolt of Madison's kiss. He felt empty and void when she pulled away from him.

Madison's eyes didn't leave Paul as she stood. She swallowed as she set her features, removing all traces of the desire she'd shown him only a second ago. She began to turn away from him, beyond his grasp. Then she took a step, and he could not follow.

"Maddie," he called after her.

She paused. But she did not turn. Her shoulders went back as though she was preparing to face a firing squad. It wasn't stormtroopers with blasters. It wasn't Dr. Vader in his white coat.

Chief Pena raised a brow as he looked at Paul. Paul supposed that was too familiar a name to call his surgeon. But then again, kissing his surgeon was likely far worse an offense.

"I know what this looks like," Paul said to the elderly doctor.

"I don't think you do, Major."

"It looks like Dr. Gray was fraternizing with a patient. But I'm not just any patient. I'm going to marry her one day."

Madison's shoulders straightened. "He's joking."

"No," said Paul. "I'm definitely not joking. But I'm not going to ask her to marry me until after the surgery, so there won't be any hypocrisy."

Madison huffed a breath as she whirled back around. "It's Hippocratic, not hypocrisy. And that's not what's happening here."

Paul looked past Madison to the man in the doorway. Chief Pena didn't look angry as he regarded the two of them. He looked pensive, as though the two of them were a complicated puzzle that he was deciding where to begin his problem-solving.

"You're a fine man, Major Hanson," said Chief Pena. "Dr. Gray could certainly do a lot worse."

"Thank you," said Paul. His chest puffed up under the compliment. But when he looked to Madison, she looked crestfallen.

"She might one day become your wife," said Chief Pena. "But, unfortunately, she can never be your surgeon."

The tingles that had started in Paul's toes crept higher. He felt them in his shins, and the back of his knees, and now higher up his thighs. He wondered if he did have the strength to stand. He needed to do something to prop Madison up. Her shoulders slumped, and her chest caved in.

"Maddie?" Paul called to her.

"Dr. Gray?" Chief Pena called to her.

Madison didn't turn to look at Paul again. She walked forward toward Chief Pena and then on past him. Paul could only lay there and watch as Madison walked out the door and followed the chief down the hall.

CHAPTER EIGHTEEN

"What were you thinking, Madison?"

Madison had been looking out the window. She'd spent most of her life in the city, where artificial lights bloomed from every corner. It had been near impossible to see the stars. But here, in the middle of the country, where towers didn't rival the skyline, she could see every single star.

Her father had brought her out to Montana a couple of times. Normally it had been on a training exercise. He'd plant her in a hotel or on the base. Madison spent her days watching the wildlife roam free. She would lay on her back at night and look up and lose count of the stars.

Those bright orbs twinkled at her now. They tried to coax a smile out of her. They almost caught one. Until Doug interrupted her thoughts.

"You could lose everything. And for what? Him?"

Madison turned away from the window to face off against Doug. They were inside Chief Pena's office. The chief sat behind his desk, his fingers steepled, not looking at either of them. Doug stood near the door with his hands clenched, his cheeks red.

Madison was standing, as well. She doubted she'd be in the room long enough to get comfortable in the chair. Chief Pena's silence unsettled her, making her want to pace.

She took a step away from the chief's desk and toward Doug. She didn't teeter in her heels. She stood tall. She stood a half of an inch over him. But somehow she felt even taller.

"My love life is none of your business," she said.

"Love?"

The word was a gust of wind between them both. Madison realized she'd never once considered marrying this man. Had they ever exchanged the L-word between them. It had never occurred to her to love Doug. She wondered if she ever could have?

It didn't matter anymore. Her heart was thudding more over Paul's surgery. That was the only thing that mattered; Paul needed to have that surgery.

Madison turned away from Doug and back to the chief. "You can't take me off this case."

Chief Pena didn't look angry. He didn't even look irritated or censorious. He looked thoughtful.

"I'm the best orthopedic surgeon you've got."

"Excuse me!" interjected Doug.

"All three of us know it," Madison continued, ignoring her ex.

Chief Pena placed his hands flat on his desk. His chin raised, and he nodded at her pronouncement. Madison felt a wellspring of relief.

"Are you telling me there's nothing between you and Major Hanson?" Chief Pena asked.

That wellspring of relief dried up in an instant. Madison opened her mouth to try and deny her feelings for Paul. A tidal wave of warmth rushed in to fill the spaces left behind.

"It's just harmless flirting," she tried.

"I haven't kissed any of my patients this week," said Chief Pena.

Doug exploded off the wall he'd been leaning against. "You kissed him?"

Madison ignored Doug. She was trying not to remember that kiss she'd shared with Paul. Her lips still tingled from that impact. She couldn't deny that's why she was fighting so hard to stay on this case. She needed to ensure the care of every single one of Paul's nerves. A man who could make her hair follicles tingle with just a brush of his lips needed special care.

"Would you have me believe you have no feelings for him, Madison?" asked Chief Pena. "Nothing outside of the normal care for a patient?"

Madison had to swallow a few times to tamp down the feelings that wanted to burst out of her. "I... he..."

With each word she spoke, she had to swallow again. She had to swallow hard because of the emotions bubbling inside her chest. Madison knew she had to quiet it down so that she could speak. It wasn't just Paul's life on the line here. It was her life, too.

She looked at the scalpel in a case on Pena's desk. Her hands itched to reach for it. She could remember the feel of the first scalpel she'd held. She'd picked up the instrument and felt a certainty. Her fingers never twitched when she held a scalpel because she was sure.

She remembered her hand inside Paul's. He'd given her fingers a squeeze. She'd felt the overwhelming urge to lace their hands together. It was the first time she'd felt so certain outside of an OR.

Madison looked up at the chief. He smiled knowingly at her. She sighed in defeat. Then she turned to Doug.

"Doug, if you ever cared anything for me, I need you now."

CHAPTER NINETEEN

*P*aul was tired. He was tired of lying down. He was tired of waiting around.

He felt no tingling in his toes. No hot and cold sensations in his legs. All the sensation was in his heart. His heart beat so fiercely, so rapidly that Paul was certain it was going to burst out of his chest. Maybe that would make Madison come back sooner.

With a glance up at the door, he saw that that wasn't happening. Paul was done waiting. He hefted his left leg up. With a grunt, he slid it off the edge of the hospital bed. It took an effort to keep his balance, but he managed. Finally, he was able to swing his right leg over the side of the bed.

He looked down to confirm that his toes were touching the cold ground. They were. But he felt nothing.

He felt nothing in his feet. Nothing in his legs. Nothing in his chest… except an ache.

Madison hadn't come back to his room last night. He hadn't seen her at all this morning. He had no clue what her fate had been with her boss.

Was she kicked off his case? Was she still employed at the hospital? What if they'd forced her to leave town altogether? He had to find her.

He began a rocking motion. Pressing his fists into the uncomfortable hospital mattress, he gave a heave, but not the ho. He looked down again to make sure his feet had contact with the floor.

They did. Not that he could feel the cold of the linoleum. It was no matter. He was going to stand. He was going to find the woman he wanted to sweep into his arms. If she wasn't welcome here any longer, then he wasn't staying either.

Taking in a deep breath, Paul leaned back, readying himself to both heave and ho, when the door to his room creaked open. Paul's head jerked up, readying to launch himself at Madison. Unfortunately, coming into the room was the last person in the world Paul wanted to have in his arms, or even in his vicinity.

"What are you doing?" demanded Dr. Lamb.

"About to go for my morning run," said Paul. "What does it look like?"

"Do not get up."

Lamb held out his hand like a stop sign. As if that would've stopped Paul.

"If you fall down and get a concussion, she'll blame me."

"She?" Paul looked over Dr. Lamb's shoulder. But he didn't see her. "Where is she?"

"She's not here. It's part of the deal."

"Part of what deal?"

"The deal she made to get me to perform your surgery."

"I don't want you to perform my surgery. I want her to do it."

"That's against the rules. Doctors can't operate on loved ones."

Dr. Lamb crinkled his nose as he spat out those last two words. Paul didn't care that he'd mangled them. The words were music to his ears.

"Loved ones?" Paul asked.

Lamb fixed his features, but irritation and disbelief shadowed his eyes. "It's just an expression."

"She said she loved me?"

"It's just an expression," Lamb insisted. "It's a good policy because, clearly, her personal feelings are impairing her professional judgment."

"Madison said she has personal feelings for me?"

Lamb let out a sigh of defeat. "I don't know what she sees in you. You don't seem very bright. For example, it's not wise to antagonize the man who is about to cut into your back with a sharp knife."

"Oh, I'm not worried about you."

"You should be." Lamb tried for menace, but he looked like a disgruntled Ewok with his mane of blond curls.

"Well, I'm not. You're too focused on winning the game."

"She was focused on the same thing at one point."

"She still is. You're just playing different games now. You're playing at that doctor game—what's it called? The one where you buzz the sides if you don't have a steady hand."

"It's called Operation, and I never buzzed the sides in that game."

"Madison's not playing that. She's playing the Game of Life. And she's swept the whole board."

"Yeah?" said Dr. Lamb. "Well, you just better hope I don't buzz the edges of your insides with my scalpel."

"You won't. Like you said, if I get hurt, she'll kill you. And I have every confidence she could take you."

Lamb nodded as though Paul was right.

CHAPTER TWENTY

$\mathcal{M}$adison paced the length of the hall. Her heels clacked against the linoleum. The sound of boots accompanied her pacing.

Luke walked in the opposite direction of her. She and Paul's best friend would meet in the middle, about-face, and head in the other direction. When they met the wall, they'd turn and repeat the process.

"The two of you are driving me crazy," said Elaine. "He's going to be fine."

"I've never been on this side of the OR," said Madison. "I'm always the one holding the scalpel."

Luke held her hand. Elaine grabbed the other. They paced together as a unit. It was the first time Madison had walked with others beside her. It was the first time she'd been in a waiting room. When her father had passed, she hadn't even been in the same state. She'd been all by herself, as no family remained. Not even Aunt Bess. Just like when she'd taken that walk home, she'd been all alone.

She wasn't by herself now. Luke and Elaine weren't the only two people in the waiting room. The room was filled to the brim with people from the Purple Heart Ranch. Soldiers, wives, children, and others who worked there.

Madison had met Paul's new employer. A female cattle rancher who stood tall in stylish boots. Brenda Vance waited patiently for news from the surgery, just as she was waiting patiently for her new horse wrangler to make it to his first day of work. Brenda didn't doubt that Paul would recover and be on the job soon. She must get that certainty from her pastor brother, who kept nodding calmly at Madison as though he was receiving word from up high that all would be well soon.

Paul had so many people who cared about him. Each person had come up and embraced Madison as though she was someone special, someone important.

How had this happened?

She'd only arrived here a few days ago. Only knew Paul for such a short amount of time. And, now, it felt like she was ensconced into the center of his world. It was a place she never wanted to leave.

It was a place that felt like a memory.

It was a place she wanted to call home.

It didn't matter to her if Paul ever stood again. Madison wanted to rest her head against this chest. She wanted to curl into his embrace. She wanted him to kiss her again. And then again, and then some more for the rest of her days.

The doors to the OR opened. A single doctor came out. His expensive loafers made no sound against the shiny floor as he walked toward them.

Madison held still. She knew every look on Doug's face. Right now, he had on a poker face that she'd never seen.

"He's resting," said Doug. "I believe the operation was a success."

There was a sigh of relief from everyone. But not Madison. She demanded to see Paul's charts, wanting to check Doug's every step and stitch.

"Dr. Gray, you can check my charts later. Right now, he wants to see you."

Madison dashed around Doug. But then she stopped. She turned and gave him a hug. "Thank you."

Doug didn't squeeze her back. He patted her awkwardly, in the way a surgeon not used to the gratitude of his patient's family.

When Madison came into the room, Paul was resting with his eyes closed. She walked quietly, slowly, toward him. Her heart rate jumped with every step. It felt like she was being shocked with paddles with each beat.

The rules had prevented her from operating on a loved one. She'd followed the rules. Because Paul was a loved one. Madison was desperately in love with this man.

His eyes opened. "Hey," he said with a lazy grin. "Either I survived. Or this is heaven. Doesn't matter which as long as you're here."

"We're still here on earth."

Madison took his hand. Her fingers curled around his until they were laced together. That certainty she always felt when she'd held a scalpel came over her when his long fingers pressed against hers.

Madison knew she would be a surgeon for the rest of her life. Maybe not chief of Orthopedic Surgery immediately. But someday. She knew that as certainly as she knew she would be with this man for the rest of her life. Not someday. Right now.

"You owe me a date," said Paul.

"Already taken care of. Dinner will be served later tonight when you're ready to eat."

"You bought me dinner?"

"No, I didn't buy it. It's on your hospital bill."

Paul chuckled, and it was the most beautiful sound she'd ever heard. But the laughter died from his throat, and he sobered. "Did you lose the promotion?"

Madison shrugged. "For now. But Doug won't stay long. He's a city boy."

"Aren't you a city girl?"

"My roots are country strong."

"With those heels?"

"Hey!"

His grin spread wider. His hand lifted to her cheek. There was still a blood pressure cuff attached to his right arm. The nubs of ECG leads were visible beneath his thin hospital gown. Madison heard the beeping of the monitors speed up. The sounds kept pace with her own racing pulse and heartbeat.

"So, you're going to stick around?" Paul asked. "You're not going back to the city?"

"Maybe for a day trip to get a nice pair of designer cowboy boots," she said as she leaned into his hand. "Otherwise, I'm good right where I am."

"Maddie?"

"Hmmm?" She nuzzled into the center of his palm.

"Since you're not my doctor anymore, it's not against the rules for me to steal a kiss."

Her eyes blinked open, and she gazed at this man who had stolen her heart while she'd been trying to read his medical chart. "Can't steal what someone gives to you."

Madison leaned into Paul. She pressed him back to the pillows when he tried to meet her halfway. When her lips met his, she was kissing a wide grin. It tasted delicious. It tasted of hope, of happiness, of love.

"That was amazing," Paul said with a sigh. "It made my toes tingle."

They both glanced down at the bottom of the bed. The sheet moved as his wriggled the toes of both his feet. It was a great sign, it meant he would stand. For now, Madison allowed him to sweep her into his arms as she deepened the kiss.

HIS GRACE UNDER PRESSURE

THE BRIDES OF PURPLE HEART RANCH
BOOK 12

CHAPTER ONE

$\mathcal{I}$t was all in his head.

The hiss of embers that sizzled at his right shoulder. The shards of debris that rained fire down on his back. The dark, curling smoke licking at the heels of his boots.

Eric Prince knew the explosion was just a dream in his head. A vivid, technicolor dream filled with IMAX theater-quality surround sound. Because he'd lived this nightmare. The dream was a memory.

He turned on his mattress. Instead of a warm cushion, he felt the gravel of the disjointed road as he fell face-first into the dirt. He twisted in the sheets. Instead of a cool blanket, he was wrapped in hot embers from the blast.

None of that was the worst of it. The worst part was the silence that stole over him after the dust settled.

Prince jerked awake to bright sunlight shining on his face. There was a chill to the morning air. He lay bare in the bed, having kicked off his blanket at some point during the dream. All was quiet and serene outside his window. The deathly silence had followed him into the real world.

Rising from the bed, he heard the faint shriek of the protesting box springs. Stretching his arms over his head, he felt the pop and crackle of healed injuries from his years in the military. Like his spirit, Prince's body didn't voice any protest. He and his bruises simply soldiered on.

He showered and dressed quickly, avoiding looking into the small mirror of his bathroom. He had to live with his wounds. That didn't mean he had to look at the scars.

After stepping into a pair of pants and pulling on a T-shirt, Prince stepped out of his room and onto the deck of his houseboat. Up above, the sky was a clear blue. The sun's rays were muted by a few clouds. Below the sun, water-filled his vision for as far as the eyes could see. The morning tide rose and fell as it lapped against the side of the vessel.

Under his feet, he felt gentle rocking, which had been the only thing that could lull him to sleep after his last and final deployment. Ever since he was a kid, the houseboat had always felt like a large cradle to him. When he was younger, it was his favorite place in the world. Now it was his home.

It was a quiet day on the marina. Most days were here. There were hardly any residents that lived on the water. Though the state of Montana was landlocked, there were a few choice lakefront properties. Prince didn't live on one. He lived on the lake, docked to the marina of this small town.

Prince had been born in this town, but he had no roots. All ties to this place and these people had been severed long ago. When he'd been injured in the line of duty, and his injuries prevented him from returning to the work he loved, this place was all he had left.

It was a busy day for him. A trip into town and down Main Street always was. He tried to make as few visits from the marina into his town as possible. But as the waters grew colder, the fish didn't bite so readily. Prince would have to stock up the cupboards unless he wanted to starve.

On the grassy knoll that buffeted the waters, he saw a large group of teens playing volleyball. Their mouths opened wide as they laughed and joked with each other, the way that friends did. The way that he and his military buddies once did before a blast had ripped their lives to shreds.

Younger kids ran in and out of the water just up to their shins, splashing cold water on one another. Prince could see an older woman standing nearby. Her mouth was agape, and her features were pinched in annoyance. She cupped her hand around her mouth, and her lips began moving. A moment later, the kids trudged out of the water, disappointment clear on their faces. Their own lips were flapping in what Prince was sure was an argument against stopping their fun.

"Hey!"

Prince came to a halt. He blinked a couple of times as the man standing in front of him came into clear view. Arnie Mackenzie, the Marina Manager, had been working the docks longer than Prince had been alive. On the old man's face, Prince read bewilderment. Arnie must have been calling after Prince for a while before he noticed.

Prince carefully arranged his features into one of disinterest. In his youth, he'd had a reputation for being a hothead and a troublemaker. Though he'd never shown that attitude out here on the docks.

"I said there's a storm coming in a few days," Arnie spoke slowly, opening his mouth wider than necessary for normal volume.

A tingling crept up the back of Prince's neck. The feeling was worse than the memory of the blast embers piercing his skin. Did Arnie know?

Self-consciously, Prince ran a hand through his hair. It was longer than military regulation. He'd started growing it out after his diagnosis. His dark hair was now long enough to cover his ears.

"Son, you know if there's anything you need…"

Prince allowed the rest of the sentence to drone out. It wasn't hard to do. The silence from his nightmare hadn't stopped ringing in his ears. It never did. Likely never would.

"Thanks, Mr. Mackenzie," Prince called out before heading toward the street.

He chanced a glance over his shoulder, but the man wasn't following him. Nor was he calling out to Prince. Mr. Mackenzie had turned back and was walking down to the marina.

The tension seeped out of Prince's shoulders like water swirling down a drain. He wanted to curse the cold-blooded fish for not being able to hack a few drops in the temperature. If not for their inconsiderateness, he'd be scaling his lunch instead of mingling with people.

Up ahead, a gruff dog sniffed at a trash can on the sidewalk. The animal's fur was matted as though it had taken a bath in the bay's waters and then run through the dirt. Its tongue lolled out the side of its mouth as though it grinned when it pulled a half-eaten sandwich from the garbage.

It looked up when it heard Prince approach. It didn't look rabid, just dirty. There was no collar or tags on the beast. One strong wind would likely knock the animal over.

Still knowing all of this, Prince gave the animal a wide enough berth. The dog was no match for a trained Tier One Operator, such as himself. Prince had taken down insurgents with rifles, knives, and even his bare hands without blinking.

Yet when this mangy mongrel sniffed the air around Prince and then sat back on its haunches, Prince's hands began to shake. Heat licked up his back as though from an oncoming blast. Prickles traced over his skin like the ghost of embers from an explosive.

In the military, bomb-sniffing dogs were trained to sit when they scented an explosive.

Prince tried to shake himself loose of his thoughts. This was a stray mutt, not a trained animal. It was sitting because it was looking to be petted. This was not a warning that a bomb was in the trash.

The dog opened his mouth. It's jaws working as it called after Prince. Prince heard not a sound of the animal's barking as he quickly walked away from it.

Six months in a military hospital, three months on the Purple Heart rehabilitation ranch, and Prince was still not healed. That bomb had stolen more than his career. It had stolen a chunk of his flesh and nearly all of his hearing. The only thing he wanted from this life now was peace and the quiet that would inevitably consume him.

CHAPTER TWO

The screech of the microphone was the best sound to come off the stage in the last couple of minutes. Ariana Carol's entire body tensed as Betsy Vance tried in vain to hit the high note in Whitney Houston's *Bodyguard* anthem. But the long note that the amateur tried to trill out scratched the back of her throat.

It was like the squeeze of a lemon on top of chocolate pudding. It was like giving a balloon a hug with the five fingertips of one hand while the nails of the other one scratched down a chalkboard. Ari had to stop in the center of the dance floor for a second and make sure that her soul wasn't splintering, much less the windows of her family's karaoke bar.

Luckily, all was intact in Carol on the Bay. The seashells on the walls did swing a bit as though the vibrations from the speakers had crashed into them. A few of the portraits of great singers seemed to shake, or rather shudder as the song came near to the end.

Meanwhile, Betsey's tone-deaf friends applauded and catcalled for her to aim for a higher note. For her part, Betsey inhaled and belted out how she would always love the man in the song. At least her boyfriend, Jared Robins, who sat at the table with their group of friends, had the right mind to cringe.

As Betsey brought the song home by hitting it out into left field, Ari regained her sense of equilibrium and headed to the section of tables on the opposite side of the establishment. Dr. Green and her husband, Nurse Tony, were regulars, as were most of the town-folk gathered this afternoon. They all had grown accustomed to tuning out the bad singers that came to the microphone and committed aural crimes against the music industry. Or perhaps their ears had crusted over from the blood-letting that had come through the speakers years ago.

"Good afternoon, Ari," said Dr. Green. "We'll just have the usual."

Ari didn't bother writing their usual down. She was already carrying Dr. G's Diet Cherry Cola and Nurse Tony's hot tea with lemon and two sugars. Their tuna melt with extra cheese and crab cakes without the bun were already on order. Ari set the drinks before the couple, along with straws and napkins.

"Thanks, Ari," said Nurse Tony.

Ari nodded before turning on her heel.

She made her way to the table behind the Greens with a coffee pot in hand. She topped off the mug of Harvey Rich. The gray-haired man's belly was as rotund as Santa's. His cheeks nearly as rosy. He looked up at her with a grin.

"You're looking lovely today, my dear."

Ari nodded, returning the man's grin.

The door opened, allowing a ray of the sunlight to shine into the dimly lit bar. It was another of her regulars. August Cassidy bobbed his head at Ari, before sliding into his usual booth. Ari gave the man a nod, already writing up the ticket for his order of steak -medium rare- and fries. She'd have his beer out in just a minute.

"You know," said Dr. G, stopping Ari as she walked back past their table. "You could do so much better than anyone who comes in here and gets on that stage."

Ari didn't nod. She offered the woman a demure smile. But as she turned to go, Dr. G gave her another tug.

"I'm serious, Ari. I heard you sing when you were younger. Do you remember that, Tony? The girl had the voice of an angel."

In response, Ari inhaled deeply and let the breath out slowly.

"Shame what happened all those years ago," Dr. G went on. "You know if you ever want to see somebody, we have some great psychologists on staff these days."

At least she hadn't offered a speech therapist. There was nothing wrong with Ari's voice. She simply chose not to use it.

Finally, with another silent nod, Ari made a quick getaway to the back. The doors to the kitchen slapped her bottom just as Betsey was bringing the song home, trying to make the last couple of notes of the song trill like a butterfly's wings. Instead, the sound was more of the buzzing of an annoying fly.

"Why do we insist on these amateur afternoons?" Adelle Carol slapped a steak on the grill before Ari handed her the order. Her red hair was pinned atop her head, but a few tendrils curled down around her neck, framing her face. "I swear every Thursday afternoon I go home with a hangover like I drank a bottle of tequila."

"It brings in more locals, which brings in more cash, which keeps you in designer threads," said Alanna. Her short red curls radiated from her head like she was the sun.

"Sometimes, I wonder if it's worth it." Adelle tugged at the apron covering her silk shirt. But not before glaring at the grill. It would be a fool drop of grease that dared mar any of her outfits. Adelle was likely the only short-order cook in all of Montana that wore heels and fine linens in the kitchen and somehow walked away without an expensive dry cleaning bill.

"Of course, it's worth it," said Alanna. "This place was Dad's dream."

"No, the three of us on a stage was Dad's dream." Adelle sprinkled a pinch of her special seasoning on the steak. The meat sizzled as though it was pleased with the adornments she'd dressed it with.

Ari winced at the thought. The Carol household had been filled with song and music since before the day she was born. The brick hearth of the fireplace in their living room doubled as a stage with the three sisters using pokers as microphones. Ari had been forever sandwiched between her sisters, belting out a song. Those performances had all stopped ten years ago.

"But Daddy also had those weird dreams of an octopus and eels coming after us," said Alanna.

The three sisters burst out into laughter. Even the sound of their laughter was harmonious. If Ari could ever bring herself to get back up on a stage, much less speak in public, the sisters would make a killing with their voices.

But that path was no longer open to them. Not since The Incident ten years ago. Ari shuddered to think about it, to think about him. So she shook herself and began loading up her plate of orders.

"Ari, baby," said Alanna, "you know I gotta take off early today."

Ari put the plates back down and turned to glare at her sister.

Alanna didn't look the least bit contrite. She was looking in a mirror and fixing a seashell barrette in her curls.

"I have a date," she said as an excuse.

Ari blew air out of her nose. She pursed her lips together. She was irritated enough to have words with her sister.

"It's a slow afternoon," said Alanna. "That train wreck on stage is almost over. There probably won't be anyone in here other than the regulars."

Ari knew Alanna was right. But still, just the mere idea of interacting with someone who didn't know her, or her tendency not to respond, set her hives a buzzing. But this was a family business, and they all had responsibilities. Her sisters indulged her. They had given up part of their dream for her. When Ari wouldn't go back on stage after her humiliation, they had lost out on a recording contract. They'd tried going on as a duet, but without Ari's voice, something had been missing.

They still sang together in the privacy of their home recording studio. But Ari knew she would never sing in public again. So, all they had left was this bar that their parents had left them before retiring to Florida.

Ari huffed out a breath as her sister bussed her on the cheek. Before Alanna could pull back, Ari enacted her revenge. She swatted at Alanna's perfectly tousled hair. Alanna called after Ari, but Ari was quick. She grabbed the serving tray and dashed out of the kitchen.

Unfortunately, another of the amateurs had taken the stage. On the karaoke machine's screen, the words for Celine Dion's *My Heart Will Go On* was queued up. Ari groaned as she turned her back on the stage.

She served up the Greens's dishes and Mr. Cassidy's drink. She walked by the rest of her regulars topping off their drinks and bussing the tables of the one's who'd left. By the middle of the song, as she was wishing she'd gone down with the Titanic, she noticed that a newcomer was sitting in her sister's section.

Ari plastered on her friendliest smile, grabbed for her pen, and headed over. As she got closer, she noted that the man looked familiar. Not familiar enough to be a regular whose order she might have memorized.

That wasn't something to worry over yet. All the specials were written out on the menu. Everything else on the menu was pretty self-explanatory. They lived on the lake. They sold mostly seafood.

She got by most nights with newcomers simply smiling, nodding, and waiting patiently. But as she drew nearer to this man, her smile began to falter as her memory sharpened.

He sat frowning at the singers on the stage. His features were sculpted perfectly like he could've been the David's handsomer older brother who hadn't had time to sit for the sculpture. His dark hair could use a trim as it fell over his ears. He had a few days worth of scruff on his face, but not a full beard yet. Still, it made him look rugged, dangerous. It wasn't until he frowned in distaste that she stumbled.

Ari had seen that look of disdain before. She saw it often in her dreams. In her nightmares, she would be standing on a stage, singing her heart out. With just one glance at the boy in the audience and his features screwed in this very manner, her voice had squeaked. Then it had left her. And it never came back.

Ari had run off the stage that day to the soundtrack of his jeering laughter. Was he about to laugh at her now? Was he about to point and jeer once again?

She wanted to run, but she stood there frozen. Just like that fateful day at the Christmas gala all those years ago. And then the boy from her nightmares turned and looked at her.

The sneer fell from his face. His gaze softened. His mouth went slack. He said the two words Ari had longed to hear for years.

"I'm sorry."

Too bad it wasn't enough. Because she still stood there, speechless in front of Eric Prince. The boy who'd stolen her voice away.

CHAPTER THREE

It was his stomach that drove Prince into the bar and grill just off the marina. That and the thought of another meal from a can. He'd spent much of his youth eating cafeteria food at the private military school his father had enrolled him in the day after his mother's funeral. Then he'd spent the next years of his life eating the gruel in Basic Training and then on base.

As he made his way into town for his shopping trip, the smell of grease and salt fairly lifted him up by the nostrils and led him through the doors of Carol on the Bay Karaoke Bar. Luckily, it wasn't too crowded inside. Even luckier was that a whole section of the place looked entirely unoccupied.

A few customers sat on the right side of the establishment. Likely locals as it was an early Thursday afternoon. However, there was a large group gathered around the front at the stage. Perhaps these were college students out for a laugh. He hoped they weren't serious with these performances. Not that he could hear their voices all that well. What he did hear was off-key.

Prince reached to his right ear and turned his hearing aid down. He could still hear the racket in his left ear, though it sounded like it was coming from farther away. That was fine with him. Prince stole into the unoccupied left side of the restaurant.

He didn't remember this place being here when he lived here. But then again, he didn't remember a lot about this place. As part of his father's military career, his family had moved so often when he was younger. Then hopped around bases in the states and abroad until he was fifteen. This had been the last place where his family had owned property. The house had been rented out, and Prince had told the occupants to stay as long as they wanted. The rent was more than enough for him to live off of. That and his disability checks. He could live out the rest of his days quietly. Especially if he kept turning down his hearing aid or simply didn't wear it.

Prince was a music lover. But it didn't appear that the people in front of the stage were. Not if they thought that off-key rendition of the *Titanic* movie classic wasn't heading towards an iceberg.

Looking over at the right side of the restaurant, it would appear that the other patrons agreed. They turned their backs on the singer and continued their conversations. With his hearing aid off, Prince could hardly hear any of it. Which was bliss.

It was times like these he felt he had an advantage on those who weren't hearing impaired. He could hear a hum of noise on his own, but it was hard to make out any single words. Especially over the constant ringing ever-present in his ears.

Prince closed his eyes and tried to get lost in the hum that typically haunted him. His world wasn't truly silent. But he could let his attention drift with no one watching him.

Only, it felt like someone was watching him. He opened his eyes and saw a pair of shapely legs standing near him. It had been a long time since he'd checked a woman out. Why would he bother flirting if he wasn't guaranteed to hear her response to his witty lines? Or worse, mistake what she said.

His gaze traveled up those legs to find softly rounded hips hidden beneath a mini skirt. Her coral pink shirt had the logo of the restaurant on her chest. His eyes moved slowly as they traversed her clavicles. That part of a woman had always been his favorite, especially when kissing. He liked playing in the rises and dips of the flesh and bone there.

Her neck was long, like a swan's. Fire red hair brushed her shoulders. That combination shouldn't go; red hair and a pink shirt. But she stood there looking stunning in the color.

There were freckles on her neck and cheeks. The sprinkle of dots rested above a full mouth, that was parted. Were her lips moving? Had he missed what she'd said?

Prince looked up into her eyes. Though he was sitting down and inside four walls, he felt he'd gotten lost. Her eyes were the blue of the ocean. He could sail on those waves in and out of days, over weeks, months, and years. If she'd let him.

The way her gaze was pinched as she looked down at him, he suspected that a witty remark was not going to grant him permission to come aboard. Likely because she'd already said something to him and he hadn't responded.

She held a pen and pad in her hand. He glanced again at her shirt and realized she was a waitress. Then he realized he was staring at her chest and glanced away.

"I'm sorry," he mumbled, barely hearing his own voice.

The menu was on the table. He grabbed for it and pulled it forward, though he didn't look at it. He turned his body so that she wouldn't see him reach for the device in his ear and turn it back up.

CHAPTER FOUR

He didn't remember her.

Ari stood there frozen, staring down at the man who had wreaked so much havoc on her life. Eric Prince, or Prince as everyone called him because during the times he was here, he walked around like he owned the town. But also because it was his last name.

Prince was even more handsome as a grown man than when he was a teen. He'd lost the lankiness of youth and filled out. Considerably.

His shoulders were so broad they took up most of the booth. She could see the definition of muscle under the thick fabric of his shirt. He'd had the beauty of a gazelle when he was young. Now he looked like a bear. Complete with the shaggy, overgrown hair topping his head, and the scruffy facial hair covering his chin and upper lip.

And he didn't remember her.

In fact, it looked like he'd found her wanting. Those green eyes had taken her in—taken all of her in. From her shoes to her head. And when he'd reached her eyes, he'd grimaced.

Even all these years later, she found he looked at her as though she was lacking, that she was a joke, that she wasn't good enough. At least this time there wasn't a group of his cronies around to witness his derision. Most of the kids Prince had run with when he was younger were gone. Except one who still hung around even though not many in town enjoyed her company.

But none of that mattered. Because Prince did not remember her.

"I'll take a burger and fries," he said. He scratched at his ear as he did so.

Ari balled her fingers into a fist. Not to get violent. Unlike Prince, she didn't have a mean bone in her body. She pumped blood and feeling back into her hand so that she could write his order down. But she couldn't remember how to spell the word burger. Her pencil tip broke when she tried to write fries. Because here she stood taking an order from Prince, the villain in her life's story, the man who'd locked her in a tower of silence and left her to wallow in a wordless world, and he didn't have the decency to remember who she was.

For the first time in years, Ari wanted to use her voice. She wanted to raise it loud. She wanted to shout at him. But she didn't. She couldn't.

Prince looked up at her then. Were his green eyes darker than she remembered? When she'd gazed after him as a preteen, she'd remembered thinking his eyes were the bright green of seafoam washed ashore. Now they appeared to her the dark color of seaweed that's hard to detect out in the water until it ensnares a swimmer's foot and threatens to bring them under.

His dark gaze held onto her. There was a haunted look at the edges of his eyes. There was a hint of fear there that she knew well. An anxiety that at any moment someone could lash out and hurt her. Not with a physical strike, but with an uttered word.

But that was impossible. This was Eric Prince. He didn't care what anyone said or thought about him. She'd watched him thumb his nose at authority when she was a young girl. He hadn't even come to apologize to her after The Incident, even when the mayor had insisted on it. And by that next week, Eric Prince was gone. Sent off to military school. He'd never returned, not for holidays or visits with his parents.

Yet here he was, sitting in her family's bar, with a hint of vulnerability on his face. If Ari was a woman who did speak, she'd be at a loss for words.

From across the room, the current singer was getting a little zealous with the microphone. High-pitched feedback protested her machinations. The sound screeched, sending a treble shrill through the speakers.

Ari winced at the sound, raising a hand to her ears. But her hand never reached her face. Before she knew it, her back was flung against the wall behind the booth. Two hundred and twenty pounds of virile male was pressed against her.

Prince had her against a wall. His arms covered her head. Her head pressed into his chest. His legs boxed her in, cutting off any and all means of escape. She was trapped against the wall by her greatest enemy.

So why did she feel safe for the first time in years?

Prince raised his head, eyes darting around the bar. Gone was the lost look he'd had just a moment ago. In its place was a wild gaze that frantically searched the room as though there was danger.

No one else noticed them. The group at the stage was too busy catcalling and whooping for the awful singer at the mic. The usual patrons had already shaken off the glaring electronic feedback and were resuming their meals.

A thought hit Ari at that moment. Had Prince been trying to protect her? Was that why he was using his body to protect hers? Because he thought there was a clear and present danger?

There weren't any dangers here in town. Not unless she counted the newspaper bandit who routinely stole the coupons from Mr. Garcetti's Sunday paper. Or the parking fairy who went around and fed low street meters. Surprisingly, that was indeed a crime. But one that would never be prosecuted.

What would possess Prince to think they were in danger of anything except a headache from the awful singing? For that, he could've offered her an aspirin, not used his body to protect her; the girl whose life he'd ruined and forgotten about.

From the cradle of his arms, Ari watched as Prince's eyes zeroed in on the sound system. She watched as realization dawned that it was a speaker that had launched an attack, not a person. The vulnerability came back in force. Heat spread from his eyes, darkening them from a light green to a darker one. The vulnerability pinched the corners of his eyes, making a nest of crows there. It spread to his nose, which wrinkled as though it smelled something foul. And finally, the vulnerability landed on his mouth, where his lips pinched together.

Prince shut his eyes, letting out a gust of air. It tasted bitter when it hit Ari's tongue. She glanced up at his unguarded face, and that's when she saw it.

In his ear, there was a plastic device. A node that fit snuggly into the hollow with a piece wrapped around the outer cone of his ear. A hearing aid.

Of its own accord, Ari's hand rose to his face. Her fingertips brushed his cheek, feeling the bristles there. They were soft, not hard and prickly like she imagined.

Prince's eyes opened. Slowly, the pools of dark green lightened as he gazed down at her. He breathed in slowly as he searched her face. Still no recognition of who she was dawned there, but she saw something else break in the light of his pupils; interest.

Ari's fingers kept their upward trail. Her thumb brushed up his jawline, feeling the strong set to the bones there. When her index finger touched the tip of his ear, Prince jerked back and out of her reach. His needy gaze shuttered, like cold metal clanging down. The need iced over into anger.

He let her go, so quickly that Ari stumbled. He didn't reach out to catch her, and so she braced herself using the wall at her back. Without another word, Prince turned on his heel and stormed out of the bar.

CHAPTER FIVE

The boat rocked as Prince stormed onto it. Houseboat living wasn't for everyone, especially those that were prone to seasickness. Even though the structure was buoyed, the residents would still feel the motion beneath their feet.

Right now, Prince felt like his entire person was off-kilter; his body, his mind, and his dark soul. The world outside was steady. Even the boat with its subtle rocking was solid ground to the turmoil raging inside. The only thing off balance was him.

What had he been thinking about going into that place and taking a seat? If he was so hungry, he could've ordered at the bar and left. What had possessed him to sit down in a booth and then...

He raked his fingers through his hair. When he got to the ends, he tugged, hoping that would bring about his good sense. The problem was he had none left.

The walls of the boat felt like they were closing in on him. The ring of the bells in his ears grew louder. He was about to have another episode, but at least he would be alone when the anxiety grabbed hold of him.

Post Traumatic Stress Disorder came in many forms. The cruel mistress had many tentacles wrapped around Prince. She visited his dreams. She often stole into his waking hours. And she had stolen his hearing.

Going into the Armed Forces, Prince had known that he might be asked to pay the ultimate price for his country. He'd been willing to do that. What he hadn't expected was the possibility of a never-ending tab after his time was up.

He might learn to manage his PTSD symptoms. But they would never go away entirely. A flare-up in private was one thing. An episode out in public was unacceptable.

Prince left the confines of the houseboat and marched down the pier. The sun was just starting to set. The sight was beautiful; cool blue meeting warm flames and casting a purple glow.

He saw none of it. All he could see were her eyes; a blue so deep he'd felt he was floating. His attention had been captivated by the flames of her red hair. The strands had been bright enough to burn. He'd felt warmed through just standing near her.

When her soft fingers had touched his skin, he'd thought he might be hallucinating. By then, he'd come to realize that there was no danger. There had been no bomb, only the feedback from the microphone caused by the awful singing on stage.

For a second, he'd wondered if that had been part of the dream. Because what other reason would this fiery angel be in his arms. And then she'd reached for the shameful device in his ear, and the spell had been broken. Reality had come crashing down around him. Luckily, no one else in the bar had seen. Only her. Too bad he harbored a desire in his heart to see her again.

That wouldn't happen. He doubted he would ever show his face in daylight again, definitely not at Carol on the Bay Bar and Grill. Though the smell of the food still reached him from its place near the marina.

Prince gazed down the path that would lead him back there. Perhaps he should go back? Perhaps he should apologize for his behavior? That's what a normal person would do.

Movement caught his gaze. Prince looked over to see the dog from earlier standing in his path. The dirty beast wagged his tail. His tongue lolled out of his mouth.

A twitch in its hind legs told Prince the animal was preparing to sit. Prince shut his eyes so that he wouldn't see the move. He didn't need to have another episode. He didn't need to remember the last time a dog had sat down on its haunches before a bomb went off. And so he turned his back on the dog and made his way down to the water.

Just a year ago, Prince's life was going the way he'd wanted. He was on an upward trajectory in the military. He was in command of his own team and being considered for advancement. And then his entire world had blown up.

Prince shook his head. He didn't want to think about that. But no sooner than those thoughts fled did the redhead come back into his mind.

That poor girl. She must be freaking out. She must be telling the entire town how Eric Prince has lost his mind as well as his hearing.

Something in him urged him not to be so sure.

The beautiful redhead hadn't looked at him like she was afraid. She hadn't screamed. There were many frequencies that Prince couldn't hear, but the sound of a woman in terror was not one of them.

Her fingers had brushed against his face. So gentle. He couldn't remember the last time he'd experienced such gentleness. He ached for it. So much so that his feet nearly did an about-face to take him back to the bar.

And what? Have a conversation with her? It wasn't like he couldn't hear her, especially if he turned his hearing aid on. She hadn't spoken to him, hadn't uttered a word. Suddenly, Prince ached to hear the sound of her voice.

A tap on his shoulder jerked him into action. He reached back, grabbing a handful of fabric. His fist was cocked, ready to throw a punch.

It wasn't an assailant that he was confronted with. The man in Prince's hold weighed less than half of him and was at least a foot shorter. Definitely not a threat.

Yet he'd immediately gone into attack mode here in his quiet, sleepy home town. And Prince thought he could have a casual conversation with the pretty waitress? Yeah, right.

His latest victim's lips quaked. Not in fear. In that nervous laughter of someone who was uncertain. The man looked vaguely familiar. The woman standing behind him, however, was a known entity.

Prince ran his hand through his hair again. It was his cover to turn his hearing aide on.

"Once a soldier, always a soldier." Ursula Spade's voice had grown sultry in her adulthood. She was as poised and polished as she had been back in high school. Her brown skin gave off a glow in the setting sun. Her long braids snaked down her back, coiling over her shoulder as she tilted her head and regarded Prince.

"I'm sorry, Ursula," said Prince. "And I apologize to your husband."

"Prince, it's me," said the man. "Your old buddy, Jett."

Prince stared at the man, but no recognition dawned. He didn't remember much from his time in this town. Except for the places he'd hide to get away from his father and a few reckless nights with Ursula.

"It's me; Jett Elison. Don't you remember?"

Prince's brows rose as he took the man in anew. Jett had trailed behind him in the short spurts when Prince had lived here. They were the same age, but the man looked like the years had not been kind to him. Just in his late twenties, Jett had a touch of gray at his temples, and the hair at the center of his head was thinning.

"Right, sorry," said Prince. "It's been a long time."

"Yeah, last time I saw you was at the Christmas Gala almost a decade ago." Jett chuckled, slapping his knee like an old man would. "Remember that?"

Prince did not. He lifted the corner of his mouth in a noncommittal grin that he let people take however they wanted.

"You've been fighting all these years overseas," said Jett. "What's your body count?"

The corners of Prince's mouth dropped into a frown. He got that question from civilians a few times. Mainly it was a male who hadn't made the decision to serve but played a lot of shoot 'em up video games.

Ursula stepped in front Jett and took Prince by the arm. "Ignore him. He's still not house trained. It's good to see you."

Prince couldn't say the same. Ursula looked older than her years as well. He could see past the makeup she used to contour her features to appear otherwise. He couldn't remember what had attracted him to her. Probably because she had had that same vicious attitude as he'd had as a kid.

Hurt people, hurt people.

Prince had hurt enough people in his life. Now he was too broken to heal. He just wanted to be left alone.

"Where are you staying these days?" asked Ursula. "We can go back to your house and get reacquainted."

Prince didn't have a single desire to spend any time with this woman. If there was one thing he remembered about her, it was that Ursula had been a social climber. Her goal had been to reach the top of the food chain. Prince decided to show her where he was positioned on the ladder of success.

"My place is over there." Prince pointed at the marina where his home was docked.

Ursula's shark-like smile slipped when she saw the boats. "You live on a houseboat."

She took a step back. She began mumbling about catching up later as she had somewhere else to be. Which was fine with Prince. He was no longer the same boy that he'd been with her. The man he'd become had no interest in getting mixed up with a woman like her. He wished he could get tangled up in a redhead with soulful eyes and soft hands. But just like he hadn't heard her voice, Prince doubted he'd ever see her face again.

CHAPTER SIX

*A*ri inhaled deeply, taking her breath into her diaphragm like her father had taught her. She waited for the swell of the music to rise. Then she opened her mouth and added her voice to the song.

The notes trilled from her perfectly. Her voice laid on top of the guitar's strings at the song's opening. When the drums came in announcing the chorus, Ari let the lyrics roll out of her. She had the urge to close her eyes and get lost in the song, but she had to look at the lyrics on the paper to keep her place.

The song wasn't a Top Forties hit, or even an oldie. But it was a goodie. It was one of her sister's new tracks. Ari had no problem lending her voice to Adelle's demo reels. Inside their home studio, there was no one watching but her sisters.

Here her voice was safe from a jeering audience. There was no one about who'd look at her with derision to make her forget herself or doubt her ability. Yet in the sanctity of the studio, the music stopped.

"Ari, you missed that note," Adelle said from behind the glass of the sound booth. "You need to fill your lungs with more air to belt that bit out. Let's do it again."

Ari rolled her eyes as she looked into the two-way mirror. Her sister's head was down, futzing with the soundboard, so Adelle didn't see Ari's ire. Not that she would care.

"Also, I need you to speed up the chorus. I want the pace to be more staccato."

"All right, I'm on it," Ari said the words into the microphone. Her singing voice was all power, but her speaking voice was still soft from years of non-use.

Though Ari could take direction and criticism from her sisters, it didn't mean she liked it. This was another source of income for them. It was the only way that Ari could comfortably use her voice to share with others. So, she took the direction and began again.

Adelle started the track from the beginning. Ari took in her sister's direction. Inhaling an even deeper breath where Adelle wanted a more resonant note. Speeding up where she wanted a faster pace.

After a moment, Ari got lost in the song. The notes rolled from her tongue effortlessly. She closed her eyes, but the moment she did so, she saw his face, and she choked.

Once again, the music came to a glaring halt. Silence filled the sound booth, along with Ari's shallow breaths.

"Ari, what's going on with you today?"

"Nothing. I'm good. Let's go again."

Ari hadn't told her sisters about her encounter last night. No one had witnessed her little tête-à-tête with Eric Prince. The man had disappeared without a trace after this new incident.

Now Ari had two incidents with the man. Both encounters had been life-altering. The first had left her mute. The second had left her wanting.

Ari couldn't get over the fact that the man was back. There wasn't much about him that was the same. Except his frown. But that expression had been fleeting, and only when he'd looked at the stage. Not when he'd covered her with his body.

"Ari, you missed the note again."

Ari scrubbed her hands over her face. It didn't erase the feel of being in Prince's arms. It didn't wipe out the look he'd given her, that longing look mixed with desperation.

Last night, after they'd closed up and she was alone in her bedroom, Ari had thought long and hard about what must have happened to force such a change in Prince. She knew he'd gone into the military, and so she had reasoned that he must be suffering from PTSD.

That and the fact that he was sporting a hearing aid. He hadn't worn one in his youth. Not back when he'd always sported the buzz cut made notable by men in the service. So something must have happened that caused him to lose his hearing while in in active duty.

That still didn't explain his second reaction. His first reaction had been to the sound feedback. His instincts should've been to duck for cover. That hadn't happened. Instead, his second reaction had been to protect her.

"You are just spacey today."

Ari blinked a couple of times, bringing her sister in focus. Adelle squinted at her through the two-way glass. Her fingers were off the sliders and knobs of the soundboard. Her arms were crossed over her chest, clearly waiting for an explanation.

In answer, Ari lifted a shoulder. Even though she spoke to her sisters, she didn't always feel the need to. They were sisters. They could communicate without words. Plus, she didn't want to explain exactly why she was spacing out.

"Did you hear that Eric Prince was back in town?" said Adelle.

Ari held perfectly still. Then, knowing that that would only draw further scrutiny, she shuffled the music pages on the stand. All the while, not meeting Adelle's gaze.

"His dad died last year," Adelle continued when Ari didn't answer. "He didn't even come to the funeral."

Ari had remembered that. Lieutenant Prince was not the nicest man in town. He wouldn't be missed, but the town still paid their respects. Ari had been on pins and needles the day of the funeral, expecting to see the younger Prince stroll into town. When there had been no sign of him, she'd decided to think the worst of him like everyone else. It fit with thier narrative that Eric Prince was just a bad seed who didn't care who he hurt. The boy who would jeer at a little songstress' first on-stage performance, causing her to lose her confidence and a bit of her dignity, would easily be a no-show at his own father's funeral.

"He's not at the old family house. It's still being let by renters. I thought he'd kick them out and sell it."

"So, you think he's just here for a short while?" Ari asked, trying to make her voice sound disinterested. She wasn't sure if she affected the right tone for the emotion. Scales were easy because she practiced them. Speaking tones were hard when she didn't use her voice in that way on a daily basis.

Adelle shrugged. "I don't see why he'd stay. From what I hear, he's been around the world, a Navy Seal, or something. There's nothing for him here. Hopefully, he takes himself back underwater and never bothers us again."

When Ari tried to remember the cruel grin of the boy who had tormented her, all she could see was the pleading in the grown man's eyes. All she could remember was the feel of his arms, trying to keep her safe.

Ari cleared her throat to force out words. "I'm gonna head out to work on that note."

"You're off to your private nook on the lake? Just don't be too long. I heard a storm is coming."

Ari nodded as she headed out the door.

CHAPTER SEVEN

*P*rince pulled at the window pane. The pane jammed, not giving. Since the day he'd boarded the boat to make it his home, he'd kept most of the windows open. But there was a storm coming at some point today, and he needed to get all the windows closed.

There had been a few rainfalls since he'd been back. However, today's storm was predicted to be severe. Enough that he needed to batten down the hatches of his home.

The window in his bedroom finally gave. It was the last one. Inside the boat's interior, the silence felt a little different. No matter whether his hearing aid was off or on, Prince could always hear the sound of the water. It was the only thing that droned on against the constant ringing from the blast. It was the only thing that lulled him to sleep at night. Even though every time he closed his eyes, all he saw behind his lids were the red of the flames from the explosion.

"Save them," a gruff voice pleaded. "Save my wife and child."

That was the other sound Prince heard on repeat. That voice accompanied the record playing on a loop. The bomb of the explosion was like a bass drum. The ringing of the silence that followed was the constant strum of guitar strings. And that desperate plea was the lyrics of a song Prince would never forget.

"They are my world."

Prince gave his head a shake, trying to interrupt the earworm that had plagued him this last year. He never sang along to this sad tune. The lyrics had never made sense to him, not with the father he'd had.

Out on the docks, it was not very cramped. The few boats stored at this part of the marina were spaced far enough apart that Prince didn't fear another ship would damage his or vice versa. Still, he went about checking his mooring to ensure the vessel was secured.

He'd learned all he knew about boats from his father. Lieutenant Derrick Prince had always seemed more pirate than soldier to Prince. He coveted the treasures in his horde and would make anyone who disobeyed his orders walk the plank -metaphorically speaking. A backhand across the face was a swifter punishment that Lt. Prince's wife and child endured when his orders weren't minded.

Seeing that the ship was attached, Prince set about his final task of clearing anything untethered from the deck. He stored his fishing gear inside, along with a lawn chair he rarely used. Though he lived out on the water, he preferred to stay inside the boat most days. Away from prying eyes. The last thing he wanted was visitors from his old life, like yesterday.

Ursula was not a good memory from his past. In fact, there were no good memories here in this town. He should think about unmooring the boat, lifting his anchors, and sailing away. But where to?

Did it matter? He had no one left. His mother had died a decade ago after one too many plank walks at the end of his father's hand. His father's alcohol ridden body had finally mutinied on him last year.

Prince had been in recovery on a German base at the time. His superiors had tried to find a way to get him to be present at his father's funeral, but Prince hadn't cooperated. He had enough memories of seeing that man while he was in pain. He didn't need his last sight of his father to be while he was recovering from a bomb blast.

Prince had also lost touch with what was left of his team. The injuries of the other two men of his team who had survived weren't bad enough that they'd been knocked out of commission. They were both still out in the field operating. When they had made time to call, Prince simply hadn't had the heart to answer, knowing that hearing the conversation would be a struggle.

He could've stayed on the Purple Heart Ranch. The rehabilitation ranch not too far from where he lived now. The place was packed to the fences with Wounded Warriors like him. That place had felt the closest to a home. But there was an edict there that to live on the ranch for more than three months, he'd have to get married. As if any woman would consent to marry him.

The thought of red flames touched his mind's eye. Not the flames of the blast. This was a crown of silky red hair that smelled of strawberries.

Prince shook his head. He should not be thinking of her. So why were his feet moving out the door?

He walked back up the marina. He didn't protest as his feet carried him into town. The fluorescent open sign for Carol on the Bay was on. Prince stepped up to the door. The glass showed that the place had a number of customers for the lunch hour.

A redhead popped out of the kitchen. She looked very much like his waitress. But her hair was cut short and radiated out from her head like a cloud. It didn't fall in long waves down her back. It was not his waitress.

He felt movement behind him. A couple was ambling toward the door. Prince stepped back and opened it for them. He saw their lips move to form the words thank you. He offered the couple an unpracticed smile. Once the door closed behind him, he turned and left.

As he walked back toward the water, the storm clouds were still off in the distance. He had time before it hit. He climbed to a hidden cove just off the lake. This had been his secret hiding place when he was a child trying to escape shouts and hits. Here the only thing that crashed were the waves when the wind blew. The only thing that shouted were the birds up ahead.

The bomb blast had done the most damage to the tympanic membranes of his inner ear. Seventy percent of that kind of damage from IED blasts recovered within six months with spontaneous healing. The blast had happened a year ago. For once, Prince wasn't in the top percentile of his class.

He had to face the facts. His hearing was never coming back. He would spend the rest of his life like this. Not experiencing the world in a full spectrum of sound. His hearing was now a shade of gray.

The wind blew, crashing the waves below him. The birds cried as they dove for food. There was something else hovering over the sound.

It was the sweetest melody Prince had heard in a long time, perhaps ever in his lifetime.

He stepped away from the rocks of the cove to peer around. His head canted like a bird's searching out the sound. He strained his hearing, urging himself to find the source.

And then he saw her.

CHAPTER EIGHT

The waters of the lake had always been Ari's favorite accompanist. The waves crashing around her fell in time to the beat of the notes she sang. The lyrics held true with every swell of the waves, every surge of lake water returning to tickle her toes.

In this private little spot of the lake, Ari could sing her heart out and not worry about detection. The rocks hid her person. The waves hid her sound. The birds were her backup singers, though they never sang the same song.

Which was good because this song her sister had written was really hard. Ari had never gotten stage fright when it was just her and her sisters. But the number of times she'd messed up the timing of this song this afternoon had unnerved her.

Was she losing her voice in earnest? Or maybe she was just losing her mind? Because it definitely wasn't the lyrics of Adelle's melody running through her mind. Ari's thoughts kept turning back to her run-in with Prince.

She should've asked Adelle where the man was staying while in town. Not so that she could happen by and see him. So that she could avoid him, of course.

What was he even doing here? When was he leaving? Had he changed at all?

Ari knew the answer to that last question. Prince had clearly changed in his time away. Physically—definitely. Behaviorally—maybe?

The bar wasn't set that high for the man. Eric Prince couldn't have had a worse attitude than when he was younger. She knew he'd lost his mother soon after The Incident. And that his father was prone to outbursts. Thinking back, she'd never seen Lt. Prince smile once. He always looked stern and miserable.

What must it have been like to grow up with a father who raised his voice and never smiled? Even now as a grown woman, Ari was lucky enough to see her father's smile every week. Well, sometimes she saw his grin during their online video chats. Most times, the camera was pointed at his chest or his forehead. Or her parents had forgotten to turn the video on. But she always heard his strong deep baritone tell her and her sisters how much he loved them. They often sang together online.

They would be here soon for the Christmas holidays, and Ari couldn't wait to be wrapped up in her dad's embrace. She wondered if Prince had ever experienced his father's embrace? She doubted it. She wondered if Prince had anyone to visit with the approaching holidays?

A wave crashed into her shins, and she shook the thought. She needed to let go of this sympathy for him. The man didn't even remember ruining her life, and here she was planning his Christmas dinner. A dinner she couldn't even talk to him at.

Ari let go of thoughts of Eric Prince and turned back to her work. She was done with her sister's song. It had taxed her brain and her vocal patience. She decided to sing a song she'd written herself.

The lyrics were about being an outcast. About a girl who was trapped looking in on a different world from the outside. This outcast girl wanted to shout, to be heard, to be part of that other world. But her voice couldn't carry beyond the sea.

Ari belted out the notes with the waves harmonizing to back her up. The birds overhead lent their cries to her desire to be part of that other world. When she finished, she was breathless. Her heart pounded. Her ears rang. She felt full, like she had gotten the acceptance she'd wanted by belting out her secret desires in that tune.

Behind her, she heard something that sounded like a gush of air. When she turned, she found that she wasn't alone. Eric Prince was standing behind her. His entire attention on her.

Suddenly, Ari felt like she was back on that stage ten years ago. She stood frozen, gaping at him. Only this time, he wasn't snickering.

His gaze was wide. There was something like awe in his dark, green eyes. His lips were parted as though he was saying wow, and had been saying it for a long time.

He hadn't heard her? Had he? He was deaf. Wasn't he?

But she knew that wasn't entirely right. He'd heard the feedback at the restaurant. Those last notes that she'd just belted out to the waters were louder than that. Which meant he had heard her.

"Please, don't stop," Prince said. His voice was rough. Not out of anger or annoyance. It was as though he wasn't used to using it often.

"I…" Just that lone syllable escaped Ari's lips. That was more than she'd spoken aloud to anyone outside of her family in years. "I…"

Nothing more would come out. Because Ari didn't know what to say. Because she didn't remember how to use her voice. Because she was dumbstruck standing before Eric Prince, who was asking her to not stop singing..

It was all too surreal, and if that wasn't enough, a flash of lightning lit up the sky. The clouds overhead darkened. The heavens opened up and poured buckets down on them.

In seconds, Ari was drenched through. The bombing sound of thunder rolled in, announcing that her private performance was over. It was dangerous to be out in the open like this. She had to find cover.

Then there were arms around her. A jacket flung over her head. A warm body pressed into hers.

"Come with me," Prince shouted over the downpour. "I'll keep you safe."

And then he was guiding her. Practically carrying her. Ari had no choice but to follow where he led.

CHAPTER NINE

Her body felt small against his. Lush, like a pillow he wanted to snuggle into. Curvy like a road whose bends he wanted to explore. But there would be no exploring or snuggling going on. She was soaked through, and the lightning above them proved that she was in danger.

Prince pulled from his training. He took on this mission with a seriousness he hadn't had for a long time. This was what he was made for; protecting the innocent. This redhead with the voice of an angel was innocence personified.

He wanted a battle ax to down the flora in their way. He wanted a bugle to sound his victory when he got her to the docks. He lifted her up onto the houseboat and ushered her inside to proclaim his victory over the elements.

She didn't offer a peep of protest. Not that he would've heard her if she had. Even with his hearing aid in, the rain drained out any hope of his hearing her even this close.

Once he got her inside, all that he could hear was the sound of her shivering. Her teeth clattered, barring any sweet sounds from escaping her lips. Her lips were tinged blue, which was a bad sign. It would take too long to heat the interior of the boat up.

"We need to get you out of those clothes."

Her eyes went wide at the suggestion. She crossed her shivering arms over her soaked shirt. Her pinched look spoke volumes as her mouth set in a firm line.

"No." Prince held up his hands, shaking his palms as though to shake off the thought. Water droplets sprayed on her forehead as he voiced his denial. "I don't mean I want to get you naked. Not that I don't imagine you look fantastic out of your clothes."

Now her brows furrowed and she took a step back from him. Her gaze darted around the dimly lit interior of the boat.

Prince shut his mouth. He slapped his hand against his forehead. The wet smacked reminded him that the job was not done.

He gave her a wide berth, keeping to the walls as he made his way to his bedroom. Once the small couch and table were between the two of them and his bedroom door was in reach, he turned the knob and opened the space.

"I'll lay out a change of clothes and a towel for you in the bedroom. Which you can go into alone. There's a lock on the door. I wouldn't try anything. I'm not that guy."

She had no reason to believe him. She didn't know him from Adam. He didn't know her from Eve. But he wanted to. He wanted to know her name. He wanted her to sit down at his small coffee table and offer her a meal. An apple would probably be a bad idea.

She took a deep, shuddering breath. Then let out an equally quaking sigh. She glanced up at him, appearing to take his measure.

Prince's back straightened. Shoulders back, head up like he'd been taught back at military school and later had reinforced during his years in the Armed Services. He held still for her inspection, hoping that he passed muster.

Apparently, he came up to snuff. She took a tentative step toward the bedroom. Prince could hear her shoes squishing against his hardwood floors. He could hear the clatter of her teeth as she breathed. He could hear her shallow breaths as she inhaled and exhaled.

Most days, he could barely hear himself think. But this woman, he heard her every move. What was it about her?

She stopped a few feet before him. A shade casting over the lovely blue of her eyes. One of her brows lifted, as though punctuating a question.

Had she spoken? He didn't think so. His gaze hadn't left her lips.

She cleared her throat. Prince heard that loud and clear. And then finally, he caught her meaning.

He moved away from the bedroom door. Once his back was pressed against the opposite wall, she went through the open door.

Prince squeezed in behind her, giving her as wide a berth as was possible in the small room. He grabbed an old army t-shirt and a pair of shorts. It was the best he could do. That and his towel he laid out on the bed; a paltry offering for a siren such as herself.

He showed her the lock on the door. He stepped through, shutting the door behind himself. He wondered if she'd locked it. The sound would be too quiet to reach his ears. He didn't dare to test the door handle to find out.

Outside, the storm raged on, rocking the anchored boat. The moorings held fast. The water pelted the closed windows. Lightning lit the sky.

Prince puttered through the boathouse. This place wasn't in any shape to receive visitors. He put the kettle on and pulled the one mug out of his cabinet.

A crack of thunder sounded outside. It was in the distance, but it was getting closer. A new thought occupied Prince's mind.

What would happen when it was upon them?

He didn't always fare well in storms, especially not those with loud noises. Even as a child, storms had never sat well with him. Likely because they brought out the beast in his father. Prince and his mother would often shut themselves in a room to escape one of Lt. Prince's episodes.

Now Prince was prone to episodes of his own. And here he was trapped with the one person whom he wanted to appear normal to when normal was the last thing that he was.

CHAPTER TEN

ri let out the breath she'd been holding since Prince shut the door to his bedroom. She couldn't believe she was standing here, in the middle of Eric Prince's bedroom. She'd never stood in the middle of any man's bedroom.

There wasn't much to Prince's private sanctum. There was a small double bed that looked like it could barely contain the man's bulk. She would bet he had to tuck his arms under his head and curl his toes to keep them on the mattress.

The sheets were serviceable. Thin, but clean. She doubted there was enough thread to keep him warm on the nights when the temperature dropped on the lake. Especially during the winter months.

Peering around, she noted that his closet was mostly bare. What was in there were the greens and browns of military wear. There was not a hint of the designer clothes he'd worn when he was the town's rebel without a cause.

That was pretty much it. No pictures of family or friends. No books with placeholders sticking from the pages. No television or radio. There was nothing to entertain a grown man inside these four walls.

Back in Ari's room, her walls were splashed with color. Every surface was crammed with the knickknacks she found in the town's shops, or ordered online, or made herself. She had a television, a computer, a laptop, and an old record player to keep her entertained.

Though she didn't like to talk to others, she preferred her world to be filled with sound.

She wondered if Prince had fallen on hard times? Or maybe this was all a choice? Likely the latter. There was the matter of the hearing aide hidden beneath his overgrown locks of hair. His world had probably turned more internal with the loss of one of his senses. But wouldn't that be all the more reason to rely on another sense, like sight or touch?

It was none of her business. She was simply here until the danger passed, and then she was leaving this silent drab place and returning to her world of music and color.

Ari gathered the towel Prince had given her and began scrubbing at the cold moisture clinging to her body. She looked again at the bedroom door, noting that it was firmly closed. She didn't think he'd barge in on her. Not after saving her from the storm.

But a voice niggled in the back of her mind. Eric Prince hadn't been an honorable kid. He'd been a hellion on the streets when he was young, playing pranks, sneering at authority, poking fun at anyone who wasn't in his inner circle. Only, there wasn't a trace of that boy in the grown man on the other side of the door.

That man had reached out and protected her not once but twice now. He didn't want to see her come to any harm. Which was hilarious because he was the cause of her silence all these years.

She'd spoken to him. True, it was only one word, one syllable. But it was more than she'd managed in years. Maybe that's why she was here. Maybe it was time for that to change.

A therapist had once told her that she needed to confront her fear. By the time Ari had been given that lesson, her fear had gone off to military school and then to a real live combat zone.

He was on the other side of the door now.

Could she do it? Could she confront him? With her voice?

Ari stripped off her wet clothing. She made certain to hold the towel around her body so that she was never exposed. When she slipped into the clothing Prince had provided her, the shirt engulfed her. The fabric came down to her knees, covering the shorts he'd left her.

She was surrounded by his scent, the smell of summer sand, a cool fall breeze, and newly cut spring grass. Ari shivered as the last of the cold from the rain left her. Enveloped by his scent, engulfed in his clothing, she felt naked.

Her shoes were too squishy to put back on, so she left them off. That was what made her feel the most vulnerable, having her bare toes exposed as she walked across the hardwood floor. Ari took a deep breath and opened the bedroom door.

She found Prince standing in the small kitchen area. A tea kettle whistled that the water in its belly had warmed. He wore different clothing than from before. He was dry, but his hair still damp. Prince's attention wasn't focused on the teapot. His gaze was on her.

He took her in, his eyes sweeping over her from the wet mass of her hair, down to his shirt that hung formlessly on her body, and then to her bare toes. Ari pressed the balls of her feet into the hardwood, trying to ensure she stayed upright under the assault of his intense gaze. His green eyes had darkened again. She began to wonder if they had ever been a lighter shade.

She pointed to the kettle, which was now screaming its readiness. She wondered if Prince couldn't hear it, or if he was simply taken by her. It had to be the former because she was a bedraggled sight.

With some difficulty and what might possibly be reluctance, Prince tore his gaze from her. He turned the burner off, which hushed the kettle.

With uncertain movements, he poured the steamy water into a mug. His motions were jerky and measured, as though he didn't want to make a mistake. He kept stealing glances at her as he added one then two cubes of sugar. With a look her way, he held up the milk, but Ari shook her head.

Cradling the cup in the palm of his large hand, he took the steps to bring it to her. His strides were exactly how she would imagine a soldier would make his way to a target. Because that's what she felt like. A target he was aiming for.

He moved one hand from the mug to indicate where she should sit. The couch was small, more of a love seat than a sofa. She took one end, and he folded his large form down onto the other. Before handing her the mug, he brought it to his mouth and blew the steam away.

Ari couldn't stop her smile at his actions. He was still trying to protect her. First from sound. Then from rain. And now from heat.

"My name is Prince."

She'd been staring at his lips. They'd stopped their puckering and now moved to make words. Ari glanced up at him, looking straight into eyes that held no trace of the past.

There was recognition there. But it didn't go any further than a day in the past. He only knew her as she was today, not a decade ago.

Did she need to rehash the past with him if he didn't remember it? Could she just let what had happened go and start anew today?

Ari took a deep breath and let it out. She opened her mouth to tell him what he'd done to her all those years ago. She wanted to remind him that he'd ruined her life. None of that came out. Only one word did.

"Ari."

CHAPTER ELEVEN

*P*rince watched intently as her lips parted. Her teeth moved apart slightly. Her tongue dipped and rose. He felt a gush of air leave her mouth and brush over his upper lip. He was mesmerized.

Unfortunately, whatever sound she may or may not have made was entirely unintelligible to his ears.

He warred with himself. He hated that his weakness was exposed to the one person whom he wanted to appear strong before. The need to know her name won out.

"I'm sorry," he said. "I didn't hear you. Can you repeat that?"

She took a deep breath, as though giving him her name was just as difficult for him to hear it.

Prince took a deep breath as well. He knew that in order to make this go her way, for him to hear her better, he'd need to take his eyes off her beautiful face. He'd have to give up watching her lips make the sound and turn his good ear to her so that he might hear her better. And so he turned his head to the left side and gave her his good ear.

"ARI!"

Prince ducked his head, covering his ear with his arm. He should've warned her not to shout. But it was too late. At least the mission was accomplished. He now knew her name.

When the pounding in his head subsided a bit, he lowered his arm and lifted his gaze to her. Ari covered her mouth with her hands. Her brows were raised, looking at him in horror.

"It's okay," he soothed. "I'm okay."

He heard the low moan of anguish that came from behind her hands. Any residual pain he might have felt in his damaged eardrum dissipated at her angst. He wrapped his fingers around hers and tugged her hands from her mouth.

"I'm fine," he said. "I promise."

She allowed him to peel away her fingers. When he did so, her perfect lips were set in a frown. He even found that beautiful about her. He wondered what battle he'd have to wage, what war he would need to win in order to earn the right to kiss those lips?

"Ari," he sighed her name. "Did I get it right?"

Ari opened her mouth. Only to immediately shut her lips. Instead of speaking, she gave a furtive bob of her head.

"It's beautiful."

Ari lifted a brow, as though to question his sincerity.

Prince smiled sheepishly. He was caught. Ari was a unique name to be sure. He'd known two guys with that name, but he'd never heard a woman called that before. Perhaps it was short for something? He didn't think now was the best time to ask. However, he wanted to see her lips move again. So, he asked.

Instead of answering him and opening her mouth to speak, Ari pursed her lips together. She lifted a hand or tried to. Both of her hands were still being held in his own. Prince let go of one hand but held fast to the other, cradling her slim fingers in his large, rough ones.

Ari lifted her hand to his face. Her fingers hesitated when they reached his ear. She met his gaze, asking permission. Like a dog seeking affection, Prince dipped his head until he met her fingertips.

Ari's index finger brushed the cone of his ear. Just like a dog, Prince shuddered at her touch. He was prepared to flop on his back and beg for a belly rub.

But Ari jerked her hand away. Worry creased her brow. Did she think she'd hurt him?

"It's fine," he said, seeking her hand again. "I'm fine."

Prince brushed the hair covering his left ear. Though the loss was most significant in the right ear, the doctors had insisted he wear them in both as both had been damaged. There was no outward scarring on his head. Just a few wounds on his back from the blast. Those had all healed over. Only his loss of hearing remained.

Ari's gaze latched onto the device in his ear. She swallowed, her long, elegant column of a throat working as she studied the hearing aid. More than anything, he wanted to hear her voice in his ear. Already, the memory of it was growing dim in his mind.

"You don't have to shout," he said. "Just come close when you speak."

That wasn't entirely true. She simply needed to speak at a normal volume. Prince got the impression that, despite her boisterous singing voice, Ari was a soft-spoken woman. Possibly even shy. Which didn't fit with her job as a waitress.

But this was a small town where everybody knew everybody. Prince barely remembered anyone from this town. He hadn't cared to. Though few had forgotten him and his family.

He wondered how long Ari had lived here? She had to be a few years younger than him. He would've never forgotten a face such as hers, definitely not her voice.

Ari leaned close to him. Prince felt her soft breath on his cheek. It took everything in him to not reach out and grab her, to pull her into an embrace, and hold her close. It would be insane. He'd only just met the woman. Yet he knew that he didn't want to be parted from her anytime soon. Being near her was the balm his wounded soul had been in search of since he'd woken from the bomb blast.

"My name is Ariana."

Prince inhaled the sweet smell of her hair. The rainwater hadn't taken the scent from her. The wet strands were the exact color of the blast from his nightly terrors. He felt not a hint of fear as he gazed at them.

"You have a beautiful voice, Ariana," he said. His was voice just above a whisper into her ear.

Ari pulled back. But only enough to look him in the eyes. There were golden flecks at the edges of her eyes. Made sense that she would sparkle from the inside out.

What was she searching for, he wondered? Whatever it was, he vowed here and now that he would endeavor to be that man for her.

CHAPTER TWELVE

*I*t had been years since someone had told Ari that she had a beautiful voice. Because it had been years since anyone outside of her family had heard her voice. And now, the man who had sent her into silence praised the sound of her voice.

"Thank you," she said.

With each word that escaped her lips, Ari was surprised to hear the sound of her voice. She'd tried hard to speak in the days and weeks after The Incident, but she'd choked every time she opened her mouth. With each word she'd spoken in the last couple of minutes, her throat functioned effortlessly. The words seeming to want to gush out and greet this man.

For his part, Prince's gaze was so intent upon her lips. Ari knew that each of her words was spoken quietly. She still wasn't used to using her voice with others. She'd never thought she'd use them with him. She might be able to talk to him, but he couldn't expect her to do it loudly.

Prince's smile told her that he understood her every syllable. His gaze, which continued to track her mouth's every move, told her he was eager for more. His breath, which it became clear he was holding, told her that he anticipated a new word to drop any second like she was dropping a new album that he was first in line for.

This had to be the most surreal day of her life. Ariana Carol was sitting with Eric Prince, sitting close enough that if someone happened upon them, they'd think that she and Prince were lovers. He held one of her hands in his. Her other hand rested on his shoulder after it had inspected his ear for any damage her shouting might've caused him.

He didn't look hurt. He looked at her as though she was what he said she was. He'd said she was beautiful.

The interest was clear on his handsome face. If she had any doubts, then the way his gaze kept dipping to her lips when she wasn't talking would definitely clue her in. The feel of his thumb making lazy circles over her knuckles would certainly alert her to his intentions.

Eric Prince wanted to kiss her. Ari didn't have to have ever kissed a man to know the signs. And Ari had never kissed a man. No one had ever gotten close enough to try. Because no man could get past her first line of defense -the whole not speaking thing.

But she'd spoken to him. She wanted to speak to him more. And tell him what? That he was the cause of her suffering.

A loud crack of thunder sounded outside the boat. The crack reverberated inside the walls, and the boat rocked. Prince squeezed her hand. Hard.

Ari yelped from the spark of pain. She tried to pull her hand away. But Prince's grip was firm. His eyes were closed. Pain was etched into the grooves of his handsome face.

Another crack of thunder sounded. This time closer. Water sprayed at the windows. The untouched mug crashed to the ground, spilling its contents and shattering on the hardwood floor.

Prince's arms came around her, pulling her flush against his chest. Just like in the restaurant when the feedback had screeched. He covered her with his body. His hand tucked her head under his chin as he used his body like a shield for her.

His breathing was labored. She could feel his chest pounding against hers. He gripped her to him, but no longer hard. His hold was now protective.

Ari's heart caught in her throat. She couldn't imagine the horrors this man had faced for the protection of others. Her hands were trapped between them. She found some space between his muscled abs and her soft middle to snake both of her hands around his back.

Up and down, her hands went on along his spine. Her mouth was on the side of his good ear. She took a deep inhale. And then she began to sing.

It was a lullaby her father had sung to her during storms. Ari sang the tune softly into Prince's left ear, having learned her lesson the first time. By and by, the storm moved past. The thunder moved on. The rains lightened.

Ari knew that Prince had calmed before the storm was over. She kept singing, kept running her hands up and down his back. His hold on her lightened. He did not seem willing to let her go. But every song inevitably came to an end.

Ari closed her mouth as she ran out of lyrics. Prince didn't let go of her in the silence. She didn't try to pull away.

The world had stopped. Nothing existed outside of these four walls and the two of them.

Prince's fingers grazed her forehead. The pads of his fingers were rough, but his touch was nothing but gentle. She wanted to curl into him like a kitten. When he spoke, it was so quiet that she almost didn't hear him.

"The storm has passed," he said.

That it had. But Ari felt like she had been shipwrecked. She had been pulled apart, rung dry, and rescued by the man who held her safely in his arms.

CHAPTER THIRTEEN

*P*rince knew how to disassemble and reassemble an AK-47 blindfolded with only the touch of his fingers. More times than he could count, he'd thumbed the curve of the magazine, had traced the lines of the cleaning rod, had brushed the coiling springs of the bolt. Handling that lethal weapon had nothing on holding a woman in his arms.

To be sure, he'd masterfully unraveled his fair share of girls in his time. Holding Ariana close to him, inhaling the strands of her hair, feeling her flesh warm at his touch, Prince was at a loss.

He worried he was holding her too tight. He worried if he loosened his hold that she might escape. That was the last thing he wanted. Holding Ari like this, he felt she was the only thing holding him together.

For the past year, Prince had struggled to hear most sounds. Storms and thunder, he struggled with the most. Not because he couldn't hear them. It was to the contrary. The weather events never failed to penetrate the barriers in his ears. Once the sounds infiltrated, they inevitably brought him back to his time in a combat zone.

The crackle of lightning could always split the ringing in his ears. The rumble of thunder out blasted the sounds of rock and building crumbling around him. Every time a storm passed over him, Prince would be transported back to the nightmare of combat in his waking hours. And every time, he would be helpless to shut it out.

Until now.

It was in part due to holding the precious treasure he'd marauded. It was mostly due to Ari's soothing lyrics. She sang quietly, but her songs resonated into the heart of him. Her voice rose up inside him, reaching his ears and tuning the storm out.

His entire world shrank down until there was only this woman in his arms. He would face an army of insurgents for her. He would stare down the barrel of a gun to protect her. He'd run headfirst at any infidel donning a suicide vest if it meant she would be safe.

Prince burrowed his nose in Ari's hair, breathing deeply. Her sweet scent soothed away all of his fears and anxieties, better than any prescription he'd been offered by the VA hospital. The feel of her heart beating against his chest calmed any stressors that had once plagued him. There were only the two of them and this moment.

For the first time in a year, all was blessedly silent and quiet. Ari's song had come to an end. The storm had passed. The peace remained.

"It was a bomb."

Ari stirred in his hold at his admission. She didn't try to pull away. Her head moved against his chest in acknowledgment that she'd heard him.

Prince didn't talk about what had happened to him with anyone. No one except the psychologist on the Purple Heart Ranch. Dr. Patel had been easy to talk to. Likely because the man was a pastor as well. Prince hadn't been raised a religious man. But he'd met his fair share of clergy when he'd joined the military, surprised that so many men and women of faith were prepared to take up arms.

Many soldiers believed they were doing God's work. It was the Creator who had given mankind the edict to maintain law and order and keep the peace. Prince had gravitated toward each man and woman of faith and eventually developed his own relationship with God. Prince was certain there was a lesson in the blow he'd been dealt on the battlefield. He just hadn't found it yet.

"We were out on a routine patrol. Me and my team of five guys and a bomb dog."

"A bomb dog?"

Prince took a moment to inhale. His heart rate had increased, and there was sweat trickling down his spine at the memories he was allowing free. But just the sound of Ari's sweet voice in his ear brought him peace.

"The military trains dogs to sniff out explosives. When they smell the chemicals, they're taught to sit and whine. The bomb dog sat down outside of a building. Inside was a family of three strapped into suicide vests."

Tension rattled through Ari's shoulder. Prince took the opportunity to pull her closer. He didn't want her to know all the horrors of war. He did want her to understand how he came to be the man he was today. He just hoped that man could prove himself worthy of her.

"The husband had refused to join the insurgents' army, and so they'd marked him and his family for death. The bombs were on a timer. My specialty is in EOD; that means Explosive Ordinance Disposal. The husband insisted I get his wife and child free first."

Save them. Save my wife and child. They are my world.

"I tried, but… there wasn't enough time to free him as well."

His voice broke. Soft hands cupped his face. He looked down to find Ari's blue gaze on his.

Prince hated the sight of pity. That's not what her eyes told him. Her gaze was filled with strength and compassion. He felt it pour into him, allowing him to continue his story.

"I said a prayer with the man as the time ticked down. At that moment, I knew that his God and mine were the same. The devil was the cowards who would use a woman and child to fight their battles and further their cause."

Prince took a deep breath. The anger bubbling up in him made the ringing in his ears louder. He wanted to clench his fist and punch something. But he had the soft flesh of Ari in his arms.

"Running away from him was the hardest thing I've ever done in my life. And you know what? The man didn't ever cry. He just kept praying. Not for himself. For his family. He prayed that his wife and child would be all right."

"And they were. You saved them."

Her words were softly spoken directly into his ear. She'd found the perfect volume for him to hear her. Ari's voice and her breath against the cone of Prince's ear sent a shudder down his spine.

"We got them out in time." Prince leaned the side of his head against hers. The movement was so intimate for two people who didn't know each other.

No -that statement felt false. He might not know the details of Ari, but he felt he knew her.

"His family is alive because of you," she said.

That thought rarely penetrated through Prince's guilt, until Ari said it. Very few things had penetrated until he'd heard Ari's voice.

"I can still feel the heat on my back from the blast. It shook the earth under my feet, and I fell. The sound of it still rings in my ears. The ringing never stops. Except when you were singing. Or even now, when you're just speaking to me. The sound of your voice… it feels like it's healing to me. I know that sounds crazy but…"

Prince looked down. An unreadable expression settled across Ari's features. She searched his face. Prince didn't blink while she did so. He wanted her to know that he would never hide anything from her. Including the feelings he was having for her, feelings that were funneling deeper with every moment.

"I should get home." Ari pulled away from him. "My family will worry."

Prince reached for her hands, bringing them back to him. Even just that distance between them was unbearable. He didn't want to frighten her. Neither did he want to lose the treasure he'd found.

"I want to see you again, Ariana."

CHAPTER FOURTEEN

$\mathcal{A}$ ri's feet squished as she walked up the steps to the back door of the restaurant. Prince had insisted on walking with her as far as the marina, but she'd stopped him there. He'd reached for her then. His hand came to graze her forearm.

At the last second, he'd balled his fist and put his hand behind his back. But he hadn't turned from her. He'd gazed down at her, staring at her mouth as though he wanted to kiss her.

Ari's chin had lifted. Her lips had parted. And then she'd shut her mouth.

Prince had pursed his lips. His once open gaze had retreated behind a wince. They'd been in each other's arms only moments ago. Now it was as though they were looking at one another from across an ocean.

A kiss would've been insane. They weren't dating. Yet

Ari slipped off her wet shoes as she came into the back door. The floor was hot from the heat from the stove. The restaurant's kitchen smelled divine, like a spice mixture whose aroma warmed Ari on the inside. The warmth of her sister's cooking had nothing on what she'd felt when she'd been inside Eric Prince's arms.

Ari was going on a date with Prince tomorrow. She'd said yes. She'd actually *said* the word to him. Her voice hadn't shaken or quivered. It had been a resounded agreement. He'd been the one holding his breath when she'd spoken. He'd been the one vulnerable while she'd taken his measure. His smile when she'd acquiesced to his invitation had been palpable. She'd had Eric Prince uncertain, unsure, at her mercy, and she had granted him a boon.

Ari was coming to believe she'd come out of that storm and walked into an alternate version of her life. She was having a hard time reconciling the man who'd rescued her from a downpour today with the boy who had made fun of her all those years ago.

She should've told him about their shared past when they were on his boat. But she couldn't. Not after he'd shared the story of his private pain.

Prince had had an awful effect on Ari's life. But she hadn't died as a result of it. And he was no longer that reckless boy. He'd risked his life to save others for years with his service in the military. That was something to be commended.

Or was she just making excuses?

Ari didn't know what to think. All she knew was that she wanted to see him again. She wanted him to lean in to hear her words. She wanted to sing to him again. She wanted him to hold her against his broad chest. She wanted him to kiss her.

"Where have you been?" Adelle's voice broke through Ari's dreams of kissing. "And what are you wearing?"

"I got caught in the rain."

The storm had passed. It had left Ari in disarray. A peak out of the passthrough door told Ari that there were a fair amount of customers at the tables and bar.

"Are those a man's clothes?"

Ari opened her mouth to respond. But to say what? That she's spent the afternoon with Eric Prince, who had done a one hundred and eighty in the behavior and attitude department. Oh, and he didn't even remember how he had ruined Ari's life.

After The Incident, Ari's sisters had been readying to go on a warpath of their own. But Prince and his family were already gone before they could sound the horns. As a military family, they moved around the country a lot. It was Prince's mother that had ties to the town, but she'd died shortly after The Incident happened. And then, Prince was gone. Shipped off to military school they'd heard.

Alanna and Adelle had never been able to enact their revenge. But her sisters never forgot the evil Prince or his dastardly deed. So, Ari kept quiet about her current attire. Adelle didn't push. These were times when having been mute for most of her life worked for her.

Ari ducked into the back closet. There she changed out of Prince's shirt and into one with the restaurant logo on it. There was also a spare pair of yoga pants with a grease stain that she stepped into. She'd have to keep the squishy shoes on, though. The insides were uncomfortable, but the nonstick soles would keep her from slipping on the floor.

Once she was presentable, Ari joined her sisters at the bar. It was a little busier than she'd seen through the passthrough. Mostly regulars, but a few out of town visitors were present. With the holidays around the corner, family and friends were starting to gather. The karaoke machine wasn't due to start up for another hour, so there was blessed quiet. Enough to hear Miss Lucille call from down the bar.

"Alanna, I ordered a drink not five minutes ago. And Princess needs a bowl of water. She's parched from the walk over."

Miss Lucille patted at a non-existent stray hair from her perfectly coiffed bun. Then she patted the white pouf of her twin, the little, four-legged, Bichon Frise in her arms. Princess, Lucille's emotional support dog, was carried everywhere the elderly lady went. Today, Princess' collar perfectly matched Lucille's pink pumps.

"Just a second, Ms. Lucille," Alanna called from the other end of the bar. She was thumbing through the driver's license and identification cards of a group of college kids who were reluctantly handing them over.

"You know how Princess gets when she is parched."

"I'll take care of it." Ari grabbed a tumbler from the cabinet and a bottled water from the fridge. She knew better than to offer the four-legged princess tap water. The dog would simply refuse to drink it, and its owner would give her a mouthful.

But Lucille was quiet when Ari brought the cup over. Princess had no barks for Ari either. Both human and pooch stared at her. They weren't the only ones. Alanna and most of the regulars were looking Ari's way.

"You just spoke," said Miss Lucille. "Well done, dear. Well done, you."

There were other cheers from the regulars, and even a few claps of approval. In addition to feeling like she was under a spotlight, now Ari felt like she was a dog who should be yipping for a treat. Ari pushed the glass toward the dog lover and backed away from the bar. She backed all the way through the passthrough door. But her sister was on her heels, identification cards, and customers forgotten.

"What was that?" said Alanna.

"What was what?" said Adelle looking up from her pots and pans in the back.

"Ari just spoke to Miss Lucille."

"What do you mean she spoke to her? Like waved hi?"

"No, like spoke to her with words in front of the whole restaurant."

Adelle sat down her spatula and rounded on Ari. "Did you do that?"

"It's not a big deal," said Ari.

"This is a big deal," said Alanna. "What's happened to you?"

"Nothing's happened," said Ari.

"Something's happened," Adelle insisted. "This is a breakthrough. Finally, after all these years, what that creep Eric Prince did to you is finally wearing off."

"Don't say his name," hushed Alanna. "Don't even bring him up. We don't want her to relapse."

"You know he's in town," said Adelle.

"Well, he better stay away from here. Especially now that our Ari is finally healing. I'm so proud of you."

Her sisters wrapped her up in a double embrace. Ari's voice was caught in her throat as their arms wrapped around her and squeezed. How was she going to tell her sisters that the very cause of her voice loss just might be the cure? Even before that, how was she going to see Prince again without them finding out before she was ready to tell them?

CHAPTER FIFTEEN

*P*rince slowed his steps as he walked down the marina. He checked his reflection in a storefront window. His shirt was free of wrinkles, though he kept tugging at it. His pants were spotless without the grime of dirt or mud on them, though he kept brushing at the fabric.

The bags under his eyes had lost some weight after the fitful sleep he'd had last night. In his dreams, Prince didn't see the red of a bomb blast. He didn't hear the pleas of a father to save his family. Neither did he dream of his own father and the pain and anxiety the lieutenant could bring about. Instead, Prince dreamed of thick tresses of red hair waving in the wind. He heard an angel's voice crooning in his ear.

Just the thought of Ariana settled his soul, be he awake or asleep. When he'd woke from a restful night of sleep, he'd been restless. He'd paced around the houseboat all day, finding little to occupy his thoughts but her. He'd looked online to see when her family's restaurant would open. It had been a struggle to wait thirty minutes until after opening time to leave the houseboat in search of her.

Prince didn't want to seem too eager. The problem was that he was all too eager. He'd tried to slow his steps on the way here, but his feet kept speeding up. She'd agreed to see him tonight for dinner. That didn't mean he couldn't happen by her place of work at lunchtime.

There were only a few cars parked outside Carol on the Bay this morning. Which might mean that if Ari was working, then she wouldn't be too busy. Perhaps she could come and sit and talk with him. Or not talk, if that's what she wanted.

He'd come to know that the woman was shy. That was fine by him. He'd never been the greatest conversationalist. He simply liked being with her. He knew he would be content just to sit beside her. Maybe hold her hand. Maybe have her croon a few lyrics in his ear.

"Hey! Prince!"

The shout came close to his ear. Prince winced, hunching his shoulders up defensively as he turned. When he looked around, he came face to face with Ursula.

"How? Are you? Today?"

Ursula stood a foot in front of him. She shouted her words, slowly. Enunciating each loud syllable, as though she was an American overseas in a foreign land trying to be understood by the locals.

"I'm fine, Ursula," he said in a normal tone.

The few people out on the streets this early turned to stare. At least they weren't pointing at the near deaf man. Their confused gazes were on the shouting Ursula.

"Good," she shouted as she leaned in.

Prince stepped back. "I'm hard of hearing, Ursula. I'm not completely deaf."

Not yet anyway. The doctors had warned him it was a possibility. Prince was still not willing to accept the fact that his full hearing would never return even so many months after the bombing.

Ursula pursed her lips as though she didn't understand his words. He knew he'd said them loud and clear. He hadn't missed anything she'd said. The people the next town over had likely heard her.

"You don't have to shout," Prince clarified.

"Oh. Okay. Well, it's good to see you."

He could barely hear her now that she was speaking at a normal volume. It wasn't a hearing thing. Prince just wasn't interested in anything Ursula had to say. He wanted to get inside. He wanted to get to Ari.

"Since you're here, why don't I let you buy me lunch. You know, for old times." Ursula stepped into his space then. Her arm snaked around his, bringing to mind tentacles ensnaring his body. "We could catch up. Maybe start some brand new times."

Prince pursed his lips as he regarded Ursula. She'd been an early bloomer as a teenager, filling out in all the right places. She was still a beautiful woman. But there was an oldness to her face that had nothing to do with her age. She was a beauty queen preserved in a jar. But her canner had filled the jar with pickling juice. She looked pruned around the eyes and mouth. Likely from all the disapproving stares, she doled out to those she deemed beneath her.

Prince had once looked at others as though they were beneath him. Because that's how he'd been taught to view others. It was how his own father had seen him. But Prince's time in the military had taught him to view himself as part of a team, as part of something bigger.

Now when he looked at others, his first thoughts were not of worth. It was to ask if this was friend or foe. An innocent or an enemy. Ursula looked every bit the enemy foe.

Prince didn't ask himself the cliché question; what had he seen in her? She had been his reflection when they were younger. He wasn't that lost, angry boy anymore. Life had dealt him a blow, but it had also brought him a boon.

That boon was Ariana Carol.

"You're not taking me here." Ursula chucked her finger to the door of the bar.

"What's wrong with here?" asked Prince.

"Neither of us would be welcome in there," Ursula scoffed. "Wait? Don't you remember?"

"Remember what?"

"The Christmas Gala? Right before you left?"

Prince didn't remember much from his time here. He certainly didn't remember any Christmases. Any time his family was forced to spend time together, it never started or ended well.

"You remember Ariana Carol and what you did to her?"

The ringing got louder in his ears. What he did to her? What had he done to her?

"She never sang again after that. I don't think she ever spoke again."

The door to the restaurant opened, and a redhead poked her head out. The woman was the spitting image of Ari, but not quite. It was the same short-haired-not-Ari he'd seen the other day at the restaurant. This not-Ari didn't offer him a shy smile. Her blue gaze shot hot daggers at him enough to make the former EOD Specialist flinch.

"I know you two aren't thinking of coming in here," said the not-Ari in a voice deeper than Prince's Ari. The tenor of her voice scratched at Prince's inner ear.

"As if we'd eat your garbage chowder, Alanna. Come on, Prince."

Ursula's tentacles suctioned onto Prince's arms. He was so disoriented that when she tugged, he followed. Prince felt his feet moving as his mind tried to work out what just happened. Both now and in the past.

What had he done to Ari?

CHAPTER SIXTEEN

*A*ri took a deep inhale. Her shoulders lifted with the breath. Her chest expanded as her lungs filled. Her ears were perked, listening for the note that would announce her entry. After much fanfare of keys, drums, and strings, the note came. Ari threw back her head and belted out the lyrics.

This time, the lyrics of Adelle's song poured from Ari without missing a single beat or word. Ari took a breath to fill her lungs. The next stanza came from somewhere deeper than her diaphragm. It came from her heart. Maybe even her soul.

Her voice trilled perfectly over the ridges. It reached the high note and then dipped down to a low note, a difficult feat that Ari handled with ease. As the song decrescendoed, Ari heard loud applause and boisterous whoops coming from the other side of the sound booth. Adelle was on her feet, hands clapping, fists pumping, grin beaming bright.

"That was amazing, Ari. You nailed it. You killed it. You murdered that song, brought it back to life, and sent it to outer space."

Ari grinned too. She'd finished the song in one take. That was a rarity with her overachiever producer of a sister who usually had Ari in the booth for half the day, if not more, doing take after take.

"With your vocals alone, this is going to sell. And then I'm probably going to have to fend off producers who want to know about the singer."

Ari shrugged. Just a day ago, the thought of singing live for judgmental record producers would have made her throat close up. Today, she didn't even give them a second thought. Her mind was on singing the song again later tonight. This time for an audience of one.

"What has gotten into you?"

Ari blinked, allowing the image of Prince to dissolve and bringing her sister in focus. Adelle studied Ari like her sister was the meters on her soundboard. Ari was sure that the energy coming off her was spiking into the red zones.

"You've been different these past two days."

Ari ran a hand through her hair. She felt different. She woke up this morning wanting to shout a greeting to the sky instead of keeping quiet.

She looked into her sister's eyes. The three Carol girls were the best of friends. Though there were two years in between each of them, Adelle, Alanna, and Ari had grown up close. More than just family or blood. Her sisters were her true friends. Ari hated keeping secrets from them. But she still wasn't sure how to tell them about Prince.

Alanna had a more forgiving heart. She might understand Ari's decision to date the man who had traumatized her all those years ago. Though Adelle wrote the most heartwarming ballads, she was also the kind of woman who would call a thing a thing and not romanticize reality. Ari could just hear her oldest sister accuse her of Stockholm Syndrome.

But that's not what this was. Prince was different. Ari was different. Together she felt they were making each other stronger.

"If I didn't know any better, I'd say you met someone."

"I have," Ari admitted.

Adelle whipped around, eyes wide. "You what?"

"I met someone."

"Here? In town? Or online." Adelle's gaze narrowed. "Oh, Ari, what have I told you about internet dating. Men never put up their true profiles. You might be chatting with some slob in his mother's basement or a baby daddy looking for a nursemaid to his five kids."

"I didn't meet him on the internet. He lives here."

"Here? In this town?"

Ari nodded.

"Who?"

Ari bit her lip.

"We don't keep secrets in this family."

"I know. But this is new. I just... can you just give me a little space. Just to see where it's going."

Adelle studied Ari, her gaze slowly softening. But then she shook her head. "Nope, spill."

"Adelle!"

"You've never been in a relationship before. You need your sister's guidance. Spill it."

Ari clamped her mouth shut.

"Oh, that won't work. Not with us. When we get to the restaurant, me and Alanna will get it out of you."

There went that plan.

Ari had a twenty-minute reprieve while they walked to the bar. During that time, Adelle proceeded to guess. She called out names. None of them Prince's. She pointed to strangers on the street. Luckily, Prince wasn't out about town today.

When Adelle pointed to Jett Elison, Ari openly gagged. Adelle threw her head back and laughed. Jett thought he was the most eligible bachelor in town, but he still lived in his mom's basement and worked the same job at the movie theater that he'd worked back in high school. Free popcorn might've been a draw to teen girls, but not grown women.

"It's not a soldier from the Purple Heart Ranch, is it? You are not desperate enough to become a mail order bride."

The Purple Heart Ranch was a good fifty miles from here, but everyone knew the stories from there. Handsome soldiers with wounds internally or physically finding a woman to marry them to stay on the family-zone ranch. Each love story started out platonically only for the couple to fall madly in love days later.

Ari had never visited the ranch. Prince was a vet. Maybe if they came up with a story like what was happening on the rehabilitation ranch, her sister might accept that angle.

Adelle was quickly running out of town residents the closer they got to the bar. Ari wasn't going to be able to keep this secret long. Besides, it had been ten years. Surely her sisters were all over the childhood antics of their youth. The Incident had happened to Ari, not them. She had chosen to forgive Prince, though he didn't know she'd forgiven him. He couldn't even remember what had happened.

"You will never guess who had the nerve to darken our doorsteps."

That was how Alanna greeted them. It looked like Ari would have another few minutes of reprieve while her middle sister went through the town gossip. The list of perpetrators couldn't be that long.

"Eric Prince."

Ari gulped. Her back was to her sisters, so neither of them saw the expression on her face.

"Are you kidding me?" said Adelle

"And you'll never guess who he was with. Ursula Spade."

Now Ari did turn.

"Don't worry, Ari. I told them both not to show their faces around here. Can you believe the nerve? After what they did to you."

Ari wasn't listening any longer. Prince had been out with Ursula, his old girlfriend from while he'd lived here? And they'd come here to the bar together?

But why? Had this all been some prank? Something in her heart told her that couldn't be right.

Ari's shoulders slumped. She felt like she couldn't get enough air into her lungs. She needed to get out of the bar.

"Ari? You okay? See, even now, he's still having this effect on her."

"No," Ari insisted. "I'm fine. I just need some fresh air."

Ari dashed out the back door before either of her sisters could say another word. Or worse; see her tears.

She was able to hold the tears in all the way down to the marina. She held it together until she made it to her secret place near the lake. But when she lifted her head so that the tears could fall, she saw that she was not alone.

CHAPTER SEVENTEEN

"Why didn't you tell me?" Prince demanded the moment he saw Ari.

Her steps came to a halt, and then he saw the tears. He had her in his arms in an instant. Were the tears his fault as well? Or had someone else hurt her?

He didn't care. He just needed to make her pain go away. To make it all go away for her.

Her tears didn't fall as she laid her head on his chest. He would've known. He would've felt their wetness. He would've felt her heaves and sighs.

Instead, Ari stilled. She didn't stiffen. She felt at ease in his arms, peaceful even. But how was this possible when he'd hurt her? He needed to be close to her at the same time that he could barely bring himself to look at her. Prince pulled away so that he could see her face.

Ari opened her mouth, but nothing came out. Prince knew that he hadn't missed a single word. He was staring at her so intensely he would've seen any sound leave her mouth.

She stared back. There was a heaviness in her eyes that hadn't been there before. Or maybe it had, and he hadn't seen it because he'd been too focused on what he wanted, on what he was feeling. Had he ever truly looked at her?

How could he not remember hurting her so badly all those years ago? His words had set off a bomb that ruined her life. A bomb of his making. And he didn't even remember crossing the fuses.

"Why didn't you tell me?" he asked again. He lifted his hand to her face but stopped. He ached to cup her chin and pull her lips to his. To kiss away the unshed tears in her eyes. Instead, he let her go.

Ari took a deep breath. She parted and then pursed her lips. Even now, she was having trouble speaking, all because of the wounds he'd inflicted on her so long ago. When she spoke, her words made no sense.

"Where's your date?"

Prince frowned. Had he heard her right? He stepped closer, giving her his good ear. "Say that again."

Ari took another deep breath. Her shoulders went straighter, her chin jutted higher. "Where's Ursula?"

Prince shrugged, still not following her words. What did Ursula have to do with anything? Unless Ursula had been tormenting Ari all this time. Prince wouldn't put it past the woman. Hurt people, hurt people.

"Did she say something to you?" Prince reached out for Ari's arm, but she jerked it away.

"She didn't need to. Why would you bring her to my family's bar on your date? You can't be that cruel."

Prince needed to sit down. The world was spinning, and he had nothing to hold onto. "You think I'm dating Ursula?"

Ari's chin wobbled. Prince knew she was angry, knew it was because she misunderstood. But he couldn't help himself any longer.

He cupped her cheek in his palms. He pressed his forehead to hers. He breathed in that sweet scent that belonged only to her.

"I was coming to see you. I ran into Ursula on the way."

Again, Ari pursed her lips. It was as though she wanted to believe, but she was too afraid. Prince wiped his thumb over her lower lip and felt it tremble.

"Ursula isn't the woman I want to be with. I'm not the boy I was when we were together. She and I have nothing in common. I don't care if I never see her again in this lifetime."

Slowly the tension seeped out of Ari. Her eyes closed, taking away the unshed tears. Her lips still trembled. Only now, he tasted relief on her breath. That still left Prince's initial question to her unanswered.

"Why didn't you tell me what I did to you?"

Ari winced. The unshed tears came back. They glistened at the corners of her eyes. She opened her mouth again, but only an unsteady breath came out.

"I hurt you," said Prince. "I blew up your life. You've been suffering all these years because of me."

Ari's lips moved. But words continued to fail her. Because he had stolen her voice.

"The worst part is I don't even remember it."

Prince shut his eyes, trying to blot out the shame of it all. Ari's hands came to his cheek. He wanted to shrug off her touch. He didn't deserve it. But he could no sooner ask his heart to stop beating than deny her touch.

"You're right," she said, into his ear. The perfect volume. Or perhaps, he was simply so in tune to this woman. "It was your fault."

The quietly spoken words were like a gong in his head. They rang him dry. He should let her go, but he knew his fingers would never cooperate.

"But, I forgive you."

Prince shook his head. He didn't want her forgiveness. Here again, he'd watched someone else blow up while he'd gotten away unscathed.

"I forgive you," Ari repeated. This time she said it directly into his ear. A whisper. An absolution.

Prince couldn't help himself. His arms came around her, and he pulled her close.

"You're not the same hurt, little boy," she said. "You're a different man now."

How he wanted to believe her. How he wanted those words to be made of facts and not wishful thinking.

"The truth is that I've found my voice with you," Ari went on.

Prince pulled away to look down at her, needing to see her face as she gave him this benediction.

"I blamed you all this time. But the truth is, you never took anything from me. I was afraid when I got up on that stage. It was so easy to sing around my family because I knew they loved me."

Could that be why she could sing to him? Because what he was feeling for her was love? He wasn't sure he even knew how to love. But if he was going to try, it would be with this woman.

"Everyone pointed a finger at you, and I let them. It was easier than admitting to my fear. I stayed silent while they kept blaming you. Because I didn't want to talk, I didn't want to sing."

"Ari—"

"No, I'm not done telling you off."

Prince hushed. Her voice was sharp, a note Prince had yet to hear. He liked it just as much as her sweet melodies.

"What you did all those years ago was childish, and rude, and mean spirited. But I'm to blame too. I forgive myself, and I forgive you, too. Now, you're going to accept that, and quickly, because there are bigger fish to fry."

He would accept it. He would never deny this woman anything. He couldn't imagine anything bigger that they could face than this.

"My sisters," Ari said. "You're going to have to win them over if we're going to really do this."

CHAPTER EIGHTEEN

eads poked out of shops as she and Prince walked hand in hand back into town. People Ari had known all her life stopped and stared at the two of them. With her hand in his, Ari didn't feel the need to duck her head and hide. Instead, she lifted it and waved.

"Hi, Mr. and Mrs. Montgomery," she called out to the pet shop owners.

"Good afternoon, Ms. Harper," she waved to the owner of the town's sweet shop.

"You're having fun with this, aren't you?" Prince whispered in her ear.

Ari loved the feel of his lips against the cone of her ear. Was that what he felt when she did that to him? No wonder he constantly dipped his ear to her mouth. She was seriously considering picking up the habit. But only with him.

She gazed up at him under the twinkling of the Christmas lights. Decorations were in full swing now that Christmas was just one week away. All around, Ari saw announcements for holiday-themed events. As well as the annual town gala.

Each year the town held the gala to raise money for a worthy cause. This year, the charity supported the local animal shelter. For the life of her, she couldn't remember what the cause had been the one, and only time, she had attended.

As she tried to think back on that night, the details kept slipping away from her. Had Prince truly laughed as loudly as she'd heard? Had her voice squeaked as much as she'd imagined?

Ari could no longer be sure. The only thing that she was sure of was that the man walking beside her, holding her hand, was as steady as a rock. She had not a single doubt in her mind that Prince would let her fall, or run off, again. Ari just hoped he was strong enough to withstand what was about to come his way.

She pushed open the door to Carol on the Bay Bar and Grill. It was just after lunchtime, and dinner was a few hours away, so there was hardly anyone about. That wasn't a good sign. It would be better for Prince if there were witnesses in the dining area. But only Judge Trexler sat in the corner, eating a bowl of chowder as he read the day's paper.

Well, that was probably good. Her sisters would be less likely to commit murder with an official on the scene. Maybe? Hopefully?

Her sisters were both behind the bar as Ari and Prince made their way across the floor. There wasn't a tumbleweed in sight, but Ari swore a dust bunny rolled across the pristine floors. An old country song played softly on the jukebox. The crooner wailed about how somebody done somebody else wrong.

Adelle sharpened a knife. Even from this distance, the knife already looked pretty sharp. Its blade gleamed sinisterly with each step Ari and Prince took.

Alanna held a white rag in one hand, while she polished a beer mug with the other. The way the mug's handle was wrapped around Alanna's knuckles brought to mind a steel knuckle ring that a street brawler would bring to a fistfight.

"Didn't I tell you you're not welcome here, Mr. Prince?" said Alanna.

"He's with me," said Ari.

Neither sister glanced at Ari. Their predatory gazes were fixed on Prince. They continued readying their weapons.

"I don't know what kind of voodoo you've done on my sister—"

Ari cut Adelle off. Not because of what she was saying, but because Adelle's voice was low. Low and menacing, which was good if she wanted to scare a normal hearing suitor. "He can't hear you."

"What do you mean he can't hear me? He doesn't talk to people like me?"

"No, he's wearing a hearing aid."

The knife stilled in Adelle's hand. Alanna set the mug down. Both women cocked their heads to the side as though to peer at Prince's ear.

As always, Prince's overgrown hair covered any evidence of the device in his ear. He lifted his hand and smoothed back his hair, revealing the tiny piece of plastic in his ear.

"He can't hear us?" said Adelle using her normal volume.

"I can now," said Prince. He wore a friendly smile on his face. "I've been to one too many heavy metal concerts."

No one laughed at the joke. Mainly because the Carol sisters couldn't abide metal bands. Shouting over the base and drum beats was not their idea of a good time.

"Prince lost his hearing in a bombing overseas. He saved a family in the process."

Yes, Ari realized she left out the part about the father whose life was lost. This was going to be a day of looking at the positives. That father had sacrificed for his family because that's what families do. She only hoped her family would come to see the good in the present and not dwell on the pain of the past.

"Listen," said Prince, stepping forward. "I realize I've dealt a huge blow to your family in the past."

So much for that plan. Ari stepped up beside him. She didn't think Adelle and Alanna would launch any weapons at him with her beside him.

Maybe?

Hopefully?

"I was an awful kid. I don't deserve your sister's forgiveness. But she's insisted on giving it to me. I'm going to spend the rest of my life being worthy of it."

Did he say the rest of his life? Ari didn't have the ability to question it. When Prince looked down at her, her heart laid down in a puddle in her chest.

"Did he just say the rest of his life?" asked Adelle, suspicion coating her tone.

"He just said the rest of his life," said Alanna, adoration sweetening her tone.

Prince winced, like a man caught in a scope. "Well… I mean… We've only just started… but…"

The look he gave Ari was one of shaded desire. But he couldn't hide it from her. She saw past the shadows he tried to cast and glimpsed his true desire.

"I think the rest of my life is a good place to start," he said. "That is if you'll allow me the honor of taking her out on a date?"

Ari turned to her sisters.

"Yes," said Alanna.

"No," said Adelle at the same time.

Their answers didn't surprise Ari. Alanna was a hopeless romantic. Adelle was, well, just hopeless when it came to romance that wasn't in lyrics.

Both Ari and Alanna turned to Adelle. The staring contest was epic. With two on one, Adelle finally relented.

"Fine," she hissed. "But know the whole town will be watching you. And if you make a single mistake."

Adelle stabbed the sharp knife into a wooden block on the counter. Ari felt Prince gulp. Inside she was dancing a jig. That had gone better than she'd ever expected.

CHAPTER NINETEEN

rince tugged at his tie. It was now so loose around his neck that it was coming off. He gave it a final yank, unraveling it from his person and tossing it in a nearby trash can.

He'd dressed up for his date with Ari, but he looked nothing like himself. The dress coat he'd worn was itchy. The shoes pinched.

He'd ditched the coat before leaving the houseboat. The tie didn't make it to the front steps of Ari's house. He'd have to suffer in the shoes. But at least he felt more like himself in clean slacks and a buttoned-down shirt without the coat and tie.

Ari had seen him in far worse dregs, and she hadn't said anything against him. She hadn't said much. Because she'd lost her voice.

Prince stopped the line of thinking before it could continue down a dark path. She said she'd forgiven him. He'd decided to take her word for it. He'd decided he'd take anything she'd give him.

He was thankful that she came to the door to greet him and not one of her sisters. He'd girded his loins for another run-in with the pair. He was already nervous enough. He'd been on his fair share of dates in his lifetime. But never one this important.

"Hi."

Prince saw her lips move, but he didn't quite pick up the sound. She was back in shy mode, and that was fine. He was simply thrilled to see her.

"You look beautiful," he said.

A light blush darkened her cheeks. Prince offered her his arm. He doubted he'd ever done that for a woman before. Mainly because most of the women he'd dated over the years he'd picked up at bars just off base. Those women were looking for a very specific time with him. They'd trail after him out of the bar and into the dark of night.

Here and now with Ari, it was early afternoon on a bright day on the bay. The weather was unseasonably warm as they walked down the main street of town. Christmas lights twinkled in the sunshine. Normally Prince would scowl at the colorful points of light as they reminded him of holidays with his family. Today, they didn't bother him so much because he walked next to the brightest thing he'd ever seen in his life.

Ari leaned into his side as they walked hand in hand. She tilted her face up. He realized too late that she was aiming for his ear to speak when he turned his face to meet hers.

She missed his ear entirely. Her lips were just a breath from his. He stared at the pink flesh. Hunger quaked in his belly.

With great difficulty, Prince lifted his gaze until he stared directly into her eyes. It was the first time in his life that he hid nothing from another being. He wanted to give himself to her, to be whatever she needed. He wanted to tell her that with his lips, but without using words.

However, that was not how he'd planned this date to go. This was the first time he'd woo a woman when he was out of uniform. He wouldn't buy her a drink and then leave before she woke in the morning.

He'd let the truth slip the other day about wanting to be with Ari for the rest of his life. That journey would start this day, one step at a time. If he played his cards right, at the end of the day, when he walked her back to her front door, then he would see if he earned that kiss.

And so Prince turned his mouth from Ari and gave her his good ear.

It took a moment for Ari to speak. He heard her clearing her throat a few times. "Where are we going?"

"To Coastal Creations. They have an ornament making station today."

"But you don't like Christmas."

Prince turned to face her. "You like Christmas. I like you. That's all I need."

Again, that beautiful blush of color tinted her cheeks. He wrapped an arm around her waist and pulled her close as they walked. That wasn't part of the plan, either. He had meant to only keep her hand in the crook of his elbow. But he didn't see a problem with picking up the pace toward forever.

They made it inside the shop, which looked as though Christmas had exploded against the walls and spilled onto the tables. The shop was crowded with kids, and adults, families, and friends. The place was noisy and a bit chaotic. Both Prince and Ari froze in the doorway.

He wasn't one for being in crowds, and he knew she got tense in social situations where she might be required to talk. Maybe this was a bad idea. When he turned to steer her out of the door, Ari stayed him with her hand.

She looked in his eyes. He knew that she could tell what he was thinking. She pressed her lips together, in that determined way of hers that he was coming to love. She wrapped her arm around his bicep and tugged him to one of the few empty spots at the back of the shop.

"Well, if it isn't Ariana Carol," said Whitney, the owner of Coastal Creations. "It's good to see you out. And who do we have here?"

Prince opened his mouth to speak, but Ari beat him to it.

"You remember Eric Prince?"

Whether Whitney remembered Prince or not, her gaze was fixed on Ari. The novelty of her speaking wasn't wearing off any time soon.

"It's nice to meet you, Whitney," said Prince, forcing her attention off Ari and onto him. "Do you think we can get a kit to get started?"

Whitney cleared her throat and nodded. She brought over two boxes and set them before Ari and Prince. Then with another grin, she turned and went to deal with a rowdy table near the front of the shop.

When she was gone, Ari took a deep breath. Prince took her hand. Her fingers trembled slightly. Again, he wondered if they should've just spent a quiet afternoon on his boat.

"Thank you for bringing me here," said Ari. "I haven't participated in events like these since my parents left."

Pride filled his heart as she gazed up at him. Along with a burst of protectiveness. He wanted to be this woman's hero, her shield, her… everything. For now, he would be her helper as they set about crafting a lobster ornament with a fluffy red hat. There was no need for words between them as they passed the tools back and forth between themselves.

The chatter around them died down from a chaotic buzzing into a more harmonious hum. Prince could make out words spoken together in a number of different voices. Looking up, he saw that the people gathered in the shop were singing.

Soon Prince could make out the sound of Ari humming along. Her voice was quiet, only loud enough for him to hear. A few people slid glances their way, but Ari didn't seem to notice them. She only had eyes for Prince.

"You realize you two choose the spot with mistletoe?"

Prince didn't know who said that to them, but he'd heard them loud and clear over the boisterous singing, over Ari's quiet humming. More and more, he was coming to believe there might be something to the notion of selective hearing.

He looked up to find a weed wrapped in twine hanging over their heads. For the third time today, Ari blushed. It was the warmth spreading across her face that did him in.

Prince couldn't wait until the end of the date. He didn't even care that they had an audience. He dipped his mouth to hers and stole their first kiss.

CHAPTER TWENTY

ri had grown up watching the awkward goo-goo eyes of girl likes boy on the Disney Channel. Later she'd clicked over to watch chaste first kisses on Nick Teens. And finally, she'd landed on the heavy petting and then fade to black on the WB Channel.

She'd seen many a first kiss and make-out session. But she'd never experienced any of it for herself. She certainly never expected it to happen while sitting in the back of the town craft shop.

It was just a light brushing of Prince's lips against hers, but she felt rocked off her world. She was thankful that she was sitting because she couldn't feel her toes any longer. She had no idea what to do with her hands. It was just as well because she couldn't feel her fingers.

All she could feel was the press of Prince's lips against hers. His top lip was warm. His bottom lip a soft pillow.

Ari had hardly slept last night because she was so anxious for this date to happen. She'd been most eager to get to this particular part of the date, the part when he would kiss her. But wasn't that supposed to come at the end?

Not that she was complaining. She'd much rather do this for the rest of the date. She sighed as his lips moved across hers, no longer light as a feather. A touch more insistent now as they pressed on. She had no idea what else Prince had planned, but she was happy to scrap it all, stay here, and keep her mouth pressed to his.

Prince wrapped her up in his arms as he sipped at her lips. Ari's dangling hands were caught between them. Her palms pressed against his heart. She felt the organ quicken at her touch, like a ballad remixed to play in a dance club.

Ari had been in Prince's arms before. He'd been an unexpected shelter from sound feedback. Then a warm sanctuary from a storm. Now, he was the only refuge she sought, would likely ever seek.

The Christmas caroling died down until all she could hear was the soft sound of his sigh. The world went quiet as the feel of his heartbeats reverberated through her palms and pulsed in her ears. Nothing else pierced her senses but this man.

The feeling came back into her hands and the sound to her ears when Prince began to pull away. She reached out to him, catching the lapels of his shirt. Ari pulled at him, but Prince didn't budge. He covered his hands with hers and chuckled. His laughter wasn't the only merriment she heard.

More chuckles, some giggles, a couple of ewws, and a few indignant clucks of tongues sounded all around her. Everyone in the shop was looking at her. Pointing at her. Shaking their heads or laughing at her.

The scene brought Ari back to the time when she was on the stage ten years ago. She'd stood in silence as eyes stared at her. She'd missed the note. It had been a hard one to reach, but she'd insisted on trying for it. She nailed it most of the time in rehearsal, but there were times when it fell flat in her throat. On stage at the gala ten years ago had been one of those times. And then all she'd heard was this chuckle. Just like she was hearing now.

Ari looked at the man who'd laughed her off the stage. The cold, white terror wasn't there. Prince's smile was soft. His laugh was light. He looked at her with adoration mixed with amusement.

He chuckled again, and it flooded her body with the most delicious warmth, like hot chocolate chasing after a warm sugar cookie just out of the oven. Ari couldn't remember why that first chuckle all those years ago had affected her so? With his chuckle today, she wanted to ignore everyone around them and sing at the top of her lungs that she was falling for this man.

"I think we should probably go," Prince said. "We're causing a scene."

Ari wanted to go, but not because everyone was staring at them. She wanted to go so that she could be alone with Prince. She wanted to press her lips to his again without an audience.

She ducked her head into Prince's side as they gathered their ornaments and headed for the door. She could still hear him chuckling as they walked out of Coastal Creations. But that chuckle was a delight now. She wanted to hear it every day of her life.

Ari lifted her head to see Prince looking down at her. His gaze landed on her mouth. She was about to get her wish. He was going to kiss her again. She didn't care that there were people walking the street.

Let them look. Let them stare. Let them point or even chuckle at the two of them. Let them—

"What do we have here?"

Prince frowned, as though he hadn't heard the words of the intruder. Ari could tell he'd heard the tone. Or maybe he'd sensed the dark cloud crashing around them

Ursula Spade stood blocking their path on the sidewalk. She was dressed today in purple and black fringe. The strips flapping at the end of her skirt made Ari think of octopus tentacles. Ari had the urge to step back. Prince pulled her into his side. His arm was strong and sure around her waist.

"What? Are you slumming, Prince?"

"No, I'm taking my girl out on the town. If you'll excuse us, I owe my sweet a cookie."

Prince pointed at Sweet Caroline's where people were gathered inside to sample holiday cookies. He took a step toward the shop, bringing Ari along with him as if she was attached to his hip. Ari had forgotten how to use her legs. She felt like she was floating beside this man.

Ursula wasn't done. She stepped in front of them, darkening the sidewalk as she did so. "You're serious? You're dating Clams Up Carol?"

It had been years since Ari had heard that name. Mainly because Ursula was the only one who used it. The girl had loved tormenting Ari all throughout school, long after Prince had left for good.

"Well, I suppose that makes sense since you're deaf, and she doesn't speak," Ursula went on when neither of them took the bait. "You two are perfect for each other."

Ari wished for a witty comeback to enter her mind. Whenever she was made fun of, which was only by this woman, she did clam up. She'd put her head down and walked away.

She didn't have to do that any longer. She'd found her voice. She would tell Ursula off.

"Yeah," Prince grinned down at Ari. "We are. She is. Ari is perfect."

And just like that, Ari was tongue-tied. The man had done it again. With just a few words, he'd rendered her mute with just a look.

She could've spoken, but she had no words for that woman. She couldn't even remember her name. Prince's gaze was once again all Ari could see. She only had words for him.

At that moment, Ari knew she was never going to clam up again. She felt like she could sing in the middle of the street at the top of her lungs. And she wanted to prove it.

CHAPTER TWENTY-ONE

"This was your idea, wasn't it!"

Prince's head jerked back at Adelle's accusation. Her voice was shrill, high-pitched enough he was sure the stray dogs outside heard it. So his hearing aid had picked her up loud and clear.

"No, it was my idea," said Ari, coming up to Prince's side.

She hadn't been far from his side all day, but he had noticed she'd been a bit distracted as they sat in Sweet Caroline's eating Christmas cookies. She'd barely sipped at her hot chocolate when they'd stopped by the Chocolate Emporium on the last stop of their date. That's when she'd told him her bright idea.

Prince didn't think Ari's plan was a good idea, either. Ari's chin was lifted in determination. With her head tilted up, her face looked like a perfectly shaped heart. Her cheeks were flushed pink with her halo of red hair framing her face like a Valentine. Cupid himself couldn't have denied such a beauty.

Ari wrapped her fingers around his. He knew then and there that no matter what this woman chose to do, he'd stand by her. He'd step in front of her. He'd take on the fire of her sisters if that's what Ari commanded him to do.

"You're not doing this," Adelle demanded.

Prince looked around the bar for any sharp objects. All he caught sight of was a dirty dishrag and a lemon peeler. He didn't put it past Adelle to figure out a way to wield both as possible weapons.

"It's already done," said Ari. "I've already signed up. I'm going to sing at this year's gala."

"Sweetie," said Alanna, her voice laced with care and reason, "you remember what happened last time you were on that stage?"

Alanna glanced over at Prince. Adelle glared at him. Ari gazed up at him. There wasn't a flicker of fear or regret in her blue eyes.

"Of course, I remember," said Ari. "I've thought about it every day for the last ten years."

Prince let out a low sigh. He wished he hadn't heard that last tidbit. But he had.

Just the idea of hurting this woman made him sick to his gut. He'd done it without lifting a finger. He'd done it with a careless glance and thoughtless laugh.

Ari's fingers were on his chin. She gently tugged until he faced her. "I'm not that little girl anymore. I've got my voice back. Part of that is because of you. I want to show you all that I'm past it."

"I don't need you to prove anything to me, Ari," he said. "I think you're perfect the way you are."

Her smile warmed his heart. He wanted to kiss her again. He wanted to kiss her always. But they weren't alone. Not that they'd been alone back in Coastal Creations. Prince was sure this particular audience would cast him out to sea if he manhandled the treasure before him.

"I don't like this idea, Ariana," said Alanna. "But I'll be there to support you. And so will she."

Adelle rolled her eyes. She crossed her hands over her chest. But in the end, she let out a puff of air. "Of course, I'll support you. I'm your family. It doesn't mean I'll have to like it."

Ari let go of Prince's hand and went to her sisters. They enfolded each other in a hug, each with an arm around the other's back. Prince hung back and stared. He wasn't used to this kind of affection in families. He'd never been hugged by his father. At some point in his childhood, his mother had stopped embracing him. Likely when he'd begun to favor his father in looks.

Alanna looked up then. She frowned at Prince. "What are you doing over there? This is a group hug."

Prince pointed to his chest. His brows raised in question. They wanted him in the mix?

"Yeah, you. Get in here."

He walked the floorboards on sea legs to join them. Ari's hand on his back was a balm. Alanna's hand was foreign but welcome. Adelle rolled her eyes, but she didn't reach for any weapons. So, he supposed that was a show of affection.

The girls squeezed tighter. Prince allowed himself to get lost in the shared embrace. He could get used to this. He could get used to all of it. Having a family, having people have his back. He hadn't experienced that since the service. But he'd left that life behind.

A memory shook loose while the women held onto him. He'd seen this group hug before. But there had been a different man in the midst.

Mr. Carol was a larger than life man. Tall and barrel-chested like Prince's dad. But the perpetual smile on the man's face set him apart from Lt. Prince. Mr. Carol had embraced his family in a group hug before Ari had taken the stage that year. Prince remembered looking at the family as though they were a cartoon, a caricature of life.

Earlier that evening, he'd been sitting on the bathroom floor with his mother, trying to bandage a cut to her cheek below the black eye his father had given her.

"It's okay," Vanessa Prince had said. "It was an accident. I'm fine."

The two of them hadn't spoken any more about it. They never did. Prince didn't offer his mother any comfort. He simply dressed the wound. Soon as he'd finished, his father had darkened the doorway. Lt. Prince had demanded dinner. His mother rose and went to the kitchen, as though nothing had happened. That was the way in the Prince household.

Prince had left out before dinner was on the table. He'd met up with Jett and Ursula looking for trouble. The only thing happening in town that night was the gala.

After the family hug, Ariana had taken the stage. The beauty that rang clear in her voice irked something inside him. That girl was loved, she'd likely never known pain or disappointment, and it showed in her voice. Prince was antsy to get out of his seat. He couldn't stomach another moment of the unattainable images her voice brought to his mind.

He was glaring at her from his seat. He saw the moment he caught her eye. She'd fumbled on the note, and the dream of a perfect world she'd been painting with her voice went silent. Because it wasn't real. It would never be real. He'd snorted into the silence, fueling the discomfort that everyone around him was experiencing. Then he'd outright laughed, because that feeling, that uncertainty, that anxiety of not knowing what would happen in the next moment, that was the reality of this world.

The mayor had pulled him aside and given him a tongue lashing for his behavior. Prince had ignored it. His gaze had stayed fixed on the Carol family as they'd embraced the little songstress. A group hug to soothe her hurts.

The memory assaulted him like a PTSD episode. He shuddered from the impact of the flashback buried deep in his consciousness now coming to light.

"You okay?" Ari gazed up at him, complete trust and adoration in her eyes.

All these years later, she still hadn't been touched by any true tragedy. Nothing other than him. He would never hurt this woman again. Not with a look, or words, or a laugh. He would be her biggest fan, her loudest cheerleader, her protector against anyone who dared to make her frown. For now and always.

"I'm fine," Prince said to her, still in the cocoon of the familial embrace. "You're going to be brilliant up there."

CHAPTER TWENTY-TWO

The week had gone by in a flurry. It was the happiest of Ariana's life. Each morning, Prince arrived at her house to walk her to work. He'd stay for breakfast then disappear during the day to work on his boat. He'd return just before her shift ended, and then they would spend the evening together.

They'd walk along the lake and listen to the water lapping. They'd sit out on the deck of his boat and watch the sunset. A few times, they stayed at her house and had family dinner.

Alanna welcomed Prince into the fold without missing a step. Adelle always made certain he could see her from the kitchen sharpening her knives. But she left the knives in the kitchen and didn't bring them to the dinner table. So… progress.

After dinner, she'd go down to the studio in the basement and practice the song she planned to sing at the gala. Prince would always accompany her. Adelle was there often as well.

Ari had selected the same ballad she'd chosen as a kid. With the creeks and croaks of adolescence gone, she was able to hit the high notes of the song each time. She was ready.

Although seven days later, on the night of the gala, there was a tickle in her throat. Her neck felt sore. Her shoulders heavy.

Ari's fingers shook as she entered the mansion where the gala was being held. The town's bed and breakfast was done up in forest green with silver and red accents. White lights fell like snowflakes all around the room.

In a corner of the room, was a small display for the local pet shop, Happy Paws, which was the recipient of this year's gala. Violet Montgomery chatted up Ms. Lucille. Violet held the leash to a mangy looking dog who couldn't take his eyes off of Princess who was held in Ms. Lucille's arms and looking down her nose at the poor dog with no tags.

"I can't wait to hear your song, Ari." Mayor Strickland stood before her, squeezing Ari's hands. It didn't appear she felt them trembling. Mayor Strickland gave Prince a wary glance. She nodded at him and then moved on.

More people wished Ari luck and the traditional breaking of limbs. Ari nodded at them all, not wanting to waste any of her voice. More people had been coming up to her this week, trying to engage her in conversation.

The fear of losing her voice was no longer there. She spoke to a few of the town folk each day. Never a lot of words. Simply because she didn't have that much to share. Her world revolved around her sisters, the restaurant, and now Prince.

Prince walked beside her. His hand found and wrapped around hers. The moment he did, the trembling stopped.

"Say the word, and we can go home, Ari."

That wasn't from Prince. It was from Adelle. She was walking on the other side of Ari. Adelle wasn't holding her hand, and so she could see it shaking.

Ari had practiced this song every day the last week. She could hit every note. She knew every word. She was ready.

As they came near to the raised platform at the end of the room, Prince pulled her into his arms. Ari inhaled his scent; saltwater and strength. "I know you need to do this."

"I do," she said directly into his ear.

"I'll be right here in the front row," he said. "I'll also be cheering the loudest when you nail it."

Ari grinned at that. She pulled away from him, feeling empowered. Prince planted a light kiss on her lips, and, just with that light touch, Ari was ready to sing an opera.

Mayor Strickland climbed the one step up the platform to announce Ari. As Ari prepared to take that single step up, her fingers began to tremble again. She clasped her hands together to stop them.

There was a tug to her other hand. It was Prince. He leaned down and pressed a kiss to her forehead. "Just sing to me," he whispered in her ear. With another press to her temple, he let her go.

Ari climbed the step. Hands still clasped together. She looked out at all the faces she knew. They were all friendly. No one expected her to fail. This was her town, her community. These were the people who had known her all her life. When she'd decided she wouldn't talk any longer, no one had forced her to try. Even now, no one forced her to greet them. They all accepted her the way she was. She could do this.

The sounds of the recorded piece began to play. Ari counted the notes before it was her time to come in. She closed her eyes. She took a deep breath. On a shaky exhale, the first lyric passed through her lips… and the note struck the perfect chord.

CHAPTER TWENTY-THREE

*P*rince was lost in the sound of her voice. He had been in raptures all week while she'd practiced. Her voice had grown stronger and stronger each time. He didn't want to live his life without her voice ringing through his ears.

Not only because it was the only thing ringing clear in his ears. Not because whenever she sang, whenever she spoke, whenever she was near, the other ringing stopped. Because it was no longer about his ears. It was about his heart.

Eric Prince was in love with Ariana Carol.

He decided then that he would go back to therapy. He would do whatever the doctors said to hold onto the auditory abilities he still had. He would try any new technique. The thought of losing Ari's voice was not a life he wanted to live. He would fight for his hearing, right after he let her know that she had his heart.

Upon that raised platform, Ari was beautiful, a vision as she belted out the notes. Her lips trembled as she held a high note. Those were lips he'd tasted every day. He was jealous of the song. He wanted to make her tremble that way. And he would. Prince couldn't wait to press Ari to him after this song.

He'd told her to sing to him. Was she thinking of him now? Her eyes were closed. Her head thrown back as she belted out the lyrics.

Finally, her eyes opened. But they didn't land on him. They landed on something past him. Her note faltered. From the corner of his eye, Prince spied the reason.

Ursula.

Unlike everyone else in the crowd, Ursula scowled at Ari. Prince had seen that scowl many a time. She'd aimed her scowl at Ari the last time they'd all been in this room. He'd been right there beside her, an accomplice in the act.

Not tonight.

Prince turned his gaze back to the woman who had lit up his life. He willed Ari to look at him. And then she did.

Ari's voice grew stronger as she came to the last stanza of the song. She was finishing strong, just like he knew she would. He couldn't be prouder of her. It was a victory for her, one he shared in.

As the last note left her diaphragm, another commotion caught his attention. Prince couldn't hear anything, but he sensed something was wrong. He'd been in enough combat situations to know when there was a disturbance present.

In the corner of the room, a ball of fur was stirring. He recognized that dog. He'd seen it just last week at the marina. Though now it was free of dirt and grime, like it had been rescued.

No, not quite rescued. The dog was a rescue looking for a new home as part of the gala's pet adoption mission. The dog's keeper was so entranced with Ari that she wasn't minding the leash in her hand. The dog easily slipped its tether. It raced toward the stage. Stopping just before Ari, the animal sat down on its haunches.

Prince's vision swam. Part of his brain told him he wasn't in a combat zone. There was no danger here in his hometown. But another part of his brain knew that was a lie. There had been violence behind the closed doors of his home all his life.

What if there was a threat? What if Ari was in danger? He would not take that risk, not with her.

He stopped thinking. He acted. Prince's body was in motion, lunging not for the dog. He dove for Ari, ready to shield her body with his own.

She'd just finished the final note. The crowd all around was applauding. The clapping came to a screeching halt as Prince and Ari crashed down to the floor of the platform.

There was no explosion in his ear. There was a chorus of shouts and screams. But no bomb blasts.

Prince lifted his gaze. He looked behind him. The dog sat wagging his tail, tongue lolling out of his mouth in the same spot on the floor.

The crowd of people stared at him in shock and horror. He couldn't hear what they were saying. It was all a mumble. What he did hear was Ari's cry of pain.

"Oh, God, Ari. I'm sorry."

Her arm was red. Twisted at an unnatural angle. She brought it protectively to her chest as he rose from her.

Finally, the awful reality settled over him. There had been no bomb. There had been no threat. The only danger was him. But the cruelest part was yet to come.

"It's okay," she said, her voice hoarse with pain. "It was an accident. I'm fine."

CHAPTER TWENTY-FOUR

"I have to advise against it, Ariana. That's a pretty good sprain you've got there."

Ari set her chin into a firm line at Dr. Green's words. In setting her chin, she also pushed her shoulders back. Which hurt the sprain in her arm.

"All right, fine," said Dr. Green, shaking her head. "But you'll need to sign the AMA paperwork. I'll send in one of the nurses."

Ari had no qualms against signing the against-medical-advice paperwork. What she wanted was to get to Prince. He'd looked lost, guilty, shame-filled when they'd rolled her into the emergency room. He hadn't responded to anything anyone said to him. He'd simply stared at Ari as if through the fog of war.

"Going AMA? Just another bad decision on your part."

Ari looked up at the person in nurse's scrubs. It was not Nurse Tony as she'd assumed it would be. Standing in purple scrubs with sea creatures on them was none other than Ursula Spade. Ari had forgotten that the woman worked here. It seemed unfathomable that someone who cared only about herself would be put in charge of the care of others.

"Just hand me the paperwork, and I'll sign." Ari reached her good hand for the clipboard in Ursula's hand.

"To go and chase after a man who beats you?"

"Prince did no such thing, and you know it."

Ursula clucked as she flipped through the papers on the clipboard, still not handing it over to Ari.

"What happened was an accident."

"You know, that's what his mother used to say. She was in here all the time when my mother used to work here. Black eyes, bruises all over her arms, a few broken bones. All accidents."

Ari snatched the clipboard out of the woman's hands. The move jostled her bruised arm, and she couldn't hide the wince.

"He's just like his father-"

"No, he's not," said Ari, tossing the signed paperwork aside. "He's not the same boy you used to know. He is a good man. He's a hero. He thought I was in danger and—"

"And so he hurt you." Ursula shrugged, but the cruel smile on her face had not a hint of concern. "Sure, I'll let the social workers know that's your statement for the next time."

Ari stormed past the woman. But Ursula's words trailed after Ari. The whole town might have that opinion of Prince. Well, she would just have to prove them all wrong.

"Ari, what are you doing?" Adelle was walking into the entrance as Ari was preparing to exit. "You're not leaving. The doctor said you have to keep that arm still."

Ari ignored Adelle's demand as she made her way through the hospital's exit. The parking lot was small enough for her to find the car. When she looked down at her arm in the sling, she realized she wouldn't be dodging her sisters any time soon.

"Can you drive me, please?" said Ari.

"To him?"

"Yes," Ari hissed. "Where else would I be going?"

"Home, maybe? To rest that big old wound your boyfriend gave you."

"Not you, too." Ari pinched the bridge of her nose with her good hand. A throb emanated from her elbow, making her want to sit down and rest. But she couldn't. Not yet. She had to make sure Prince was okay.

"He didn't even stay at the hospital with you."

"Fine." Ari turned from the car. "I'll catch a cab."

"Ari, get in the car."

Ari turned back to her sister. Adelle's lips were pinched as tightly as Ari's. The two glared at each other.

It was rare for Ari to put up much of a fight, especially when Adelle was the opponent. She was not backing down from this. She knew she would have to convince the whole town, including her family, that what had happened last night was an accident. But first, she needed to see how the man at the center of the storm was dealing with his demons.

"Fine," said Adelle. "I'll drive you."

Ari slid in the passenger seat, taking care to not let her arm touch the door. Dr. Green had given her something for the pain, but the pills couldn't erase the memory of the look of absolute horror and shame on Prince's face.

Ari had seen the look in his eyes before he'd charged the stage. It had been the same look as he'd had back in the restaurant when he'd pushed her up against the wall after the sound feedback. He'd been trying to protect her then. She knew he'd been trying to protect her at the gala.

"I just need it said that I am not for dating a soldier with PTSD," said Adelle. "Because that's what this is, isn't it?"

"Cut the guy some slack. He's been fighting for our country."

"He just took a chunk out of my sister."

"He would never hurt me," said Ari.

"He just did."

"He was trying to protect me," said Ari. "In the Army, dogs are used to sniff bombs. When they sit, that means they found an explosive."

"So, you can never have a pet dog?"

Ari decided to revert to her old ways and keep quiet. She had her hand on the handle of the door and was jumping out before they parked at the marina. Relief flooded her when she saw the houseboat still docked there. She had been truly frightened that he would leave.

She didn't bother knocking. She flung the door open. He wasn't inside. She found him outside on the deck. In his hands was the boat's anchor. He'd pulled it up from its place deep in the lake. He was preparing to leave.

CHAPTER TWENTY-FIVE

he rope that connected to the boat's anchor was long. Pulling it up had felt like it had taken an eternity. The anchor was meant to keep him safe, to keep him secure. Holding it in his hands, Prince felt lost, adrift, like he was going to float away at any second.

"Prince?"

He stiffened at the sound of her voice. He didn't turn around. He didn't want to see the damage he'd caused her. "You should still be in the hospital."

"I checked myself out because I'm fine."

Her voice was soft, steady. But that single word was a bomb in his mind.

He turned then. His eyes wanted to go to her face, to drink in the loveliness that was Ariana Carol. But his gaze slid to her arm. From what he could see around the sling she wore, the skin there was red and splotchy. At the center was an angry purple bruise. A bruise by his own hand.

"You are not fine, Ari."

"What happened last night wasn't your fault."

First the *fine* bomb. Now the aftershocks of passing the blame. Prince's hands tightened on the anchor, letting the sharp edges cut into his flesh.

"You're leaving?" she said. "You weren't going to tell me?"

"I'm going to get as far away from you as possible."

Ari had been moving closer to him, as though preparing for a sneak-hug-attack. Now she stepped back. Her left eye flinched, as though he'd slapped her.

"Don't you understand, Ari? I hurt you."

"It was an accident."

"It wasn't the first time. The last time I hurt you, the wound festered for ten years."

"I didn't want to sing. I was scared. I used what you did as a convenient excuse."

Prince shook his head. It didn't matter. "Then again last night—"

"Did you do that on purpose?" Ari asked.

"No. I would never."

Prince took a step to her. In doing so, he dropped the anchor. It splashed back into the water. The rope unwound as it sank deeper and deeper into the lake's depths.

"You would never hurt me on purpose," she said.

Ari was within arm's reach. How had she gotten so close so fast? He was a trained soldier. He should've seen the danger of her coming at his heart from miles away. But he'd let her infiltrate. Because he wanted to be turned to the other side.

"You are not your father." Ari laid a hand on his heart. The organ leaped to her gentle touch. "You keep trying to protect me. But there are no enemies present."

"My head's not right, Ari." His hands came up and gripped her shoulders. He wanted to push her away, but his arms wouldn't straighten to strong-arm her. Instead, Prince pulled her into his chest as though she were the lifeline, his anchor.

"Having family members that aren't right in the head is not new to me," she said. "You've met Adelle."

That brought a chuckle out of him. Prince wanted to pull her tighter to him, but he was ever conscious of the very real wound he'd dealt her. The purple bruising he spied looking down into the sling brought him back to reality.

"There's the very real probability that I'll lash out in some other way," he said. "Nightmares, walking flashbacks, and then there's the hearing loss to contend with."

"There's a VA hospital not too far from town. We'll go together. You're not alone."

Ari tilted her head back and looked up at him. Her blue eyes were so clear, so full of care. Prince's arms wrapped tightly around her, knowing that he was never letting this woman go. She was his family. She was his world.

"The first time, I ran away," she said. "I ran, and I hid. Last night I faced my fear. I got up on that stage, and I conquered it. Don't run away from this. Stand with me and face it."

"I love you," he said. "I know it's too quick—"

"It's not," she said. "I feel it too."

"Nothing is worth causing you pain."

"If you leave, I will be in pain."

"Then it looks like you're stuck with me." Prince dipped his head to hers and captured her mouth.

With thier kiss, it was as though she sang into him. The lyrics of the love song went straight to his heart, leaving him lightheaded. He couldn't hear her sigh of pleasure, but he felt it on his lips.

"Ouch."

Her cry of pain, he heard loud and clear. Prince pulled away from Ari. Glancing down, he saw her injured arm between them.

"That's it," he said. "No more kissing until you're healed."

"Sorry, I couldn't hear you."

"You heard me loud and clear." He stepped away from her and turned her by the shoulders. "It's to bed with you."

"Well, soldier, if that's your order."

Prince couldn't hide his chuckle. He could see now that the woman whom he thought was shy and reserved was going to be a handful. But loving Ari was a risk worth taking.

EPILOGUE

"**O**migosh, Ari! You didn't! Is this! Omigosh!"

Adelle flew into Ari's arms, knocking her sister over as they sat huddled in a sea of wrapping paper on Christmas Day. It would appear that Adelle liked Ari's gift to her, a vinyl of Esther Rolle's album *The Garden of My Mind.*

Ari worried that Adelle's squeals would set off Prince's new hearing aid. When she spied her boyfriend on the other side of the room, he wasn't paying the sisters any mind. Prince was engaged in a deep conversation with her father.

Her parents had arrived a few days before the holiday. Their reception of Prince had been lukewarm the first day. By Christmas Eve, they were bringing him into the conversations more and more.

Which wasn't always a good thing. Now Prince was privy to tales of Ari trying to make friends with a lobster as a kid, insisting that the crustacean could talk back to her. That was one of many embarrassing tales her family told her new beau.

Prince took it all in stride. His shoulders eased with each meal he was invited to. His laugh came more freely. Ari didn't hold her breath that the man would open up and share awkward tales of him as a child. Speaking about his family was, and would likely always be, a sore subject with him.

Ari was simply happy that he had chosen to stay and face his issues head-on, with her at his side. He'd already seen a counselor at the VA Hospital. And they'd gone back to the Purple Heart ranch to participate in a couples' group for partners suffering from PTSD.

They'd floundered in their first meeting with the group. What with Prince being a man who didn't like to discuss his feelings, coupled with his hearing disability. And what with Ari being a woman who didn't like to speak in public. But they'd fumbled through it hand in hand, together.

This was going to work. Case in point, her dad was now smiling at Prince. Prince stuck out his hand in an offering for her father to shake it. Her dad smacked his hand away and brought Prince into a hug.

Yes, this was going to work.

"Isn't it time for Ari's present," Alanna singsonged. The seashell hair combs Ari had given her sister were pinned up in her hair, making her look like a mermaid on land.

"I think I opened all of mine," Ari said.

"There's one more," said Prince.

Ari watched as he went to the front door and pulled in a large box. The box shook. Then it barked.

Ari's gaze lifted to Prince with a question. "Is there a dog in there?"

"Open it up and see," was his response.

But Ari hesitated. Why would he be giving her a dog? The animals were one of his triggers.

As though he read her mind, he said again, "Open it up."

Ari pulled the lid of the gift box off. Sure enough, a dog's head poked out of the top. It sniffed at her hand and then gave it a tentative lick. Looking closely, Ari realized that this was the same dog from the gala. The same dog that had come and sat at the edge of the stage and caused the commotion that led to her arm being in a sling.

"I don't understand?" said Ari.

"He didn't get adopted," said Prince. "He has special needs. First, he's not the prettiest mutt in the world. His back paw is injured. He has severe hearing loss in one ear."

Ari gazed up at the man she loved. That fluttering feeling that was always present when he was near rose from her belly to her heart. Inside her heart, where Prince had taken up a large chunk of space, she felt more room being made.

"You want me to have him?"

"You're pretty good with wounded animals," he said. "But I thought he could be our dog. We just have to give him a name for his collar."

Ari looked down at the collar around the dog's neck. The name tag there was blank. But there was something else hanging on the collar. That something else glittered.

Ari gasped. Behind her, her family sniffled and sighed. Her father nodded at her, as though letting her know that she had his permission. Ari knew exactly what the dog would be called at that moment. She looked up at the co-owner of their new pet and said the dog's new name out loud.

"Yes!"

The Rancher takes his Best Friend's Sister

The Rancher takes his Runaway Bride

The Rancher takes his Star Crossed Love

The Rancher takes his Love at First Sight

The Rancher takes his Last Chance at Love

The Silver Star Ranch Romances

His Pledge to Honor

His Pledge to Cherish

His Pledge to Protect

His Pledge to Obey

His Pledge to Have

His Pledge to Hold

a Flying Cross Ranch Romance

His Vow to Love

His Vow to Treasure

His Vow to Adore

His Vow to Trust

His Vow to Respect

His Vow to Defend